D0001238

HARL'EM REDUX

A David McKay Mystery

PERSIA WALKER

BLOOD VINTAGE PRESS

Published by Blood Vintage Press 2011

Printed in the United States of America

ISBN-13: 978-0-9792538-7-4
ISBN-10: 0-9792538-7-4

ACKNOWLEDGMENTS

This work owes a profound debt to the writers of the Harlem Renaissance ... Countee Cullen, Rudolph Fisher, Langston Hughes, Zora Neale Hurston, James Weldon Johnson, Nella Larsen, Claude McKay, Vivian Morris, and Wallace Thurman, among others. Their short stories, novels, memoirs, essays, and articles fired my imagination. Their writings were windows against which I pressed my nose, eager as a child, to spend many pleasurable hours viewing their world.

Thanks also to historians David Levering Lewis, Carl T. Rowan, Michel Fabre, Tyler Stovall, Steven Watson, and Lionel C. Bascom. Their informative, perceptive, and very enjoyable works on the Harlem Renaissance provided a wealth of information—more than I, with my skills, could do justice to. For whatever insufficiencies this text might contain, debit them to me, not my sources.

A special round of applause for Julie Castiglia, my agent, for her determination and steady guidance, and for Andrea Mullins at Simon & Schuster for making the editing process a genuine pleasure. Between these two dynamos, I was well taken care of.

My heartfelt gratitude to Debbie Geiss-Haug, Sonia Ehrt, Michelle Bonnardot, Michelle Moore, Kathy Raymond, Dina Treu, Ilse Nehring, Gabriele Heblik-Hochholzer, and Swarthmore College Professor Charles James. And a special thanks to Henry Ferretti. They've been steadfast friends, forgiving unreturned phone calls, missed get-togethers, and general unavailability. Without their humor, patience, encouragement, and feedback, this novel might never have been completed.

Most of all, I want to thank my mom, for her love and faith, and my little troopers, Tyler and Jordan, for so generously sharing their mom with David and Annie, Gem and Lilian, Nella, Rachel, and Sweet.

–Persia Walker
November 9, 2001

DEDICATION

For Essie, Tyler and Jordan

HARLEM REDUX

Sunday, February 21, 1926 - 10:30 P.M.

The room was dark, except for one silvery ray of moonlight. An icy wind slipped in through the open window, swept around the room, and caressed her with chilling fingertips. She came to with a start. The darkness shocked her. The silence told her she was alone. How long had she lain there?

Her hands had been folded across her chest. She felt throbbing spurts of warm liquid spilling onto her breasts, drenching the soft cotton of her nightgown. And she sensed the approach of that final darkness. The urge to close her eyes, to give in, was overwhelming. The room seemed to revolve. Slowly. Her eyelids drooped. An inner voice asked:

Are you really going to lie there ... and bleed to death?

Her eyes snapped open.

No.

At first, her hands seemed mercifully numb. But within minutes, the pain had grown more pronounced. Soon, it was agonizingly refined. The tortured nerve endings in her slashed wrists screamed with voices that echoed inside her, quickening and clarifying her thoughts.

I have to get help.

She tried to move her legs, but they were like logs, heavy and inert.

Find another way.

Pressing her elbows to her side, she twisted her upper torso and rocked back and forth. Her body rolled once, twice, then over the edge. The bed was high; the fall was hard. She landed with a heavy thump and for a moment lay stunned. Her heart pounded; her thoughts struggled for clarity.

There was no way she could use her hands. They were half-dead clumps of flesh. But her legs had been jolted back to life.

Elbows still pressed to her side, she rolled over onto her chest, drew her knees up under her, then pushed herself up with her elbows. Leaning on the mattress to brace herself, she could stand.

The effort cost her. She sagged against a bedpost. Trying to hold on, she threw her forearms around the carved wooden beam. Her limp hands dangled, dripping their warm liquid. Cold sweat slipped down from her forehead and upper lips.

The darkness crept nearer.

Time had played a trick on her. She wasn't in the house on Strivers' Row, but elsewhere. The air didn't smell of jasmine and tobacco, but of the sea. She was in the Hamptons, in Nella's house. There came the sound of a life-and-death struggle, a gunshot. She again saw a pair of dead, staring eyes.

"No," she whispered. "No. I won't let you do this."

She held on and the darkness receded. She knew where she was. She could make out the shapes of furniture by the moonlight—could even see her own shadow as she clung to the bedpost. But she felt seasick, as if she were clinging to the mast of a swaying boat. Her stomach heaved and she bent over, vomiting on herself and the bed. She clung to the bedpost as another wave of dizziness passed over her, then straightened up with a moan. Wiping her mouth with the back of her forearm, she smeared her face with blood.

Time's running out.

She could make it to the bedroom door.

Fifteen steps. That's all it would take.

But she hesitated. She did not know what—or more accurately, who— might be waiting for her on the other side. In a bizarre way, her bedroom meant safety. She heard a thump. Her heart lurched. Was it a footstep in the hallway—or just the house settling on its foundation? She swallowed and took a deep breath. She would have to make it down the stairs, creeping along with the help of the banister, then make it into the parlor before she could reach the telephone. If she fainted along the way, on the steps or at the parlor entrance, then ...

No, not the door.

What then?

An icy breeze stroked her cheek.

The open window. Get to it. Scream. Call out—that's the way to go.

She counted backward from three, focusing her energy. At zero, she let go of the bedpost and took a step toward the window. Her legs were weak and shaky. Her knees trembled, but they didn't buckle. She took another tottering step. And another. That window had never seemed so far away; her body never so unwilling.

She was nearly across the room when it happened.

She tripped over the hem of her gown and toppled forward. Her head hit the corner of an antique linen chest. A sharp pain lanced through her skull and the moonlight, dim as it was, grew dimmer.

No, not now. Please, not now.

But her vision blurred and the light grew duskier. She lifted her head a wobbly inch or two, her eyelids drooped and her head sagged to the floor.

She might have drifted away permanently if it hadn't been for the wailing scream of a racing police siren. The sound expanded in the air, ballooned inside her head, until it seemed to explode inside her skull. She lay blinking in the dark, telling herself it was all a bad dream. But the cold floor under her face was real. So was the blood that had congealed and crusted on her face and arms and chest. She was awake and she had to get going. She didn't know how much blood she'd lost, but she assumed she'd lost a great deal. If she passed out again, she wouldn't wake up.

She was too weak to stand again, so she half-crawled, half-dragged herself across the floor. An eternity passed before she reached the base of that window. She rested, panting, and looked up.

The casement sill was little more than a yard above her head, but it might as well have been a mile. Her head throbbed. Her heart knocked. She wanted to sit and be still.

Get to that windowsill. Find the strength.

Curling up, she leaned one shoulder against the wall and inched her way up. It was taking forever. She was swimming up from way down deep. She held her breath, struggling against a vicious, relentless, downward pull. Clear droplets of agony slipped down from her temples. Would she ever reach the surface?

Then she was up. Fully upright. She leaned into a blast of frigid air. It cut to the bone, but it felt good. So very good! To be standing. To be at the window To *still* be alive.

Pushing aside a porcelain vase on the windowsill, she flopped down on the narrow ledge and looked out. The small dark street seemed empty.

No! There has to be someone. Please, Lord, let there be someone. Help me this once, damn it. I'm begging you, begging you to help me. Now!

She noticed a light shining in a second-floor window across the way.

"Help! Help!" she screamed, but the wind, merry and malicious, kissed the words from her mouth and whipped them away. "Pleeease! Somebody! *Anybody]* HELP MEEEE!"

Again the wind, ever careless and cruel, swallowed the sounds of her pleading, took them so fast she barely heard them herself.

She pushed herself to hang out the window. Down the street to her left was a man walking his Doberman. He was stooped with age and bundled against the cold; his cap jammed down over his ears.

"Hey, mister! Mister, please! Up here! Send help! Please, mister, *please!*"

The man did not respond but the dog paused, perked up his ears, and howled. The wind that swept her words away served up the dog's mournful wails with mocking efficiency.

"Please! I don't wanna die! I DON'T WANNA DIE!"

The dog barked harder, louder, belting agitated yowls that rode the hellish gusts of wind up and down the street. Hope pulsed through her. The Doberman pulled on his leash, strained in her direction. The dog's owner yanked him back. He cuffed him on the nose. And dragged him off down the street. Away from her.

"NO!!!"

Her elbow touched the vase. She turned without thinking and gave it a shove that sent it plunging out the window. She watched it turn and tumble as if in slow motion, saw it crash and explode into minute pieces. She looked down. Had they heard?

They were gone. So quickly. Gone. As though they'd never been there.

Her legs gave out. She crumpled to the floor, her outstretched arms smearing trails of blood on the wall. Her head sagged.

"Oh, God ... no," she wept. "Don't let this happen. This can't happen."

Then she felt the curtains. Made of lightweight silk, they billowed about her face, as familiar, as gentle, cool, and caressing as a loved one's touch. She closed her eyes. An eerie calm crept over her. Odd, how the pain was receding. If only she could rest. Sleep.

No! She wanted to live, to hold on. She loved life. She refused to let it slip away. Not like this. Not while she was young. Not when she finally ... had nearly everything ...

But the darkness was getting hard to fight. She had never felt so tired. Her inhalations grew fainter. Her eyes slid shut. From behind her closed eyelids, she saw her inner lights fade individually, felt herself float away, bit by precious bit, as her blood-starved organs shut down, one after another. She was about to die and she knew it. Summoning her strength, she raised her face to bathe it in the moonlight. She held it there with stubborn determination for several exquisite seconds. Then her last inner light faded and with a moan she slumped down, a bloody but still beautiful corpse gazing blindly at the bleak night sky.

1. THE LOST SON RETURNS

Lilian's older brother had been away for years, but he had altered little, at least on the surface. He was thirty-five. Silver already touched his temples, but his hair was otherwise still dark and thick. Quite tall and lean, he had an oval face and clear olive skin with a strong fine profile. He had retained the lustrous dark eyes that had melted many a feminine resistance. Time had magnified their eloquence. Maturity had deepened them and experience saddened them. He was aware of his effect on women, but he tended toward solitude, and though he enjoyed female company, he always feared that in the end, a woman would ask for more than he could give. Or worse, that he would give all he had, then see her pull away in disappointment and leave him.

Well-built and poised, David McKay had a reputation for dressing well with tasteful understatement. His clothes were of excellent quality, but close inspection would have shown them to be worn. There were no holes or tatters, hanging threads or missing buttons, but the clothes, like the man, gave off an intangible air of fatigue. Even so, he was usually the handsomest man in any crowd. That day, his dark gray cashmere coat was buttoned high against the early spring chill. He wore his fedora tipped low to one side, just enough to cast a shadow, but not enough to hide the sad gleam in his eye.

Like his sister, David preferred to stay out of the limelight. But his air of quiet distinction was noticeable to even the most casual observer. It was all the more evident that chilly March Thursday because of the mute pain in his eyes. The early evening's dusky skies emphasized his pallor. Sorrow had grayed his complexion. Tension had cut furrows into his handsome face. He was bone-weary. From shock, grief, and lack of sleep. His sister was dead and buried some three weeks, but he had only learned of it the day before.

He had forgotten much of the past twenty-four hours. The last moment he did recall was when he got that note while eating lunch at his desk in Philadelphia, that telegram summoning him home. He had an excellent memory. It could be useful, but there were times when it absorbed information he would have rather forgotten. The words to that telegram, for example, would remain etched in his memory until the day he died. It had turned his world upside down. When he left his law office to head home and pack, he was as disoriented as a man who suddenly finds himself walking on the ceiling.

Lilian was a part of him. It was nearly impossible to accept that she was gone. He swung between anguish and numbness. His mind struggled to accept her death even as his heart rejected it. Her presence hovered in the air about him, a gentle warmth that carried a hint of the light powdery perfume she wore. Whenever he looked at a crowd, he thought he saw her face.

It had never occurred to him that Lilian might die. He had not seen her in four years, but he had always been able to visualize her writing poetry at her desk or reading a newspaper before the parlor fireplace. Those images had comforted him. He had summoned them in times of doubt. Lilian: stable, dependable, clearheaded, and never changing. Whether she agreed with his life choices or not, she had been there for him.

It wasn't only her death that stunned him; there was the manner of it: The telegram said she had committed suicide. When had Lilian's life become so unbearable that death seemed to offer the only relief? And why?

She had mailed him a letter on the first of every month for

some two years, starting in January 1923. Her letters had never reflected dissatisfaction with her life. They were always warm, colorful missives, filled with innocuous but witty gossip or news about her writing career. Her letters had arrived with efficient regularity until a year ago, in March 1925, and then ended abruptly. He told himself now that he should have become worried at her sudden silence. He should have made inquiries. That last letter had begged him to return home. He hadn't answered it.

Now he longed for one more chance to hug her, to tell her how proud he was of her, to confess and explain the unexplainable. But he would never have an opportunity to do that—never. And that stunned him.

Struggling to confront the inescapable, he tried in vain to reconcile the immense contradiction between her dramatic death and her deep devotion to discretion during life. She was a proud, gentle woman, known for her exquisite discipline, delicate tastes, and exceptionally even temperament. Were someone to ever write her life story, a most likely title would be *Pride of Place.* She was a reclusive person, raised with a deeply ingrained awareness of her responsibilities toward her family, her class, and her race—in that order. A conscientious conformist, she strove to keep her name synonymous with propriety, refinement, and perfect manners. She scrupulously guarded her privacy and avoided contact with anyone whose behavior might attract inappropriate attention. It was a horrible irony that the most private of all acts—the act of dying—had made her the source of tabloid scandal.

He had lost all sense of time during the train ride from Philadelphia. Fear had lengthened the trip into an eternity. And fear had shortened it, propelling him toward his destination much too quickly. He had gotten hold of a copy of the *New York Times,* but neither the latest corruption tales involving the Democratic Party machine at Tammany Hall nor the political circus of the Sacco-Vanzetti case could distract him. His terrorized mind fought to stave off the coming appointment with his very personal reality. A vague protective hope that some terrible mistake had been made rode with him, kept him company the entire way, but this false friend abandoned him the moment his train pulled into Manhattan.

That was less than an hour ago. Now he stood on the doorstep of his family home on Harlem's elegant Strivers' Row, deeply disoriented, his one suitcase at his side, and it seemed that the family maid was the only person there to greet him. But the sight of her loved and familiar face warmed him.

Annie Williams's wizened face lit up when she saw him. Her hands went to her cheeks and her dark eyes widened in surprise.

"Mr. David? Is it you? Is it really you?"

David gave a barely perceptible nod and the whisper of a smile. He sensed her astonishment melt into joy, momentarily eclipsing her grief, and felt the knot in his chest loosen. God, how he'd missed her. She'd been there as long as he could remember. His eyes went over her. She was ginger-brown, like her favorite spice, a thin, wiry woman of strength surprising in someone her size and age. She was in her late fifties. Most of the time, she appeared younger, but mourning for Lilian had taken its toll. Her eyes were sunken and ringed by circles of dark gray.

He wrapped his strong arms around her in a hug. Her soft breath buffeted his ears as she whispered gratitude to God for having answered her prayers. Finally, she stepped back, swiped at her tearful eyes with her apron, and took a good look at him.

"Where you been, Mr. David? We sure did miss you. Coulda used you 'round here."

"Movement business," he said, glancing away.

"It was so horrible when you didn't come back. We thought you was dead and gone. Nobody seemed to know nothing. Them Movement people even offered a reward. But they just gotta lot a kooks writing in. Nothing worthwhile. 'Magine, Miss Lilian knowing where you was all the time. I ain't faulting her for not saying nothing—I'm sure she had her reasons, but—"

He managed a small smile and forced himself to look at her. "I asked her to be discreet."

"Well then, I guess I can't say nothing—but it sure woulda lifted a coupla hearts to know you was all right."

She ushered him into the house. Until that moment, he'd wondered if he would actually manage to set foot in it again, but with her to welcome him it wasn't so difficult.

I'm acting like a child, he thought.

And like a child, he let her ease off his coat. She brushed her hand over it and hung it in the vestibule closet.

"I was going through Miss Lilian's things after the fun'ral. That's when I found your address. I wish I'da known where you was before. Maybe it woulda made a diff'rence. Then again, maybe not. I just know I sure is glad you here. I'm so glad you come back."

Her eyes went over him devotedly. It had been years since he'd seen so much love for him in anyone's face. He walked into her arms. They held one another again and it was hard to tell who was comforting whom.

In her own way, Annie had helped raise him and his twin sisters, Lilian and Gem. She'd seen them through their first loves and first heartaches. She'd rejoiced with them when they won school prizes and comforted them when they lost. He knew that she was as proud of the McKay children as she would've been of her own. As she hugged him, her flat, spade-like hands patted him on the back.

Like I'm a child, he thought. *And I'm glad of her comfort, like a child. All these years of living away, and the moment I return here, I'm—*

"C'mon, Mr. David. Let me fix you something to eat."

He nodded and followed her as she led him down the corridor. She moved with unfamiliar slowness, as though the weight of her years were bricks on her back. Her left shoulder was a tad bit higher than the other from a slight curvature of the spine he hadn't noticed before, and she walked with a slightly perceptible limp. He did not remember her being so frail, so worn.

What else had changed? He cocked an ear. He didn't know what he was listening for, but he knew what he heard:

Emptiness. No sounds of life, of love or laughter. Just a roaring emptiness that fills every nook and cranny. A hollow silence that echoes every thought, every heartbeat.

He looked around, at the paintings on the walls, the flower-bedecked tables that lined the hallway. All seemed familiar, yet remote. His eyes knew what to expect, but none of the sights seemed to touch his heart. He was detached and distant and it reassured him to feel that way.

This is like a place I only dreamed of.

But then his gaze fell on the dark gleaming door to the left of the library. This was the door that had guarded the heart of the house. This was the door that had haunted his childhood dreams and even now—

His breath caught; his shoulders rode up. He counted his steps and kept his eyes straight ahead. The hallway seemed to twist and lengthen. It was taking an eternity to cross that door. Every footfall echoed in the thudding of his heartbeat. Finally, they were past the door, beyond it. The hallway snapped back into shape. He exhaled.

They entered the kitchen. It was warm and comforting, familiar in its rich mixture of smells. His joints were stiff after the long train ride. He eased himself down into a chair at the kitchen table and let his tired eyes drift over the spotless room: up to the clock on the wall, down to the gas stove, the enameled sink and the refrigerator. His breathing slowed.

How many meals have been prepared in here . ..

This kitchen was Annie's domain. She'd made it her own, made it a place for more than just physical nourishment. Annie's kitchen was a source of warmth, a place for truthful conversations. It was a place to break down and weep or bust out with a big laugh, to be temporarily free from concern about what was or was not becoming in a colored family of status. Never before had he been so intensely aware of the role Annie's kitchen had played in his life. Never before had he so envied the boy he'd been.

She moved about the room, singing softly to herself. He watched her go about boiling water and heating something in a pot on the stove. Nothing more was said as the contents of the pot simmered. In a short time, she placed a cup of black coffee and a deep bowl of rich vegetable soup before him. She went to the pantry and fetched him bread and butter. He ate in silence. For a while, the only sound was the clink of his spoon scraping against the side of his bowl.

She poured herself a cup of coffee and sat down at the table across from him. He felt her eyes dwell on him with affection. He could imagine what she thought she saw: a good man possessed of a kind and compassionate nature, a man who performed brave deeds. He could imagine her talking to her friends. He could just hear her describing how it was before he went away.

"Always so nicely dressed in his debonair British suits. Never a hair outta place, shirts perfectly pressed, razor-sharp crease in his pants, black shoes so shiny you could see your face in them. 'Fine David McKay,' the young ladies used to call him. Them girls was crazy about my David, with his soft hair. But David never had no time for any of them. He was too busy studying. Wanted to be a lawyer. That's what he done, too. After he come back from the war, he went off to Howard University and got hisself a fine education. Then he got a job with the Movement. They sent him on down south. He went to get to the truth behind them lynchings. It's dang'rous work, going down to them there hot spots. Those ol' crackers would just as soon lynch a colored man as look at him. That was back in '22. There sure was a lot to keep a colored lawyer busy back then. Still is. Sad to say, there still is."

David thought about a little town in Georgia and his brief sense of well-being vanished. A chill touched his soul. He'd virtually disappeared after joining the Movement. He had kept his whereabouts secret from all but Lilian. He looked at Annie. Had she read his letters? No, it wasn't likely. She was inquisitive, but she could be trusted to respect private matters. Furthermore, he'd been careful to keep his letters lean.

Finishing his soup, he laid his spoon and napkin neatly to one side. Silence permeated the room, thick and waiting. His mind was filled with questions. So many questions. They mobbed his mind like grief-stricken relatives clamoring around an accident scene, all seeking the impossible, the essentially unattainable—an explanation, an answer, a satisfying solution to that one question survivors are always driven to ask: Why?

"What happened?" he asked. "What brought her down?"

Annie wrapped her hands around her coffee cup. It was old and chipped. He realized with a start that the cup was the one he'd given her as a Christmas present when he was ten years old. He'd spent all of his first allowance on it.

"I don't know if I can give you the answers you need, Mr. David. I seen a lot in this house, and I got my thoughts. But they's just the notions of an old woman."

He'd never known her to lie or bite her tongue when the truth needed telling. "It's me, Annie. Whatever you want to say, however you want to say it, just go ahead."

She looked away, out the window, where a couple walked past pushing a baby carriage. The young husband said something and his wife gave a high-pitched giggle. Inside the kitchen, it was quiet, so quiet that David could hear the sound of his own breathing. He waited. He could be patient. As a lawyer, he'd learned to be patient. Her eyes swung back to his. *Do you really want to know?* she seemed to ask.

Yes, he thought. *I want to know.* "I need to know," he said.

Her roughened hands trembled. "Well... a lot's done happened since you been gone, Mr. David ... an awful lot." Her words pierced him.

"Go on," he whispered, his voice suddenly hoarse and tight

and unwilling.

"I don't know where to start. It's hard when I think back on all I seen and heard." Her voice trailed off. "Miss Gem come back for a while—"

"*Gem* is here?"

"No, she gone. Been gone. She didn't stay long. Just long enough to try to cause trouble." An expression of disapproval flitted across her face. "Anyway, she left again after a few months. And ain't nobody heard nothing from her since Miss Lilian died."

"Does she know?"

"She should. I sent a telegram. She never sent no answer. Never showed her face. I don't know what to make of it. Nobody does."

He had his own opinions on the matter, but he kept them to himself. "Go on."

"Well, that young Miss Rachel—you know she was gone for a while— well, she come back, too."

His heart gave a little twist. He kept his face unmoved.

"And then ... as for Miss Lilian ..." Annie paused.

"Yes?"

"She got ill. Her mind went. And ain't none of the doctors knowed how to help her." Annie folded her hands together. "But I'm getting ahead of myself. The biggest change, the one I'd better begin with, is how Miss Lilian up and got married."

David's eyelids raised involuntarily, then lowered like shutters yanked down over a dark window. *Married.* He shivered and wondered at his own reaction. Surely news of a marriage was to be welcomed.

It was also to be shared.

Why didn't she tell me? She never once wrote a word about it, not even dropped a hint. All those letters of pretended openness. By saying nothing, she lied.

He was suddenly furious. And instantly ashamed. How

could he be angry with the dead?

"I wondered if she'd written and told you," Annie said. "Didn't think she had. She didn't tell nobody."

"You mean she eloped?"

"It'll be exactly two years ago next month. She kissed him in March, married him in April. Knowed him for one month. Met him at a fancy-dress dinner them civil rights folks at *Black Arrow* magazine had down at the Civic Club. You musta heard about it."

Yes ... The dinner had caused a lot of talk. It was widely written about in the Negro press. The dinner introduced the cream of Harlem's black literary

crop to influential white publishers. It was held at the Civic Club because the Fifth Avenue restaurant was the only classy New York club that admitted patrons regardless of color or gender. It was the perfect meeting place for distinguished black intellectuals and eminent white liberals. As a writer and editor at the Black Arrow, Lilian would have been there.

He loosened his collar. What kind of man had finally elicited Lilian's love? She had made female friends quickly and maintained them easily, but men she had kept at a cool distance.

"So who was the lucky guy?"

"His name is Sweet, Mr. Jameson Sweet. He's gone on business. He'll be back Sunday. Maybe you know him? He works for the Movement, too."

A light flickered in David's deep-set eyes. Regret, anxiety, and fear rumbled like freight trains through his chest. He had known he was taking a risk in returning, but the danger was closer to home than he had anticipated. He felt Annie watching him, her eyes quick with intuitive intelligence, and forced himself to remain calm. He must take care. She was as gentle as a dove, but as sly as a fox.

"Mr. David, I got your old room waiting' for you," she was saying softly. "I gave it a good going over when I knew you was coming'."

"No, it's better if I stay in a hotel."

"This is your home."

Not anymore, he wanted to say. "It's better if I go. I can't stay long, no way—"

"Oh, but you got to stay."

He gazed at her. "No, Annie. I've got business down in Philadelphia—"

"You got business here, too. *Fam'ly business.*"

"Annie—"

"Miss Lilian's gone and Miss Gem's 'cross the ocean. I'm just an old woman and I got no say. You the only one left to set things straight."

His eyes narrowed. "Set what straight?"

She measured her words. "Mr. David, you and I, we both know ... well, we both know that things ain't always the way they seem." She looked at him as though that explained it all.

It didn't. As far as he was concerned, it most definitely didn't. "Yes ... and?"

Her expression became somewhat impatient. "Mr. David, I'll put it as simple as I can. More than one fox got into this chicken coop while you was gone."

"You mean Lilian's husband—"

"I mean he's sitting pretty in this here house, *real* pretty."

A pause, then: "Just what kind of man is he?"

"A hard man, a determined man. And he ain't the sharing kind." She reached across the table and laid a firm hand on his wrist. "Now Miss Lilian never meant for this here house to pass outta the fam'ly. You know that."

What she said was true. This beautiful house had been his father's pride, the crowning glory of a lifetime. A stately, turn-of-the-century Italianate building on tree-lined 139th Street, it boasted twelve rooms, casement windows, and iron filigreed balconies. Set on Strivers' Row, with its air of manicured exclusivity, the house was a monument to Augustus McKay's real estate acumen. It was a coveted symbol of the McKay family's status among Harlem's elite—and a lightning rod for the hate and envy of others.

"Mr. David, you can't be willing to give up your daddy's house—-just like that." Annie snapped her fingers. "You can't be."

He gazed steadily at her for a long time. She meant well, but she didn't know. How could she? He had forfeited the right to call the house his home. He was in no moral position to reclaim his birthright. He doubted he ever would be. The small jaw muscles on either side of his face began to bunch. He had but one question.

"Did he hurt her?"

"Things ... like I said ... ain't always the way they seem."

He considered the matter. "I'll stay until I've talked to Sweet. Maybe he and I can reach some agreement."

She leaned toward him, her eyes burning. "Mr. David, it's time for you to take your place. Here. You got a point to make. Make it now. Later might be too late."

She led him up the stairway, humming a spiritual as she climbed. She moved slowly, but he moved even slower. His suitcase seemed to grow heavier with every step.

Part of him was relieved. He had been waiting for this summons for a long time. The night before, he had dreamed that by returning home, he would be walking into a trap, that his family, Strivers' Row, Harlem—they were all bundled to-gether—would swallow him, smother him. He had seen mocking phantoms, knowing smiles, and pointing fingers. Tossing and turning, he had entangled himself in his bedcovers, rip-ping the sheets as he struggled to break free. When he'd finally jerked upright, he was panting and disoriented, drenched in cold sweat. He'd stared blindly into the dark, his agitated heart-beat thudding in his ears. He had known he couldn't run for-ever. Known he would be summoned back. Someday. Somehow

"It's so nice to have you back, Mr. David." Annie swung

open his bedroom door and led him into the room. "I freshened it up for you real nice."

She offered to unpack his bag for him, but he shook his head. He watched tensely as she bustled about, plumping pillows that had already been plumped, smoothing a bedspread that had already been smoothed. Then she glided past him with a warm smile and was gone, drawing the door closed behind her, leaving him alone with his ghosts.

He understood what people meant when they spoke of time standing still. The room seemed to be exactly as he had left it. Even the extra pair of navy blue socks he had laid out but forgotten on the dresser top was still there. He left his suitcase by the door, crossed the room, and yanked his closet door open. It too was as he had left it: empty, except for an old black suit and his army uniform. He stroked the lapels of the army greatcoat and fingered a cuff.

It had been seven long years since the war. Since the Hell Fighters marched up Fifth Avenue. Since the city had given a dinner in their honor.

Damn, we were so proud then, so proud. And so hopeful. To think of all the dreams we dreamt ...

Faces of the men he'd known flashed before him. Joshua Lewis, Ritchie Conway, Bobby Raymond ... He'd lost contact with all of them. He would have liked to believe that most had fared well, but from what he'd seen since returning in 1919, he doubted it. A week after coming back, his best friend, Daniel Jefferson, had died while still in uniform, and it was an American mob, not a German soldier, that killed him. Danny had had the temerity to tell a white woman in Alabama that he was a man who had fought for his country and deserved better than to be called "boy." He was dead within the hour.

The war over there was nothing—nothing compared to the one over here.

David fingered his medal, still pinned to the front of his jacket. He had won the French Croix de Guerre for facing down a German raiding party on his own.

Medals are for heroes, he thought, *heroes ...* and dropped his hand from the medal as though it suddenly burned him.

His eyes moved to the black jacket. June 1921. His father: an old man, propped up by thick pillows, dying from tuberculosis; an old man with a grasp of iron and a will of steel.

"You go finish up at Howard. Be somebody. Make a difference and fight the good fight. And always, always protect your sisters."

Then there was his father's funeral service at Saint Philip's Episcopal. As befitting a man of Augustus McKay's social and financial stature, the service was weighty, dignified. An impressive convoy of expensive cars accompanied his coffin to the cemetery. Afterward, there was a small gathering at the house "for the right people."

When the last guest was gone, David and Lilian huddled near one another on the parlor sofa, sharing a pot of tea, relieved at the quiet. Gem flounced into the room, gay even in funereal black. She saw her brother and sister sitting together and was instantly jealous.

"Plotting, plotting. Something nifty, I hope?"

David gave her a look that silenced her immediately. She actually flinched. He was hard hit by his father's death and showed it. He and his father had never gotten along. Whether David could admit it or not, there had been several times when he had wished his father dead. But once the old man was gone, David missed him. Gem, however, was quick to push her grief aside, assuming she felt any. Her mind was on one matter and one matter only: money. She suggested that Lilian and David buy out her share of the house. She was sure they would agree, and they did. It was the first and last time the three of them agreed to anything with alacrity. Gem took her money and vanished within days. David and Lilian supposed that Gem had gone west, since she had mentioned Los Angeles, but they couldn't be sure. Indeed, they didn't much care.

The day we laid Daddy in the ground marked the last day we stood in the same room together. Not that we planned it that way. Not that we would've ever guessed it would turn out that way.

He and Lilian returned to their respective universities: He to Howard law in Washington, D.C.; she to study French literature as a Cornell undergraduate in Ithaca, New York. She would earn a Phi Beta Kappa key. Whether or not their chauvinist father had wanted to admit it, Lilian was the family brain. Gem had had the talent to develop into a gifted and memorable if radical poet, but she had dissipated her ability. After two years of cutting the rug and doing the bumpity-bump, dancing her semesters away, she'd quit her studies at the University of Southern California.

But if Gem failed to live up to Daddy's hopes, then so did I.

Standing in his room that March evening, he felt a familiar surge of shame. Yes, he had kept his promise to Augustus, but it had been to the letter—not in the spirit—of the old man's wishes. Over the past four years, he'd wandered far from his father's mansion. Could he find his way back? He had no choice. He had to, if he was to understand Lilian's death and regain control of his father's house.

David closed the closet door. He went to the window, parted the curtains, and looked out. The street seemed deserted, except for an old man walking his Doberman. David stood there thoughtfully for a minute or two, then let the curtain drop, went to the door, and left. A few steps to the right and down the corridor and he was in front of the master bedroom. He put his hand on the doorknob, but then hesitated. This was the room in which it had happened. He dreaded the sight of it. Yet he felt compelled to view it. Perhaps standing in this room would help him accept the reality of her death ... her *suicide.* He twisted the knob very gently and slowly pushed the door open.

The strong smell of fresh paint rushed out from the closed room, stinging his nostrils. Catching his breath, he paused on the threshold. He didn't know what he had expected to feel, but it wasn't the odd sensation that overcame him. He felt as though he were standing before a museum diorama set up to replicate Lilian's room. This subdued, muted place could not be real. It lacked the familiarity, the hominess of Lilian's room. It could not be the genuine article. *But it is,* he told himself.

In the cold light of that March evening, the room was dim. Lilian's combs, brushes, and hand mirror were laid out on the dressing table. Her hairpins were neatly aligned on a little mirrored tray. Delicate perfume bottles by Lalique were arranged to one side. The bed's counterpane was obviously new, as were the curtains at the windows. On the night table next to her bed lay her Bible, closed but with strips of red, yellow, and blue ribbon inside it to hold her place. Family photographs of their parents and of her with Gem and himself were artfully arranged atop the chest of drawers opposite the foot of her bed. A sad smile touched his lips. Even a picture of a stray puppy Lilian had adopted as a child was there.

He let his eyes drift over the dresser top once more and frowned. Something was missing. At first he didn't know what it was. Then it hit him. All those photographs of Lilian and the family, but not one of her husband. Why not? Why, if she'd loved him—if they'd had a good marriage—were there no photos of him on display with the others in her room?

"Mr. Jameson moved out after it happened," said a voice behind him. David turned. It was Annie. "He took another room," she said.

David nodded. He could understand that. He certainly wouldn't have wanted to continue to sleep in a room in which his wife had bled to death. He took a few steps into the room. Annie followed him, and they paused at the foot of the fourposter bed.

"Is this where she did it?"

She nodded. "Mr. Jameson had a new mattress brought in." She gave a little shudder and hugged herself. Her gaze went to the base of the windowsill. "Sometimes ... sometimes I ask the

Lord why I had to be the one to find her. But I suppose it was better me than someone who didn't love her. I was there when she came into the world. It was only right that I be there when she left it."

Bending down, David brushed his fingertips over the new counterpane. A pale ivory, it would have pleased Lilian. He turned to Annie. "Tell me about it, about how it was when you found her."

Annie paused, then said: "She suffered a bad death, Mr. David, a real bad death. They say you shouldn't never touch nothing, so I left the knife right there on the bed where it was, but I did close her eyes. And I laid a blanket over her. Then I called the police. And sat down in the room to keep that last wait with her. I thought about all the years gone by and the thousands of kind things Miss Lilian done for me. I'da never imagined her going like that. She was such a lovely young woman, so very sweet. She was a lady, a real fine lady."

David's gaze went again to the photos. "That, she was ..."

"Them cops sure took their sweet time coming. It was just the death of another colored woman to them. They didn't know nothing about how wonderful Miss Lilian was. And they wouldna cared. Me, I didn't mind the wait. I didn't like seeing her that way, but I knew it was likely the last time I'd see her at all."

"The funeral, was it nice?"

"Oh, yeah." She smiled. "It was sumptin' to see. And so many people showed up, so many. They had to close the doors to Saint Philip's to keep the peace. But that was to be expected. Seeing as how your family is so known and all, that was just to be expected."

"I wonder ... how many of those people actually cared about her."

She was thoughtful. "You know how people can be, Mr. David. You know how they can be. Lotsa folks who didn't have no time for her when she was sick, and lotsa others who never knowed her—well, they all just had to come ... just had to come an' see when that sweet child died."

2. HARLEM ON MY MIND

David paused on his doorstep, pulled his hat down lower, and wrapped his coat tighter. He would take a walk. To stretch his legs. To see how Harlem had changed. And to forget what Annie had told him. *A lot's done happened since you been gone.* He shuddered and forced his thoughts in another direction. His gaze traveled up and down the street, registering the familiar homes of his neighbors. After a minute, he turned up his collar, went down the front steps, and started toward Seventh Avenue.

It was a curious sensation to be back. There was, above all, a sense of the surreal; that sense, once more, of time having stood still. The trees appeared a mite bigger, but nothing else on the block had changed. It was still serene and immaculate. No matter the weather or the light, the trim, neat houses of Strivers' Row looked regal and well-to-do. As they should. After all, they were designed for the affluent. That the homes should land in the hands of blacks was a development that David H. King Jr., the original builder, had probably never foreseen.

When in 1891 King commissioned New York star architect Stanford White to design the series of houses along the north side of 139th Street, King envisioned homes for wealthy white families. At first, that's what they were, homes for white millionaires, such as the first Randolph Hearst. But a depression hit Harlem's inflated real estate market in 1904 and opened the way to black residency. By 1920, a good number of New York's most prominent blacks—the Rev. Dr. Adam Clayton Powell Sr., James C. Thomas, Charles W. Anderson, and others—had moved to Harlem. Already by 1914, even modestly affluent blacks could afford to buy Harlem real estate. By 1917, white brokers were begging for white investor interest in Harlem by advertising how cheap property had become. And by 1920, superb properties such as the King Model Houses had begun to pass into the hands of black professionals. As black families moved in, white ones moved out. The houses along what would be known as "Strivers' Row" went for a song.

"A twelve-room house. Fit for a king. For nine thousand dollars," Augustus beamed in announcing his purchase. "Nine thousand dollars. It was worth it."

The McKays were the sixth family to arrive. Dentist Charles H. Roberts and Dr. Louis T. Wright, Harlem Hospital's first black doctor and later its chief of surgery, soon became the McKays' neighbors. Then there was Vertner W. Tandy, widely recognized as the first black architect to be licensed in New York State, and Lieutenant Samuel J. Battle, Manhattan's first black police lieutenant. Eventually, Strivers' Row would become a popular address for black theatrical stars: composer Eubie Blake, orchestra leaders Fletcher Henderson and Noble Sissle.

Back courtyards, gardens, and fountains connected by an interior alleyway ran the length of the block. The houses on the north side of 139th Street, including the McKay house, were neo-Renaissance, made of thin, reddish Roman brick. The pale cream-colored houses running along the south side were neo-Georgian. All displayed the same spare but expert use of classical details. All were set back from the pavement to emphasize privacy. And all had rear entrances that kept the unsightly business of housekeeping where it belonged—out of sight.

The residents of Strivers' Row were a proud lot. They strove for excellence; hence the street's nickname. They kept their trees neatly tended and their hedges closely clipped. Entrance railings and balustrades were painted, windows and front steps washed, brass doorknobs and knockers polished.

Over time, the Row had become a tiny oasis of spacious ease and prosperity surrounded by a desert of danger, despair, and decay. When David stepped around the corner of 139th Street and Seventh Avenue, he entered a world of poverty, of rotting garbage and ragged children. The juxtaposition of rich and poor never failed to give him a jolt.

Seventh Avenue, that broad thoroughfare that slashes through the heart of Harlem, was well-peopled even that cold evening. Tall trees with thick trunks spread their gnarled branches over the wide dark street. Beige and brick-brown tenement buildings, four and five stories tall, rose up on either side, like mammoth shadows in the evening light.

He headed downtown, taking long, even strides, doing his best to appear at ease. He walked neither quickly nor slowly. His expression was neither curious nor indifferent. His eyes examined everything but dwelled on nothing. He saw a world of cracked pavements and battered trash cans. He passed rows of dilapidated buildings and he knew, without having to enter them, what they looked like inside: Dark, dirty hallways. Broken windows. Rusted pipes. No heat. No hot water. Rats and roaches, ticks and water bugs. Many of the folks who lived in those buildings slept ten to a room.

Most of black Harlem's residents had originally fled Georgia, the Carolinas, Virginia, and other points south, seeking jobs and safety from the pervasive threat of the lynch man's noose. They'd come north, dreaming of the Promised Land, and ended up living a nightmare. Some people could barely afford "hot beds," mattresses they switched off with other shift workers. Many couldn't even find jobs. Harlem's biggest department stores depended on blacks as customers but refused to consider them for hire.

Seeing the myriad ebony, brown, sepia, and amber faces that now peopled Harlem's streets, it was odd to think that not so long ago, Harlem was white. Only about thirty years earlier, in the late 1800s, it was Russian and Polish Jews fleeing the pogroms of Eastern Europe who had given Harlem its color. Even as recently as fifteen years earlier, Russian Jews had dominated the census figures. Then, there were the Italians—the area from Third Avenue to the East River was "Harlem's Little Italy"—and the Irish, the Germans, the English, the Hungarians, the

Czechs, and others coming from the Austro-Hungarian Empire. Harlem did have a smattering of Native Americans and a small but stable black population—the descendants of freed slaves—but by and large, the neighborhood's complexion was pink.

All that had changed, seemingly in the blink of an eye, and Harlem was now indelibly brown. Years later, people would forget that Harlem was ever white. Those few who remembered would sometimes still wonder what had happened.

King's decision to build the homes on what would become Strivers' Row was part of a turn-of-the-century construction boom in Harlem. The anticipated building of new subway lines into Harlem had turned the neighborhood into a target for speculators. Developers snapped up the remaining farmlands, marshes, garbage dumps, and empty lots that still constituted a good part of the area. Between 1898 and 1904, brownstones rose up on every corner. But by 1905, the party was over. There were too many apartments and too few renters. Even after the Lenox Avenue subway was completed, high rents discouraged the anticipated influx of new residents. The real estate market broke and people panicked. They needed tenants and needed them badly.

Meanwhile, downtown in mid-Manhattan's miserable Tenderloin district, the construction of Pennsylvania Station was destroying the area's few all-Negro blocks. Colored families being forced out of their homes wondered: Where to next?

In stepped Philip Payton Jr., a Negro real estate broker. His Afro-American Realty Company brought the white owners of Harlem and the colored families of the Tenderloin together. White owners might not have been thrilled to rent to blacks, but they preferred it to ruin. Some decided to take any Negro tenant who would pay the high rents being demanded. Hundreds, then thousands of blacks moved to Harlem. The neighborhood swelled with poor people burdened with inflated rents they couldn't afford and grand apartments they couldn't maintain.

David had spent more than half his life in the rat-infested Tenderloin and clearly remembered his family's move to Harlem when he was nineteen. He understood the hope that Harlem had represented to New York City's black residents. It was their chance to build a community—a respectable, decent community. Now, as he gazed at the tenements around him, he wondered how far that dream had been realized.

Harlem's residents were caught between low salaries and high rents, yet many people saw it as the largest, most dynamic black enclave in the United States. And in fact, the community was alive with success stories and colorful characters: bootleggers and racketeers, literati and blue bloods, barefoot prophets and uniformed liberators.

As David waited for a streetlight to change, his gaze drifted over the street life around him. There were so many half-forgotten, familiar sights. Mamas tired after a long week's work dragged toddlers with one hand and hugged grocery bags with the other. Tail-wagging dogs strained against leashes to gain the nearest fire hydrant. Stray cats with scarred faces and ripped ears huddled alongside the entrances to alleyways. Hip young men with cool ambition in their eyes hustled by. Others, with deadened dreams, sat on stoops or leaned languidly against street lamps. Street vendors hawked toys, perfume, dresses, stockings, and watches. Their goods spread out on torn blankets, they proudly displayed a profusion of glittery items one might desire, but would never use. And an abundance of dreary items one could use, but would never desire.

He'd been away a long time. What he saw was both familiar and foreign. Part of him was baffled and bewildered. But another part, a deeper part, understood and accepted, without doubt or dismay. He walked for hours. Nostalgia slowly drew his unwilling soul into her lonely embrace. These were the streets he'd roamed, the alleys where he and his friends had played. He remembered the days when 134th Street was the northern boundary of Negro Harlem, when a black man knew never to cross Lenox Avenue, no Negroes lived on or near Seventh, and none dared to appear unarmed on Irish Eighth. He remembered so much, but realized he'd forgotten even more. This was indeed his town, but it was no longer his home.

What he needed, he decided, was a drink. What about Jolene's? It was a lap joint, not far away. Back in his first days home after the war, when he and his friends wanted a break from the cabarets, wanted something a little dingier, dirtier, and down-to-earth, they would hit Jolene's. Gem had sung there sometimes, living out her fantasy of being a torch singer.

Jolene's was a dive on the edge of Harlem's "low-down" district, on 135th and Fifth. It was run through the back door of a grocery store. A body could stroll into that store any night until five in the morning to find Birdie Williams perched on his stool behind the counter. Signs in the window advertised five-pound bags of sugar for twenty-two cents, half a pound of bacon for a dime, and three cans of dog food for thirteen cents. You could also buy a bottle of Pepsi for a nickel, but if you were a regular or knew the right words, Birdie would let you go downstairs, where you could get happy with some hooch. If you thought you could get in because you were a Somebody, then you were wrong. Birdie kept a sling razor ready just to show you how wrong you could be.

When David pushed open the door to the store that night, he found Birdie cleaning his fingernails with the tip of a nasty-looking blade. Birdie looked up and saw David, and a surprised grin spread over his broad face.

"Well, hot damn!" Birdie jumped up and came around the counter. He pumped David's hand and slapped him on the back. "Man, oh man, I ain't seen you since Hannibal was a child. Where the hell you been?"

"Laying low. Taking it easy."

"Shit, I heard you got lost down—"

"That was just talk, man. Just talk."

Birdie perched on the edge of the counter. "Sorry to hear

about your sister. Was a damn shame."

"Thanks."

"Staying long?"

"Just visiting."

David glanced around. He saw nothing but two bags of sugar and a lonesome can of dog food, the sum total of Birdie's efforts at pretending to run a legitimate operation.

"So who's playing tonight?"

"Sweet Lips and his boys. We had Ethel in last night."

"No lie?"

"She just happened by."

"Too bad I missed that."

"Next time, brother. Next time." Birdie went back behind the counter and pulled a long chain connected to a bolt on the back door. "Go on down."

Jolene's was simply a raw cellar behind a door at the bottom of a steep flight of rickety steps. It was as damp and dark as a rotten boat. A wall of smoke greeted David as he entered. The air was heavy with the stink of cheap whisky, sweat, and a busted toilet. But the smooth, bluesy sound of Sweet Lips' sax almost made the stench worthwhile.

David ordered a drink, knocked it back, and grimaced. He hated cheap liquor and this stuff was raw enough to clean a car engine. He glanced around. Half of Harlem was there. About two dozen tables were jammed into the small room; most were crowded with five or six people. The rest of the folks were perched on wire-legged chairs. Guys in silk-striped shirtsleeves and gals in bright dresses with low-cut necklines were laughing and jiving, telling tall tales and smoking reefer. Dancers filled the tiny open space before the band, but it was too crowded for them to do the bump or the mess-around, so they were shuffling in place, dancing on a dime.

"Hey, David," a coarse voice called from behind him.

David turned back to the bar. It was Jolene, Birdie's older brother. Birdie wasn't bad looking, but as Gem once put it,

Jolene was "uglier than a witch's tit." He was short, fat, and bald. He wore a patch over one eye—he'd lost the eye in a knife fight—and his other eye tended to roam, sort of like an eight ball looking for a pocket. You never quite knew if he was really looking at you when you talked to him.

"Birdie told me you was here," Jolene said. "So, what's Mr. Yella Nigger himself doing in my humble gut-bucket?"

"Keeping you humble."

"Well, you can just press the pavement, jack." He reached out and shook David's hand. "Glad to have you back."

David accepted the handshake coolly. He and Jolene had never gotten along. Birdie was all right, but Jolene hated light-skinned Negroes. It was as simple as that and he'd never tried to hide it, so David was surprised at the warm welcome.

Well, people do change, David thought and put the matter out of mind.

Sweet Lips was working with a torch singer that night. She walked out on the floor with great leisure and self-assurance, then stood there with haughty nonchalance and waited. The dancers sat down. The babble of voices subsided. She began her song.

Waiting at home, now
For him to come home.
How long's it been ... since he's been gone?
Watching the nightfall
Hearing my heart call.
I don't know what I'm gonna do, oh Lord
No, I don't know ... what I'm gonna do.

"Sing, Stella! Sing!" the people cried. They tossed wadded dollar bills at her feet and rapped on the tables with glasses to demand more.

"Pretty, ain't she?" said Jolene.

David glanced back at him. Jolene was chomping tobacco and ogling the singer with his one good eye.

"Yeah," David said. "She's pretty. Pretty enough to make a

preacher lay his Bible down."

"Name's Stella." Jolene rolled his cyclopean eye in David's direction. "Now, don't get no ideas, Mr. Yella Nigger. She's mine."

"Is that what she says?"

Jolene spat and a muddy-brown substance flew across the counter. "Don't matter what she says. That little sheba's all mine. You lay a hand on her, I'll slice you open."

David raised his hands in a peaceful gesture. "Hey, I don't want her."

Jolene leaned across the counter. "You insulting my Stella? What the hell you say?"

"I don't want her 'cause she's yours. Should I want her just to give you a reason to 'slice' me up?" David had to smile. If nothing else, Jolene was good for a laugh. "Jolene, you crazy. You know that?"

Jolene gave him an evil look. Then a little smile crept over his hideous face. "Well, you crazy, too, nigger. Playing with me like that."

Stella did a couple more numbers, then the band took over. She sauntered over to the bar and got a drink. Her eyes fell on David and lit up. "Well, lookey, lookey what we got here."

"Nice to meet you, too."

Her forehead dimpled with a frown. "You know, you look mighty familiar, baby."

"Ain't that my line?"

"Seriously. I seen your face before."

"He got a sister," Jolene said. He was looking evil again. "You know her. Gem—"

"You Gem's brother?"

David nodded.

"Well, if that ain't a monkey's uncle. She used to come in here. Liked to sing a song or two."

"Yeah ... But that was years ago."

"Not that long. She was in here last year. Looking mighty

fine, too. She's back in Paris, I hear."

"Paris?"

Stella smiled. "You ain't heard nothing from her, huh? I dig that. Well, I don't know if you're interested, but I was talking to Shug the other day—"

"Shug?"

"Shug Ryan. He blows a pretty mean sax. Shug and Gem used to hang out in Montmartre. He just come back from over there. He mighta seen her."

David wasn't sure he wanted to talk to Shug, but he asked anyway: "Where can I find him?"

"Hell if I know." She shrugged, turned to Jolene, and put her glass down on the bar. "Set me up, babe." Then she glanced at David's empty glass and his sad eyes and smiled. To Jolene, she said: "Gimme the bottle. My friend here and I, we gonna make a night of it."

David saw the look on Jolene's face and Stella saw it, too. David didn't want a fight, but he was too tired and wrung out to care. Stella laughed and flung an arm around Jolene's meaty shoulder, then planted a kiss on his scarred cheek.

"Don't make no trouble," she whispered, "or I'm gonna be gone with the morning light."

Jolene did as he was told.

It was past four in the morning when David left Jolene's, melancholy and drunk. As the lively sounds of Jolene's faded behind him, images of Lilian's room returned. And that curious sensation it had given him of a museum exhibit—staged, detached, sanitized—gripped him once more. He shivered. How he dreaded going back to that house.

A lot's done happened since you been gone.

Stella had invited him to enjoy her hospitality, but while expressing his appreciation, he'd refused. Now, he wondered if that had been wise.

My life, he thought, *is just a series of missed opportunities.*

He only hoped that he'd walked enough, drank enough, smoked enough reefer to exhaust himself. He wanted to sleep like a rock. *No, like a dead man,* he thought, and chuckled at his morbid humor. He made his way back to Strivers' Row. After letting himself in, he managed to hang up his coat and was about to climb the stairs to his room when his gaze fell on the door, *that* door, the one next to the library. He stared at it, like a moth drawn to a flame. One moment, he was standing by the newel post; the next, he was facing the door. His hands hung at his side, balled into fists. Beads of perspiration sprung up on his forehead. His right hand went out. He touched the doorknob ... then hesitated. What would he find behind this door? Indeed, after all these years, what in the world was he looking for? Reconciliation? Peace?

He gripped the knob and twisted it.

It wouldn't budge.

He blinked, confused. Then, taking a deep breath, he gripped it harder, jiggled it and tried to turn it again.

It held fast.

He fell back, baffled. He didn't remember the door ever being locked. Running a hand through his hair, he tried to clear his thoughts.

But, of course. I locked that door the day Daddy died. It's been closed ever since.

He closed his eyes. Suddenly, he was so tired. Here in this empty house, this house that was so full of ghosts and memories, how would he ever find rest? As in a daze, he spread his hands over the door panel and pressed his face against it. The polished dark wood felt cool and smooth. He let his mind drift back ... back through the years to the times when he and his sisters had been summoned to this office, to one particular afternoon in which he alone had been called.

"You're my heir and I expect great things! Great achievements!"

Images from that afternoon flew toward him like slivers of a splintered mirror. He spun around and pressed his back against the door.

"You've been given an edge in life. What've you done with it?"

"I've done my best."

"Your best? Well, your best could've been better!"

David clapped his hands over his ears, but the words echoed inside his head. It had been five years since his father's death. *Five* years. Why hadn't the old man's voice died with him? Why did it live on to haunt him?

You've been given an edge, an edge ... Your best could've been better!

He tore away from the door with a cry and stumbled toward the stairs. On the third step, his strength left him and he sank down. He rested his head against the cool wood of the banisters and closed his eyes.

A lot's done happened, done happened, done happened ... A lot's done happened since you been gone ...

He drew himself up, staggered up the stairs, down the hallway, and into his room. He sagged down onto his bed, still fully clothed, and closed his eyes, exhausted.

But sleep eluded him.

He lay awake, his eyes burning in the dark, and the voices followed him. They came from either side, chanting in a rhythm that threatened to drive him insane.

And always protect ... always protect ... always protect your sisters ... And always (she suffered) ... and always (she suffered) ... (and always) She suffered a bad death ... a bad death.

With a groan, he turned over and punched the pillow. In the morning, he'd ask Annie to tell him the full story of what had gone on in the house.

3. ANNIE'S TALE

"For a good part, the story of Miss Lilian is the story of Miss Gem. You never could mention one without the other. Diff'rent as day and night, but just as connected. Looking back, I some-times wonder whether Miss Gem's return marked the begin-ning of Miss Lilian's end."

Annie placed cream and sugar on the kitchen table, but David decided not to use them. He needed coffee and he needed it black. His head hurt and his eyes were bleary. He hadn't been able to touch the grits, biscuits, and sausages she'd made. He'd called himself seven kinds of fool upon waking. Going to Jolene's had seemed like a good idea last night, but he was sure he'd never do it again. The price in pain was too damn high.

She took a seat opposite him, added a little cream to her cof-fee, and stirred it with an even rhythm. Her voice, as quiet as a coming storm, slowly filled the room.

"Lotsa folks say the trouble started when Miss Gem went back to Europe. I say it began a lot sooner: the moment she ar-rived. From the day that girl stepped foot in this house till the day she left, she ain't meant nothing but trouble. Miss Gem come back for a purpose. I could see that the minute she walked in the door. She had that look in her eye. That look, if you know what I mean. I don't know what she done all them years in Paris, but whatever it was, it sure left her looking lean and hun-gry."

Lean and hungry, David repeated to himself. *Gem was always hungry. Somehow, we all were. Funny about that. Or maybe not so funny when you think about it. That we should be as rich as any colored family needs to be, yet still hungry.*

"It was Halloween," Annie was saying. "Miss Lilian got to the door before me. She didn't even bother to ask who it was. She was expecting a bunch of kids, some trick-or-treaters, I guess. When she saw who it was, she lost her voice. Couldn't find nothing to say.

"Miss Gem stood there like a ghost that everybody's done put out of mind, even if they ain't quite forgotten about it. The wind was at her back—whipping her hair up, like a black cloud. She'd been gone five years—*five years*—but didn't look a day older. Maybe she was a bit thinner, but she still had that smooth, creamy skin. And she had this sable coat, thrown over her shoulders. Wore it like a queen, she did. Rich and sophisticated—like a Eur'pean. Miss Gem knew she was sumptin' to look at. *Knew* it. It was in the way she held herself: just so. And in the way she looked down at Miss Lilian.

"Y'know it's hard to b'lieve that they started out as iden'ical twins. I ain't never seen two women given the same material work so hard to do sumptin' diff'rent with it. 'Course, Miss Lilian was lovely in her way, too. It's just that her way weren't Miss Gem's way."

No...it wasn't, thought David. Lilian also had the slight but shapely build of a dancer and the paradoxical air of being fragile yet strong. She too had the oval face, fawn-colored complexion, and lustrous chestnut hair typical of her family. But Lilian downplayed her looks. Her full lips were sweet and generous, but she was puritan in outlook. She rarely put on makeup. She wore her long hair in a tight bun. And she treated clothes as a pragmatic matter: Fashion was a secondary indulgence. Her outfits were neat, tailored suits; her perfume, clean and light.

"Well, Miss Gem was a-looking at Miss Lillian like a lion on the hunt. Miss Gem threw her head back and laughed. You know how she likes to flash them pretty teeth. Then she teased Miss Lilian. Said: 'Cat got your tongue, sister dear?'

"Miss Lilian asked Miss Gem, just as cool as you please, 'What're you doing here?' Miss Gem didn't like that. She got this funny look on her face and said, 'It's wonderful to see you too, dear.' She took Miss Lilian's face in her hands and kissed her twice, once on each cheek. Lawd, Lawd! You woulda thought Miss Lilian was being clawed, the way she yanked her face back. She looked down at Miss Gem's suitcases—two large ones standing on the doorstep—and Miss Gem caught her.

"'You'd better make up your mind fast,' she said.' The neighbors'll start talking if they see me standing here like this.'

"Well, that did it. You could see Miss Lilian didn't like it, not one bit, but she stepped aside and made for Miss Gem to come in.

"'You ain't changed a bit,' Miss Gem said. 'Still a fool for appearances.'

"Then she put her hand on her hip and strutted on by. Miss Lilian asked Miss Gem what time her ship had got in, but I think she really wanted to ask Miss Gem when her ship was *leaving*. Either way, Miss Gem ignored her. Just gave a little wave of her hand. She stood under the light of the vestibule chand'lier. She coulda been an actress standing in the spotlight. Her face glowed; her eyes sparkled. Miss Gem always did have a flair for the dramatic. She just stood there, quiet-like, looking round. Then she whispered sumptin' about not much having changed. Turned to me, told me it was good to see me. Then she gimme them little pecks on the cheek them Eur'peans pass for kisses. I know they treat the help different over there, but Miss Gem knew she was back in Harlem, where a smart colored woman don't try to lord it over the help."

David smiled at that. Gem knew better than to strut in front of Annie. If anybody in the house could yank Gem's chain it was this old woman. He raised his cup to his lips and took a sip of coffee, enjoying its bitterness. "Did Gem say exactly where she was all those years?"

"Miss Lilian tried to ask her, but Miss Gem just waved her away again. Said she'd tell her all about it later; she just wanted to enjoy being home at first. Said she was dying to look 'round. Wanted to know if her old room was the same. But she didn't even wait for Miss Lilian's answer. Miss Gem went to the foot of the stairs and looked up. She pushed her coat off her shoulders, just let that beautiful coat land in a heap at her feet, then she run on up the stairs, never once looking back. Left me and Miss Lilian standing down here with her luggage on the doorstep, like we was bellhops or sumptin'.

"Miss Lilian turned to me and told me to clean up the downstairs thorough. She grabbed my arm, led me to the parlor, clucking like a worried hen, and pointed out stuff she wanted put away. It didn't take long to see what she was up to: clearing out all signs of a man in the house. That's all it was.

"I said to Miss Lilian: 'You can't keep Mr. Jameson a secret. When you gonna tell her?'

"Her jaw got tense and that look come on her face—you know the one I mean—sort of pained and worried. 'Not now,' she said.

"'You got to tell her sometime,' I said.

"She shook her head. 'Maybe Gem won't stay that long,' she said. 'She might leave before he gets back.' Then, she gimme a hug and told me she'd take the luggage upstairs herself.

"Miss Lilian put off telling Miss Gem about Mr. Jameson for as long as she could. And that was only about a week. She got away with it that long 'cause Mr. Jameson was outta town. Miss Lilian was real careful about not letting Miss Gem into her bedroom neither, where she coulda seen signs of him. But by-and-by, Miss Lilian lost hope that Miss Gem was back for a quick visit. I don't know where she thought Miss Gem might go, seeing as how Miss Gem didn't know nobody in Harlem no more. She'd been away too long.

"Now cain't no woman hide the fact that she got a man living with her. 'Specially when everybody up an' down the street know about it. I don't know who that sister of yours thought she was fooling. But even if nobody hadna said nothing, Miss Gem woulda figured it out all by herself. That woman's got the nose of a cat. She can smell a man hanging round like an alley cat can smell a rat.

"Well, Miss Gem had me and Miss Lilian running 'round, serving her like she was the Queen of Sheba. One night she come back 'round four o'clock in the morning, hissy as a snake. She'd been hanging out at Hayne's Oriental and somebody'd asked her what she thought of her sister's new husband. Naturally, she ain't knowed nothing but nothing about what they was talking about. So, they laid it on thick. I ain't never seen nobody as angry as Miss Gem at that time of morning.

"Well, she woke Miss Lilian. Me, too, for that matter. I was in my room, but I could hear them. I reckon the neighbors heard them too, the way they was carrying on. Miss Gem told Miss Lilian she was a fool.

"'Don't you realize he married you for your money?' she said.

"Miss Lilian said she didn't care.

"'Well, you'd better start,' Miss Gem said. 'Everybody's laughing at you. Everybody knows he ain't no good.'

"Miss Lilian asked Miss Gem, since when did she care what everybody says. 'You never cared before,' Miss Lilian said. 'And for once I don't care neither. Everybody thinks they know he doesn't love me. I know for certain he does.'

"Then they sorta got quiet. Dropped their voices like. And I'm glad they did, 'cause I didn't wanna get involved no way. I don't have no trouble staying outta other people's business. Not that anybody ever asked my opinion. But I'll tell you sumptin': Laying in the dark that night, I got a sense of foreboding, the likes of which I ain't never had b'fore. It sat like a rock, here in my chest."

She wedged her fist tight up under her bosom. "It was fright'ning to lay in bed and listen to them voices. Voices that sounded like the folk they b'longed to was dead. Voices that made you think of ghosts. Ghosts that kept on fighting into the grave."

David shifted uncomfortably. He was a lawyer and lawyers like facts. He didn't like superstition and any reference to it unsettled him. But what unsettled him more, if he were honest, was the way her words echoed inside him. He was frightened all of a sudden, and he wasn't quite sure why.

"What happened next was written on the wall," she said. "Anybody with eyes to see woulda known what was coming."

She picked up her cup and ran a finger over the nicks on its rim.

"Mr. Jameson come home the next day. Miss Lilian was out running errands. Miss Gem come downstairs looking for Miss Lilian and found Miss Lilian's husband instead. He was in the parlor, sorting his mail. Miss Gem stopped short in the parlor doorway. She was wearing a frock, red like cherries. I seen her. We'd just got some new flowers for the vestibule and I was standing there fixing them. I must say she looked very pretty that day, very pretty standing there. She was watching Mr. Jameson, waiting for him to see her.

"He was sitting at your daddy's old writing desk. He didn't notice her at first 'cause he was concentrating on a letter. Had his pipe in his mouth. That man smokes a nice pipe. Uses fine tobacco. Actu'ly, Mr. Jameson's pretty fine hisself. I got to give the devil his due. He's the kinda man every Mama warns her girlchild about.

"Well, I could see Miss Gem just licking her lips. She cleared her throat— real delicate-like but loud 'nough for him to hear. Mr. Jameson looked up, said hello, and went back to his mail. Then he swung his head back 'round again. His eyes liked to pop right outta his head.

"'Lilian, what have you done to yourself?' he said.

"Miss Gem gave him time to take in every pretty detail. Then she sort of floated on in and gave him her hand. Introduced herself, real lady-like. Said it was 'so nice' to meet him, just as sweet as she could be.

"Now, I must say, Mr. Jameson's got the manners of a gentleman. He stood up quick as lightning. And Miss Gem, she broke into a smile as wide as the Mississippi.

"'I *like* tall men,' she said, real soft-like. 'You remind me of Daddy.'

"'Do I, now?'

"'Yes, you do.'

"They shook hands for just a li'l too long, if you know what I mean. Then the front door slammed and they jumped apart. Miss Lilian come in. Fresh as a June breeze. Cheeks all rosy.

She was a-glowing. Didn't have no idea of what was coming at her. But when she saw them two together, she got right pale. Her face got all pinched. She tried to act like it was all right, made a big show of hugging and kissing him. Miss Gem stood by, patient-like, her arms folded cross her chest. She kept her face all pleasant and polite. Miss Lilian wrapped her arms 'round Mr. Jameson's waist. She said she was happy he and Miss Gem had fin'ly met. But she didn't sound happy. And she told Miss Gem it was nice of her to keep Mr. Jameson comp'ny while she was out. Miss Gem said it was no trouble, no trouble at all."

Annie rose from the table and went to the stove. She picked up the coffeepot. "You want some more?" she asked him.

"No." He shook his head. "I've barely touched what I've got." He let her pour herself a cup, then asked: "So, did Miss Gem try to ..." He paused, searching for the words. "Try to, you know ..."

Annie nodded and her lips tensed. That look of knowledge and disapproval once more flitted across her face. She brought her cup to the table and eased back down onto her chair. "Once she'd met him, Miss Gem was real polite to Mr. Jameson. She didn't show nothing of her true feelings. Nothing happened: no fireworks, no nothing. Miss Lilian let out a breath of relief. That was one naive child. I coulda told her it was the quiet b'fore the storm. Miss Gem was just biding her time.

"Oh, she was proper and correct when Miss Lilian was round, but the moment Miss Lilian was outta sight? Hmmm-hm! Miss Gem used to follow Mr. Jameson 'round with her eyes whenever they was in a room together. She'd say li'l cutting things at the dinner table and look over at Mr. Jameson like they was sharing a secret. She'd find a way to touch him, get close to him, every time she saw him. She'd brush up 'gainst his shoulder if they happen to come in a room at the same time. She had sumptin' in mind all right.

"Miss Lilian saw what was going on, but she wouldn't let it

get to her. She did say sumptin' to me. Once. We was in the kitchen. She wanted to know about supplies for a dinner party she was planning. I don't right recall how we got on the subject. Maybe I asked her about the seating. Anyway, she said to make sure Miss Gem's place at the table was as far down from Mr. Jameson's as possible. She musta caught my look, 'cause she turned her eyes away sorta embarrassed. Then, she said, 'I know there's nothing to worry about, Annie. Gem's trying to rile me. She wants to prove that my man's no good. But we not gonna play her game. He's not about to give her the satisfaction, and neither am I.'

"Miss Lilian tried to sound brave, but her voice shook. She weren't nowhere near as confident as she made out to be. She knew Miss Gem wasn't one to give up easy. Now I know lots of women woulda put their sister outta the house. But Miss Lilian wasn't like that. I don't b'lieve it ever crossed her mind. Still, there was a lotta talk going round. Some people said Miss Lilian was a fool. Said she'd invited the fox into the chicken coup, and was working hard on keeping it there. But Miss Lilian said her marriage was her business. And she was *not* gonna let the gossips get their way."

"Why didn't Sweet do something to set Gem straight? Say something?"

"Well, actu'ly, he did. I gotta say he tried. It was about a month later, in late November. Miss Lilian went to a lit'rary conference in Chicago. Mr. Jameson drove her to the train station.

"That morning, I washed the windows, starting with the downstairs, and worked my way up to the second floor. It got to be 'round lunchtime. I was heating up some chowder—I love me some soup, 'specially in the wintertime—and the doorbell rang. It was Miss Gem. She'd gone out and forgotten her key. I let her in. She went on in to the parlor. I went back to the kitchen. I was breaking my last cracker over my soup when I looked up to check the time, and I sees Mr. Jameson's car pulling up to the house. I let Mr. Jameson in, then came on back in here, finished eating, and did the dishes real quick. The wash was next, so I headed upstairs to get the used linen and dirty clothes. I had to go past the parlor. Them doors weren't shut all the way. I couldn't help hearing. Mr. Jameson had joined Miss Gem in the parlor. Now Mr. David, I ain't never eavesdropped before. Ain't never spied on nobody. But that day, sumptin' told me to go on and do it. Soon as I saw them two was in there together, I put my eye to the crack in the door and had me a good look-see.

"Miss Gem had found herself some bootleg liquor and was curled up on the sofa with a glass of it. Mr. Jameson was leaning up 'gainst the fireplace mantel. He was telling her that Miss Lilian had missed her at breakfast. Miss Gem shrugged like she didn't care and said she'd see her sister when she got back. Mr. Jameson didn't like that attitude, didn't like it at all. But he didn't say nothing, just took out his cigarette case and lit a Lucky Strike. He smoked for a li'l while, all the time studying Miss Gem. Finally, he turned round and tapped his ashes in the fireplace. Then he gave Miss Gem sumptin' to think about.

"'I'm only going to say this one time,' he said. 'And one time only. I won't let *anyone* make my Lilian unhappy. I don't intend to make her unhappy myself. She's one of a kind.'

"'She certainly is,' said Miss Gem.

"'I bless the day she married me.'

"'I'm sure you do.'

"Mr. Jameson liked that answer even less, but he let it go. Miss Gem, she grabbed her drink from where she'd put it on the floor and swung her legs down off the sofa. She sallied on over to the table where she'd stashed her bottle, poured herself another drink, and made one for him, too. Then she sort of sidled on over to him and pressed the glass in his hands.

"Why wasn't he smoking his pipe, she wanted to know. Said she liked his pipe. Told him he prob'ly only smoked it to impress women. Well, Mr. Jameson told her that if that was the case, then she'd best take note he wasn't interested in smoking it 'round *her*. Miss Gem gave a little laugh and scolded him for being so direct. Anyway, she said, the only reason he wanted Miss Lilian was the money her daddy left her. She told Mr. Jameson that he and Miss Lilian didn't have nothing in common. Said that *even if he did* want her sister, there weren't no reason why he shouldn't want her more.

"Mr. Jameson took a long, hard look at her. Said she must take him for a fool, but he was gonna have to disappoint her. He loved Miss Lilian, he said.

"'You mean you love her money,' Miss Gem said.

"Mr. Jameson got angry. Said he didn't care what she thought, but she'd better get one thing straight: Couldn't nothing happen—not between her and him, not between him and Miss Lilian—if he didn't say so. He was her sister's husband and she'd better get used to it.

"Then he told her that he understood if she was jealous. Said she had reason to be, since Miss Lilian had 'out-classed' her and all. Miss Gem got so angry, she threw her glass at him. Mr. Jameson stepped aside and the glass broke at his feet. He laughed at her. Well, Miss Gem couldn't take that. She went crazy, tried to hit him, but he caught her.

"'Don't,' he said. 'Don't you ever do that again.'

"He never raised his voice, but you knew he meant business. She told him she didn't never let nobody laugh at her. He lowered her arm and kissed her wrist, real gentle-like. Then he asked, 'Is that better?' Well, it musta been 'cause she got her lazy smile back. She leaned into him. He stroked her face. He cupped her cheeks. Then his grip got tighter. He squeezed so tight it hurt to see. She tried to pull away, but he yanked her back. Then he kissed her. Well, I'm calling it that, but what he done ain't had nothing to do with no affection. She fought him—leastways, at first she did. Pounded him on the chest and such. But then she started to give in. Started to put her arms around him. And the minute she did that, he let her go.

Pushed her away. She fell back, hit the mantelpiece. Mr. David, there was tears in her eyes. That man actually made Miss Gem cry. He got to her. Looked at her with about as much feeling as a butcher's got for meat. Said the only kinda loving he'd ever have for someone like her would be hard and quick—when he wanted it and how he wanted it."

"For *'someone like her'?*"

"Sure 'nough. She swore to him that he'd regret it. He shrugged. Said maybe he would—maybe he wouldn't."

Annie sipped her coffee and was silent, thoughtful. "The strange thing of it is, after a while I got the feeling Miss Gem genuinely cared for him. It started as a game, just to spite Miss Lilian. But then Miss Gem fell for him. Fell hard. She changed after he put her down like that. She started treating Miss Lilian with more respect. No more of them sly looks at him.

"It was just after that, that Miss Gem and Miss Lilian started spending more time together. They'd go on shopping trips. Come back laughing and giggling like they was schoolgirls. I wondered what Miss Gem was up to. Later on, I started to think that maybe she was poisoning Miss Lilian 'gainst Mr. Jameson."

"Why'd you think that?"

Annie looked at him. "'Cause of what happened later."

And just what was that? David wondered. He could try to get Annie to clarify her statement, but why rush her? He'd find out soon enough what she meant. Pressing his fingertips to his eyebrows, he massaged the muscles over the bridge of his nose. Poisoning Lilian against her husband would be something Gem would do. If she couldn't have Sweet, then she'd take away the woman he really wanted—and ruin Lilian's feelings for the man she'd finally found. David looked at Annie and his eyes hurt.

"What then?"

"Miss Gem went out and got herself a man of her own, a West Indian guy. Everybody in the neighborhood was talking about it. They said he was a gangster. Well, you never know now, do you? She brought him 'round here a coupla times.

Seemed like a nice 'nough fellah. Li'l bit older. Quiet. Good to look at. But smooth. Maybe too smooth, when I think about it.

"Everything seemed so nice for a while. Miss Gem and Miss Lilian was getting along. Miss Gem was going out all the time with her fellah. Miss Lilian was busy with her poetry readings. Then, it all fell apart.

"Miss Lilian took ill. Got the tremors. Her hands would start to shaking. She got so she could barely hold a cup. She started complaining about her eyes, too. Said her vision was getting blurry. One minute everything would be fine and clear. The next, she was as blind as a bat in a ray of sunshine. Mr. Jameson took her to the doctor, but the doctor said he couldn't find nothing. Told Miss Lilian it was her nerves. She was working too hard, he said. She'd been taking on extra work since her boss left and she was writing poems, book reviews, and the like. Doctor said she'd have to cut back, go to bed and get some rest.

"Well, she tried. But it didn't do no good. She'd start having nightmares the minute her head hit the pillow. Sometimes, she'd wake up screaming, babbling about voices in the dark. Mr. Jameson, he told the doctor to give her a sleeping potion. But them spells come on her so sudden, nobody knew what to do. And they'd go way quick as they come. One minute, she could see; the next she couldn't. One minute, she was sitting at her desk, typing away; the next, her hands were shaking so bad she couldn't hit the keys. And her heart—she said it'd beat so hard, she thought it was about to jump outta her chest.

"We was all desp'rate, trying to find ways to help her. We was so busy with Miss Lilian, wasn't none of us paying no attention to Miss Gem. She seemed fine enough with her fellah. But then sumptin' went wrong there, too. Folks say he jilted her. I don't know about *that*. I ain't heard nothing about them supposed to be getting married. But he sure 'nough dropped her. They had a big blowup. Right out in public. Everybody was talking about it. She left town right after that. Said she'd had enough of New York. At least, that's what Miss Lilian said. She the one went out there and talked to Miss Gem. Nobody else did."

"When was that?"

"Last year. 'Round this time. Strange how Miss Gem took off: Not a word to nobody. Gone. Into thin air, much the way she came." Annie felt around in her apron pocket, pulled out a small white handkerchief, and blew her nose softly. "After Miss Gem left, Miss Lilian started drinking. Having blackouts. Sometimes she'd lose track of hours. Didn't have no idea where she'd been or what she'd been doing. Leastways, she *said* she didn't know. But I knew. She'd go places when Mr. Jameson wasn't home; come home late at night. I smelled smoke on her clothes and liquor on her breath.

"God forgive me if I'm wrong—but I think it was Miss Gem who got Miss Lilian started down that road. She's the one taught Miss Lilian about smoking and drinking. To this day, I wonder why Miss Lilian listened."

Maybe, he thought, *just maybe Lilian thought she was missing out on life.* He didn't know why he thought that, but something inside him told him it was so.

Bitterness touched Annie's face. "She dropped all her old friends, got right secrety. And she tried to fire me. Me, of all people. After all I done for her. After she'd promised me a place till my dying day. Well, she had to bring me back a week later. Miss Lilian didn't say nothing about why she'd changed her mind. But *he* told me the new girl had burnt a hole in his best shirt. Said he liked a smooth-running house. He was the one told her to fetch me back. She didn't want to do it, but he forced her to."

David's dismay deepened.

She sighed. The tightness around her eyes softened. "It was sad, so sad, how Miss Lilian changed toward the end. Forgetting things and all. Her hair turned white. She was scared of her own shadow. She'd have fits. Tear all her clothes outta her closet. One time she couldn't find a frock she wanted. Mr. Jameson suggested she wear sumptin' else. She got so angry she grabbed up the shears, started ripping her clothes up. Said she hated her clothes, hated her life. Then she looked at *him.* Ran at him with the shears. He caught her just in time. Shook her. Her eyes cleared and she broke down. Started weeping like a baby."

David was by nature a silent man, so he had listened to Annie's account for the most part without interrupting. Now he continued to regard her for some time without speaking. The more she told him, the less he understood. The babble of inner voices seeking answers had only intensified, their questions multiplied. A sliver of pain darted through his head. He rubbed his temples. He was so terribly hung over. He turned his gaze to the window. Vaguely, he noted a rumble of thunder in the distance, like the faint rolling of drums. It was hard to believe what he was hearing about Lilian.

"But what caused it all?"

"Coulda been Miss Gem's up-and-going like that. Mr. Jameson sure didn't seem to know what to do. He said nobody, but nobody, could figure it out. Not none of the doctors, anyway."

"Was she taking medicine?"

"Yes, but I don't r'member no names. Just sumptin' to calm her nerves."

The rain fell suddenly. Fat drops beat a hard ratta-tat-tat against the windowpanes. The only light in the kitchen came from the soft pearl gray of the storm clouds outside. They could have been sitting in a small, shadowed cave.

Inwardly, he shuddered. *Lilian, dear Lilian. How was it possible?* Leaning on the table, he rubbed his eyes. *A lot's done happened since you been gone.* He groaned. *Yes, it had.*

Some two years ago, in April 1924, Lilian had impetuously married a virtual stranger, moving with amazing alacrity. That same year, Gem returned. She was at the house for roughly five months, before suddenly, inexplicably, taking off again. Lilian had written him for a whole year without once mentioning either her new husband or Gem's return. She had lied to him by omission, and betrayed Annie's trust by trying to fire her.

That wasn't Lilian's way. It wasn't her way at all.

He'd been so grateful for the bits of news she was sending him that he hadn't noticed what she was leaving out.

Now that's a lie.

The truth was, he'd sensed that something was wrong. Sensed it. And when the letters stopped, he could've asked why—

But I was too busy hiding my own damn secret.

He raised his head. Now he knew that Lilian had had her secrets, too.

But why hide her marriage and Gem's return? Why not write and say she was ill? It was unlike her to be so secretive. Perhaps she didn't want me to worry.

That would have been like her: self-sacrificing, determined to resolve her problems alone. Only Lilian had remained loyal to herself, to her home, to their father's vision of what it meant to be a David. Only she had really tried. He had more in common with Gem than he wanted to admit. They'd both become wanderers. Both had rejected their upbringing and tried to reinvent themselves.

But he was ashamed of his new identity. He lived in a personal hell of his own creation—and from what Annie said, he suspected that Gem did, too.

He could imagine Lilian's shock when she opened the door and found Gem standing on the family doorstep. They hadn't heard anything from Gem since December of 21, when she'd sent a postcard from Paris after six months of silence. At the time, they'd wondered whether she was paving the way toward asking for more funds, but as far as he knew, nothing more had been heard from her. Not before that Halloween night.

Gem's return meant that her money was gone. She had set sail for home and the one sure touch for easy cash. But someone had gotten to the till before her: a watchful husband. Gem might have figured that it would be difficult to manipulate Lilian, but easy to seduce Sweet. She had never had to do more than crook her finger to make a man come running. But Sweet was different. He had refused to budge. For once, Lilian had it all: the man and the money.

Sister Gem was down on her luck. Is that why she hightailed it back to Europe?

Perhaps. But it was unlike Gem to give up easily. Especially when it came to men and money. He would've expected her to make another play for Sweet. Instead, she had reconciled with Lilian. That was surprising.

But then she left, although she knew that Lilian was ill. Now that was not surprising, not surprising at all. And her silence since Lilian's death, it fit her pattern also.

He resented Gem's absence, but he was relieved by it, too. He preferred to handle this matter alone. She might have been able to help him, but he doubted she would have been willing to. She might have been the only one, other than Annie and Sweet, who could help him understand why Lilian died. But Gem knew how to set his teeth on edge and enjoyed doing so. She was fickle and unreliable, two qualities he despised. She had an easy charm he found suspect. She had never once thought about pleasing anyone but herself. And she had nothing but contempt for her family.

Had Lilian given Gem money to go away? Not exactly paid her off, but ... Gem must've gotten the money from someone. From whom else, but Lilian?

"I wasn't in the house when she did it," Annie was saying. "She told me she was going to stay with friends for the weekend. Said she'd be back Monday afternoon. That's when Mr. Jameson was supposed to be back, too. So I went and visited my nephew. I'll wish to the day I die that I'd stayed here. She musta done it sitting on her bed. The mattress was soaked. Blood everywhere. On the walls, the bed canopy, the floor. Pools of blood. Dried hard, dried black. I don't remember much more. She was wearing a white gown, I think. Or it had been white. And she was sitting under the window, looking up to Heaven. Her eyes, those beautiful sweet eyes, was wide open. And she had these deep cuts, one in each wrist. I'll never forget that. All it took was them two wounds, just them two wounds, and Miss Lilian's life poured out."

4. LILIAN'S GRAVE

She was buried in a municipal cemetery at least an hour's drive away in Brooklyn, amid a sea of white and gray headstones. Standing at Lilian's graveside, David gazed out over the memorial park.

She was never fond of Brooklyn. Except for Coney Island, she had no use for the place. That she should end up here, of all places, here ...

"It was the only place Mr. Jameson could find for her," Annie had told him. "It's a shame Miss Lilian couldna been buried in consecrated ground, closer to home."

It's a shame she's here at all.

Crouching down by the grave, he reached out to touch the hard mound of earth. Slowly, his hands balled into fists. It was such a struggle to believe that Lilian—gentle, proud, and deeply religious—would take her own life. *What brought you down, little sister? What brought you down?*

A breeze, unseasonably warm and gentle, caressed his hair. His nostrils caught a faint whiff of perfume, lightly sweet and powdery. He imagined he heard her voice.

Remember me, she seemed to say. *Forget what others tell you. Remember me, as you knew me.*

He'd been five years old when Lilian was born. From the moment he laid eyes on her, he'd given her his heart. His parents were touched and amused, but perplexed by his singular affection for Lilian. She was a twin. Why did he love her more than Gem, who was as sweet and huggable as her sister? How could he, as small as he was, even tell the two tiny girls apart? He shrugged— he didn't know. He simply never mistook one for the other.

Snatches of memories floated to the surface of his mind. Images of life with Lilian: holding her up in the shallow end of the public swimming pool as she splashed about; stealing chocolate chip cookies for her from Annie's kitchen; standing side-by-side at their mother's graveside. They had been so close. How could he have let four years go by without seeing her?

The last time he *had* seen her, she had been conscientiously teaching English to bored high school students. It was her way of living up to their parents' edict of giving back to the community. He had visited her classroom one day and, quite honestly, found her a tedious, uninspiring teacher. He had come away wondering whom he should feel sorrier for, Lilian or her students. He thought her effort misdirected, but he admired her for it just the same. During summer breaks, Lilian would escape to Provence. She had friends there who rented her a small cottage. She wrote during those summers, but she seemed to have given up any hopes of a serious literary career.

Then her situation changed.

From Lilian's letters, he knew that she had met Helga Bennett during one of those summers in southern France. Bennett was just launching the *Black Arrow,* which was to be not only a literary journal, but also the official voice of the Movement. Bennett was so impressed with Lilian that she invited her to join the staff. She became Lilian's mentor, but was herself inspired by Lilian's enthusiasm and vision. They both dreamed of a day when Harlem artists would receive the same recognition, prizes, and contracts that white writers did. Lilian wanted to read books about her people, written by her people. By that she meant books about well-bred, refined colored people. There was, she said, enough being written about the downside of Negro life, about the crime and the poverty. Someone had to tell the story of the educated colored people, too. Someone had to speak up for the Negroes who were doctors, lawyers, philosophers, professors.

"We live as a minority within a minority," she once wrote him. "It's time our voice was heard. That would advance the cause of the entire race."

By the time of her death, Lilian was a senior staffer at the *Black Arrow* and making her own mark as an author. The Nubian Art Players had performed her unstructured play, *Shadowlands,* the year before. She had written one novel and was working on another when death claimed her. Her first book, *Lucifer's Parlor,* was a social statement about Irish and Negro life in the Tenderloin. Her second work, *Lyrics of a Blackbird,* dealt with betrayal in a genteel Harlem family. Her first book was well received. He was confident her second one would have been, too.

Someone had placed fresh roses near her headstone. The flowers were a pleasing soft shade of pink. He brushed them with his fingertips. The blooms were stiff in the cold air. They would discolor and shrivel soon. He closed his eyes. The pain in his head had become a steady pulse. There was again that breeze from nowhere. He blinked and looked up at the sky, but saw nothing there. No miraculous face in the clouds, not even a sudden ray of sunshine to ease the bleakness of the day. What had he hoped for? Leaning forward, he examined the farewell on Lilian's gravestone, mouthing the words.

"Lilian McKay Sweet, 1897-1926. To my Lilian, I will miss you."

He assumed that Lilian's husband had written the words. Sitting back on his heels, he wondered. *Who indeed was Jameson Sweet?*

5. The Book of Rachel

When David returned home, he found Annie sitting at the kitchen table. She had a nearly empty bag of string beans to the left and a big pot of beans and water to the right. She grabbed up several beans from the bag, lined their ends up, and snapped their tips off with a smooth twist of her wrist—*blat-blat-blat*. She tossed the last of the beans into the pot and dropped the tips onto some newspaper sheets.

"How was it?" she asked.

"Fine. It's not a bad place, that cemetery. Just far from home."

She nodded. "Too far."

She shoved her chair back and stood up, wiping her hands on her apron. Then she rolled up the newspaper, put it into the bag, and set it aside for garbage.

"I'll just let these soak for a while," she said, putting the pot of beans on the stove. "Sit down. Rest your feet. You left without eating breakfast this morning. I just made some coffee and I baked a pie, apple, 'cause I knows that's your favorite."

"Oh, Annie, I—"

"It ain't no trouble. That's what I'm here for, to take care you." She wiped up the table and motioned for him to take a seat. He did. She took down a plate and fork and poured him a cup of coffee. "Before I forget, Miss Rachel stopped by to see you last night."

He bit back his surprise and forced a smile. "How'd she know I was back?"

"Oh, everybody know you back, Mr. David. Everybody know that."

He kept his smile plastered in place.

She fetched the pie, set it on the table, and served him a healthy slice. "Miss Rachel helped me nurse Miss Lilian when she was sick."

"Did she, now?" He picked up his fork. "What did she say?"

"That she wants to see you."

Keeping his face devoid of expression, he reached for his cup and took a sip. A question hovered on the tip of his tongue. "Did she ever marry?"

Annie looked at him. "No, Mr. David. She never did."

He flushed at the knowledge in her eyes. Mercifully, she left him, saying she had shopping to do. Alone, he drained the coffeepot. But, although it was delicious, he barely tasted the pie. One name echoed in his mind.

Rachel.

She lived in a tenement building on 130th Street, on Harlem's southern edge, in an area called "Darktown," presumably because it had been an area for black residency since the 1890s, when the rest of Harlem was still white. It was a crowded building. Most of the apartments were filled beyond capacity. She was the only resident who could afford the luxury of living in her apartment alone.

She sat on the couch near her parlor window, a small, delicately slim creature in a warm tailored frock. Flipping the pages of a thin photo album, she studied the photos one by one. Pictures of her and the McKay children: of her and Lilian; of her and David; of her, Lilian, and Gem. Studio photos taken over time, paid for by the McKays.

The friendship between the McKays and the Hamiltons went back some twenty years, when both were living in the Tenderloin. The two families had lived only blocks apart. They attended the same church and Rachel went to the same school as the McKay children. Rachel spent many afternoons after school playing with Gem and Lilian. Her mother worked. Mrs. McKay was at home. The arrangement was practical.

No one thought of long-range consequences.

Like the McKays, the Hamiltons started out poor. Unlike them, the Hamiltons stayed that way. While Augustus McKay, a waiter, sunk every extra dime he had into real estate, his buddy Bill Hamilton, a better-earning mortician, drank and gambled away his dollars. Augustus's fortunes took a decided upswing in 1907 when the Pennsylvania Railroad purchased some of his Seventh Avenue property for more than one hundred thousand dollars. Three years later, in 1910, when the twins were four-teen and David nineteen, the McKays left the miserable, over-crowded Tenderloin and bought property on West 134th Street, joining other prominent blacks in Harlem. It took the Hamiltons, now consisting only of Rachel and her mother, an-other nine years to achieve the move uptown, and when they did, it was to squeeze into a grimy four-room apartment on West 130th Street with four other families. By then, David was back from the war and the McKays were on the move again, too—this time, into their home on Strivers' Row. Over the next few years, the McKay property would rapidly rise in value, and the building housing the Hamiltons would just as decidedly decline.

Despite the economic fissure dividing the McKays and the Hamiltons, the friendship that began in the Tenderloin en-dured. Rachel remained one of the few people outside the McKay family who could tell the twins apart. For nine years, she doggedly made the trip uptown to visit Lilian. The instant affec-tion she'd felt for Lilian in the first grade deepened, as did the instant antipathy she'd felt toward Gem. As for her feelings for David, they were clear even to the blind.

Rachel closed the picture album with an air of finality and put it back on her bookshelf. She looked at her clock. How would he react to her message? Would he come by to see her? Going to her dresser, she eased out the top drawer and dug out a hand mirror. She had spent the better part of the morning preparing for his hoped-for visit. She had marcelled her hair and put on her best dress. It was a cream creation called "cham-pagne beige." She had bought it from a "hot" man. People said hot men sold stolen goods. Rachel neither asked nor cared. Like most Harlem women who bought from hot men, she spent little mental energy on the ethics of buying possibly pilfered mer-chandise. If she thought about it at all, she shrugged and said the stores priced the clothes too high anyway, so if something "fell off the truck" or was "rescued from a warehouse," it was a way of robbing the rich to give to the poor. What she did know, and knew for sure, was that hot men enabled her to dress well and inexpensively. Her earnings were meager as a nurse at Harlem Hospital.

Rachel regarded what little she could see of herself in the mirror coolly, looking for the person she imagined and hoped David would find. Her short hair was groomed using Madame C. J. Walker's products. Her fingernails were scrubbed and meticulously self-manicured.

Some Georgia plantation owner had passed down vivid green eyes. Otherwise, Rachel's dark-skinned African forebears had prevailed. Her charcoal complexion unmistakably marked her as one of their own. She knew that people often murmured that she would have been quite pretty if she were not so black, but they raved over her eyes.

Rachel often wondered how an emblem of sexual and racial degradation had become a badge of honor. It was perverse to idolize the legacy of a white slave-owner's lust. But all rational analysis aside, Rachel loved her jade eyes, too. Her sooty complexion was another matter.

She knew the frustration that compelled some dark-skinned women to try to lighten their complexions. Her friends went from slathering their faces with bleaching creams to swallowing arsenic wafers. She scorned such solutions. She knew they weren't effective; her pride would've kept her from using them even if they were. Unlike her friends, Rachel didn't blindly worship light skin, but she did see the practical advantages of having it. If she caught herself wishing she'd been born with beige skin, it wasn't necessarily because she found it beautiful but convenient. "Whiter" meant "righter" in the world she knew.

Take the McKays. Their buttermilk beauty added much to their prestige. Even during the Tenderloin days, the McKays seemed set apart. They were admired and envied. Invitations to their home were rare and highly coveted. Everywhere they went, they were warmly received.

Once upon a time, she dreamed of becoming a David. She had loved David since they were children, but she'd never dared hope for his love in return. Four years ago, it seemed as though he had fallen in love with her. They'd met secretly. She'd given him her heart, her body. She'd trusted him completely. Then one day he had gone away, on Movement business, and failed to return.

Desperate, Rachel went to see an old West Indian conjure woman and paid her some hard-earned cash. The woman told her to take a pair of David's shoes and sprinkle a little "come on home powder" on top of the toes. If he'd gone south, then she should swing the shoes around and set them down with the toes pointing north.

"He'll be back in seven days, honey."

Rachel had a time getting a hold of David's bedroom slippers—that's all he'd left behind—but she managed to do it. She sprinkled the slippers generously and followed the conjure woman's instructions to the letter.

"But it didn't help. He didn't come back," Rachel complained, returning to the woman.

"Well, somebody somewhere is working mo' powerful magic than you."

The old woman chuckled and shut the door in her face. Rachel was nearly broke, but she cared little about the money. She wanted David back.

Now he was again in Harlem. She shook her head at her earlier foolish fantasies. She wouldn't make the same mistake twice. Life had taught her hard and bitter lessons. It simply didn't pay to be naive.

David climbed the steps to Rachel's building uneasily. As Lilian's best friend, she could probably help him, but would she be willing to? What had his disappearance meant to her? They had been young. He could barely remember the person he'd been when he'd last seen her. The life he'd led, the pain he'd felt and witnessed since then, had changed him irrevocably. Rachel represented a life he had been forced to leave behind. Surely, she must see that neither of them could take their love affair seriously. That it was better to consign it to the brief but intense passions of youth. That it was better not to ask whether it could have endured.

He carried a bouquet of pale pink roses, difficult to find that time of year and expensive. After a moment's hesitation, he rang her bell and went in the building's entrance. He found her second-floor apartment easily and had just raised his hand to knock when the door was yanked open. His breath caught at the sight of her. She had changed.

She was still very pretty, but so thin. Gray circles ringed her eyes and faint hollows touched her cheeks. The years had added an air of fragility. Something inside him fluttered and his vision of her reverted to what it once was. No longer was she the woman he had abandoned, with all the guilt that entailed. She was, first and foremost, a dear friend. And he had missed her. Suddenly, he was glad, very glad, that he had come. Her face broke into a heart-wrenching smile and she threw her slender arms around him.

"I'm so sorry about Lilian," she whispered.

Seated on her sofa, the two them shared a warm drink and homemade apple betty. Rachel had displayed his flowers prominently in a vase on her coffee table. Glancing around, David admired the soothing atmosphere of her apartment. She had chosen her furniture with an eye for comfort as well as beauty. He saw too that she had been influenced by his mother's tastes, but discerned that she had adapted them to fit her own personality. How could Rachel live so well on a nurse's salary? Smiling gently, he told her that he was glad to see her. He'd heard that she'd gone away.

"I had to come back," she said. "Two years ago. I had to. Just like you."

His smile faltered. "It's not the same. You came back because you wanted to. I returned because I had to. Lilian's death is the only reason I'm here."

He saw the flash of pain in her eyes and instantly regretted his words. She knew he had not come back because of her. No need to remind her. Once again, his eyes went over her. The bleakness in her gaze; the sag in her shoulders: What had happened to her? He started to ask, then stopped. If he inquired about her last four years, she might inquire about his.

She asked if he planned to move back into the house. Her voice was full of hopeful expectation, but when he shook his head, she seemed more relieved than disappointed. "So you'll be selling your half to Sweet?"

"I don't see why I should."

"But if you don't want to live there—"

"That house was Daddy's pride. I'm not giving it up."

"I see."

Did she? He'd never been able to fully read Rachel.

She gazed down thoughtfully at her small, neat hands, which lay folded in her lap. "So how long *will* you be staying?"

"Not long."

She gave him a long, intent look. Behind her beautiful eyes battled love and pride. "And there's no way you can move back?"

"No way at all. As soon as I'm done, I'm catching the first thing smoking."

The forced casualness sounded false even to his own ears. Her face took on a set expression. He was reminded that Rachel had a firmness of character that was startling in one who looked so frail. She could express herself in cool, precise terms when she wanted to. When she raised her chin, he knew what was coming.

"If Lilian's the *only* reason you're back, you might as well leave right now. You can't change what happened."

"I have to know why she did it."

"You never will—"

"I have to try to understand."

"Or try to ease your conscience?"

Her remark stung, as he knew it was meant to. He felt himself grow warm.

"Thank you," he said, "for putting it so succinctly."

Her expression softened. "I'm not judging you, but that don't mean I got to help you deny the truth neither."

"I'm not asking you to."

"Aren't you?"

He smiled grimly. "Perhaps you're right. But I didn't come here to talk about myself."

"Who then?"

"Lilian's husband." His eyes traced her lovely profile. "Do you know him?"

"He's a good man. Kind. Loyal." Her eyes flickered over him. "The kind of man a woman can depend on."

He ignored that. "So he loved her?"

She nodded.

"Treated her right?

"You mean ... did he treat her better than you treated me?"

Their eyes locked.

"You don't give a man a break, do you?"

"Only when he deserves one."

Utter silence.

"Rachel, I know I hurt you," he said huskily. "I never intended to."

"Then why did you?"

He regarded her with regret. How could he answer? What could he say? As always, when words failed him, he found another way of communicating. Without thinking, he reached for her. He put his arms around her and hugged her. She resisted for a moment and then put her arms around him, too. They clung to one another. Her cheap perfume, acrid yet seductive, enveloped him. She had worn the same scent when he'd last seen her. He paused in his thoughts, remembering.

Life was much simpler then. We were both so hopeful.

"I'm sorry," he whispered. "More sorry than you'll ever know."

"But why? Why'd you stay away so long?"

"Don't ask," he said. "I can't answer."

She pulled away. He reached out to caress her cheek but she averted her face, then turned back to gaze at him with suspicion. Taking his left hand, she laid it on top of her own and studied it. She turned it this way and that, with the air of a gypsy fortune-teller. With her fingertips, she stroked his palm and traced a line along his fourth finger. She found no traces of a wedding ring, but still she asked: "Who is she?"

"I've stayed alone."

She searched his face with wide, clear eyes that not only sought the truth of his feelings, but also revealed her own. He had the momentary illusion that if he peered into her eyes, long enough, deeply enough, he would learn all there was to know about her. But then, he asked again about Lilian, and the illusion died. Rachel's face clouded over; her lovely eyes became dim.

"There's nothing to tell. Lilian just got sick. That's all. She just … got sick."

"I can't accept that. There's more. There's got to be."

"David, I know you feel bad, but you can't start chasing demons. Listen," she said with a rush of feeling. "Sweet was always here for Lilian. She had herself a good man." A trace of bitterness crept into her tone. "It's okay if you were out there having a good time, baby, 'cause believe me, at the end, she didn't even know you were gone."

"You're not being fair," he said and felt like an idiot saying it.

"Well, neither are you."

Her eyes challenged him and he started to respond, but then something happened: He remembered how much he'd enjoyed her peppery temper. After a moment, he laughed gently and conceded. "You're right."

She looked at him. Then her anger faded as quickly as it had come. A smile came to her lips, too. "You hungry?"

He nodded.

"C'mon, then. Let's have lunch."

He helped her set the table and noticed the floral design on her china. It was familiar. "These were my mother's dishes. Her everyday service."

"I always liked them. After your daddy died, I asked about them. Lilian said I could have them. She didn't mind and Gem didn't care. Don't you remember?"

He didn't, but it mattered little. The dishes and the silverware she gave him to lay next to it conveyed a feeling of comfort. The tension between them eased. As she worked to prepare the meal, she exuded an air of serenity. She had the face of an ebony Madonna: gentle and sweet, but solemn. He noted the calming beauty of her dress. She seemed at peace with herself. He envied her.

The air of contentment that filled her kitchen as she cooked stayed with them. They left the topic that had brought him to see her and spoke of pleasant matters. She had seen a new exhibit of sculpture by Meta Warrick Fuller. Fuller's work was brilliant. Did he know that Fuller, a black woman, had actually studied in Paris with Rodin?

When given free rein to choose her topic, Rachel made a spirited conversationalist. Her inquisitive mind had refused to accept the limitations of her formal training and sought to expand itself. She was well read. Her knowledge of contemporary literature, philosophy, and art was more than adequate for intelligent discussion. She also had a spicy wit that cut through pretension and hypocrisy.

He looked at her laughing face and wondered, *What would've happened if I had returned?* But there was no point in thinking about it. Whatever chance they might have had was long gone. His fall from grace when he decided to stay away four years ago would be nothing compared to the condemnation he would suffer if she knew *why* he had stayed away.

And was it wise to visit her, speak with her, to sit in her kitchen and share her meal? His visit was meant to heal old wounds, not inflict new ones. He needed her forgiveness. For his sake, as well as hers. He would have to leave Harlem within twenty-four hours. The moment he clarified a few questions about Lilian's death and settled matters concerning the house with Sweet, he would board a train and speed back to the life he had built in Philadelphia.

That life was simple. It was lonely but not entirely dissatisfying. As a lawyer, he helped people. He lived modestly so he could afford destitute clients, those who might not have had a chance otherwise. He was extremely effective as a criminal defense attorney. In fact, he had made a name for himself, not as a defender of lost causes, but as an honest man who could make things happen.

His work had become his penance. Guilt drove him during the day and exhaustion put him to sleep at night. A successful court decision helped to assuage his shame, but never fully lifted it. Success also fueled his anxiety. He dreaded newspaper coverage that might bring him attention. So he always sought the small cases, the ones no one wanted to be bothered with. But too often, a case would take a twist that lent it unexpected significance. When this happened and reporters knocked on his door, he would bar himself in his small one-man office. He would think of home. He would dream of seeing Lilian and Rachel and Annie.

On Christmas Eve 1922, deeply homesick, he had written to Lilian and mailed the letter before he could change his mind. She had quickly answered. A correspondence gradually developed, sporadic and hesitant on his side, consistent and faithful on hers. After a few months, he suspected that she knew why he was staying away and what he was doing. In time, he became certain she did. But she never once criticized him nor did she pry. Her letters expressed love and gentle curiosity. Her tactful

avoidance of issues that might have pained him convinced him
that she understood and accepted his way.

Lilian was the only person with whom he had been honest,
and that was because she had never forced him to lie. He could
not expect that of Annie or Rachel. Their grief over Lilian's
death and relief over his return had temporarily abated their
inquisitiveness, but it would return if he stayed too long. He
would have to leave in order to retain their respect and affection.
He was convinced of it.

In the meantime, he meant to make the most of his short
visit by finding out everything he could about Lilian's last
months. Looking at Rachel, he thought he understood her reluctance to discuss Lilian's illness. It was, after all, an unpleasant
subject. But surely she must understand his need to know what
had happened.

"Lilian used to write me," he said, "telling me all the goings-
on."

Rachel dabbed at the corner of her mouth with her napkin.
"Did she mention me?"

"Once. She said you'd moved away."

"Is that all?"

He nodded.

Rachel picked at her food. "You know, Lilian and me . ..
well, we sorta had a falling-out. It was more on her side, really.
She dropped me. From one moment to the next."

"But you two were like a married couple."

"Yes, maybe. But Lilian did drop me. She threw her sticks
in with Gem." Rachel gave a rueful little laugh.

David laid down his fork. "Actually, Annie did say something about that. But it's hard to believe."

"Well, believe it. Somehow, Gem got Lilian to trust her. It
started with them going out all the time, shopping together. By
the time Gem left, she could get Lilian to do just about whatever
she wanted her to. Even quit her job."

David looked stunned. "But that job at the *Black Arrow*

meant the world to her."

"Lilian said her doctor had told her to quit, too. But she didn't quit when *he* told her to. She quit when *Gem* told her to. Lilian said she could use the time to work on her book. Well, I didn't trust Gem. She never wanted to help nobody. So, I went to see Lilian. I tried to tell her that Gem was probably up to something, but Lilian wouldn't listen. It wasn't none of my business, she said. She wouldn't talk to me after that. Ignored me when she saw me at the poetry meetings."

If anyone other than Rachel had been telling him this, he wouldn't have believed her. But Rachel and Lilian had been like sisters for years. Rachel loved Lilian more than Gem ever loved her, and he knew Rachel would never lie. It hurt to think that Lilian had betrayed their friendship in favor of Gem. "Betray" was perhaps too harsh a word. Gem, after all, was Lilian's sister, her flesh and blood, and it was fine if Gem wanted to be close to Lilian, to repair their relationship. But she never should've done it at the cost of Lilian's friendship with Rachel. She never should've forced Lilian to make that choice. And Lilian should've refused to make it.

"Months went by when I didn't see her," Rachel said. "Then, in the fall, Sweet sent for me. Wanted me to help Annie nurse her, just till he found somebody regular. I got to admit, I wasn't too keen on going over there at first, seeing how she'd treated me, but then we'd been friends for so long ... and Sweet was so worried. It scared me when I saw her. She wasn't the same, David. You wouldn't have recognized her."

"Annie said the doctors could never figure out what was wrong with her."

Rachel hesitated, then said, "I'm sorry, David, but they did mention schizophrenia."

Schizophrenia. He turned that over. It was one explanation. Naturally, it didn't make him happy, but—

"Okay, you say you didn't see her for months, but somebody else must've seen her, talked to her. You knew Lilian's other friends."

"I don't run in them circles. Rats and dicties don't mix. What's between the Hamiltons and the McKays is special."

"Yes, it is." He took her hands in his. "But what about the poetry meetings at the library? That was common ground."

"Lilian dropped out. Cut off everybody. The folks who saw her on the street said she was like ice. Told them she'd never liked their work. She said she'd had her fun with the literary crowd. Now she was into a better class of people. Turns out, she'd taken up with some rich ofay. You know the kind. A 'Negrotarian,' as Zora Neale would say."

David's dark eyes widened. Anthropologist Zora Neale Hurston had coined the term "Negrotarian." It reflected the cynicism of black artists who were mildly uneasy with or outright distrusted the motives of their white patrons. Some Negrotarians were devoted philanthropists; others merely sought the thrill of being trendy. Some were members of that spiritually Lost Generation—they stopped off in Harlem on their way to Paris. The more profit-oriented Negrotarians looked at blacks and saw green: They calculated money when investing in art, literature, and entertainment with fashionable African-American themes.

"So, who was Lilian involved with?"

"A woman named Nella Harding. Ever heard of her?"

He thought for a moment. Then it came to him. But if that was the woman, then—

That must've been one odd friendship.

Nella Harding, the Nella Harding he was thinking about, was the kind of person to have attracted Gem—and repelled Lilian.

"What was Lilian doing with somebody like that?"

From Rachel's expression, he could tell that she thought him naive.

"Listen," she said, "a lot of Negro writers would like to ignore Nella, but she's got Mister Charlie's ear. She's got what they call 'influence.' Big time. She can open doors with a phone call. Even someone like Lilian, who had money and connections, has to kneel before Mister Charlie, sometime. Don't you see? The jigs have got to try to use the Nellas of the world, but ain't none of us stupid. We all know that they're using us, too."

6. NELLA'S PARTY

Nella Harding's latest proud product was a prime example of what Rachel meant. *Ebony Eden* was supposedly based on Nella's experiences in Negro Harlem and it was a best-seller. Everyone was talking about it, but few would admit to having read it. The book's plot was simplistic and rudimentary: A cabaret singer falls in love with a jazz musician, only to see him constantly betray her with other women. One night, in a fit of drunken jealousy, she shoots her lover and his friend, and then turns the gun on herself.

Not a single critic, black or white, deemed the book to be of literary value. One newspaper dismissed it as "cheap romance, colored cafe-au-lait." But stores couldn't stock it fast enough to keep customers happy. One of New York's culturati had written a book, and what a book! It promised to tell all about a secret and deliciously sinful Negro world. Sales went over the top.

Blacks denounced Nella as a literary voyeur. Some accused her of having exploited the Harlemites who trusted her in order to swell her pocketbook. The more generous Nella said had tried to serve two masters at once: She had pandered to the lurid curiosity of her white readers and to the ethnic pride of her black ones.

David had read the book. His judicial mind noted that *Ebony Eden* did take in High Harlem, with its genteel brownstones and polished grammar. The book's characters were distilled caricatures of Harlem's more colorful figures. Nella even took a poke at her fellow whites: Her husband, Nikki, appeared thinly camouflaged as a white missionary who was "astounded to discover jungle bunnies" who debated contemporary German literature, were intimately acquainted with Dadaism, Kandinsky, and Bauhaus realism, and were multilingual and widely traveled. But David quickly perceived that what Nella viewed as positive in blacks was what she saw as "primitive," and that this is what she emphasized. Nella depicted a black world characterized by rapacious lust, primordial superstition, and impenetrable stupidity. David found the book worse than insulting—it was demeaning. He could understand, however, why white critics found it fascinating.

"As propaganda for the so-called 'New Negro,' the book speaks volumes," said one.

"Volumes of nonsense," said the Negro press. "For us colored, *Ebony Eden* is the equivalent of taking one small step forward and two giant steps back."

Despite the uproar over *Ebony Eden,* or in some corners because of it, Nella remained Harlem's most welcome "Nordic." With her decided gift for always being at the right place at the right time, her penetrating presence was hard to avoid. She and Nikki had become point men for fashionable white America's fascination with black Harlem. They regularly escorted wide-eyed visitors to speakeasies, rent parties, and cabarets. The Hardings liked having Harlem come to them, too. Their "mixed" parties—long, languid, liquored evenings where black artists mingled with white society—were the talk of the town. The Hardings were giving a bash at their house in the Hamptons that evening. When the operator put through David's call to Nella that day, she told him to join in.

"I'd prefer to speak to you alone," he said.

"So would everyone." She laughed. "Just come and we'll see what we can do."

As David stood before the Hardings' imposing front door that Saturday evening, unease weighed like bad cooking in his belly. He was running a risk by showing up at such a trendy gathering. Suppose someone from the Movement was there? There could be questions.

But he had to talk to Nella about Lilian. That overrode every other consideration.

Squaring his shoulders, he pressed the doorbell. A chime rang deep within the house. Within seconds, a butler opened the door and ushered him in with a gracious bow.

David stepped into a spacious entryway softly lit by clusters of small gilded sconces. There was a high, wide arch at the other end ... waves of warmth from human bodies gathered together ... voices raised in hilarity ... the babble of excited chatter.

He took a deep breath.

The butler eased David out of his coat and led him through the archway to the salon. David paused on the threshold.

To have said the room was overdone would have been kind.

It was huge, at least three times as large as the McKays'. And whereas the McKays' was restrained, tranquil, and patrician, this one was grand, golden, and glittering. The walls were covered with brocaded ice-white silk framed by slender gilded moldings. The same silk hung in deep folds at the ceiling-high windows, and it was drawn back to reveal gold lining and a trim of gold braid. Padded sofas and fat cushions, all upholstered in white with gold brocade, were placed about the room. Small table lamps with diamond tears dripping from the shades provided soft highlights and threw shadows over other corners of the room. The white, the touches of gold, and the sparkling lamps made all the perfectly tailored tuxedos and perfectly styled frocks seem even more perfectly sophisticated.

One-quarter of the people wearing those tuxedos and frocks were well-heeled blacks, easily recognizable from the theater world. The rest were whites: socialites, local politicians, and Harlem club owners.

Negrotarians, thought David, *a whole room of them, gathered under Nella's roof.*

The Hardings had decorated their party with Negro artists

who were the darlings of every critic's pen. The actress Selena Ashburn, who boasted that she could drink any man under the table, stood holding an empty flute glass in one hand and a plate of appetizers in the other. Roland Pierce, the fabled jazz musician, was talking to friends in one corner. The poet Julian Woodstock was telling a joke in another. His group also included the opera singer Sylvia Burroughs, composer Geoffrey Gerard, and Broadway comedian Fannie Howell.

No one from the Movement, thought David with relief. But then a little voice said: *No one you recognize.* He recalled that he'd had little chance to become acquainted with the New York office staff before being sent south.

David felt as set apart as a dead man walking among the living. So much vivacity and sparkling wit, it exhausted him to see it. The hum of happy voices irritated him. Anger flashed through him.

So many of them must've known her—

His sister had been dead three weeks and now these people were carrying on with asinine jocularity. As though nothing had happened. As though the world was still right. As though he weren't a man who was walking on the ceiling.

What was he doing here? How long would he have to hold out in this room of blinding, burnished, specious smiles? Not a single guest was standing alone. All stood in small conversational rings. There were no outcasts. Every guest had been carefully chosen for his or her ability to fit in. Apparently, to stand alone, as he preferred to do, would be unforgivable.

But then his observant eye picked out several tense faces hidden behind the grins of forced glee. The Hardings had indulged in a certain malevolent sadism. They'd invited the most hated critics of several artists in the room— then mercilessly abandoned them to one another.

David became aware of a warm presence nearby.

He turned at the touch of fingertips on his elbow. A sweetly scented woman had materialized at his side. Their eyes locked.

He had never seen eyes like hers: a deep sapphire blue, set under long, black lashes and slender plucked eyebrows. Captivating eyes, mesmerizing. But for all their wide-open charm, they held an unmistakable shrewdness. Despite their apparent warmth, they chilled him: a knowledgeable woman, but predatory. Her platinum-blond hair was done in finger waves that framed her face. It was a lovely face, like a doll's, but faint rings under her eyes and a certain hollowness to her cheeks hinted at an excessively indulgent life. Despite this, her hair still glistened and her ivory skin had a soft luster. Her lips, painted a deep burgundy, were the only points of intense color on her face, and they were moist and provocative. Her shimmering gown could have been liquefied gold, the way it flowed over her curves. She was, without doubt, one of the most alluring women in the room, but she left him cold. She smiled, flashing two rows of tiny polished teeth.

"I'm Nella. You must be David."

Her voice was husky. She was standing quite close to him. Her scent, a heady mixture of Chanel, gin, and cigarettes, enveloped him. She extended her hand and he took it. Her hand was small and soft—

Like a leopard's paw—with smooth, sharp nails that gleamed in the demi-light.

"Touched that you could make it," she purred. "I was very sorry to hear about Lilian. She was a lovely girl. I miss her."

"You knew her well?"

"Not really."

"But—"

"We'll discuss it later."

He examined her with astute eyes. She was the kind of person who amused herself by collecting people, throwing them into an arena, and watching them rip one another to shreds. Well, he had a reason for being at her house and it was not to perform like a slave in her personal Coliseum. She *would* speak to him. It might take time, but she would. Meanwhile, he would try to be as superficially sociable as the rest of her guests.

She lit herself a cigarette, grabbed herself a fresh glass of gin from a passing waiter, and made sure he had a drink too. Then she led him over to a corner sofa, where once settled she studied him over the rim of her crystal glass under suggestively half-closed eyes.

"I heard that you're marvelously attractive but utterly unapproachable. Does the description fit?"

"Admirably."

Her eyes twinkled. "You're a very serious man, aren't you? Don't you ever laugh?"

"When I have reason to."

"Yes, of course." She crossed her legs and became suitably serious. "You've been gone a long time, haven't you?"

"I wasn't here while Lilian was ill, no."

"And now you'd like to talk to people who knew her?"

He nodded.

"Well, I can't help you," she said. "I didn't know her that well—certainly not well enough to explain why she did what she did." She paused. "I could tell you about Gem. Would that help?"

Why was she claiming to know Gem, but not Lilian? His answer was cautious. "Perhaps."

She studied him, curiosity beaming out of one eye, calculation out of the other. "But why should I tell you anything? What do I get out of it?"

"What do you want? Money?"

She threw her head back, laughed, and gestured to the overdone room. "Good god, no! I've got more than enough of that, don't you think!" Then she leaned closer. "What I want," she whispered, "is much more costly."

Her jewel-like eyes glided over him. My, my, she was a live one. On a side table, he noticed a copy of *The Beautiful and the Damned*, F. Scott Fitzgerald's mood piece depicting the dissipated lives of a wealthy couple.

"You haven't introduced me to your husband," he said.

"He's out of town this week." She leaned closer to him. "Convenient, don't you think?"

"I suppose it depends ... on what you have in mind."

Her bright eyes grew even brighter. "You just must come and see me. One day next week. I'll be at the Fifth Avenue address." She told him exactly where. "Come, darling. I'll give you everything you want. And more."

Yes, he was sure she would.

"That's a lovely offer, but I can't accept it. I'll be leaving town."

At that, she straightened up, her cherry lips in a pout.

"Must you?"

"Absolutely."

"How tiresome."

"So, we have to talk. Now." He put his glass down on the table nearby. "I wanted to ask you—"

Nella raised a hand and pointed. Her gaze had fixed on a point across the room. "There's someone I'd like you to meet."

He followed Nella's pointing finger and saw a large man cutting through the crowd toward them. Actually, it wasn't so much that he was cutting through the crowd as that it was parting before him.

People were actually moving to get out of his way.

The newcomer's robust figure was sleekly packaged in an expensive suit. His left hand was shoved into one pocket; his right held a short, fat cigar. He bore no resemblance to his newspaper photographs. The grainy newsprint had always conveyed the sense of a crude ruffian, but in life Adrian Snyder presented the image of the polished, successful businessman. He was in his early fifties. There was nothing to hint at ruthlessness, nothing to show that here was a man whose rivals tended to end up in the East River.

Nella cheerfully waved him over.

No one knew for certain how Adrian Snyder had made his

fortune, neither the numbers runners under him nor the Feds who kept a covert eye and watched him. But no one seemed to doubt that Snyder was a major player in organized gambling. All agreed that he had impressive financial resources.

His holdings included some of Harlem's best apartment buildings, a Long Island estate, and several thousand acres of prime New Jersey farmland. He was an influential and generous patron of small businesses and community efforts. His thriving operation at the Forest Club financed the Agamemnon awards given out by the *Black Arrow*.

But, as David knew, not even Snyder's wealth could bridge the cleft of prejudice that divided American blacks from their West Indian counterparts. The intimate cliques of genteel Harlem excluded him. They coolly accepted his money but rejected his person.

He, in turn, viewed upper-crust Harlem with contempt. He could afford to. West Indian society had its own circle. Among his own, he was highly esteemed.

David and Nella stood. She made the introductions. Adrian smiled amiably at David and warmly extended his hand.

"Nella said she'd invited you. I'm glad to see that you've come."

David accepted the handshake, but he was taken aback at the man's engaging familiarity. To the best of his knowledge he had never met him before. Snyder must've read David's expression.

"I knew your sister, Gem."

David understood. "So you're the one." He withdrew his hand.

"I see you've heard."

"Of course I have."

Nella stepped in with a mild pleasantry and the three of them chatted awkwardly for several minutes.

"Oh, there are the Lunts!" she cried. "I've just got to go and greet them." She laid a light hand on David's forearm. "You'll be all right, won't you?" She glanced at Snyder and gave him a gay smile. "You'll take care of him for me? No games with cement shoes now."

She gave a mischievous giggle and scooted off. David watched her go. Had she invited him there to meet Snyder? He turned back to the gangster. Snyder's expression had changed. His demeanor of affability was gone. His face was hard and drawn.

"We have to talk," Snyder said. "Come see me."

"I don't have time. I'm leaving tomorrow."

"Whatever you got to do, it can wait."

"I'm afraid it can't."

There was a pause.

"I'm not used to hearing the word 'no,'" Snyder said.

"Then perhaps it's time you learned."

"Do you know who I am? I mean *really* know?"

"You're a crook. A rich crook. And you don't mind spilling blood to get your way."

"But that doesn't bother you, huh? You're not scared?"

"What bothers me is what happened between you and my sister."

"Humph. Funny you should say that, 'cause it's been bothering me too."

"It's a bit late to apologize, isn't it?"

The corners of Snyder's mouth curved in a brief, humorless smile.

"You've got a smart mouth. I hope you've got the brains to go with it." He studied David, then said. "Come see me. I'm paying you the compliment of inviting you, not ordering you."

He paused and an unexpected gentleness entered his eyes. "I'll even say please. For both our sakes, please change your mind."

Before David could utter another word and assure him that he would not, under any circumstances, change his mind, Snyder had turned and gone. David watched him, torn between curiosity and indignation. *What was* that *all about?*

Selena Ashburn's brassy voice boomed across the room, commanding just about everyone's attention. "Who's serving? I need a drink, damn it, and some music. Roland, where *are* you?"

The tall, loose-jointed man with an easy grin broke away from a group in one corner. "Yo, Selena," he said. "Take it easy."

"Easy, my ass. I want some music, honey. Gimme the good stuff."

Roland Pierce chuckled. "Calm down, Mama. You giving me a fright. You know that Papa's here and he gonna do you right."

He ambled over to the piano and sat down. After first tickling a few treble keys experimentally, he slid into a medley of silken jazz. Conversational clusters broke up as people arranged themselves around the piano. Nella reappeared. She clutched David's arm possessively and sighed happily.

"Negro music is marvelous, simply marvelous! I adore spirituals and jazz and the way you people sing the blues. Two years ago, Nikki and I attended our first Negro Orphan League Ball. That was it. Since then, you people have taken up all my time. I hardly see any white people anymore. But I don't mind. I do so love to help whenever, however, I can."

David gave her a look. Nella had made a name for herself by writing columns in the white press about Negro music and the people behind it. Gospel, spirituals, jazz, the blues: She praised them all rhapsodically in review after review. She astutely mixed gossip, fact, and innuendo in a colorful and potent brew. Few readers could distinguish one element from another. Nella's articles had helped the careers of a few colored artists, but more than anyone else's, they had helped her own. David allowed himself a raised eyebrow but chose to remain tactfully silent.

Roland's performance started off an evening of apparently spontaneous entertainment. Someone cleared a space and Luella Hughes performed a solo from the latest work by the Black Orpheus Ballet Group. Her sleek and sinuous movements cast a hush over the gathering. Julian Woodstock inserted a melancholy note with a reading from his *Heaven's Trumpet*. And Sylvia Burroughs brought everyone to tears with a spiritual.

Then the butler passed around a new round of drinks and Nella told Roland to pick up the pace while she turned down the lights. Roland's nimble fingers danced over the keys in a jaunty ragtime and the guests drifted back into conversation, well-lubricated by Nella's superior gin.

By then, David was also beginning to get a pleasant buzz. Nella had stepped briefly from his side. He let his gaze wander over the gathering. It happened to land on a cluster of faces nearby and his attention snapped into focus. Two men and one woman were engaged in a hefty discussion. Actually, only one man was doing most of the talking. He was tall and lean, of aristocratic bearing, with a handsome light brown face. He appeared to be in his late fifties. His head was balding, his forehead broad, his silver-flecked mustache and goatee meticulously groomed. His dark eyes revealed an incisive intelligence; his jaw suggested determination. Everything about his demeanor bespoke discipline and precision, concern and compassion; it also indicated intolerance, impatience, and absolute conviction in his own beliefs. David recognized him instantly: Byron Canfield was the author of the seminal work *The Color Line,* a collection of essays on the plight of black Americans.

He was also a magisterial officer of the Movement.

David's thoughts raced. How could he have missed seeing Canfield before? The man must've arrived during the performances.

I've got to get of here. But no—that won't do. I haven't gotten Nella to talk. I'll simply have to stay clear of Canfield. Make use of the fact that although I know him, he doesn't know me.

He could at least move to the other side of the room.

He was about to do so when one of Canfield's comments caught his attention.

"What Nella thinks is good and what I, as a colored man,

think is good, have nothing to do with one another."

"Don't dismiss the book so quickly," said the other man. "She's made white people aware of educated Negroes."

"Humph! She's made caricatures of us—rarefied versions of the 'noble savage.'"

"Give the woman her due. Her book deals with passing, segregation, the differences between DuBois and Booker T. In some ways, the book is deep."

"The book is trash. And she's a leech, a culture-sucking parasite."

"She talks about the shit we're doing to ourselves. Like how we light-skinned colored scorn white separatists, then turn around and cut against our own people. People are upset 'cause Nella hit dirt. She exposed family secrets."

"Well, it ain't her family. It's none of her business. And the more attention we give that damn book, the more people will buy it. Those fools demonstrating outside the publisher's office today—they did nothing but drive up sales. Idiots."

Remarkable, thought David. *If Canfield thinks so little of Nella and her work, then what's he doing here? It's like giving her the Movement's seal of approval.*

He felt Nella return to his side and turned to her. "By any chance, are you celebrating *Ebony Eden* tonight?"

She smiled. "You haven't read it?"

"I *have*—"

"But you don't like it?"

"There are ... points with which I have difficulty."

She appeared to be tickled by his tact. His eyes flickered over to the little group that had been criticizing her book. She caught his glance and laughed. It was a practiced, pleasant, musical sound.

"Them. I don't mind them. The fact is, you people don't trust anything we whites write about you."

"The fact is, *we people* have good reason not to."

"Is that so?" She regarded him with faint disappointment, as though she had expected better judgment from him. "But if I don't write about Harlem, someone else will. And with a good deal less sensitivity."

"Are you so sure?"

She looked stunned. How could he question her commitment, her understanding of the issues at hand?

"Harlem is a field waiting to be harvested," she said. "It's ripe with fresh, untouched material. No one has written the ultimate gambling or rackets story. No one has unveiled the seductive secrets of cabaret life. Who has even bothered to inquire into how such a melting pot of diverse African tribes can coexist? No one. Nobody has taken a bite out of all the luscious and wild fruit that's for the taking in Harlem."

It was a nice little speech. How often had she delivered it? Quite often, if one could judge by how fluidly the words with their rather mercenary logic flowed over her tongue. He was impressed by her enthusiasm, but appalled at her insensitivity.

"Has it occurred to you that what you find exotic and captivating we might consider embarrassing, offensive?"

Like a spoiled child, she stamped her foot. "I don't care."

"Exactly. You don't. We do."

She put a hand on her hip and wagged a finger under his nose. "Instead of complaining, you Negro intellectuals had better hop to it. Harvest your own fields or ambitious whites will get to it before you do. They'll gather quickly, steal away silently, and sell your life stories right out from under you.

"Just as you did."

She opened her mouth, but nothing came out. Slowly, she closed it. A new respect for him came into her eyes. He'd got to her. She smiled, her indignation fading.

"Yes ... just as I did."

He couldn't help but smile, too. She was amusing, in a way.

"I like you," she said. "You're honest. You have the nerve to tell me to my face what you think ... unlike others." She looked over at the little group. Her expression became roguish. "Come,

I'll introduce you."

Nella slipped her arm inside his, as if they had known each other for years, and David found himself propelled toward a meeting with Byron Canfield. He tried to ignore the sinking feeling in his stomach and worked to keep his expression bland.

"People," Nella called out lightly. "This is David McKay."

Three heads bobbed with sympathetic nods and stretched with empathetic smiles. The woman, a short, plump lady with neat gray hair, clutched David's hand, murmured words of condolence, then excused herself, muttering something about the lateness of the hour. Canfield shook David's hand firmly.

"My sympathies regarding your sister. I didn't know her personally, but I heard of her. From her husband. A marvelous trial attorney."

David didn't know whether to feel reassurance or panic. On the one hand, if Canfield knew Sweet, then that spoke for Sweet's legitimacy. On the other—

Before David could stop her, Nella had touched his shoulder and was saying with an odd sense of personal pride: "David here's a lawyer, too."

Canfield's inquisitive eyes flickered over him. "Really?" Something registered in Canfield's eyes, something that made David uneasy. Did Canfield know him—know *of* him? David tensed for trouble, but none came. The conversation flowed on and David was relieved to see that he would not be the center of attention.

Having wondered how Nella had lured Canfield to her party, he now caught a hint of an explanation. Apparently, Canfield had written a negative review of *Ebony Eden*. The review had been given wide coverage and somewhat dulled the glimmer of Nella's success. She'd invited Canfield to her party to discuss the matter. Or so it seemed. David wondered whether Nella's indignation was simply a subterfuge. He remembered her words— that she didn't care what black people thought about her work—and he believed them. If that was true, then her sole purpose for inviting Canfield was to dupe people into believing that Canfield didn't think so badly of her book after all.

David had another thought and it made him queasy. Had she invited him to her party to bring him together with Canfield? Did she already know of his life in Philadelphia? Or was he being paranoid? Every now and then, he caught Canfield looking at him. When David met his gaze, Canfield would smile. But the smile never reached his eyes. They remained thoughtful.

If David hadn't been so preoccupied, he would've found it amusing to listen to Nella and Canfield dicker. It was clear that Canfield, despite his opinion about Nella and her book, felt complimented by her attentions. Naturally, however, he refused to change a word of what he had written. He did magnanimously offer to edit any of her future manuscripts for "verity of content and character." But Nella's smile froze on her face at the very thought of it. David, despite his unease, chuckled inwardly. It served her right.

For a moment, Nella's attention went to another of her guests in their little circle, and Canfield turned to David. "We're neighbors, you know."

"On Strivers' Row?"

"Moved there two years ago. Why don't you stop by tomorrow?"

"I'm sorry. I have a train to catch."

"You're leaving? Too bad." Canfield rubbed his chin. "Actually, I'm sure I've heard your name before. And it wasn't from Sweet." He paused, looking at David, his eyes speculative. There was something ... something worth remembering, and he was on the verge of grasping it.

David was about to make a distracting comment, when one of Canfield's eyebrows shot up.

"Yes ... of course. It was when you joined the Movement— some years ago. That's how I know your name. Everyone in the New York office was looking forward to working with you."

Canfield's eyes narrowed. "Then you were sent out on a case and ... and—why, you're the one who *disappeared.*"

Canfield's voice carried, not across the room, but far enough to let others standing close know that something was wrong. Nearby conversation died. Nella's eyes, like those of her guests, went from Canfield to David and back again. David's heart skipped a beat. For a moment, words failed him.

"Where in the world have you been?" Canfield demanded.

The question, so directly put, was brutal. David had been dreading it for years. Now here it was, presented to him not in private, the least he could have hoped for, but before influential listeners—"inquisitors" was the word his mind supplied. He felt more than a little ill. Nella took a step away and to the side. He could see her out of the corner of his eye. A little smile played about her lips. Was this an ambush, after all? Did she know? But how could she? There was only one way to handle the situation. He adopted a pleasant, urbane expression and allowed a trace of amiable condescension to creep into his tone.

"I've been busy handling matters elsewhere."

"So, you didn't disappear?"

"Of course not."

"But no one in New York heard anything about your reassignment. I certainly would've heard something." Canfield paused. "Where did you say you've been working?"

"I didn't."

Canfield looked as though he'd been struck. He arched a heavy eyebrow and gazed at David with increasing displeasure. David met Canfield's gaze head-on.

"The Movement is large, complex," David said. "One hand doesn't always know what the other is doing. My responsibilities require me to move around a lot. You know how it is."

Canfield looked David up and down. He stroked his mustache. "No, in this case, I don't. Normally, we keep close tabs on our workers, for their own safety. And I usually know if—"

"Byron, don't be such a bore." Nella stepped to David's side and wrapped a proprietary arm around him. "I was just being polite, introducing you. But I've barely had a chance to speak to him myself. I certainly didn't bring him over here for you to grill him." She stroked David's collar. "Leave that up to me."

There was some uneasy laughter.

Canfield cracked a thin smile. "Yes ... perhaps you're right. I think it's time for me to go." He offered David his hand. "It's been ... shall we say ... very interesting to meet you."

"Likewise," David said, shaking Canfield's hand.

Turning back to Nella, Canfield thanked her for her hospitality.

"You're not bailing out on me?" she said.

"I must. I have to go to the office tomorrow."

"Work even on a Sunday?"

Canfield glanced at David. "Calls to make. Questions to ask."

Nella shrugged, pointedly dismissing him. She turned away from the group, pulling David with her. "My, my, dear boy. You got the old goat going. Just what have you been up to?"

"Nothing interesting."

"But Canfield—"

"—is a bit overcurious."

"Well, so am I." Nella's eyes moved over him intensely, as though if she tried hard enough, she could see right through him. "You've got a story, dear boy, and I want to know it."

"You're mistaken."

She eyed him shrewdly. "Smart of you to leave tomorrow."

"Why?"

"Because if you stayed, Canfield would unearth every detail he could about you. And so would I."

His heart thumped heavily, but his smile stayed easy. "It would be a waste of your time."

7. GETTING TO KNOW THE NEW RELATION

David rose early Sunday morning to the rhythmic drumming of raindrops against his bedroom window. He had slept like a man buried alive, kicking and clawing at the sheets. Now, rubbing his eyes, he threw aside the bedcovers and swung his legs out of bed. Staggering to the window, he drew apart the curtains. Dark bands of sooty clouds roamed the sky, trailing ragged tendrils as dirty as trampled cotton.

This was the day he would return to Philadelphia. It was apt weather for his return. There was a five-thirty train leaving from Penn Station. He would be on it.

But, first, he would talk to Jameson Sweet, get that ball rolling.

David felt a powerful surge of anger just thinking about it. He tried to tell himself that Sweet might actually be a decent man, despite what Annie said. He was obviously a man of accomplishment, or Lilian wouldn't have married him. But the fact that she hadn't written to her own brother about the marriage galled him—and his first instinct was to blame the man she'd married.

And no, it didn't help, what Annie said about Sweet's intentions toward the house. It didn't help at all.

For a moment, he tried to take a step back and put himself in Sweet's shoes. If he were Sweet, would he give up his place in a house like this? No, not easily. But he would see the very wrongness of trying to fully claim it. He would see that. Would Sweet?

He turned from the window, went to his washstand and poured cold water from a porcelain pitcher into a basin. He splashed his face once, twice, three times, the chilly drops splattering his bare chest and shoulders. Grabbing a towel, he dried himself, rubbing his skin with rough strokes.

He happened to look up and caught sight of his reflection in the bureau mirror. The puckered skin of an angry scar slashed across his left shoulder. He stared at it and a mental trapdoor opened. For one horrid moment, he was falling, falling into a deep, dark place.

Jonah ... Jonah, in the belly of the whale.

There had been only one time in his life when he'd been called upon to display not only physical but also moral and spiritual courage. And he had failed. Miserably. He had never forgiven himself. And he lived in constant fear that his failing would be discovered. Worse, he dreaded the possibility that he would be put to the test once more and his weakness revealed, but this time before an audience, in such a way as to ruin him. He touched the scar.

The war over there was nothing—nothing compared to the one over here ...

He shuddered, wrenched his eyes away, and tossed his towel over a chair. Dressing quickly, he left his room. Annie stood at the foot of the stairs.

"Mr. Jameson's back," she said. "He's expecting you."

"I'm glad Annie found your address," Sweet said, his voice a rolling low timbre. "I wish I could've been here sooner."

"We would've contacted you, but we didn't know how. Lilian said nothing."

She told me nothing about you either, David wanted to say. Had she ever planned on telling him? Or had she simply trusted that he would always stay away?

After breakfast, he'd told Annie that he was ready to meet "the mystery man." She started off down the hallway. He realized with growing consternation that she was heading for his father's office. She put one hand on the doorknob, turned to him, and raised the other. "Wait." Then she knocked lightly and went in. Fifteen seconds later, she reappeared. Seeing his expression, her forehead creased.

"Yes, he's in your father's office. I know it's a shock, but please try to get along with him. For now, you've got to try."

David smiled to be polite, but said nothing. Trying to get along with Jameson Sweet was neither his concern nor his intention.

The room he'd entered had a high ceiling but was dusky, deep, and narrow. Weighty tomes of encyclopedic volumes lined the walls on either side, as somber as soldiers guarding a path and pointing the way forward. Thick pile carpet covered the floor, absorbing the sound of every footfall. The air was bitter, stale, and still, tainted by the flat smell of old tobacco. He thought of his father and a sense of unspeakable regret rose within him. He had to force himself to put one foot in front of the other.

The room culminated in a rich mahogany desk set before a tall slender window. Thick drapes were drawn to block any outside light. A banker's lamp cast a soft amber glow over part of the desk. The weak light shied away from the man that sat behind it. Shadow obscured his face. For a moment, the room was filled with an unearthly quiet. All David heard was the scratching of a pen, saw was the movement of a large, masculine hand, a left hand, as it signed papers. Then Jameson Sweet leaned forward into the light, as stealthy as an animal emerging from its lair, and the two men took each other's measure.

Sweet's complexion was smooth, almost unnaturally even—*like a mask,* David thought —and the color of mahogany—*a tough, resilient wood.* Sweet's close-cropped hair was an inky black and meticulously cut. A refined sliver of a mustache graced his upper lip, as dignified and precise as the stroke of a master's paintbrush.

Like Gem, David was struck by Sweet's uneasy resemblance to Augustus. Physically, Sweet was as dark as Augustus was light. *But looks are irrelevant,* David thought. He could smell the rank odor of frustrated ambition. It had a bitter bite he'd learned to recognize among those who roam the halls of justice.

Sweet rose to his feet with grave dignity and came around from behind the desk. From his pinstriped vest to his tailored woolen pants, he was immaculately attired. He shook David's hand firmly and willingly. There was no apparent enmity in him. But his lizard-like eyes were cold. David sensed a hypnotist's gift for persuasion and an actor's skill at pretense. Here was a man who would be neither lightly deceived nor easily led into revealing more than he chose.

Sweet offered a drink, which David declined. "Thanks, but no thanks. Relax, there's no need to treat me like a guest. I am, after all, in my own home."

Sweet inclined his head in a nod. "Very well. Shall we move to the parlor?"

The front room held a sofa and a couple of armchairs, one of which was a deep royal blue. With its high, wing back, this particular chair was quite regal. When Augustus first had it brought in, the family gathered around and laughingly nicknamed it "Daddy's throne." Augustus had spent many hours in the spacious chair, staring into the flames of the fireplace, planning his investments. Lila had sat opposite him, reading, casting a thin shadow.

Sweet now placed himself firmly on Augustus's "throne." David said nothing and took a seat on the couch opposite. He could be patient. After all, Sweet's days as a pretender were numbered, whether he realized it or not.

Annie had lit a fire in the fireplace and brought them coffee. Flickering flames threw devilish reflections on their faces. Sweet lit his pipe, using his left hand. He smoked contemplatively, his eyes on the flames, and David watched him.

"When did she fall ill?"

"Around February of last year."

"What kind of doctors did you take her to?"

"Every kind that I could think of."

"Psychiatrists?"

"She saw Dr. Hawthorne once a week for six months, then refused to go anymore."

"You couldn't change her mind?"

"She wanted drugs, not therapy. Drugs to make her sleep. Drugs to wake her up. At first, they helped, but soon the effect wore off. She started drinking. She thought she could hide it, but I know what drinking looks like. And smells like. She lost weight, went down to nothing. Her face got puffy. She was tired and sleepy, kept falling down. Kept seeing things, hearing voices."

David listened not only to what Sweet said, but how he said it. Sweet's voice was melodious, full of cadence and echo. It was the modulated voice of a natural orator, an invaluable commodity for a courtroom contender. Sweet had presence. His charm was calculated and purposeful. He had passion, the dark and dangerous kind. He was indeed the type of man to fall deeply in love, but would he have fallen in love with a shy, reserved woman like Lilian?

"She seemed to get better for a little while after Gem left—Gem's being here must've been too much for her—but the improvement didn't last. And then she was worse than ever. Hawthorne suggested that I put her away, but she begged me not to. I told the doctor to get us a nurse. I asked Rachel Hamilton to step in temporarily. We'd just arranged for someone permanent to take over when it happened. Annie found her. I was in Newark that weekend. When I got home that Monday, the police were here."

"Did she leave a note?"

Sweet rested his pipe on a large crystal ashtray. He took a wallet from his back pocket, and removed a folded square of white paper from it. This, he handed to David. The note was typed:

> Tears and nightmares never persuade family and friends of the depths of your despair. But death, at a stroke, ends all doubt.

"They're the words of the French-Algerian philosopher Pierre Lorraine," David said. He pondered the slip of paper for a moment, then handed it back. "The thing is, Lilian never liked

Lorraine. But you didn't know that did you?" He regarded Sweet.

The man shrugged. "No, but I don't see where it matters."

"It matters, because I don't see her choosing to use the words of philosopher she couldn't stand for such a delicate matter."

Sweet nodded. "Yes, well, she changed. Your sister ... changed a lot."

"Yes, so I've been told." David looked into the flames, was quiet for a moment. When he spoke, it was as though his question had just occurred to him. "That weekend, why did you leave her here alone?"

"I didn't—Annie was here."

"But no nurse—not Rachel."

"No."

"Why not?"

A pause. "This is beginning to sound like a cross-examination."

"I just want to know why she was left alone. A simple enough question."

"There was ..." Sweet shifted in his chair. "Well, a mix-up. A very unfortunate mix-up. I left Lilian with Annie on Thursday. The nurse was supposed to come that Friday—but she didn't. Annie had planned to go visit family. She started to cancel when the nurse didn't show. But then Lilian told her to go ahead. She said she was going to visit friends. She'd be gone all weekend, so it would be okay for Annie to leave. I'm sure Annie wouldn't have left the house otherwise. You can't blame the old woman. She's—"

"It wasn't Annie I was thinking about."

Sweet's dark eyes glittered. "You have a helluva lotta nerve."

"You married my sister after knowing her for exactly one month."

"It was love at first sight."

"Love for her—or for this house and what her name might bring you?"

"I won't even dignify that with an answer."

"I didn't think you would."

The two men faced off, stared each other down.

Sweet spoke first. His voice was low and intense.

"I loved your sister. And yes, I love this house. I love it because we were happy here together."

"And now that she's gone, you intend to stay."

"I have a *right* to stay."

"Your 'rights' came into question the day she died."

Sweet gave David a cool appraisal. Then he chuckled. "So that's what this is all about. You don't care about what happened to Lilian. You're the one who's only interested in the house. You stayed away all these years, waiting for your chance. Now she's gone and you want to take over."

"It *is* my family house."

"It was."

"It still is." David rose to his feet. "If you loved her, and I'd like to believe you did, then nothing can replace your loss. And it would be a double blow to lose the home you shared with her. But you know as well as I do that she never intended for this house, our father's house, to pass out of the family."

"But, like it or not, I *am* family. And legally, I own fifty percent of this place. Of course, possession is nine-tenths of the law. So for all intents and purposes, this house *is* mine and you *are* a guest——"

"No——"

"Now I'm perfectly willing to purchase your half——"

"I'll never sell my share."

"And I'll neither sell nor give up mine."

David regarded him with barely concealed fury. "I would advise you to reconsider."

"Are you threatening me?"

"If anything, I'm trying to spare you a battle."

Sweet's lower lip curled with contempt. "You wouldn't dare take me on."

"Oh, but I would. With joy. But I'm trying—trying hard––to give you the benefit of the doubt. I heard that you took good care of Lilian when she was ill and if that's true, then I'm grateful. But if it isn't, then trust me, I'll find out and I'll make you pay. So I suggest you leave. *Now*. Go while the going is good."

Sweet's response was a look of disdain. He leaned back in Augustus's armchair and made himself comfortable.

"Get used to me, brother-in-law. Get used to me. Cause I'm here and I'm here to stay."

David left the parlor, went upstairs and down the hall to Lilian's room. Standing at the foot of her bed, he let his gaze pass over the dresser top again. He eyed the perfectly replaced wallpaper, the refurbished bed, and the well-scrubbed floor. His face was drawn, his eyes thoughtful. He needed to leave town, but having met Sweet he knew in his bones that there was more to Lilian's death than met the eye. Surely this room could tell him something.

He heard a cough behind him and turned at the sound. It was Annie. He saw the worry, the fear and uncertainty in her eyes, and understood. He had said he would leave when he had spoken to Sweet. Now that he had, she wondered whether he was about to go. But like every natural diplomat, she knew better than to introduce the subject of her main concern.

"Mr. David, you shouldn't stay in this room by yourself," was all she said.

He gave a brief, gentle smile to reassure her. "I'm fine. I've been thinking about what you said, about how things aren't always the way they seem."

"And?" She came up to him.

"And I find it strange, very strange ... that she chose to cut herself there, in the bed." He felt Annie's questioning gaze. "When people slash their wrists, they often do it in a bathtub filled with warm water. It contains the blood ... and makes the dying faster."

He leaned against one of the bedposts. The surface felt cool and smooth.

"Even the bedpost was covered in blood," said Annie. "Bloody handprints, as though she'd grabbed it to help her stand."

He looked at her. "Why would she struggle to get up after lying down to die?"

"I don't know. But she sure 'nough got up. There was a line of blood running from here to there." Annie pointed to a place about five footsteps away. "And on up to the windowsill." She swung her arm in a low arc and pointed to the base of the window. "That's where I found her."

He studied the area. A ghostly ache swelled in his chest. Turning around, he let his gaze travel over the newly papered walls above the bed, over the new canopy, and then back over the trail that Annie had indicated on the floor.

"Tell me about the blood."

"The what?"

"The blood. Was it in spots? Close together?"

"It was everywhere. Like I said: Dried hard. Dried black."

"And what about on the floor? Was the blood in large splatters or—"

"Mr. David, what you wanna ask me sumptin' like that for?"

"Bear with me. It's important."

She set her shoulders and still looked unhappy, but complied. "Well, the blood on the floor ... It wasn't in spots. It was more spread out, smeared-like, in a wide line, like sumptin' had been dragged—"

He nodded. It was the answer he'd expected. "And you say, it appeared that she'd been here alone?"

"Weren't no hint of nobody but her."

"No sign of a break-in?"

"None at all." Her forehead creased. "Why you ask, Mr. David?"

"Blood everywhere, you said. Usually, that means a struggle."

"You mean, like a robber?"

It wasn't at all what he meant, but he said nothing.

"A struggle .. ." She reflected. "But nothing was missing. Nothing 'cepting that vase."

"Which vase?"

"The one that used to sit in the window." She pointed. "You remember?"

"That little Japanese one? It was gone?"

"Smashed to smithereens on the sidewalk. And there was blood on the windowsill."

He went to the window. Faint pink smears still showed on the sill. Or did he imagine them? Drawing his fingertips over the new coat of paint, he was thoughtful. He drew the curtains apart and peered out. It was a crisp, clear Sunday morning, and Strivers' Row was impressively still. The best of Harlem was undoubtedly gathered together in their finest finery a little ways over and down the road at Saint Philip's to worship. The street was empty, as it would've been that night.

That night. Who would've been out on the street that night?

David perched on the edge of the windowsill and stared out. He pictured the little vase, remembering its delicacy and beauty. He thought of the love and effort that must have gone into fashioning it. He recalled how his mother had treasured it, admired it, striven to protect it from the clumsy, the curious, the covetous. She had kept it sheltered here, within the heart of the house, where only the most trusted were allowed. How and why had the vase been ripped from its place?

He could imagine it in freefall. In his mind, he watched it tumble over and over, spin out of control, then crash against the concrete pavement. He saw its fragile beauty shatter. And he saw Lilian. Also fragile. Now also shattered. A chill, as sharp as a scalpel, pierced his core. He shivered. The vague notions that had been germinating in his mind for the past days became clear.

Conservative and cautious, the Lilian he knew wouldn't have married someone she barely knew. Sensible, sane, and solid, she wouldn't have slashed her wrists. Stoic, proud, and deeply religious, she would have never shamed her family name.

Not the Lilian he knew.

Annie had come up alongside him. She was staring out the window herself now. He turned to look at her.

"Do you believe my sister killed herself?"

Annie's gaze was fixed on the hard pavement three stories below.

"As God as my witness, after I seen the way that sickness changed her, I b'lieve ... I b'lieve she coulda."

"But you don't believe she did."

"No ... I don't." With a sigh, she looked at him. "I could never help wondering why she dragged herself, used her last bit of strength, to get to this window."

"But you know the answer as well as I do."

Her eyes met his.

"She came to this window," he said, "to get help."

From her expression, he knew they had reached the same conclusion.

To get help. Like pebbles piercing the surface of a still, deep pond, those three small words would cause ripples if applied to Lilian's death. They implied, in effect, that she had either regretted her decision to die or that the decision itself had been someone else's to begin with.

"So, you're gonna stay?"

"Yes," he said and his voice was tired. "I'm going to stay."

She exhaled with relief. "I'm glad, Mr. David, so glad. Things is gonna get better with you here. I know they'll be just fine."

Her sweet words brought a bitter taste to his mouth.

You don't know me, he wanted to say. *You don't know what*

I've been doing. If you did, you'd turn your back on me. You'd help me pack my bags yourself.

8.   RACHEL AND THE MCKAYS

A few blocks away, Rachel was thinking about how small her apartment was and how much she would've loved to move. Her thoughts skipped nimbly to the McKay house, as they often did at such times, and in her mind's eye she could see their beautiful parlor—

Big enough to hold a wedding in.

And the spacious upstairs bedrooms—

Why go away on a honeymoon?

The house was wonderful, of course, nearly perfect, but as every woman knows, there's always room for improvement.

First things first. If it were up to me, I'd change them old paintings in Lilian's room, throw out the—

She happened to glance out her bedroom window and her daydreams about redecorating were for the moment forgotten. A young girl, about seven or eight, was jumping rope across the street. The child's feet kept getting entangled in the rope, but she refused to give up. She would patiently unwrap the rope from around her ankles and start jumping again. She did this repeatedly and Rachel watched, fascinated. If there was one thing she admired, it was determination.

She's just like me. One day she's going to be Somebody.

Rachel leaned on the windowsill. A sad smile played about her lips.

Isabelle would've still been too young to skip and jump like that. But in a few years, she would've been able to ... . she would've been, if she'd lived.

She blinked and wiped the sudden tears away, staring through blurry eyes at the child across the street.

Go on, girl, she whispered. *Go on. Don't never give up.*

Rachel knew the meaning of perseverance. She recalled the

days when she'd travel from the Tenderloin to visit the McKays after school. How she'd struggled to imitate the family's effortless grace. How she'd striven to emulate its sedate gentility. All to no avail. She had learned the hard way just how complex and uncompromising the African American elite could be in its membership requirements. If you could not certify pedigree and demonstrate connections, your presence was condoned but you were given to understand in subtle and polite ways that you would not be—*could not be*— considered a member.

Her clothes, for example, had always made her stick out like a sore thumb. Lilian had offered to share her clothes with her, but Rachel was too proud to take them. And so she'd worn the same clothes to school, day in and day out, for nearly two years: a pale blue shirt, in some places held together with pins; a long gray skirt; thick black stockings that were pulled down and tucked under at the toe; and black brogues that had seen much, much better days. Some of the girls at school had tried to taunt her, but Rachel had a fury in her that caused them to step back. She wasn't interested in impressing *them*. It was the McKays she wanted to impress. It was their world she yearned to be part of. And if it hadn't been for her no-good father, she would've been.

When he died, I didn't care. I was just glad me and Mama were free of him.

And when they moved, *finally* moved, uptown, she'd rejoiced, thinking she had it made.

But that was foolish, now, wasn't it?

One afternoon—it was right before Christmas—she'd gone over to the McKays'. It was 1920, the first Christmas after Lila McKay's death, and Rachel was twenty-three. Lilian had told her to come by to pick up some presents. Rachel had gone to the front door, as usual, and rung the bell. Annie opened it promptly.

"Hi!" Rachel fixed a bright smile on her face, although she didn't particularly like Annie. Never had and didn't even know why. "Miss Lila told me to stop by," she said, wondering why

Annie just didn't step aside and let her in, as she always had.

"I see, miss. Well, you'll have to go round by the back side."

Rachel looked dumbstruck. She hadn't heard right. She couldn't have. "'Scuse me?"

"I said, you'll have to—"

"I heard what you said. You don't understand. I never use the back way. Why, I'm not a serv—"

"I know, miss." Annie's tone was restrained but firm and it was starting to get on Rachel's nerves. "Most times, there ain't no problem with you coming in this way. But to day, Mr. Augustus, he got comp'ny." Her eyes dwelled on Rachel, as if to repeat: *Comp'ny. It's pretty clear what* that *means, ain't it?*

Rachel felt herself grow smaller and smaller. And her face grow hotter. She was furious to find tears coming into her eyes. Blinking rapidly, she brushed them away.

"You let me in!" she cried, balling up her puny hands into impotent fists. She saw the pity in Annie's eyes and that made her angrier. "Let me in, I said!"

Annie sighed. "C'mon 'round back, miss. Don't stand out here in the cold no more. Miss Lilian's waiting for you and I got to get back to my pie."

Rachel stared at her a second longer, then dropped her fists, defeated. "You can tell Daddy McKay that he'll rot in hell before I walk through *his* servants' entrance."

Annie smiled, unperturbed. "You want me to tell him that, miss. D'you *really* want me to?"

Rachel wanted to smack her. She almost did, but some residue of common sense took hold. "Why d'you stick up for him?" she cried. "You know that he's... he's ... that he's evil."

Annie's eyes widened just a tad. It wasn't much of a reaction, but it was something. Rachel pulled her thin coat tighter around her, whirled, and stomped away. At the end of the block, something made her pause and look back. Annie was still standing in the doorway, watching her.

Two days later, Lilian, Gem, and David showed up at Rachel's door, with presents for her and her mother.

"I'm very sorry," Lilian said. "I didn't know Daddy had told Annie to do that."

And what would you have done if you had *known?* thought Rachel. *Probably nothing.* But she saw the look on Lilian's face and knew her friend's apology was genuine. And so she relented, at least until Gem opened her mouth. Gem took one of the assorted candies they'd brought Rachel's mother, one of the choicest ones in fact, and popped it into her mouth. She was home from college, and it looked like the only subject she was studying out in California was how to wear makeup.

"Look," said Gem, giving her fingertips a quick lick, "you have to understand. Daddy had guests. Some very important people. We just couldn't let you in. Not by the front door. It would've been unseemly. After all, *we* are people of consequence. You're not."

Rachel's anger surged back. Her mother had set a teapot on the table and for one crazy moment, Rachel was sorely tempted to grab it and bash Gem over the head with it. She almost reached for it when she caught David's expression. He'd been silent so far throughout the visit. He was looking at her now with amusement. There was affection and mischief and yes, admiration too. His eyes went to Gem and then back to her and she understood.

Don't take her so seriously. None of us do.

But that was easy for him to say. He was Gem's older brother. He was one of those "people of consequence." Rachel knew at that moment that she disliked Gem because deep in her heart, whether she wanted to admit it or not, she believed that what Gem said was true.

"You're too tied up with them McKays," Rachel's mother told her later. Minnie regarded her only child with sad exasperation. "You should be proud to be a Hamilton. We ain't rich, but we's a fine family, too. We just as good as them McKays. What you wanna be one of them dicties for, anyway?

Most of them rich, light-skinned colored folk don't even know what side of the bridge they standing on. Don't know if they's black or white. 'Least you know who you is, honey. That's important. It's about the most important thing there is. It's one thing you got over any dicty any day."

A *dicty*. Yes, the McKays were dicties. But she was infatuated with them.

Rachel adored her mother, but she'd chosen Mrs. McKay as her role model. Lila McKay had been both dark and beautiful. She'd married a successful light-skinned man. She'd been cultured and gracious. Lila had lived barely eight months after moving into her new Strivers' Row home, but before her death she'd completed its decoration. In a burst of activity, she sought out beautiful pieces from the Americas, Asia, and Europe to create an atmosphere of harmony and comfort. Mixing antique and modern with a sure hand, she'd created a luscious home.

Rachel was back at the McKay house as soon as the Christmas and New Year's holidays were over, as soon as the McKays' circle of parties ended and the rounds of important guests slowed down, as soon as the imperative for her to enter by the servants' gate was lifted. And sometimes, to make up for the disastrous holidays, she was now allowed to sleep over.

Her stays at the McKay house were tantamount to visits to a small but lovely mansion. She loved how the tiered chandelier in the McKays' entryway twinkled overhead; how the polished wooden banisters of the curving stairway gleamed softly; how the smell of fresh cut flowers sweetened the air. She never ceased to wonder at the walls of delicate Japanese prints with their soft pastel colors and the fine ink drawings by French masters. She hesitated to step on the beautiful Aubusson rugs that adorned the hardwood floors, but joyfully curled her toes in the deep pile cream-colored carpet that covered the parlor floor. She sank happily into the deep chairs that furnished the library and let her eyes rove eagerly over the endless shelves laden with dark leather-bound books. When not there, she dreamed of the large airy rooms, of the massive soft beds with their long, tapering posts.

She'd lie on her narrow cot at home wondering how it would be to live permanently in such plenty. Her contact with the McKays taught her to love nice possessions at an early age. Over time, her desire would grow into a craving.

"Honey, if you ain't careful, your love of pretty things'll be your downfall," her mother would tell her. "People like us, we can't afford such fine things."

"Yes, Mama," she'd say and keep on dreaming. Most of her earnings now went toward clothes, books, and furnishings. She would've liked to wear frocks and furs from Bendel's and Revillon Freres, but this was patently beyond her. Some looks she could approximate, but others she knew better than to even try. She preferred to do without rather than settle for the embarrassment of a cheap copy.

She turned away from the window and surveyed her neat little bedroom. She thought of Annie and David and Sweet.

All of them sitting in that huge house not so far away—while here I am, stuck in this little cage.

The image flashed through her mind of her living in this "cage," forced to struggle until the last of her youth was gone, until nothing was left of her strength and she was an old crone, dying, forgotten, and bitter.

Oh, how long? she cried. *How long before things go well enough for me to get out of here?*

9. SWEET'S REAR GUARD

Some five months earlier, on the night of October 10, 1925, a mob armed with pistols and baseball bats had charged the home of a young black Chicago physician. Boston Richards had just bought the house, which was in a white neighborhood. As the mob rushed forward, he opened fire and a white man died. Dr. Richards was caught and charged with first-degree murder. But he was lucky. He wasn't summarily lynched, as he would've been elsewhere. Instead, he was jailed and tried in what became highly publicized proceedings.

Six weeks of heated courtroom drama came to a grinding halt when Richards' lawyer had a stroke and collapsed during an argument with the presiding judge. The Movement took up the matter. The case files, dozens of them, landed on Byron Canfield's desk in January. To contemporary eyes, Richards' innocence might seem obvious. But in 1925, no black was ever justified in raising a hand, much less a weapon, against a white. Canfield knew that to beat the odds and win an acquittal he'd need the assistance of the best legal mind the Movement could offer. If he'd stayed in New York four years earlier, David McKay would've come to mind. Now it was Jameson Sweet.

Months of working on the case had brought Canfield and Sweet a bond that surpassed mutual respect. Long hours of sweating over law books and plotting strategy can teach a man a lot about how his colleague thinks. Canfield decided that Sweet was one of the best legal gamesmen he'd ever known.

He could've been my son, he thought.

He and Emma had never had children. When young, she hadn't wanted to have any. An image of their barren marriage bed flashed across his mind. He sighed. He'd once loved her. God, how he'd loved her! But that was then. What it meant to love was a faint memory. It was no more relevant to his current state of mind than a faded rose pressed between the pages of a forgotten diary.

He removed his coat from the vestibule closet and took his hat down from the shelf. She came out of the living room just then and paused with one foot on the stair.

"You're going out?" she asked.

Her voice held a trace of disappointment and that surprised him.

Perhaps there is something left.

He shrugged into his coat, buttoning it up and adjusting the collar. He looked at her round familiar face and for a moment felt regret.

"Just down the street. I have to see Sweet." He yanked down a cuff.

"Right now?"

"Right now. He's in trouble."

She said nothing more and he turned away from the look on her face. It was a vague, haunted expression that arose whenever he mentioned Sweet's name. A mixture of resentment, jealousy, and longing—as though she'd been reminded of the children she'd refused to have.

Canfield stepped out of his house and looked up the street. A few doors away, Sweet had just left the McKay house. The two men met midway down the block and after a few moments of discussion decided to walk along Lenox Avenue.

Canfield studied Sweet. The young lawyer had been preoccupied lately. He hadn't been making mistakes, but his work wasn't as exact as it used to be. Of course, with Lilian's illness and now the sudden reappearance of her brother, it was to be expected.

"This is about David, isn't it?"

Sweet glanced at him. "You've met him?"

"At Nella Harding's last night."

"He does get around, doesn't he?" Sweet clamped his pipe between his teeth. "So what did you think of him?"

"Something's very wrong there—"

"He's a troublemaker. He stayed away while Lilian was alive, didn't show his face while she was ill; now he comes and wants to play the hero."

"In what way?"

"Well, he just about accused me of killing her."

"He didn't! He wouldn't have!"

"Oh, but he did. He didn't come right out and say it, mind you. He didn't have to."

Canfield shook his head. "His own guilty conscience, that's

what's behind it."

"Definitely. Didn't do anything for his sister before, so he's angry at the person who did. But if that's all there was to it, I wouldn't be bothering you."

"Well, what is it then?"

"He wants the house."

Canfield came to a halt and stared at Sweet, then shook his head. "Actually, I'm not that surprised. Irresponsibility and greed tend to go together." They began walking again. "But there's more than just run-of-the-mill greed at work here. Four years ago, David McKay left on Movement business and disappeared. God only knows what he's been up to. It would be horrible if he's done something that would destroy the credibility and efficiency we've worked so hard to build."

"I know the name of a man down in Philly. He's done some work for the Movement. He's good, *real* good. If there's anything worth knowing, he'll find it. I think we should contact him—for the sake of the Movement, of course."

Canfield glanced at Sweet. Something in Sweet's tone bothered him, gave rise to a slight unease. After a moment's consideration, he dismissed the feeling. "You're right, of course. We should do something."

"So I have your backing?"

Again, Canfield found himself hesitating and wondered why. Was it because he disliked the idea of investigating a fellow lawyer? Or because he disliked the idea of investigating a fellow race man even more?

"Well?" Sweet said.

Canfield looked at this young lawyer he so admired, feeling that glimmer of unease, but seeing nothing in Sweet's eyes to justify it. "All right," he said, "Do it."

10. GEM'S INDELICATE TALES

David was relieved to see that Sweet had left the parlor. He sank into his father's armchair, made a tepee of his fingertips, and stared into the crackling flames.

If what he suspected was true, then Lilian had been murdered. It didn't take a leap of the imagination to land on the most likely suspect. But it would take a great deal of imagination to ferret out the full truth of the matter and find proof, legal proof, of a crime. He didn't have much time. He'd been back in town only two days and already two people were suspicious of him: Nella and Canfield. It could be a matter of days before they found him out. He had to move fast. But where should he begin?

The doorbell rang, interrupting his thoughts. He heard Annie answer, then the soft tones of another woman. Rachel.

He straightened up.

Seconds later, Annie showed Rachel into the parlor, then left and shut the door behind her. David rose at the sight of her. He put on a smile. He wasn't in the mood for company, but it would be wrong not to greet her. Furthermore, she did look comely, fresh and crisp in her nurse's uniform.

"My, my. What a surprise. Your patients must love to see you coming."

"Hush your mouth," she said, but her eyes twinkled at the compliment. She handed him his leather gloves. "You left these at my place. I was hoping to get them here before you left."

"Well, that was nice of you, but I'm not going anywhere."

"You're not?"

"Not for a while."

She looked at him for an explanation, but he gave her none. Instead, he invited her to coffee. She agreed, saying she had an hour before her shift started.

"You told me that Gem seemed to exert a strange influence over Lilian," he said. "How was that possible?"

"I'm not sure myself, but ..."

Her voice trailed away.

"Yes?" he prompted.

"Well, I was just thinking that time we all went out together. It was me, Gem, Lilian, and Sweet. Lilian had some tickets for the Harlem Symphony. Fletcher Henderson was playing. The place was packed. We were all in a good mood. Afterward, somebody suggested we check out Happy Rhone's place over on 143rd. Lilian didn't want to go. But Gem pushed for it."

He'd heard of Arthur "Happy" Rhone's. It was closed now, but at the time it was the place to go if you wanted to see and be seen. It was known as "the millionaires' club," and it was posh. The interior was a sleek and sophisticated ebony-on-ivory. It was the place where Hollywood met Harlem, a namedroppers' paradise, where Nobodies and Somebodies swung to the same smooth sax.

"It's not the kind of place Lilian would've liked," he said.

"She hated it. Said it was stuck-up and snooty. Well, it was, but it was fun."

The four of them had lucked out and gotten a table with a good view of the floor show. But none of them watched it. They were too busy listening to Gem. She held them spellbound with risque, bawdy stories about her life in Paris. She had an endless supply of tales that she felt just had to be told.

"There was this silly man who claimed to be a Russian count. He could've been. Nobody, absolutely nobody gave a damn. But I thought I'd give him a turn. He had money, after all, and lots of it. For my birthday, he took me to the Chateau de Madrid. Very exclusive. Just outside Paris. But they wouldn't let him in. I was perfectly dressed, but he—well, Russians, you know."

Gem rolled her eyes. "You won't believe this: He went 'round by the kitchen and got hold of a waiter. He bribed the man to swap clothes with him. That's how we got in. He danced the tango with me in a waiter's dinner jacket. Not one of those hoity-toity so much as sniffed the difference."

She chuckled, delighted at her wit. "We ate caviar—nasty,

nasty stuff—and drank champagne till three in the morning. Then we went for a swim in a pond in the forest. I think it was breakfast time when we finally collapsed in bed. We were tired, but not too tired to, well ... shall we say ... enjoy one last tango."

She softly exhaled. Her shadowy eyes slithered in Sweet's direction, lingered a moment, then slid over to Lilian. Sweet's eyes glittered. Lilian's face was pale, very pale. Gem raised her glass to her lips, hiding a satisfied smile.

Then she went on recounting tale after tale of merry mischief and creative self-indulgence. She told of parties that began on Wednesdays and ran on till Sunday. She described a world of manic gaiety, one in which people threw champagne bottles out of windows, ran half-naked through the streets, and danced on car tops past dawn. Rhapsodizing over a supper party she attended, Gem said the champagne punch was made from fifty bottles of brut, and gallons of whiskey, Cointreau, and gin.

"Then there was the Four Arts Ball. It's a huge, wild thing given every June by art students in Paris. Thousands of people in costume—if you want to call it that. People don't really wear much more than body paint, a loincloth, and maybe some feathers on their heads. I went to one ball at the Porte d'Auteuil with a rich kid from Minnesota. Everyone was supposed to dress up like an Incan. Robby—that was his name—rubbed himself down with red ocher and strung three dead pigeons around his neck."

Sweet leaned forward. "And what did you wear?"

"Something exquisitely fashionable and stylishly simple ... bare breasts and a turquoise wig."

Sweet smiled faintly. Lilian gagged. She grabbed her glass of water, tried to drink it, and sloshed water over her chest. She jumped up so violently that her chair toppled over. Her eyes were wet; her shoulders hunched. She hugged her purse to her chest as though it were a shield.

"I have to go," she gasped, then fled the room. Sweet went after her.

"Lord help the person who's got something Gem wants," Rachel said. "That woman would scare the Devil himself if he got in her way."

Indeed. Gem had been mercilessly clever. She had chosen a public place, with a private audience, to reveal her own rebellious morality, to tantalize Sweet and embarrass Lilian with suggestive tales. Had Sweet really remained immune to Gem's charms?

"But Gem didn't stop there," Rachel said. "First, she went after Lilian's marriage to Sweet, then she went after her friendship with me. She made out like there was something between Sweet and me or that I wished there was. See, I knew Sweet before Lilian did. We grew up on the same block. His family moved there after you guys left. Lilian knew that I'd met Sweet before, but I'd never told her that we'd known each other as kids. It was a long time ago and it wasn't worth mentioning. But Gem used it. Twisted it around. Put it in Lilian's head that I liked Sweet."

"Surely Lilian didn't believe her."

"No, but that was just the beginning."

David could well imagine. He knew Gem's methods. *What a waste of human energy.*

Rachel said she had to leave. He showed her to the door. At the last moment, she stood on tiptoe and brushed her lips against his cheek. He was surprised, but pleased. She took his hand.

"Walk me to work, why don't you?"

"All right."

As he turned to get his coat from the closet, he had the feeling that he was being watched. He glanced over his shoulder and saw Annie, standing at the foot of the stairs. Guilt gripped him. He didn't know why.

"I'm just going to walk her to the hospital," he said, wondering why he felt bound to explain.

Annie nodded, but said nothing. Shouldering his way into his coat, David turned back to Rachel and gave her a quick smile, then hustled her out the door. He sensed Annie's eyes on his back until the door shut behind him.

II. PASSAGES

She stood there a moment longer, then continued upstairs to David's room. As she set about straightening up, her mind was in turmoil. She didn't like what she'd seen at the doorway, didn't like it at all. But what could she do about it?

Nothing, she thought. *He's a grown man. And cain't nobody do his thinking for him. He's got to follow his own mind.*

"But how could he ... ?" she muttered. "After all that's happened, how could he start up with that child again?"

She saw his suitcase lying side down on a chair and went to it with the thought of setting it in his closet. Without thinking, she flipped it open.

Hm-humph! Didn't even take his clothes out. He sure don't mean to stay long.

She saw one shirt, some underwear, and two pairs of socks.

Didn't bring much, neither. And his clothes—they look taken care of, but ... well, he sure don't dress like he used to.

She started to unpack the suitcase herself—

Lay everything in his dresser nice an' neat for him—

then thought better of it.

I sure don't wanna try to force him. Don't wanna upset him.

She lowered the suitcase lid and turned to the rest of the room. She'd remade his bed and was about to wipe down his desk when she saw that he'd found his old Bible. He'd left it lying open on his desk. She was surprised and pleased. She smiled wistfully.

Why, I r'member the day I gave him that. It was back in the days of the Tenderloin. His first Holy Communion Day. He was one proud li'l boy. Only nine years old.

She'd scrimped for a year to be able to buy him that small Bible ... *even paid extra to get his name written in gold on the cover.*

"You're a man, now," she'd told him. "A man in the sight of God."

The two of them had sat together, two or three evenings a week, and read it page for page. He had asked questions—

Good, smart questions—

And she'd done her best to give him good answers. And he'd believed— believed with his entire heart—in a loving God, a forgiving God.

He had such devotion, even more than Miss Lilian. Where'd it go?

When she mentioned that Miss Lilian had been buried in unconsecrated ground, his silence had said more than words.

What happened to him? Whatever it was, it just about ruined him. And kept him away. Kept him in exile.

He thought she believed he'd been working for the Movement all this time. But she knew better. Knew it in her heart. Something had gone wrong in his life.

"Terrible wrong," she said out loud.

Her gaze dwelled on the Bible.

At least, he took it out. Could be he's trying to find his way back, God help him.

The Bible was open to the New Testament. A passage had been marked. Bending for a closer look, she squinted at the fine print.

"Matthew 26:57-75," she whispered and began to read aloud. "Those who had arrested Jesus took him to Caiaphas, the high priest ... Peter followed him at a distance, right up to the courtyard of the high priest... A servant girl came to him. 'You also were with Jesus of Galilee,' she said. But he denied it b'fore them all. Another girl saw him and said, 'This fellow was with Jesus of Nazareth.' He denied it again. Those standing there went up to Peter and said, 'Surely, you are one of them, for your accent gives you 'way,' Then he began to call down curses on hisself and he swore to them, 'I don't know the man!' Immediately, a rooster crowed. Then Peter remembered the words Jesus had spoken: 'Before the rooster crows, you will disown me three times.' And he went outside and wept bitterly."

She eased herself down into the wooden desk chair and touched the pages, wondering.

Peter's denial of Jesus: What's that got to do with my David?

"'And he went outside and wept,'" she read again. "'Wept bitterly.'"

The page was well-fingered.

He been sitting here and reading—reading and reading about how Peter denied his Lord. Why? Has he done sumptin'?... Or has somebody done sumptin' to him?

She was peering into the display window of the Righteous Lady Dress Shop. From a distance, she looked pretty in a clean, simple way. Her coat was practical, but not stylish. And her little hat was modest. Her arms were full of groceries and at her side stood a small boy of about three dressed in knickerbockers. He was playing with a bright green ball. As David's gaze moved from the woman to her child, his lips bowed in a faint smile. Once, he'd hoped to have a family.

The boy bounced his ball and it rebounded high. He tried to catch it, but it escaped from between his plump little hands and rolled toward the curb. He scrambled to catch it, but every time he reached for it, it slipped away. It wobbled until it hit the curb, then bounced off and rolled into the street. He followed. His mother, her attention on the display, didn't notice.

A milk wagon swung around the corner with a screech of tires. David glanced at it and his lungs contracted. The wagon had taken the corner way too wide and way too fast and was careening down the street. The boy didn't hear or see it; he was intent on his ball. It had settled dead in the middle of the street. Now it was just beyond his fingertips. He took another step and reached for it.

David's heart lurched. Then he was running. Running hard. Giving it all he had. He had a sensation of terrible slowness, of trying to run through mud. Somewhere, as though from far away, a woman screamed. Her sound of terror was muffled, as though he heard it through a glass wall. Now he was closing in on the child, surging forward with arms outstretched, conscious of the wagon bearing down on them. He got a brief glimpse of the boy's startled brown eyes; then he'd snatched him up and was diving forward, crashing against the pavement. His head hit the ground hard. He felt an explosion of pain and fractals of color went skidding before his vision. The wagon barreled by in a puff of smelly exhaust. David lay with the boy in a heap, the child resting on his chest. He closed his eyes for a moment, stunned. When he reopened them, he found himself looking up into a pair of wide, innocent eyes. A cute little face with round cheeks and a set of miniature teeth grinned back at him.

"Ooh, that was fun!" the boy giggled. "Can we do that again?"

What a little charmer, thought David. Then the boy's smile disappeared into a look of surprise as he was yanked away. David heard a woman sobbing and scolding—the child's mother, he assumed—in a mixture of love, anger, and relief. Then there were other hands, strangers' hands, helping him to his feet, brushing him off, clapping him on the shoulder.

"You okay, mister?"

"I'm fine." David nodded. He was still dazed, though, and his head was throbbing.

"Damn them wagons," someone muttered.

"Lady, you one lucky woman," another said. "I ain't never seen nobody move that fast."

David dusted himself off. The young mother stood nearby, holding her son in her arms. Up close, he could see the dark circles under her eyes. She was young, maybe in her late twenties, and she looked wrung out.

"Oh, baby, don't you know you coulda been killed?" she was saying, stroking her son's scratched and dirt-smudged cheeks.

Unshed tears sparkled in her eyes. The boy looked at her with stupefied concern. He reached out with his small hands and touched her face. "Don't cry, Mommy. Please, don't cry!"

"You my precious angel. You all I got. If I lose you, I'll go outta my mind."

She bit down on her lip, trying to keep herself under control. An expression of horrified dismay crawled over her boy's small face. Then the corners of his lips turned down and his lower lip began to quiver. His face screwed up, his mouth dropped open, and he let out a deafening wail.

"But I wah-wah-wanted my ball!"

She tried to smile, but her lips trembled. "Toby, I've told you: If a ball goes out into the street, don't go after it. Let Mama do it." She wiped her eyes with the back of her hand. "Please, please baby. Let Mama do it. You promise? Don't never run out in the road like that again."

Fat tears slipped from his eyes, rolled down his cheeks, and fell in thick drops from his chin. "Unh-uh, I won't," he said. "I promise." He hugged his mother tight, nestling his head in the crook of her neck.

She looked up from him to David, extended a hand, and brushed David's sleeve with her fingertips.

"God bless you," she whispered.

"It was nothing." He reached out and tweaked the little boy's ear. "You're a fast one, chum."

Toby managed a weak smile through his tears.

"Too fast," his mother said. "He ain't got no sense yet."

"He'll learn."

"He'd better." Now she did give her son a little jiggle to show her annoyance, but she was betrayed by the loving expression in her eyes. He looked up at her and the faint smile he'd given David grew into a mischievous grin for his mother. She grinned back, then looked at David and her eyes were humble.

"God was with us today, but I shoulda been paying attention," she said. "I just bought him the ball. He was so excited and he wanted to carry it. I told him not to play with it till we got home, but I shoulda known better. He's just a baby. How could I expect him to understand? Then I just stopped for a minute to look at that shop window. They had a sign last week, saying they needed help. I shoulda been paying attention," she repeated. She glanced down at her son, hugged him closer, and looked back at David. "Oh, Lord," she whispered. "If you hadna been here, I ..." Her voice broke and the tears she'd been fighting to contain slipped from her eyes.

"Don't be so hard on yourself." David reached over and stroked the small head. "He's fine. And he's learned a lesson. He won't be running out into the street again. Will you, little man?"

Toby nodded his head without lifting it from his mother's shoulder. The crowd had drifted away. David put a supporting hand under her elbow and escorted her back to the sidewalk. Her groceries lay spilled on the ground.

"I'll pack your bags for you," he said.

"You don't need to do that."

Their eyes met.

"Yes, I do," he said warmly.

She smiled and briefly averted her large chocolate eyes. He realized that she was quite pretty, despite the dark half-moons under her eyes. Her face was well scrubbed and her complexion smooth. She had high cheekbones and a kind mouth.

"This is awful kind of you," she said as he gathered the errant goods—a Hormel canned ham, a box of Wheaties, some Sanka decaffeinated coffee, a box of Quaker Quick oats, and two candy bars. He returned them to their bags and started to hand them back to her, but she was still holding her son.

"I can help you carry these," David said.

Doubt flickered in her eyes. He understood. He had just saved her son's life, but he was still a stranger. In New York City, a wise woman did not let a strange man, even an apparently helpful one (in some cases, *especially* an apparently helpful one), walk her home.

"It's okay. I'll just take you to your corner, if you want me to."

She smiled, but shook her head. Putting her son down, she picked up her grocery bags.

"My ball," the boy protested.

David spied it lying in the gutter. He fetched it, pulled a worn silk handkerchief from his pocket and wiped the ball clean. Then he sank down on his haunches and offered it to the child. "Here you go."

The boy reached out and hesitated. He looked up at his mother. She nodded that it was okay to take the ball and he did so. Suddenly shy, he hid behind his mother's coat.

"Toby, say thank you," she said.

Toby peeked out from behind her coat and said, "Dankyu."

David laughed and straightened up.

"I'll be going now," she said.

Thanking David once again, she left him. Her tiny son firmly grasped her coat with one pudgy fist, his ball tucked under his other arm. David watched them go. She must've felt his eyes on her because at the corner she turned and gave a little wave. David waved back. Then she and her son disappeared from view. David dropped his arm, aware of an odd surge of sadness. The feeling bewildered him. A woman and her boy going about their lives—people he'd never seen before and would never see again: Why did the sight of their walking away make him feel so alone?

Shoving his hands deep into his pockets, he headed back toward Strivers' Row. As he walked, he had an image of the house, waiting for him with all of its empty rooms. And he recalled what he'd asked his father when he bought it.

"Why'd you buy such a big place, Daddy? What do we need all them rooms for?"

Augustus had laughed. "For grandchildren, son. Babies. The babies that you and the girls will bring home when you get married someday."

"We're a family," Lila had said. "And families need a place where they can be together."

David paused at a street corner, waiting for the light to change. Well, since his father's death, Gem had gone to Europe and he'd headed off down south. Only Lilian had remained in that big house, alone. Where were the grandchildren his parents had dreamed of? What had become of their vision of a large family, of generations gathered around the dining room table? Gem had never taken part in that dream, but he and Lilian had. Now Lilian was gone and he was the only one left. There was little chance of his marrying and having children. Not with the hell he was living.

Annie wanted him to fight for the house and he would do so, because he loved his parents, he loved Annie, and deep down, a part of him did love the house. He would fight and he would win, but in the end to what purpose?

The light changed; he was free to cross. But he remained standing there, rocked by a sense of loss. His family, he realized, was dying out.

Adrian Snyder leaned back in his chair and examined his fingernails. They were buffed to a nice soft gleam. He used a letter opener to dig a nearly imperceptible bit of dirt out from under the fingernail of his left index finger, then held his hand up to admire it. He heard a hiccup from his guest and looked up.

His "guest" sat in a chair in the middle of the room, flanked on either side by two of Snyder's biggest, baddest men, Shotgun and Slate. The guest fidgeted. He was bony and sharp-featured.

Something about him always did remind me of a ferret, Snyder thought. He hated ferrets.

The Ferret kept picking at the cloth at his knees, which he jogged up and down nervously.

"Nice pants," Snyder said in a conversational tone.

The Ferret tried to smile and failed.

"Did you buy them with my money?" Snyder asked.

The Ferret licked his lips. "Look, boss, I, uh—"

"Don't lie to me, Sully. Don't lie to me," Snyder said, still in a quiet tone. He never raised his voice. "There's only one thing worse than pickpockets and thieves and that's liars."

Sully flinched. He'd broken out into a cold sweat and his face was the color of wet putty. "Boss, I—I don't know what got into me. I swear, it'll never happen again."

"I'm sure it won't." Snyder examined a bit of loose skin on one cuticle. "So where's the rest of it? Or did you spend all twenty Gs?"

Sully's eyes shifted. "I—uh—I got it at home. In a box. Under the bed."

Snyder threw his head back and laughed. He had beautiful teeth. They caught the light and gleamed like pearls.

"C'mon, Sully. You can do better than that." He became serious again. "For your sake, you'd better do better than that."

He sent an eye signal to Shotgun, who dropped a brick-like hand on Sully's shoulder. Sully jumped and gave a little shriek.

"Okay—okay," he said, trembling. "It—it's in a box. Tied to a rope."

"Um-hmm," Snyder said. "And what's the rope tied to?"

"One of the pilings leading into the East River."

"I see." Snyder studied Sully, tapping the letter opener against one hand.

"I guess you didn't believe me when I said I can't stand liars." He paused. "I don't even tell lies myself." He drew a fingertip over the point of the opener. "You see, my boys already found the money. Wrapped in an oilskin and sunk in your toilet tank. Stupid move, Sully. It was one of the first places we looked." He gave a sigh of disappointment. "Now, I gave you two chances, two chances to tell the truth. And you fucked up. Actually, you fucked up three times, Sully. *Three* times. First when you stole from me. Second, when you lied to me. Third, when you lied to me again."

Sully was trembling. A wet stain blossomed at his crotch. Snyder saw it and shook his head with disgust. He glanced at Slate.

"Show him a slow twist."

Sully jerked forward in his seat, his face contorted in panic.

"Oh, God, no! Oh, please! It was Sheila, boss. She said she'd leave me if I didn't—"

The thin metal wire that was whipped around his neck cut him off in mid-sentence. His eyes bugged out. He clawed at the wire as it cut into his neck.

Snyder watched without expression. "She said she'd leave you, did she? Well, I'm afraid you'll be leaving her."

Sully turned and twisted, his skinny legs kicking at air. Droplets of blood oozed out along the line of the garrote. He pleaded with bulging eyes. Snyder said nothing.

Just as Sully was about to lose consciousness, Snyder signaled again. The wire was removed and Sully fell forward, clutching his neck.

"Oh, God, thank you. Thank you," he gasped.

Snyder got up and walked around his desk to where Sully sat. He towered over him.

"Look at me," he said.

Sully raised his bloodshot eyes. Snyder bent and brought his face close to the little man's. Snyder wrinkled his nose. The guy stunk of booze, piss, and fear. Sully reached out to him with bloody hands.

"Please ... please, forgive me," he rasped.

"'Course I do."

Snyder's smile was affable. He gave Sully a little pat on the cheek. A tear ran down Sully's face. His eyes shone with relief.

"You forgive me, boss?"

"It's forgotten. Look," Snyder said. "I got something for you."

He put a chummy hand on Sully's shoulder and hugged him. Sully stared into Snyder's eyes with gratitude. Snyder smiled, brought his right hand up, and plunged the letter opener deep into the base of Sully's throat. Sully's whole body jerked. He gagged and tore at the letter opener. His eyes fixed on Snyder's. Then he pitched forward. Snyder stepped aside and Sully fell to the floor with a thump. He twitched for a few seconds, then lay still. Snyder looked down at the dead man with contempt.

"You dumb fuck. I told you to never listen to my sister."

He signaled to Shotgun and Slate. "Get rid of him. He's bleeding on the rug. Then come back here. I have another job for you. His name is David, David McKay."

David's head ached from having been smashed against the pavement. His eyes hurt even from the pale light of the over-hung sky. And his thoughts churned restlessly inside his head.

A lot's done happened .. .A lot's done happened .. .A lot's done happened since you been gone .. .

Well, there was nothing he could do to change the past, but—

"Hey, mister, you wanna shine?"

David blinked and looked down. A grizzled old man with milky blue irises stood looking up at him. A battered hat sat jauntily on his round head. His lower lip hung a bit, revealing missing teeth and tobacco-stained stumps. His eyes gleamed with benevolence.

"Here, you wanna sit down?"

The old man gestured to a shoeshine stand built alongside a grocery store on the street. David saw then that the old man's hands were stained with boot black. His wooden shoeshine box stood nearby.

"No, thank you. I'm fine."

"You don't look it."

David had to smile at the old man's candor. Truth to tell, he didn't feel well. He yielded when the old man took him by the arm.

"Here, you sit down. Let me give you a nice shine."

"No, really, I—"

But the old man insisted. Finally, to be polite, David climbed up onto the mounted chair and placed his feet on the supports.

"I'm Roy," the old man said. "Roy, Roy, the Shoeshine Boy. See, it rhymes. Kinda catchy. Customers like it. You new in town?"

"Not really, no."

Roy poured some drops of liquid shoe cleanser on David's shoes, spread it around with a soft little brush, then snapped open a strip of stained gray cloth and started to rub David's leather shoes with vigor.

"Set out to see Seventh Avenue, have you? That's what all the folk new to Harlem do. Well, it's pretty quiet today, but in the summertime, it's sumptin' t'see. The gals strut they stuff and the crowds is deeper than deep. We gets all kindsa parades up and down the street. It sure is sumptin' t'see."

Roy whipped out another rag from his back pocket, twisted open a tin of black polish, used the rag to apply the polish, and began to shine the shoes: from side to side, across the toe, around the back. He was quick and strong and while he worked he talked.

"Yeah, we's had lotsa parades." His voice trailed off. "But the one I best r'members, the one that meant the most, was back in 1919, when our boys come home from that there war over in Europe." He was silent a moment. "My son went to France and didn't come back. My missus say he died for nothing, but I can't say that, don't want to say that. The hurt done nearly killed her. That and believing he died for nothing." He looked up at David with cataract eyes. "You weren't here for that parade, son. Too young to know what I mean."

"I was there," David said. "I was in it."

"You was over there? For real?"

"Yeah," David nodded. "For real."

The old man's eyes grew shrewd. "When d'you ship out?"

"Summer of '18."

"You was an officer, right?"

"A lieutenant."

Roy studied him. "You look way too young for them kind of mem'ries. But they're in your eyes ... You got old eyes. My missus would say you got an old soul, son. A very old soul."

David said nothing, but he was touched.

"I bet you got a medal," Roy said. "You look the type."

"Do I now?" David smiled. "Well, yes, I did ... I did, at that."

"It was hell over there, wasn't it?"

"Yeah ... in many ways it was." *But the war over there,* he wanted to add, *was nothing—nothing compared to one over here.*

The knife of regret stabbed him.

Forgive me, Jonah. Forgive me. At least, you've found your peace. Maybe, just maybe, one day I'll find mine.

12. A VOICE STILLED

"Excuse me, Mr. David, but I have sumptin' for you."

Annie's voice brought him out of his reverie. He hadn't heard her as she entered the parlor, her skirts rustling softly. She reached into one of her deep apron pockets, withdrew a slender rose cloth-covered book, and handed it to him.

"It was Miss Lilian's."

Taking the book, he opened it. The book's delicate pages were covered with Lilian's fine script. His face registered surprise. He looked up at Annie.

"Did she leave other papers?"

Annie shook her head. "Mr. Sweet burned everything else.

Even her last manuscript—"

"He burned her *book?*"

"Did it right after the funeral. But he didn't get this. I'd taken it. Hidden it."

He thanked her. She gave a slight bow and moved away. His suspicion and resentment of Sweet hardened. How could the man have destroyed her work? It was beyond callous; it was cruel. Or did the manuscript contain something Sweet wanted no one to see? That manuscript represented Lilian's last creative effort. It contained her last written thoughts.

But did it?

His gaze dropped to the diary. The book was new. He turned the pages one by one. She had written it as though it were a novel, recording the events like scenes from a book. Perhaps she'd intended to use it later as material. She'd begun it in October, the day Gem arrived. The last entry was dated last March. She must have stopped writing in it at about the same time Gem returned to Europe. Strange. He turned back to the first page.

Friday, October 31, 1924

Gem is back. How apt that she reappear on Halloween, the day on which ghosts return to bedevil the living. God help me. I don't want her here. Not now, when everything is finally turning out well. I must get her out of the house swiftly, but she must leave voluntarily. I can't just turn her out. People will talk.

I sat on Gem's bed this evening, watching her unpack. She has tawdry taste. There was a slinky number in glittering crimson with a deep cut in the back—*vulgar*. And the gold outfit that followed—*obscene*. And the shoes she had! Pair after pair after pair! I had to ask her if this is how she's been spending Daddy's money, on trashy outfits.

Gem turned her nose up. "Darling, my clothes come from the best collections. There's absolutely nothing trashy about them. And I'll have you know, I didn't pay for a single stitch—at least not with cash."

She chuckled shamelessly. Then she proceeded to tell me what she's been up to. Living it up, as she called it. "Having a helluva time! In London, Paris, Amsterdam, Munich, Berlin! Fantastic city, Berlin. German lovers have incredible energy. No style, but lots of energy. And stamina."

She ground her hips into the air and thrust them forward roughly. Her manner was crude. Disgusting. She laughed at my expression and twirled exuberantly. She told me about her life in Paris. Montmartre, she said, is a playground.

"There's no other word for it. A playground. You need to go there. It's home-away-from-home for us colored folk."

She had a singing gig at Le Grand Duc, she said. I've heard of the club. Only the best people go there: Nancy Llewellyn, Raymond McMasters, Geoffrey Aragon, the Bendal sisters, Maria Noone, the Baltimore Tates. All of them fought to get tables to hear her, Gem said. And between sets, they begged her to sit with them and drink champagne.

"After hours, the Grand Duc was like a Harlem cabaret. Niggers from the other clubs would come over and we'd get down. Even Langston was there! He was working at the Duc, washing dishes. After hours, he'd come out of the kitchen and join in."

Gem's eyes sparkled; her cheeks were flushed and her skin glowed as though lit from within. I closed my eyes against the sight of her. She made me feel pale and drab, stiff and regimented, claustrophobic within my own skin.

My life has been dominated by obligation. It was never my own. What did Gem do to merit such freedom? What did she ever do? Nothing. She took it as her right. Perhaps I should have done that, too. Simply taken my freedom, instead of having felt compelled to earn it.

When I consider all those years of teaching school ...

Pure drudgery. Daddy's voice would boom in my conscience every time I thought about quitting. *Duty, duty, first and foremost.* I would think of Gem and dream about what she was up to. I wanted to go out and experience life too, but I stayed put—because I thought I had to. I endured loneliness—because I thought I had to. This evening, listening to Gem, it seemed that my sacrifices weren't only useless, but foolish. An acute nausea crept up from the pit of my belly. Not once in five years had I felt this insecure—not once since Gem left. Only a few hours in the house and already she was affecting me.

I was suddenly angry, not just at her, but at myself. How could I let this empty-headed woman cause me to doubt myself? She's always had only one goal in life—to have fun—and she's never felt guilty about it. Such a goal would have never satisfied me and apparently it hasn't done much for her either. Gem has squandered her freedom. Otherwise, she wouldn't have come back. I let her prattle on about how marvelous her life in Paris was until I couldn't stand it anymore.

"If it was so wonderful there, then why are you here?"

Gem didn't miss a beat. "Because I missed you, sister dear. Missed you terribly."

"Are you sure you didn't miss my money more?"

Something flickered in her eyes. I told her about the letter I got from Aunt Clara the other day. About how well Auntie's doing. Settled in Chicago. On her third husband. He's even richer than the last, I said, related to the Johnsons. I told her that Auntie had asked about her.

"You were always her favorite. I'm sure she'd love to see you."

Gem caught my meaning. Her expression toughened and her left hand went to her hip. With her right index finger, she jabbed the air to emphasize every word.

"This is where I want to be. Here, in Daddy's house."

"*Daddy's house* no longer belongs to you. Remember? You sold your share to David and me."

"Well, I like it here. I'm going to stay—as long as I want to— and there's nothing you can do about it." She thrust her face up close to mine. "You don't have the guts to throw me out."

"Don't underestimate me. I've changed. I won't support you."

"Oh, but you will. You'll give me anything I want because you're afraid of people talking. And you know I know how to make people talk."

I stood to leave. "I won't let you destroy what I have. I've worked too hard to let you take it away. I'll see you out on the streets first."

She snickered. "Don't be stupid and don't try to scare me. I've run with the big boys. They play for keeps. And so do I."

David paused, remembering. Lilian and Gem had fought viciously in high school. Gem had been the one with the glittering looks and witty personality; the studious Lilian couldn't compete. The more people had urged her "to be like Gem," the harder she had fought to be different. She'd deliberately chosen to downplay her beauty and gain respect for her brains. They'd carried the conflict into adulthood. On Gem's first night home, they hadn't wasted time on niceties, but gone straight to the heart of the matter. They virtually declared war on one another. How in the world had they reached the point where they would go shopping together?

He found his place and read on.

Friday, November 1, 1924
Is something going on between Gem and my husband?
So, Lilian had begun to doubt Sweet's fidelity, after all ...

Wednesday, November 12, 1924

Gem and I had lunch today. Her invitation was a surprise. Expecting the unpleasant, I planned to tread lightly and listen carefully. However, the conversation took an unexpected turn. I've decided to try to reconstruct it as accurately as I can because I sense that Gem's words contain a secret that I've yet to pierce.

Gem picked the Civic Club, because of its high social visibility, of course. When I arrived, she was seated at a center table, dressed in a buff-colored wool suit with a cream chinchilla stole. A bit much for so early in the day.

"You need to relax. Have more fun," she told me and chuckled. "I know you think I have too much fun. But you should try it. You might like it. Once I had a Buddhist lover. He'd pound me into the mattress for hours. Then he'd have the nerve to meditate for ten minutes and lecture me on moderation for twenty!" Gem gave a husky laugh.

Her voice was loud and I was sure her shameful words had carried. I glanced around, expecting to see ovals of shocked faces staring at us, openmouthed. Thank God, there were none. But I was still mortified. I looked back at her, at her overdone makeup, her supercilious air. She was the same old Gem: crude despite all her culture.

"You never will change, will you?" I said in a low, tense voice.

"Why should I?"

"That you have to even ask—"

"Listen, if I have too much fun, you have too little. Look at you. You're aging before your time."

This was an old argument between us. I wasn't in the mood for it.

"All right, all right," I said, waving her words away and hoping she would quiet down. The waiter was approaching with our tea.

As soon as he was gone, Gem produced a silver flask and

before I could say anything, she had poured a dollop of whisky into my cup.

"Here. Eat, drink, and learn to be merry," she said.

I was tense and tired. My paper wasn't as well received at the Chicago conference as I'd hoped it would be. And I've been having nightmares. So I thought Gem might be right. I should relax. I took a sip. I didn't like it. I've never liked alcohol. But then I felt warmth spread through me and decided to take another sip after all.

Gem nodded approvingly. She waved her jeweled hand at the waiter and he promptly took our orders. Gem and I chatted. The conversation was going well and under the influence of several cups of tea, I began to relax. Indeed, I think now that I relaxed too much. The trouble began when Gem started criticizing me.

"You should do more for yourself. Take off those old-fashioned clothes. Doll yourself up a little."

"I'm as 'dolled up' as I need to be."

"Don't be a sap. Your face, your clothes—they're what people see first and remember last. Sometimes, I think you work to make yourself look like a zombie."

"I work to be respected. I don't want to be a bit of fluff on a man's arm."

"Like me, you mean?" She smiled saucily. "Why are you so stubbornly naive, dear? It was forgivable when you were younger, but it's tiresome now."

"Oh, please! My profession doesn't involve seducing men. Yours apparently does."

"Watch yourself, dear—"

"Getting a man was never as important to me as it is to you. I saw what Daddy did to Mama and I vowed I'd never let that happen to me. I knew that I could do without a man. Didn't want one. Didn't need one."

"Then why the hell did you marry one?"

"Men do have their uses. I wanted children—"

"You wanted sex—"

"No—you've had enough of that for both of us."

I stopped, appalled at what I'd said. But Gem smiled, unperturbed. She scooped up her flask and sloshed more whisky into my cup.

"Drink up, sweetheart. It seems to be doing you good."

I nudged my cup away. I'd had more alcohol than I intended to and now it was tricking me. Arguing with Gem was the last thing I wanted to do. The conference was exhausting. And this feeling, ever since I've been back, that something isn't right with Jameson ...

My head ached. It felt as though an evil dwarf with a pickax had gotten inside my skull and was hitting an anvil with malicious regularity. I can't quite explain it, but something gave way inside me. I just didn't have the energy to pretend.

"The simple truth is that I was tired of being alone. I was in my late twenties and still single. I knew what everyone was thinking: 'How sad. What an old maid.' So when I met Jameson, I decided to marry him."

"Just like that?" Gem snapped her fingers.

"Just like that."

"Then why don't you do the work required to keep him?"

"What do you mean?"

"I mean: Be pretty, Lil. Give him something to look at."

"Jameson loves me the way I am."

"You believe that, do you?"

"Yes. I do. I'm plain. I'm old-fashioned. That's me, and I'm not ashamed of it."

"But why? You can look as good as I do!"

"Don't you understand? I don't want to look like you!"

"Well, be plain then! It's annoying to look at you. If you lose your precious Jameson, you'll be the one to blame, not me."

I didn't like what I saw in her eyes. "Why should I lose him?"

She didn't answer, but her lips curled maliciously. I suddenly felt cold.

"You want him, don't you? That's what this is all about."

"Yes, I want him, dear. But more to the point: He wants me."

The little man in my head struck his anvil a reverberating blow. I gambled when I married Jameson. For the first time in my life, I flew in the face of general opinion. And I did it quickly, afraid to give myself time to reconsider. But I've never been able to silence a nagging doubt...

Gem was studying me with the sharp, observant eyes of a hunter, eyes that missed nothing. And I wondered once more, why does she have to be a part of my life?

I closed my eyes, shutting out the outer world. I could hear the sounds of people drawing their chairs up to their tables, of napkins being snapped open; the obsequious murmur of waiters taking orders, the clink and clatter of silverware. I felt the suffocating quality of air in a closed room, and smelled the riotous mix of spices and oils in the sumptuous dishes laid out on surrounding tables. But I heard and felt and smelled everything from a distance, as though I sat on the other side of a dampening curtain, isolated, alone with this throbbing pain, this exhaustion and this rapidly spreading dread. The only sensation that was up close and immediate was the penetrating impression of Gem's scrutiny crawling over me, probing, tasting, analyzing. Opening my eyes, I met her gaze head-on.

"I won't make it easy for you."

She laughed, but I didn't let that dismay me. I went on.

"You've always taken what you wanted—but not this time. I have Jameson; I'm going to keep him. He'll never leave. He'll stay where the money is. And that's not with you. Perhaps you'll get him to cheat. Maybe you can teach him new tricks. But he'll bring them right back to me, to me and my bed. He will always come back."

Gem's face became as glacial as carved ice, her eyes as hot as molten lava. They virtually glowed with spite.

"Don't be a fool. You may be well off, but you're not rich. Not rich, little sister. I know rich. You are simply financially healthy. And you're not beautiful. You've got the material, but you don't want to use it. There are many other women who are either incredibly ugly but breathtakingly rich—or incredibly lovely but breathtakingly poor. Jameson would leave you for either one."

Her fangs had drawn blood and from my expression she knew it. My mind scrambled for a suitable reply. My thoughts ran hither and thither—I admit it—like a trapped mouse.

The waiter brought our orders. He swung our plates down on the table with a proud flourish. Gem picked up her fork and attacked her plate with gusto, but I'd lost my appetite. I tried to isolate Gem's venomous words with a mental tourniquet, but her poison had hit my veins. Self-doubt and apprehension burned through me. The dread of losing Jameson cut my breath to a painful wheeze. I couldn't lose him; I couldn't. I couldn't bear the shame.

Gem picked up a piece of celery and snapped it in two. "Wake up, dear. In this world, you've got to fight with everything you've got."

"He'll never leave me," I whispered.

"Baby, you don't even know what's cooking under your own roof. You need me to pull your pretentious little butt out of the fire. Well, I'm going to do you a favor. I'll save your marriage for you." Gem savored my stunned silence for a long delicious minute. "That's right. I'm going to help you."

"Help me? How?"

"I'll take you shopping. Get you acquainted with the seductive side of life."

The thought disgusted me. "I don't need your help."

"You're an idiot."

I felt sick. That little man with the pickax was swinging to a steady, bitter, battering rhythm. "Since when would you be willing to help me?"

She didn't answer at once. Her expression softened and saddened. Gem, the tough woman of the world, suddenly appeared vulnerable. It was an amazing transformation.

"You asked before why I came back. You didn't believe me when I said I missed you. But it was true. Europe was magnificent, but it was also very, very lonely. Can you imagine what it's like to wander past the expensive shops of the Champs Elysees or struggle through the hordes clogging Berlin's Kurfürstendamm, year after year, and never once see a familiar face from back home?"

"But that's what you wanted."

"At first." Gem's gaze was distant. "Those first couple of years passed in a frantic haze. I was so busy, I could barely keep up. But then time seemed to slow, to stretch out. The days became longer; the nights lonelier. I missed Harlem. And I missed you." Gem's eyes refocused on me with a strange intensity. "Whatever happens, please believe that. I missed you."

Something in her tone gave me the chills. I tried to shrug it off. "All right, you missed me. That doesn't explain why you would be willing to 'save my marriage,' as you put it. If you want Jameson, then why would you help me keep him?"

"There are many men in the world, but I have only one sister. Does that satisfy you?"

"No."

She eyed me. She seemed to be measuring me, perhaps assessing just how much she could get away with.

"I want the truth. Gem."

"The absolute truth? All right, then."

She shrugged and snapped another celery stalk. It sounded like the breaking of bones.

"The fact is, I'm not interested in helping you keep Jameson, or any other man. I don't want to help you, period."

"That's more like it."

She laughed. "Truth is, I just like shopping. That's all. Especially when it's at someone else's expense. There, are you satisfied now?

I eyed her.

"Come now," she coaxed. "What difference does it make why I help you? Just as long as I do?"

She was making me feel unreasonable. She had put me in an unforeseeable and disagreeable quandary. I'd always been free to blame Gem for our estrangement, but by offering to reconcile, she'd turned the tables. The onus was on me. I felt trapped. Manipulated. Outmaneuvered. And irritably, annoyingly, against all reason, vaguely guilty—I suppose for being so suspicious and unyielding, as though Gem has never given me good reason to distrust her, as if her demonstrated gift for deceit and deception is as insignificant as the dead leaves of autumns past, to be swept aside and discarded, without a second's qualm.

Was I being unreasonable? Perhaps Gem had indeed been homesick. Perhaps she had realized that those friends of hers in Paris were nothing more than opportunists who lost interest in her the moment her pockets were empty. Perhaps.

I would've liked to believe in Gem's avowed sisterly love, but....

Well, no matter what my doubts might be, one aspect was perfectly clear: As long as there was no proof of "an ulterior motive," I couldn't reject Gem's conciliatory offer in good conscience. And didn't want to admit it, but I do need help with this marriage. So I relented.

Gem was delighted. That made me wonder anew. I still can't figure it out. And somehow, I can't free myself of the image of Gem signaling the waiter, then turning back to me with a grand smile, and saying brightly:

"Your bill."

Those two words made me shudder. Just what will I have to pay for? And what will be the price?

David closed the small book and leaned back, rubbing his eyes. He'd had no idea that Lilian was so lonely. Now he understood why she'd married so quickly. No wonder she hadn't informed him of her decision: She herself had never been at ease with it.

Like Lilian and Rachel, he wondered about Gem's sudden willingness to help. *Life does change people,* he thought. He knew that only too well himself. But had it changed Gem? Had the loneliness of her years abroad actually taught her to value her family or had it simply, as Annie put it, left her lean and hungry? And if Gem had indeed learned to care so much for Lilian, then where was she now? Why was she silent in the face of Lilian's death? Why the blatant indifference? Perhaps the reconciliation was short-lived. Did the diary hold the answer? Sitting up, he flipped it open and found where he'd left off.

Friday, December 5, 1924

Wonder of wonders ... Dr. Steve agrees that I'm going to have a child.

David read the one line twice. She was pregnant? He sat there, stunned. But where was the baby? And why hadn't Annie said something? He'd seen no evidence of a baby in the house. Nothing, anywhere. And why had Lilian never written to him about it? He wasn't keeping a list of her emerging secrets, but maybe he should start.

He looked down at the slender book. What else would

he find in there? For a split second, he was afraid to continue reading it. Would he learn something he didn't want to know?

Monday, December 8, 1924

I haven't told Jameson yet—I don't want to. This secret, this wonderful secret, is something I want to cherish alone. At least for a while, I want to enjoy it alone.

Sunday, January 18, 1925

There was a time when everything was going so well. I was writing regularly and my work was well received. Now when I put my fingers to the keys, they tremble so badly I can't type. This diary is now the only writing I do.

Tuesday, January 20, 1925

Gem has made friends with some rich whites, the Hardings. She brought them by yesterday. Horrible people. Always gushing about how "marvelous" Negroes are. But I suppose they were as sincere as ofays can be. It amazes me how white people observe so little and presume to know so much. Whites have hated and hunted us for years. Now they're fascinated with us. Their ignorance is deafening, their arrogance dazzling. Any colored man could fill an encyclopedia with what he knows about them, but it's a rare ofay who could fill a pamphlet with a little truth about us. I believe they know more about their dogs. Certainly, I don't recognize myself or anyone else I know in the black characters produced by white writers. As for white patrons: They're only out to back what they think is "pure Negro art." As if they know us better than we know ourselves. I thank the Lord every day that I don't need the white man's money. I wouldn't trust a single one of them.

Tuesday, January 21, 1925

Jameson leaves me alone a great deal. He says he must, because of his work. That's true, but only to a certain extent. The truth is, he spends as little time with me as possible. He either locks himself in Daddy's old office or makes arrangements to meet friends, and he always meets them elsewhere, never inviting them to the house, carefully avoiding any overlap between his friendships and our marriage. I once asked him why.

Don't you want me to know your friends, darling?

He only smiled. Enigmatic. Charming. Unattainable.

But darling ...

He never answered. His habit of evading my questions infuriates me. Like a cloud, he seems solid but is as insubstantial as mist when I reach for him. He's always gently kind, astutely considerate and sweetly polite when we pass in the hallway or sit down to dinner, but his manner is detached, as though I'm a neighborly acquaintance instead of his wife. He's gentlemanly and affectionate in public, holding my hand, supporting me by the elbow, making sure I'm properly seated in restaurants and at dinner parties. To all outer appearances, he's the perfect husband, but he leaves my side the moment our front door closes behind us.

We still share the same bedroom, but during the day he never enters the room when I'm in it, and on most nights, he eases into our bed only when he believes I'm asleep. Once a month, he exercises his husbandly privileges, but he's mechanical, distracted. I wonder why he bothers. Ours is a shell of a relationship, a lovely, beautiful shell.

Friday, January 30, 1925

He has never loved me. I knew it from the beginning. I hoped I could change him, but the more I do for him, the less he cares.

He's only interested in my money and his career. I'm scared to tell him about the baby. He doesn't want children.

But I'm determined to have this child, come what may.

Sometimes I think of the years Mama endured Daddy's cruelty. I always sympathized with her; now I can empathize with her, too. But Mama had it better than I do. Deep down, Daddy did love her. And she sensed it. She felt that he needed her all along, even though he didn't know it himself. And that gave her strength. I wish I could feel that way about Jameson. But I can't. My only sources of comfort are my church and this child. All my hope I put into this one small human being. And all my love.

Wednesday, February 4, 1925

Jameson loves someone else. I'm sure of it. I've discovered that I can be intensely jealous. I've searched his jacket and coat pockets for bits of paper, checked his shirts for lipstick smears, read his mail. In short, I've done everything I could think of to find evidence that he's been somewhere he shouldn't have been, with someone he shouldn't have been. But I've found nothing. I should feel relieved. Instead, I feel worse. It sounds crazy, but the very lack of evidence seems proof that Jameson is being careful to hide something—or some*one*—from me.

Saturday, February 7, 1925

It's hard to remember the way it was when we first got married. I was so deeply in love with him, so grateful to have him, that it didn't matter that his ardor was weak. I wanted to believe that he was cool by nature, but loyal and committed. I was proud to have such a brilliant lawyer as my husband. But with the pregnancy, I can no longer ignore his lack of affection. I must find the strength to tell him about the baby.

Tuesday, February 10, 1925

Jameson continues to be solicitous and overwhelmingly

kind, but today I realized that I hate him. I've heard of pregnant women coming to loathe their husbands, but my feelings don't stem from my condition. My feelings toward him have been changing for some time. I just didn't want to admit it. I wouldn't have believed that I could detest anyone so intensely.

Why did I marry such a lower-class social climber? What was I thinking of? Jameson should be grateful I even looked his way. Most women of my class wouldn't have given him the time of day, and here I went and married the man. Daddy would've never stood for it. I can't believe I made such a mistake.

I'm compelled to spend the rest of my life with him. That realization horrifies me. But the thought of losing him to someone else is worse. The shame, the scandal, would be unthinkable. Yet, I don't know how I can go on with him. The very sight of him makes me shake with rage.

Friday, February 13, 1925

If only I could get him away from me. But he's ever present, always there with his potions and medicines. I have to force myself to submit to his ministrations. I'm sure he can feel my loathing for him, but he ignores it. He's outwardly concerned, attentive and responsive to my every murmured wish. He pretends that the only problem is my "nerves," as he calls it.

I wish I had someone to talk to. If only Mama were here, but she's long gone. There's Annie, but as much as I love her, she's still just a servant and I can't see myself stooping so low as to confide in the help. I think of David. Often. But he has problems of his own. And to be truthful, I'd rather not have to admit to him that I've made a mess of my life.

Then there's Gem.

The reversal in my feelings toward Jameson, dramatic as

it is, still amazes me less than the change in my attitude toward Gem. After so many years, the two of us have come to share a closeness that I'd only heard other sisters speak of. She and I are at ease with our differences now. And we've discovered similarities that surprise us. Our rivalry will always be there, but it has lost its bitter edge. We can laugh and joke with one another.

Wednesday, February 18, 1925

I wonder whether Gem has noticed my changed feelings toward Jameson. She's very cool toward him. Sometimes I watch the two of them together. She's clearly not thrilled to see him when she runs into him. She's extremely cordial, but she seems blatantly relieved when he goes off on one of his business trips. I haven't told Gem about the baby, either. I've tried several times, but I just can't bring the words out. I don't know why. Instead, I've confided in Rachel. That choice confuses me. I went outside the family. Why? It seemed right at the time.

For a moment, David stopped breathing. *Rachel? She told Rachel?* He closed the diary, too angry to read further. *If Rachel knew then surely Annie knew, too, and neither one of them said a damn thing.* He glanced at his pocket watch, left lying on his night table. It was nearly ten. Annie was in bed—it was too late to see her now ... although he was sorely tempted to wake her— and Rachel was probably busy at the hospital. He sat for a moment, trying to get his emotions under control. *There are too many damn secrets in this house, too many.* His gaze dropped back down to the diary; he flipped it open. Only two more pages left.

Tuesday, February 24, 1925

I took a walk down by the Hudson River to see the sunset this evening. It was such a pleasure to get out of the house, away from the smell of medicines. The air was cold but crisp and clean. And the colors were magnificent. As though a mad painter had taken his brush and, in florid strokes, splashed the horizon with streaks of red, orange, violet, and gold. For one intense fleeting moment, I wished that I were as free as Gem, to simply pick up and go and never look back. But that will never be. I have responsibilities, status, property. I'm a wife and soon will be a mother. I'm rooted to my place, as firmly shackled to it as a prisoner wearing handcuffs.

Saturday, February 28, 1925

Our lives are falling apart. Snyder has broken with Gem. He did it in the most degrading way, right out in public, and now the town is buzzing about it. She has fled to the Hardings' estate in Amagansett. I feel for her and I envy her ability to escape.

Monday, March 2, 1925

Gem has sent me a message. She's still in East Hampton, feeling alone and humiliated. It isn't just the breakup with Adrian. She says there's no place for her here, with Jameson and me. I'm trying to convince her otherwise, but she doesn't believe me. It's ironic that this miserable marriage to Jameson has brought me closer to Gem. I'm almost ashamed to recall my earlier fears that she would try to take him. True to her word, she has become a loyal friend and ally. The thought of what has happened to her saddens me.

Thursday, March 5, 1925

My health seems to be worsening. Something must be very wrong with me. I'm so tired. I'm ready to collapse. My head throbs continually. The pain is almost unbearable. I seem to have lost my sense of balance and I stumble a lot. I'm afraid of falling and hurting the baby. I'm worried about my bouts of forgetfulness, too. These memory lapses are humiliating. And the dreams. Miserable, shifting images that invade my sleep. Maybe I'm losing my mind. I lay awake at night, the blood pounding in my temples, unable to raise my head from the pillow or even turn it sideways without stabbing pain. The doctors poke and prod but find nothing. Jameson wants me to see a psychologist. I don't want to. I'm not crazy. I know I'm not. I can't be.

That was the final entry, the last words of a voice now stilled. He would have to speak to the living to learn the rest of Lilian's story.

He closed the diary and weighed the little book in his hand. It was so small to contain such misery. He thought of Lilian's letters. What effort it must have cost her to sound cheerful. He recalled how her last letter had asked him to return and how he hadn't answered it. And he gave a long, deep sigh. He'd been so obsessed with his own dilemma that he had never considered, had refused to consider, that she might need him. And this ... this was the consequence.

13. THE PICNIC

"Why did you tell me he was a good husband?"

"Because he was."

"Lilian's diary tells a different story."

"Her diary? You found her diary?"

It was late Monday morning and they were sitting in Rachel's living room. Her thin shoulders were hunched and tense under her cheap white cotton shirt. She folded her arms across her chest. He felt a spark of pity for her and quashed it.

"And why didn't you tell me that Lilian was pregnant?"

"Because I ..." Her voice was barely above a whisper. "Well, I wasn't sure. I mean I ... I knew she claimed to be—"

"*Claimed* to be?"

She licked her lips. "Remember, I told you there was a time when Lilian and I didn't see each other?"

He nodded.

She took a deep breath. "Well, there were two times when we did see each other ... two times that ..." She swallowed and looked at him. "David, this is so hard to tell you."

"Just spit it out. Nothing can be worse than what I'm thinking right now."

Something glimmered in her eyes, something like hurt. "A year ago, in January, Lilian stopped by. She hadn't spoken to me in ages, but there she was. Pale as a ghost. Said she had to talk. But once she came in, she got quiet. Wouldn't say nothing. I let her be. And I made some coffee. Then the clock struck three. The kids started leaving the school across the street. We could see them through the window, all loud and laughing. Lilian started crying. And then she said she was pregnant."

"Why didn't you tell me before? Neither you nor Annie said anything about Lilian having had a child."

"Well, I guess that's because she didn't."

"You mean she *lost* the baby?" A horrible possibility dawned on him. "Did she kill herself because she lost the child?"

An indecipherable glimmer came into Rachel's eyes. Did it reveal sadness, perhaps agony, even a flash of anger? She swallowed and dropped her gaze.

"It would've made sense, wouldn't it? Losing a baby is... why, it's unbearable." She gave a little shake of her head. "But no, that's not what happened."

"Then what *did* happen?"

"I don't know," she said thickly.

"How far along was she?"

"She claimed she was in her fourth month, but there still wasn't nothing to see. She said she hadn't been sleeping. She talked a little bit about it being a boy or a girl. And then she said she was scared, that maybe it wouldn't turn out right. I told her a lot of women worry about stuff like that. But the baby almost always turns out fine. She smiled at me, sort of in a sad way. Then she got up to go. She stopped at the door and gave me a hug. She told me she loved me, but she didn't come by no more."

"But that wasn't the last time you saw her?"

"No." She shook her head. "But it was a while that went by. She'd stopped coming to church, too, you see. For years, she'd come. Every Sunday, rain or shine. But after Gem, everything changed.

"The time came for our church's Fourth of July picnic. Even the blue bloods over in Brooklyn come over for it. Lilian was one of our best organizers. Folks at church were hoping she'd show up just to say hello."

"And did she?"

"Oh, she was there all right. Holding a big plate of food when I saw her. She wasn't eating it, though. Just picking at it. Like she needed something to do. She didn't look good. She'd fallen off. Her color was bad. And her belly was as flat as a pancake."

"What?"

"She tried to act like she didn't see me. So I went up to her and asked her about the baby. She turned white—whiter than a bleached sheet. Said she didn't know—didn't *want to* know—what I was talking about. I asked her if she remembered coming by my house that January. And her face changed. It just sort of... crumpled. She looked so sad. I asked her if I could do anything for her. And then she gave me this look." Rachel frowned. "This look, David, it was hard to describe. There was hurt and anger and, well ... disgust—like she thought I was her worst enemy. Then she turned and ran. She hightailed it out of there so fast you'd have thought the tax man was behind her."

"So she did lose the baby."

"David, don't you get it? When I asked her about visiting me, she really didn't know what I was talking about."

"How is that possible?"

"It's obvious, isn't it?"

"Not to me."

Rachel took a deep breath. Her gaze went out the window, to the school across the street. "Your sister wanted a baby. Wanted it bad. Don't you know what that kind of wanting can do to a woman?"

"Are you saying she *imagined* being pregnant?"

Her mouth tightened. "Do you really want to know what I think? What I honest to God think?"

"Yes."

"All right. I can tell you right now that I *don't* think she killed herself because she lost a baby." She looked him in the eye. "She did it cause she couldn't have one."

For a moment, he sat there in utter silence. He was stunned. That possibility had never occurred to him. *Could she be right? Was that it?* He sighed. *Was that what brought Lilian down?*

"Now that you know, David, would you please, please leave this alone?"

He licked his lips and took a deep breath. "No."

"David, please—"

"I cannot. I will not."

She sagged down onto the sofa and put a hand to her forehead. He sat down next to her. His voice was quiet but penetrating.

"You might be right about the baby and her wanting one so badly. But there was another hand in this. Another reason."

"She got sick. That's all. She was sick and—"

"Yeah. Slit her wrists. I don't buy it."

"What're you saying?"

"I'm saying that all this talk of a mysterious illness makes no sense."

For a moment, she studied him and then her expression changed. She looked as though she were seeing him clearly for the first time. "I almost don't recognize you and that frightens me. All of a sudden, you're not just the grieving brother—

you're an avenging angel."

He didn't deny it. "Look, there's something wrong here. I felt it before, but I know it now. And that something has to do with Sweet."

"I told you—Lilian wanted a baby and when it came to Sweet, she wasn't confident—"

"The diary, Rachel. The diary. Lack of confidence wasn't the problem. And I'm betting you know it."

She swallowed.

"Don't worry," he said. "I'm not angry. Not yet."

"What do you want me to say? I know how you feel—"

"You don't know a damn thing about how I feel. I'm riding a rollercoaster through hell. I want to know why it happened."

"You just want to blame somebody."

"Yes, I want to blame somebody."

"But there is no one to blame! Not you, not me. Not Annie, not Sweet. You've got to accept that Lilian did what she did because she had to do it. Something in her *drove* her to it. None of us could've stopped her. Why can't you see that? My God, it'd be better if you'd just stop thinking about it."

"Don't think about it? Hell, I can't think about anything else!"

He jumped up. She grabbed his forearm. He tried to wrench himself away, but she held firm. She stood up, put her arms around him, and laid her face against his chest. He was rigid.

"Please, let this go," she whispered. "Let Lilian rest in peace. Please, please, let her go."

"I wish I could. But I can't, not yet. Not until I prove—" He cut himself off.

"Prove what?"

He paused, then said, "That he killed her."

Her eyes widened." *What?* "

"That Sweet killed her. I know he did and I'm going to prove it."

She looked stunned, bewildered. "No," she breathed, "You can't mean that."

"Oh, but I do."

Her small face paled. She grabbed him and her hands were cold on his wrists. "But why would you think that?"

"They weren't happy—"

"So what! That's no reason to say he killed her."

"He didn't love her, Rachel. I know he didn't. He loved someone else."

She pulled back. "You can't believe that—"

"Gem wanted him. And he must've wanted her. Of course, he denies it, but that's to be expected."

Her sweet face was miserable. "But the police didn't find nothing wrong. Do you think you know more than they do?"

"The police didn't care enough to dig. I do."

They argued. She accused him of being suspicious due to his own sense of guilt. He denied it. She asked him whether he was just being a snob, suspecting Sweet because Sweet was born poor. He denied that, too. Finally, she accused him of being willing to do anything to fully reclaim the house.

"Yes, I want the house back! But that hasn't got a damn thing to do with it!"

"Think about this. Please! Sweet's not just anybody. He's got important friends. Byron Canfield treats him like a son. I'm afraid for you."

"You needn't be."

"But do you have any proof? Any evidence—"

"No—"

"Then why—"

"I have my instincts. And they rarely lie."

Her expression became grave. "My God, David, has your sense of guilt driven you this far? Is the idea of murder actually easier for you to live with than suicide? Murder's ugly enough, but suicide is even uglier, isn't it? Suicide makes you feel guilty. Murder means you can blame someone else." She stroked his cheek. "Oh, I ache with you. But why won't you understand that no one is responsible for Lilian's death? No one."

"Someone *is* responsible. And no, the idea of murder isn't easier than suicide. It amounts to the same thing. My sister's dead when she should be alive. And I refused to come back when she needed me."

Rachel dropped her hand. She stared at him and her eyes were beyond sad. "You're determined to go ahead with this?"

He nodded stubbornly and his eyes narrowed. "Now if you know something, then you'd better tell me."

She turned away, fidgeting with a button on her blouse.

"Turn around, Rachel. Turn around and talk to me."

She shook her head.

"Rachel?" He lightly but firmly put his hands on her shoulders and turned her to face him. Seeing her fearful expression, he softened his tone: "Please tell me what you know. Tell me now."

A moment went by. She averted her gaze. "All right," she whispered. "All right." She wrung her hands. "I knew Sweet was trouble to begin with. He was never no good."

"You *knew* it?" he repeated. His grip tightened and he took her by the chin, forcing her to look at him. "Why the hell didn't you say something to her, warn her?"

She wrenched away. "I tried to, but Lilian wouldn't listen. She was lost the minute she met him."

He struggled to keep his mounting anger in check. "So, Lilian's diary told the truth. He never loved her."

"No." In the face of his furious stare, she squared her fragile shoulders. Folding her arms across her chest, she hugged herself. "Look David, Lilian was a grown woman. She made her own decisions—and her own mistakes. Eventually, like all of us, she came to regret some of them."

His eyes widened. "How dare you! Who're we talking about here? You or Lilian?"

Her nostrils flared and her pretty lips pressed into a bitter line.

His anger exploded. "Let me tell you something, baby, you're not the first woman who's been left and you won't be the last. Now, I'm sorry I hurt you, but that doesn't mean I'll take you lying to me."

She looked as though she'd been slapped. "Get out," she said. "Get out!" She took a step toward him, her hands balled into fists, and screamed. *"Get outta my house! Get outta my life! GET OUT!"*

"Gladly," he said and left.

14. As Thick As Thieves

He'd never intended to have a fight with Rachel, but she'd gone too far— lying to him like that. She'd known Sweet was trouble—had known it all along and lied to him. What the hell had she been thinking?

He forced himself to take a deep breath. He needed to think clearly. Anger would only muddy the waters. He forced his thoughts in another direction. Back to the diary. What else had he learned from it? He'd learned that for Gem, the return to Harlem had been a misadventure.

He'd never spent much thought on Gem or considered the possibility that she could be in emotional pain. She'd been arrogant and overconfident, and then she'd been brought low. He found it ironic that Gem, who had felt so lonely abroad, had come to feel even more so at home. But her alienation from home was a foreseeable consequence of her years abroad. The trust that she had developed with Lilian still surprised him, although after reading the diary, he found it more tenable. A sense of failed dreams ran like a common thread between the twin sisters. Perhaps it was this shared disappointment in the world that had provided a basis for mutual understanding and helped them to reconcile. But if their reconciliation had been real, and they had learned to value one another, then again:

Why Gem's silence?

"The story of Miss Lilian is the story of Miss Gem ..."

Isn't that what Annie had said?

He needed to know more about Gem, about what she'd been up to while she was in New York. He thought of Nella. She had offered to speak to him, not about Lilian, whom she claimed to have hardly known, but about Gem. Nella was a gossip, but an observant one. Despite her propensity for mixing dull fact with spicy fiction, much of what she could tell him would probably be true.

Yes ... Nella was the next one to see.

Nella's Fifth Avenue living room was a lively combination of purple, raspberry, and turquoise fabrics used generously for weighty curtains and upholstered fat chairs. A Venetian glass chandelier hung from the ceiling, vases of calla lilies decked tables, and Oriental rugs covered the floors. Her desk near he window was a controlled chaos of glass paperweights, silver dolphins, and porcelain tigers. She greeted David's unexpected visit warmly.

"I thought you were leaving."

"I've decided to stay a while."

"Why?"

"I have my reasons."

She chuckled at his evasiveness and promptly had her maid make him a highball, to get him in "the right mood," she said. He decided not to ask her what she meant. He did, however, choose to sit in a narrow armchair a safe distance away from her, rather than join her on her couch. He sunk into the armchair, feeling claustrophobic and cramped, while she stretched out on her sofa, obviously hung over. She sipped her drink, laid her head back on a lace-covered pillow, and closed her eyes.

"I do love liquor," she sighed. "There are few things finer in the world than a good drink." After a moment, she opened her eyes and stripped him with a lustful gaze. Then she noticed that his highball was untouched. "Don't you drink?"

"I prefer wine."

She raised an eyebrow. "How very, very cultured of you."

He chose to ignore both the mockery in her tone and the desire in her eyes. "Did you know Gem in Europe?"

She needed a moment to shift mental gears. "No," she said finally. "I met her here. She came to see me." She paused, remembering. "I found her utterly marvelous. Full of primitive spirit. She was perfect for my villa gatherings. She has that rare gift, you know: the ability to do nothing—and to do with style. She's a woman of unbelievable conceit, but you forgive her for it because she's so full of life. I actually think I miss her."

She sat up and reached for a jewel-encrusted gold cigarette case on the marble coffee table before her. Pearls and emeralds had been worked together to give the case an intricate, eye-catching pattern.

"An original by Cartier," she informed him.

He waited while she fitted a twelve-inch gold-tipped filter to her cigarette, then held a light for her. She was smoking Chesterfields, he noted. Strong stuff.

"Does my smoking offend you?" she asked. "Do you think it improper for a lady to smoke?"

He smiled neutrally. "I don't mind."

"How very liberal of you." Her smile was saucy and her eyes impish. "Smoking is relaxing, David. Would you like to try it? Would you like to *smoke* with me?"

His eyes met hers. "No, thank you. Some habits I prefer not to develop."

He hoped she wouldn't press him. She didn't. Her eyes teased him, but she said nothing. She merely shrugged, sighed with theatrical regret, and took a drag on her cigarette.

"I was curious about Gem, wanted to know all about her. She'd been in Europe, she said. Seeing this person, visiting that one. She laughed, saying she didn't have a memory for details. I told her I had a feeling that her memory was excellent, simply highly selective. She didn't like that."

"Did she say why she'd come back?"

"I found out for myself. Like any lovely girl, she'd had several European sponsors. Her first was a Scandinavian cultural attaché in London. Her last was a Portuguese count—or claimed to be. He actually married her."

This bit of news was unexpected. The twinge of pride he felt was even more so. His sister, a girl from Harlem, had married a Portuguese nobleman.

"You sound surprised that someone would marry her," he said.

"I'm surprised that *he* did. Gem is a beautiful woman. But beautiful women are a dime a dozen in Europe. And usually these old fogies have nothing more than fun in mind."

"I suppose he loved her."

"Apparently, he did. He bought her a villa near Lisbon, and then conveniently died. His will was generous. Gem's life would've been set. But the children from his first marriage contested the will."

"And Gem ended up with nothing."

Nella smiled at him languidly. She sucked on her Chesterfield. Lazy puffs of smoke encircled her words. "Do you know why I like Gem?"

"Because she plays the exotic."

"Because she insists upon being herself. And she isn't a complainer. Despite setbacks, and she's had several, Gem still believes that the world is a nice place to live in. How many Negro woman see it that way?"

"Very few. But then, not many have always found someone else to pay their way."

Nella was amused. "You really don't like Gem, do you? She said you didn't."

"Did she? Well, but you like her. That's what's important. You two spent time together."

"Yes, we did." Nella arranged herself more comfortably. "In

the short time Gem was here, she set a new standard for beauty. She had a permanent table at Barron's. Only the best people go there. You and I should try it."

"I won't have time."

She tilted her head and regarded him. "You're like Lilian, aren't you? A bit prim?"

"I thought you said you didn't know her."

"Touché." She smiled. "I'm trying hard to provoke you. Why won't you let me?"

"Because I'm here to discuss my sisters, not me."

"But I think you're fascinating, David. You remind me of Gem."

David raised an eyebrow.

"I never knew what would happen with her," Nella explained. "Like you, she came and went as she pleased. And she never let anyone get to her. One night, we all decided to go to some downtown restaurant—Gem, Adrian, Nikki, and I. My chauffeur had the night off and the men didn't want to drive, so we all piled into a taxi. The cabby took one look at Gem and said he couldn't take Negroes. Gem said she didn't blame him. *She* couldn't take them either. Then she told him to put his foot to the pedal and drive. *Please.*"

David cracked a smile. Nella laughed merrily. She described how she and Gem had gone around together, dragging Nikki and Snyder in tow. The women loved to visit dance halls like the Renaissance Ballroom or the Rockland Palace, but they rarely danced. She and Gem stayed at their table, observing the others. The Charleston and the Black Bottom were all the rage then. The dancers could be wild, providing spectators with great entertainment.

"We went to Small's one night with Winston Charles, the playwright, you know. The music was copacetic. And those waiters! They're a show in themselves. Twirling their trays on their fingertips! Marvelous! Winston was so taken with the place that he tried to dance on our table. Smashed several glasses.

Nearly broke his neck."

Nella and Gem shared several characteristics, thought David, *including a desire to watch and witness human foible, all the while remaining utterly blind to their own.* He could imagine Nella and Gem as thick as thieves, but it was nearly impossible to see Lilian in this same scenario. Now he thought he understood why Nella said she'd known Gem better. But why had Lilian pretended that it was she who was friends with the Hardings— when even in her diary she had confessed that she disliked them?

"Tell me more about when Gem first arrived."

"Well ... she was short on funds. She was too proud to ask me for help and, naturally, she wouldn't approach Lilian. So I introduced her to Adrian, that marvelous man—"

"You're the one who introduced her to Snyder? How could you—"

"He's the perfect sugar daddy."

"He's dangerous."

"He treated her like an empress—"

"He dumped her."

"But he loved her dearly. It's just that Adrian's not the marrying type."

"Why didn't you tell her?"

"I assumed she knew. Everyone else did." Nella was darkly amused. "Come, come. Admit it, you're relieved. You wouldn't want your sister married to a West Indian."

"I wouldn't want her married to a racketeer."

"Well, then."

"Was he was the reason she left town?"

"It wasn't quite right, the way he did it. Still, I was surprised that Gem took it so hard. She wasn't heartbroken, you know. Just humiliated. They'd become quite the couple around town. Everyone knew them. She tried to say she'd left him, but no one believed her." Nella ground out her Chesterfield. She exhaled one last stream of smoke. "I don't think she loved him at all."

"That's not the point."

"The point, my dear, is that she used him as much as he used her. And I don't think he was the only reason she left New York. He was a front."

"For what?"

"It was more for *whom.*"

"She loved someone else?"

"I never did find out who. She laughed when I asked her about it."

"Could it have been Lilian's husband?"

Nella laughed. "Jameson Sweet?"

"Did she love him?"

"No, she loathed him, absolutely hated Jameson Sweet. Apparently, he tried to seduce her in the parlor one day, but she'd have none of it. She said he was mad for her. She couldn't be in the same room with him. His eyes were always on her."

So this was Gem's version of events. David repressed a grim smile. It did not surprise him that Gem would have reversed the roles; it did surprise him that Nella, who seemed so astute, would have believed her. But then, why not? Gem was an attractive woman. It was easy to believe that all men found her appealing. He himself was having a hard time believing that Sweet had continued to resist Gem's charms.

"What do you know about Jameson Sweet?" he asked.

"Ah, *him,*" she said. She cut her eyes over at David. "You're thinking of taking him on?"

He made a non-committal movement.

"Well, good luck. Jameson Sweet is an impressive character. Extremely arrogant, but he's earned the right to be. His given name is actually Jimmy. He elevated himself to Jameson later on. An only child, his family was dirt-poor. They're from Virginia. His parents never finished school. Had no education to speak of. His father worked on the railroad, was away all the time. The mother took in wash. They were very proud people, clean, stable. They scrimped and saved to send him to school.

Sweet himself has worked like a dog since he was a child. He's a dedicated civil rights attorney, determined to make a difference. By all accounts he has a brilliant future. He's sharp, cutthroat, and as tough as nails."

"Sounds good."

Nella raised an eyebrow ... and smiled. "Don't worry. He isn't perfect, dear. He doesn't hold a candle to you—not where it counts." She frisked him with her eyes again and sighed a sigh that came from her very core. David ignored it.

"What's his Achilles heel?"

"Come now, what do you think?"

"Money."

She nodded to compliment him. "Sweet's drawn to the lush life, but he's acutely aware of the handicap of his color. He knew he could have never earned it on his own. Privately, when it comes to women, Sweet has an appetite for dark chocolate. But he never let that stop him. He went through a succession of wealthy female friends, sometimes discreetly crossing the color line ... before he found Lilian."

She watched him as she said this, but he knew his face expressed nothing. Lawyers learn fast to conceal their reactions. Inwardly, of course, his emotions were in flux. She was confirming what he'd supposed. That relieved him; it also worried him. Having his suspicions about Sweet's character only increased his sense of urgency. He had to find proof of Sweet's guilt and find it quickly.

Then, there was the matter of Nella herself. Her ability to ferret out information both impressed and appalled him. After grinding out her last cigarette, she had immediately taken out another. He held her lighter for her.

"So what happened after Gem's breakup with Snyder?"

She leaned back and stretched out. "Gem came to me, desperate for a place to hunker down until the uproar blew over. She felt that everyone was talking about her. I assured her it really wasn't quite that bad, but Gem is certain the world re-

volves around her. She wanted to use our house in Amagansett.
It's quiet there, very peaceful and beautiful. The perfect setting
for a lovely woman who wants to withdraw from the world."

She exhaled and streams of smoke flowed out of her narrow
nostrils. Then she rounded her cherry-bud lips and blew. A
smoke ring emerged and floated upward.

"That was the last time I saw her. I'm not even sure she
stayed at the house a full two weeks. After about eight days, I
received a note, saying she'd decided to catch a boat back to
Paris. By the time the note arrived, she was gone. Left without
even dropping by to see me." Nella actually sounded injured.

"Who gave her the money to leave?"

"I haven't a clue. Maybe she sold some of that marvelous
jewelry Adrian gave her."

Nella sat up and ground the smoking cigarette into an ashtray. Standing up, she walked over to her window. David joined
her. She had a captivating view of Central Park and lower Manhattan. Together, they looked down on Fifth Avenue. A mixture
of cars and carriages snaked down the avenue. It was an impressive vista, but he didn't really see it. His thoughts were of Gem
and Paris. The City of Light seemed unreal and unimaginably
distant. What was she doing over there, so far away?

"Perhaps it was neither Jameson nor Adrian that caused her
to leave," Nella said. "Gem was born with wings on her feet.
Not even she knows what she's searching for. But she *is* determined to have a good time finding it."

Yes, that sounded like Gem. She had never had time to stop
in any one place for too long. She'd been running, running, for
years. But then, David caught himself, so had he.

"I haven't heard much from Gem since she went away,"
Nella said. "I used to get the occasional postcard, but they
stopped a while ago. They always said essentially the same thing:
that she's going to hell in a basket, and loving every minute of
it."

She turned to him and her eyes searched his. "You come

here and dredge up memories ...Why, you've almost managed to make me sad."

She moved closer to him. Her perfume, a rich heavy musk, filled his nostrils. Then her fingertips were on his crotch, stroking the bulge in his pants. She massaged him and he felt the warmth of her hand even through the material. He looked down at her working hand; then back up at her. There was no mistaking the question in her eyes. And no mistaking the answer in his.

"What's the matter, Nella? Nikki been away too long?"

"We made a deal. Remember?"

He took her hand by the wrist and moved it away. She yielded with good humor, but raised a warning finger. "I'll let you slide—this time. But the next time you want answers, be prepared to pay on delivery. And the bill's still open for what I've told you so far." She raised an eyebrow. "With interest."

"Good-bye, Nella," he told her and walked out.

Back on the street, he crossed Fifth Avenue and started walking uptown, his shoulders hunched against the cold. It was early evening and the air was frosty, yet many people were out. Black nurses wheeled along their young white charges, chauffeurs walked pampered poodles. David felt so detached from it all, as though he were watching a news reel in which he had no part. Every now and then he had the odd sensation that something had cracked inside him. He could feel pain in his bones. In his fingertips. He wondered how Rachel could accept Lilian's suicide so easily and be so ready to move on. She did not seem concerned with the why of it. Perhaps it was because she was a nurse: She had learned to deal with death on a daily basis. He wished bitterly that he could be like her.

And he thought of Gem, of her callous indifference to the news of her sister's death. She was no doubt too busy living the busy, madcap life of an ex-pat, no doubt with the same no good friends who had abandoned her.

You'd think she would've learned.

All those years of struggle abroad—she'd run back to it! When he thought of what she'd been through!

She had tried to settle down with the unlikely figure of a Portuguese nobleman, but fate had been against her. Stripped of her status and wealth, Gem had returned to New York. She had hoped to squeeze money out of Lilian, but had run into the obstacle of a husband. She had tried to seduce him, but that had failed, too.

Then she had shifted in an unexpected direction. After having tried to destroy Lilian's marriage, Gem had ostensibly tried to shore it up: She had helped Lilian improve her appearance and found herself another man.

Why the about-face? Had she really changed?

Gem was apparently penniless when she arrived, but she had found the money to leave. How? From where? Or who?

Nella couldn't say.

Nella ...

Her story was a bit contradictory, wasn't it? For example, she confirmed that Gem left soon after her breakup with Adrian Snyder. At the same time, Nella claimed that Gem's departure was unrelated to her failed affair. She was convinced that Gem loved someone else.

A Mr. X.

Who could that be? To his way of thinking, if Gem wasn't in love with Snyder, then it must have been Sweet. But Nella was adamant that Gem hated Sweet. She believed Gem's version of what had happened in the parlor that day. David, however, was certain that Nella was wrong. Gem had reversed the roles. Nella had been astute enough to sense that Gem loved someone, but not enough to see through Gem's ability to rewrite history.

David's forehead creased with thought.

Sweet was undeniably the type of man Gem was drawn to. And he had rejected her. That would have only served to boost her desire for him.

The creases deepened.

Hell hath no fury like a woman scorned: a particularly apt saying when applied to Gem. Yet she had apparently swallowed Sweet's rejection. She had done nothing more than publicly humiliate Lilian and rewrite the tale to favor herself. Given Gem's ruthless nature, David would have expected her to mount an all-out campaign to bring Sweet either to her bed or to his knees—or both. That she had done so much less—in fact, done nothing—puzzled him.

Gem had been accepting when he would have expected her to fight. She had swallowed rejection by two men, then simply fled town. Unthinkable.

And Lilian, dear Lilian, had acted totally out of character, too. She had rejected the intellectuals and artists whose respect she had worked so hard to attain, then befriended a woman she would have normally disdained. She had gone out smoking and drinking, then tried to fire Annie, a servant she loved. She had told Rachel she was pregnant, but instead of being happy, she had cried. Then she had repressed the memory—or pretended to—when she saw Rachel at the church picnic. But whether she had truly forgotten her claim or pretended to, she was not pregnant last July. So she had either lost the baby or, despite her claim of the doctor's confirmation, never been pregnant to begin with.

Annie, Rachel, and Nella: Speaking to them had produced more questions than answers. David ran his fingers through his hair distractedly. He was so deep in thought that he barely noticed when a black Lincoln pulled up alongside him. He was oblivious to the hidden hands that drew aside a dark curtain inside the car window and slightly rolled down the window itself. When he finally did look down, it was into the muzzle of a gun.

15. AN OUTSIDER AMONG OUTSIDERS

"Get in."

David felt a rush of adrenalin that sent his pulse racing. He sensed the blood drain from his brain and with it, his ability to think. His first impulse was to run, but his legs were as immobile as lead. His eyes darted over the street in an automatic search for help. There were plenty of people, but—

"If you make a move, I'll blow you away."

The window had been rolled down enough for him to see the speaker, or at least to see his eyes. That wasn't much, but it was enough to convince him that the man meant business.

He got in.

They blindfolded him and took him on a long, swerving drive. If the purpose of the whole exercise was to disorient him, it succeeded. Blind instinct told him that in forty minutes of driving, they hadn't traveled forty minutes' worth of distance, but he couldn't be sure. In fact, he decided he didn't want to know. If his safety depended on a certain degree of ignorance, he was willing to play along.

Once at his destination, he was led to a room that smelled of sandalwood. Perfumed hands removed the blindfold. The hands belonged to a lovely woman who smiled at him, then vanished. His eyes went to his host, who sat behind a large, handsome desk, sipping bootlegged brandy and smoking a cigar.

"There was no need to kidnap me," David said.

"Sorry. Sometimes the boys get a little eager."

"Why did you want to see me?"

Snyder shrugged eloquently. "Curiosity, partly. Gem would never say much about her family. Naturally, that kindled my interest." He gestured toward an armchair. "Sit down."

"I would rather stand."

"A drink?"

"No, thank you."

David took in the room's spare Danish furnishings, the eclectic mixture of thirteenth-century Flemish and modern West Indian art on its walls. Two walls were lined with shelves of books. There were bound volumes of United States history, Virgin Island history, Danish history, German philosophy, and Western economic thought. His gaze went back to his host. This was a man who could effortlessly order another man's death, but he saw no immediate aggression in Snyder's black eyes: they were cold, yes, and watchful, but thoughtful, too. His rimless spectacles made him look more like a banker than a numbers king. He exuded the assurance of the self-made man and the charisma of one who knows how to build a following. He was a mobster, but intelligent, educated, and cultured. That, David would grant him.

Snyder rose from behind his desk and went to the leather conference chairs arranged in one corner. He gestured toward one of the matching chairs.

"We have to talk. Please, sit down."

David acquiesced. Snyder pressed a button. Another attractive young woman appeared with a tray of two fresh brandy glasses. Snyder urged one on David.

"By the way, you shouldn't be angry at Nella for having introduced me to Gem."

David was surprised at Adrian's bluntness, but he appreciated it. "She meant well, I'm sure, but—"

"There's always that 'but' with you dicties, isn't there?"

"I don't care about your being West Indian. I do care about your ... business connections."

"That would concern someone like you."

David's memory stirred. *Someone like you.* The phrase struck him as familiar but he was unable to place it. After a moment, he shoved the matter to the edge of his mind, where it hovered briefly before fading away.

"I enjoyed Gem's company very much," Snyder was saying. "I never intended for it to end that way."

"Then why did you break up with her?"

Snyder hesitated.

"Why did you *humiliate* her?" David pressed.

Snyder's dark eyebrows hovered like storm clouds over his face. "Because ... she asked me to."

David's eyes narrowed.

"We were a scandal to respectable Harlem," Snyder said. "She always said she didn't care. But when I asked her to marry me, she said no."

"Because you're West Indian?"

"She said that had nothing to do with it. And I believed her."

"Why?"

"Because she said she wanted people to think that *I* had dropped *her*."

This was news. This was indeed *unexpected* news. David said nothing, but he was thoughtful.

At the look on David's face, Snyder sighed. "I know. It's hard to believe, that anyone would leave me—that anyone would have the temerity to leave me—or worse, that I would let them. But it's true. It was her, not me. And I loved her. I loved her enough to let her go."

David inclined his head. "Even if this is incredible enough to be true, she couldn't have wanted you to publicly humiliate her."

"But she *did*. She wanted a breakup and she wanted it big. She said that she wanted to give the folks something to remember her by."

David could think of only one explanation. He gave Snyder a long, keen look. "Was there someone else?"

Snyder paused, the merest fraction of a second. "I would've known."

"Why else would she break up with you?"

"I don't know." A hurt look flitted across his face. "She laughed. She kissed me, and asked me to leave her. I thought it was a joke. But about a week later—we were at Barron's—she pitched a fit. The world was there. Everybody who was anybody at the jump that night knew what was going on. She cried. She screamed. I had to play along."

"She left town after that?"

"Yes. Didn't even say good-bye."

"So you didn't give her the money to go?"

Snyder looked surprised at the question, and thoughtful. "No, actually not. Of course, I used to give her change, but she always spent it—"

"Then how could she afford passage? Nella told me that Gem was broke. You say you didn't give her the money. Well, someone had to."

Snyder took a slow and thoughtful swallow of his brandy. "You really think she was two-timing me?"

"I think there are a lot of questions that need answering."

"I hope you believe I've told you the truth."

"Yes," David nodded. "I do. Gem's the kind of woman who does the leaving, not the type who's left. I'm not wondering whether you've told me the truth—but *why* you've told me. Not many men want it known that a woman left *them*."

"I'm not telling the world. I'm telling you."

"Again, why?"

"I thought you'd be glad to know."

"I am. But why should you care? You don't know me from Adam. So why would you want to do me favors? Why would you give a rat's ass what I think?"

Snyder didn't answer.

David studied him. He believed him, but he didn't trust him. "Did you ever meet Lilian?"

"A couple of times, when I was out at the house."

"And?"

"She was one of the most sensible women I've ever met. Not my type. Not that it matters." He paused. "What does matter, if I may say so, is that she wasn't her husband's type, either."

David's eyes met Snyder's. "Was Gem?"

"Yes," Snyder said reluctantly. "She was."

"And did Gem like Sweet?"

"She had absolutely no interest in him."

"Are you sure?"

"Very. Gem knew I wouldn't have tolerated two-timing."

David raised an eyebrow. Why should Gem care what Snyder would tolerate when she planned to break up with him? Surely, he saw that.

"Okay, let's be frank. You brought me here for a reason. And you told me the truth about your breakup—for a reason. You want me to find out what went wrong between you and Gem. Isn't that what this is all about?"

"I want to know what happened. It sounds crazy, but I can't get her out of my mind." Snyder leaned forward. "Tell me, have you heard from her? Why isn't she here?"

"Because she doesn't want to be."

"Did she write and say that?"

"She didn't have to."

Snyder's well-clad shoulders sagged. He picked up his glass of brandy and swirled the amber liquid, gazing into it. When he looked up, his eyes held a strange light.

"What's your story, David?"

"Does it matter?"

"You tell me. You've been gone for years. Now, you're suddenly back. You claim you've been working for the Movement, but nobody there can place you. No one knows who you are anymore."

"It's better that way."

"Everyone's talking."

"Let them."

Snyder smiled. "You don't plan on staying long, do you?"

"No."

David downed his brandy, set his glass on the table, and stood up. Snyder accompanied him to the door. He signaled to his man.

"Make sure he gets home." Snyder turned back to David. "I can understand why Gem doesn't like you. But I do. Let's just say that I know what it's like to be an outsider among outsiders. If you should decide to stay, or ever need help, my door is always open to you."

Adrian Snyder, a murderer and crime boss, a man with whom respectable Harlem refused to associate, offered David his hand in brotherhood. And David, thinking of the odd code of honor that sometimes *does* exist among thieves, accepted it.

Snyder's men again blindfolded David and this time drove him home. By then, it was after six. Night had fallen and the ride was swift panoply of changing shadows. David stared into the darkness, thoughtful.

Snyder's claim that it was Gem who left him was surprising, but the more David thought about it, the more it made sense. At least, it fit her personality. So much of what people had been telling him didn't. Gem was quick to leave a man—as soon as she found another.

So she must have had another sugar daddy waiting in the wings. Who else, if not Sweet? But if it was Sweet, then where was she? Why wasn't she there, with him?

Maybe, Nella was right. Maybe, there was some other Mr. X.

He would have to be someone big to get her to leave Snyder. But Snyder was pretty big himself. If she snagged a bigger fish than the numbers king, she wouldn't have hidden it. She sure wouldn't have gone to the trouble of making herself look bad.

So why did she do it?

He couldn't figure it. Leaving a man was one thing. But pretending to the world that he'd left her—that was another. Snyder saying that Gem had done that was like claiming he'd seen an elephant fly.

The problem was, David believed him. At least, he thought he did. He didn't know what to believe anymore. The more questions he asked, the more half-truths he heard. And the less he knew what to believe. It seemed as though everybody was either lying to him or holding back: Lilian never saying a word about getting married or Gem returning; Annie, who must've known, keeping mum about Lilian's pregnancy, real or unreal; and Rachel canonizing a devil like Sweet. He hated to think that the only people who had told him the truth—the full truth, as they knew it—were Nella and Snyder, a white woman and an island man. By everything he'd been taught, they were the kind of people you disbelieved on principle.

His thoughts were confused and ran in circles. As he gazed out the car window, watching the streets fly by, one thing was clear to him, however. And that was that he had to find an-swers—and soon. If he stayed too long, then people—people like Canfield—would start asking questions of their own, ques-tions he didn't dare answer.

So he would assume it was Sweet. *It had to be. She just hooked up with Snyder and strung him along until she landed Lilian's hus-band.*

But that didn't explain why she wanted a public breakup.

And her saying that she wanted the folks to have something "to remember" her by––that sounded like a good-bye—not just to Snyder, but to everybody. Like she was already planning on leaving town ...

Did she believe that she and Sweet would run away together? But why would she? He wasn't the type to give up his career and they both wanted the house and the money that went with it.

Maybe he made promises he never intended to keep. Maybe he gave her the money to leave.

Or maybe it really wasn't Sweet after all—
But then, damn, who could it have been?

16. CLARIFICATIONS

Early Tuesday, David went to see the family physician. Dr.

Steve Johnson had delivered David and his sisters. Known to them as "Dr. Steve," he was short, chubby, and dapper. He had a habit of looking at patients over the top of his glasses. When David was a child, Dr. Steve's dark, merry eyes had reminded him of Santa Claus.

"I heard you were back," Dr. Steve said. He shook David's hand and offered him a seat. "It's good to see you. I'm so sorry about Lilian."

"It was a shock."

"I can imagine."

"I want to know what caused it. Did you see her during that last illness?"

"No," Dr. Steve shook his head. "No, I didn't. The last time I saw her was more than a year ago. She was pregnant and fairly healthy."

"Pregnant?" David felt his stomach tighten. "How far along was she?"

"In her third month."

"Was it a normal pregnancy?"

"Up to that point, it certainly was. But I never heard from her again, so I don't know how the rest of it went. It broke my heart to read about her dying like that. Odd, how the papers didn't mention a surviving child. What did she have? A boy or a girl?"

David paused. "There was no child."

Dr. Steve looked at him with disbelief. "But that's impossible. Was there a miscarriage?"

"Not that I know of."

Dr. Steve cleared his throat uncomfortably. Abortion was unmentionable.

"Well, then I don't understand."

"Neither do I," David said. "Neither do I."

David returned home. So Lilian *had* been pregnant ... but there was no baby. Only a couple of explanations were possible. She wouldn't have had an abortion, because she wanted the child. Not unless she told Sweet and he forced her to it. David felt sick with anger at the thought of her in some filthy room with a back-alley cutter. But in all fairness, he couldn't accuse Sweet of that. Not yet.

According to Lilian's diary, she'd never even told Sweet about the pregnancy. Perhaps she'd had a miscarriage. But if so, then surely she couldn't have kept it a secret. Sweet would've learned about it. But if he *had* known, then he would've mentioned it, wouldn't he? He would've had no reason not to. On the other hand, Annie had said nothing. And she must've known. She must've.

But had she?

Now back at home, he went looking for her and found her in the kitchen. She was wiping down the top of the stove, humming to herself. She stopped when she looked up and saw his expression.

"What's the matter?"

"Did you know that Lilian was pregnant?"

Annie moaned and got a pained look on her face.

David felt his temper rise. He fought to keep his voice steady. "So you did know. And you said nothing to me?"

Her forehead creased with worry. "How'd you find out?"

"Her diary. And Dr. Steve just confirmed it. Why didn't you tell me?"

She sighed and shook her head. "I just didn't know what to say. Truth is, she never said nothing to me. I caught her being sick in the bathroom. And she was tired all the time. I guessed what was going on. I tried to help her, but there wasn't much I could do."

"But the baby ... She didn't have it, did she?"

"No, she didn't. And I don't know why. I don't know what happened. One week she was sick every day. The next, she was fine." Annie snapped her fingers. "Just like that and she was okay. Months went by. There was no baby. No nothing. She never mentioned it no more."

"And you didn't ask her?"

She gave him a strange look. "I had a feeling it'd be better not to. I had a feeling... it was too late."

He felt a terrible disquiet. "What does that mean?"

"I don't know, Mr. David. I just had the feeling that whatever was gonna happen had happened, that it was, well... over and done with."

It was a strange answer, one more intuitive than rational, one that chilled him. He started to ask her more but then stopped. She'd said exactly what she meant. She didn't know how to say more.

So he asked another question, on another subject, and framed it carefully.

"After that scene in the parlor, are you sure you didn't notice any particular ... closeness ... between Miss Gem and Mr. Jameson?"

"No," she shook her head. "Definitely not. There weren't no closeness between them two. Miss Gem certainly had an affection for Mr. Jameson. She sure did. But that man didn't care nothing for her. He was polite, but cool."

He felt he could trust Annie's observations in most instances, but this time he was unsure. Sweet would have taken great pains to hide his feelings for Gem, especially from Annie.

"He says he was in Newark that weekend."

"That's right. Mr. Jameson said he had a conference. He *said* he'd be gone till Mond'y. He left Thursd'y. When he come back, Miss Lilian was already gone." She gave him a shrewd look. "Now, there ain't no way anybody *reason'ble* would say Mr. Jameson had anything to do with it. But ..."

"Annie, you've never liked Mr. Jameson, have you?"

She hesitated. "Mr. David, you know I'm not one to judge people. But I distrusted that man the moment he walked in the door. It was how he looked at the house. He stared so hard. At the furniture, the silverware, even the paintings on the walls. I couldn't understand why Miss Rachel put that man in Miss

Lilian's path. There was greed in his face. Greed. Just like the moneychangers Our Lord Jesus threw outta the Temple."

"Do you remember the name of the hotel Mr. Jameson stayed at that weekend?"

She squinted, trying to recall. "The Newfield, I think." She nodded. "Yes, it was, the Newfield."

"And where's Mr. Jameson now?"

"He done left for work already. But he'll be back later."

He needed to talk to Sweet. But maybe he could use the fact that Sweet wasn't home to his advantage. Leaving Annie, David went to his father's office door, put his hand on the knob, and turned. Naturally, it resisted, but this time, he expected it to. With a little effort, he could pick the lock. And a little while later, he did.

"What'd you say the name of that hotel was?" the driver asked.

"The Newfield," David said.

It was twenty minutes later. The break into Sweet's office had yielded results, but not the results David expected. Now he was out looking to check Sweet's alibi.

The hotel was a modest but attractive establishment. The woman behind the counter was polite but uncooperative. She refused to confirm or deny that Jameson Sweet had had a reservation at the hotel on the night David mentioned.

"We respect our guests' confidentiality."

"Listen, his wife died that night and I'm her brother. I just want to make sure he was where he said he was."

The woman's eyes became knowing. She looked to be in her mid-fifties, plump and gossipy. "You mean, you think he was stepping out on her?"

"I don't know what to think. That's the problem. All we know is that she's gone and there's a question ..."

The woman nodded. "My baby girl had a cheating husband. It was terrible." She considered. "Look, I've got to go in the back for a second to check on something. People think I've got eyes in the back of my head, but I'll tell you a secret: I don't. So I won't have no idea of what you're up to while I'm gone. Just make sure you've cleared out before I get back. You hear?"

"Thank you."

With a wink, she turned her broad back to him and bustled into the back office. David spun the register book around and flipped the pages back for several weeks. He found Sweet's signature for the weekend that Lilian died. David scanned the room numbers and saw that Sweet had shared a room with another Movement official, Charlie Epps. David quickly copied Epps's name and address.

He took the hired car back to Manhattan and found Epps's building on 145th Street. It was midday. There was a small chance that Epps had come home for lunch. David rang the doorbell and waited. No reply. He rang again, long and loud, and waited. Still, no reply.

Disappointed, he turned away and went down the two steps leading to the street, then headed home.

17. Speaking of Secrets

Annie met him at the front door. "Mr. Jameson's back. He's sitting in the parlor."

"Good," David said. "I want to talk to him."

Sweet sat on Augustus's throne, reading a best-seller, *The Man Nobody Knows* by Bruce Barton. He glanced up when David entered and gave him a slight nod.

David leaned against the fireplace mantel. "So, Sweet," he said casually, "did you know that Lilian believed she was pregnant last year?"

Sweet looked up. He appeared to be stunned. *"What?"*

"Lilian told Rachel she was expecting a child."

"That's impossible. Lilian never said anything to me about it."

"Maybe she was afraid to."

"Why? I would've been thrilled." He frowned, apparently

thinking it over, and then shook his head. "No, there was no pregnancy. There couldn't have been." He spoke more to himself than to David and his tone held the urgency of a man who as trying to convince himself more than another. "A pregnancy," he muttered. "That can't be true."

"How can you be so sure?"

Sweet regarded David with resentment. "She would've told me. I was her husband."

"Yes, you were, weren't you?"

"What do you mean by that?"

"Just how well did you get to know Gem?"

Sweet's dark eyes took on a hard glint. "Not so well."

"How well?"

"Not as well as you'd like to imply."

"Gem is a stunning woman—"

"But obvious. It was easy to see what she was after."

"And did you give her ... what she was after?"

Sweet snickered. "Your train is running on the wrong track."

Annie came in with a coffee tray. David asked about Gem's absence.

"Strange that she hasn't responded to word of Lilian's death. I heard that they became close."

Sweet was quiet for a moment, then he laid his book aside.

"As far as I know, they *did* become close. Lilian told me she was receiving regular news from Gem."

"Letters?"

"Postcards."

"I'd like to see them, if you don't mind."

Sweet hesitated. *Did he burn them, too?* David wondered.

"Of course you may see them," Sweet said with glacial politeness. "But I'm not sure where they are. I'm not even sure she kept them."

Annie spoke up. "I b'lieve she did. Miss Lilian used to always read them at the desk in the library. She had a special drawer she liked to put them in. I can fetch them if you like."

Sweet smiled thinly. "That's all right. I'm sure I can find them."

David accompanied Sweet to the library. Sweet went to the desk, pulled out one shallow side drawer. "Ah, here they are." He removed a small stack of postcards held together by a pink ribbon, handed them to David, then walked a little distance away. David sorted through the cards, then slapped the little packet against his palm. He ran a speculative eye over Sweet.

"Gem didn't write these cards. She has a lovely script. She's very vain about it. Whoever wrote these cards is barely literate."

"Lilian said these cards came from Gem. If Gem didn't write them, I don't know who did."

David looked down at the packet of cards. "When did they start coming?"

"About a month after Gem left. Look, David, Lilian had many secrets. Now she's gone and she took them with her. And I, for one, am glad to let them be."

"Are you?"

"I said I am."

"Well, I'm not."

A tic leapt near Sweet's right eye.

"Speaking of secrets," David said, "I've come across Lilian's diary."

"Her diary?" Sweet repeated tonelessly.

"It adds a whole new perspective to things."

"How interesting. Perhaps you'll let me look at it."

"Put it like this: When the time is right, I'll be sure to tell you what I've gotten from it."

David went upstairs to his room and gathered several handker-chiefs. Then he went to Lilian's room and headed for her private bathroom. There were shelves and a small medicine chest. The shelves carried only bath soaps and beauty ointments. He turned to the wooden medicine chest and opened it. Nothing. It was bare.

He's cleaned it out, thought David. *There was something in there he didn't want anyone to see.*

A hand touched his shoulder and he jumped. Then he saw that it was just Annie.

"Good grief," he said. "What're you doing here?"

"'Scuse me, Mr. David. Didn't mean to scare you." She nodded toward the medicine chest. "He emptied everything outta there soon as the police left, the day she died."

David sighed. She put a hand on his wrist. He looked up and she crooked a finger, as if to say, *Follow me.*

Fifteen minutes later, he had thrown on his coat and set out for Seventh Avenue. His long muscular legs covered the distance quickly. Soon, he was standing before the Renaissance Pharmacy on the corner of 138th and Seventh. He shoved open the swinging glass doors and headed for the prescription counter. He had to wait until the pharmacist finished with a couple of elderly customers. Then he told the druggist what he wanted. The pharmacist did not comment. He simply extended his hand. David turned over a small bottle. He was told to come back on Thursday. The information he had requested would be waiting for him.

As David headed home, he thought about the other discovery he'd made that day, the one in his father's office.

18. LYRICS OF A BLACKBIRD

Lilian had started writing when she was ten. She'd kept a diary even then. The contents of her journal she'd kept secret, of course. But her poetry and short stories she'd shared. Sometimes with Rachel; mostly with David. While Gem and Rachel and Trudy Maxwell from up the street and Sally Mabel Stevens from down the street were all outside playing hopscotch, Lilian was indoors, busy with her "scribbling," as Augustus called it. He wasn't too thrilled about Lilian's fascination with the written word, but he tolerated it. Lila defended it. She was very proud of her daughter and encouraged her, but Lilian didn't particularly like to show her mother her writings. It was David she sought out. It was his opinion that made a difference.

"What d'you think?" she'd ask.

"You've got talent," he told her one day when he was twenty and she fifteen. He'd just finished reading a story she'd given him entitled, "The Man with One Green Eye." It was about a colored man who had one brown eye and one green one. He couldn't see out of both eyes at the same time, so he had to walk around with a patch on one eye all the time. He'd switch back and forth between eyes every day, "to give each eye an equal chance to see the world its way."

David could see the pride in her eyes, but she kept her expression serious. "That's very nice of you to say I have talent. But I *know* that. I need constructive criticism, David." She held up a small warning finger. *"Constructive."*

And so he tried, as best he could, to give her some. "But I'm not like a teacher. I don't know the rules."

"You're better than a teacher. You're my brother."

He laughed and said, "Okay, your brother says this story's good enough for you to try to get it published."

Her eyes did shine then and her mouth sagged open. "You mean it?"

"Wouldn't have said it if I didn't."

"But, David, what magazine's gonna publish something from a colored girl?"

"Don't have to be a magazine. We'll try a newspaper. How about the *New York Age?*"

"They print short stories?"

He shrugged. "I don't know. If they don't, they'll change their mind when they see yours." He smiled. "There's always a first time."

She threw her arms around his neck and hugged him. "I've got the best brother in the whole wide world."

The newspaper did indeed publish "The Man with One

Green Eye" and over the years it printed a couple of Lilian's poems, too, each of them after they'd undergone David's constructive criticism. And so he took personal pride in her literary accomplishments.

He now eased down in the chair before his desk. He pulled open the bottom drawer on the right and took out a package. He had found it in Sweet's office—Augustus's office. The package, wrapped in plain brown paper, was addressed to Lilian McKay. When he'd hefted it in his hand, he'd sensed the consistency and weight of a manuscript. *Lilian's last manuscript.*

The return address was Knopf Publishers. Her manuscript, sent back either because it was rejected or accepted but needed corrections, had arrived the day before.

How had Sweet managed to get his hands on it? Usually Annie was on hand to accept all the mail, but the package could've arrived while she was out shopping. It didn't matter. What mattered was that he, David, had now gotten *his* hands on it. Sweet probably would've burned it. He would make sure Sweet never would.

David laid the manuscript on his desk. His heart beat a resounding staccato. *Her last words—last creative endeavor.* Quickly, he cut the twine holding the package together and ripped open the paper. Sheaves of typed pages were revealed. The tide page read: "Lyrics of a Blackbird, by Lilian McKay Sweet."

Lilian had written him that *Lyrics* concerned secrecy and betrayal in a family on Strivers' Row. Beyond that, he knew nothing. Would it tell him more about Lilian's frame of mind before her death?

He began to read and once he started, he couldn't stop. On the surface, the plot was simple, but it held an underlying complexity that reverberated to his core.

It was the story of Georgia and Frank Johnson; their daughter, Helen; their sons, Mark and Joel; and their housekeeper, Alice. Alice and Georgia had started out as best friends, sharing a room in the Tenderloin with five others. Alice worked hard, but she could never keep two cents together. Georgia wasn't rich, but she had a little inheritance from her father, a white man who had never publicly acknowledged her. Despite her white blood, Georgia was as blue-black as the midnight sky. And Alice, who had no white ancestors she knew of, was as yellow as a sunbeam. It was Alice who met Frank Johnson, but it was Georgia who married him. An ambitious, self-righteous man with a touch for making money, Frank knew a good deal when he saw one. He may have loved Alice, but he needed Georgia's cash. Her little dowry gave a nice boost to his first real estate investment. But all did not flow smoothly.

Soon after Frank married Georgia, Alice learned that she was pregnant. Georgia offered to take the baby, a little girl with pale skin and silken curls, and raise her as her own. Alice could stay near the child—if she was willing to work as the servant. Under no conditions was she ever to tell Helen that she was her mother. Five years later, Georgia gave birth to twin sons. They too were cream-colored. But unlike Helen, they weren't so light as to pass for white.

As the years went by, Georgia realized that her husband's love, such as he was capable of, had stayed with Alice. And she suspected, though she could not prove, that their affair had never ended. She hated Alice—and she knew that Alice hated her. She saw that Alice was desperate to claim Frank and Helen as her own, but she didn't realize just how desperate. Not until it was too late.

Alice poisoned Georgia in the hopes that Frank would finally marry her. But Frank refused. He would never marry her now, he said. What would people say? A man of his stature, marrying the maid? Furthermore, he'd loved Georgia. Didn't she know that he'd grown to love Georgia?

The afternoon light slanting through David's bedroom window grew gray, then darkened with the sunset. He paused twice to adjust his lamp, but otherwise he read the manuscript straight through. After turning the last page, he went and stretched out on his bed. He closed his eyes, feeling drained.

Things ain't always the way they seem, Annie liked to say. *She should know,* he thought, *she should most certainly know.*

19. THE LIES OF KINDNESS

There was a knock on David's door—"Yes?"—and Annie stuck her head in. "Miss Rachel's here to see you."

David got up and followed her downstairs, his thoughts running in parallel tracks, one leading to Annie, the other to Rachel. He wondered about what he'd just read and he wondered what Rachel wanted.

The latter was standing in the parlor, before the fireplace, nervously staring up at Augustus McKay's portrait and wringing her hands. She started and turned at the sound of David's entrance. Her face broke into a bright, edgy smile.

"I'm glad I caught you. I won't stay long. I just had to come by and say something after I ..." She paused and looked away. "I wanted to apologize. I didn't mean to do anything wrong. I—"

He raised a hand to still her. "It's okay. I guess we both said things ... things we didn't mean." He gestured for her to sit down on the sofa and sat down beside her. "I still don't understand, though. Why didn't you tell me the truth about Sweet when I first asked you? Did you just want to get back at me?"

She lowered her gaze. "Maybe I did. But mostly .. ." She raised her eyes to meet his. "Mostly it was because I didn't want to cause you pain."

"Cause *me* pain?"

"We can't bring Lilian back. It doesn't help to run around with extra heartache. I thought it'd be better for you to believe that Lilian was happy in her marriage." She was apologetic. "I'm sorry. I just wanted to help."

He heard her weariness and his anger toward her faded. He tried to follow her logic. Yes, it would've been nice to think that

Lilian had a good husband, to believe that she'd received support from at least one of the people she loved, trusted, and depended upon. It would've been nice to believe that not everyone who mattered—her husband, her brother, and her sister—had failed her. *It would've been nice,* he mused, *but it wouldn't have been true.*

To Rachel he said, "Just help me find the truth, that's all. It'll be better that way."

"Okay, I'll do whatever I can. I loved Lilian. She was the closest I'll ever have to a sister. And I hate to think that I didn't do everything I could to help her." She laid a hand over his. "And now to help you."

"Thank you."

"What're you gonna do now?"

"Keep on digging. You know about my having been to Dr. Steve. After I saw him, I went out to New Jersey—"

"Jersey? What's out there?"

"The hotel Sweet said he was staying at the night Lilian died. I wanted to see if they remembered him being there, or if not, find out the name of the man he shared his room with."

"And did you?"

"They wouldn't say, but I got the roommate's name. Unfortunately, he wasn't in when I tried to see him. I'll have to go by later."

"And suppose he says that Sweet *was* there all that night?"

"We'll cross that bridge when we come to it." He smiled. "Anyway, I have an ace up my sleeve."

"What's that?"

"I went to Lilian's room looking for the medicine Sweet gave her. Naturally, he'd cleared everything away. But Annie had set some aside."

"You mean Annie suspects something, too?"

"You could say that."

"But what did you want the medicine for?"

"To have it tested."

She looked at him with concern. "Oh, David, you're working so hard at this."

"I have to. The least I can do for Lilian, now that she's gone, is to clear up any questions about her death."

She went into his arms and the pain swelling his chest eased. For one intense moment, he wanted nothing more than to pretend that the last four years had never happened. He crushed her to him with a slow, deep sigh.

"Come home with me tonight," she whispered.

"I can't," he said. "I—"

"Please, don't make me beg."

"I'll only hurt you and I don't want to. Not ever again."

"Please. I'll take what you can give. I know I can't keep you." She caressed his cheek. "Let me be with you while you're still here. Let me at least have that."

Her eyes smoked and her lips found his. Her fingertips caressed the base of his throat and with nimble fingers she freed the top buttons of his shirt. Then she drew a fingertip over his lips and kissed him. With a husky groan, he gripped her shoulders and kissed her back, savoring her taste, her smell, her softness. Vaguely, he heard the doorbell ring. Moments later came Annie's voice.

"Mr. David?"

Rachel started; David dropped his hands. He felt a surge of adolescent guilt. Quickly redoing his shirt, he said, "Yes, Annie? What is it?"

"There's a messenger from Miss Nella Harding," she said and moved to one side.

A uniformed chauffeur stepped smartly forward. He whipped out a white envelope and presented it to David.

David took the note, read it—"Have urgent information you might consider invaluable. Come now."—then refolded it.

"I have instructions to drive you, sir, if you so require."

David threw a quick glance at Rachel, then turned back to the driver. "No, I—"

"It's OK, David," Rachel said. "It seems to be important. You should go." She stood up and smoothed her skirt with short embarrassed hand strokes.

"Are you sure?"

"Yes, I'm fine. You needn't worry about me. I'll—"

"It's late and dark. I'll take you home."

She hesitated, then said that would be nice.

It was a short distance to Rachel's house. During the two-minute drive, she stroked the leather seat covers and every now and then gave David a shy smile. When the car pulled up in front of her building, she started to open the door on her side, then stopped at the restraining hand David put on her wrist. She looked at him, not understanding. He nodded toward the chauffeur. "Wait."

The chauffeur was getting out. He walked around the car and opened the door for her. She glanced at David, smiled, and got out. Then she turned around, leaned back into the car, and kissed him.

"Promise me one thing," she said.

"What?"

"Let me help—really help. If you want me to go anywhere or talk to people and ask questions, you'll ask me. Okay?"

He cupped her face and kissed her again. "Okay."

She drew back and the chauffeur closed the door. She stood on the curb, waving good-bye. She cut a small, lonely figure in an oversized coat. David returned her wave until the car turned the corner and she was gone from view. He thought about what had nearly happened and whether he would let it happen again.

Then he put all thoughts of Rachel aside and he focused instead on *her*, Nella.

20. PLAYING WITH FIRE

"Here," she said. "I've come up with something special for you. Something I think you'll like." Nella pressed a tall, chilled glass into David's hand. "Drink up."

He eyed the glass suspiciously. Its contents were a murky white. "You wouldn't be insulted if I were to ask you what this is?"

"I would be, so don't." She took her own drink and stirred it. "Some things," she said with a wicked grin, "are better left unsaid."

"Some things, perhaps, but this isn't one of them."

"Why don't you trust me? You really should."

"I should?"

"Yes."

"Why?"

"Why not?"

He didn't bother to answer. He lifted the glass to his lips and took a cautious sip. It *was* good. He commented with raised eyebrows. She raised her drink to him in a silent toast, then drank half of it straightaway.

"Prohibition is such a bore, don't you think? I do hope they get rid of it soon. Nikki thinks it's marvelous, though. He says liquor is so much more fun when it's forbidden."

"Aren't you worried about drinking around a sworn upholder of the law?"

"Darling, I never worry—about anything. It's against my principles. Just last week, Nikki and I were visiting a judge friend of ours. He treated us to some of the most delicious highballs we've had in ages. If I'm not worried about drinking with a judge, why would I worry about drinking with you?" She sipped and smiled. "You're a perfectly marvelous man, David. You do know that, don't you? I just can't understand why some lovely little Negress hasn't snapped you up."

"Nella, I'd like to sit and chat, but I can't. It's late and I'm tired. Now, you summoned me here. You said you have information—"

"It can wait—"

"Then I guess I'll be going."

"No, you won't."

She crossed the room, her dress rustling, and went around behind the sofa where he was sitting. He felt one of her hands ease onto his shoulders. She began to massage the side of his neck. His hand snapped up, grabbed hers, and held it away.

"It's time to pay up," she whispered. Bending down, she nuzzled his earlobe. "I've got a taste for chocolate, that special David brand of cream. A connoisseur's special. A gourmet's delight. Be with me, David. Here. Tonight."

"I can't do that."

"Can't? Or won't?"

"Does it matter?"

With a hiss, she tore away and slinked across the room. "I told you from the beginning: I don't give information for free. We had a deal and you're going to stick to it. One way or another, you're going to pay."

She had carelessly left her Cartier case lying on the divan near one window. She scooped it up, yanked out a Chesterfield and lit it from a taper burning in a tall golden holder. She took short, angry puffs and stood staring into the flame.

What was she thinking? What was she up to?

"I do love fire," she said suddenly. "It's beautiful, mysterious, and"—her eyes cut over to him—"very, very lethal."

He felt increasingly uneasy.

"Take this tiny flame," she said. "Think how quickly it can grow when fed. How quickly it can consume a man and bring death."

She turned and threw those last words directly at him. He rose to his feet. He was too caught off-guard to answer. The wound ran too deep, the wound and the shame. He went pale.

"That's the problem with you light-skinned Negroes," she said. "Everything shows on your face. You don't know how to hide anything. I dare say, in some ways, the really inky spades are much better off."

"What do you want?"

"I've told you."

"This is not the way to get it."

She came up to him. "Don't try to act virtuous, darling. I know you like vanilla."

He blinked, now puzzled. "Why would you think that?"

"Your life in Philly. You have a weakness for white women, don't you?"

He stared at her in bitter disbelief, then almost laughed out loud. "Is that what you think it's all about?"

It was her turn to look disconcerted. But she tried to sound confident. "Well, obviously. Everyone knows that colored men—"

"What *everyone knows* doesn't amount to a hill of beans." His dark eyes flashed. "I have never licked vanilla—and I never intend to."

She shrunk back. Her delicate nostrils flared. "I see."

"Do you?"

"More than you realize." She turned away, obviously stung and trying to hide it. "Don't think I'm interested in you personally, darling. I'm interested in your *type*. I write. People aren't real to me. They're *characters*. Gem will definitely make a star appearance in my next book. And so will you. I knew you had a story the moment I saw you. Your modesty, your asceticism: What lay behind it?"

"I'm no one special."

"Of course you are—you're the star of my next book. Shall I tell you its title? *Duplicity*. It deals with denial and deception. It's about double lives and double meanings. Do you think the title gives away too much? Maybe I'll pare it down."

He didn't appreciate the joke. "I'm not the man to try this with."

"Believe me, I'm not your enemy. I could destroy you with a phone call and you know it. The right word in the wrong ear ..." She snapped her fingers. "And that would be that. But why should I harm you? I like you."

"You have a strange way of showing it."

"I'm not a hypocrite. Neither are you. That's one reason I like you. But I have to show you who has the upper hand here."

"May I remind you that slavery went out more than sixty years ago? You can have your dogs sniff out my trail, but you cannot haul me in. You don't *own* me."

"Are you sure?"

His expression hardened. She went on.

"As cliche as it might sound, it's fair to say that your fate is at the mercy of my pen. If you're nice to me, I'll make sure no one knows who I'm writing about. Think it over."

"There's nothing to think about. A little notoriety never hurt anyone."

"It would destroy you."

"I would survive."

"Not without help." She sighed, exasperated. "My God, why do I like you so much? Think, David. *Think.* Someday, they're going to find out, whether I write about it or not. Someday, you're going to need my help. The moment you came back to town and confirmed where you'd been—the moment you stepped foot on that train in Philadelphia—you put yourself in danger. You can't stay in Harlem—not for long—not without a protector. I can be that person. I can be your advocate."

"And what would Nikki say? Or do you have a *deal* with him too?"

"Don't be cynical. It doesn't fit you."

"Nella, I am not for sale—not at any price. I'll get what I need from someone else, some other way."

"There is no one else. There *is* no other way. And payback is always a bitch."

"Your bill is paid, lady. I got information on my sister and you got information on me. We are *even.*"

He grabbed his hat and went to the door.

"You make it hard to be your friend," she said.

Something in her tone stopped him. He paused in the

doorway and turned around. He saw her standing there in the middle of her vast, overblown room and it was as though a veil had lifted. He saw her for what she was: Not just a spoiled dilettante craving illicit attention, but a lonely figure surrounded by the cold baubles of wealth. He understood her frantic partying, drinking, and socializing with blacks: Like him, like Gem, she was trying to escape her demons by taking flight into an alternate reality. He also knew the answer to his earlier question: Nikki had indeed been away too long, and if he guessed right, that was often the case.

David slowly recrossed the room. They stood for a moment, facing one another. Then he took her by her shoulders and a little light of hope entered her eyes. He drew her to him and then kissed her very gently——on her forehead.

"Good night," he said. "And sweet dreams."

She leaned against him and moaned. But when he pulled away, she didn't try to stop him. At the door, he turned back once more and gave her a little smile. This time, he tipped his hat and said:

"When Nikki comes back, would you tell him something for me?"

She looked at him, a little sad, a little surprised. "Yeah. What's that?"

"That I said you're a hell of a woman ... and that he's a fool." He thought of Rachel. "He can take it from me: It takes one to know one."

21. THE LOST WEEKEND

On Wednesday morning, Annie knocked on Sweet's office door. "Mr. Jameson, this here letter just come for you."

He nodded, giving her permission to approach. He still hadn't made up his mind what to do about her. She moved about the house with the familiarity of a family member. Her presence was pervasive. He'd realized early on that if not handled properly, she could be a threat. He'd hoped to make her closeness to Lilian work to his advantage. He'd even rehired the old woman after she had been fired. Now, Annie would be loyal to him too, he'd thought. She'd seen how sick her mistress was. She could testify to Lilian's mental state as having deteriorated to a dangerous level. Should the need arise, she could also testify to his husbandly devotion. Who'd be a better character witness than the woman whose dedication to Lilian was long-proven?

Of course, he'd only need such a witness if questions were raised. But why should anyone doubt that Lilian had committed suicide? Lilian's own behavior made her suicide likely. Lilian was a witness against herself.

He'd been shocked when Annie found David's address and he'd never anticipated David's tenacity. Worst of all—and he could've kicked himself for this—he'd never foreseen David's attachment to the house.

In hindsight, it seemed obvious. Once Annie found that address, the battle for the house was inevitable.

Sweet told himself that he really wouldn't have any trouble if the matter went to court. His legal claim was straight and clear. But he would—*naturally*—prefer to avoid court if he could.

Sweet took the letter, thinking that this could be the answer. He dismissed Annie with a curt nod, watched her leave, then ripped the envelope open. It was a response from the operative in Philadelphia. He leaned forward into the light and read the opening lines. They were good. He smiled. Very good.

Charlie Epps seemed to be out of town. He was certainly never home. It was Thursday. David had been by Epps's house three times now—morning, noon, and night—and never gotten an answer.

He'd been back to the Renaissance Pharmacy, too, but the drug analysis still wasn't ready. In the meantime, he'd had another couple of nasty run-ins with Sweet and he'd received the distinct impression that Sweet was up to something. He was tempted to simply have someone come, pack Sweet's things, and move them to a hotel room. But as inviting as the idea might be, it would be only a temporary solution. He needed something permanent. That led his thoughts back to Lilian ... and Gem. He telephoned Nella and she agreed to see him late that evening.

"Let's make a new deal," he said at her apartment. "You think you've found a story in me—but your story doesn't have a context and it doesn't have an ending. I'll give you both. I'll talk to you, if you talk to me."

"So you *are* willing to sell yourself."

"To sell my history, yes. But *not* my name."

She reflected. "All right, but there's one thing you should learn about me. I have ears everywhere. So don't try to hold out on me."

His jaw tightened, but he said nothing.

"I heard about your meeting with Adrian," she went on, "and I know what was said. I also know that you went to Newark to check Sweet's whereabouts the night Lilian died, and that you're having a druggist test the medicine Sweet gave her. One plus one equals two, my boy: You've got it in for Jameson Sweet."

He refused to give her the pleasure of showing either surprise or dismay. Instead, he asked: "Did you suspect what Snyder told me?"

Her eyes narrowed. "It surprised the hell out of me. The little bitch lied to me—and I believed her."

"You still know Gem better than anyone else—even better than Snyder. Can you figure out why she left him? Snyder loved her. He's attractive, urbane, witty. He has money and position—"

"But he would've never gained acceptance among Harlem's elite—"

"All the more reason. Gem is a rebel and she loves mavericks. Why did she reject him? And why did she insist that the breakup be so public?"

"I really couldn't say—but even if I could, I wouldn't tell you, not until you tell me what's going on inside that handsome head of yours. What have you got against Sweet and how did you get it?"

"I believe Sweet killed Lilian. His motives: greed for Lilian's money and love for Gem; his method: an as-yet-unidentified poison; and his opportunity: one lonely weekend when everyone, including his victim, thought he was away at a Movement conference."

"Your proof?"

He glanced away. "I don't have any. Not yet."

"So you have nothing but bitter suspicions."

He looked back. "Suspicion, supposition: Without them, no investigation would ever begin."

"Listen to me. Lilian is dead. You can't bring her back. You want to prove she was murdered and you want to blame Sweet. That's all very well, but if you're honest, you'll admit that there's more evidence—hard evidence—for suicide than for murder. Let's just say for the sake of argument that Lilian *was* murdered. Do you really want to dredge up the whole thing? It would mean a lot of unpleasant publicity. How do you think the Movement would feel about having one of its most talented attorneys accused of such a miserable crime? Given your history, do you think Harlem would stand by you or stand by him? Then take Sweet. He's a dirty player. If I could find out about you, so could he. Is that what you want? What would it do to that proud family name of yours? Lilian's death would be forgotten in the scandal over your crime."

"I have to get at the truth."

"The truth? Don't disappoint me by turning into a hypocrite. People who live in glass houses should never throw stones."

"Are you really telling me that I should let him get away with it?"

"I told you: I'm your friend. I only want to make sure you know what you might be getting into."

"I do know."

"I don't think so."

There seemed to be no point in staying longer. She wasn't going to tell him anything. He took up his hat and coat and thanked her for her time. He was almost out the door when she asked: "Do you like bedtime stories? I'm good at them."

He turned around; she chuckled wickedly at his expression.

"Don't worry. I've lost interest in you. You're no good to a live woman, anyway. You're too busy with the dead. Sit down. Over there." She waved imperiously toward the divan across the room. "If you won't let me tuck you in, at least let me give you something to dream about."

David glanced at the divan, then at Nella. Slowly, he crossed the room and sat down.

"Listen carefully. What I'm about to tell you could save you a lot of trouble."

She lit herself a fresh Chesterfield and played with her lighter.

"After Gem left, I became curious about Lilian and her husband. I invited them to dinner. Gem had told me that she and Lilian were identical twins, so I should have been prepared. I wasn't. I was shocked and intrigued. I'm afraid my manners weren't very good. I stared at Lilian the whole evening. At first, it was as though Gem were there, but of course, she wasn't. She was thousands of miles away, across the sea. It didn't take long to see the differences. As Gem said, it was mainly a matter of personality. Lilian was shy and diffident. She let her husband speak first and never contradicted him. A couple of times, she opened her mouth to comment and he silenced her. It took no more than a glance and she would simmer down. It was terrible. I could have hated him myself—almost. But I have a weakness for good-looking men. And when they can be disarmingly charming, well then ..."

Nella flicked a bit of ash from her dress.

"Anyway, Nikki invited Sweet to sit by the fire and enjoy a coffee. Lilian and I retired to another room. I hoped that she would open up when we were alone. But she was even more reticent, if that's possible. She answered my questions with monosyllables and wouldn't look me straight in the eye. I decided there must be something seriously wrong. I told her that if there was anything I could ever do for her, she should call me right away. She nodded but said nothing. I left it at that.

"I was surprised to hear from her about two months later. It was in May, I believe. Remembering my promise, I asked her if anything was wrong. No, she said, there wasn't. She sounded quite gay, actually. She asked if she could come out and visit. I was thrilled and very curious. I told her I was giving a party in Amagansett that evening. She was welcome, of course. Given what Gem had told me about Lilian—and what I'd seen myself that evening—I didn't think she'd come. You can't imagine my surprise when she did. She was dressed beautifully. Her style was entirely different from Gem's, but it was every bit as effective. She had a touching innocence that made one want to protect her. In her own way, Lilian could be as devastatingly manipulative as Gem. It was a wonderful discovery.

"It took a while for her to warm up to me, but eventually she did. I liked her very much. Lilian was a lovely woman. But she never toughened up. She was very gay during the times I saw her.

"We used to talk about Gem and wonder what she was up to in Paris. Lilian had a natural gift for mimicry. She used to do marvelous impersonations of Gem for me. I think she could sense how much I missed her sister. It didn't seem to bother her. She was never jealous of my affection for Gem. I admired her for that. It was another difference between the two sisters, a difference that put a plus next to Lilian's name. Gem would've never stood for being in second place. But Lilian was simply happy to have a place at all.

"I've often wondered why the two turned out so differently. Objectively speaking, Lilian was every bit as pretty as Gem. But she lacked something. Perhaps it was the self-love, that extra drop of poisonous narcissism that makes Gem so pitiless and yet so attractive to men and women alike.

"Lilian and I saw one another off and on for several months. I always invited her to my soirees. If Jameson was out of town, she would come. I told her the invitation included them both, but she merely laughed and said my parties were meant for her alone. Then the time between her visits lengthened.

"Nikki and I went to Europe last July. I tried to contact Gem during a long stopover in Paris, but I wasn't successful. When we got back in September, I sent a note to Lilian but she didn't respond. I was a bit concerned, but with one thing and another, I got busy and didn't get around to trying again. Months went by. I started hearing from Lilian again in December. She came out to the house once, in January. She'd missed both my Christmas and New Year's Eve parties. I couldn't believe she'd done that, but she said Jameson had made other plans. Looking back, I remember thinking she didn't look well. It was nothing specific, just a general sense that something was off. After that visit in January, she promised to come again. That was how things stood until a month ago.

"Late that Friday morning, Lilian called sounding confused and depressed. Jameson had left that day on a business trip and she was alone at home. She was incoherent. She claimed the place was haunted. She begged me to let her come out to Harding House. Of course, she could, I said. She asked if Nikki or I could go and get her. We couldn't. Nikki was out with the car. She was quiet, and then she said she was sure she could get there on her own. She did arrive—hours later. I was horrified when I saw her. She was exhausted when she stepped out of her car. She looked like death warmed over. I know it's a terrible choice of words, but you get my meaning. Her face was bloated and gray.

Her clothes hung off her carelessly. She looked nothing like the exquisite Lilian I knew.

"I wasn't quick enough to hide my shock. She didn't say a word. Just grabbed her suitcase, ran into the house, and shut herself in our biggest guest room. I went upstairs to her. I was afraid she wouldn't let me in, but she did. She was lying on the bed. I urged her to spend the weekend with us. I'll never forget her answer.

"'Whether I stay or not, I'm going to die, Nella. I'm going to die. But we've all got to die sometime, don't we? Some of us just have a better notion of when.'"

Nella shivered.

"She was talking like a madwoman. Yet her tone of voice was absolutely sane, even sensible. Lilian seemed convinced that a ghost was haunting her house and would kill her.

"I offered to help her unpack. When she didn't answer, I took it upon myself to start. But when I opened her suitcase, I found that she'd packed just one outfit, a cocktail dress, a bright red one with a glittery top. I couldn't understand why. My husband and I hadn't spoken of any party. We hadn't planned on having one. The dress was totally inappropriate. And it was the only bit of clothing she'd brought. Otherwise, she had only what she needed for her hair and face."

Nella pulled a Chesterfield out of a jeweled box on the table. She let David light it for her, and then stretched out. She stared at a large painting of Cape Cod on the wall opposite her.

"Lilian came down for dinner that evening. We served steak. She ate like someone starved. Said she was thrilled to have some real food, finally. Nikki and I exchanged glances. She consumed enormous amounts. I lost my appetite watching her.

"After dinner, she told us she had to go take her sleeping powder—I didn't know she'd been taking any. She said she was going to bed, but then she asked me to sit and talk with her until the medicine took effect. I was quite willing. I hoped she'd tell me what had happened to change her so quickly. So, I went upstairs with her. I couldn't believe how much sleeping powder she took. It was incredible. Suddenly, her mood changed. She said she wanted to be alone and sent me from the room.

"I went back downstairs. My husband and I talked for a while. Then we both went up at around ten. Her door was closed and there was no light shining from under it. We went to sleep thinking—hoping—all would be well. Then began a night I will never forget.

"I heard her screaming at around three that morning. She was shrieking out her own name. I ran down the hall and wrenched open her door. She was sitting stiffly upright in bed. Her eyes were wide and staring. Fixed on the window opposite the bed. Her hands were pressed over her ears. She was shaking her head from side to side. And she was babbling, imploring someone she thought was in the room. It wasn't me; she wasn't seeing me. I couldn't make out her words. They were utter nonsense. But she was afraid. Scared out of her wits. She kept saying her own name. But it had turned into a terrified whimper. I ran to her and shook her. She fought me and God forgive me, I slapped her. That seemed to bring her out of it. She collapsed in my arms, weeping. And begged me to stay with her until daybreak. I sat with her for two hours. She refused to speak. She lay with her eyes wide open, staring at the ceiling. I tried to talk to her, but she acted as though she hadn't heard me. At one point, she closed her eyes. I thought she'd fallen asleep, but the moment I tried to leave her, she reached out a hand and grabbed me. She was as thin as a rail, but she had the strength of two men. At around half-past five, she finally fell asleep.

"I crept back to my own bed, exhausted. I slept late, but Nikki was up early. When I woke, he told me that Lilian had come downstairs, eaten a hearty breakfast, and then gone back to bed.

"Lilian spent most of Saturday in bed reading or in the bathroom soaking in the tub. That evening, she came downstairs with her bag packed and announced that she had a very important appointment. She didn't say what it was. I can still see her. She went to the door, suddenly turned around and said: 'I love you, Nella. You're the only other one who lets me be me.' I was so stunned, I didn't know what to say. Before I could answer, she went out.

"Nikki and I didn't know if she intended to come back or not, but she reappeared that evening, after about three hours. I heard a car drive up at around ten-thirty and went to my bedroom window. It was Lilian, getting out of a taxi."

"A taxi?"

"There was no sign of her Packard. I ran downstairs to let her in. She was smiling and cheerful. She was all dressed up in her red dress and she seemed very energetic and decisive. She didn't give me time to put questions, just kissed me lightly on the cheek and dashed up the stairs to her room. And then the night before was repeated. It was ghastly: the whole thing, at three a.m., the crying out of her own name. That night, she asked me to bring her water for more sleeping powder. I was afraid she'd kill herself if I did, but Nikki told me to go ahead and do it. She took another big dose, slept again.

"Nikki and I like to have a good Sunday brunch. Lilian ate well and with enthusiasm. She seemed to be her old self again. Afterward, she said she was tired. She went upstairs and when I checked on her later, I found her sound asleep. She slept around three hours. When she woke up, she said she felt better, so much better in fact that she wanted to go home. Jameson wasn't back yet; I was afraid for her to be at home alone. I tried to talk her out of it, but she wouldn't listen. She had firmly decided to go home. She said that a Dr. Hawthorne—I take it he was her therapist. Clearly, she must've been under treatment. Anyway, this Dr. Hawthorne had found a nurse for her and the woman would be at the house Monday morning. She also said she had a lot to do before Jameson got home. I agreed ... reluctantly. Nikki said he would drive her. They left at around six that evening.

"When Nikki got back hours later, he was very upset. Lilian had cried the whole way home. She'd talked about going back with him. Several times, he'd wondered whether he should turn the car around and bring her back. But when they drove up to the house, she'd suddenly become calm. She took out her keys and got out. She asked Nikki to go through the house with her, to make sure that no one was there. He did. The house was empty. But she didn't believe him. She said that her sister was there, that she could smell her. She asked Nikki to check again. But again, he found no one. He left her standing by the parlor window, gazing out into the empty street. And that, dear David, was the last time either of us ever saw her."

David closed his eyes and leaned forward, resting his head in his right hand. He suddenly wanted a cigarette badly. Never mind that he didn't smoke. And he would have been happy to down one of Nella's bizarre cocktails. He could almost believe that Lilian had killed herself, had seized a butcher knife from the kitchen cutting block, gone back to her bedroom, and systematically sliced down deep into her own flesh. He could almost envision it.

Almost.

Nella gave him a piercing look.

"You still don't want to accept that Lilian killed herself. But you must. Forget about Sweet. Forget him. I'll tell you something more: I was curious about where Lilian went that evening, so I contacted the taxi companies working the area near my house. Sure enough, a driver did remember bringing a young colored woman to Harding House. He had picked her up at a cheap hotel. The cabby gave me the name of the place. Only one word to describe it: squalid, absolutely irredeemably squalid. I don't want to imagine what Lilian was doing there. I spotted her Packard in the parking lot. The keys were still in the ignition. Unbelievable. Anyone could've driven off with it. I think the proprietor had been using it himself. He was very reluctant to part with it. The car is in my driveway in the Hamptons. You can pick it up the next time you come out. The hotel owner also showed me the room in which Lilian spent three hours that evening. I found a letter. It isn't addressed to anyone and it isn't very coherent, but I can show it to you."

Nella went to a small side table and slid out a narrow, shallow drawer. She withdrew a piece of folded blue paper and handed it to David. Other than the hotel's moniker, the page was nondescript. It was covered in a small nervous scrawl. The handwriting was barely legible. It was difficult to recognize as Lilian's.

> It's her fault. It's her fault.
> My sister, that sister of mine.
> She's trying to kill me, to slay me,
> With her dead, blind eyes.
> She chokes me with sadness.
> Her plainness, her grayness,
> Are a suffocating shroud.
> But I am a bird that will survive.
> I will fly, far away, high up on high.
> She will see. I will destroy her.
> I will survive.

David shuddered.

Nella nodded grimly. "Finally," she said. "You understand."

A little ways uptown, Sweet was handing Canfield a letter. They were sitting in Canfield's study. Canfield read the missive, his expression deepening from curiosity to displeasure to fury. Finally, he looked up.

"Good God, is David out of his mind?"

Sweet took back the letter. "He would seem to be."

Canfield regarded the missive grimly. "The Movement will have to make a formal statement, cutting him off."

Sweet looked pleased. "Were it up to me, I'd have him disbarred."

Canfield looked up at him. "Just what *are* you going to do with this information?"

"I don't want to destroy the McKay name, or damage the family. When it comes down to it, I *am* part of that family now. And I respect Augustus McKay's memory, even if his own son doesn't. So I wouldn't want to harm it. But David McKay can't be allowed to go on like this. And I won't let him drive me out of the house." Sweet tapped the letter against his palm. "For the moment, I'll hold on to this for a little insurance. When the time's right, David and I will have a talk. Right now, I have to go to Chicago to take more depositions. I can't put the trip off and I'll be gone about ten days."

"Yes, the Richards case. We can't afford to let anything distract us from it. Try to talk to the widow."

"That'll be almost impossible."

"The key word is 'almost.' Find a way." Canfield drew himself up. "And don't wait too long on the McKay matter. Now that I know what he *is*, what he's been doing, I can't afford to have him associated with the Movement." He gestured toward the letter. "Your operative will bring the evidence when he comes?"

"Oh, yes," Sweet said. "He'll bring evidence. He'll bring plenty."

22. TO BE WITH RACHEL

Upon leaving Nella's, David decided to walk home. It was nearly ten o'clock at night. Fifth Avenue was cold and damp and for the most part empty. The street lamps glowed with a ghostly light through the fog that had descended over the avenue.

It was a good stretch from Nella's apartment to Strivers' Row and not all of it was through hospitable territory. Negroes still took their lives in their hands when walking through parts of Manhattan. Even so, he decided to walk that night; he hoped it would clear his head.

He had to admit that the picture Nella had drawn of Lilian strengthened the contention that Lilian killed herself, but he was not free of his suspicions of Sweet. Not by a long shot. He was being stubborn and he knew he looked like a man on a personal vendetta, but he was not prepared to give up. Not yet.

He kept up a good pace and in a relatively short time he'd reached lower Harlem. Soon after that, he was passing 130th Street. He immediately thought of Rachel. He recalled that last lonely image of her standing at the curbside, waving. Without thinking, he turned down her block.

She answered the door still wearing her hospital uniform. She was obviously tired but she pushed aside her fatigue when she saw him. Her soft eyes filled with concern. "Have you eaten?"

He shook his head.

She started banging about in her small kitchen and soon the air was fragrant with sizzling bacon. She dug out some potatoes and onions and fried them. David told her to stop. "I don't want to cause you work." She smiled and kept on cooking. David ended up helping her. They ate and afterward, as they were washing the dishes, he told her what Nella had said about Lilian's lost weekend.

"It was horrible, listening to her. And the thing is, I'm sure she's telling the truth."

"Would she lie?"

"No," he said with a sigh. "I don't think she would." He rubbed his eyes. They were still irritated from the onions. "It doesn't really mean anything, what she said, you know. Even if Lilian was a bit ..."—he searched for the word—"a bit confused that weekend ... it doesn't mean that she killed herself."

"Have you talked to the man who stayed with Sweet at the hotel?"

"No, but I will. And I'm still waiting on the man at the drugstore to tell me what was in that stuff Sweet was giving her."

"You're sure the news is gonna be bad—I mean good, good

in the sense that it *was* poison?"

He paused, then said: "I think it very likely, yes."

She looked away. "But suppose he doesn't find what you're looking for? Does that mean you'll be ready to stop looking? To move on? Does that mean you'll be leaving?"

He cupped her chin and turned her face to him. Her eyes twinkled like emeralds. He recognized unshed tears. On impulse, he put down the dish-towel and took her in his arms, wishing that he could reassure her, but how could he, without lying? He felt her soften against him and felt himself respond. He remembered how soft and supple she'd been. They had moved instinctively to the same inner song, so closely intertwined they could have shared one skin. Her body fitted perfectly to his.

Too perfectly, he thought, and released her. "I'd better go."

"Stay." She gripped his hand. "Just a little while longer. Please."

"Rachel ..." He gazed at her and felt his desire harden, but he shook his head. "I can't."

She kissed him, muffling his refusals. His resistance weakened. Before he knew it, he was returning her kisses, his hands pressing into the small of her back. After a while, she interlaced her fingers with his. "C'mon," she said and drew him down the hallway.

She had a small bedroom. The bed itself wasn't much more than a glorified cot, but like the rest of her place, it was very feminine, very inviting. To a man coming out of the desert, it looked like paradise.

He tried to turn off his thoughts, tried not to think about how he'd feel later, and for a time, he succeeded. But when it came down to it, he couldn't go ahead. Poised over her, he stopped. He gazed down at her, tightened his jaw against the throbbing in his groin—and made himself think. He closed his eyes and breathed deeply. He became aware of the thudding of his heartbeat and concentrated on every inhale-exhale.

Rachel moaned beneath him. "David?"

When he thought he was calm, he opened his eyes.

"David?" she said again, this time a little worried.

He kissed her, then rolled away and sat up on the edge of the bed.

"What's the matter?" she asked, pushing herself up on one elbow. "What's wrong?"

His hands began to shake. Soon, his whole body was shaking.

"David?" She put a hand out and touched his elbow, more than a little worried now.

"I'm all right," he said. He inhaled deeply, trying to get his trembling under control. "But I can't—I can't do this. It wouldn't be right. I gotta go." He patted her hand. "Rest, now. Sleep, if you can."

"The hell I will." She half-raised up.

He stood and started getting dressed.

"You can't leave me like this," she cried.

His response was to finish getting dressed and walk to the door. There he paused, with one hand on the knob. With a low groan, he dropped his hand, went back to the bed, planted his fists on it, and leaned over her.

"Don't you understand?" he said. "The problem isn't that I don't want you. It's that I want you too damn much. I can't be messing around and still concentrate on what I got to do."

He grabbed her face and kissed her hard. Then before she could say anything more, he was gone. The sound of her weeping followed him as he took his hat and coat down from the wall hook by her door. He ran down the stairs, cursing himself. Crossing the street, he headed toward Lenox Avenue and forced his thoughts back to the business at hand.

23. QUAGMIRE OF DOUBT

His reawakened feelings for Rachel disturbed and dismayed

him. He felt vaguely that he was taking advantage of her. The next morning, he scolded himself for having given in to his desire to see her, for having let himself be swept away by his need for—

Standing over his wash sink, his thoughts came to a full stop. His need for *what?* When he'd first gone to see her, he had told himself it was to heal old wounds and to possibly gain information about Lilian. He had attributed his second visit to his desire to share his suspicions about Sweet and correct— that is, clarify—what she'd told him earlier. Last night, he'd told himself that she would calm him after his disappointing day.

He splashed his face with cold water.

The fact was, he was finding excuses to visit her. He had crossed the borderline that separates properly ending an old relationship from the territory of building a new one. And he had done it without due thought.

He toweled his face.

Do I really want to start up something new with her?

How could he? Nothing in his personal situation had bettered. In fact, he could practically count the hours before his departure.

But what if you could *stay?* a little voice asked him. *Would you want to be with her then?*

It was a question he couldn't answer.

He ate a hasty breakfast in the kitchen with Annie, then collected his dishes and brought them to the sink.

"Is Mr. Jameson still here?" he asked.

"No, he's gone again," she said. "Another one of them business trips. He won't be back for days."

She sounded tired. He glanced at her. The circles under her eyes were more pronounced than usual.

"You all right?"

She gave a wan smile. "I'm fine, Mr. David, really I am. Just had a little trouble sleeping."

"Well, maybe you'd better go lie down."

"Soon as I finish here."

"I'll take care of it."

"No, I cain't let you—"

"Annie, I've been doing my own washing and cleaning for a long time now. I'll take care of it."

She looked grateful. "Well, all right. If you think you can manage." She started out, then paused. "Oh, I almost forgot. Miss Rachel called for you late yesterd'y."

"Thanks. I saw her last night."

She turned back to him, an unhappy look on her face. "You saw her?"

He nodded. She gripped the back of a chair.

"'Scuse me, Mr. David, but do you think that was wise? I mean, you coming to depend on her a lot, ain't you?"

"She's a good friend, a very good person to lean on."

"That's just what I mean. Nobody should be leaning on her too hard. That child's got her own worries and woes."

"Yes, I know."

She gave him a peculiar look. "You know? Just what d'you know?"

He felt uneasy. "I meant ..." His voice trailed off as he realized that he in fact knew nothing about Rachel's difficulties. He'd been too busy taking his troubles to her to wonder whether she had cares of her own. The vague sense of selfishness that had haunted him that morning and the evening began to take on weight and shape.

"D'you know anything about what's been going on in that child's life?" Annie asked.

"No, I've been too pigheaded to ask."

She shook her head and turned away.

He put a tentative hand on her shoulder. "Annie, what's the matter?"

"Nothing." She wouldn't look at him.

"Tell me what's wrong. Please."

"I cain't. Mr. David, I just cain't."

"You've got to."

Annie hesitated, then she said, "Just r'member what the Good Book says, Mr. David. What ye sow, so shall ye reap. R'member them words." She sighed and rubbed her wrists. "I think I'll lay down now. These old bones just ain't what they used to be."

David was nearly out the door when the telephone rang. He had a sense of impending disaster the moment he realized who was on the line.

"What's this all about, Doctor?"

Dr. Steve cleared his throat. "After our last conversation, I went over my notes on Lilian. It seems there *was* some question about whether she was indeed pregnant—"

David was stunned. "What?"

"Your sister was displaying all the signs of early pregnancy when she came to see me. But pregnancy wasn't the only explanation for her symptoms. I agreed with her that she probably *was* pregnant, but I cautioned her that I could not be sure. Not at that time. And I told her to come back."

"Why didn't you tell me this before?"

"Because I did believe that Lilian was pregnant. Now, however, looking back, I realize that it was partly because she was so sure herself—many times a woman knows these things. But you yourself told me there was no child. We both know she was not the kind of woman to have had an abor—a termination. And surely, someone would've known if she miscarried. So what else can I conclude?"

David leaned on the wall. "Doctor—"

"I'm sorry. But given what I later heard about Lilian's state of mind, there is the chance it was a hysterical pregnancy that simply went away by itself."

David rubbed his eyes. "Do you actually think that's possible? Knowing Lilian, you—"

"I know what you mean. Normally, she wasn't the type to have hysterics, but, at the end, she wasn't ... well, she just wasn't normal, was she?"

There was a silence.

Then David drew a deep breath and sighed. "Thank you," he said and hung up.

For a long moment, he stood there, lost in thought. Then he grabbed his coat and headed out.

When Charlie Epps answered his doorbell, David thought that maybe his luck was changing. Epps turned out to be squat, round, and partially balding. He had beady brown eyes and full cheeks. He was nibbling on a ham sandwich with buckteeth when he opened the door. He acted friendly enough until David explained the reason for his visit and started asking questions about Sweet.

"Who'd you say you are?" Epps asked.

"I'm a lawyer. And I'm inquiring into a family matter."

"Is Sweet in some kind of trouble?"

"Not that I know of. Why would you ask?"

"No reason." Epps shrugged indifferently, but his eyes shifted uneasily. He put the sandwich down on a plate left lying on the living room coffee table. "What exactly did you want to know?"

"Whether Sweet was in his hotel room the entire night of Sunday, February twenty-first. Was he?"

Epps folded his arms across his chest. "This sounds like something serious. I don't know if I should be talking to you. Does Sweet know you're here?"

"Is there a reason why you wouldn't talk to me? Do you have something to hide?"

"Of course not."

"Does Sweet?"

"Look, man, I don't want to get involved in—"

"Just answer my question, that one question, and I'll leave."

Epps coughed and rubbed his throat.

"Well, what's your answer?"

Epps averted his eyes. "Sweet never left his hotel room that night. He went to bed at nine with a stack of briefs. I couldn't sleep because his lamp was on half the night." He looked back at David. "Now please go."

"Are you absolutely certain that Sweet was in the room all night?"

"Mister, I don't know who you are or what you want, but you've gotten all you're going to get out of me."

David left. Epps's statement had disappointed him, but when he thought about it, he couldn't say that it surprised him. Sweet was clever. He would have made sure that he had a sound alibi in the unlikely case that anyone raised questions. So he had either gotten Epps to lie or convinced Epps that he was still in the room for the hours he presumably left it.

I've got one more chance at bat, David thought. Epps's statement counted as a strike. And Dr. Steve's call certainly chalked up as another one.

Two strikes. Three and I'm out.

Of course, if Nella's description of Lilian's lost weekend was counted ... well, then he'd already struck out.

But I don't count it, he thought. *There was too much room for Nella's opinion.*

His lips tightened. The fact was, he'd run up against a wall. Hit it full speed running. His intelligent face was grave. He had proven neither method, nor motive, nor opportunity. He was angry and frustrated—and scared.

Am I wrong? he asked himself. *Am I wrong to suspect Sweet?*

Did he really think Sweet was guilty? Or did he just want him to be? Without a doubt, Sweet had been a lousy husband, but was he a killer?

Back in his room at home, David forced himself to reflect. True, he had no proof, but his suspicions had a solid basis, didn't they? What about the questions his talks with Annie,

Rachel, Nella, and Snyder had raised? The contradictions?

What contradictions?

He wasn't even sure what they were anymore. The gravest of them all— Lilian's pregnancy—was apparently no contradiction at all. It was the question of her pregnancy that had formed the underpinning of his suspicions. Without a confirmation of the pregnancy he had nothing. He was sinking into a quagmire of doubt. It was getting harder and harder to think.

Were his suspicions valid? Or were they simply the effort of a weary mind and even wearier heart to blame someone else for his failure to answer Lilian's call for help?

Has your sense of guilt really driven you this far? Rachel had asked, *Is the idea of murder actually easier to live with than suicide? Murder means you can blame someone else ...*

He would have to tell her. He went downstairs to head out again and saw Annie.

"You haven't had lunch yet," she said.

"I'm not really hungry."

"I can fix you sumptin' real quick."

"That's all right. I'm going to see Rachel. Maybe we'll have a bite to eat together."

"Miss Rachel?" she repeated. "You going to see Miss Rachel *again?*"

He was reaching for his coat. Her tone stopped him. "What's on your mind, Annie?"

Her nostrils flared just a bit. "'Course it ain't my place to say ... but I hope you ain't meaning to start up sumptin' you can't finish."

Relieved that her concern wasn't over something more serious, he gave a wry smile and took down his coat. "I'm not."

"That young woman done been through a lot. Please don't go making no promises you know you can't keep."

"We're friends. That's all. Friends."

"Does that mean what I hope it mean?"

"It means that I won't hurt her."

Her stern expression softened, somewhat, but he could tell that she still wasn't satisfied.

"I know I hurt her when I went away," he added. "I know she hoped for more, but..."

"But what?"

"But sometimes," he hesitated, then looked at her. "Sometimes we can't have what we want."

She studied him. "In them four years you was gone, what happened to you? What'd they do to you *out there?*"

He forced a smile and gave her a kiss on the cheek. "Nothing important," he said lightly. "Nothing that a man can't learn to live with."

24. Isabella

He felt a pang of guilt when Rachel opened her door. She looked exhausted. Evidently, she'd just returned home, hadn't even had time to remove her coat. The dark circles under her eyes were pronounced and her heart-shaped face was pale. After he'd left the night before, she'd been called back in to work part of the overnight and early morning shifts, she told him. Two of the other nurses had called in sick.

"I'm sorry," he said. "I should go."

"No." She stayed him with an outstretched hand. "Come in. Please. Seeing you is good for me."

She went to the kitchen. Rapidly, she put up water for coffee and took out chocolate cake. Finally, he got her to sit down. He spoke in low, intense tones of his failure to prove a case against Sweet.

"Sweet's hotel roommate claims that Sweet was in his room the whole night Lilian died. All of a sudden, Dr. Steve says he's *not* sure Lilian was pregnant."

"Oh, David ... what you've been through."

"When I add all that to what Nella said, I... I have to say I..." His voice trailed off.

"Maybe it's for the best. You've done all you can. Now you'll have peace of mind. Now you know it *was* suicide. I mean—you do see that now, don't you?"

He was silent.

"David McKay, you're one of the most stubborn men I've ever known. You've got to accept what happened. You've got to let Lilian go. That's the only way to survive this. Your thoughts belong with the living, not the dead."

Nella had said something similar. Why couldn't he let go? Admit that he might be wrong? The fact was, he did want Sweet to be guilty. He needed him to carry the blame.

"Promise me you'll forget about Sweet," she begged. "For your own sake, you've got to promise me that you'll move on."

"Rachel... I can't."

There was a long uncomfortable moment.

"What are you going to do now?" she asked.

"I don't know."

She studied him with bleary eyes. Then she rose from the table with the slow, stiff movements of a sleepwalker. "I'm very tired now. I'd like to sleep."

She was kicking him out. He stood up. He looked at her narrow shoulders hunched miserably under her thin coat, remembered what Annie had said, and felt ashamed.

"I'm sorry," he said.

She turned away from him. He laid a light hand on her shoulder. At his touch, she gave a dry sob. He put his arms around her. She turned, laid her face against his chest, and openly wept.

"It was so horrible," she sniffled. "All those months with Lilian and then her dying that way. And then I heard that you were coming back. And it sounds terrible, but I thought that maybe her death was meant to be, that it was worth it, if it could bring you back. But then you said you weren't going to stay. I don't want you to leave Harlem, but I can't make you stay. I don't want you to stay, not if it's going to be this way. Not if all you can think about is getting Sweet."

She babbled on, like a heartbroken child. The kitchen clock ticked loudly. The sounds of laughter floated in from the street. *Happy people, normal people,* David thought, glancing out the kitchen window. *Do such people still exist?* Sometimes, it seemed to him that he was mired in sadness, that everyone he knew was struggling with tragedy. Perhaps it was his work in Philadelphia; perhaps it was only his own skewed view of the world.

Gradually, Rachel calmed down. The remaining traces of her perfume, mixed with the hospital odors of sweat, disinfectant, and sickness, wafted up to him. He kissed the top of her head. She moaned and looked up. Her green eyes intrigued him. Sometimes, they were as clear as dewdrops; at other times, as opaque as a forest at midnight. Right then, they were tired and reddened, and they wore an expression that made him yearn for a sweetness he had no right to taste. He felt himself swelling. He moaned. Even the agony of saying no was beginning to feel good. He was tempted, so tempted to cross that line. If he didn't get away soon, he'd burst—

"Stay with me," she whispered.

Somehow, she'd managed to slip off her coat, and now his was coming off, too.

With nimble fingers she unbuttoned his shirt and rolled it back over his shoulders. Spreading her fingertips over his chest, she covered it with hot, moist kisses. She began to lick him, the tip of her tongue fluttering lightly over his nipples. Her lips traced a line of fire, downward, while her fingers undid his belt, burrowed inside his pants and touched him there ... there ... and *there.* His eyes slid closed; his breathing grew ragged. What was the point? Why couldn't he—for once—just let go?

He sensed her slide to her knees. When he realized that she was parting his fly, he clasped her by her shoulders and drew her up. She looked at him, wondering. Had she done something wrong? Was he going to leave?

No, he shook his head. "I want to be here, with you," he

said and caressed her with his eyes. "It's just that ... I didn't think we could ever have this again. I didn't really think ..."

A wealth of relief and happiness flooded her face. He stroked her cheek.

"Let's take our time," he whispered. "Let's take it slow ... and easy."

With his right hand, he cupped her cheek and kissed her lips. When he drew back, he saw that her eyes were closed, her lips slightly parted. He drew a fingertip over one of her eyebrows and she opened her eyes. They were like green flames now. Taking her face in both hands, he slowly ran his tongue along her upper lip, then made his way down her chin. Tilting her face upward, he gently sucked on her throat.

Moaning, she pressed herself against him. Her body quivered. Then, she pulled away. "Wait," she whispered and left the room. He heard the sound of running water. When she came back, she took his hand and led him to her bathroom. He saw that she'd filled the tub, a deep claw-footed one. She'd also set lighted candles on the tiled floor. Their small flames cast flickering shadows on the bathroom's yellowed ivory walls.

Slowly, they undressed one another. She had him lie back in the tub. Then she stepped in with him and knelt between his legs, facing him. When he reached for her, she pressed his arms down.

"Relax, baby."

Tenderly, she lathered him with a sponge and a bar of soap scented with sandalwood. Gently, as though she were handling a child, she lifted his arms and soaped his armpits, then moved down over his chest. His erection arched over his stomach like a bird about to take flight. He reached to cup her breasts, but she swatted him away, and then she began to wash him with calm efficiency, a woman reclaiming her lost lover as her own.

For a time, he watched her slender hands at work. Then he closed his eyes, slid deeper into the warm water, and gave in to the sweet sensation of her hands moving over him. Now and then, she would kiss him and where her lips touched him, he ached.

He would never feel as captured by a woman as he was by Rachel. As she bathed him, he imagined a cleansing that went deeper than the skin, one that took him back to earlier times, before shame and exile.

He moaned as she cradled his balls and lathered them. He closed his eyes and let his head fall back, and then he felt her mouth envelop him. A sharp stab of pleasure shot through him. He looked down. With her tongue, she was caressing him from base to tip, tip to base. She looked up, saw his expression, and smiled her Mona Lisa smile, then gave him one last lick. Still on her knees, she took his right hand and placed it between her thighs.

He curled his fingers into her soft dark triangle. Her breath caught as his middle finger slipped inside her and she bit her lower lip. For a brief moment, she closed her eyes and shivered from head to toe. Then her eyes opened to dwell on him, as warm and inviting as the Caribbean. Silently, she leaned forward and kissed him long and hard on the mouth. All of her pain, her longing, went into that one kiss. He drew her to him, sliding her forward through the water, and kissed her eyes, her lips, her throat. Then he washed her, too.

They dried one another with short, rapid strokes of the towel, then went to her bedroom. Once there, they got close, loving hard, loving deep, sweating to make up for lost time. Once he woke her to lick honey from between her thighs. When the day had given way to early evening, she laid her face on his chest and asked:

"So, is your honey-stick sore?"

"It aches, all right."

She chuckled and played with him lazily. "You were a hungry man."

"Four years without a dip in the pot can do that."

"Four years?" she repeated with wonder, turning his exhausted member this way and that. "Why? Were you sick?" She looked up. "Or were you in jail?"

He saw the morbid interest in her eyes and felt only faint surprise. He'd always suspected that she had a dark side and yes, he was attracted to it. He chuckled.

"Yeah, I saw the inside of a couple. But not in the way you mean."

She twirled some of his chest hairs around her right index finger. "Does loving me cause you pain, David?" She pulled on the hairs a little, watching his skin lift, and whispered, "Do you feel ashamed?"

He shook his head.

She smiled sweetly at him, then gave his chest hairs a swift, sharp yank, ripping some out by the roots. He jerked up and grabbed her hand.

"What the fu—"

"Do you feel ashamed?"

Their gazes locked. She stared him down.

"Yeah," he said, finally. "I guess I do."

Her feline eyes appraised him. "But still, you love me." Her grip on his hairs loosened, and with a contented little smile, she lowered her head and nuzzled her cheek against his chest.

He let himself sink back against the pillow. One hand he threw across his forehead; with the other, he stroked the top of her head, drawing her hair back from her face. "Why d'you ask?"

Her voice, when it came, sounded as though it was floating from somewhere deep within him.

"Because ... it's no good when the loving's easy. It's got to hurt... and hurt bad. That's the only way a body knows it's for real."

Years later, looking back, he would wonder at the power of pain, at how some people are more attracted to anguish than to ecstasy, how for some they are one and the same. But at the time, he only perceived that Rachel connected with him on a level that no other woman did. And that he was grateful to have someone with whom he could express, without explaining, the pain he otherwise had to hide.

He found that he'd forgotten his keys and had to ring the doorbell. Annie shook her head at the sight of him. Hers was the expression of a teacher who had seen his homework and was none too pleased. It was in the set of her mouth, the way her eyes moved over him. She hung up his coat, gave him another dark glance, then headed off down the hall. He pursued her and put a light restraining hand on her arm.

"Hey, Annie, what's the matter? Come on, look at me."

She turned around, her arms folded across her bosom, her lips pressed tight. "Yes?"

"What's the matter?"

She looked at him hard. This was more than disapproval. It was fury. "Mr. David ... Her smell's all over you. You reek of her."

Normally, he was slow to anger, but her words threw his switch. "And what of it?"

"Looka here, I sees you running over there all times of day, disappearing early in the morning and coming back at night. Now I don't know what you doing, but I can guess and it don't seem right, not after all that's happened."

He took a deep breath to try to calm down. "Annie, I love you and I respect you, but I won't let you mind my business. Now I know you're upset about Lilian—so am I—but that don't give you the right to—"

"This ain't got nothing to do with Miss Lilian. And you know it."

He stared at her, not comprehending. "I know *what?*"

She looked at him skeptically.

"Annie, tell me what-all I'm supposed to know!"

She studied him, still mistrustful, then relented. She told him to follow her into the kitchen, had him sit down. She talked; he listened. Twenty minutes went by. By then, his throat had gone dry, and he was shaken to the core.

"Are you sure?" he asked.

"Go back 'n see her. Talk to her. But no matter what she says, please r'member this: There's some things a woman never forgives or forgets. Miss Rachel may not want to carry her mem'ries round with her—I'm sure she don't—but she ain't got no choice. Them mem'ries is cut into her heart, burned into her soul. She'll never come free of them. Hear what I say, Mr. David, hear what I say. Them mem'ries will be a part of her till the day she die."

And so they would be. Rachel would never forget the day when the sun turned dark in her inner sky and bitterness settled like a permanent night over her heart. It was the twentieth of January 1923. David had been gone exactly three months. She'd visited Lilian. They were in the McKay family parlor. Rachel had sat nervously on the edge of the fireplace armchair. She was weak after days of vomiting. Her eyes were reddened from nights of crying. She saw that Lilian couldn't bear to look at her. They were old friends, but Lilian was ashamed and embarrassed. She obviously wanted her out of the house as quickly as possible.

Lilian took a step toward her, then faltered. Her expression was grim, but decided. "I'm sorry, Rachel. You're like a sister to me, but I can't help you. You're asking for something I cannot give."

Rachel's heart thumped painfully. "But why?" she pleaded. "Just tell me where he is."

"No."

Rachel's small hands balled into fists. She willed back the tears she feared were about to spring to her eyes.

Lilian's pale pink lips pressed together firmly. "Rachel, you're to blame for the trouble you're in. No decent woman would've let a man go as far as you did."

Rachel cringed inwardly but she forced herself to speak up.

"It's not like I got this way by myself. David was there, too. I didn't force him to love me."

"My brother was only reacting like a healthy man. It's always the woman's place to keep matters within proper limits." Lilian's control snapped. "You should've known better."

"We were together only once."

"And this had to happen?!"

"You think I did this on purpose to make him marry me?"

Lilian gritted her teeth. "I have nothing against my brother marrying you, but I won't let you use him. I don't believe he loves you. If he did, he would've come back."

Rachel wailed, "He'd come back if he knew—"

"I'm doing you a favor, Rachel. You don't believe it, but I am."

"It wouldn't be the way it was between your parents—"

"How dare you!"

Rachel saw that she'd said the wrong thing. What could she do? Finally, she begged. "If you won't tell me where he is, will you at least tell him about me, about... ?"

Lilian's eyes narrowed. A little smile appeared on her lips. "Yes," she said. "Of course I will."

"But I knew she was lying," Rachel said. "I knew it before the words even left her mouth." Rachel's eyes moved over David's face. "I mean, she did lie, didn't she? You never knew, did you?

"No," he said. "I never knew."

His eyes burned in his head. He had left Rachel to face this alone. As for Lilian—he struggled to understand—how could she have done this?

"Didn't she do anything to help you?"

"She offered me money, in your name. To finance a new start, she said. *Elsewhere.*"

Of all Lilian's secrets, this was the worst. That she had known where he was, known that Rachel and his child needed him, but failed to tell him.

"She only wrote me that you'd left town."

"I didn't take Lilian's money. Mama bought me a bus ticket—a one-way ticket—to Chicago. She thought it'd be better for me if I went away. She was afraid the gossip would hurt me. But nothing could cut deeper than knowing you were gone. After that, nothing mattered. But I couldn't stay. I had to think of Mama, too. She gave me all her savings. I went to the station by myself. But I didn't go to Chicago. I went to D.C. Somehow, I had a notion you were there. But you weren't. At least, I couldn't find you. I bought a cheap ring. Found a rooming house. And said I was a widow."

"And the baby?"

The expression in Rachel's eyes softened. "A little girl. I named her Isabella."

Pain blossomed inside David like a blood-red flower. "And did you put ... Isabella ... in a home?"

Rachel smiled dreamily. "She was so pretty. Sometimes I can still feel her soft little cheek against mine."

He had a sinking feeling. "Rachel, where's the baby?"

Rachel's smile abruptly faded. "Dead. Caught pneumonia. Died right before Christmas." Rachel's eyes became wet. She blinked and swallowed hard. "Maybe it's better she's gone. She wouldn't have had much of a life. But I loved her. God, I ache for her. Mama said Isabella suffered for my sins, but I wonder what kind of God would punish an innocent baby. Sweet Jesus, she was five months old."

Rachel clenched her teeth and shut her eyes. Her small fists flexed and curled in her lap.

"I was afraid to ... I didn't have the money to ... bring her back here. I had to bury her there. To leave her down there with nobody to visit her. Sometimes I dream about getting the money together to go back. Just once. Just to put some flowers ..." She bit her lip. "I left the same day as the funeral. Came back here. Mama fell ill three months later. She was gone within a week."

"My God, Rachel ..."

He moved to put his arms around her, but she drew back. She was stiff with renewed anger. Her pretty face was bitter.

"Lilian came to see me. My mama was dead. My baby was dead. And now, she wanted to know if there was anything she could do. I told her, no. No, thank you."

Rachel swallowed. She drew a deep breath, raised her head a notch and forced a smile. "But you know something?" She swiped away a tear. "I am not bitter. I'm not gonna *let* myself be bitter. I'm gonna stay glad, so glad that I had Isabella. Given my life, I just have to be grateful that I had her at all."

And then she did let him hold her. She let him rock her gently back and forth, but she refused to shed any more tears.

He convinced Rachel to lend him her sole picture of Isabella. She relinquished it only after he promised to return it. Later, ensconced in his armchair before the parlor fireplace, David fingered the small rectangle, studying it. His fingers trembled. His little girl had had his eyes, almond-shaped, dark and liquid. Her small lips were pert and soft like the leaves of cherry blossoms. She was a beautiful child who stared into the camera with a sense of expectation and curiosity about what life would bring. The magnitude of his loss hit him. He felt gutted. So much had happened while he was away. How could he have ever thought his disappearance wouldn't matter?

"You want another cup of coffee, Mr. David?"

Annie's gentle voice brought him back. She stood next to him, pointing at his still half-full cup on the nearby side table. "It's sat a long time. Probably done gotten cold. You want a fresh cup?"

Yes. He needed warmth, to drink it and hold it, to stave off the cold that was creeping around inside him.

"Thank you," he said, then asked: "Why didn't Lilian tell me that Rachel needed me?"

"The first of the Seven Sins," she said promptly.

Pride, he thought. *Puritan pride. They were friends. Like sisters, for years. But when it came down to it, Lilian didn't think Rachel was good enough. And it didn't matter that Rachel was carrying my child. She didn't just turn her back on her friend—but on her own flesh and blood ... because of pride.*

He fingered the small photograph, still thinking of Lilian.

Just one more sign that I didn't really know her. No more than I know Gem.

His thoughts slowed.

Gem ... .

Who was he to judge her? After what he'd done? After what Lilian had done? Gem was his one remaining blood relative. They'd never made much effort to get along, but now—he wanted to. Suddenly, he was determined to.

But first, he had something else to do. A plan fully formed had presented itself to him. And to his tired mind, the plan made sense. He'd failed his father, his sister, and his child. What was done was done and they were gone. He hadn't done right by them, but he could still do right by Rachel, do what he should have done to begin with.

Marry her.

Yes ... that's what he had to do. A sense of relief, as well as of inevitability, swept over him. He saw with startling clarity that he was not in love with Rachel. He felt at most a deep affection for her. She could certainly make him desire to touch her more than any other woman he had ever known, but lust had nothing to do with love. He saw that while part of his decision to marry her grew from a sense of guilt, another part stemmed from his awareness that she was a tie to his roots. They were bonded by a common history, one of shared pain as well as pleasure. After living for four years as a stranger in a strange land, he was desperately lonely and needed someone with whom he could be himself.

His plan required him to give up his life in Philadelphia, but he knew with sudden, brilliant clarity that he would not miss it. What he desired most was a new start. He could do that with Rachel. When he left town this time, he would take her with him.

The idea of marrying someone he was not in love with seemed familiar. Why? Then he thought of his mother and Lilian. Inaccessible husbands, neglected wives. One-sided marriages were the McKay way.

He'd long ago stopped trying to understand his parents' relationship. Or rather, he thought he *had* understood it and because that understanding brought him no comfort, he'd finally left the matter alone.

Lila had suffered under Augustus. She was lithe, pretty, and accomplished. But her skin likened to chocolate, not honey; her hair to wool, not silk—and those were the deciding factors. She adored her tall, light-skinned husband. There was no sign, however, that he loved her. Quite the contrary: His eyes filled with resentment when she entered the room. He dismissed her love but demanded her loyalty. Any respect he showed her was due to her station as his wife, not her worth as an individual. And any need on his part to love or be loved was satisfied in the arms of the high-toned mistresses he took on with a vengeance.

"Why do you have to humiliate me?" David had once overheard his mother cry. He'd been walking past his father's office door. It was shut, and normally, you couldn't hear a thing through it. But his parents must've been standing just on the other side. Augustus was trying to get Lila to leave. She'd broken into his inner sanctum and he wanted her out. She had no intention of going, not without saying her peace. David listened with a sense of shame.

"I can't take it much longer—"

"You'll take whatever I give you. You wanted me. You got me. Now, leave."

"Augustus, please—"

"Leave!"

David hurried away, ducking into the parlor just in time. He peeked out. His mother stepped outside his father's office. She turned to look at Augustus and he shut the door in her face. As David watched, she bent her head and wept. She muffled her cries with a handkerchief.

His blood pounded in his head. He was filled with hate and shame—hate for his father and shame that he couldn't protect his mother.

Why did Daddy marry her? If that's the way he's going to treat her?

She straightened up and held her small head erect.

That's right, Mama. Don't let him get you down.

Was there ever a time when it had been good between them? When his father had treated her with love and respect? David searched his memory for instances and found precious few.

His mother went toward the kitchen, then paused on the threshold and turned back. Her face had a peculiar look when she did that. He'd noticed that she never entered the kitchen when Annie was in there. She and Annie rarely spoke to one another, exchanging words only when it was necessary.

She started back toward the front of the house. David withdrew into the parlor and went behind the door. He didn't want her to see him standing there, *spying on her.* Through the crack between the door and its frame, he watched as she passed and went up the steps.

He'd once heard his father mutter that marriage to a "high yella" would've helped him businesswise, would've brought him good social contacts. No doubt Augustus believed that and the wisdom of the times backed him, for it dictated that everyone in the race "marry up." But if that was the case, then one had to wonder, why *had* he married Lila?

David had heard rumors and he'd done simple arithmetic. It took a woman nine months after marriage to bear a child. Why had she needed only six with him?

So what if he married you because he had to, he wanted to say, as he watched her climb the stairs. *That doesn't give him the right to treat you this way.*

That was the message he wanted to give—and one day would. But he had to find the right words. The wrong words would hurt her, would make her feel cheap, and God knows that's not what he wanted to do. He wanted, if anything, to relieve her of the burden of keeping a secret. A secret he already knew. *Mama, it's okay. I understand,* he wanted to say. *Someday, Daddy's going to know what he had in you. Someday, he'll be sorry.*

He'd stood there with clenched fists, thinking that yes, in time he'd find the right words ... the words and the courage. But time ran out before he found either one.

Lila died under the wheels of a trolley car on Thanksgiving Day in November 1920, eight months after they'd moved to Strivers' Row, one week after he'd overheard the scene in his father's office.

On the eve of her funeral, David watched as his father approached Lila's casket in the parlor. Augustus broke down. His tears ran freely. In his remaining months, he wandered through the house, a tired, insignificant-looking old man. Without Lila's love and adoration to inflate him, he seemed to shrink. He withdrew, disapproving of any "outsider" who stepped through the door, and filled the house with his mournful spirit. He held his children to him with a dark magnetism that silenced all thoughts of resistance. By June, he was gone, too.

David now resolved that his marriage would be different. He would give his wife attention and affection. He would do his best to be a good husband. His past neglect of Rachel would ensure his future care of her.

His mind made up, he decided that the marriage would take place as soon as possible, but his plan for a fresh beginning would have to wait. Even if he did manage to accept the idea of Lilian's death as a suicide, he still wanted Sweet out of the house. Once Sweet was gone, a decision would have to be made about the place. Glancing around the room, David knew he would never sell the house, but he couldn't live there either. He hadn't lived in it long before going south, but in that short time, it had accumulated too many memories. And goodness only knows how long he could stave off questions about his past if he remained in town. He would retire Annie—she would hate that, but he had no choice—rent the house (with Annie in it, if necessary), and he and Rachel would start anew.

Later that day, he went to Annie in the laundry room and told her: "I just thought you should know. I plan to ask Miss Rachel to marry me."

Annie was folding towels. She was quiet at first, getting used to the idea, he supposed. Then she looked at him. "Do you love her?"

He was quiet for a moment. "I care for her."

She took a deep breath and went back to folding. "So, it's really 'cause of the baby?"

"Sort of." He folded his arms across his chest. "And because I need someone. I can't stay in Harlem—don't ask me why—and when I leave, I'm going to take her with me." He touched her elbow. "Don't you like her? I thought you'd be ... well, happy, to hear that I'm going to do right by her."

"Two wrongs don't make a right," she said and went back to folding a bath towel, taking extra care to match the corners. "I'd like to see you marry somebody you love. I know that girl's been crazy about you since she first laid eyes on you. She so fulla love for you, she cain't see straight. And right now, it prob'ly won't much matter to her that your feelings ain't the same. I mean—you ain't lied to her or nothing, has you, saying something you don't mean?"

"No, I've been honest."

"Well, I guess she don't know it yet—or she don't care—but she'll find out. It can be awful hard on a woman living with a man that don't love her. All them feelings going out and nothing coming in ... it's kinda like starving."

He thought again of Lila and Augustus, of Lilian and Sweet. "I'll take good care of her. It doesn't have to turn out badly. Maybe the love'll come later."

"Maybe ... But maybe, it won't." She looked at him. "You really think it's gonna come with you?"

"I don't know."

"Well, you best be thinking long and hard about it, Mr. David, 'cause when you say them words 'I do,' you cain't never take them back."

She picked up another towel and spread it out flat on the countertop. "And what you gonna do about the house?"

He licked his lips. "I wanted to talk to you about that. Annie, like I said, I can't stay here—but I'm going to make sure Mr. Jameson's out of the house."

"He ain't going nowhere if he finds out you ain't gonna stay here."

"He'll leave. One way or another, he'll go. What I want to talk to you about is what happens after he's gone."

She blinked, her eyes wide with sudden understanding. "Don't tell me you gonna sell this place—"

"No ... No, I'm not. But I am going to have to rent it out."

Panic flashed across her face. "Oh my God, you gonna put me out?"

"No, of course not."

Stunned and hurt, she put a hand to her mouth. A little sound escaped. She blinked and turned away. He put an arm around her shoulder.

"Don't worry, please. No matter what, you're going to be able to stay here."

She just shook her head, soundlessly.

"I am *not* going to put you out," he repeated. "And I'm not going to let anyone else do it either."

She put a trembling hand on the counter to steady herself. "Oh, Mr. David, you don't understand. You just don't understand." She turned her wrinkled face toward him. Tears shimmered in her eyes. "This house," she whispered. "This house—I done spent more'n halfa my life taking care of you and your fam'ly. I don't wanna work for nobody else. I *won't* work for nobody else."

"Annie, calm down."

"You just don't understand."

"I do understand—"

"No, you don't. You don't understand nothing—not nothing."

She turned away. He let his hands drop and sighed.

The problem was, he did understand. He understood oh, so well.

25. THE PROPOSAL

The sun hung low in the sky with a dull, metallic gleam. The air was cool and damp and looked like it would stay that way forever. It was that time of year when it's hard to believe there ever was or ever will be another summer.

David began his day with another visit to Lilian's grave. He stood there for a long, long time. A tidal wave of grief and despair surged inside him. He tried to contain his pain, his hands clasped tightly before him, but as the emotional pressure in his chest swelled and expanded, he felt as though he might explode. Closing his eyes, he let the pain wash over him. He rolled with it, like a man tossed and tumbled by the sea. His chest constricted; he couldn't breathe. And like a man adrift, he wondered if he would ever reach shore again. Finally, the pain subsided. Numbness set in. He sank down on his haunches by the grave.

"I'll never stop fighting for you, never," he whispered, "but I have other responsibilities, too. What we did to Rachel—it wasn't right. She deserved better. I wish we could change the past. But we can't. And now there's no turning back. You must understand. There is no turning back."

There was no answer, just a still and mournful silence.

Rachel had the day off. David picked her up late that afternoon. They walked through the park path along Riverside Drive. Couples strolling along hugged one another against the cold. Others took turns pushing prams. A few children rode battered bicycles while their friends ran alongside. David thought of Isabella. She would have been three years old, able to run, climb, get into mischief, and keep up a constant chatter. Then he caught himself. He was yearning for a child he would never hold. Putting one hand on the small of Rachel's back, he guided her to the edge of the path. It was a quiet spot, from which they could clearly see across the Hudson River.

The water was a filthy blue-gray. And the skyline beyond it was less than significant. Yet the scene had its own melancholy beauty. David's gaze dwelled on the water. The Hudson had always fascinated him. Its swift current had stirred his young man's heart with thoughts of travel. It had beguiled him with hints of life beyond the horizon, of days filled with adventure, danger, and delight. There were fortunes to be made and worlds to be conquered if only one had the guts to step beyond the shore. The river, the river: It promised the freedom to wander, but never once mentioned the loneliness of exile.

"Rachel, you've told me it's time to look toward the future. You're right."

He felt her tense.

"You're leaving?" she asked.

"Yes... but—"

"Don't worry. I won't try to keep you."

He took her hands in his and brought them to his lips. Her fingers were cold. Exhaling puffs of warm air on them, he massaged them gently.

"I want to buy you some gloves. The warmest I can find."

"That's very kind, but you don't need to."

She withdrew her hands from his and put them into her

pocket. Her sudden coolness dismayed him. He tried to remember all the sweet words he'd rehearsed, but could recall none of them. So he went straight to the heart of the matter. He reached into his coat pocket and brought out a small jeweler's box covered in blue velvet. He opened it to reveal a ring, a tear-shaped diamond on a slender gold band. Her eyes widened at the sight of it.

"I'm asking you to be my wife. I promise, here and now, to honor and respect you, as long as we both shall live." He took a deep breath and his voice broke. "Marry me, Rachel. Believe in me. Trust me, again. And the loving won't have to hurt for it to be real."

She swallowed hard. Tears welled in her eyes as she looked at the ring. "It's beautiful... but I can't accept it."

His heart thudded. "Why not?"

"You're only proposing out of guilt."

"I should've asked you long ago."

"You're only asking now because of Isabella."

"Isabella was simply the kick I needed."

Silent and skeptical, she turned her face away. He cupped her chin and made her look at him.

"Rachel, I know life's been hard on you, but it's been hard on me, too."

"Hard on *you?* You're a McKay. You have a name, money."

"But I don't have you. And that makes all the difference. Now how about it? You gonna make an honest man of me?"

For a moment, she didn't answer. Tears slid down her face. Pride and desire, those old foes, battled it out behind her eyes. Then she smiled and nodded jerkily.

It was all he needed.

She gasped as he slipped the ring onto the fourth finger of her left hand. He grabbed her up and kissed her face, her eyes, her lips, and the tip of her nose. He picked her up and swung her around. His heart had never felt lighter, his soul freer. He had finally done something right. He would be able to leave all the madness of Harlem and Philadelphia behind him.

"We'll go somewhere, start fresh."

"You mean not live on Strivers' Row?"

"No. Once Sweet's out of the house, I'll rent it. We'll find a new place. Start over."

For the first time in years, he felt hope. He was so engaged with his vision of their future that it took him a while to notice that her smile had faltered.

"What's the matter?"

Rachel hesitated. Her gaze went out over the Hudson, to the world beyond the river's shore. "I was thinking about what leaving Harlem might mean. I don't know if I can do that."

His smile died. "You can't mean that."

"But I do."

"Don't you ever want to experience life outside of this place?"

She was quiet. "I did. Once. I never want to step foot outside Harlem again."

"It'll be different this time. You'll be with me."

"No, it's not what you're thinking. I don't know if I can explain it. I need this place, somehow. Seeing the people in the neighborhood going about their daily lives. I don't know—I feel strong here."

He had never expected her to refuse to leave Harlem. There were black communities elsewhere that had something to offer. Yes, he could understand that like thousands of Harlemites, she might be indifferent to white New York. She might admire items on display in its downtown shops, applaud shows at its theaters, browse through books in its libraries, and every now and then sip coffee at one of its restaurants. She might even peruse its newspapers and cluck her tongue over "the doings of white folks." But then she would promptly use the newsprint to wrap potato cuttings in. Never once would she consider herself a part of the silver metropolis. Hundreds of wealthy whites might stream toward black Harlem to visit its cabarets, but essentially white New York had nothing to do with her, or she with it, and she liked it that way.

David could understand all that. But it surprised him that she had absolutely no curiosity about life outside New York. Did she actually intend to live her life within the strict confines of Central Park to the south, Fifth Avenue to the east, St. Nicholas Park to the west, and 145th Street to the north?

It was as though she'd heard his thoughts.

"This is my portion, David, and I'm satisfied with it." She faced him, her eyes darkly somber. "We have a home here, a place to build on. The house on Strivers' Row might have bad memories now, but we can fill it with love. Think, David. We have friends here, a community. And we're so lucky we do. We're living in the heart of the world's most exciting Negro community. So no, I'm not gonna leave it. And if you thought about it, really thought about it, you'd see that neither should you."

He gazed at the horizon with profound longing. He should have anticipated her desire to live on Strivers' Row. She was a realist. The house was one reason why she was attracted to him; the house, the status and the stability it stood for. That didn't bother him because he was sure she loved him. He had sensed her adoration since the first day she had seen him, when they were children, so many years ago, long before his family became rich. He wished intensely that she had been prepared to go away with him, but why should she? What could he offer her but vague promises and undefined dreams? His shoulders slumped but his smile was valiant.

"All right, we'll stay here, Rachel. I promise you the house and all that goes with it. If that's what you want, that's what you'll have."

He felt like a prisoner who'd been given a glimpse of freedom, then yanked back into his cage. He then saw the delight and joy in her eyes and that comforted him.

"One more thing," she said. "I want you to accept that Lilian's gone. You can't bring her back. You'll get Sweet out of the house—I don't want him there either—but otherwise, you'll leave him alone. No more trying to say that he killed Lilian. Agreed?"

She squeezed his hand gently and looked up at him. He was quiet, his head bent, his jaw clenched. There was a long silence. This was not what he had intended. She kissed him.

"I don't want you to spend our married life chasing down Sweet," she said. "I don't want you wasting *our* time."

He looked at her.

"I have a right to ask that of you," she said. "God knows, I've waited for you long enough."

He smiled dryly, but he thought to himself that she was right. He had kept her waiting, too long. And how much of a life could they have with him always looking back? On the other hand, how could he let Sweet get away with ...

He sighed roughly. Rachel drew a fingertip across his chin. He gazed down at her. He did care for her. And he wanted to make her happy. Perhaps she was right. Perhaps it made no sense to continue to rake up the past. Perhaps ... it was indeed time to let Lilian rest in peace. With an effort, he pushed his misgivings aside and took Rachel in his arms.

"All right. It's agreed."

They headed back to her apartment. She invited him in, but he turned her down. Noting the concern on her face, he hugged her again. Then he was gone. He needed to do what he did best—be alone.

26. IN THE BELLY OF THE WHALE

If she only knew what that promise might cost us.

Public shame and social ostracism: The McKay family name, which represented such genteel dignity and pride of race, would become muddied with cowardice and mired in moral disgrace. The doors to the elegant homes and elite salons she so desperately wanted to enter would be slammed in their faces. They would not be able to walk down the street without encountering stares of disdain.

She might even leave him. What irony! He would stay in Harlem to give her pleasure, but it was this very decision that would cause her pain. Nevertheless, he would try. He owed her that much. He had abandoned her when he left Harlem those four years ago, not that he had planned to leave her, to leave anyone, when he went away that October day. It was the seventeenth of the month, 1922. He had expected to return after a couple of weeks' work, but it hadn't happened that way.

His assignment had taken him to Charlottesville, in Boone County, Georgia. He could still hear the train wheels screeching as the locomotive ground to a halt, the confused babble of hurried, excited voices as people climbed off, met friends, and tried to find their way.

Charlottesville was a rich little town in the southernmost part of the state, near the Florida border. David's intent was to investigate the lynchings of five Negroes—four brothers and one of the men's sons, an eleven-year-old boy—two weeks before.

Passing himself off as a white reporter for the *New York Sentinel,* David found it easy to get the locals to talk. They didn't try to hide their part in the lynchings, but talked volubly, sometimes with pride. They enthusiastically described the torture, mutilation, burning, and hanging of the five victims as though they were relating a day at the circus. Many took out their "souvenirs" from the lynchings: the burnt stump of a wooden stake, a bloodstained stretch of rope, charred bones, and pickled body parts removed while the victims were still alive. At the same time, however, none of the whites he spoke to would name names. If he pressed for the identities of the mob leaders, a funny look would flit across their faces, a sudden suspicion, and he'd find the conversation ended.

Certain facts were not in dispute: Over the course of three days, October 8 through 10, 1922, mobs executed Hosea Johnson, his brothers Solomon, Jeremiah, and Ezekiel, and Ezekiel's son Caleb. The men were accused of having murdered a white farmer, Ray Stokes, and of raping Stokes' wife, Missy.

There was no doubt that Stokes had been killed, but was it premeditated murder? Had his wife indeed been raped? And if so, what, if anything, did the Johnsons have to do with these events?

The Johnson brothers were family men. Stable. Hardworking. Even the whites conceded that. After the men were killed, their homes were burned to the ground. Their widows and the remaining children, a total of twelve, were whipped, then driven out of town with only the clothes on their backs.

Talks with the locals also quickly gave David a picture of Stokes. Big and burly, Stokes had owned a large plantation in Boone County. He was known for beating and cheating his Negro workers. After a while, no blacks would voluntarily agree to work for him, so Stokes found a way to force them to. He would visit the courthouse and check the docket to see what black man had been convicted and couldn't pay his fine or was sentenced to work on the chain gang, Stokes would pay the fine, get the man released into his custody, and have him work off the debt on his plantation.

Hosea Johnson fell under Stokes' shadow in just this way. His thirty-dollar gaming fine had been beyond his means. Stokes put his money down and had himself a new man. Johnson labored on Stokes' property until the thirty dollars had been worked off. Perhaps the situation would've turned out differently if matters had ended there. But they didn't.

Johnson's wife was pregnant with their fifth child. Money was more than tight and work was hard to come by. So when Stokes offered to "let" Johnson work additional hours, Johnson agreed. Days went by and Johnson's labor added up to a considerable amount of service. After a week, Johnson asked Stokes for his money; Stokes refused. Witnesses said the two men argued. That was on October 7. That evening, Stokes was found dead on his front porch, an ax embedded in his meaty chest.

The call went out and men swarmed to the Stokes plantation. Suspicion immediately targeted Hosea Johnson. Somebody mentioned how close the Johnson brothers were and pointed out that they'd all had trouble with Ray Stokes. No doubt, the brothers had committed the crime together.

Men were deputized and went looking for the brothers, but word of Stokes' death and the ensuing manhunt had spread; the Johnson brothers and their families had disappeared into the woods.

On October 8, Solomon and Jeremiah Johnson were captured about five miles outside Charlottesville. They were lynched on the spot. Hung upside down, they were literally ripped apart by a furious fuselage of more than five hundred bullets.

Sheriff Parker Haynes caught Ezekiel that afternoon and placed him in the nearby Putnam city jail. That evening, Hayes and the county court clerk took Ezekiel out of jail, ostensibly to transport him to the county seat at Lovetree for safekeeping. Haynes told David that a mob had "ambushed" him near the fork of the Dicey and Lovetree roads, just two miles from their destination. Outarmed and outmanned, he said, "I had no choice but to stand by and watch."

Ezekiel was handcuffed and slowly strangled. First, the lynchers chopped off his fingers. They then strung him up and choked him till he was on the verge of death. Three times they strung him up and three times they let him down and revived him, to give him "a chance to save his immortal soul by confessing." Finally, they just let him swing. He died maintaining his innocence.

They left Ezekiel on display for two days, as a lesson to the colored and entertainment to all others. Crowds in autos, buggies, and on foot strolled by to point and snigger.

Meanwhile, the hunt for Hosea continued in vain. After two days of searching, people assumed that he'd successfully fled the area. On the afternoon of October 10, a black man named

Moses Whitney burst into Haynes's office and told him that Hosea was hiding out at his house. Hungry and exhausted, Hosea had come to him for food, Whitney said. He'd given Hosea some grub, promised him supplies, then given him a place to sleep. As soon as Hosea had dropped off, Whitney had slipped out of the house.

The sheriff's men surrounded Whitney's house. There was an exchange of gunfire but Hosea was taken alive. He was attached by rope to the back of a car, dragged down Crabtree Boulevard, the busiest street in Charlottesville, then taken out to a place called the Old Indian Cemetery, on the edge of town. There, they hung him upside down, doused him with kerosene, and set him on fire. David visited the place. It was beautiful and still, and it was hard to believe it had been the site of such recent evil. The only testimony was the scorched remains of an isolated tree.

David tried to see Mrs. Stokes, but was told that she was still suffering from shock. He was able to gather information from servants, however. It was Mrs. Stokes who had found her husband's body. As soon as she saw him lying there, she'd run screaming to her father-in-law's house. The family physician, who happened to be a dining guest at the home of Stokes Sr., quickly sedated her.

David noted at least two discrepancies. A hysterical Missy Stokes had run screaming that Hosea had axed her "Christian man," but she'd said nothing about Hosea having attacked *her.* Then there was the fact that she lay unconscious for nearly two days. Nevertheless, City Superintendent Sharkey Summers claimed that he'd talked to her the morning after the murder. "She told me what the nigger done to her," he said in one newspaper article. He became one of the leading advocates for the burning of Hosea Johnson.

Local newspapers claimed that Hosea had confessed to the murder and the assault before he died. David read and reread the reports. The papers had fed the lynching mania. Not a sin-

gle one had urged due legal process for the accused when captured. All had predicted with malevolent glee that Hosea Johnson would be hung and burned, virtually passing sentence and
preordaining the mode of his torture and execution.

Nor had any report attempted to explain the death of Ezekiel's son, Caleb. One wrote that "the nigger child's death was
too insignificant to explore."

David talked not only to white locals, but also to black residents. At least, he tried to. Most had fled into the woods and
were only slowly daring to return. They professed absolute ignorance of what had occurred while they were gone. Others admitted that they'd seen and heard enough to have something to
say, but they refused to speak.

Over a three-day period, David canvassed about forty ramshackle homes on the black side of town. Most wouldn't even
open their doors. Finally, he gave up. There was a late afternoon
train. He'd be on it. Back at his hotel, he wrote his report,
packed his bags, and headed for the railway station. It was there
he happened upon a man who *would* talk. And the man's name
was Jonah.

"Caleb was a bright youngster," Jonah said. "He was there when
they dragged his papa from the woods. Later, somebody heard
him say that he'd write to the Movement, tell who it was done
what. That night, they came back for him."

"God," murmured David.

At the railroad station, Jonah, a porter, had whispered instructions to meet him at Miss Mae's Rooming House. Then
he'd gone back to work, hauling luggage. David had gone ahead
to the house and Jonah had showed up ten minutes later.

"The next train ain't till tomorrow," Jonah had said. "But
you can stay here tonight."

Miss Mae's was a little two-story construction, not much
more than an oversized hut. David had had his doubts when he
saw it. But Miss Mae eased his concern the minute he stepped

inside the door.

"What a fine young man!"

She welcomed him, a stranger, with outstretched arms. She was so thin, it hurt David to look at her. He gratefully accepted the hug and the pat on the shoulder she gave him, and gently hugged her back.

"You just come on in and rest yourself," she said. At the sight of Jonah, her smile grew wider. "Jonah! You come on in here. I ain't seen you for way too long."

Before David could blink, Miss Mae had sat the two of them down and laid out some thin peach pie and watery coffee. It was a meager spread, but it was all the woman had and David was touched by her generosity.

Miss Mae sat at the table with them. She refused to eat, but said: "Y'all take as much as you want." Her voice was as soft as a whisper. She looked at David and her eyes twinkled with curiosity. She wasn't fooled by the lightness of his skin. "You one of us, ain't you?"

David smiled and nodded.

"So, where you from?"

"He's from up north," Jonah said.

David sipped some coffee to wash down the hard, crusty pie. "I'm working for the Movement. Took the train down from New York. I'm here to find the truth about what really happened."

Miss Mae and Jonah exchanged glances. David sensed a palpable sadness enter the room. Jonah rubbed his chin. He was thoughtful.

"In a way, what happened here," he began, "weren't nothing special. Nothing we ain't seen b'fore. It was bad. Yeah, it was real bad. But bad happens to us colored all the time. It happened here, but it coulda happened in the next town over. Y'understand?"

He looked at David, who nodded.

"There's a lot of Charlottesvilles waiting to happen," Jonah said, his brown eyes mournful. "Us colored folk ... we's born under the hangman's noose. We never know when he'll come a-knocking. Could be, he never comes. Could be, he comes on the morrow, any time, any day. And we accept."

He fell silent, staring at his large hands, which he clenched and opened, clenched and opened. David looked at them too, thinking of their size ... and their impotence in the face of the white man's rule.

Jonah looked up at David. "We cain't do nothing about nothing down here, so we accept. We just ... accept." He dropped his hands to his lap, and there was something very close to despair in his eyes. "My name is Jonah and many times I wonder ... will I end up in the belly of the whale? I just hope the Lord'll deliver me if I do."

"Hush your mouth," Miss Mae said. "Ain't no need to be scaring this young man. He a stranger—"

"That's right," Jonah said. "He a stranger and he don't know nothing about what's going on down here. But he need to."

"That's why I'm here," David said with confidence. "It's my job to ask questions. Get answers. And, hopefully, change things."

After eating, he and Jonah had moved to the front porch. Now Jonah was sitting in Miss Mae's creaky rocking chair, hunched forward. David was perched on the wooden railing, his arms folded across his chest, his face grim.

"The reports say Hosea admitted to killing Stokes and assaulting the man's wife. Is that true?"

"He ain't gone nowhere near Missy Stokes, but yeah, it's true he said he killed the white man."

"They tortured it out of him?"

"Didn't have to. He fessed up all right. Free 'n' clear. Told Whitney all about it."

"Whitney? The one who turned him in?"

"That's right."

"You believe what Whitney said, considering the fact that he turned him in?

"Yeah, I b'lieve it. Most times, you cain't b'lieve a thing Whitney say, but this time I b'lieves him. See, Hosea said he killed Mistah Stokes all right, but he said it was an accident. He went back to see Mistah Stokes about the money. Mistah Stokes told him that if he chopped him some mo' wood, he'd give him his money. Hosea said he wasn't about to do that. Mistah Stokes got angry. Took out his gun and aimed to shoot. Hosea—he threw his ax at the man and run. He say he heard the man grunt, but he ain't look back, so he didn't know that he'd killed him."

"And what about this business with Missy Stokes? Did he say anything about that?"

"He say he guessed she was in the house, but he ain't never seen her. Said he just threw that ax, turned tail, and headed for the woods."

David looked at Jonah for a moment. Everything Jonah had said made sense. He asked the main question that no one so far had dared answer.

"Who was the mob leader?"

Jonah hesitated, then he told him. David sighed. It was as he'd thought. He dropped his hands to the railings, and shook his head, reflecting on what he'd learned. Then he looked at Jonah and thanked him.

"I hope it'll help," Jonah said.

"It will. And don't worry, I won't name your name in my report. Nobody'll learn from me that we had this conversation."

The two men shook hands. They'd been talking for more than an hour. David had missed his train. He didn't want to spend another night in town, but it looked as though he'd have to. He cast his eyes to the western horizon. The winter sun was setting. Brilliant streaks of red, orange, and gold were layered behind the trees. His gaze took in the lush green foliage crowding the edge of Miss Mae's yard. In stark contrast to the decrepit rooming house, it was a rich display. As he looked, a branch swayed, leaves rustled, and a twig snapped. He frowned, his gaze hardening into a stare.

Jonah, following David's look, said, "Maybe we better go inside."

David glanced at him, then back at the bushes. They were still and silent. "Yeah ... maybe we'd better."

Night fell. Jonah had wished David good luck and gone home. After updating his report, David had retired to the upstairs room Miss Mae had given him. His sleep was troubled. He was standing in a narrow street, caged in by rickety buildings on either side. He could hear a low rumbling, a churning sound, like an approaching river. It was getting nearer. He looked up— just in time to see the rising wave of water rushing toward him. He had to get out of the way before he was crushed. He started to run—

And jerked himself awake. He lay there for a moment, stunned. Gradually, he realized that the rumbling he'd heard in his dream was still there. He sat up in bed, his ears straining to understand the sound. He was aware of his heart beating heavily, of cold sweat trickling down from his armpits. He crept to the room's sole window and peeped out.

By the ghostly light of a full moon, he saw dusty clusters of white men swarming up the town's main street. It was the muffled sound of their running feet that he'd heard, and the blurred murmurs of their agitated voices. They carried homemade torches. All bore arms: everything from shotguns and pistols to iron clubs and bullwhips.

David dressed quickly in the dark. Miss Mae was standing on the landing when he left his room. Her sad, wrinkled face was drawn. She held a candle; it threw flickering orange shadows over her shrunken face. Her bony shoulders shivered under her thin shawl.

"Don't go out there," she whispered. "Please!"

"Don't worry. I'll be all right."

He gave her a hug, and then raced down the steps and out into the street. He'd never felt such fear, not even under fire in Europe. Yet a desperate need to know drove him on. He followed the growing mob. The crowd, which included women and children, had stopped at a clearing at the farthest end of the Old Indian Cemetery, where the grass grew thin, not far from the tree where Hosea had died.

David looked around. The area had a few other trees, but they were young—nothing sturdy enough to support a man's weight. That gave him hope—a hope that withered when he looked at the faces in the crowd. He saw grim, maniacal expressions, pale eyes that glittered with homicidal determination. The air crackled with pent-up anticipation and repressed exhilaration.

Then the ground began to vibrate. Then came the rumble of galloping horses and the cries of men raised in exultant triumph.

David turned.

The crowd had parted. A single white rider appeared, galloping at full speed, kicking up a billowing cloud of reddish-brown dust. Out of the cloud emerged the form of a ragged bundle, dragged by a rope attached to the rider's saddle horn. Soon, other riders appeared. And men on foot who waved their arms. The horsemen thundered through. They dragged their victim to the center of the clearing, jumped down and untied him. David's recognized him. His heart thumped.

It was Jonah, bloody and battered.

Four men lugged in two short wooden stakes. They pounded them into the ground—not too deep, because they were in a hurry, but deep enough to make them hold. They stretched Jonah out on the ground and yanked his hands over his head. His wrists they bound to one stake; his ankles to the other. Meanwhile, people in cars were arriving. They parked in a semi-circle and left their headlights on, illuminating Jonah in a glaring, ghostly white light. From the cars erupted men with cameras and tripods. Within minutes, the atmosphere had gone from grim to festive. A party was about to take place and a torture-murder was the main attraction.

In a spasm of terror, Jonah twisted and yanked at his bonds. Onlookers jeered, enjoying his struggles. He bucked and pulled, but the stakes held.

Finally, he let his head drop back and closed his eyes. He lay there, his chest heaving. Then he raised his head again and looked around. His gaze jumped backed and forth across the crowd and then ... they found David.

David felt something inside him spasm and a pain shot through him that reached his fingertips. Just a few hours earlier, he and this man had been sitting at Miss Mae's together. *Will I end up in the belly of the whale?* Jonah had asked. Now, Jonah's eyes, full of wrenching despair, held the answer.

One of the whites followed Jonah's stare. "Hey, I know him!" he yelled, pointing to David. "He's the one been hanging around, asking questions."

"He the one I seen at Miss Mae's," another cried. "He was sitting and jiving with the niggers just like he was a one of them."

"Maybe he *is!*" the first said. "A Yankee nigger!"

Angry murmurs rumbled through the crowd. The mob seemed to contract, then it surged toward David like a murderous claw. He couldn't move. His instincts said run, but his legs wouldn't carry him. He could never outrun that crowd. His eyes went to Jonah. Their gazes locked. It couldn't have been more than a split second, but David would never forget the agony, the dignity and fellowship in Jonah's eyes. *Save yourself,* Jonah seemed to say, *and live to tell my story.* David heard Jonah's message in his heart. He did not remember opening his mouth, but he heard his own voice, anguished, broken and husky.

"I'm not a nigger," he whispered. "I'm not ... one of *them.*"

"You spoke to him at the railroad station. And then you was

at that ole nigger woman's house. I saw ya!"

David's chest heaved. "He said she wasn't feeling well. I went to help. But I don't know him ... don't know him at all."

"You's a lying uppity yella nigger!"

"Come down here to spy on us!"

"Let's burn the bastard!"

"Yeah!"

David tried to swallow, but his throat had gone dry. With a leaden finger, he slowly tapped the collar of his well-cut jacket. His voice was heavy with shame. "Would a colored man be dressed so fine? Speak so well? Would a colored man stand here and watch while another colored man dies? Wouldn't I be running ... if I was a colored man, too?"

Hoots and snickers went up.

"Hey, we's wasting time," a voice cried out. "We already got a nigger to burn!"

"Yeah!"

"Let's get to it!"

The mob lost interest in David. The people began to turn their backs on him. On impulse, he took a tentative step forward and asked: "But what has this man done?"

One of the white men slowly turned. He was tall, nearly skeletal and had a fanatic's gleam in his eyes. He held a coiled bullwhip. "What d'ya mean, what's the nigger done?" he hissed. He looked David up and down, and his gray eyes glinted with renewed suspicion. Gesturing toward Jonah with the bullwhip, he said: "Niggers don't need to do nothing to die, but this one's done a-plenty. He's been spreading lies about them nigger deaths."

"Take him to the sheriff," David said. "Whatever you think he's done, he deserves a fair trial."

More laughter, but bitter this time and laced with poison.

"Damn! Where you come from anyway?" the lanky man asked. "A fair trial? It's the American way, right? Well, hell, down here, son, *lynching* is the American way. Y'see the niggers down here—*our* niggers—they gets a hot tongue—a very hot tongue—when they forgets their place."

The lyncher turned back to the crowd. Laughing amiably, he slowly uncoiled his bullwhip. Then he spun around and brought the lash down across David's left shoulder. David reeled backward with a cry. The material of his jacket tore and his shoulder reddened with blood. The lyncher pulled the whip back with a resounding crack, and then flicked it forward. It wrapped around David's ankles like a thick snake. The lyncher yanked and David's feet went from under him. He lay in the dust, sprawled on his back. The lyncher stood over him.

"Now I don't b'lieve in whipping no white man. But I will if I have to. If you know what's good for you, you'll just settle down and enjoy the show. This here's gonna be a good one."

A babble of malicious chuckles and comments went up. The mob surged back to their victim. Children were sent to scavenge for twigs, urged on by their parents' pointing fingers. It was a game to see who could gather the most. Some of the children were no older than three. Jonah watched mutely as they ran hither and thither, laughing and giggling. The oldest staggered back quickly, their thin arms weighed down with twigs, their small faces suffused with pride. Kneeling down next to Jonah, they arranged the branches snugly at his side.

How can they do this? David wondered. *They're old enough to realize that he's a human being, old enough to know better. Don't they know what they're doing?*

What they were doing was their parents' bidding, as the cheering yells of the adults testified.

The hedge of kindling grew higher.

One of the men raced forward with a small knife. Another darted forward. He too, held a blade. David, confused, thought they were going to stab Jonah. But no, the men knelt down on either side of him. They yanked on his ears, pulled them away from the side of his head, and sliced them off. Jonah arched at the pain and bit back a scream. The first man stood and gave a great yell, waving Jonah's right ear in his hand. The other man soon did the same with the left ear. Others scurried forward, their knives held ready. They stripped the skin from his face and hacked away at his fingers. Through it all, Jonah never once gave them the satisfaction of a cry or an appeal for mercy. Only once, as the dull knives were being used to doggedly—and slowly—cut off his fingers, did David hear Jonah speak, and then it was to moan, "Oh, Jesus."

"Clear away!" came the sudden yell. "We're gonna set to it!"

The souvenir hunters ended their bloody work. Other men came forward. One laid down his shotgun, grabbed hold of Jonah's jaw, and forced open his mouth; another poured in kerosene. As Jonah lay there choking and gagging, a third dropped in a lit twig.

The flames bubbled up in Jonah's mouth for a moment, then shot up with a whoosh. The crowd cheered. Jonah's exhalations were literally on fire. And every time he inhaled, he sucked the flames deeper into his body.

God, no! David inwardly cried. *They're burning him! My God, they're burning him! For having talked to me! They're burning him alive!*

Jonah's agonized face contorted in silent screams. Cherry-red flames licked him and kissed him and he writhed in their embrace. Meanwhile, the flashbulbs popped, blitzing the area with white light, as photographers took pictures for later sale as postcards. And the children stared, wide-eyed, while their parents grinned and pointed, to see Jonah's blood vessels burst and his blood boil in the heat.

David watched, impotent and overwhelmed, and as he watched he prayed, prayed harder than when he was in the woods of Belleau and the Germans were racing toward him.

God help him. Help him help him, please.

From the west came the soft rumble of faraway thunder, and gradually, the crowd fell silent. Most stared dumbly. One or two had even turned away, sickened. Others still looked, but had shielded their eyes and peeped through their fingers. Now, there was nothing but the sound of the crackling flames. The air was nearly unbreathable, heavy with the stench of burning flesh. And Jonah, unbelievably, still twitched.

David cried to his God in anguish. *Jesus, please!*

Jonah's struggles suddenly stilled and a bolt of lightning tore the sky. It cast the faces of everyone in that mob in a ghostly glow. In that flash of cold, blue light, they all appeared dead.

We're all walking corpses, thought David. *We all look like we're out for a night on the town in Hell.*

The last of the carnival atmosphere was gone. A vague unease settled over the mob. The people glanced at one another, then looked away, suddenly unable to meet one another's eyes. They shuffled in place. For one split second, something very like terror rippled through the crowd. David could feel it. He could see it. People began to sidle away. One by one, they left. Men pulling away wives, mothers dragging away children; in some cases, shielding their children's eyes from the very sight they'd brought them to see.

David stayed. He kept witness until the bitter end.

Jonah's torso arched and his legs drew up as his muscles contracted in the heat. After about forty eternal minutes, his roasted body was reduced to an unrecognizable smoking mass. The flames sputtered and popped, briefly flared up again, then went down.

David turned away. He was alone. The others were long gone. He stumbled a short distance, then collapsed on a boulder and vomited. The war in Europe, despite its vast horrors, had not prepared him for what he'd just seen: the specter of God-fearing, churchgoing, patriotic Americans burning a fellow man to death.

For talking to me. For telling the truth. His breath came in hitches. *I was a fool. All us colored who fought for this country—we were fools.*

He felt worse than a fool. He was ashamed to be black. *We're a race of victims. Always at the mercy of some white man's whim. That's what we are. Always at the mercy of some white man's whim.*

Then he heard another voice, a voice that would come to haunt him.

You did nothing. Nothing. But stand by and watch.

Self-hatred surged through him and he spilled hot tears. If he were honest, if he faced the truth, he would have to admit that he was less ashamed of what he was, than of what he had done.

You betrayed the Movement. Betrayed it and everything you swore to uphold.

There was nothing I could do!

Nothing? Nothing but stand by and watch?

He couldn't have saved Jonah. What could he have done against a mob? Saving himself was the least—and the most—he could have done. But an implacable voice, a voice that sounded so much like his father's, condemned him as guilty of unforgivable cowardice.

David bent his head and gave in to gut-wrenching sobs. He was a strong man. He'd seen a lot during the war and survived it all. But the lynching was something else. That single atrocity did what a year in the trenches had failed to do: savage his hope for humanity, his belief in his country, his faith in his God—and his respect for himself.

Suddenly, the rains came, hard and heavy, drenching him to the skin. Casting his eyes to the sky, he held out his hands, palms upward. He felt the slanting rain splatter against his face and laughed harshly. *So, now you send the rain. Too late, my Friend, too late.*

He clenched his fists, closed his eyes, and whispered a bitter prayer. *You're guilty too. You know that, don't You? You and I, we both did nothing. Nothing but stand by and watch.*

He dragged himself to his feet and staggered back through the muddy streets to the rooming house.

Early the next morning, he went to see Sheriff Payne and told him what he had seen—and what he'd learned. He'd already filed his report, one that named names, the city superintendent's name among them.

"Leave town," was Payne's polite advice. Saying it was for David's safety, Payne had him escorted to the station and put on the next train that came through. But five men were waiting at the next stop—Payne among them. They dragged David off the train, down into the dust.

"You one lucky white bastard," Payne said. "We hates Yankee nigger-lovers down here, almost as much as we hates niggers themselves."

He delivered a ferocious kick to David's side. One of the men standing alongside slammed the toe of his boot into David's lower back. The others moved to join in, but Payne held up his hand. Bending down, he grinned in David's face with brown, tobacco-stained teeth.

"Don't worry. I ain't gonna let them kill you. I wouldn't do that to one of my own. But you gots to learn how we do business down here. You gots to learn not to stick your nose where it don't belong." Straightening up, he nodded at the others. "All right. Get to it, boys. I ain't got all day. Just don't kill the sonuvabitch."

David awoke days later in a hospital in Lovetree. Railroad workers had found him lying by the side of the tracks. The doctors and nurses had assumed he was white and treated him better accordingly. Broken spiritually, mentally, and physically, he did not correct them.

After leaving the hospital, he drifted. One morning, he woke up in a filthy flophouse in a city he did not know. He did not remember where he had come from or when he had arrived. His reflection in the small mirror over the washbasin indicated that it had been weeks since he had shaved. His new beard was hard and matted. His hair was newly touched with gray. He cleaned himself as best he could, then left the flophouse and began walking.

He learned that he was in Philadelphia. He walked for hours. Finally tired, he decided to rest on a park bench. A black woman sat there, neither old nor young, but visibly bent under the weight of sorrow. Her sobs were silent but her shoulders heaved. He half-turned, intending to walk on. But something told him not to. Something in that woebegone figure drew him back. In her hunched figure was the personification of his own desolation.

She looked up. Alarm flickered across her face at the sight of him. His face was clean but unshaven and his clothes were dirty and disheveled. He realized that he appeared disreputable, so he spoke quickly.

"I don't want to bother you, lady. I just want to ask if I can help."

She drew back and shook her head, but she seemed reassured. Her thoughts apparently went back to her troubles. Her gaze drifted away and her head bowed again. He took a step toward her.

"Maybe it would help to talk. I'm good at listening."

She ignored him. He hesitated, then slid onto the bench next to her, not too close, but not too far away either. He waited patiently. Minutes passed.

"My boy," she said in a sudden whisper. "They've got my boy."

He waited, but she said nothing more. "Who's got him?"

"My boy," she whimpered. "He ain't but fourteen. The police. They gonna put him away."

"What do they say he's done?"

"Robbed a store. Killed the owner."

He took this in. A Negro teenager in a situation like that barely stood a chance. "You got a lawyer?"

"No money for one." She hugged herself and rocked back

and forth. "No money. And no way to get none."

He was quiet. A squirrel scampered down the trunk of a nearby oak tree and found a tidbit in some last-minute pre-winter scavenging. The little animal grabbed it up and scampered away with a switch of bushy tail.

"I'm a lawyer," David heard himself say. "I could defend your son."

She looked at him, surprised, doubtful, and a bit alarmed. "You's a crazy man, ain't you?"

"I admit I don't look like a lawyer." He smiled apologetically. "But I am one. And if you want me to, I'll talk to your son. My talking to your boy wouldn't hurt him, now would it?"

"No ... I suppose it wouldn't." She scrutinized him. "And you say you's a lawyer? You sure?"

"Yes, very sure." His soft eyes twinkled.

They talked a little more about the details of the case and she seemed to feel better. She gave him her name, her son's name, and where she could be reached. He scribbled it all down with a pencil stub on a piece of paper he'd found in his pocket. As he stood to go, he clutched that bit of paper like a man adrift who has found a life raft. He was flush with a new sense of purpose. She looked up at him, her face a mix of worry and hope.

"Why," she asked, "would you want to help my boy?"

He was the one who looked away then. How could he explain that she was doing him a favor? He gave a little half-smile. "Because ..." He shrugged, "because I can."

"Well, maybe you can." She was thoughtful. "Being a white man makes a difference in this city. Maybe you can make them listen."

His smile froze. It had never occurred to him that she might take him for white. He started to correct her, then stopped. She thought he was white and that gave her hope. Why disappoint her? He was an experienced pretender. The Movement had given him the moral mandate to pass as white in order to investigate lynchings; he'd abused that trust when he disavowed Jonah. Now, he might once again put his lies to good use. He suppressed a bitter laugh. Passing was becoming a curse.

"I can't promise you anything."

"You promise to do the best you can?"

He nodded.

"That's enough. That's all anybody can do."

He won that case. It became the first of many. They came to him because he was dedicated, inexpensive, and apparently white: an unbeatable combination.

The switching of identities required no effort. He simply let people take him for what he appeared to be. Many times, he wished he hadn't had the freedom of choice, for it was a temptation and a responsibility. His father had always been adamant about "standing tall as a colored man," about identifying himself, but what would his father have said under the present circumstances? What purpose would he serve in destroying his credibility and with it, his ability to help the people who needed him?

Most of his clients were small-time offenders. He was their main hope and the main one they lied to. He became used to them evading, denying, obfuscating—telling anything but the truth. By and large, they were gauche, uneducated, unemployed men—either too reckless to realize that they would end up in jail or too desperate to care. Most had never had a chance to be anything other than what they were.

When David had an odd moment to reflect, he would compare their lives to his sheltered upbringing. After what he had done with his life, he was in no position to criticize them. Streetwalkers, alcoholics, and thieves: It was an education to serve them. His previous life took on the blurred appearance of a dream. He changed his name and severed contact with everyone from his past, everyone but Lilian. He felt alive, challenged, and productive. This was his path to redemption—even though it meant living in exile, living a lie.

Now Lilian's death had summoned him back to Harlem,

back to Rachel. He would never find the strength to leave her again. And given what he now knew, he wouldn't be able to live with himself if he did.

He thought about his furnished room in a Philadelphia boardinghouse. The house sat back from lovely, inviting, well-manicured lawns, but the room itself was desolate and plain. It contained nothing for him to return to: a thin bed, a table, and a dresser; a sink attached to one wall; a closet with two extra suits, some simple ties, and his one luxury—a second pair of shoes. The room was a monk's cell, a place to sleep. Alone. Night after night, alone.

He was concerned, however, about his clients, about the cases he had dropped. There were depositions to be taken, briefs to be written, court dates to be kept. He could not abandon his clients. He would write letters to them and to the courts, offering some explanation. And he would write his colleagues, asking them to take over his cases.

He turned his thoughts away from Philadelphia. It too now belonged to his past. It was his future in Harlem that worried him, and his marriage. Would it be strong enough to overcome the difficulties it would no doubt face?

27. TOBY'S MOM

He found himself on the corner of 137th and Lenox, in front of a slightly battered-looking establishment called the Mayfair Diner. On impulse, he stepped up to the door and went inside. He simply wanted somewhere to sit down. The place was half-empty with the late lunch crowd; there was one waitress, wiping a table at the farther end. She seemed familiar. He recognized her when she turned around. It was the woman whose son he had saved, Toby's mother. She came toward him. Her tired expression softened at the sight of him and his heart felt oddly lighter.

"Well, if that don't beat all," she said. "Take a seat."

He slid onto a stool at the counter. "How's your boy doing?"

"Fine. He asks about you."

"Nah."

"Sure he does. You his hero."

David smiled. "Thanks."

"What for?"

"For making me smile."

She cocked her head to one side as she poured his coffee. "Had one of them days, huh?"

"You could say that."

"Well, don't worry. Whatever it is, it too will pass. That's what my papa used to say."

"Did he now?"

"Yes, he did. And he was a wise old coot."

David chuckled. "Where're you from?"

"Virginia. My folks was sharecroppers."

"Big family?"

"There was nine of us kids. We was poor but we had a good time together. I guess you could say, we didn't know no better."

"Been here long?"

Her smile faded. "I come up here with my sister a few months ago—but she went back. Sister couldn't take the city. She wanted to take Toby back with her, but he's mine and I'm keeping him. His daddy don't want him. He up and took off. I can't have him thinking that his mama don't want him, neither."

Was this the way Rachel would've spoken about him if Isabella had lived? He would've wanted Isabella, though. If he'd had the chance, he would've protected her, given her everything he had.

"You really are having a bad day," she said, looking at his face. "How about something to eat?"

He shook his head, glancing at the stitching on the pocket of her shirt. He hoped to see her name but it was simply the name of the diner. "Just a cup of coffee."

For the next twenty minutes, he watched her move up and down the counter, exchanging lighthearted banter with the other customers: truck drivers, busboys on break, drunks, and drifters. He saw the way she managed to bring a crooked smile to even the saddest face. Finally, she paused in front of him.

"Anything more I can get for you?"

"Just more coffee, please."

His gaze fell on her hands as she poured. In her rough skin and broken fingernails, he saw a lifetime of sewing and scrubbing, cutting and chopping. He watched her move away and again wondered what her name was. He could imagine her hands kneading dough for fluffy biscuits, patting a baby's bottom, massaging her man's back. She would give comfort and strength. She looked like a woman a man could trust, someone he could bare his heart to.

He blinked, suddenly aware and faintly disturbed at the course of his thoughts. He stood, signaled her. She caught his gesture out of the corner of her eye and moved down the counter toward him. He took out his wallet and gave her ten bits. She quickly returned with his change. He waved it aside.

"Keep it."

She touched the money and looked up at him. "This is way too much."

"It's way too little for the price of a smile."

She studied him with light amusement, as though she didn't know what to make of him. He liked what he saw in her eyes and he liked the way it made him feel—like a man standing in sunshine after spending years in the rain.

"Good luck," she said. "I got a feeling you need it. Maybe even more than I do."

She tucked the money into her apron pocket. He watched her move away, then turned to go.

"Hey," he heard her call to him. He turned around. "I get a break in five minutes," she said. "You wanna take a walk?"

He paused. "Yeah, okay."

She looked suddenly shy, perhaps realizing how "forward" she'd been. "Okay."

He slid into a booth to wait and looked out the window. Some members of Marcus Garvey's Universal Negro Improvement Association were parading down the street. The men were dressed in military-like uniforms with generous applications of gold braid. Many of the women wore long pale dresses with wide cloths tied about their heads like missionary sisters. These people were trying to keep up the spirit of Garvey's Back-to-Africa Movement, but the UNIA was in tatters, and their leader, the Black Moses—a short, charismatic Jamaican who had galvanized thousands of Harlem's poor with talk of returning to their ancestral homeland—was himself locked in the Atlanta federal penitentiary, serving a five-year sentence for mail fraud.

"I'm ready," David heard a soft voice say and turned around. She was bundled up in her coat and had stuck her little cloche hat on her head. She looked adorable.

"All right," he said. "Let's go."

As always, the Avenue was crowded. It was even more so that day because of the parade. Though small, the parade was enough to attract attention. They joined the onlookers for a minute, admiring the UNIA's smart color guard, then turned away and headed downtown. On the left, they passed the Renaissance Casino & Ballroom.

"You ever go to a dance there?" she asked.

"A long time ago."

"It's real nice, ain't it? I heard they got receptions and basketball games and everything."

Directly across from them, on the corner of 135th, was Small's Paradise, the place where Nella's playwright friend had danced on the tables. Not a block away was Saint Philip's. The last time David had been there, it had been for his father's funeral. They reached the corner of 135th and paused for a stoplight.

"NAACP secretary James Weldon Johnson used to live

around here," he said. "I met him once."

"What's he like?"

"Got a good sense of humor." The light changed and they started across the street. "Fats Waller and Florence Mills live only a couple of blocks down the way."

They walked in comfortable silence, pausing at the corner of 133rd. To the left and right stretched "Jungle Alley," the main drag of expensive Harlem cabarets. David's memories came to life. The Nest Club, Kaiser's, Barron's: Once he'd been a regular at them all. Farther down Seventh was the Lafayette Theater. There was no better place to see tap-dancing greats Bill "Bojangles" Robinson, Honi Coles, Bunny Briggs, Chuck Green, and Baby Laurence.

Then there was the Band Box Club, just off the Avenue on 131st. A man could go there and hear the purest jazz he could hope for. And what about the Tree of Hope? Folks said it had magic. Entertainers hoping for a break would rub it. On a good night, a man could see any number of stars under it: jazz singer Ethel Waters, Fletcher Henderson, and Eubie Blake. Across the street was Connie's Inn. Bill "Bojangles" Robinson and Earl "Snakehips" Tucker entertained hundreds of guests on Connie's raised dance floor nightly. Below Connie's was the Barbecue, the best rib joint in Harlem.

David took a deep breath. There was talk everywhere about Harlem enjoying a heyday, and if he could believe his eyes, that was certainly the case. But what no one wanted to talk about was the poverty lurking behind the glitz.

"I'm glad to be here," she said suddenly, "but Harlem ain't an easy place to live. Ever since I been up here, I been hearing talk about the 'New Negro,' but what does it mean? I feel the same and I don't see where nothings changed. There's a lot of white folks stepping up here to go clubbing. But what do we get out of it? A few jobs and nothing more. The places they go, we cain't go. There's a lucky few—some colored writers and painters and singers I hear tell about. But there's always a lucky few that breaks through, whose star gets to shine a li'l brighter. But what about the rest of us—the reg'lar folk? When'll it be our turn?"

He smiled at her. "What would you do if you had the chance?"

"I'd paint," she said. "Every now and then, I'd paint." She laughed. "But them's all dreams. My pappy, he said dreams is like water: Too li'l of them and you dry up. Too much of them and you drown." She shook her head and looked up at him. "Don't get me dreaming. I can't afford to do that." She looked down at her work-worn hands and sighed. "No, I can't afford to do that."

28. FOR RICHER, FOR POORER ...

David married Rachel two days later in a City Hall ceremony, then took her to the Bamboo Inn for a small celebratory dinner. When he brought her home, there was no party, great or small. Rachel would have preferred one, but she acceded to his wishes for privacy and quiet.

"I want to be with you alone," he said.

"Perhaps we can have a party later. Introduce me to society?" she asked.

He hesitated, then agreed. He carried her across the threshold of the front door, then eased her down. She slid to her feet as agile as a kitten. She stood for a moment, just looking around, then piled her coat and purse on Annie's waiting arms. David caught the disapproval in Annie's eyes and made a mental note to talk to Rachel. Now, however, was not the time.

He followed his new wife as she walked through the parlor, touching things here and there.

"So beautiful," she whispered. "These are all ours ... for as long as we both shall live."

Turning to him with an adoring smile, she threw her arms around his neck and gave him a deep, lingering kiss. He groaned. Loving Rachel was addictive. Bending, he grabbed her up and carried her up the stairs to his room. Once in bed, she opened his shirt and covered his bare chest with hard kisses. She ran her fingertips lightly over his body, playing it as though it were a familiar instrument, as though she had loved him every night in her dreams. Then their clothes were gone and the world fell away and he was lost, lost in tidal wave of need that for a time suspended all the fear and doubt and self-recrimination that plagued him.

"It's hard to believe that I'm finally here ... with you," she whispered afterward.

He kissed her naked shoulder and gathered her in his arms. "Are you happy?"

"Very." She gazed into his eyes. "And you?"

"Quite."

"You're so quiet."

He smiled. "That's because I'm sated with love."

She slapped him playfully on the cheek. "You and your fancy talk. Don't make fun of me."

"Never," he laughed out loud, and hugged her.

It felt good to be here, with her, to be able to forget, at least for a while, the nagging fear that someone would learn his secret. And yes, it also felt good to not think about Lilian.

Rachel sighed happily and gazed around the room. "It's a bit dark in here. Lilian's room's brighter. And bigger." She inclined her head. "You ever think about moving in there?"

"No. And if I ever *had* thought about it ... well, I wouldn't want to do it now."

She nodded. "I know. I can understand that." She was quiet for a minute and then: "But the room ... it's just too nice to go to waste."

He half-raised up. "Rachel, I'm not moving in there. That's where my sister died. Eventually we'll do something with the room—it will not 'go to waste'—but we are not, I repeat *not*, moving into it."

"Shhh. I didn't mean to upset you. I was just asking, that's all."

He eased back down. "It's just difficult, you know? Just difficult."

She leaned down and kissed him. "Know what I'm thinking about?"

"I have no idea, but I'm sure you're going to tell me."

"I was remembering these boys at school when I was eight."

"Not even one day married and you're already thinking about other men?"

"Hush. These boys—I wish they could see me now. They told me I was dog dirt. Got me in a corner one day and tried to do nasty things to me. Then they yanked my hair and made fun of my clothes. And there was this rhyme they kept singing over and over.

Cat on the scene, cat on the scene.
Yella sits pretty in a black limousine.
Brown sits humble in a Model-A Ford.
They going somewhere. Oh yes, my Lord.
Monkey on my back, monkey on my back.
Black gals climb on a donkey's back.
They never getting nowhere, eating out a sack.
They never getting nowhere, just ugly and fat.

"It was the first time I realized that my own people can cut deeper than any ofay." She paused. "I never expected nothing from whites no-how. I trusted my own people. But they was the very ones who tried to knock me down.

"I remember looking for a room to rent. So many times a Negro landlady took one look at me and slammed the door in my face. And then, when I was trying to find a nurse's job, one supervisor said to me: 'Children is afraid of dark skin. We can't afford that.' Can you imagine?"

He stroked her back. "Rachel, a lot's been done to our people to make us hate ourselves. Sometimes we colored folk ... we're our own worst enemy."

She snuggled up closer to him. "Well, I'm protected from all them evil people now. I got you."

He sighed, thinking of the danger his past represented. It was time he told her. He opened his mouth to speak, but she hushed him with her fingertips.

"I don't want to talk no more. Not right now. I don't want no more looking back."

They snuggled deeply under the blankets together. She began to dream aloud of the parties she'd give. She named the names, like the Nails up the street, of the people she intended to invite.

"We'll have luncheons, bridge parties, and formal, white-tie dances. And we need a new car. And a boat. And didn't Augustus buy a summer house in Martha's Vineyard?"

He listened with half an ear, his thoughts elsewhere. "Sweet's due back in about a week."

She looked up at him, realizing that he hadn't been paying attention. She didn't seem to be annoyed, though. Getting Sweet out of the house was a real concern. She understood that.

"I'm sure he'll want to move out," she said. "Now that you've decided to stay, he won't feel comfortable."

"Perhaps. Perhaps not."

"I'm sure you can handle it." She gave him a kiss on his chin. Then, apparently full of confidence in her beloved husband, she closed her eyes and went to sleep.

But he lay awake, worrying.

I should've told her. And I should've done it before we got married. When she could've made a choice, when she was still free to—

C'mon, an inner voice said, *she would've married you no matter what and you know it.*

Yeah, but—

And she still wouldn't have wanted to run away. She's a fighter. Be glad you've got her in your corner. No, my friend. She's not your problem. You're *the problem.*

David rubbed his eyes. He'd arranged by telephone with his secretary in Philadelphia to shut down his office there. He would also give her a list of colleagues who would be willing to take over his cases. His life in the City of Brotherly Love was over. Now he had to deal with the question of just what kind of work he could do here.

The same kind you did in Philadelphia. Defend the indigent. Just under your own name, as yourself.

Only to have it all destroyed by, how did Nella put it? The right word in the wrong ears? How much time would he have to build up anything *anyway?* He would've liked to rejoin the Movement, but how could he? With his past hanging over him and with Sweet in the Movement?

Speaking of...

Was he really going to let Sweet get away with his part in Lilian's death?

He sighed. *Be patient,* that inner voice said. *Sometimes it takes years to gather proof and evidence and put them together in a way that means a conviction.*

And what about Rachel? he wondered. He'd promised to drop the inquiry.

That little voice laughed mirthlessly. *Are you kidding?*

29. THE LIZARD LOUNGE

Over breakfast the next morning, he watched Annie and Rachel avoid one another, circle one another like cats in an arena. It was subtle, but it was there. Rachel would tell him what she wanted, and it was up to him to tell Annie. Meanwhile, Annie acted as though Rachel didn't exist.

He took a deep breath. Annie wasn't happy about his decision—*stated* decision—to drop his inquiry into Lilian's death, and though he hadn't mentioned Rachel's part in it, Annie seemed to sense the connection.

He watched her move about. She was indeed much slower than she used to be.

She looks exhausted, he thought. *But after more than half a century of cooking and cleaning for others, she has every right to he.*

Since reading Lilian's manuscript, he'd watched Annie and listened to the words behind her words. He knew little of her life before she'd joined his family—to him it seemed that she'd always been there—but he did remember a story she'd once told him about her childhood. He was twelve and angry that Augustus had made him stay home to do extra homework. Annie had brought milk and cookies to his room. There, she'd sat down with him.

"Want to hear about my tenth birthday?" she said. "I'll never forget it. I was so excited. I'd been dreaming of this doll I'd seen in a store window. She had this long blond curly hair and a pretty dress. I'd never seen nothing like her. I didn't know how much she cost, but I do r'member thinking: Mama's gonna get me that doll. I just know she will.

"Well, the day of my birthd'y come and I bounced outta bed real early. And there was Mama, and Uncle Clement. And sure 'nough, they had a big box, wrapped up all pretty. Jumbo size. I couldn't believe it. And then I opened it."

Annie sighed. "You won't believe this—I didn't at first. It was a bucket. A bright, shiny, spanking new washerwoman's bucket. And while I was trying to get over *that,* Mama went and fetched my second birthd'y present. Guess what it was. A mop. That's right. A mop.

"I was ten years old and my Mama was giving me a mop and a bucket for birthd'y presents. That hurt. That cut deep. Up till then I'd always gotten a toy, even if it was just a rag doll. And I woulda been happy with another rag doll. Mama knew she didn't have to gimme that 'spensive doll, but why'd she have to go and gimme a mop and a bucket?

"Well, I took one look at her face and I knew. It was the end of my childhood. Mama said I'd been playing long 'nough. I cried. Told her she was being mean. Said she wasn't being *kind* to me. I'll never forget her answer. Not as long as I live.

"'I am being kind, honey,' she said. I's being as kind as a mama can be. I'm giving you the most important thing I got to give: a way to survive. I'm gonna teach you how to fend for yourself. Gonna make sure you learn. And I'm gonna start right now.'

"And you know what?" Annie smiled. "My mama was right. If she hadna taught me how to cook and clean, I wouldna found this here place with you and your sisters. Mama *was* being kind, as kind as she knew how. And I learned, from that day on, to always appreciate kindness—no matter what form it takes."

Kindness. Would she say that kindness was what Lilian's manuscript was all about?

He remembered the cautionary ending to Annie's tale: "Sometimes, you gotta be a little cruel to be kind. And sometimes, what people claim for kindness ain't nothing but cruelty."

He looked at Rachel across the table and recalled what Lilian said in denying her help: *I am doing you a favor.* And then he reflected on his own decision to marry Rachel although he wasn't in love with her.

Was he guilty of a milder form of cruelty masquerading as kindness?

As Annie pottered about, stacking the used dishes on a tray, Rachel's eyes followed her. The moment Annie left, Rachel asked:

"You ever think about letting her rest?"

"You mean, retire her? Not really, why?" Of course, he had. Why was he lying about it? Because he felt guilty. That's why. And protective of Annie.

She shrugged. "I just don't think it's right to make such an old lady work so hard, carrying groceries and wash baskets and such. She's done her share for your family."

"That she has. But she'd be miserable if she wasn't working." He took a sip from his coffee, then set the cup down. "You don't like Annie, do you?"

She looked surprised. "What gave you that idea?"

"I don't know. It's just a—" He shrugged. "A feeling."

"Well, it's all in your mind. Oh, I had my run-ins with her in the past, but that was then. I was young and silly. Annie's a member of the family. And she's a great help, but I do think you take advantage of her."

"All right then, I'll talk to her about it. See what she wants to do."

It was something to say. He knew full well what Annie wanted, but he wasn't about to tell Rachel. He didn't know much about women, but he knew a territorial cat-fight when he saw one. And if he got caught up in it, it would be *his* blood that was on the floor.

He looked at his new wife across the breakfast table and smiled. For her, the world could hardly be more perfect, but he still had certain steps to take in order to rebuild *his* life. Marrying Rachel had been one step; regaining control of the house would be another.

Reestablishing contact with Gem would be a third.

Rachel did not greet this news warmly. Her clear eyes darted over his face. "But why would you do that? Why contact Gem all of a sudden?"

"Because she's the only family I have."

"But you've never liked her."

"Well, it's time I learned. She's the only sister I've got left."

Rachel appeared stupefied. Her reaction to his decision to find Gem surprised him, but he thought he understood it. She had never liked Gem, and all brides tend to be on guard against in-laws. Well, once Rachel saw that Gem would not be a threat, she would calm down.

She would have to.

The idea to find Gem had seized him with incredible power. He *would* find her, even if it meant sailing to Paris. The time and money would be worth it. He would not try to convince her to return. Just seeing her would be reassuring.

Reassuring?

Finally, he was prepared to admit it, that he was worried about Gem—indeed, had been for some time—but he'd been so fixed on Lilian he hadn't wanted to acknowledge it.

It began with those postcards.

Yes. They disturbed him. And Snyder's words and Nella's admission that she couldn't reach Gem in Paris, they troubled him, too.

The old fearful questions tumbled out, one after another. Why did Gem demand that public breakup with Snyder? Why didn't she respond to Nella's calls? Gem was flighty and free-spirited, but she'd always make time for a rich friend, especially one as generous as Nella. Why hadn't Gem responded to word of Lilian's death?

The answer was there, but he turned away from it. No, he didn't want to think that something had happened to Gem, too.

That afternoon, David paid a visit to Birdie's grocery store and went downstairs. "Jolene, you got an idea where I could find Shug Ryan?"

Jolene leaned across the bar. "Try the Lizard Lounge, up on 140th. Shug likes to shoot pool when he's in town."

Stella came up and caught what Jolene was saying. "The Lizard Lounge? Don't send him up there. Them some nasty jigs."

Jolene shrugged. "It's his life, Mama." To David, he said, "A broad named Bentley runs the place. Tell her I sent you. And tell her quick, b'fore one of them saps gets itchy."

It would've been generous to call the Lizard Lounge a "hole in the wall." David only found the place because he trudged up and down the east and west sides of 140th Street, from one side of Harlem to the next, checking out each door along the way. The place had no sign to mark it and that in itself told him what to expect inside.

The Lizard Lounge apparently consisted of a long, narrow room with no windows and one door. Through the haze of smoke and the murky light, David could barely see, but he could feel several pairs of eyes on him. Why would a sax player be hanging out in a dive like this? Usually, musicians went to places that catered to entertainers. As his eyes adjusted to the light, he made out the six pool tables, with green baize lampshades dangling over them.

And then he saw the patrons.

The Lizard Lounge was a hangout for vicious hustlers, red-eyed gangsters, and men who were experts at giving pain. It was the kind of place where a man could literally get his throat cut for batting an eyelash at the wrong time. He figured he had better follow Jolene's advice and find Bentley.

He scanned the room for a woman. There was only one in sight. She was sitting at a fold-up wooden card table on the far side of the room. She was fat, about fifty, with black and gray finger waves and large cheap golden earrings. She was playing Solitaire, laying out the cards methodically, and just as methodically, watching him. He felt the eyes follow him as he walked over to her. Felt them like tips of daggers pressed against his skin.

"Evening," he said. "You Bentley?"

"Who's asking?" She slid a hand under the table.

"Jolene told me to look you up."

Bentley's jaundiced eyes widened and a sound like a hiss left her mouth. Before he could blink, she'd whipped out a gun from under the table and rained it on his chest. He stepped back and slowly raised his hands in the air. Very slowly. Only the breadth of the card table lay between them. If she cut loose, there was no way she would miss.

"Yo, lady, chill," he breathed.

"Jolene ain't never sent me nothing but trouble. The last time, trouble was packing a switchblade. He tried to bury it in my ribs."

"I don't know nothing but nothing about that."

Her eyes narrowed. "Sure you don't."

He sensed two men behind him. He glanced back over his shoulder. One had pale green snake eyes; the other was fat and soft-looking but crusty, like enough that had been left sitting on the counter too long. Bentley smiled at David, revealing brown, rotting stumps for teeth.

"Baby, don't you know who you messing with?"

"I guess I'm about to find out."

Her broad nostrils flared. She nodded to the two men. They took him through a back door he hadn't seen to an alleyway. The moment they were outside, Snake-eyes bashed him in the head from behind. Pain scissored through him as he dropped and twisted. Doughboy aimed a kick at David's ribs and David rolled on the ground, gasping. They pulled him to his feet. Snake-eyes gripped David from behind and held him, while Doughboy tore into him with his fists. Doughboy was fast and vicious despite his looks. He pulled back for a killing blow and that was when David ducked.

Doughboy's fist connected with Snake-eyes' nose. There was the thin crunch of broken bone and Snake-eyes yelled, stumbling backward. David whirled and slammed his fist into Doughboy's throat. The fat man sputtered and sagged to his knees. By then, Snake-eyes was back on his feet. He had a blade. David glanced around, saw a dusty lead pipe, and grabbed it. It took two good blows before Snake-eyes went down. David didn't know if Snake-eyes was alive or dead. He didn't have time to think about it. Doughboy was gone. That meant that reinforcements were on the way. David dropped the pipe. He had to clear out. Fast.

The moment Birdie saw David he raised his hands. "Hey, David, I'm sorry. If I'da known—"

"Let me go downstairs."

"Can't do that. He's my brother."

"Well, your brother's gonna have a rat's pack of trouble if he don't haul his sorry ass up here."

"I—"

"I don't wanna shut you down, Birdie. But he shouldn't have done that. Now get him up here."

Birdie nodded. "Okay. No hard feelings between us, I hope."

"Naturally not."

"So you stay up here and keep a lookout for me while I go get him, okay?"

David smiled. "Sure."

Birdie went downstairs. The moment he was out of sight, David left the grocery store and went around the back way. A set of parallel iron stairs ran alongside the building and down to the cellar doorway. A minute later, the cellar door flew open and Jolene came busting out. David snatched him by the collar and slammed him against the building's brick wall. Jolene sputtered and clenched at his throat, staring at David with one bulging eye.

"It was just a joke. I ain't mean no harm."

"You've got a strange sense of humor. It could get you killed one day."

Jolene fumbled at his pants pocket. David slammed him again. Jolene threw his hands back up.

"Easy, man. Easy. You wanna know where Shug is, right? A bird told me he'll be playing a rent party tonight."

"A bird told you that, huh?"

Jolene nodded. Beads of sweat had popped out at his temples. "No lie this time."

"So where's the jump?"

"Card's in my pocket."

Jolene gestured downward with his right hand. David dipped into Jolene's pants pocket and drew out a cheaply printed square.

"It's a woman named Lulu Smits," Jolene said.

David nodded, "Lulu, huh?" and read the card.

Hey, papa, come on and shake that thing.
Bring pretty mama and let it swing.
We gonna hop and pop and rattle the room.
We're gonna shimmy and shally and shatter the gloom.

David tucked the little card into his breast pocket. Now, what to do about Jolene? He was inclined to inflict a bit of pain.

Jolene cringed. "Man, don't cut me," he begged. "Please don't hurt me."

David shoved Jolene back against the doorway, looked at him with disgust, and released him. He felt dirty from having touched him. David turned to go. He had taken two steps when some minuscule sound warned him to turn around. Jolene was coming at him with a switchblade. David sidestepped the lunging blade, then pivoted and swung around in a neat movement. He put his fists together and brought them down like a hammer between Jolene's shoulder blades. The ugly barkeep went down with a grunt. David stood over him. He deliberated for a moment. Then he gave Jolene a deeply satisfying kick in the ass for good measure.

30. NEIGHBOR, NEIGHBOR

It was still way too early to go to Lulu's, so David headed home. He wanted to get cleaned up before going to the party, anyway. He'd just turned the corner onto his street, when he ran smack into Byron Canfield.

"My God, can't you look where you're going?" Canfield brushed off his coat sleeve as though he'd collided with something dirty. Then he realized he was speaking to David. "Oh, it's you!" He looked David up and down, noting his slight dishevelment. "Yes, well ... I did hear that you'd stayed."

The derision in Canfield's tone was unmistakable, as was the hint of unsavory knowledge and superiority. And the look in his eyes—that, too, was unpleasant.

David was tempted to curse his luck at this chance meeting but realized that it had been inevitable. As a young lawyer, just starting out and still hoping for a career within the Movement, he'd wondered what it would be like to try a case with the great Canfield, a man as known for his arrogance as for his intellect. David now realized that such a collaboration would've been unprofitable. He realized that the antipathy between them wasn't simply the product of the present situation, but stemmed from disparities that went much deeper. Remembering his manners, David donned a polite smile.

"Circumstances forced me to change my plans," he said.

"Did they, now? Well, fancy that. So you're staying?"

"For a while, yes."

Canfield nodded to himself, as if to confirm some private thought.

"Well then, there's no reason you can't come by for dinner," he said. "We'll do it immediately. Tonight. You're not busy, are you? Even if you are, you'll cancel."

David understood that he was not being invited but summoned. He briefly entertained the idea of firmly but politely saying no. He was tired, he felt ill: Any one of a hundred excuses would do. But Canfield would know them for what they were, a way of avoiding him. And Canfield's curiosity, already aroused, would grow stronger.

David found himself recalling one of his teachers at Howard: Professor John Milton. Milton was a gifted strategist and an enthusiastic instructor. He was full of good advice and pithy mottoes. David could hear him now, saying, "If you want to know your enemy, then go visit him: Just drop by, sit down, and enjoy a nice, long chat."

"Thank you for the invitation," David now said. "I'm looking forward to it."

They shook hands and Canfield turned to go. Then he hesitated and turned back, as though he'd remembered something.

"Oh and by the way," he said, "you needn't worry."

"Worry?"

"Yes. There won't be anyone there tonight—no one except you and my wife and I."

David's pleasant expression froze. He clamped down on the chill and fear that Canfield's words had given rise to and forced himself to use a normal tone of voice.

"A small gathering? How nice. I'll bring my wife."

"You're married?" Canfield seemed surprised. "But you were single the last time I met you, weren't you? My wife prides herself on knowing about everything that occurs on Strivers' Row. I don't see how she could've possibly missed hearing about your wedding."

"It happened rather quickly."

"Well, well... you're full of surprises."

"My critics have never accused me of being boring."

"I'm sure I would agree with them."

They parted, David having agreed to show up for dinner at eight. Rachel was delighted at the invitation. The Canfields were exactly the type of people she wanted to impress.

"Have you met Mrs. Canfield? Is she nice? Do you think they'll like me?

"They'll adore you." David kissed her. "Just be yourself and you can't go wrong."

As he escorted her to the Canfields' that night, he watched her admire her new neighborhood.

"It's so beautiful here," she whispered. "So very, very beautiful. And quiet."

He only smiled in response. As always, he was caught between guilt and pride that his family lived there.

"Isn't it amazing that colored folk ever managed to get into such nice buildings?" she said.

"Yeah, I can remember Daddy's joy when he bought our house."

"I hope I can fit in here. I've been waiting for this all my life, but now ..."

She looked up at him. She seemed so fragile. He hugged her and kissed her forehead.

"Don't worry. You'll do fine."

Dinner was pleasant enough, but David was glad to see it end. Afterward, Emma Canfield led him and Rachel into her parlor while her husband went off, looking for a favorite wine in his pantry.

The Canfields were the perfect example of a Strivers' Row couple. They were educated, traveled, refined. They saw themselves as influential, but benign and modest. They were also hopelessly out of touch with the concerns of Harlem's poor.

"I don't understand those people out there," Emma said, gesturing toward her windows. "It's as though they want us to become what they are. They've got this blind hatred of us. Just because we read and keep our property clean, they say we're snobs. We're not snobs. We just enjoy knowledge and we want to live well. It's as though they've accepted the popular idea that the only genuine Negro is an ignorant, dirty Negro."

David felt Rachel tense. He glanced at her. Her lips were bent in a smile, but her eyes regarded Emma with resentment. She wanted to speak up. She was biting her lip to keep silent. He took hold of her hand and gave it a squeeze.

Like most of the doctors, lawyers, and educators who composed the bulk of Strivers' Row residents, the Canfields were committed to doing everything they could to make sure that their street would not be sucked into the slum beyond. They had convinced themselves that they could provide a shining example to other blacks of how a winsome neighborhood could be maintained. But the effort was failing dismally, and they were bewildered by the reaction they were getting. The more manicured Strivers' Row became, the more mockery it drew from

Harlem's poor. The more elevated the Row became, the greater the cleft between it and the rest of the neighborhood.

David, perhaps because he'd lived for so long among Philadelphia's poor, understood what Emma could not.

"Mrs. Canfield, let's be honest," he said. "If the people who don't live on Strivers' Row resent the people who do, it's at least partly because the people on the Row deserve it. The people 'out there,' as you put it, simply resent the sight of Negroes who not only live well, but don't seem to care that others live poorly."

"We do care," Emma cried. "But there's no way we can help them if they won't help themselves. No one helped us. My husband and I—and all the rest of us here on the Row—why, we have what we have because we worked for it and worked hard. Nobody gave us anything. Nobody urged us on. And now that we have something, it's our own people who want to tear us down. I don't understand it."

David raised an eyebrow. Actually, he agreed with her—to a degree. At the same time, he found it ironic to hear her, a relatively rich woman, echo Rachel's poor woman's complaint. He glanced at his wife and saw the repressed anger in her eyes and the tight smile on her lips and he wondered whether it was her being intimidated or disciplined that kept her from saying the words that surely must've been on the tip of her tongue.

Emma set her bone china teacup down on her glass coffee table with a rattle and fixed David with her jet-black eyes. She was a matronly woman of about fifty. She had a round, soft figure and a pretty face. One would have thought her the soul of tolerance and generosity from the sweetness of her expression, but the hardness of her eyes reminded David of granite. She was assiduously groomed and everything about her displayed an exacting perfectionism. She was, David thought, the perfect match for Byron Canfield, from the top of her perfectly coiffed head to the tip of her polished kid leather shoes.

"Strivers' Row is about more than black-tie dinners, bridge parties, and balls," she said. "It's proof that not only whites but blacks can make it. If we're smart enough, stubborn enough, tough enough. It proves that DuBois is right, that the best of us, the 'Talented Tenth,' will succeed if we commit ourselves to American ways and reject that Back-to-Africa nonsense. We try to be role models and an inspiration. I wish they'd think of us that way."

David glanced at Rachel again. Her smile had grown tighter. He thought he understood why she didn't feel free to speak up; Emma's imperious smugness was intimidating. But he couldn't sit there and smile. Emma's arrogance was beginning to make him feel suffocated and her lack of commonsense compassion was definitely making him bristle.

"But how can we be role models when we're increasingly cut off from the community?" he asked. "Most of the people on the Row don't know a single soul who lives out there."

"And why should we? They're shiftless, lazy. If they worked, they could have what we have. Or nearly as nice. If their houses are dirty, it's because they dirtied them. And if they're living five and ten to a room, it's—"

"It's because they can't afford the rents, Mrs. Canfield. Open your eyes."

"Those people—"

"Are our people," he said gently. "And they need us. Harlem's not just the well-feathered beds of Strivers' Row. It's the hot beds of shift workers. It's battered tenements, cramped kitchenettes, and bleak rented bedrooms. It's the wheelers and dealers on Seventh; Mr. Jones's barber salon on 125th, and Mrs. Johnson's beauty salon on 122nd. Harlem is storefront churches and jackleg preachers. It's people finding faith wherever and however they can: young folk visiting the conjure man on Friday and the jump joint on Saturday; it's old folk giving up their nickels and dimes to the preacher on Sunday, singing and praying and singing some more at the First Baptists, Good Saviors, and Little Bethels that dot nearly every Harlem street."

"You just don't understand. My husband says you've been

away a long time—"

"Yes, I have—but maybe that's why I see so clearly."

Emma's response was cut off by her husband's arrival. Canfield came in, proudly displaying a red wine bottle.

"Found it," he said. "A lovely Beaujolais I brought back from France during the war."

"You should be honored," Emma told David. "My husband is very discriminating about who he offers his wine to."

David smiled politely and buried the words that had sprung to his lips.

With Canfield's presence, the topic of conversation changed. Eventually, it turned to the ideological dispute that was threatening to splinter the Movement. Its leaders were divided as to whether the Movement should fight for total integration or accept compromises along the line of "separate but equal." For the February issue of the *Black Arrow*, Canfield had written an editorial suggesting that it might be wise to accept limited racial segregation. When Walker Gaines, the Movement secretary, saw it, he had a fit. He wrote a scathing counterstatement that attacked segregation "in any form" and committed the Movement in perpetuity to a war against it. Gaines had expected his piece to be published in the March issue, but Canfield had blocked it. Gaines was now accusing Canfield of considering himself beyond reproach. David, like many others, had been stunned by Canfield's essay, and he'd watched in dismay as the ideological debate crystallized into a power struggle between the two men. Now, he found himself listening to Canfield as he set forth his position.

"Cultural nationalism," Canfield said, "is the most important goal our people can aim for. It can be seen in the light of the Zionists' desire for political separation."

David felt Rachel shift next to him. She had moved from being intimidated to feeling bored. Canfield warmed to his subject.

"Cultural nationalism relates to ethnic pride as well as political strength. It's an important concept and rather radical, because it bespeaks a certain amount of self-imposed 'segregation.'"

David felt another prickle of annoyance. "But segregation is what we're fighting against—"

"We can't denounce segregation in theory without denouncing the Negro church, the Negro college, or any other purely Negro institution."

"It's one thing for us to choose ethnic privacy; quite another to be forced into—"

"Simple-minded people try to avoid the issue by distinguishing between voluntary and involuntary segregation. But to put it rather colloquially, we can't have our cake and eat it, too."

David's temper surged. "Sometimes 'simple-minded' people are the most perceptive. *They* have a mental clarity that many intellectuals seem to lose. *They* don't lose sight of priorities and they don't cloud the issues with irrelevancies. Desegregation is, and was, one of the Movement's primary goals as a means to an end."

"You're mistaken. Or misled. The Movement has never 'defined' its position on segregation, merely taken concrete steps to oppose it in its baser forms."

David looked at Canfield, wondering if he had heard correctly. Then he leaned forward, and took a deep breath.

"Mr. Canfield, I have to be blunt. If the Movement isn't openly opposed to segregation, then it's lost all meaning." His eyes met Canfield's. "And its leaders have lost all credibility."

Canfield stared at him. "How dare you—"

"Any first-year law student—no, any man in the street— knows that the black man's desire for ethnic privacy in his lodges and his churches does not exclude his right, his basic human right, to integration and equality in the public sphere."

"David, please," Rachel said.

She touched him on the elbow. He shrugged her off—he was beyond caution—and pressed on.

"For the time being, we've got to live with Jim Crow's rule, but it's an anathema. It must go. You wrote of accommodation, Mr. Canfield, of compromise. Well, you can forget compromise. The Devil doesn't make compromises. Neither can we. It doesn't matter whether you or I survive to see Jim Crow die. We have to fight it—to crush it—or we're all lost. Black and white, we're all done for."

Blistering silence. The two men gazed at one another with open enmity. Finally, Canfield cleared his throat.

"Thank you for that little lecture. It's good to know that you haven't lost your dedication, or your energy for debate. One wonders, you know, about a man who's been away for so long."

Clearly, it was time to leave. David stood and drew Rachel up alongside him. He thanked the Canfields for their hospitality and bade them a good night. Rachel spoke up the moment they left.

"What did you have to insult him like that for? He's a powerful man. He could've been our friend."

"With a friend like that, a man doesn't need enemies."

"So what if you don't like him. I don't particularly care for his wife, either. But she knows all the right people. She could make sure that we're invited everywhere. Now, I'll have to—"

In that instant it hit him that Rachel hadn't been intimidated at all. She'd held her tongue because of her social ambitions. That angered him even more and he rounded on her. "Rachel, you're my wife and I want to make you happy. But I will not play the hypocrite, not even for you."

"But if you'd just—"

"No, I won't. So, don't." He held up his hand. "Just don't."

31. LULU'S HOME JAM

Lulu lived in the poorest section of Harlem. 'Shatter the gloom,' her card had said. Well, where she lived, one constant source of gloom was the constant fear of being short on the rent. If you didn't pay the rent by Sunday, you'd be out by Monday. So you'd do just about anything to raise that money. That included rent parties: opening your home to strangers and charging admission, from a dime to a half-dollar.

Lulu's place was on 131st Street and Eighth Avenue. David got there at around one in the morning. The door downstairs was broken open. Broken glass, discarded bottles, cigarette butts, newspapers, and one curiously flattened dead cat littered the entryway. From the back of a dark, narrow hallway emerged the distant sounds of a party in full swing. David could make out a piano playing ragtime. He followed the sound to the stairs at the back of the hallway. Lulu's apartment was on the third floor. The apartment door was ajar. Inside, he found an incredibly fat woman sitting at an itsy-bitsy table behind the door.

"Come on in!" she said. "Make yourself comfortable! Corn liquor's in the kitchen. Fifty cents a pitcher. You alone, son? I'm sure we can find you some comp'ny."

The room was hot and funky. It stunk of smoke, sweat, and booze, collard greens, chitlins, hog maws, mulatto rice, and hopping john. Scores of folks had paid their nickels and dimes to get in. The place was jumping, packed with young studs looking for mischief and pretty young things out for fun. There were painters, truckers, policemen, and drag queens. David recognized poets, novelists, even a local politician or two. He glanced back at his hostess. She was watching him with amusement.

"Don't be shy, sugar, we got something for everybody."

"I'm looking for a sax player. Name of Shug Ryan. He playing here tonight?"

"Baby, I got a box-beater and that's that. If Shug was supposed to come, I don't know nothing about it." She held out a grubby hand. "So you staying or what?"

He paid his quarter and moved into the crowd. It turned out to be a five-room apartment. A poker and blackjack game was up and running in one bedroom; a "private party" was going on in the next. The parlor and dining room had been nearly cleared of furniture. The music had changed to a slow, bluesy number. A sole red light bulb cast a lurid glow over dancing couples, who shuffled in place, grinding their hips together. From the shadows along the edge of the dance floor came pants and whispers, grunts and groans. The floorboards sagged and creaked as the dancers slow-dragged around the crowded floor.

The box-beater—or piano player, as he'd be known in more polite society—was a narrow, thin man with tired eyes. He swung into a mad folly of light notes tripping over one another. A fat light-skinned girl with dark eyes and long straight black hair climbed atop a chair. She twisted her top so it exposed her midriff and pushed down her long skirt until it sat on her fleshy hips. Raising her arms, she started to rhythmically jiggle her hips to the music. The piano player picked up speed. One loose key flipped off the keyboard. David couldn't help but think that if that old piano had been alive, it would've rocked on dancing feet. He smiled, shook his head, and tapped his feet. After a while, the music started to wind down. David went and bought two cups of liquor and had one waiting for the box-beater when he took a break. The piano player smiled readily when David asked about Shug.

"Yeah, he's here. Over there, in the corner. C'mon. I'll introduce you."

Shug Ryan was in his early forties, a short, bald man with a high forehead and flabby cheeks.

"Let's go in the kitchen," he said.

David bought Shug some corn liquor and asked a few questions about Paris, thinking he'd gradually lead the conversation back to Gem. Shug was eager to talk. He'd hated the Paris scene as much as he'd loved it.

"Don't get me wrong. It's hot, all right—just sometimes, a tad too hot. Us niggers would head into them nightspots in Montmartre. Pockets full when we got there, pockets empty when we left. Drinking that cheap champagne, making it with the white girls. Them chicks knew how to wheedle free drinks and food out of a man. They'd get hold of a fellah and have him jim-clean before the night was through. But we didn't care. We wanted fun. Wanted to be *out there*. We was like kids in a candy shop." He smiled. "We'd get all hopped up, smoking that bamboo, tucking into some snow—whatever and whenever we wanted it." Then he shook his head and said to himself again, "Yeah, them streetcorner Sallies fleeced us clean."

"What made you decide to get out?"

Shug took a drink from his cup and set it down. "Well, it was like this. My friend Julian Campbell was playing with the group Jukebox '29. One night, he fell down dead while blowing his horn. Had a stroke. Right in the middle of a set. The life did him in. He was young, but the life killed him. Well, that brought me up straight. It sure did. I caught the next boat back."

"How long you been back?"

"about a month."

"How's your luck holding?"

Shug grinned. "Ain't got nothing but holes in it, man. Nothing but holes."

"So, did you see Gem McKay over there?"

"Nah, man. Ain't laid eyes on her in more'n a year."

"But I thought you were friends with her."

Shug hunched his shoulders and raised his hands in an I-don't-know gesture. "Hey, a woman like her don't have no friends. You know that. You say you her brother, so you got to know that."

"Well, if you didn't see her, did you at least hear about her? Where she was, how she's doing?"

"Far as I know, ain't nobody heard nothing. And I do mean nothing."

David tucked ten bits in Shug's hand and turned away. He felt a deepening sense of dread. He'd been so sure that Shug would give him the information he needed. So sure th—

Wait.

Shug *had* given him something, something important. It was odd—*No, downright strange*—that Shug hadn't heard anything about Gem. He was part of her crowd.

David felt a chill.

Of course, there was always the possibility that she'd left Paris, gone south to Marseilles or off to Madrid or Barcelona if she'd found a new friend.

But what if she didn't leave Paris?

Wasn't it time he admitted what had been right before his eyes?

The increasingly overwhelming signs that she never even got there at all?

32. OUT ON THE TOWN

They'd been married for two days. Every minute that ticked by was borrowed time, time counted against the moment his secret was revealed. Whether that time could be counted in months or weeks or even days, David didn't know. That was all the more reason to make the most of it. He decided to surprise Rachel with a night out. So earlier that day, he'd reserved tables at a cabaret. When she returned home from work that day ("When are you going to quit?" he kept asking. "I can't right now," she'd say, "They still need me"), he told her to get fixed up.

"We're stepping out," he said. "But first, let's see if you like this."

He pulled out a slender blue box. It was tied with a gold ribbon. He set it on the bed and her face lit up like a child's at Christmastime. He sat nearby and watched her. She tore the ribbons open and lifted off the cover. When she saw what lay within, her mouth formed an O of surprise.

"My God," she whispered, and covered her mouth.

A string of pearls gleamed on a bed of blue velvet. She reached out to touch them, then drew her hand back.

"Go on," he said. "They're yours. Try them on."

She couldn't. She couldn't move. With a smile, he got up, took the necklace from the box, draped it around her throat, and fastened it. He put his hands on her shoulders and steered her toward the mirror. She stared at her reflection, that of a very beautiful—and wealthy—young wife. She stroked the pearls and regarded her image with wonder.

He laughed and hugged her. "And now, my dear, you're supposed to say, 'Oh, David, you shouldn't have.'"

Her gaze moved to his reflection. "Am I supposed to say that?"

He nodded.

"All right," she said, warming to the game. "'Oh, David, you shouldn't have.'"

"And then I say, 'But aren't you glad I did?'"

"And then," she turned to face him, nuzzled him, kissed him, "And then … I get to show you just how glad I can be."

An hour and a half later, they were walking east across 139th Street toward Lenox Avenue.

"Where we're going," he said, "used to be one of my old stomping grounds, Jack Johnson's Club Deluxe. Of course, it's got new owners now, and a new name, but I'm sure it's just as fine."

They turned north. When they reached the corner of Lenox and 142nd Street, they saw a long queue of limousines pulled up in front of the club's marquee. People in ermine and top hats pressed around the entrance, waiting to get in. Rachel and David joined the crowd. He noticed that a few glances were thrown at Rachel, then at him, but he thought nothing of it. After all, Rachel was a pretty woman and the new clothes she'd bought did her justice. The crowd moved forward and soon they were just inside the entrance. He missed the hesitant look the doorman gave them.

An usher came up, wearing an unctuous smile. He was young, white, and skinny, and already starting to bald. He glanced at Rachel and his smile disappeared.

"May I help you?" he asked.

"Why, yes," David said, "we have reservations—"

The usher's eyes again went to Rachel. "I'm afraid that can't be."

Rachel tensed.

"What do you mean?" David said, perplexed and irritated. "You took my reservation."

"You must be mistaken. We've been booked out for weeks, months—"

"Years?" David added.

The usher shuffled uncomfortably.

David said, "This is ridiculous. I—"

"Perhaps it would be better if you spoke with the manager." The usher bowed himself away, leaving David and Rachel standing there.

"David, let's leave," she whispered.

He put an arm around her shoulder. She edged closer. The usher reappeared, this time with a large, fat, bullet-shaped man, who was also white. The usher gestured toward David and Rachel, then stepped back. The big guy surged forward with a definite I'm-in-charge attitude. He had Mob written all over him, from the loud checks of his sack suit to the scowl on his face. He jabbed a thick thumb in the direction of the cowering usher behind him.

"My man here tells me you folks got some kinda problem."

"No problem," David said. "We just want our table."

"You've made a mistake. All our tables are taken."

Rachel's grip on David's arm tightened. "Please, let's go."

"No." He turned to the fat man. "If there's been a mistake, then you've made it. I was here yesterday. I made reservations and your man said everything would be fine. Now we're going to sit at our table. If somebody else is sitting there, you'll just have to ask them to leave."

The fat man glared at David. "Buddy, you're the one who's

leaving. You wanna hang out with a spade, that's fine with me. But you can't do it here." Two muscular men appeared at his elbow. "I suggest you don't ask for trouble."

"David—" Rachel tugged at David's arm. "It's not worth it. They'll have us thrown in jail—or worse." She threw them a terrified look. "Now please. I just want to be with you. It doesn't have to be here."

"Rachel—"

"I don't want to stay here!"

As they left the Cotton Club, they were silent. He could've kicked himself. He should've known better. He'd heard that some of Harlem's best clubs had gone white, but it hadn't really registered. He looked at Rachel. The worst part was that he didn't know what to say to her. He didn't know how to make it better.

I'm protected from all them evil people now. I got you.

He stopped, took her in his arms, and hugged her. "I'm sorry, Rachel. I should've checked. It was my fault."

"It's nothing, David. It don't matter. Don't matter at all."

But looking down deep into her eyes, he could see that it did.

33. AUGUSTUS

That next evening found Rachel and David sitting in the parlor, reading. He was deep into J. W. Johnson's *Autobiography of an Ex-Colored Man*. She peeped at him over the top of her magazine. He'd asked her if she wanted to go out again that night and she'd said no. She could tell that he'd been relieved, but he felt guilty. He assumed that she was still upset over the Cotton Club business. She was, but that's not why she wanted to stay home. In fact, he was more upset about the Cotton Club than she was. She simply wanted to stay home because she had this sudden desperate desire to keep him all to herself. She didn't want to share his attention, not with anyone, not even an admiring social circle. She knew this was unreasonable, but the impulse was so strong it didn't have to make sense.

He glanced up, caught her staring, and smiled, then went back to his book.

I can't believe he belongs to me ... that I'm here with him ... and that no one, but no one, can ever order me away again.

Her eyes rose to the painting over the mantelpiece. Augustus McKay's portrait looked down at her with stern disapproval. She felt a little chill crawl up her spine. For a moment, she actually thought the eyes in the portrait were alive. They seemed so full of displeasure at the sight of her.

I bet you're rolling over in your grave to see me here. Well I am here and you can't do nothing about it.

Her memories of Daddy McKay were vivid. He'd been one of those successful colored men who were not only proud of their achievements but acutely aware of their responsibility toward other "less fortunate" members of their race. As far as she was concerned, he'd been obsessed with "the race issue." He'd systematically subscribed to every protest magazine and religiously read every sensationalist newspaper printed by the Negro press. He was always ready to discuss, debate, and deliberate on the injuries and humiliations done to his people.

"Rachel, I don't want you over there so often," her mother had told her one day. "Don't be hurt when I say this, honey, but I don't think Daddy McKay likes you."

At the time, Rachel was fifteen. She put down the book she was struggling to read—*Jane Eyre* it was—and scowled. "Well, I don't like him neither."

"Then what you going over there for?" Minnie asked, letting her knitting sink to her lap.

Rachel felt a surge of impatience. Her mother would never understand. "Leave me alone, Mama. I can't explain. Just let me be." She picked up her book and tried to find her place.

Minnie was hurt. "Lord, Lord, help my child," she whispered, just loud enough for Rachel to hear.

With an irritated sigh, Rachel laid *Jane Eyre* aside. She went over to her mother where she was sitting in the rocking chair, hugged her, and gave Minnie's sunken cheek a kiss. "I'm sorry, Mama. I didn't mean to be rude."

Minnie gave a wan smile and squeezed Rachel's hand. "That's okay, baby, but you be careful."

Rachel nodded, although she really wasn't sure what her mother was warning her against. Daddy McKay might not like her, but he'd never harm her. She was, after all, the family's pet "uplift" project. Her dark skin and her poverty made her perfect for that role, though absolutely unsuitable for any other.

She had nothing but contempt for the man.

What a hypocrite.

He railed against "social inequality" but he believed in social "distinction." He would have scornfully refused any invitation from a white, had he ever received one. Certainly, no white was ever made welcome in his home. He swore that every wretched black sharecropper deserved as much respect as any world leader. But he looked down his chiseled nose at his people's earthy spiritualism, their hearty meals, their love of bright colors and light-hearted tomfoolery. He viewed their everyday ways with detached contempt. He never permitted criticism of black art, music, or literature, but he had no personal affinity for his people's songs, their dances and softly cadenced speech. He despised and distrusted white people, but he admired their clothes and emulated their manners. Like other elitist "brown" men of his time, he lived in a world of "society" events and self-serving perceptions that insulated him from a harsh reality while rewarding him the status the white world denied.

"Don't worry, Mama," she said. "Daddy McKay ain't violent—just weird."

"That's not what I meant," Minnie said, but Rachel wasn't listening.

"He likes to have these meetings," she said.

"Meetings? What kinda meetings?" Minnie was quick to be

suspicious.

Rachel smiled and for a moment, she looked much older than her years. "Oh, they ain't got nothing to do with sex or religion, if that's what you're thinking."

Minnie gasped. "Why, Rachel Hamilton, you—"

"They's got to do with something much worse—politics."

"Politics!"

"Yes, ma'am. He gets David and the twins together once a week—and if I'm there I get pulled in, too. We get to sit in his office and ..." She let her voice trail off and gave a shrug that said, *What goes on in Daddy McKay's office ain't worth the effort of describing.* But now that she'd mentioned the meetings, Minnie wanted to know about them. In detail.

"Sit, and yes—then what?"

Rachel sighed. "Don't be such a worrywart. We listen. That's all. We just get to listen. For at least an hour, while Daddy McKay rants and raves about the sins of white folk and the responsibilities of black ones. His children have a mission to advance the race, he says. He's given them money and education—"

"Well, that's true."

"And he expects something for it."

"'Spects what?'" With a raised eyebrow.

Rachel smiled, bemused. "Why, he don't expect nothing much—just that his children become big, important Negro leaders, members of the Talented Tenth."

"The Talented what?"

Rachel looked at her. "Oh, you heard of that, Mama. Why, that's a theory of Mr. W.E.B. DuBois. He says that there shall arise a Talented Tenth of the Negro people and they shall lead us to the Promised Land."

Minnie failed to catch the cynicism in Rachel's voice. "Is he some kinda false prophet, this Mr. DuBois?"

Rachel shrugged. "I don't know. To me, he's just like one of them white folk that think the better-offs should get more and the rest of us should keep struggling."

"He ain't black, is he?"

"Sure 'nough is, Mama. One of them light-skinned educated race men, done studied in Europe."

"Humph," said Minnie. "Well, that explains it." She picked up her knitting.

Rachel suppressed a chuckle. "You know something, Mama? I think you got more wisdom in your pinkie than Mr. Du-Bois's got in his whole head. But a lot of people respect him. They think he's done good things for our people."

"Has he, now? Well, I ain't never heard of him. And from what you tell me, I can't b'lieve he's interested in doing anything for poor folk like me." Minnie paused to catch a dropped stitch. "What d'you do when Daddy McKay's carrying on like that? What d'you say?"

"Nothing," Rachel answered. "He'd never ask our opinion about nothing. He just wants to hear himself talk. So, yup." She sighed. "That's all I do ... is listen."

And that's hard enough.

Even if he did ever ask her opinion about anything, she'd be crazy to actually try to talk to the man. To tell the truth, he not only irritated her, he amused her. Who'd have ever thought to find so much racial ardor in a family that was by and large insulated against the ravages of racial prejudice? Of course, sometimes she *did* tire of his speeches on the ignorance, arrogance, and malevolence of white people. Sometimes, she wanted to stand up and cry out: *What do you know about it, really?*

Instead, she always sat quietly, appearing to listen dutifully, while her thoughts and eyes wandered elsewhere—elsewhere inevitably meaning David McKay.

And now, finally, unbelievably, she was his wife.

Her eyes went back to him and she thought of Isabella. *She looked so much like him.*

He looked up again, to find her eyes on him. Concern crossed his face. He closed his book, putting a finger between the pages to hold his place, and leaned forward.

"You all right?"

For a moment, she looked as though she were about to cry. "I'm fine."

He laid his book on the side table and went to sit next to her. She snuggled into his arms and raised her face.

"You do love me?" she whispered.

"Hm, hmm ... Of course I do." He kissed her on the top of her head.

"Then tell me. Say the words."

His forehead creased. "What's wrong, Rachel?"

Her eyes searched his. She saw what she suspected and something painful pinged inside her. She dropped her gaze and looked away.

"What's the matter, baby?"

"Nothing. I was just being silly. There's nothing the matter at all."

34. NELLA COMES CLEAN

"You weren't quite truthful with me before—"

"I don't tell lies—"

"But you don't always tell the whole truth either."

It was Sunday. David was seated in Nella's immense living room with a glass of suspicious contents pressed into his hand. She put a platter of sweets on the coffee table. Choosing what appeared to be a chocolate-covered cherry, she popped it into her mouth whole.

"Just what is it you want to know?"

"How to find Gem."

"I told you—"

"You told me that while you were in Paris, you tried to contact her."

"I told you that I was unsuccessful."

"But you didn't tell me that you didn't give up."

She stared at him, stunned. "How did you know?"

"You're a stubborn woman. The kind who doesn't change her mind once it's made up."

An admiring smile slowly spread over Nella's face. She did not answer directly, but ate another cherry and chewed thoughtfully. "Remember our deal. Information for information."

"Yes, yes, I remember," he said mildly. "Now please, do what you do best. Talk."

"David, you have a way with you—a way that ..."

She clenched her jaw and pressed her lips together. Words failed her. She lit herself a cigarette and jabbed the air with it. "If anyone else ever spoke to me that way, I'd have him thrown out on his ear. Not even Nikki—"

"Nella, you don't have to throw me out. Just answer my question and I'll leave."

Her eyes narrowed. "I'll let that last little quip slide, but don't—"

"Nella, please—"

"All right, all right." She held up a hand, then took a deep breath. "You're right. I didn't give up." She plopped down in the seat opposite him, evidently unhappy. She took a minute to collect her thoughts, and then began.

"After several attempts to contact Gem, I decided to go see her, to drop in on her unannounced. I knew it would be in bad taste. But I felt entitled. After all, she hadn't taken the time to even answer my notes. The boy I'd sent told me there was a girl who accepted the messages. Clearly, the girl wasn't Gem, but he said she seemed capable enough. He didn't doubt that she was passing my notes on. It was Gem's fault that she was about to get an unexpected visitor.

"I took a taxi to the address on the postcards Gem had sent me. I was very surprised when the driver pulled up in front of the place. It wasn't at all what I'd imagined. For one thing, it was dirty; slummy in fact. The driver assured me that this was the address I'd given him. He was getting anxious about his money, so I paid him and got out. Then, on second thought, I turned back, gave him a little something extra, and asked him to wait.

"A young woman answered the door. I assume she was the one who'd taken my messages. She was rather tall, but stooped and starved-looking. Her clothes were fashionable, but they didn't fit her well. They looked like the cast-offs of some wealthy, chic girlfriend. The young woman herself wasn't chic at all. Her makeup was poor. Her jewelry were cheap imitations. The worst a long pearl necklace à la Chanel; it clanked when she moved. And her fingernails ... they were broken and dirty and polished this bright garish red that was chipped and peeling.

"My opinion of her must've shown in my face. She drew herself up and tried to play la grande dame, but she was too young and too ignorant for the part. She told me in guttural French that Gem wasn't there. She wasn't exactly impolite, just brusque. Something about her made me curious. Her eyes kept flicking from side to side, glancing up and down the street. Obviously, she wanted me away from her door as quickly as possible. I think she wanted to shut the door in my face, but she was afraid I'd make a scene. I practically forced her to let me in.

"I followed her down a short hallway that opened into a small parlor. The room had a very low ceiling and one tiny window. It was like being in a dark hole. The place stunk—a repellent mixture of garlic, cheap perfume, and stale cigarettes. The room had dirty white walls with cracked and peeling paint. There was a lumpy red sofa, a couple of tables and a lamp, and not much else. She probably worked as a cheap fortune-teller. I noticed some battered Tarot cards laid out on a table.

"We seemed to be alone. She rolled herself a cigarette. I was sure that she was hiding something. Slyly, she admitted that she was. She wanted money. Naturally she asked for too much. We haggled. She was greedy, but I'm very, very stingy. Most rich people are.

"Finally, she came out with it. Gem had never been there, she said. She'd been collecting Gem's mail and messages for months. I showed her a postcard I'd received. She admitted she'd written it herself. She said Gem had been paying her to regularly make up messages and send postcards to certain people in the States, had given her a list in fact. She showed me the letter from Gem that told her what to do. I made her give it to me. Here, I can show it to you. I brought it back."

Nella jumped up and walked briskly out of the room. David waited impatiently. When she returned, she handed him a sheet of once-white, once-very-expensive stationery. There were only three sets of names and addresses written on it: Lilian's, Nella's, and Snyder's. The page itself had been handled a great deal. Fingerprints smudged it and one part of it buckled under an old brown coffee stain. Nella caught David's look and shrugged.

"That's the condition it was in when the girl gave it to me."

"Why didn't you tell me all this before?"

Nella sighed. "I didn't see what relevance it might have to Lilian's death. But then it occurred to me that Gem's silence might be causing you pain. I don't want that. If you hadn't come today, I would've sent for you. I realize that many people don't think well of Gem, but I like her. Gem isn't that callous. She hasn't said a word because she doesn't know about Lilian. I'm sure she would be here if she did."

Interesting how two people can interpret the same thing differently. Nella was dismayed by Gem's silence. Nothing more. She didn't find it alarming—at worst, inconvenient. He almost wished he could feel the same way, too.

"Well then, where is she?"

Nella shrugged. "I haven't the faintest idea. But I'm sure she's fine. It's obvious, don't you see? Gem doesn't want to be found. She's played a little trick on us. It's just her way. She'll pop up sometime. We must be patient. We have no other choice."

But we do, he thought. *We do.*

His worry about Gem had reawakened his doubts about Lilian's death, doubts he had never fully put aside. He rubbed his temples. *I'm tired,* he thought, *so damn tired of trying to believe in explanations that make no sense.* He thought of Lilian's disappearing pregnancy and Gem's faked postcards; of Lilian's hatred of Sweet and Gem's breakup with Snyder; of Lilian's friendship with Nella and Gem's refusal to answer Nella's calls.

Things ain't always the way they seem. His inner voice, echoing Annie's words, spoke to him now more loudly than ever. But the words were indistinct, muffled by conflicting thoughts and distracting opinions.

Back home in his room, David reviewed all the questions he had raised and the few answers he had found. Visualizing the details of what he had learned as puzzle pieces, he mentally shifted them around, trying to interlock them, breaking them apart. Gradually, he discerned a pattern. One by one, the pieces slid into place.

Why had it taken him so long to see the obvious? He knew—undeniably and completely—that Lilian had indeed been murdered. He knew who had killed her. He understood why Gem had given up her attempts to seduce Sweet; why she had offered to help Lilian; and why she had staged that raucous breakup.

He thought about Sadie Mansfield, a former client. She had cut her wrists after her husband left her. He would never forget her body. Her wrists were covered with the small incisions she had made as she worked up her courage to die.

With rapid fluidity, his thoughts flew to a book he had once read in his father's library. French sociologist Emile Durkheim had written that suicide victims always give their act a personal stamp, one that reflects their temperament and the special characteristics of their circumstances.

David found a sheet of paper and a pen. He wrote first the name "Pierre Lorraine" and underlined it heavily. After a moment or two, he wrote the word "conceit." Then after a space, the question: "Why not take the easy way?"

He sat quite still for about three minutes. In his mind, he could hear Rachel asking him, "But why would Sweet kill her?" and his answer, "Because he not only didn't love her—he loved someone else."

He thought of Nella and vanilla. And his heart gave a hard little thump. Something heavy and cold landed in the pit of his stomach. He had been close to the truth before, very close—but two false assumptions had kept him from it. He saw it all now. He had the solution, he had it—but how he wished he hadn't.

There was a knock on his door. Annie stepped in. "Mr. Jameson's back. I just thought you might like to know."

"Thank you."

She turned to go, then hesitated.

"Yes?" he asked.

"Mr. Jameson—he don't know about you and Miss Rachel. Maybe you better tell him—b'fore she comes home from work."

"Yes," he said slowly. "I'll be sure to talk to him—about that and many other things."

Going downstairs, he found Sweet relaxing with a newspaper in Augustus's throne. Sweet was humming the popular song "I'm Sitting on Top of the World."

David stood in the doorway, watching him. Sweet shifted uneasily. Perhaps he felt a cold wind at his back. He looked up, saw David, and rose to his feet. The two men stared at one another.

"You don't miss my sister at all, do you?" David said.

Sweet looked at David as though he were mad. He opened his mouth to reply, but David raised a hand. "Please. The last thing I need is to hear more lies."

David entered the room. Sweet watched him warily. David remembered how impressed he'd been with Durkheim's insights. He'd never foreseen that he would have to recall Durkheim's words twenty years later to solve his sister's murder. He spoke thoughtfully, explaining in a methodical tone.

"I returned because I was told that Lilian had committed suicide. That she'd become mentally unstable and taken her life. I was told that Gem had suddenly reappeared after five years' absence and just as suddenly left again. So I was told, and so I was supposed to believe. But none of it made sense. None of it reflected the people I knew my sisters to be. So, I asked questions. Annie, Rachel, Nella Harding, you. On the surface, you each told the same tale, but when I looked closer, listened harder, I found too many contradictions to ignore. The Lilian I knew was not the Lilian people described."

Sweets expression was faintly contemptuous. "I told you— her illness changed her."

"No illness could explain these changes."

"Which changes?"

"Lilian's pregnancy, for one."

"It was imagined—"

"Her doctor, at least initially, confirmed it."

Sweet looked genuinely stunned. "He couldn't have. She would've told me—

"She wouldn't have told you and she didn't tell you—for reasons we're both aware of."

Sweet's lizard-like eyes narrowed. "I refuse to believe there was a pregnancy. But go on. You spoke of several—what was the word?" He paused. "Oh, yes. Contradictions."

"Suffice it to say there were enough to make me wonder. When I first started asking questions, Annie warned me that things aren't always the way they seem. The more people I talked to, the more applicable that warning seemed to be."

Sweet smirked. "You think I killed her, don't you? You feel guilty about her suicide, so now you want to say *I* did it."

"No. Not at all."

Sweet's surprise was obvious.

David inclined his head. "Naturally, there was someone else who could've killed her—someone who like you would've benefited, or hoped to benefit, from her death."

Sweet tensed.

David kept his voice calm and restrained. "I know that Gem was interested in you and that you rejected her when she approached you openly. Gem found herself another lover, Adrian Snyder. She showed how much she disliked you when Lilian was around and offered Lilian the benefit of her sisterly advice. Finally, she ran weeping to the Hamptons after her breakup with Snyder. But nothing was as it seemed: Gem neither despised you nor loved Snyder. He didn't break up with her—she broke up with him. And she wasn't ashamed of the breakup. She wanted people to know about it. They had to believe she had good reason to suddenly leave town.

"While the gossips were still atwitter, Gem packed her bags. She fled the cold grayness of New York for the stillness of Harding House. Nella's described it to me; it sounds like a lovely place. Relatively isolated, set on an outcropping of private beach, with a small private dock and a boat for short excursions. It fitted Gem's needs perfectly. The water was too cold to swim in, so Gem probably sat on the beach the first couple of days, letting the hours slip by peacefully, watching the sun sink lower over the horizon. I can see her hugging herself, as the air grew chill with the setting sun. She prepared simple suppers and ate them alone. She probably read for a while, before going to bed. She spent several days like this, in self-imposed isolation. Then one night, lying in the dark, let's say she watched a cloud pass over the moon. And she knew it was time to do what she planned next.

"She telephoned Lilian, invited her to visit. When Lilian arrived, Gem went on to the next step of her plan—a plan that was exquisitely simple and brutally direct. She killed her own sister—shot her, stabbed her, I don't know—and hid her body on Nella's property. Then she dressed herself in Lilian's clothes, drove back to Manhattan, and took Lilian's place."

Sweet said nothing, but he looked dismayed.

David went on. "This would explain why the last entry in Lilian's diary was dated just after the breakup. It would explain why no one had a chance to see Gem before she left. Why Lilian was suddenly no longer pregnant. Why she lost interest in her friends and sought out Nella. It would explain a great deal. And it would explain it with sense."

"But that couldn't be! It couldn't! Don't you think I'd know if Gem had been pretending to be my wife?"

"A good question," David said. "Very good."

Stillness.

Sweet cleared his throat. "This is ridiculous. I know it was Lilian. If it had been Gem, she would've been healthy. But the woman who came back from Harding House was as sick as ever."

"You said she was well for some time after Gem supposedly left."

"Just for a short time—"

"Enough time for Gem to develop Lilian's symptoms."

"Preposterous! Impossible!"

"Think about it—about the mental strain Gem was under. She'd gotten Lilian to confide in her, so she felt sure of her familiarity with Lilian's life, but there must've been many perks to Lilian's personality, areas about Lilian's life, that Gem didn't know about, and they must've tripped her up. What was worse was conforming herself to the ways and habits she did know about. It was an ironic twist: Gem the free spirit had trapped herself in a situation where she had to adopt the ways of the sister she'd scorned, the woman she'd killed. As time went by, Gem must've felt imprisoned by glass walls. And she felt guilt. Intense, unbearable guilt. Yes, she'd been cold enough to kill her own sister. But she wasn't cold enough to live with it.

"Gem was haunted by Lilian's dying gaze. That would explain a letter Nella Harding found, a letter that reads like a poem. 'It's her fault. It's her fault. My sister, that sister of mine. She's trying to kill me, to slay me, with her dead blind eyes ...' Gem was the family poet. She's the only one who would've written those words. I think she dreamed constantly about what she'd done. She was tortured by nightmares. That's why, on a visit to Nella's house, it seemed as though she was screaming out her own name.

"When you urged Gem to see a psychiatrist, she panicked. She couldn't afford to let a stranger probe her mind, but she couldn't hold out. She probably told the good doctor what she thought he wanted to hear. She knew exactly what to say to make him cluck or sigh or tsk or simply nod his head in empathy, sympathy, or feigned understanding. What a dear old fool, she probably thought. And that was fine, because she found it entertaining to manipulate him, but then he became a 'tiring old fool' when she began to suspect that he was seeing through her, was indeed learning more about her through her lies than any of the few truths she volunteered. So she broke off her therapy. She turned to liquor."

"Gem would've never committed suicide. She's the most self-loving woman I've ever met."

"And one of the most self-destructive. Liquor and guilt can bring anyone down."

David paused. "Still, I agree with you. Gem did not kill herself. She didn't die by her own hand any more than Lilian did."

Sweet's dark eyes were bleak and grim. Several uneasy minutes passed by.

"You might've gotten away with it, Sweet. But you're a sloppy killer."

Sweet started, and then caught himself. "Lilian wasn't the only one with mental problems, I see."

"Yes, well ... All of us McKays are cursed with a rather creative intelligence," David said mildly. "Unfortunately for you, you aren't. You didn't do your homework. You didn't study your victim enough."

Sweet said nothing, but he swallowed once.

"Is your throat dry?" David asked. "Nervousness—fear—will do that to people. Make yourself a drink."

Sweet licked his lips, but he didn't move.

"I once read that every suicide chooses his death, marks his death," David said, "in a way that reflects his special temperament. Seen in that light, it was a bad idea for you to have shown that suicide note to me. Neither one of my sisters would've written something like that.

"You quoted Lorraine. I'm sure you thought you were being brilliant. But Lilian hated Lorraine. Why would she quote a writer she so disliked? I mentioned that, but you didn't react. You didn't understand. You didn't realize what your ignorance told me.

"Then I realized that it wasn't Lilian, but Gem who was found upstairs, and that made the note seemed even odder. Gem would've never written such a thing. At most, she might've grabbed a page of stationery and in her pretty script, scribbled, 'See you in Hell.' She would've never typed it. Neither Gem nor Lilian would've thought to write anything so personal on a machine."

Sweet's eyes were riveted to David's face. He listened, unwillingly captivated, as David continued.

"Gem's thinking patterns never interested me before. I never found her scintillatingly unpredictable. She was one of the most boringly predictable people I've ever known. Why? Because she was unerringly selfish and vain. She always chose the easiest way out. And she always wanted to look her best. So why would she choose such an ugly, not to mention painful, way to die? Why didn't she use the drugs that were right there? Why would she instead take a knife and butcher her own flesh? It didn't make sense."

There was a momentary pause, then David added, almost as an afterthought: "There was also the matter of the slashes."

"The what?" Sweet stirred. "The slashes?"

"On her wrists. Suicide victims usually make one or two shallow cuts while working up their courage. But Annie described two clean wounds."

"But the shallow cuts were there. Annie just didn't see them."

"But you did?"

"Yes—I did. You can't trust that old woman's memory. The shock of finding Lilian's body probably drove everything else out of her mind."

"I see. So you want me to believe that the discovery shocked Annie, but it didn't shock you?"

"I didn't mean——"

"Of course, you did."

"Don't twist my words."

"I don't have to. They speak for themselves. Every inconsistency reflects a certain truth."

That nervous tic leapt near Sweet's right eye.

"I've thought a lot about that weekend when my sister supposedly killed herself," David said. "She told Nella Harding that you'd be gone the entire time. You certainly went to a lot of trouble to make it look that way, setting up an alibi, including a witness. The man who shared your hotel room claims you were there all Sunday night. But we both know he's lying. It's easy to buy false testimony. But given time and determination, it's also easy to break it. I'm sure Epps will think twice when he learns he's part of a murder investigation."

Sweet didn't answer, but his eyes were venomous.

David walked circles around him. "You hid while Nikki Harding searched the house. And came out after he left. Gem suspected that you were here and she wasn't happy about it. She'd come to fear you. She wasn't sure why. In her confused state, the best she could do was talk about ghosts.

"You waited until she'd gone to sleep. Then in the night, you crept up on her. As she slept, you took her hand. You uncurled her fingers and—" David raised his hand and, with a swift slicing motion, mimed the flash of a blade over flesh. "The pain woke her. Her eyes snapped open. She saw her blood squirting from her wrist. Perhaps she clapped her other hand over it, but the blood would've just bubbled up between her fingers.

"Maybe you went so far as to tell my sister that it was time for her to die. You held the knife away from you so it wouldn't soil those nice new clothes her money had paid for. Maybe you tilted the knife, turned it this way and that. No doubt some of the blood trickled down onto your hands. Maybe you looked down at them, admired them. For their strength. For their ability to destroy a woman."

The twitch at the corner of Sweet's eye was pronounced. He strode to the writing table, pulled out a hidden glass and bottle and poured himself a drink. He gulped half of it down, turned, and eyed David with intense distaste.

"Tell me more. I'm sure there is more."

"You're the kind of killer who takes pleasure in explaining how clever he is, so you explained to her what you would tell the police. You would say you found her dead. That she'd been depressed but had refused help. That she'd apparently taken matters into her own hands. That's all you'd have to say. They would call it suicide for you.

"You went on to tell her how everyone would believe you. That no one would suspect. After all, you're the man who loved her, the good husband who'd stayed at her side. They'd believe anything you said. And my sister listened, mute from the pain, the terror of finding herself trapped with a monster. Maybe she found her voice and asked you, 'Why?' You had the money, the house. Why weren't you satisfied?

"I can imagine your answer. You thought you were talking to Lilian. She was a wonderful woman. But for a man like you, she was too quiet, too thoughtful. You would love another kind of woman—someone who plays the game of life as you do: a fighter, a dirty player. You wanted Gem. And you were prepared to kill in order to be with her. The great irony is, you killed the very woman you loved."

Sweet paled as the meaning of David's words sunk in.

"I'm sure my sister pleaded for her life. I know she fought. For all she was worth. Blood everywhere, Annie said. On the sheets, the canopy, the walls. Drugged or not, Gem would never have died easily. You must've had to drag her down, pin her down like an animal, to do what you did."

Sweet's eye twitched again. He half turned away.

"Yet you two deserved one another," David said. "Both ruthless and greedy, disdainful of humanity and unable to love anyone other than yourselves. Gem, unwilling to risk another rejection, determined to have you at all costs. You, driven by a sick love for the woman you couldn't have and contempt for the one you did."

Several seconds of hostile silence followed.

Then Sweet tossed back the last of his drink. He set his glass down on the writing table with a thump and turned to face David. His eyes were dull and cold now. Slowly, he raised his big hands in the air and began to applaud loudly, mockingly.

"An excellent performance," he said. "Too bad you didn't sell tickets."

David's smile was frosty. "Would you like that? A public display? That's what I want, too. You, charged with premeditated murder in a very public courtroom."

"What proof do you have? None. If you did, you'd be talking to the police right now." Sweet was contemptuous. "Where do you get the nerve to accuse me? Where were you when Lilian needed you? I was the one who carried her, who soothed her nightmares and cradled her when she slept. I was the one! Not you!"

Sweet drew himself up. "You have no right to play judge or jury. I know about you. Don't think I don't. I contacted an operative down in Philly, a good, no-nonsense kind of guy. Fast, efficient, accurate. I thought he'd have to look far and dig deep, but he said you were easy. It seems you're a local hero. Marvelous press clippings."

David's expression became stone-like.

Sweet laughed. He was enjoying himself. "That's right. Your secret is a secret no longer, my friend. Soon, everyone who is anyone will know your game. You and your accusations. What a hypocrite!"

David looked Sweet up and down, then shook his head. "You really don't understand, do you? This isn't about me. I don't care what you say about me, as long as you end up behind bars. It might take time, but I will make you pay for what you did."

Sweet's nostrils flared.

David said, "Pour yourself another drink. You're going to need it." He gave Sweet one last look of contempt, then turned to go. At the doorway, he paused and turned back. "Oh, and one last thing."

Sweet, caught holding the liquor bottle, looked up.

"While you were gone, Rachel Hamilton and I got married. You know her, I believe?"

Sweet blinked as though he'd been hit. His face drained of expression. "You ... and Rachel?"

"She's at work. I want you gone before she gets back. Pack your bags and get out."

Sweet sank down in the chair. For a moment, he was silent, his face darken with emotion. He cast his eyes around, looking at his beautiful surroundings. But there was no pride of possession, only a look of bitterness and something else. Something akin to ... despair.

Finally, he brought his gaze back to David and got to his feet. He balled his huge hands into fists. "I warn you. I will not let you send me to prison. I'd rather die first. I've always been a man to choose my own destiny. Neither you nor anyone else will dictate my end." With that, he walked out and headed down the hall to the office.

David watched him go with a grim, set expression. A long fight lay ahead. No doubt, Sweet would make good on his threats. He would tell the world about Philadelphia, but David found that he was relieved. He was tired of running and ready for a fight. If public humiliation was the price to pay to see Sweet in jail, then he was willing to pay it.

His first concern was Rachel. He had to protect her. The uproar over his past would hurt her—more than it would hurt him. He cared nothing for the stifling *café au lait* society that would bar them, but Rachel would hunger for entry. He'd had years to prepare for a day of reckoning, but Rachel would be caught like a deer in headlights.

He had to send her somewhere safe, where the vicious tongues would be still. Aunt Clara's in Chicago. His father's younger sister was practical, tough-minded, and independent. And she loved a good fight.

Aunt Clara always said that the best defense is a good offense. He had to find proof that Sweet killed Gem. He'd considered having Gem's remains exhumed. Of course, Sweet would fight it, but David felt that he could box it through. He rubbed his jaw. An exhumation would demonstrate the switch in identities, but would it yield proof that Sweet wielded the knife?

First things first. He had received word that the druggist's report was ready. Finally, but finally, he might receive some empirical evidence to use against Sweet. He paused. Of course, that could be a double-edged sword, couldn't it? He paused. He would have to take the bad with the good, that's all. He'd just have to take the bad with the good.

The druggist greeted David with a smile. He was a kindly man with short gray hair and a gray goatee. "I've got to some good news for you," he said, when David stood before over the counter.

David felt himself inwardly relax. Finally. Progress.

"There wasn't nothing wrong with that medicine you

brought in," the druggist said.

David was stunned. "Are you sure?"

"Oh, yeah. No doubt about it. It's harmless stuff. Bet you're glad to hear that, huh?"

David didn't answer.

Now, the old man frowned. He peered down from his raised counter and asked, "Just what'd you think you'd find?"

What indeed?

David said nothing. With mixed feelings, he paid for the analysis, and turned away. He was gravely disappointed. That report would have been helpful in pushing through to have Gem's remains exhumed. Without it, he would simply have to find something else. He had intentionally told Sweet about his suspicions in order to rattle him. He hoped Sweet would do something rash, something incriminating, and he would be there to catch him.

At the same time, he was deeply relieved. The results meant that at least one nasty, brooding suspicion could be put to rest. And for that, he was grateful.

As he headed back to the house, his thoughts stayed with Rachel. She would soon be at the epicenter of a storm. He would have to prepare her, find a way to tell her in a coherent way, *a way she'll understand,* about Jonah and Philadelphia.

He happened to see a flower shop. On impulse, he crossed the street, went in and bought her a dozen roses. They were lovely, but the moment he walked out with them, his heart sank. Rachel would know that something was wrong the moment he gave them to her.

36. HEAVY BRACELETS

In hindsight, David would remember sensing a new heaviness to the air when he opened his front door and stepped inside that evening. But at the time, all he noticed was a particularly bleak silence.

"Rachel?" he called out. No answer. That was odd. She should have been home by then. Perhaps, something had happened at the hospital to delay her. "Annie?" No answer there, either.

He laid the flowers on the vestibule side table and hung up his coat. He wondered if Sweet were still there, in Augustus's office. If not, then perhaps he could get in there again, have another look around. Perhaps, he'd missed something that first time in. This time, he'd be more thorough. This time, he'd make sure he found something that would help topple the pretender from the throne.

He started past the parlor, headed for the office, but then he noticed that the parlor doors were oddly half open, neither fully closed nor open, and his eye caught an even odder flash of color, low down, where it shouldn't have been. He paused, took a step back and inclined his head for a better look. For a split second, he didn't move. Then he strode to the parlor doors and shoved them apart.

Jameson Sweet lay on the floor, his head a crimson mess. He was on his back, his arms flung out on either side, his eyes open and one knee bent. He looked like a man crucified. A gun lay in the curled fingers of his right hand.

David closed the doors behind him. He went to the body, knelt beside it. He reached out, felt for a pulse in Sweet's throat, even though he was sure he wouldn't find one. Sweet was dead. No doubt about it. David's gaze went to the gun and he recalled Sweet's words. *I've always been a man to choose my own destiny. Neither you nor anyone else will dictate my end.*

He heard the sound of the front door open and close and seconds later, Rachel calling out. "David? Are you home?"

He heard her moving about the vestibule. Quickly, he got up and went to the parlor doors. He slid them open just wide enough for him to slip through, then shut them behind him.

She smiled at the sight of him. She was holding the flowers. "Oh, they're lovely. You bought them for me?"

"Of course, who else?"

She came up to him, started to kiss him, then drew back. "Why, David," she frowned. "What's that on your shirt?"

He looked down. Somehow, he'd gotten blood on himself. He must've wiped his hands on his vest without realizing it. He looked up at her and she must've seen something in his face, because the joy drained out of hers, and she said, "What's wrong? Has something happened?"

He swallowed, tried to think. "There's ... there's been an accident."

"Accident?" she repeated. "What kind of accident?"

He didn't answer.

"Is it Annie?" she said. "Has something happened to Annie?"

"No," he said darkly. "It's Sweet." He watched her. "He's dead."

Her eyes widened. "No!" She dropped the flowers and her hands covered her mouth. Then her gaze moved from him to the doors behind him. "In there?"

He nodded.

She reached around him to open the doors, but he blocked her.

"Rachel, it's not pretty."

"*Pretty?*" she cried. "I don't care about pretty! I'm a nurse. I've seen ugly that you can't imagine. Now, let me in."

"He's gone, Rachel."

"I want to go in."

They stared at one another grimly.

"All right," he said.

She was right. She had seen a lot of ugly. Of course, she had. Maybe as much as he had on the battlefield. Maybe even more. But what she perhaps didn't realize was that it's one thing to see a stranger in violent death and quite another to see an acquaintance.

He turned and opened the doors for her. Then he stepped

aside, so the whole scene lay before her.

She froze in the doorway, staring in momentary wide-eyed shock. Then she turned back to him and said in a horrified whisper, "My God! David, what have you done?"

He felt the blood drain from his face.

Before he could answer, she ran to Sweet's side. Just as he had done, she placed two fingers on the side of Sweet' throat and felt for a pulse.

"It's impossible, Rachel. You can't do anything. He's gone."

"No," she cried. "He can't be." She put her ear to Sweet's chest, listened for a heartbeat, and obviously found none. When she straightened up, her face, and throat and the bodice of her white nurse's uniform bore his blood.

Then she saw the gun and reached for it. David rushed forward to stop her, but too late. She'd picked it up. Her fingerprints were now on it. She stared at the gun, a small deadly thing, then with a cry, dropped it as though it had burned her.

David went to her, gathered her in his arms, and drew her away from the body.

"What ha-happened?" she wept. "What did you do?"

"Nothing. I found him here."

She looked up, searched his face.

"Are you saying he killed himself?"

"It—well, it looks like it."

"But that makes no sense! Why would he do that?"

He didn't answer.

Anguished sobs broke from her throat. She buried her face in David's arms, whimpering. He looked over her shoulder. A bullet had drilled a devastating wound into Sweet's right cheek. The projectile had exited on the left side, at the top of his head, and taken a good part of his skull with it. The resulting explosion of blood and brain matter had splattered nearby furniture and soaked the carpet beneath him.

No one deserves to die like that, he thought, but he couldn't deny his sense of relief. The nightmare was over. His secret was safe. Now, he and Rachel would be able to live out their lives in peace.

"We have to call the police," he said.

"We can't. You—everyone knows how you felt about him. They'll think you killed him."

"Hush."

"And if they find out I found you here with them?" Rachel gulped. "What—what'll I say?"

"Tell the truth."

David hugged her. The coming police interview would be difficult, but once it was done, they would be free.

She sat next to him, stiff with too obvious fear, as he gave his statement. A homicide detective, a man named Peters, listened with the ill-concealed cynicism of a man who was used to being lied to. Peters was gray and tough-looking, like a faded bulldog, of medium height with a balding head, ruddy jowls, and bloodshot blue eyes.

"Are you aware of any reasons," he asked David, "any personal problems that might've led Mr. Sweet to take his life?"

David paused. What was he to answer? To say yes would open a Pandora's box. Everything about his sisters might come out. To say no would undermine his credibility.

"I didn't know my brother-in-law well. But I believe he'd been in a critical frame of mind since my sister's recent death."

Peters turned back to Rachel. "Did you ever see Mr. Sweet looking depressed, hear him talk about suicide?"

"He talked about his wife. He couldn't come to terms with having lost her."

"She committed suicide, too—"

"After a long illness."

"They were close?"

"Yes."

Peters leaned forward. He looked from Rachel to David. "Did either of you touch the gun?"

David shook his head, then glanced at Rachel. She gave him a questioning look and he answered with a nod.

"Yes," she said hesitantly. "I did. I tried to see if he was alive and then I saw the gun and I ... I just reached for it."

Peters inclined his head. "So were your hands on the gun when it went off?"

"No," Rachel drew back. "I told you. I wasn't here when it happened. I only saw him, later, after he was dead."

David gave her hand a reassuring squeeze.

"What's behind your question, Detective?" he asked.

Peters smiled blandly and snapped his notepad shut. "Just looking for the truth. We'll have to test you both for gunpowder residue."

Rachel started. She turned to David. "But I—"

"It's normal in situations like this," said Peters.

David comforted her. "It's procedure. Don't worry. You have nothing to fear."

"No," she murmured. "Of course not."

Peters returned the next day and asked for Rachel. Annie told him Rachel was resting, so he asked to speak with David. She left the two men in the library. David rose from his armchair to shake hands with the detective and asked him to sit down. Peters spoke without preamble.

"Your wife tested positive for gunpowder residue."

"Of course she did. She said she picked up the gun."

"But she didn't say she was holding it when it fired."

David straightened up. He was surprised and indignant. "Are you accusing my wife of murder?"

"There's also the matter of her fingerprints."

"You can't be serious. Whatever test results you have, they came from her having touched the gun when we found him. I told you, she wasn't even here when it happened."

"The test—"

"I don't give a damn about your test. I'm the one who found

the body. I was there. Not her. And I saw the kind of wound he had. It consistent with suicide: close contact, to the head."

"That it was. But there's another problem. The muzzle must've been pressed against his cheek. Most people shoot themselves in the temple."

"That's razor thin—"

"Let's say Mr. Sweet was sitting down—or he was standing." He waved his hands to stave off argument. "It doesn't matter. Either way, it would've been simple for her to come up behind him. He would've been dead before he knew what hit him."

"A big man like that? You're saying a big man like Jameson Sweet would just let someone creep up on him, put a gun in his face, and fire?"

"If he trusted her enough not to look behind him."

"That's ridiculous. My wife had no reason to kill Sweet. She tried to save him."

The two men studied one another.

"Don't try to arrest her."

"I have a warrant."

"You don't have a case. You don't even have a motive."

"We have Byron Canfield."

David's eyes flashed. "What does he have to do with this?"

"He says Mr. Sweet had hold of a secret that could've destroyed you. We've checked it out and his story is solid. Your wife offed Mr. Sweet to protect you. To protect your name. Your money. And her status."

David understood now. Canfield was using this opportunity to get back at him. He wouldn't have thought Canfield capable of such enmity, or underhandedness, but there it was. He'd poisoned Peters against them. That had to be it. That was the only explanation.

David stood. "You—"

"David?"

Both men turned. Rachel stood in the doorway. Framed by the archway and an aureole of soft late afternoon light, she seemed ethereal and delicate. David went to her. Peters rose to his feet.

"Mrs. McKay, I have to ask you to come with me."

"No!" she cried and clutched at David.

He stepped between them. "If you take her, then you'll have to take me, too."

Peters looked at David. "I could charge you with obstruction—"

"You can charge me with murder if you want to. Just don't take her."

Rachel looked frantically at David.

Peters said, "Do you mean that?"

And David answered, "I do."

Peters looked at David with a calculating hunger.

"Think about it," David said. "This is the best offer you'll have all day."

"I can't just forget about the gun residue test."

"We both know they're notoriously fallible. Look, man, I'm offering to go with you. We both know I make the better suspect. After all, I was the target of the scandal."

The detective's eyes narrowed. "May I take that as a confession of guilt?"

"No," David said. "You may not. Just because I've offered myself on a silver platter, doesn't mean that I'll give you the means to roast me."

The metal handcuffs were cold and heavy and cut into his skin. Annie watched silently from the kitchen doorway, her eyes full of pain. Rachel's wails followed him out the house. Then Peters slammed the door behind them, cutting off the sound of her cries.

Two police officers were waiting by a squad car. They came up to him, one on either side, gripped him by his elbows, and led him from the house to the waiting car. It was late afternoon, bright enough for the world to see his disgrace. He was painfully aware of the parting of delicate French curtains up and down the street, of highbrow noses pressed against window-panes and wide eyes staring. Humiliation overwhelmed him. Although he had volunteered to be arrested for a crime he had not committed, he was sick with shame. That they should see him this way. That his life should have come to this. Yes, he was innocent of this crime, but he was guilty of another—and soon everyone would know it. As Sweet said: *Everyone who is anyone will know your game.*

One officer grabbed him roughly by the back of his collar, forced him to bend down, and shoved him into the backseat. The car reeked of stale cigarettes, cold sweat, and dried semen. An odious mixture. The cop climbed in next to him. David looked at him, at his resentful, muddy brown eyes and blotchy complexion.

"It stinks in here."

The young officer grinned at him. "You'll get used to it."

David turned his face away. He tried not to think of the stench and peered out the grimy window of the police car instead. The world whisked by. He caught glimpses of a young woman in a wheelchair with a small girl on her lap, a teenage boy pedaling a rusted cart, an old man in tattered clothes shuffling along with the help of a cane. For a moment, he forgot about himself. What about those people? Look at the burdens they had to bear. What would be their end? An awareness of the brevity of life pressed itself upon him. The words of a psalm Lila had loved rose within him.

Lord, make me to know my end. And what is the measure of my days, that I may know how frail I am. ... Do not be silent at my tears, for I am a stranger with you, a sojourner as all my fathers were. Look away from me that I may be radiant, before I go away and am no more.

Years had passed since he'd thought of those words, but now they returned unbidden. Why? He thought for a moment and he knew. Death, in its psychic form, awaited him. He stood on the edge of a mental precipice. His arrest, his incarceration, the trial and the public excoriation that would undoubtedly follow would push him over the edge. Life as he knew it would end.

But would that be so terrible?

He had been blessed in many ways. Life had been generous to him. It had granted him more advantages than it did most people, black or white. And to what benefit had he used them? That woman in the wheelchair, the teenage boy, and the old man: Their struggles—disability, poverty, and age—had been forced upon them. His problems were of his own making. He'd made too many wrong decisions. He had failed at every determining moment. Why hadn't he fought for Jonah—even if it meant dying at the hands of that mob? Wouldn't it have been better to die with honor than to live in shame? Wouldn't it have been better if when he'd seen that woman in Philadelphia, upon offering to help her, he'd had the guts to tell her who and what he was? And why, dear God, why hadn't he answered Lilian's last letter?

If he'd made the right decision at the right time, he would have been able to return. He would have been there to support Rachel and save Isabella. Maybe, he could have dissuaded Lilian from marrying Sweet. He could have protected his women.

He could have made a difference.

He felt the heavy handcuffs cutting into his wrists, pressing into his back, and his shame left him. An odd calm washed over him. Life, he told himself, had once more been generous with him. It had granted him a chance to make amends.

They took him to the City Prison down on Centre Street. They led him to an interrogation room and seated him in a chair before a long, battered wooden table. The room was dark, except for one glaring light, which was angled so that it shone directly in his eyes. He winced, blinded. Several officers stood over him with their shirtsleeves rolled up. They asked him his name and told him to tell them what had happened. He told them everything—beginning with the day he returned, ending with Sweet's last words that he would not allow himself to be jailed. They urged him to confess to murder. They demanded. They cajoled. They threatened. He refused. Then the beatings began. Still, he refused.

The "interrogating" and fingerprinting lasted well past midnight. They threw him into a small, narrow cell that reeked of urine and vomit. He was grateful, however, to have a cell alone. When the guard extinguished the light, it was pitch-dark. David couldn't see his hand before his face. Feeling his way in the dark, he stumbled into the cot shoved up against one wall. The mattress was thin and hard and it stank of mildew. He lay down, his body a mass of bruised and aching parts, his right eye swollen shut. Staring into the gloom, he waited for panic to set in, but he felt eerily calm. A warm liquid numbness that began in his fingertips spread slowly to the rest of his body. He closed his eyes, sure that he would be unable to sleep. But he did, uneasily.

37. THE CONFESSIONAL

Early the next morning, he was chained to two other men and hustled to the Criminal Courts Building for a hearing. He looked and felt horrible. His hair was dusty. His swollen eye was purplish and tender. He had a nasty taste in his mouth and his clothes stunk of rot after a night on the cell's filthy mattress.

He was charged with murder in the death of Jameson Sweet. Bail was out of the question. As he stood before the judge, he glanced around the courtroom, looking for Rachel. She was nowhere to be seen. Yes, he had told her to stay away and he was glad she had listened. But he was saddened. He missed her. Annie was there, however. And so was Byron Canfield.

Later that day, David sat on his thin mattress, reading. A pile of newspapers lay scattered on the floor at his feet.

"RACIAL TREASON: DAVID LIVED AS A WHITE IN PHILLY!"

screamed the headline of one paper. *"POLICE: MOVEMENT LAWYER SLAIN BY NEGRO PASSING FOR WHITE!"* proclaimed another. *"MCKAY'S DOUBLE LIFE: DID HE KILL TO PROTECT HIS DIRTY SECRET?" SAID A THIRD.*

The Negro press was full of his arrest; more accurately, they were full of Canfield.

"Young Sweet was like a son to me," Canfield was quoted as saying. "I showed him the ropes, brought him along. We had just returned from Chicago, filled with joy over our landmark victory in the Boston Richards case. Then this happened. Sweet's work on the Richards case was impeccable. His death is a loss to every colored man, woman, and child.

"David McKay, on the other hand, is a source of shame for us all, most especially for those here at Movement headquarters. We placed our faith, our trust, our hopes in him. He fell lower than any of us could have ever imagined. He murdered a man to keep his dirty lies a secret. He killed in order to steal the money and the house, to which Jameson Sweet had a legitimate right. We are cooperating with the prosecution in every way to purge our community of such a cowardly monster."

The man makes good copy, I have to admit. David smiled grimly. He shuffled through the other papers. Apparently, Canfield talked to anyone who would quote him, and most of the Negro newspapers did. *So much for being innocent until proven guilty. As a lawyer, you'd think Canfield would at least honor that.*

A guard appeared at his cell. "Get up. Someone's here to see you."

Surprised, David laid the newspapers aside. Was it Rachel? He'd love to see her. But what would she think when she saw him? They'd given him a basin of cold water, and he'd done his best to wash and shave, but he still felt grubby. To make matters worse, he now wore a jailhouse uniform. He hoped his appearance wouldn't shock her.

He touched his bruised eye. *Does it hurt to love me?* she'd asked. Well, yes, he sighed. It did.

Heart thumping, he tucked his shirttail tightly into his pants, ran his fingers rapidly through his hair, and went through the opened gate. The guard escorted him to a tiny visiting room. David stepped inside and stopped. A muscle in his chest twisted painfully.

She sat on the other side of the wall of iron bars that divided the room. She was as lovely as always, but looked wrung out. She paled at the sight of him. He smiled to reassure her. Crossing the room, he slid onto the seat opposite her. The guard warned him to keep his hands in his lap, and then stepped back.

David leaned toward her. "How are you?"

She gave a wan smile. "The reporters have been annoying and the neighbors are gossiping up a storm, but I'm okay."

"You look wonderful. But you shouldn't have come."

"I had to." Her eyes glowed with loyalty. "The stories in the papers about Philadelphia. Why didn't you tell me?"

He sighed. "I wanted to. I intended to—but everything happened so quickly."

"It don't matter, you know," she said. "None of it matters to me."

"I'm so sorry."

"Don't be. You did what you had to do to survive. I'd rather have you this way than not at all."

"I've been a fool. All those years wasted. I wanted to come back, but I couldn't."

"Shush—"

"I have one hope. One chance. I've got to face up to what I've done. If I survive that, I'll be free, really free, to live my life with you. To stay here, at home, where our roots are."

He looked around at the dingy institutional walls encompassing him. "A man has a lot of time to think when he's here. I've thought a lot about what you said that day, Rachel. The fact is, you were right. The world out there will deceive a man. It can bring him down. What I've been looking for, I had right here." He gaze went back to her. He tried to smile, but failed miserably. "What a husband, huh?"

"Oh, David," she moaned. "But they have no proof against you!"

"This is 1926, baby. They don't need proof to try a colored man. To execute him, either." If only he could hold her, at least touch her hands. He had to get her through this situation as smoothly as possible, to protect her from the scandal as best he could. "Rachel, promise me that you'll stay away when the trial starts."

"But I want to be with you—"

"You will be. In here." He touched his chest.

Tears shimmered in her eyes. She reached out to him. The guard stepped forward and gave a warning signal. She let her hand drop. "I'm going to be there, in that courtroom every day," she whispered.

"No."

Tears spilled down her cheeks. "Yes."

Annie visited him. "I can't stay long. They won't let me." Her wise face crinkled with a sad smile. He assumed that she had heard the gossip from the neighbors and read the newspaper reports. She must be so disappointed in him. She answered him as though reading his thoughts.

"You oughta know I'm not here to judge. I want to listen and listen well. Tell me if what I've heard is true."

David looked up at the room's sole window. How to explain? The light inside the small visitors' room darkened as clouds moved over the sun. It rained. Heavy, pelting drops that beat furiously against the windowpane. Finally, he began. He spoke at length and Annie listened without interrupting. If she was shocked at what he told her, she kept it to herself. Every now and then, lightning would snap overhead and thunder would roll; a storm cloud would burst and needles of rain would come slanting down to punch against the windowpane. It seemed as though it would rain forever. David talked until he could say no more. It all came out: the years of running and pretending, his efforts to make amends.

"It wasn't just the evil of those supposedly God-fearing people that got me. It was what I saw in myself. God, I'll never forget the moment when I realized what I'd done."

The visitor's room had taken on the air of a confessional. A contemplative silence had settled over it. The rainfall quieted. Even the rumble of thunder seemed to come from far away. Annie looked at David's wretched face.

"Son, what do you think life is? Don't you know that in many ways, it ain't nothing but a battle with yourself?"

"But I saw something in myself that horrified me."

"You think you the first one that's happened to? What about all them people out there drinking and cussing and carrying on? Who d'you think they running from? People start out with all kinds of high-faluting ideas. And then things happen, bad things, to test a man's grit. And don't nobody know how they gonna react till their time comes."

"I was so sure of myself when I set out, so sure of what I was capable of—"

"When you left here, you didn't have the faintest idea where you was going. Or what you'd do when you got there."

David remembered how he'd responded with confidence when Jonah and Miss Mae expressed their fear. They must've thought him a fool. He gave a rueful smile. "Maybe you're right. Being knocked down can clear a man's head of a lot of nonsense."

"You had a choice: to lay down and die or get back on your feet. And you chose to get up. Some folks might not agree with how you did it, but you did it and I'm proud that you did."

His eyes shone. He blinked rapidly. "I love you, Annie."

"And I love you." Her eyes dwelled on him for a bit, then she said, "I got a present here for you." Reaching into her purse, she pulled out his worn childhood Bible. "Take it and read it. The Lord'll stand by you if you stand by Him."

He looked at it, knowing that his faith was long gone. "Thank you. You'll have to give it to the guard. He'll pass it to me."

Annie leaned toward him. "I know you feel alone, but trust in the Lord. You got friends, son. Not just me. Powerful people. Some of them in the strangest places."

David thought about Snyder and what he'd said. *I know what it's like to be an outsider among outsiders.* And what about Nella? Despite her manipulative ambition, she had sincerely tried to help him. And he sensed that he could always count on her for eccentric but oddly dependable support. A West Indian rackets king and a wealthy white socialite: The prejudices of his time rigidly classified them as his enemies, but they had shown themselves to be his allies. He, of all people, had been forced to learn once more that in life so little is as it seems.

"You done traveled a long hard way, and you got a ways to go. But I b'lieve you'll be all right. I do b'lieve you'll be just fine. Just remember: Everybody gets tested. And sooner or later everybody fails. Discovers something about themselves they don't wanna know. Everybody's got secrets, young man. Everybody."

His eyes dwelled on her and his expression saddened. He had a heavy feeling in his chest. For once, it had nothing to do with his own guilt. "Even you, Annie?"

There was a long silence and then the edges of her smile began to tremble. She sighed. "How long you been knowing?"

"I found a copy of Lilian's manuscript. It was all there." He paused. "Why didn't you tell me? After Daddy died, you could've said something."

She didn't answer for a long, long time. "I wanted to. All these years, I wanted to. But I made a promise—"

"You made a pact with the Devil."

"I knew he'd give my son the best."

"But to make you a servant—"

"Hush. It was the only way. He'd married my best friend. It was over. It was done. You was on the way. And you was all I had. I didn't wanna give you up. And I didn't wanna have to raise you alone. When Lila found out, she had the idea. And I agreed."

It's a hard thing for a man to realize that the people he has most loved and trusted have lied to him all his life. It takes strength to resist the temptation to be bitter. He thought of all the times he'd seen her and his father together.

"And did you still love him? Did you two keep on loving each other through all those years?"

"No." She shook her head. "When he married my friend, that was the end of anything that coulda been between us. All I cared about was you getting his name."

Was this how Rachel felt when she was carrying Isabella? He thought of the parallels between Augustus and Annie, and himself and Rachel. Were sons always destined to repeat the sins of their fathers?

"How did Lilian find out?"

"I don't know. She never said nothing. But there were days I caught her looking at me—and I knew. It was the same way you started looking at me after you went into Mr. Jameson's office. I didn't know what you'd found, but I was pretty certain what you'd learned from it."

David drew a deep breath. "It's time for the lying and pretending to stop, don't you think? It's time for a little honesty—from all of us."

There were tears in her eyes as she whispered, "Yes ... yes, it is."

"Remember me?" the old man said when David was shown into the visitors' room.

"'Course I do. You're Roy—"

"That's right! Roy, Roy, the Shoeshine Boy. How ya doing,

soldier boy?"

"Fine," David said, then thought about it. He gave a sheepish grin and gestured toward his surroundings. "Well, not so fine, actually."

Roy shook his head. "Ain't this a mess? When I saw your face in the paper, and read what happened, I just had to come. How can they treat a fine soldier boy this way?"

David slid his seat closer. "Listen, I'm glad you're here. I couldn't sleep last night and I got to thinking about what you said, about the war ... and your son and all."

Roy's sunny expression dimmed. "Sorry about that. I was just flapping my lip. Went and put my foot in it."

"No, I'm glad you said what you said, about your wife thinking your son died for nothing and what that does to you. As you know from the papers, my sister recently died and the hardest part of it all is the notion that she died before her time. But that's not what I wanted to talk to you about. Not directly. You see, I had a time too when I was bitter about having fought in that war, about having risked my life for Mister Charlie."

"But you're a hero. You got a medal."

"I was in the wrong place at the right time—if you can imagine."

"And you ain't bitter no more?"

"No. I realized last night that I'm not." David paused, trying to find words to explain. "I was twenty-seven when I signed up, too old for any romantic notions about the battlefield. Our civil rights leaders were telling us that colored patriotism in the trenches of Europe would mean social equality for us at home. I didn't believe it. We colored folk fought in the War for Independence and every war since then. Our courage had never been acknowledged or rewarded. I didn't understand what made DuBois and the others so sure it would work this time. How could they ensure that we wouldn't just come back to broken promises? And there was nothing going on to make a man feel better.

"There was that mess over in East St. Louis. All those colored folk killed—hundreds dead and thousands more torched out of their homes. That was in July. In August, a riot tore through Houston. The colored soldiers stationed outside the city got tired of putting up with the white boys' nonsense. Seventeen white folk died. To avenge them seventeen, Mister Charlie hung thirteen blacks, court-martialed sixty, and jailed scores for life. But you know all this. Kill them or lock them up: That was the way to keep colored men in line. Understanding why the riot happened was the last thing on the white man's mind. So, things couldn't have been much worse."

"But you and my boy, y'all signed up anyway."

"I believed we couldn't let a chance go by without at least trying. The army had set up this training camp for colored officers at Des Moines. DuBois was urging educated colored men to go there. But once I was there, it didn't take long to see that those white folk were giving the higher commissions to the fellows with little or no education. They viewed educated colored men with suspicion and treated us with contempt.

"That fixed it for me. My dying over there wouldn't mean a damn thing over here. I'd be just one less nigger to deal with. As for civil rights, white mobs would go on lynching, killing, burning with impunity; the ballot box would remain off-limits; southern university doors would remain closed, and good jobs would be a luxury for a lucky few. Me and the other fellows at the camp, we used to ask ourselves why we should go overseas and risk our lives for a democracy we were denied at home. We never found a good answer. But we went anyway.

"Army life confirmed my worst fears. They confined us colored men to camp. Made us go through hourly checks. We were a threat to white women, they said. We were lazy, stupid brutes, they said. But we were strong and they worked us like dogs. Sometimes fourteen hours a day. We were poorly fed, physically abused, mocked, and humiliated. They forbid us to consort with French civilians and they told the French to have nothing to do with us. We were sexually depraved, they said, cowardly, incompetent. And the French, they didn't know any better, so they listened.

"I remember that first French village my company entered. The village folk were scared to death. But we won them over. We worked hard at it, doing all we could to help. And it worked. We won their trust. We won their friendship. Best of all, we won their respect. They invited us into their homes. They shared their food, their stories, their losses, and their luck with us. And they appreciated what we did for them. It was so different from here in the U.S., where the white man says nothing we do is good enough.

"France was an eye-opener. I'd never dreamed that black and white could coexist like that. Some of those French folk were even willing to fight Mister Charlie to defend being friends with us. I remember one time when a riot broke out in a club. A white American officer had insulted a colored Frenchman for talking to a white girl. The girl's brother understood some English and caught what was said. Those French people took off after those soldiers. Nearly tore up the place. Don't get me wrong. I knew that France wasn't perfect. They gave the Senegalese something to complain about. But there was no sign of the endemic, systematic, and deadly contempt that the white folk here got for us.

"When it was over, the white boys left us all the clean-up work. My last memories were of the military cemetery at Romagne, near Verdun. It was the eve of General Pershing's visit. Those white boys refused to help bury their own men, the guys who'd died in the battle at Meuse-Argonne. We colored had to do it. We'd rise at dawn and go back to the battlefield, collecting the dead. We bent our backs from dawn till dusk. From Romagne, we went on to Beaumont, Belleau Wood, Fay-en-Tardenois, and Soissons. God, those names I'll never forget. Twenty-two thousand white crosses we planted. The white boys got to go home. We were left to do what they refused to do. We were the last to go.

"Of course, by then, lots of the fellows didn't even want to come back. They'd had enough of this country. They were going to stay in France. Study. Open clubs. They wanted me to stay with them, but I had other ideas. I had a promise to my father to keep. But it wasn't just that. I really thought I could make a difference. I'd seen the way it was in France. I knew it wouldn't be easy to make changes here in the States, but I thought it was worth a try. I was naive. I know that now. But what I wanted to tell you, Roy—what I want you to tell your missus—is this: Before he died, those French villagers gave your son, gave all of us Negro soldiers, a gift. And it was this: a vision, a taste, of what it's like to be viewed with respect and treated like a man. Something most of us would've never had if we'd stayed here. Now, I don't know how your son died ... but I know he didn't die for nothing."

There was a silence. Roy's lips began to tremble. He pressed them together, then put his hand over his mouth. He closed his eyes and his chest heaved. Tears leaked out from under his eyelids. He produced a torn but clean handkerchief and swiped his damp face with it. He looked at David with grateful eyes. "I came here to comfort you. Now you's the one comforting me. Thank you." He smiled through his tears.

Roy left soon after that and David was returned to his cell. His memory stirred, he was swamped with images from the summer he'd returned, the "Red Summer" they called it, referring to the streams of Negro blood sent flowing down American streets. By the year's end, bloody race riots had erupted in two dozen cities or counties, scores of blacks had been lynched and burned, and the Ku Klux Klan had resurged in popularity. David had read the reports, sickened. Still invigorated by his memories of France, he had planned to attend Howard, and then join the Movement. But as he contemplated a newspaper photograph of a black man's scorched remains hanging from a tree, he knew there wasn't a snowball's chance in hell of re-creating the openness he had seen in France in the United States, at least not in his lifetime. But he promised himself that he would do what he could. He vowed to work until he dropped to at least make it safe for black men, women, and children to walk the streets of American towns. As for what happened to that vow, that was the most painful thought of all.

David's next visitor couldn't have been more of a surprise: Toby's mother. She drew her chair close to the grate separating them. Her gentle eyes were actually amused. She couldn't believe he had killed Sweet, she said, but she didn't know what to think about the rest. Had he really led a double life? He explained and when he was done, she simply nodded.

"Well, I suppose a man's got to do what a man's got to do. And sometimes that means wearing a mask to survive."

He smiled at her pragmatic way of seeing the situation, but his conscience rejected it. It seemed that while part of him yearned for redemption, another part strove for condemnation, and the more his friends forgave him, the more he demanded punishment.

"What happens," he asked, "when that mask becomes your second skin? You forget how to live without it. You forget what your own face looks like. What's worse, you're not sure you want to know. And when a chance comes to take it off, to tell the world, 'This is me. This is who I am,' you pass it up. Life behind the mask has become too safe, too comfortable. That was me."

"You know, you think too much. It's always bad to think too much. I got a sister who's passing. She ain't found nothing comfortable about it. She the loneliest person I know. At least you did it to help people. She ain't into rested in helping nobody but herself. Everybody in the fam'ly know what she's doing and why she's doing it. And we still love her. We just don't never see the need to talk about it." Her eyes went over him. "You got to stop looking back. You done your best. The Lord don't ask for more."

For an instant, she reminded him of Annie. "I don't know what the Lord asks for. I used to think I did, but that was ..." He grimaced. "I was a child."

"My pappy used to say we got to love with the heart of a child and think with the mind of a man."

"Your pappy wasn't talking about abandoning his friends. Lying about his identity."

"No, he was just talking about surviving." She looked at him and shook her head. "I done known a lot of people in a lot of trouble, but you take the cake. I got to admit, though, you'd look good in stripes."

He could feel a smile coming on. "Could be I'll be wearing them for some time."

"Don't think so."

"No?"

"A man like you got a plan."

"Have I now?"

"Um-hm. Men like you, they always got a plan. So, what you gonna do?"

He thought about it. It was getting harder to hold back that smile. He gave a wry grin. "Well, like you said, a man's got to do what a man's got to do. And a man can't live his life looking backward, now can he?"

"Not if he don't want to get an awful crick in his neck."

He couldn't hold it in anymore. He laughed out loud, grateful for her mischievous humor. He asked her to tell him about Toby, something she was happy to do. He liked the way her eyes lit up when she spoke of her little boy. The minutes allotted them passed quickly and soon it was time for her to leave. She would attend the trial, she said, whenever she could, and nothing he could say would dissuade her. He needed friends and she meant to be among them. He watched her go with a new warmth in his heart. It was only then he realized that he'd again forgotten to ask her name.

Nella stopped by. She was bold and to the point. "So tell me the truth, dear boy. Did you shoot him?"

"Would you blame me if I had?"

"Not a bit. But you didn't, did you?" She sighed. "How unfortunate."

"Why?"

"It would make my book oh so much juicier if you had."

Snyder puffed on his cigar and fixed David with a paternal eye.

"You didn't have to kill Sweet, you know. I can understand why you did it, but I wish you'd left him for me."

"I didn't kill him."

"Too bad," he said, but it was with an amused expression. "It always amazes me that I like you. But I do. And now I know why. When I first looked at you, I sensed an old wound—a deep wound—and I sensed the strength that went into hiding it. You're a strong man."

"Am I?"

All of the amusement left Snyder's eyes. He was suddenly dead serious. "I don't trust men who don't feel pain. Men who don't risk pain are cowards, and those who can't carry it are weak."

"Well, if that's the case, then my muscles should be busting through my shirt."

38. EVERY WHITE MAN'S NIGHTMARE

The leaders of the Movement demanded that the accused murderer of Jameson Sweet suffer the full brunt of the law. David McKay had not only destroyed one of the Movement's best legal minds, but sullied the reputation of the Movement itself. Calling upon their white allies, the Movement's officials put the heat on police and legal authorities.

On Monday, April 5, one week after David's arrest, a grand

jury needed just twelve minutes to indict him. The trial was scheduled to begin two weeks later, on April 20. In the interim, both the prosecution and the defense scrambled to prepare.

Byron Canfield became the prosecution's mainstay. In a major deposition, he recapped how David had disappeared years earlier, then "conveniently reappeared" following Lilian's death. He described David's evasive answers at Nella Harding's party and repeated Sweet's complaint that David wanted to eject him from the house. Finally, he related the results of Sweet's private investigation into David's life and Sweet's plans to expose David's duplicity.

Peters subjected Annie to hours of grueling interrogation. She was uncooperative, sometimes flatly refusing to answer. He threatened to jail her until she reconsidered. Annie was sent away with a proud mien and her lips sealed, but twenty-four hours in a cold, damp cell weakened her. With tears in her eyes, she "admitted" to having urged David to fight for the house and said, yes, she'd overheard him argue with Sweet on the day Sweet died. But she was sure she "heard Mr. David leave a long time before Mr. Jameson got shot. Miss Rachel was in the house when that happened. Mr. David wasn't." That last statement was given short shrift. She went home sure that she'd put a noose around her own son's neck.

David didn't learn of Annie's ordeal until it was over, but Rachel was there when Peters took Annie away and she saw the old woman's sorry state when she came back. For the first time since the nightmare began, Rachel stepped forward to speak to reporters. With taunting, angry words, she denounced the way Annie had been treated and proclaimed David's innocence. When reporters asked Peters for a response, he dismissed Rachel's statement with a shrug. "A woman," he said, "is expected to stand by her man."

The scandal raged, and it spread beyond Harlem. White-owned publications with national circulation picked up the story; even the *New York Times* and one of the Washington papers expressed interest. As Mason Rugby, an influential white editor, put it:

"This is not just an everyday murder, in some filthy Harlem back alley. Here we have a top attorney in the national civil rights movement slain— not by white men, but by one of his own: another civil rights attorney, the rich scion of a Harlem success story. Jameson Sweet wasn't just any victim; David McKay isn't just any accused killer. They represent the *creme de la creme of cafe au lait* society—the hopes of the Negro people, the best that the black man can produce. Yet all they could do was try to kill each other. What does that say about the Movement? What does it tell white America about the so-called New Negro? I'll tell you what it says: It shows that them niggers can't blame us whites for all their problems, can they?"

The scandal divided not only Harlem, but the conservative black societies of Atlanta, Philadelphia, Chicago, and Washington, D.C. They were riveted and horrified. Everyone, it seemed, had an opinion. Not one fancy parlor—or funky pool hall for that matter—was free from debate.

Passionate syndicated columns for and against David ran side-by-side with confused reports that presented rumors as facts. The newspapers continued to quote Canfield heavily, and he was merciless. He had David tried and convicted before his first court date. For his part, David neither hid nor scurried. He let reporters see him. He gave quiet, lucid, concise statements. By the time he was to appear in the packed courtroom, he had attracted much sympathy, especially among women, but few believed him—male or female—when he maintained his innocence. As the time approached for jury selection, the very newspapers that had inflamed the public now expressed concern as to whether a panel free of prejudice could be found.

Nevin Caruthers, a superbly educated and privileged black man, offered to act as David's attorney. In his mid-fifties, Nevin was of short physical stature but immense presence. His salt-and-pepper hair was closely cropped and his mustache was copious but carefully groomed. His walk was robust and energetic. Behind his eyeglasses, his dark brown eyes reflected a gentle heart and perceptive intelligence.

"I was a friend of Lilian. I admired her work. Lord knows, she could be temperamental, but she was a talented woman. I won't see her brother go down without a fight."

District Attorney Jack Baker, a ruthless cross-examiner, formed the prosecution. He was hungry for a high-profile conviction that would bring him closer to his goal: the New York State governorship.

Nevin warned David that Baker would crucify him.

"This is not about whether you killed Jameson Sweet. This is about Philly. You've done what most every colored man at one time or another wishes he could do but would never admit to. You committed the unforgivable. And you got caught doing it."

"When the time comes, let me testify," David said. "Let me tell them why."

"Nobody gives a damn about why. They only care that you did. *You* are every white man's nightmare. Someone who looks like them, sounds like them, but isn't one of them. Someone who can pretend to be the Man Next Door. Character. It's all about character. The prosecution is going to do its best to paint you as a devil and Sweet as a saint."

"Canfield and the papers have already done a good job at that."

"We have to reverse those images. We'll remind them that you're a war hero. We'll bring in witnesses who'll testify to the compassionate work you've been doing in Philly. Friends, people you work with—"

"No, not that. I won't let you."

"But why not?"

"I won't have them involved. It's bad enough that they'll be mocked because I tricked them—"

"If they're your friends, they'll want to help."

"I can't ask them to."

"Maybe you can't, but I can."

"Don't do it."

Nevin leveled a steady gaze at his client. He saw despair and regret and something else, too. "David, are you afraid that none of the people you helped, that none of the friends you made, would stand by you if given the chance?"

"They're good people and they would. But I'm not going to ask them to."

Nevin shook his head, frustrated. "All right. We'll leave it alone for now. But we do need character witnesses. It's crucial. So you think about it."

He looked down at his notes, scribbled a comment, and sighed. "While we're on this difficult topic, we might as well broach another. Your best witness, you know, would be Rachel."

"No."

"I figured you'd say that."

"No one will believe her. She's my wife."

"She was present when you struggled with Sweet. She can speak to his suicidal intent. People will wonder why she doesn't testify on your behalf. Even if they're set against believing her, they'll want to hear her. Her appearance in court is crucial."

"I won't have her exposed like that."

Nevin rubbed his forehead and sighed. "David, I—"

"My answer's no. Now let's move on. I take it the second part of our strategy has to do with dressing down Sweet?"

Nevin looked at David and shook his head. He paused to re-arrange his thoughts, then went on. "If you don't want Rachel to testify, we have to find another way to convince the jury that Sweet chose to die. That means, we've got to provide a motive for suicide. A good, strong motive that'll compensate for the lack of physical evidence, like a note. To show motive, we've got to shore up your contention that Sweet killed Gem. Make them believe that he preferred to die rather than face a humiliating trial. The fact that the prosecution will put Sweet on a pedestal could then work in our favor. Sweet was a man with a lot to lose.

Many proud men in his position have taken the same way out."

39. On Trial for Stealing Honey

Gray skies heavy with rain clouds darkened lower Manhattan on the opening day of the trial. A loud, angry crowd assembled before the courthouse. Authorities decided to bring David into the building through a side entrance. They posted twenty policemen in front of the courthouse and sent another ten inside to guard the courtroom.

With a blow of his gavel, Judge Sylvan Richter called the session to order, and District Attorney Baker took center stage. A skeletal man with parchment-colored skin and raven-black hair, Baker had small, marble-like eyes that seemed curiously dead behind round, rimless spectacles. He launched his case by calling Dr. Hubert Thatcher to the witness stand. Thatcher was broad and squat, with bulbous eyes and pencil-thin lips. His nose was so flat that it barely rose from his face and his nostrils were merely horizontal slits. With his pale, waxy skin, oddly tinged green, he resembled a large toad struggling for dignity in a tight black suit.

Thatcher began by testifying as to the time of death. His first statement was not a matter for contention; his next one was.

"I can say without doubt that the blood and human tissue found on David McKay's right hand and coat collar belonged to the victim, Jameson Sweet."

"Did you conduct a laboratory analysis?" asked Nevin in cross-examination.

"I didn't need to," said Thatcher. "Everybody can tell a Negro's blood just by looking at it."

Nevin checked a smile of satisfaction and glanced at Baker. A look of irritation flashed across the D.A.'s face. His first expert witness had just revealed himself to be both a racist and a sloppy technician, the second quality being by far the worst.

Nevin turned back to Thatcher.

"Could David McKay have picked up the blood and tissue through contact with another person at the death scene?"

David's breath caught. How could Nevin do this, when he'd pleaded with him not to involve Rachel?

Thatcher's eyes shot over to Baker hoping for a hint as to how to answer. Finding none, he looked back at Nevin. A thin layer of sweat enhanced the waxy sheen of his forehead. "I suppose it's possible. But I, uh ... I find it highly unlikely."

"But it *is* possible?"

Thatcher hesitated. "Yes, it's possible."

Thatcher was dismissed. Baker then sought to demonstrate that David was the last person to see Sweet alive. He called a reluctant Annie to the stand. Since she was a hostile witness, he was given leeway in questioning her. She answered with brief sentences and her eyes never left David. An expression of relief crossed her face when Baker sat down and Nevin rose to cross-examine her. He gave her a chance to emphasize that she was sure, "Mr. David was outta the house when it happened." But on re-direct, Baker asked her whether she'd actually seen David leave and she had to admit that she hadn't.

Next came Byron Canfield. He told his story with devastating simplicity. David was forced to listen to an amalgam of circumstantial evidence that maligned and misrepresented him.

To back up Canfield's testimony, Baker summoned Frank Nyman, the white private detective Sweet had hired. David took one look at Nyman and sensed danger. Nyman was the kind of witness who could do damage. He was small, wiry, and scruffy. He was poor and made no attempt to hide it. He had chosen to wear a shapeless black suit and dusty shoes. His tie was crooked and his shirt none too clean. His hair was unkempt and a shock of it, black mixed with gray, fell over his narrow, lined face. His heavy-lidded eyes were as black as pitch. His lower lip was full and fleshy, and his upper lip, thin and cruel. He was indisputably ugly and more than slightly seedy, but David saw at once that none of that mattered. None of it made a damn bit of difference because Nyman was also utterly charming. In fact, his ugliness made his charm all the more disturbing. It allowed him to sneak up on you, to take you unawares. Humor flashed in his eyes, wisdom rested in the corners of his lips, and an easygoing lassitude rode his shoulders every time he shrugged. Despite his rough, uncouth manner, or perhaps because of it, he was entirely credible. He knew exactly what was expected of him and he delivered. He seduced the members of the jury and they never knew what hit them.

As David listened to Nyman testify, his heart sank. Nyman's comments, though succinct, were colorful. With a few vague words and several fairly explicit gestures, he implied much while saying little. *An out-and-out con man's trick,* David thought, *but the judge and jury bought it.*

At one point, Nyman hinted that there was much he could tell about David's "relations with white females," but he would prefer not to "out of respect for the ladies present."

Nevin objected. This testimony had nothing to do with the murder charge, he said. Baker countered that the testimony was directly relevant since it elaborated on the personality of the accused. Richter found for the prosecution. He not only approved further testimony along the same lines but ordered Nyman to "give details." First, however, he said, the courtroom would have to be cleared of women and children. There was a flurry of movement; the courtroom doors opened and closed behind little feet and straight skirts. Then Richter told Nyman to continue. The private detective obliged with a graphic description of how David had "preyed on innocent white women who had no idea they were being seduced by a Negro."

There was a hush in the courtroom, then a murmur, then an angry hum. David thought of bees when they discover an intruder who's trying to steal some of their honey.

Richter banged for silence. Again, Nevin moved to have Nyman's lascivious descriptions stricken from the record, and again Baker objected. Richter denied Nevin's motion to suppress, and whites in the all-male courtroom erupted in vigorous applause.

"My God, Nyman's destroying me," David whispered to Nevin.

He patted David's hand. "Don't worry. The prosecutor's entitled to a few good moments."

David shot Nevin a troubled look. "Let's just make sure he doesn't have too many of them, shall we?"

Nevin gave David a reassuring smile. "I got some good news this morning that'll give this case a whole new complexion." He chuckled at David's expression and patted his hand.

Despite his outer calm, Nevin knew that David's concern was justified. Nyman had been convincing. It was time for damage control. For more than an hour, he cross-examined the private detective, trying to get him to admit that much of his report was regurgitated hearsay. He did get Nyman to concede that some of it was based on secondhand gossip, but Nyman wouldn't budge about the core of his report: David McKay's pretense of being white was a well-documented fact.

"There's no end to the proof," Nyman said.

He'd collected Philadelphia newspaper reports on David's cases and statements from white friends and colleagues who were shocked at the mere suggestion that the man they knew might be black.

Nevin thought it wiser to stipulate that David had indeed lived as a white man in Philadelphia—arguing against a given fact would simply decrease David's credibility—but he asked the jury to remember: "This does not constitute proof that he killed Jameson Sweet."

David's guilt seemed to be a given, however, for the city at large. Front-page speculation, innuendo, and rumor continued to characterize news coverage of the trial. Someone in the D.A.'s office leaked a copy of Nyman's provocative report to the press. Many newspapers thought Nyman's direct testimony too offensive to quote extensively, but they reprinted his written report in full. Once again, as the trial went into its second day, officers posted outside had to stand off a mob.

Baker called Peters to testify about the crime scene itself, to tell what he saw when he entered the McKay parlor that day. Peters delivered his statement in a dry tone that contrasted vividly with the gruesome details he conveyed. Baker asked Peters how he had come to arrest David McKay. Peters looked David straight in the face and said: "The defendant admitted to knowing that Sweet had the goods on him, but he only gave himself up when he knew his wife would have to take the fall."

Not only the whites but also the black viewers in the courtroom shook their heads.

Baker had Peters describe Sweet's fatal wound, but he noticeably failed to ask about any gunpowder residue on the hands of the accused or fingerprints that might've been found on the murder weapon. Nevin asked, though, in cross-examination, "Whose fingerprints were lifted from the gun?"

Peters licked his lips and joggled one knee. This was a question he would've preferred not to answer.

"Detective?" prompted Nevin.

Peters cleared his throat. "There were two sets of prints. One belonging to the victim; one belonging to the defendant's wife."

"Are you telling me that the defendant's prints weren't found on the gun at all?"

"No, they weren't."

"A little louder, please. It's only fair if those people in the back rows can also hear you."

"No," said Peters a bit louder, in a faintly squeaky tone. "David McKay's fingerprints were not found on the gun."

There was an instant of heated murmuring before Richter stopped it with a bang of his gavel. Baker began his redirect.

"If David's prints weren't on the gun," he asked Peters, "then why did you arrest him?"

"Because he was on the scene; he had the best motive and, of course, the best opportunity."

"Once more, Detective: Was this the typical wound of a suicide?"

"No," said Peters with renewed confidence. "I've never known a suicide to shoot himself in the cheek. It's usually the temple. Almost always, the temple."

Late that afternoon, Nevin began to present his case. Nella had offered to testify as a character witness in David's defense.

"I'm going to let her," Nevin said. "She's a prominent person."

David had his doubts. "Nella's not just prominent. She's white and she's a woman. What all-white male jury will heed a white woman defending a colored man? Do you think they'll listen, especially after what Nyman said about me? She means well, but her testimony could do more harm than good."

Nevin conceded the danger, but said: "We need her. She's not just the best witness we've got. She's nearly the only one."

Nella took the witness stand and surprised David and his attorney with a blithe lie. "David McKay generously offered me his biography some time ago to use in my next book. He wouldn't have killed Sweet to conceal his life story—he'd planned to have it published anyway."

"Did you know she was going to say that?" David whispered to Nevin.

"No."

As Nella stepped down, Nevin whispered miserably to David, "She tried."

David smiled gratefully, fleetingly at Nella as she switched past. She bent to give him an encouraging tap on the elbow. He did not agree with her having lied, but he was touched by her effort to help him.

"You didn't have to."

"Of course I did. I owe you. Thanks to you, my book's going to be a bestseller."

40. LIES AND WHISPERS

Annie decided to stay home the next day. The arthritis in her knees was sometimes so painful, she had to bite her lip to keep from crying out. It was especially bad when she first eased out of bed in the morning. On rainy days, she could barely walk. David knew nothing of her condition. She had never told him and never intended to, partly because she feared that he would retire her, but mostly because she felt he had enough troubles to deal with. Relaxing on the window seat in the parlor, she thought once more of that passage she had seen marked in his Bible.

He's tried so hard to make good, Lord. Won't you help him?

She wanted to help him, too, but she didn't know how.

Show me ... please.

The doorbell rang. Annie jumped at the sudden sound. The bell rang again. Parting the curtain, she peeked out the window with a suspicious eye. Since David's arrest, strange people had been stopping by the house, some threatening to put a curse on the family—*what's left of it,* she thought grimly—others offering to help with spells, voodoo, witchcraft, and such. *I don't hold with none of that stuff.*

A boy of about thirteen or fourteen stood at the front door. He wore a brown cap and blue jacket and was holding an envelope. He looked harmless enough. As the bell rang again, she stood uneasily and went to the vestibule. She hesitated, looking at the door, still undecided. Finally, she answered it, her mind set to give the stranger a good tongue-lashing. Before she could say anything, the boy politely whipped off his hat and spoke. He had a message from the Renaissance Pharmacy. He thrust the envelope into her hand, then stood nervously fingering his cap, obviously hoping for a tip. She found a nickel in her apron pocket and gave it to him.

After he left, she stood in the vestibule, studying the envelope's contents. She couldn't read all that fast and many of the words were unfamiliar, but she understood the gist of it. Her face lightened with interest, then darkened with puzzlement. When she was done, she stood quite still for a minute. *Thank you, Lord,* she whispered, then hurried to her room and fetched her coat.

In court that afternoon, Nevin called Adrian Snyder to the stand. David looked at Nevin, surprised.

"You're calling *him* as a character witness?"

Nevin patted David on the shoulder. "Have faith."

David held his head high but inwardly battled despair. His star character witnesses were living scandals: a suspected crime figure and a white woman known for socializing with blacks. Leaning into his hand, David rubbed his forehead wearily. He sensed waves of hostility and contempt flowing from Canfield. The aristocratic old lawyer had pointedly placed himself in the first seat directly behind the prosecutor. David resolved to ignore Canfield. His ears picked up the melody of a Negro spiritual, sung softly in the courtroom behind him. He glanced over his shoulder. Annie sat four rows behind him. She must have just arrived. She hadn't been there earlier. And sitting next to her—his eyes widened—was Toby's mother. She gave him the thumbs-up sign. His heart lifted. He looked back at Annie. She gave him a smile. It was sweet, sudden, and oddly dazzling. It warmed him. He glanced at Rachel. She sat in the first row, slightly to one side of him, so she could see his face easily. She smiled at him, too, but he saw fear in the tightness around her eyes. He returned her smile, and then returned his attention to the theatrics of his trial.

Nevin took Snyder through a brief description of his courtship of Gem, and Gem's decision to end their relationship. Baker objected.

"This testimony is irrelevant."

"Your Honor, the relevance will become clear," said Nevin. "I'm trying to lay the foundation for causal evidence."

Richter looked from Nevin's mahogany-brown face to Baker's alabaster-white one. Then he brought down his gavel, sustained Baker's motion, and brusquely ordered Nevin to move on. A frustrated Nevin was forced to dismiss Snyder. He called his next witness.

"Homicide Detective Bill Rogers."

A short, portly white man in his late forties waddled to the stand, identified himself, and took the oath. He worked in Amagansett, he said.

"Now is it true that you were summoned to Harding House last night?" asked Nevin.

Rogers nodded.

"Please tell us what you found."

"Mr. Snyder there and some of his men said they'd gone fishing on the Hardings' estate. They reported finding a skeleton, and sure enough, they had—mired in the waters off the Hardings' private dock."

A wave of gasps and whispers rolled across the courtroom. Richter banged his gavel. He beckoned to Nevin and Baker. Richter, a broad-faced man with rolls of fat under his chin, scowled down angrily at both men.

"Just what the hell is going on here?" He looked at Baker. "Did you know about this?"

"No, Your Honor."

"Baker, the report is on your desk," said Nevin hurriedly. "We couldn't get it to you sooner. We only learned about it ourselves this morning."

Richter glared at Nevin, then asked, "What does this have to do with the case at hand?"

"Everything," said Nevin. "Jameson Sweet's death was simply the culmination of a series of murderous events that began with the victim found yesterday."

Richter looked down at Baker. "You going to object?"

Baker looked worried, but shook his head. "No, Your Honor, but I reserve my right to do so."

"All right. Get on with it."

Nevin turned back to Rogers. "Can you describe the remains?"

"The skeleton had been in the water for some time, probably a year. It was a woman, not too old, not too young."

A wave of murmurs stirred the courtroom.

"Colored or white?"

"Can't say."

"How'd she end up in the water?"

"Put there."

"Didn't fall in?"

"She was bound and weighted down. Probably dead before she hit the water. Looks like the bullet we pulled from her sternum's gonna match the bullet we took out of Jameson Sweet—"

Baker jumped to his feet. "Objection, Your Honor. Testimony is irrelevant. I move to have it stricken from the record."

Nevin went to Richter, his arms raised. "Please, Your Honor. This man's testimony substantiates my client's claim. It will show that Gem McKay murdered her sister, Lilian, then took her place—only to be killed by Jameson Sweet, who committed suicide when faced with his crime."

Richter turned to Rogers. "Is there any way to identify this woman?"

"Not definitely."

"Any way to prove that she was Lilian McKay Sweet?"

"Not likely."

Richter banged his gavel. "Objection sustained."

"But Your Honor—" cried Nevin.

"Objection sustained!"

Nevin gritted his teeth. *That was our trump card,* thought David. *That was it.* Behind him, Annie sang softly. David closed his eyes. He had never been so tired in his life. Nevin dismissed Rogers.

"We're not finished yet," he whispered to David.

"Let me testify."

"No."

"Please—"

Nevin ignored him. He straightened up and in a ringing voice, said: "In as much as neither my learned opponent, the prosecutor, nor anyone else can prove what happened in the McKay parlor that day, I move for a dismissal of the charges against David McKay, based on lack of evidence."

Richter raised his bushy eyebrows in disbelief. With a great sweeping motion, he raised his gavel high, as though it were the hammer of Thor, and brought it down swiftly with a thunderous blow. "Motion denied!"

Nevin pressed his lips together and bit back a response.

The court took a ten-minute break. Rachel hurried to get to David's side, but he was swept out of the courtroom before she could reach him. A phalanx of guards surrounded him to keep the reporters at bay. She tried to press her way through the jostling crowd, but was pushed back.

Annie was waiting for David in the crowded hallway. She waved frantically from the edge of the crowd, trying to catch his eye. He was almost past when one of those odd momentary partings in the crowd allowed him to catch sight of her. He sent a guard to bring her to him.

"I gotta talk to you," she whispered.

Out of breath from the effort to get through the crowd, she stumbled and nearly fell. David grabbed her under one elbow. Nevin showed them to a private room with guards posted outside, then started out. Rachel emerged from the courtroom just in time to catch a glimpse of Annie and David, their heads bent together, before Nevin closed the door behind him.

The moment they were alone, Annie told David about the envelope. It contained a note from the druggist, and something else, too: a report. She handed him a sheet of paper.

"They said they made a mistake. They got your medicine mixed up with somebody's else's. But this here"—she tapped the paper—"this here's the report they shoulda given you."

David looked at her with anxious eyes, then at the paper she'd pressed into his hand.

"A homemade mixture expertly made," it said. *"Can be used to treat bad nerves, but overuse will cause tremors, blurred vision, fatigue, headaches, and loss of balance. Hallucinations, anxiety, a pounding heartbeat, stroke and death."*

He felt for the chair behind him and sat down heavily. Finally, but finally, he had the proof he'd sought. But at what price? He recalled his relief at the mistaken findings. Now this! He'd had his suspicions, of course. He'd felt that something was off all along. But he had hoped and prayed that he was wrong. Dead wrong—

There was a knock on the door. Nevin came in.

"It's time to go back in."

David nodded. He pushed himself up and stood unsteadily. His olive complexion was ashen and his hands shook. He folded the sheet of paper clumsily and shoved it into his inner breast pocket. A look of concern came over Nevin's benign, round face.

"C'mon," he said and rushed them back to the courtroom.

Nevin called a forensics expert to counter the state's testimony about the wound that killed Sweet. The witness, Harold Schmuck, a sallow, dry little stick of a man, was obviously proud of his expertise. He took great pains to answer each question in excruciating detail. He multiplied words impressively but ineffectively. He was a bore and painful to listen to. David saw that the jury had not only lost interest but was becoming hostile. Why was Nevin keeping the man on the witness stand? It was obvious to those few people who were listening that Schmuck refused to take sides. Given the nature of Sweet's injury, he said, it was open to fair interpretation whether the wound was self-inflicted or not.

"The bullet entered the victim's right cheek at a forty-five degree angle, producing an ovoid entrance. The barrel of the gun was held directly to the victim's skin. There was some searing and blackening of the skin at the lower edge of the wound. There were also particles of soot and unburned powder in the wound track itself. However, as I said, that was only on the lower part of the wound. The upper external wound area was characterized by a radiating pattern of soot. This was the direct result of soot and gas having moved outward from that point where the barrel did not actually touch the skin."

"So what does this tell you?" Nevin said.

"That while the gun was held firmly against the victim's head, it was held held at a fairly low angle, with the gun pointing upward."

"Would you say that the victim shot himself or that another shot him?"

"It could have been either way. If it was another, however, the person was no more than five-feet-five inches tall. It would have been difficult for someone taller to have shot the victim at that proximity and from that low an angle."

David heard that and felt that another nail had been slammed into her coffin. He wondered if Nevin had caught the significance of Schmuck's testimony. He didn't seem to have. He was proceeding along with the testimony.

David glanced at the jurors. Their faces were blank with boredom. None of them had registered the meaning of Schmuck's words, either.

Then again, why should they? For them, Schmuck's argument weighed like a well-balanced scale that tipped sometimes this way, sometimes that. *Unfortunately,* thought David, *the decisive weight tipped the scales most certainly against him.* As Nevin had told him privately, "The problem for us is that Sweet left no physical sign, no proof, not even a hint that he intended to do away with himself. He neither said anything to anyone nor left a note to clearly demonstrate pre-meditated suicide. And accidental suicide would be equally hard to prove. What we need," concluded Nevin, "is paper evidence."

David closed his eyes. The pathologist droned on, his statements punctuated by Nevin's brief, precise questions. David only half-listened. His head ached. He thought of the druggist report in his pocket. *Here's your paper evidence, Nevin—here it is.* He felt nauseated.

Annie and Nella had given him the answer. Right at the beginning, they had told him what to look for. Annie had described how Sweet told Gem that he could never love "someone like her." And Nella had told him that Sweet liked dark women. That should've told him immediately that Sweet's words to Gem meant that he could never love someone light-skinned. And when he met Sweet himself, he had sensed immediately that Sweet would want a woman with street smarts, a fighter.

There had been so many signs, but he'd refused to heed them. He hadn't wanted to. The direction in which they were leading him was too painful to follow. He had chosen to look away. And that first erroneous druggist report had helped him do it. It had reassured him. But this one—there was no mistaking the meaning of this one. *A homemade mixture—so well made it must have been done by an expert.*

A fighter. An expert. A killer less than five-feet-five inches tall.

His thoughts went back to the parlor that day. He had seen the gun in Sweet's right hand and suspected it for what it was. He'd flashed on seeing Sweet sign documents with his left hand, smoke with his left hand and known the gun's placement to be false.

And yet he had moved to protect her. Why? Was it because he wanted to believe that she had done it to protect him? Why else would she have pulled the trigger? Why else?

Sitting behind him, Rachel was tense. She had caught the significance of Schmuck's comment all right and she was wondering if David had, too. She was also more than a little worried about what she'd seen out in the hallway, that glimpse of David and Annie with their heads bent together. What did it mean? Did it mean anything? He'd barely glanced at her since returning to the courtroom. Something was wrong. Was her luck running out? No ... it couldn't be. Not when it had held out this long.

She thought of Sweet, of that last wretched conversation with him, and again saw him dead on the floor. She hadn't wanted it to end that way. She could say with all honesty that she'd tried every trick in the book to dissuade him from his plan. Nothing had worked.

He'd been upset. Had wanted to clear out, and had wanted her to go with him. Naturally, she'd refused.

"Don't be silly. It's worked out perfectly well. We both got what we wanted."

"Got what *we* wanted? I didn't get what I wanted—I wanted you! Who do you think I did it for? For you, woman! You, not me! It was you who wanted the big house, the fancy clothes. And not just any house. It had to be the McKay house, the McKay money."

"You love money as much as I do. And you hate the McKays as much as I do. You've always hated dicties."

"But my hate didn't drive me out of my mind. My love for you did that. Damn it! I risked everything for you. I killed for you." He shook his big fists at her. "How could you choose that yellow nigger over me? How could you? And after what he did to you?"

Her sweet face screwed up with contempt and though she was the shorter one, she managed to give the impression of looking down on him.

"Don't you understand?" she hissed. "David is the one I want, the one I have *always* wanted. How could you have ever thought I loved you?"

Sweet's face twisted bitterly. "Woman, don't do this to me."

"You disgust me, 'cause you're no better than me! But you don't know it. Darkies like us—the world is never gonna let us amount to anything. We can't do nothing for each other but bring each other down. We need to marry up to survive. You with your obstinate pride, your talk of Negro dignity—you're a fool. A stubborn, stupid fool. I could never let myself love a man like you. Now go away. Build yourself another life while you have the chance."

"What chance? He knows. Don't you understand? He *knows.*"

"He doesn't know. He suspects. And he only suspects you—not me."

"Rachel." Sweet's chest heaved. "We go together or not at all. Either you come with me or I tell everything."

"You would do that to me?"

"I'd have to."

She was quiet a moment, then said, "I see." She turned away. She could hear him breathing heavily behind her, waiting for her decision. Her shoulders sagged and she seemed to deflate. All the fight appeared to leave her, like hot air seeping from a balloon.

"All right," she said in a listless tone. "When do you want to go?"

"Right now."

She was standing at the writing table. Her large purse lay on top of it. She went into it and took out her compact. While she dabbed her nose, she watched him in the mirror and noted how far away he stood. "Won't I have time to pack?"

"No."

She went back into her bag, dropped the compact, and found the other item she wanted. It had taken her an hour that morning to find where Gem had hidden it in Lilian's bedroom. She had started looking the moment David left to see Nella. *Time well spent.* She felt Sweet come up behind her and left her hand hidden within her purse. He gripped her shoulders.

"It's better this way," he whispered. "You wouldn't have been happy here. With him."

"No, perhaps not." She turned to face him, her right hand dropping deftly behind her back.

"We belong together," he said. "We're two of a kind, you see."

He took her in his arms and she raised her face for him to kiss. He closed his eyes and she, at the last moment, pulled away—just before she put the gun to his cheek, and fired. For a split second, he looked surprised, then all expression was gone. She sagged to her knees at his side. She'd just curled his fingers around the handle of the gun when David appeared.

Lies and whispers. Whispers and lies. Where would we be without them? Was that a line from a song she'd heard? If it wasn't, it should be.

Sitting in court, she stared at David's profile. How many more days would she have to drag herself to this damn courtroom? She was sick of the reporters, the neighbors; sick of having to play the loyal wife; of having to visit her "beloved" in that stinking jail. When would this stupid trial end?

Her eyes went to the jury members, two rows of pale strangers: They had the power to convict David, to put the period at the end of his sentence. She smiled grimly. Only once the jury spoke, could her life—the life she dreamed of—go on.

41. A VERY PUBLIC FLOGGING

The trial ground onward with grim inevitability. Nevin took stock of the situation. There seemed to be no way to prove that Sweet had killed himself. He had tried to introduce evidence that Sweet's death was the brutal end to a chain of homicidal events, but the strategy had backfired. Baker had objected to the introduction of the allegation, and Richter had bent over backward to oblige. The judge had ruled out any testimony that extended beyond the immediate murder of Jameson Sweet, yet in effect had given Baker leeway to use the allegation to bolster his own case. David's belief that Sweet killed Gem, Baker said, provided David with an additional motive to commit murder.

David, too, had done his share in tying Nevin's hands, with his adamant refusal to let Rachel testify or seek help from his friends in Philadelphia. As a result, Sweet's reputation remained pristine; David's was ruined. The hundreds of backbreaking hours he had logged in Philadelphia were dismissed; the lives he had salvaged forgotten.

Nevin now turned to David and said in a fierce whisper, "All right. We play it your way. You get to testify. But remember: If you say one wrong word—just one—you're dead. Those good citizens on that jury will lynch you. And they'll do it legally. They'll fry your ass in the electric chair at Sing Sing. A flick of the switch and you'll be as dead as a nigger hanging from a southern tree."

David rose slowly. He straightened his tie and walked forward. Climbing the steps into the witness stand, he placed one hand on the Bible offered him and swore to tell the truth, the whole truth, and nothing but the truth.

Nevin led David through a formal restatement of his innocence and a description of his confrontation with Sweet, and then paused dramatically.

"Your Honor, members of the jury, and honored guests, because the claims against my client hinge on his alleged motivation, I think it would be appropriate to hear my client himself speak to this matter." Nevin turned to the prosecutor.

"Does my learned colleague concur?"

Baker nodded. "No objections."

Nevin turned back to David. "You're up to bat now," he whispered. "Don't strike out."

David looked out over the courtroom. He was intensely aware of Rachel. And of Canfield. The influential lawyer resembled an eagle waiting to pounce. David decided to look beyond them to Annie and Toby's mother. To Nella and Snyder. And Roy, crowded into a seat in the back. David took in all the faces of those present, the faces of poor people, people educated not by books but by hard knocks. It was these people, as much as the white jury, who would decide his future. Even if he convinced the jury, but failed to sway the folk, he was doomed. For himself, he was unconcerned. But his parents deserved better. They had worked hard to make something of themselves and the family name. His friends and all those who had written to him in jail or otherwise extended their support—they too deserved better. Holding his head high, he began.

"When I left Harlem four years ago, I never intended to be gone long. I thought the job would take a week, two at most. But my life was about to change. I just didn't know it."

Every soul in the courtroom hushed. They had been waiting for this. Most of the black onlookers were southern. David's words evoked pictures they had hoped to forget. As he touched the crucible of his tale, they listened uneasily.

"After the lynching and the beating, I drifted ... just wandered for weeks after leaving that hospital. I don't even remember arriving in Philadelphia. One day, I met a woman. Her son was in jail. I offered to defend him. She took me for white. I started to correct her, then thought better of it. Her mistaken belief increased her sense of hope. Why take that away?

"Well, I won that case and more came to see me. That's how it all began. I did not decide to pass for white. I did decide to let people see what they wanted to see."

David turned to the jury. Some of the men looked away; others frankly met his gaze—with varying degrees of interest, sympathy, belligerence, and accusation.

"I lived as Daniel Kincaid. No one but Lilian knew where I was. I explained the name change as a discretion that was necessary for my work. I think that as time went by, she began to suspect what was happening. But she never once criticized or denounced me.

"I started a law practice, representing poor colored who couldn't afford good lawyers, who thought they were getting a sympathetic 'white' attorney. I thought about revealing the truth. I came close once or twice, but hesitated: What purpose would this particular truth serve? It would destroy my effectiveness as an attorney—and thereby allow others to question the moral and legal validity of every court decision I had won. It would not only endanger my former clients, but end my ability to help future ones. And so I kept mum.

"I helped a lot of my people. I know I did. But the gratitude in their eyes was a dagger in my soul. I had confirmed their belief in the white man's power, for better or for worse. If they had won their cases or gotten good sentences with the help of an obviously colored attorney, their faith in a Negro's ability to determine his own fate would've been strengthened. I had robbed them of that. I cheated them. It was subtle, but it was there. And it was wrong.

"Most of all I harmed myself. I thought my decision would set me free, but I just exchanged one burden for another. I wanted to walk without fear, but I was never more afraid in my life. I thought I could finally be me, but that's exactly who I *couldn't* be. I wanted to be free, but I had to repress the best part of me. I wanted to be seen as an individual, not as a racial symbol. But when my clients looked at me, that's all they *did* see—a symbol of benevolent white domination."

He paused and gathered his thoughts.

"I'm not proud of what I did. But I must add that I don't fully regret it either. I don't regret having wrenched back some of the authority that's been bullwhipped from the Negro in this country. I certainly don't regret having used it to relieve my people's pain. For once, the color prejudice of the legal system worked to the black man's favor."

David extended his gaze to encompass the courtroom. There was shame, sympathy, anger, frustration, and bewilderment in the brown faces he saw. He thought he detected, hoped he detected, expressions of support, too. Perhaps not all of them agreed with what he'd done; but every single one of them had to understand why he'd done it.

"I'm accused of having killed Jameson Sweet because he threatened to unveil me, to shame me before the world. I admit he repelled me. This man tortured my sisters, plotted to murder one, and ended up murdering the other. That I couldn't forgive. But when he said he had discovered my secret, I felt grateful. He had freed me from a burden I was tired of carrying. I needed Jameson Sweet to live. So no, I didn't kill him. I have never knowingly been destructive toward anyone. No one but myself."

The courtroom was still and it was a silence no one dared break. In that profound silence, David hoped that his words had penetrated the hearts of his listeners.

Eventually, someone coughed. The rough sound, though slight, broke the spell. The onlookers stirred; they began to murmur among themselves. Richter banged his gavel and recessed the trial until the next day.

David returned to his single jail cell uncertain as to whether the truth had significantly helped his case, but deeply relieved at having told it. He looked forward to a restful sleep that night, but Rachel's spirit kept him awake.

He'd confronted her the evening before. He didn't know what reaction he'd expected, but it was not the one he received: She'd laughed and her pretty mouth had curled with spite.

"If you're waiting to hear me say I'm sorry, you'll be waiting a long, long time."

Her green eyes were as incandescent as gems and just as hard. Had he only imagined that less than one month ago, they had shone with love for him?

"Our wedding night. The love we shared. The vows we made. They meant nothing?"

She gave him a pitying look. "You should know better than to ask. Lies and whispers. Whispers and lies. Where would we be without them?"

Nevin turned to Baker: "Your witness."

The district attorney rose. He leaned forward, planted both fists on his desk, and nailed David with an unblinking stare.

"Thank you for yesterday's exciting narrative. We were all caught up in your tale of woe. Now let's clarify a few points."

The jury turned to David.

"Mr. Kincaid or Mr. David—which do you prefer?"

"It doesn't matter."

"Doesn't it? In this courtroom, we're inclined to take a serious view of aliases. However ..." His attitude suggested that he would be generous and let the point slide. With a long finger, he checked his notes, then looked up. "Mr. David, it would appear that when those men in Georgia approached you, you lied about being a Negro?"

"They would've killed me if I'd—"

"You lied, did you not? A yes or no will do."

"Yes."

"Thank you. And when they asked if you knew their victim, a man who had befriended you, you lied then too?"

"Yes."

"And later, in setting up your Philadelphia law practice, when identifying yourself to the authorities, you also lied?"

David hesitated. "I didn't fully tell the truth."

Baker's tone hardened. "You knew that everyone believed you to be white and treated you as white. You permitted, if not outright encouraged, that belief?"

David took a deep breath, knowing that he was about to hand himself over to his enemies. "I did nothing to correct it. No."

That admission was all Baker needed. A master at verbal savagery, he scourged David with ridicule, contempt, and innuendo. He twisted David's words and interrupted his answers. He took obvious pride in putting him to the verbal lash. David took the flogging with dignity. He gritted his teeth and bore it, but that only incited Baker to more. Nevin tried several times to object, but David signaled him to sit down. He would not cringe or dodge or deny, but gradually, despite his determination, his strength left him. The merciless brutality of the questions—the inflexible manner in which he was allowed to answer—all wore him down. Like a bullwhip, the questions came faster, fell harder, cut deeper, and dealt a sharper sting. He was virtually being flayed alive. His admissions, like blood, began to pour from him.

"So in effect you lied to the courts?"

"Yes."

"Lied to your clients?"

"Yes."

"Lied to your colleagues and friends?"

"Yes! Yes!"

"And once back here, when asked what you've been doing, you said—"

"I said nothing—"

"You let people believe you've been working for the Movement, but this too was a lie?"

"Yes, a lie."

"And isn't it true that you would be back in Philadelphia if it weren't for your marriage? Wouldn't you still be deceiving? Concealing? Living your lies?"

"I would be living—another life. Yes."

Baker moved in for the kill. "The fact is, Mr. David, you've lied to your family and friends, to your clients and colleagues, day after day, month after month, year after year—*for four years.* Do you know what the truth *is* anymore? Do you even *care?*"

David gripped the railing of the witness stand. "I give you my word. I didn't kill—"

Baker slammed his fist down. "Why should we believe you? Why should we trust you? Why, when it seems that you do nothing but lie?" He looked at the judge. "No more questions, Your Honor. We are finished with this *witness.*"

Nevin stood. "Redirect, Your Honor?"

Richter nodded.

Nevin leaned on his desk—the onlookers leaned forward in their seats. With a sonorous voice, Nevin intoned: "This then is the truth: That you accused Jameson Sweet of having killed your sister; that he said to you: 'I will not let you send me to prison. I'd rather die first,' that you left him alive, and when you returned he was dead?"

"That's what happened. That is the truth."

"On your oath before God?"

"On my oath before God."

"Thank you."

Nevin sat down heavily. His kind face was grave. The cross-examination had been damaging. There was no doubt about it. The judge dismissed David with a curt nod. David stood stiffly. The stares of the jury seemed to burn into his back as he walked to his seat.

"You did well," Nevin told him. "You did fine."

42. WAS IT COWARDICE OR COURAGE?

Baker's summation was delivered with consummate skill. He reminded the jury that it was the defense that had introduced the possibility of a second powerful motive, "David's obsessive belief that Sweet killed his sister," and that it was a Negro civil rights official who had brought police attention to the racial aspects of the case. David McKay's own people saw him as a traitor to the Negro race and a shame to humanity, Baker said. In bringing in a verdict of guilty, members of the all-white jury need not fear accusations of racism. They need not be concerned with allegations that David lacked a fair trial. Nor would the fine city of New York suffer claims "against its reputation as a place of refuge for the honest and hardworking, no matter what their shade or hue." None of these matters need concern the jury. What the jury did need to consider was the calculated cruelty of the crime and the deceitful personality of the defendant.

"Through his words and deeds, David McKay has shown himself to be an opportunist, a chameleon who changes colors the way others change clothes. He lies and thinks nothing of it. He abandons his family and thinks nothing of it. He sees a good friend burned to death, stands by, and does nothing about it. Would such a man stop at murder? I think not.

"David McKay is a spoiled Negro. A spoiled Negro? Two terms some would say are mutually exclusive. But there it is. He had more than any decent Negro could hope for; yet he wasn't satisfied. Cowardice, greed— would a man with such qualities stop at murder? I think not.

"Jameson Sweet, on the other hand, was a hardworking man, a good example to Negroes everywhere. He overcame daunting disadvantages to become an attorney. He was a giving man, a brave man, dedicated to making life better for his people. He was a loving husband who patiently nursed his ailing wife— only to be cut down by her self-serving brother."

Baker leaned on the rail separating him from the jury. He looked each member of the panel in the eye, taking his time. His normally stern visage was softened by the hint of a sad smile.

"It's up to you," he said. "You have the power to make David McKay pay." He raised his fist and brought it down on the railing in an intense, silent blow. The touch of compassion in his expression was gone, replaced by one of hate. "Make him pay! *Make him pay! MAKE HIM PAY!*"

Nevin paced slowly, thoughtfully, back and forth before the jury box. An impressive figure and a gifted speaker, he had inherited his father's eloquence as a Baptist preacher. Nevin knew exactly what he wanted to say. His slow pacing was meant to give the jury members time to recover from the dark emotions stirred by Baker's speech. Every trial attorney knows that the fight for the jury's vote entails a battle for its heart as well as its mind, the first often superseding the other. When Nevin sensed that the jury members had settled down, had focused on him, he began.

He opened by thanking them for their time and patience, and he expressed confidence that they would reach a fair and well-considered verdict. As he moved to the core of the matter, his tone was conversational, reasonable, and quietly but intensely passionate.

"Evidence," he said. *"Evidence.* That is the *crux* of the matter. Remember: In this country, a man is innocent until proven guilty. Proven by *evidence.* Only two sets of fingerprints were found on the gun that killed Jameson Sweet. Did either of them belong to David McKay? No, they did not. Did one of them belong to Jameson Sweet? Yes, they did.

"I repeat: *Evidence.* Look to the evidence. But how can we? There is *no* evidence that David McKay shot Jameson Sweet. There is, however, evidence that Jameson Sweet shot himself."

Nevin's voice took on the rolling cadence of the pulpit preacher. His walk became more vigorous as he strode the span of the jury box. He was no ordinary attorney; he was a craftsman. His soaring, vital voice drove on. Steadily and precisely, he depicted the fallacies of the state's case.

"The charges against David McKay were based on his alleged motive: to keep his double life a secret. Since the trial began, a second alleged motive—to avenge his sister's death—has been brought to bear. These motives remain unproved. Yes, David McKay wanted to retain his privacy, but Nella Harding testified that he had already agreed to let her publish details of his life. Yes, he wanted his sister's killer punished, but it was a legal, a judicial punishment he planned to seek. Gentlemen of the jury, this case boils down to the word of the state against that of the accused.

"My learned colleague, Mr. Baker, sees no reason to believe David McKay. David McKay is a liar, says Mr. Baker: David McKay has lived a lie for four years. Has denied his own people for four years. This man, implies Mr. Baker, is a murderous coward. But I remind you: This man is a war hero. This man has faced what no member of this jury will ever face: the blood-lust of a lynch mob."

Nevin leaned on the jury box. "Who among you would have acted differently than David McKay? Who is ready to cast the first stone? David McKay did not turn from his people—he turned from injustice. Shall I repeat his words? He said, 'I did not decide to pass for white. I did decide *to let people see what they wanted to see.*'"

"I ask you: What kind of moral code requires a man to constantly identify himself as a target for racial hatred? Or to make himself a willing victim for the proponents of genocide? Tell me, men of the jury, which one of *you* would have stepped forward to endure the hangman's noose or the burning pyre?"

Nevin paused to let his words sink in. "David McKay's initial denial of his racial identity was born of terror. But his long-term decision to no longer brand himself as either black or white stemmed neither from fear nor cowardice, but from despair. Despair at the murderous stupidity of lynch mobs; despair at the haunting political impotence of the black race; at the rigidity of America's caste system and the knowledge that the democracy you fought for overseas will turn a blind eye when you're lynched at home.

"As you know, in this country, a man's worth is irrevocably determined by his racial identity. David McKay thought his decision to be *neither black nor white* would free him from America's whole mad obsession with race, and in his sense of racial responsibility, he worked privately, feverishly to help as many of his people as he could. How could anyone see a man who cares that much, who labors that hard, as a murderous coward?"

Nevin paused once more, to make sure he had everyone's full attention. "A life of cowardice or courage: Which has this man led? That is truly the crux of the matter. For, as I repeat, there is no evidence against him in the matter of Jameson Sweet. There are only allegations against his character. So, was it cowardice or courage? I ask you, good men all, to look into your hearts and find the fair, honest and compassionate answer."

David thought of his clients in Philadelphia. Now he knew how they felt when they were on trial: the helplessness and frustration at the beginning; the despair and resignation toward the end. He had always tried to give them hope. He had asked them to have faith. He realized with a sinking heart that retaining faith was the most difficult of all things to do. He found himself praying as he hadn't prayed in years, for hope, for faith, for courage to endure what he was sure would befall him.

They took him to another room in the courthouse to await the jury's decision. He asked Nevin to leave him alone, then sat down on one of the hard wooden chairs furnishing the barren room and stared out of the barred window.

43. When Love Turns to Hate

Inevitably, his thoughts returned to Rachel. She had offered to serve him choice bits of truth on each successive visit.

"What shall I tell you today?" she would ask. "What do you want to know?"

"Tell me," he'd said the evening before, "about Jameson Sweet."

"Jimmy? Now what's there to say about him?" She played at being surprised. But her mocking tone was softened by a bittersweet smile.

"He was your sheik, your sugar daddy?" he asked.

"And my friend." Her look was teasing. "Jealous?"

"No," he said mildly with a little shake of his head.

"Just curious, huh?" She was suddenly bitter. "You never loved me."

"No, but I cared. For a while, I cared very much."

"And now?"

"Does it matter?"

She eyed him. Her heart-shaped face was tight with anger.

"No," she said coolly. "It don't matter. Don't matter at all."

"I didn't think so."

Her eyes narrowed. "You want to know about Jimmy? Well, he loved me. Adored me. Always had. From the time we ran the streets as kids."

"You never talked about him."

"Why should I? I knew the kind of people I wanted to be with—and he wasn't one of them."

For the first time since he'd known her, David saw the naked ambition in her eyes, the sense of ruthless calculation that drove her. He did not fault her for it; given her life, he even understood it. Nevertheless, it repelled him.

"I saw less of Jimmy as I grew older. Years went by. Then I ran into him two years ago, right after I moved back from D.C. Jimmy knew about the baby. Seems like everybody did. I was tired, broke. Jimmy tried to help. After Mama died, he offered me everything he had. He thought he could make me forget. But he was wrong."

Her soft voice was heavy with hate. "I wanted to make you people hurt the way you hurt me, and I wanted Jimmy to help me do it." Her voice trailed off, as she remembered. "He tried to talk me out of it. He promised to deliver the sun and the moon and the stars, if I'd just give up my idea. But I wouldn't. Finally, he gave in. He loved me too much to let me try it alone."

David had never expected to feel sympathy for Sweet, but for a moment he felt something quite close to it. He rearranged his normally expressive face into a mask, but he found it impossible to keep the rage from his eyes.

"What was your plan?" he asked in a dull voice.

"It was simple: Jimmy was to marry Lilian, fake her suicide, then wait a while and marry me."

"As simple as that?"

She arched an eyebrow. "Yeah, as simple as that." She smiled provocatively. "You're very handsome when you're mad."

"Is that what you told Sweet before you shot him?"

The smile disappeared. She was furious. "What d'you care what I said to him? What I *did* with him on the parlor sofa—before he died?"

He gave a slow, studied shrug. "You're right. I don't give a damn what you two did together. I just want to know about my sisters. You introduced him to Lilian, didn't you?"

"Well, what of it? She wanted to marry a dark-skinned man. To make herself look good. To prove her commitment to the race by marrying 'a real Negro.' My, my, she was something. A pathetic snob who knew nothing about men." Scorn distorted Rachel's pretty features.

"But Rachel, when you learned that she was going to have a child—"

"That changed nothing."

"You still planned to kill her?"

"Of course." She gave him a hard stare and a strange light entered her eyes. "I wanted her dead. You hear me? Dead. You think I should've had pity on her 'cause she was carrying a baby. But she didn't have pity on me. Lilian as much as killed my child—our child, David, our child. I didn't owe Lilian a damn thing. Isabella would've lived—if only she'd gotten good food, good medicine—if only she'd had you."

Something convulsed inside him. His blood pounded in his face. "Tell me the rest," he said thickly.

She gave him one last resentful look. Then her features composed themselves. Her passions, so dramatically evident one second, disappeared the next as though some mental door had swung shut behind them. Within a minute, her face was calm.

"Everything was going fine. Then Gem arrived. That worried us, but we decided to go ahead with our plan. We didn't know Gem had plans of her own. Not until later, when Gem told Jimmy what she'd done to Lilian at Nella Harding's house."

A look of injured self-righteousness swept over her face. "You think I'm cold-hearted. Well, what about Gem? She killed her own sister: shot her in the heart. Right on Nella's dock. Gem said she'd wondered how it would feel to kill. But it was no big deal. She said she'd had more fun shooting rabbits. So there."

David knew that she expected a response; he gave her none. He believed what she said about Gem, of course. He believed her one hundred percent. It was more or less what he had figured out. But that made the confirming details no less painful to hear.

And Rachel knew it.

Telling him how Gem had murdered Lilian was part of her revenge. She wanted to wound him and she was doing a good job of it. He felt as though she were raking his heart with claws, but he was determined not to let her know it, so he met her vicious tongue with silence. He knew that she would be unable to hold out and he was right. Her own need to tell him everything drove her on.

She began speaking in a low, vehement tone. And he listened—he had to. He was truly a captive listener. He had sought the truth and now he had it, delivered in its most brutal form. She told him how Gem had stripped Lilian's body on the spot.

"That's when she saw Lilian's belly. It was a little too round. She touched it and nearly rocked on her heels. A baby. Gem thought back on how Jimmy had acted—how he and Lilian had acted together—and it hit her like a thunderclap that maybe Lilian hadn't told Jimmy about the baby. It was a slight chance. Slighter than the crack in an ant's behind. But still there. And if Lilian *had* told him ... Well, Gem figured she'd have to have herself a little accident. Maybe a fall down the stairs.

"Anyway, she didn't waste time worrying. She dragged the body to the edge of the dock, tied it up with some rope and rocks, and rolled it off the pier. The next morning, she put on Lilian's clothes and drove back in Lilian's car.

"Jimmy didn't suspect—at first. But Gem was a lousy actress. Too conceited. Didn't like having to pretend to be somebody else—especially when that somebody was Lilian. Finally, Jimmy said something. She admitted everything. Even bragged about it.

"Jimmy said he'd turn her in. But she said she'd say he helped her. It would've been his word against hers. Then she told him he'd be smarter to just play along and let her 'keep Lilian alive.' No one would be the wiser. You were the only one who could tell the difference, but you'd been gone for years. Gem was sure you'd died in some southern cornfield. No one else could guess. Not even Annie. Gem didn't know about me. So, Jimmy and me let her think she was getting her way. We decided we'd just wait a while, then kill her, too."

David was past being shocked. Still, he stared at her, wondering. Her face was familiar—her eyes, her nose, her delicate throat—but he felt as though a stranger sat before him. Where was the desirable woman he had married? Had she ever existed? Usually, he had good instincts for people. Why had he never perceived the bitterness, the ruthlessness that simmered within her? There *had* been times when he had sensed something … something not quite right. That was the best choice of words he could come up with. But his remorse had blinded him. His sense of guilt and regret had disabled him. *Now I'm free of such constraints,* he thought bitterly. His mind was once more free to follow a logical train of thought, no matter where it led him.

"Was it your idea to drive Gem out of her mind using drugs?"

Rachel's smile was smug. "We'd done it to Lilian. I stole the drugs from the hospital. Jimmy mixed them with Gem's food, put them in her drinks. Then he brought me into the house. To help 'take care of her.' We waited a year. A whole damn year. Long enough for everyone to know she was sick. I got tired of it, so I said: 'Jimmy, go do it.' He picked the weekend he was supposed to be in Newark."

"And what about his alibi? The roommate who Sweet said

was there all night—did Sweet buy him?"

"He didn't have to. Charlie Epps. Good ol' Charlie. He don't know if Jimmy was there all night 'cause he wasn't there himself. He spent the night having fun with a lady friend. Naturally, he didn't want the missus to find out."

"So Sweet was supposed to be *his* alibi?"

She laughed. "He didn't know he was going to be Jimmy's alibi, too."

"Clever," was all David said.

Her smiled faded. "I'll tell you who was clever—I was." She leaned forward, her small hands curled into fists. "Jimmy came back here, did what he had to do, and drove back to Jersey. It went down fine. Then Annie found your address. As soon as I knew you were coming back, I decided to go to work on you. Jimmy didn't like it. But somebody had to keep an eye on you." Her tone became syrupy sweet. "I knew you'd trust me."

His temples throbbed painfully. How many times had she misled him? In how many ways had she masked her lies? She'd been so fearful when he shared his suspicions against Sweet and so relieved when he found no evidence to support them. He recalled how she denied the importance of her history with Sweet; praised Sweet as a husband; dismissed Lilian's pregnancy as imagined; and tried to dissuade him from seeking Gem—all because she herself had ordered Gem's death.

He listened, outwardly calm, as she told him that at the beginning, she had simply wanted to keep him in line—and get him to leave Harlem as soon as possible. She had pressed him to accept Lilian's death as suicide. But then she had seen that he was determined to dig deeper, and that had frightened her. Horrified at his discovery of Lilian's diary, she'd tried every argument to dissuade him from taking on Sweet. And when that didn't work, she'd had to do some quick thinking.

"I decided to tell you what you wanted to hear."

"And when you offered me your loving—"

"It was a little insurance. I had to get you to trust me again.

But yes, I wanted you." She leaned toward him. "I'm not as terrible as I sound. Part of me, the part that was scared of being found out, couldn't wait for you to leave Harlem. The other part, the part that still loved you, ached at the thought of it. Every time you came by, I thought it might be the last time I'd ever see you.

"When you showed up, asking about Isabella, I was shocked. And then when you proposed .. ." She shook her head. "I just couldn't believe it. It looked like the Lord was finally gonna answer my prayers. Everything I ever wanted was right there for the taking. I could have it all. Not just the house, but the McKay name. I was so happy ... and then, I remembered Sweet."

She felt, she said, as though she were walking a tightrope. On the one hand, she hoped desperately that he would never uncover what Sweet had done, for that would mean her own unmasking; on the other, she hoped that he would get rid of Sweet for her, so she could fulfill her dream of living with him on Strivers' Row. She only killed Sweet, she said, because Sweet forced her to.

"Letting me go to you was Jimmy's biggest mistake. He never guessed that I'd fall in love with you again."

"Rachel ... I don't think you have the faintest idea what love means."

Was that pain in her eyes? She looked stung. "Don't judge me. Your family put me through hell. I know what you think of me. I can see it in your eyes. You think I'd use anyone and anything to get my way. You see something wrong with that and maybe you're right. But your family ain't no better. That pile of money you sitting on, your daddy didn't get it by doing good deeds. Anybody and everybody'll tell you that. Maybe that's why he was so fixed on making you into some kind of social hero."

"My father never plotted to kill—"

"He put people out on the street. In the middle of winter, in ice and snow. Whole families, children and old people. When they couldn't pay the rent, he'd take the best of their furniture, sell it and trash the rest. Now don't act like you don't know about that."

Yes, he did know about his father's cruelty. Thank God, he also knew about Lila's kindness. She'd made it her business to quietly find new homes for every single family Augustus evicted. Everyone in the neighborhood knew about it; everyone but Augustus.

"Perhaps you have a point," he said firmly, "but we were talking about you."

"Fine. I did what I had to do to survive. But I didn't use you, David. I gave you what you wanted. A way to ease your conscience. You felt guilty about Isabella. But it wasn't me making you feel guilty. That was you. It wasn't even me who told you about Isabella in the first place. That was Annie—"

"You knew she'd eventually tell me—"

"It wasn't her place. Me, I would've never said nothing. I got too much pride for that. When you asked me to marry you, I even turned you down. I gave you a chance to back out. Whatever else you can say about me, you can't say I used you and you can't say I used my baby's memory to get you."

And that, David realized, was, to a certain degree, the truth.

44. Good Men All

The jury deliberated for four hours—*One hour for every year I was away,* David mused—and returned its verdict mid-afternoon. As the twelve men filed in and sat down, David noticed that they avoided looking his way. Bad sign. His chest tightened. Nevin touched him on the elbow and they rose to hear the decision.

"In the death of Jameson Sweet, we, the jury, find the defendant, David McKay, guilty of murder in the second degree."

Guilty.

The word echoed within him. It meant the death penalty.

He closed his eyes and bowed his head. Mayhem exploded behind him. He heard cheers and whistles, catcalls and boos. Amid the uproar, he barely heard Nevin's whispered promise: "I'll get it reversed on appeal." There was the bang of Richter's gavel and a stern demand for quiet. The order was ignored. Richter banged his gavel again and again. David forced himself to take a deep breath and straightened up. He glanced behind him and saw that a fistfight had broken out in one corner of the room. Guards pulled the men apart. Richter was furious. He declared a twenty-four-hour cooling-off period and said he would postpone sentencing until the next day.

David listened with half an ear as the judge ordered his return to the Tombs. Annie, Nella, and Snyder had rushed to his side. Nella's sapphire eyes glittered with what looked suspiciously like tears. Snyder squeezed him by the shoulders. Toby's mother stood by her chair, afraid to approach. Roy shook his head sadly, his eyes watery.

David felt numb. All around him was pandemonium. People wagged their tongues and slapped hands as if settling bets. Others looked sadly at David and shook their heads. Reporters pushed and shoved and finally climbed over one another in a mad dash to file updates.

David caught Canfield's eye. The aristocratic lawyer sat stock-still, his back ramrod straight, his disapproving face as hard as chiseled stone. He rose and approached David. Nella and Snyder dropped back. Canfield looked David in the eye.

"I never thought I'd rejoice to see twelve white men put one black man behind bars. But men like you shame us all." His rigid demeanor momentarily softened. "Thank God your father isn't here to see this."

David's bit back a response. Granting a glance to the little group at David's side, Canfield gave a curt bow, clicked his polished heels, and turned away. David watched him blend into the crowd and disappear.

Then he saw Rachel. There, in a corner, by the door. Their eyes locked. He saw her relief at the verdict and he remembered her words, *If you're waiting to hear me say I'm sorry, you'll be waiting a long, long time.* He felt another spurt of anger and reminded himself to be patient. Her time was coming. And soon. He would make sure of it. He forced himself to give her a courteous nod. She responded with a smug, feline smile and blew him a kiss, then turned and sashayed out the door.

Nevin gave David a grim pat on the back.

David turned to him and said. "We have to talk."

Nevin raised an eyebrow and said, "Yes, I think we'd better."

Nevin told David he had already begun work on an appeal. He would soon have it ready to lay on Richter's desk. He was claiming several points of error in the trial. He was maintaining that the jury was biased against David from the beginning. At least two of the jurors had been heard to make racist remarks. A juror named Jack Dawson had reportedly said, "[It] does my heart good to see a nigger go down. If they choose me for the jury, ain't no way I'm gonna let that nigger go." A number of people had overheard a second juror, "Sling" Monahan, say it was a shame the state was "gonna waste 'lectricity frying a spade. Just string him up and get it done with."

Nevin was also contending that the virulent news coverage and raucous crowds gathered outside the courthouse had poisoned the atmosphere and intimidated the jury, excluding any possibility of a fair trial. He maintained that Nyman's gossipy testimony about David's alleged sexual adventures should have been excluded. The testimony was inflammatory and unsupported, he said.

And he was concluding his appeal with the refrain that the prosecution's evidence as a whole was weak, circumstantial, and "of questionable taste."

Nevin explained all this the moment he, David and Annie were back at the Tombs. Then he said, "But that's not why we're sitting here, is it?"

"No," David said.

Nevin looked tired and worried. "It was Rachel, wasn't it?"

"You caught Schmuck's comment."

"Of course." He studied his client. "Was that your first ink-ling? Or have you suspected her all along?"

"Not all along, no, but ... at one point, a while back, I ..." David wiped his face with his hand. "Nevin, sit down. This is going to take a while."

Nevin exchanged a look with Annie. She frowned, said to David, "You mean you didn't tell him?"

"Tell me what?" Nevin said with impatience.

"About the druggist report," David said.

"The what?" Nevin's voice went up a notch.

David hesitated.

"Go on," Annie said. "Say something or I will."

David returned her look, but began.

Nevin listened grimly until David was done, and then asked, "Why didn't you tell me about this sooner?"

"Yes," Annie said. "That's what I wanna know, too. Him knowing all that, it coulda helped him set you free."

David shook his head. "The report wouldn't have been enough. Introducing it as evidence might've even done more harm than good. It doesn't prove that Rachel did it. It doesn't even prove that Sweet got the drugs from her. Baker would've argued that Sweet could've gotten the drugs anywhere. He might've even argued that Lilian drugged herself. What he defi-nitely would've argued is that my believing that Sweet drugged her proved that I had a grudge against him, that I felt I had rea-son to kill him."

Annie looked to Nevin.

He reflected, then reluctantly agreed. "I hate to say it, but David's right. Still," he sighed. "I wished you'd said some-thing. You got any more secrets?"

"No," David shook his head.

Annie pressed her lips together unhappily. She looked from one man to the other. "Well, what are we going to do? I hope you two ain't planning to just sit back and let her get away with it."

"No, I have a plan," David said.

"Oh?" Nevin raised an eyebrow. "Exactly what did you have in mind?"

Annie leaned forward. "I want to hear this."

In baring her embittered soul, Rachel had shared so much with him, so many ugly details. He'd spent hours going over her words, hearing her voice repeating them again and again. Finally, he'd found it, the one detail that he could hang her by.

Now, the time had come for him to share it —— and to share how to use it.

45. The New Mistress of the House

The next morning, Annie walked into her kitchen and found Rachel going through the cupboards. Annie halted in mid-stride. Her mouth sagged open. Rachel turned, saw Annie, and put her hands on her hips.

"This kitchen is a mess. It has to be redone."

"'Scuse me?"

"This kitchen," repeated Rachel bitingly, "is a mess. I'll show you how I want it—"

"But I've got my kitchen just the way it should be."

"This is not your kitchen. It's my house and my kitchen."

Now, Annie put her hands on her hips, too. "Look here, I done run this kitchen for years. I cooked your meals here when you was just a young visitor. And I did it just fine—"

"Well, I'm not a visitor anymore. I'm the mistress of this house and I want changes."

"But Miss Rachel, Mr. David don't like it when someone else is in this kitchen—"

"Mr. David isn't here. He's gone and he's not coming back.

This is the beginning of a new day—my day—and you'll do what I say."

Annie crossed her arms across her chest. Her dark eyes swept over Rachel.

"All right, I'll take my orders from you. But first, tell me one thing."

Rachel waited.

"How could you say you loved him?"

Rachel's eyes widened. Her hand flashed out to slap Annie, but Annie caught Rachel's arm in midair. Her strong, callused hands closed around Rachel's bony wrist and forced it down. Rachel tried to yank herself free, but Annie held tight.

"Miss Rachel, I done watched over Mr. David since his mother died, so I got the right to ask a mother's question. One mo' time: How could you say you loved him?"

Annie's eyes were hard. Rachel stared back at her, defiant, but she couldn't hold out against the old woman's strength. Rachel's gaze faltered. Her angry pride buckled and a shadow of shame flitted across her face. She looked down, struck silent, and Annie, with a look of contempt and pity, released her. Rubbing her wrist, Rachel stumbled to the doorway. She halted on the threshold and turned. Her face was drawn and haunted; her voice hoarse.

"You ask a mother's question; I'll give you a mother's answer. I used to love David. But that love is dead and gone. I left it buried with a baby in a D.C. graveyard."

Annie put a hand to her chest, but after a moment took it away. Rachel had a right to her pain, but she'd been wrong to let her disappointment and grief embitter and twist her. She'd been wrong to do things that any sane person would have a hard time forgiving.

Rachel stalked out and Annie wondered if that would be the end of it—for now—but minutes later, she heard disquieting sounds overhead, sounds of drawers being opened and slammed shut.

"Lord, help us," Annie whispered. "What's she up to now?"

She went upstairs as fast as her rheumatoid legs could carry her and found Rachel in David's bedroom. Rachel was hastily packing her few things. Annie stood just in the doorway, bewildered. What was going on? Was Rachel actually moving out? For a moment, Annie felt a glimmer of hope.

Then Rachel looked up. "You can stop thinking what you're thinking, 'cause I'm not going nowhere. I'm taking over the master bedroom."

"But Mr. David don't want nobody in there."

Rachel slammed the lid of her second suitcase shut. "Old woman, you better learn to listen to me." She pointed to her two bags. "Now, take this stuff for me."

Annie took a step back. "No, ma'am. You wanna move in there, you gotta do it by yourself."

Seething, Rachel grabbed her bags and dragged them out of the room. Annie followed her down the hall to Lilian's old room. She watched Rachel from the threshold. "Mr. David—"

Rachel spun around. Fury contorted her pretty face. "Get out!" She shoved Annie out of the room and slammed the door. Standing in the corridor, Annie heard the sound of things smashing and thumping.

She took a deep breath and cracked open the door.

Rachel stood in the middle of the room, her narrow chest heaving. Her gaze fell on Lilian's beautiful collection on brushes on the dressing table. She crossed the room and raked them all into a trash can. In a fit, she went through the room, tearing down every sign of Lilian, every photo, perfume bottle, book—she tossed them all to the floor.

And when she was done, she stood in the middle of that empty, sanitized room, looking lost and alone. Then she sank to the floor and wept.

46. A WAY MUST BE FOUND

David welcomed his new visitor with polite words that belied their antagonistic past. "I'm sure you never expected to find yourself here. Thank you for coming."

Byron Canfield inclined his head. "I can't imagine what you would have to say to me—not unless it's to finally clear your conscience with a full confession."

"Actually, that's sort of what I had in mind. A telling of truths."

Now Canfield was interested. "Well, then. Let's hear it."

And so David told him. Everything. From the who to the what, the why, and how of it, he told it all. From Gem's duplicity to Rachel's conspiracy and Sweet's final fall.

To his credit, Canfield listened. He listened without interruption, but by the time David was done, Canfield's face was dark with rage.

"You," he sputtered. "I've never known such a liar! Jameson Sweet never would've—"

"He would and he did."

"You have no proof, no real proof. It's all circumstantial."

"So was all the proof against me."

Canfield's nostrils flared. "You're here because you're guilty."

"No, I'm here because I did something that our society fears more than murder. And we both know it."

Canfield threw his arms up. "I'm not here to argue with you."

"No, you're here, because deep down, you sense that something's wrong, too."

Canfield set his jaw. He reflected, then shook his head. "This business about the druggist's report, it means nothing. He could be mistaken. He was mistaken once. He could be mistaken again."

David conceded the point, not because he thought it was

valid, but because he felt that an important part of getting some-one to yes entailed allowing them a limited no.

"There is more," David said.

"There can't be. There's no such thing as evidence of some-thing that didn't happen."

Under normal circumstances, Canfield had a brilliant legal and logical mind, but those circumstances weren't normal. David knew he was listening to the stubborn denials of a man in paternal grief. So he ignored them. He had to. He had one chance and this was it.

So he waited for Canfield to quiet down, then he told him what to look for and where to find it.

Canfield flatly refused. He dismissed David's words as those of a desperate liar. "You would do anything—*anything*—to smear Sweet's memory! Have you no shame? None at all?"

"And have you no curiosity, no sense of justice?" David spoke with intensity. "Look, for me, Sweet was a monster, a man who viciously destroyed my sisters. To you, he was someone else entirely. Don't you want to know the truth, the whole truth, no matter what it might be? Or deep down, are you so afraid that you'd rather not know it at all?"

"I won't even dignify *that* with an answer." Canfield got to his feet and drew himself up. He stalked out, cloaked in self-righteousness.

The rest of that afternoon went by, with no further word from Canfield . While David had anticipated Canfield's proud knee-jerk response, he'd also hoped desperately that the elder attorney would reconsider when alone. But as the hours ticked by, David wondered if he'd played his last card and lost.

He knew that upon sentencing he would be transferred im-mediately to Sing Sing. and put on death row. He would be placed in the death house. A prison within the prison, the death house not only housed the electric chair, but its own kitchen, hospital, visiting room, and exercise yard as well. Like all death row inmates, he would be kept in isolation and under constant suicide watch. His physical existence would be reduced to the confines of a cell seven feet high, six and a half feet long and three feet wide. There, he would wait and hope, hope and pray, while Nevin launched a wearying court battle, one that could last months. If he lost, then Rachel would go free and the long days would begin to race by with accelerating speed, until one day the guards came for him and strapped him in and the executioner threw the switch.

He thought of Rachel and grew angry, then of Toby's mother and felt himself grow calm. He'd never learned her name, he realized, and felt another tinge of regret. Then he closed his eyes. He could see her face, hear her voice. She cheered him.

So, what you gonna do? She'd asked. *Men like you, they always got a plan.*

Yes, he had. But was it working?

He counted the hours, the minutes, watched the sun go down and the sun go up and passed a sleepless night. Then, at twelve noon, on the second day, he heard the sounds of men approaching. Seconds later, two guards appeared.

They had come for him.

47. A MAN OF THE SUPERIOR SORT

On the morning her husband was to be sentenced to die for a crime that she had committed, Rachel McKay quit her job at Harlem Hospital and went on a Fifth Avenue shopping spree. She spent more money in those three hours than she normally earned in a year. Later, that afternoon, as she stood before Lilian's mirror, she congratulated herself on a plan well done. Now, she could enjoy the rewards of victory, a victory she felt she fully deserved.

At the moment, that reward included a new mink coat. As soon as she'd gotten home, she'd stripped herself down and slipped it on. Now, except for her jewelry, she was naked beneath it. She hugged the coat to her, loving how the smooth satin lining caressed her breasts, her belly, her hips, her thighs. She rolled up the coat's collar and buried her nose in its rich brown fur. Ah, this was good, so very, very good. *Better than sex even!*

She looked into the mirror and fingered the pearls David had given her. She held up her right hand to marvel at the sight of it, bedecked with a new diamond ring. How the thick dark fur caused the pearls to glow and the diamonds to twinkle! She looked rich, now——really, really rich. She had finally stopped being a victim. She had finally taken the bull by the horns and set matters right.

And this was the payoff. It was better than she'd dreamed, better than she'd ever imagined.

Downstairs, the doorbell rang. Surprised, she wondered who it could be. Probably another one of those damn reporters. They had constantly pestered her since David's conviction. *Will there be an appeal, Mrs. McKay? Do you still believe in your husband? Hell, no,* she wanted to say. It had taken all of her self-control to bite her lip modestly, to do her best to look shy and smile sadly.

"Miss Rachel?"

She swung around. Annie stood in the doorway. Rachel decided that she hated her. She would replace her as soon as possible. "What is it?" she snapped. "I told you I don't want to be disturbed. If it's one of those newspaper people—"

"It's Mr. Canfield. Mr. Byron Canfield."

Rachel raised an eyebrow. Now this was a surprise. What could *he* want? Should she refuse to see him? Yes, that would be best. After all, it was his fault that David was behind bars. "Tell him to go away."

Rachel turned her back on Annie and returned to admiring her reflection. *Perhaps, I should go back and get that black sable I liked, too.*

"Miss Rachel," Annie said, still there. "I knows you don't wanna hear no advice from me, but when a powerful man like Byron Canfield says he wants to talk to you, it's best you do just that, let him talk to you."

Rachel swung back, a sharp rebuke on the tip of her tongue. But a thought stopped her. Maybe Canfield's visit didn't have nothing to do with David at all. Maybe the old geezer had an eye for the ladies. Maybe, with David gone, he was looking to give her a little company. A nasty little smile played about her lips. She almost giggled. Everybody knew he was one of the most important Negro men in all America, a real big shot with the Movement. He knew just about everybody. If she got in good with him, her life was made. But better not be too nice to him at first. Got to play the hurt wife, mourning for her wronged man. Oh, yes, she could do that well.

"All right. Show him into the parlor. I'll be down in a minute."

Byron Canfield prided himself on being a realist. He knew that no one was perfect, himself included. But he preferred to believe that he was of the superior sort—the kind of man who rarely made mistakes and when he did, moved quickly to correct them. That afternoon, he found himself at the McKay house on a mission he would've never foreseen. Nonetheless, he was looking forward to it with relish.

Rachel entered the room. She was exactly as he remembered her: lovely to the eye, with an air of fragile delicacy that would evoke the protective instincts of any warm-blooded man. Coming forward, she shook his hand. "You're an unexpected guest." Her smile was charming but restrained.

"Lovely home you have here. Exquisitely done."

Rachel's smile warmed. "Thank you," she said. "I enjoy decorating."

He was quite aware that it was Lila McKay, not Rachel, who had decorated the house, but he was of the opinion that most people gladly accept even the most blatantly undeserved compliments.

"May I offer you something to drink, Mr. Canfield? Tea or coffee, perhaps?"

He demurred. "Thank you, but I won't be staying that long. It's bad enough I drop in without an invitation——"

"Oh, no, that's fine. You're welcome ... *anytime.*"

Had he heard her correctly? The slight breathiness, the sudden softness in her voice when she spoke that last word: had it really contained an invitation or had he imagined it? He gave a sharp glance that found her eye and there he saw his answer. She didn't even try to hide it.

For a moment, the thought crossed his mind to take her up on it. Oh, it was there for less than a tenth of a second, but it was there. Then he caught himself. He realized what he was thinking and that realization appalled him. Moreover, it gave him a deeper understanding of just what he was dealing with.

He smiled at her and said, "How kind of you."

They took seats and for ten minutes chatted amiably over this and that. Then he came to the apparent point of his visit.

"I hope there are no hard feelings, Mrs. McKay. Of course, I was very upset at the death of Jameson Sweet and I only thought it right to inform the police of what he had told me. But you must believe that it was done without any personal animosity."

Rachel accepted this polite little speech with an equally polite and forgiving murmur. "You needn't worry yourself over it. I understand."

"Thank you." He paused, then drew a deep breath. "Yes, well, I think I've taken up enough of your time." He got to his feet.

She stood and pouted prettily. "Oh, so short a visit?"

"I'm afraid so. But ..." He paused.

"Yes?"

"Before I go, there is one small matter I'd like to mention."

"And that would be?"

Rachel regarded him steadily, expectantly. He had to admire her poise, her self-possession, and the hypnotic effect of those emerald eyes.

"Simply this," he said and went into his jacket pocket. He withdrew a thin envelope and handed it to her.

She took it, but hesitated.

He nodded. "Go ahead."

The envelope was unsealed. Upon opening it, she found a ticket bearing her name for an ocean liner to Italy. Her brow furrowed with momentary puzzlement, then darkened with sudden suspicion. She looked up at him sharply. "What's this?"

"The other ticket, by the way, the one in Jameson's name, it's in my office safe."

She said nothing, but her face paled, just the slightest bit, and the hand holding the ticket tightened.

He continued. "I didn't learn of the tickets until yesterday. They were forgotten in the confusion over his death. Apparently, he intended to go away." Canfield eyed her. "And he expected you to go with him."

"That can't be. You're mistaken." She said it mildly enough, but something definitely unpleasant slithered in the depths of her eyes.

"My dear, you needn't deny it. The evening he died, he messaged his secretary and asked her to make travel arrangements—for two. He gave her your name."

"Really, Mr. Canfield, I—"

"Jameson was like a son to me. And like a father, I suspected certain things but lacked the courage to confront him. There were opportunities, but I missed them and I'll always regret it. He was distracted. His work had begun to suffer. I thought it was his wife's illness. Now I know there was another reason."

"You've overstayed your welcome. Please leave." She drew herself up, looking every bit the indignant mistress of the house.

He was unimpressed. "David McKay's statement that he accused Jameson of killing Gem is part of the public record. It's a fairly complicated story and the newspapers botched most of the details. I didn't see any point in learning them myself—not until I heard of Jameson's travel plans. Then I sat down with Nevin Caruthers. He related every detail of the whole indelicate tale. He also showed me an analysis of the so-called medicine Jameson was giving Lilian. I made a call to Harlem Hospital and had a very interesting conversation with your former superior. It seems there's been an unexplained shortage of the very same drugs—"

"You can't believe—"

"I'm afraid I do." He was assured, intent, and very determined. "Jameson was a tough attorney, but a weak man. I can't blame him. Seeing you, my dear, I can well understand how you got him to do your bidding."

"Leave!"

"The ticket is still valid. If I were you, I would use it. At least, I'd try."

"I am staying here." She arched her small head regally. "You have nothing against me. Nothing! You're just trying to intimidate me."

"Of course, I am." He said it almost kindly. "My dear, have you any idea what will happen to you if you do stay? You will be arrested. Nevin Caruthers and I will work to the bitter end to see you convicted. Should we fail and you retain your freedom, then you may of course spend your life in this house. But no one will visit you. No one will open his door to you. I will see to it that you are socially dead to everyone who matters. When I'm done, you'll be buried alive, grateful for the company of jail-house prisoners."

She sank back down in her chair, stunned. For a long moment, she said nothing. Then she looked up at him, her expression showing not only frustrated anger, but genuine puzzlement.

"Why," she whispered. "Why would you do this?"

How could she even dare to ask? But this was her particular brand of sickness, wasn't it? She was incapable of comprehending such matters. If she had been, then she never would have done what she did.

He nearly didn't answer, but then decided he would. Whether she understood or not, he had to speak. He had to release some of the pain that was clenching his chest, the rage that was nearly suffocating him. But his voice betrayed none of this, none of the fury that was directed at himself as well as at her.

"Why? Because you destroyed a wonderful young man. Jameson had his failings. He was perhaps too ambitious. Too bitter. But he had pride—in himself and in his people. He had vision. You betrayed him. Worse, you made him betray himself. And for that, I will never forgive you."

"But—"

"I was too late to save Jameson, but I owe it to myself—and to the Movement—to save McKay. He's a good man. I underestimated him. Now he's behind bars for a crime he didn't commit, and you and I are to blame. I intend to make amends. And I will *make sure* that you do, too."

He could see her thinking it over. He could sense the fear and uncertainty beneath the outer bravura.

For a moment, she looked as though she might just give in.

But then, she rallied. Her fine eyes narrowed. Her lips tightened and she drew herself up straight. She got to her feet and with slow, deliberate movements, held up the ticket for him to see. Then she tore it in half and tore it again. She kept on tearing until she'd reduced it to bits of chaff. Then she threw the mess in his face.

"There!" she said. "You've got no proof against me. You've got nothing, nothing at all."

He brushed himself off with languid strokes. "Your little fit of pique, though certainly amusing, was useless." He smiled with grim graciousness. "Do you actually think I'd give you the only proof of your ticket? I have the receipt in my office. It not only lists the tickets and who they were made out to, but shows who bought them and when."

Realizing the implications, she took a new tact.

"So what?" she cried. "So what if he did buy me a ticket? What does that mean? Nothing! Who's to say I told him to buy it? Who's to say I even knew about it? No one! That's who! No one!"

He didn't answer, just looked down on her with contempt.

"You don't know me," she said, "but I am a survivor. And I'm telling you right here, right now, that you can take your threats and stick them where the sun don't shine. Because I *will* make friends, Mr. Canfield—and very grand friends, too. I'll *buy* them if I have to. I can do that, you see, now that I have the McKay name and the McKay money to back me!"

As much as he disliked her, he had to admire her spirit. She was a little spitfire.

"As for you, Mr. Canfield," she jabbed in the chest with a strong index finger, "you can go to hell, for all I care — you and all your dicty friends. Y'all can take the first train to damnation." And she stared at him with blistering anger, her hands balled into tight little fists.

He regarded her with evident distaste, but for a long moment kept a cold silence. It was a mien that always worked with hostile advocates in court and it worked with Rachel now. The heat of her anger cooled, and with it her bluster faded, leaving her with the chill of uncertainty.

"Well," she said uneasily, folding her arms across her chest. "Are you going to leave or what?"

He said nothing.

"You come here, all big and mighty, trying to throw your weight around, threatening to call the cops—"

"I never threatened—"

"You were about to, but I'm warning you. If you don't go right now, then it'll be me calling the cops, and you they'll be taking away."

It was a weak threat, predictable. He batted it away with less effort than he'd use against a fly. "You wouldn't," he arched an eyebrow, "really do anything that stupid, would you?"

She opened her mouth to speak, but he interrupted her.

"Actually, as much as it pains me to admit it, you're right. The evidence *is* circumstantial and is unlikely to carry enough weight to save him or ..." He let his voice trail away, the rest of his sentence evident.

He appreciated the surprise on her face. She hadn't expected him to capitulate. Not so quickly.

"So," she said.

"So," he continued. "I'm prepared to make you an offer."

Surprise deepened to shock. The look on her face provided bitter amusement. She was so easy to read. If you knew what to look for, if you hadn't yet fallen under her spell, then her face was an open book. He could see that she was suspicious but worried. And curious despite herself. She didn't want to show interest, but she couldn't help herself. Because, deep down, she knew she was in trouble. If he was offering her a way out, a *real* way out, then she had to hear it.

"What kind of an offer?"

He almost felt sorry for her. Almost.

"Tell me why you did it, and how. Tell me that and I'll ..." He paused, as though he couldn't quite bring himself to say the words.

"Yes?" she prompted.

"Leave you in peace. I'll do nothing more against you."

She was deeply suspicious now. "That's all you want, just me to say how and why?"

"No, it's not all I *want*."

"But it's what you'll take."

"Yes."

That brought a smile to her face. She even got a little cocky again.

"And why I should take this oh-so-generous offer again?"

"Because if you don't, then I'll do just as I said. I'll strangle you alive, socially. And yes, I'm sure you *could* buy friends. But they wouldn't be powerful, not nearly powerful enough, to stand up against *me*. Getting those kinds of friends, my dear, cultivating that kind of power, they take time, a great deal more time—and *money*—than you'll ever have."

Her nostrils flared. But she had enough control to bite back an angry response. She pressed her lips together in a hard, thin line. And she thought it over. He watched her with a practiced eye, the veteran of much tougher backroom court deals than she could imagine. But he had to give it to her. She was strong. She'd had to be, to get as far as she had.

Finally, she gave him a sideways look. "And if I gave you your answers, you'll keep quiet?"

"That's right. I won't say a word."

"You'll leave me alone, not poison nobody against me?"

He nodded.

She was tempted. He could see that, but she still had her doubts.

"Let me tell you something, Mr. Canfield: I'm thinking you're trying to trick me. You're thinking you're going to tell me one thing, then do another. Maybe take what I say to the police. Well, it's not going to work. And you know why?"

"Yes, I do. I still won't have any proof."

She was brought up short when he said that, when he robbed her of a bit of her thunder. All she could say was, "Well, I'm glad you realize that. But maybe you should realize something else, too: If you ever do take it into mind to tattle or spread vicious lies, then I'll sue you. I'll sue you for everything you've got. I'll find me a sharp lawyer and take it all away."

"Of course," he said, mildly.

Her lips curled at the sarcasm. "All right," she said. "Let's get to it. What do you want to know?"

"The truth: Did you really have Jameson Sweet kill Gem

McKay?"

Her jaw worked, but she didn't answer and her eyes edged away.

He leaned forward. "Well?"

She paused another second or two, then she with an air of grit, she looked him in the eye and said with pride, "Yes. Yes, I did."

"And then did you shoot and kill Jameson Sweet yourself?"

Again came that firm, "Yes, I did."

Canfield realized then that despite everything, he'd still hoped, in some small dark place, he'd still hoped that she would continue to lie and that would've allowed him to believe in the lies he'd clung to.

"But why?" he asked now. "Why did you do it?"

She looked him up and down.

"Someone like you wouldn't understand."

"Try me."

She gave him a smile dripping with saucy contempt.

"Well, if you really want to know, it was their fault. They're the reason your Jamison died."

"Who?"

"The McKays."

"You're not serious."

"Oh, but I am." She turned, went up to the fireplace mantel and looked up at Augustus McKay's portrait. She drew her fingertips along the lower edge of the frame almost lovingly, and her voice was sweet when she said, "None of this would've happened if he'd just been nice to me."

Canfield shook his head. "But he took you into his home, into his family—"

She rounded on him. "Took me *in?*" The sweetness was gone. There was only bitterness, bitterness and rage at old festering wounds. "He didn't damn take me in. Not in no damn way. He kept me around as a 'social case.' Someone he could teach them to look down on. Feel sorry for. Daddy McKay couldn't stand me. I wasn't good enough, smart enough, fine enough."

"So this was all about revenge?"

"Call it what you want. All I know is that now I've got everything he built. His name, his money, his *house*. I fought for it. I earned it. And I'm gonna keep it."

He studied her for several long seconds, then drew a deep breath. It was nearly over now. He had only one more question.

"And Jameson?"

"Him?" She dismissed him with a shrug. "Trust me. It wasn't all that hard to convince him. After all, he was a man, wasn't he?"

It was what he'd expected. But it still cut to hear it. "Thank you," he said, swallowing his anger. "I appreciate your candor. It always helps to hear it from the source."

She regarded him with a smirk, and perhaps a little admiration, too. Her voice became husky. "I like a man who can stand to hear the truth."

Again, there it was. The invitation. He felt it in the intimate way her eyes raked over him, saw it in the way she coyly licked her lower lip. Was she serious or was she mocking him? It didn't matter. He'd accomplished his goals. It was time to go.

"Well, the truth is one of those odd things, isn't it? In the end, no matter how painful, it's always easier to bear than a lie."

She shrugged. "I'm happy you think so." She came up to him, laid her fingertips on his chest, light and caressing, in a manner so different from how she'd touched him earlier. "You're sure you're satisfied? Sure I can't satisfy you in some other way, maybe do a little something else to seal the deal?"

He took her hands away and quite deliberately brushed himself where she had touched him. She fell back a step and stared at him. For a moment, her face showed only anger. Then came the evident realization that she'd gone too far. He took pleasure in knowing that he'd gotten through.

"Good-bye, *Mrs.* McKay," he said and started out.

He felt her gaze on his back and then her words tearing at him.

"You will keep your word?" she cried out.

He paused, nearly at the parlor doors, and turned for one last disgusted look. "Yes," he said. "Yes, I will. You'll have no more to fear from me, but ..." And here he paused, preoccupied, as though he'd just thought of something.

"But what?"

He looked at her. "Well, I'm afraid I can't say the same for the others."

She blinked. "What others?"

"Why them."

He turned and gestured toward the parlor doors. They slid open and Rachel gasped. David stood there. Detective Peters, Nevin Caruthers, and Annie was there, too—as well as two uniformed policemen.

Rachel's shocked gaze flew from them to Canfield, then again to David and Annie, to Peters and Nevin. Her eyes widened in realization. And her lovely face paled with panic. How long had they been there? How much had they heard? Her hand flew to cover her mouth, but it was too late. It was all there, in their faces. They'd been standing there whole time ... had heard everything. She gripped her hair, staring from one to the other, seeking signs of compassion or sympathy, and finding none.

"You see, my dear," Canfield said, "you did it all for nothing."

That snapped her out of it. It struck her pride. For a second, her face hardened and she straightened up, pulling herself together. She threw Canfield one last venomous look of hate, then dismissed him.

Her gaze went to David and, like a chameleon, she changed. Her expression softened. She went from proud and haughty to helpless and defenseless. Her gaze excluded everyone else in the room. It was David she needed to talk to. Only David. She could always get what she needed from him.

Her beautiful eyes lit with desperate hope. They sparkled with the tears of the misunderstood. She ran to him and flung her arms around him.

"Oh, David, I'm so glad you're here! Please, help me! You don't know what this man's been saying to me. Why, he's threatened me. He's—"

"Rachel." David gently but firmly disengaged himself.

She reached for him again, but he gripped her by the shoulders and held her away.

"No," he said. "It's over."

"Please!" she wailed.

He gazed down into her panicked face and compassion rose in his eyes. With a deep sigh, he folded her into his arms and she clung to him, sobbing.

"Oh, baby, baby," he said softly. "I'm so sorry."

"Oh, I just knew you'd understand. I knew it," she whispered.

He didn't answer.

She looked up,. "I mean, you do, don't you?"

"Oh, yes," he said. "Yes ... I do." He smoothed her hair.

She closed her eyes and relaxed against him in obvious relief. For several seconds, he held her, and rocked her, as though she were a child. Canfield, watching, saw her open her eyes. She caught him and gave him a little smile of triumph.

"You feel better now?" David asked.

She nodded and sniffed, casting her eyes downward.

David cupped her chin and tilted it upward to make her look at him, then lightly thumbed her tears away.

"Rachel, I need you to understand something."

She was wide-eyed and innocent. "Yes? What is it?"

"I'm sorry for how we made you feel—"

"Oh, David—"

She tried to rush into his arms again, but he held her at bay.

"Hush, now," he said. "You've got to listen."

She worried her lower lip, then gave a small nod. "All right."

"What you've got to understand, baby, is that my being sorry for what we did to you is one thing." He paused. "And letting you get away with what you did to us is another."

For a moment, she stared at him in puzzlement. Then understanding dawned and her lips parted in disbelief. She frowned and shook her head.

"No! No, you can't meant that. You're not really going to—"

"If you'd only been honest with me, come to me. Now ... well, now, it's just too damn late."

With those words he released her. He took a step back and gave a nod. The two uniforms flanked her. One reached for her and she pushed him away.

"Oh, God, David, no! You can't do this. I won't let you. Do you hear? I won't *let* you! *You owe me! YOU OWE ME!*"

He had only three words for her: "Bye, baby. Bye."

Handcuffs appeared. She recoiled in horror and looked around, wild-eyed, seeking a way out. But suddenly, the others were all there, forming a circle around her, closing in on her. She had no way out, nowhere to go. Her threats turned to pleas.

"David, please! You know what they'll do to me. You can't let them! *You can't—*"

She gave an anguished sob. The officers gripped her by the wrists and she tried to wrench herself away. She dug in her heels. She struggled and squirmed, but it was no use.

"Oh, no, *David! NO!*"

They clamped her in handcuffs and took her away.

48. CELEBRATIONS

Days of exhausting celebration followed David's release. Upper-crust Harlem welcomed home its lost son with backslapping, handshaking, and toasts to his good health.

"We believed in you all the time," his neighbors said.

"Sure you did," he answered.

Canfield, backed up by two other leading Movement officials, offered him reinstatement. David politely thanked them and turned them down. He preferred to labor outside the established but strife-torn civil rights organization.

Amid all the festivities, he made time to honor his sisters. He saw to it that Lilian's remains were given proper burial. He visited what he now knew to be Gem's grave and whispered words of reconciliation. He also ordered a new headstone and invited Snyder and Nella to a small, very private service in Gem's memory. Afterward, David escorted Nella to her car, then drew Snyder aside. He shook the gangster's hand.

"I want to thank you. Canfield told me how you stepped in and got the D.A. to listen."

"Baker was a tough nut to crack."

"Canfield said you cut a deal. Hope it didn't cost you too much."

"I gave him what he wanted; he gave me what I wanted."

David looked at him.

Snyder smiled. "You don't want to know too much."

"No," said David, "I guess, I don't, but ... tell me, anyway."

"Look, it was a straight exchange. You were a big fish; I tossed him a bigger one."

David waited.

"A dirty judge," Snyder said.

David raised an eyebrow. "Not one of yours?"

Snyder laughed. "Hey, I like you, but not well enough to give up one of my own. No, this was one of the competition's."

Later that afternoon, David approached the door to his father's office. He hesitated, and then reached for the doorknob. Taking a deep breath, he gave the knob a slight twist. In his heart, he still expected it to resist him. He was surprised when the lock clicked and the door swung inward. With his knuckles, he nudged it open and went in. The office was as gloomy and musty as he remembered it, but it had lost its dark magic. It no longer oppressed him. He saw it for what it was: an old room with old things, simply that and nothing more. Walking to his father's desk, he leaned on it. The wood grain felt warm and welcome beneath his hands. He walked behind the desk, swung the wide chair around, and eased down into it.

It felt right.

David stood up. He swept open the curtains and threw up the windows. Light and air streamed in. And then he took a deep breath, inhaling hope.

❦ ❦ ❦

EPILOGUE

After the long, stubborn winter, the air had finally gained that balmy touch that signifies spring. The streets were alive with people. Harlemites were bursting out of their cramped apartments, pouring into the streets, searching for life, liberty, and a spark of adventure. The air crackled with vitality and tingled with a steady current of pride. David sensed its strength and felt a part of him reach out for it. Suddenly, Harlem seemed to have so much to offer. That afternoon, it assaulted his eyes with brilliant colors, teased his nose with delicious aromas, and soothed his ears with the rolling notes of jazz careening from radios propped in open windows. David felt nourished by the rich diversity of humanity around him. Bits of conversation floated to him, delicious jokes and improbable tales, his people's words, their idiosyncratic phrases—the lyrics to a song he instinctively knew how to sing.

Across the street, an old man pushed a wide broomstick in front of his grocery store and waved his fists at a pair of youngsters who tossed a bread wrapper at his feet. At the next light, two young women ran giggling across the street. A little down the way, three little girls were having a good time with a game of double-dutch, their pigtails flying and skinny legs pumping in time to the dancing rope.

Once upon a time
Goose drink wine
Monkey did the Shimmy on the trolley-car line.
Trolley car broke
Monkey choke
And they all went to heaven in an old tin boat.

On impulse, David made for the Mayfair Diner. Grabbing his favorite waitress by the hand, he took the dirty dishes from her and paid her boss to give her the day off.

"You're crazy," she cried. "Where are we going?"

"Nowhere and everywhere."

Together, they swung down Seventh. They happened to see two men unloading a large refrigerator from a small truck and paused to observe them. David noticed two women standing on the stoop of a building nearby. They were watching the men work.

"I wanted me a new fridge. Wanted it something bad," one said. "Couldn't get it out of my head. But my ol' man, he said we didn't have no money. Well, I knows that was partly true. We did and we didn't. To tell the truth, these last two winters was so cold, we ain't need no fridge. Just used to set the food out on the windowsill. Still, I had it in my head that I was gonna get one like them rich white ladies got."

The refrigerator's apparent new owner had thrown a cheap coat over her baggy housedress. Perfectly aligned rows of hair clips covered her head. Her legs were bare and she wore flat cloth house slippers. Her upper lip was sunken in as though she'd lost several of her upper teeth. Her attention was fastened on the deliverymen.

"Hey, y'all be careful with that," she yelled, then turned back to her girlfriend. "Anyways, I know the only thing my Joe care about is his beer. So Tuesday last, I up and puts his beer in the oven for a bit, turns the oven on real low. Don't take much. Didn't want it to explode. Wouldn't you know, by the time Joe comes home, that beer's warm enough to take a bath in! He took one swig, liked to gag. Man, don't you know he went out an' bought a new fridge the very next day! Got one of them fine things they had to order special. That's why it took so long to get here."

There was a suspicious noise from the truck. The woman took one look at what the deliverymen were doing, dashed down her steps, and went running across the street, slippers flapping, arms waving, all the time screaming warnings, threats, and advice.

David had to laugh. He hadn't laughed in a long time and it felt good. He felt a flash of exhilaration that stunned him. Yes, Harlem was poor and it was battered, but it never quit. The sense of racial pride that had died at the lynching surged back. These were *his* people and they were a tough lot. He was proud of their creativity, their humor, their endurance and absolute determination to survive.

A great weariness descended upon him and dread rose within him when he thought of the world beyond Harlem's doorstep. He recalled his lonely room in Philadelphia. He was indeed tired of living as a stranger in a strange land. He had learned much and seen even more during his foray into the white world. It wasn't as wonderful to be white as some might think. It was still a whole lot more convenient than being black, but he could renounce that convenience handily. He was mighty relieved to be home and back in his own skin. The sight of Harlem's battered streets and proud inhabitants struck a deep chord within him. He hadn't walked these streets in years. But they had welcomed him back, risen to greet him. He had regained his faith, his name, and his place in the world. And he had regained them in Harlem. This was where he belonged. Here, where his roots made him strong. The streets of Harlem, those dusty streets of trampled dreams, were an integral part of him.

His heart beat with Harlem's rhythms. His voice sung to its melodies. He inhaled deeply. He needed this place. This little bit of broken concrete. This place called Harlem.

He turned to his companion and took her hand. "I've got one question for you—just one."

"Yes?"

"What's your name, lady?"

Her smile was warm. "Cora," she said softly." My name ... is Cora."

EXCERPT FROM BLACK ORCHID BLUES

BLACK ORCHID BLUES

"The best kind of historical mystery: good history, good mystery, all wrapped up in a voice so authentic, you feel it has come out of the past to whisper in your ear." ––Lee Child, author of *Worth Dying For*

"*Black Orchid Blues*, a historical novel set in 1920s Harlem, is better than any pulp I ever read. It's simply terrific!" ––*The Globe and Mail*

"Put a Bessie Smith platter on the Victrola, and go with the flow ...." ––Library Journal

"Smart and sophisticated. Walker hits all the right notes in this dark blues riff." ––Reed Farrel Coleman, three-time Shamus Award-winning author of *Innocent Monster*

"Lanie (Price) is a brilliantly drawn character, stubborn, smart, annoying, sometimes petty, often foolhardy, deeply compassionate." ––*Caribbean Life*

"A gripping crime novel with characters who'll stick with you long after the story ends." ––SJ Rozan, Edgar Award-winning author of *On the Line*

"Walker's exuberant third Harlem Renaissance mystery [is a] dark, sexy novel." ––Publishers Weekly

Queenie Lovetree. What a name! What a performer! When she opened her mouth to sing, you closed yours to listen. You couldn't help yourself. You knew you were going to end up with tears in your eyes. Whether they were tears of joy or tears of laughter, it didn't matter. You just knew you were in for one hell of a ride.

Folks used to talk about her gravely voice, her bawdy banter and how she could make up new, sexy lyrics on the spot. Queenie captured you. She got inside your mind, claimed her spot and refused to give it up. Once you heard her sing a song, you'd always think of her when you heard it. No matter who was singing it, her voice came to mind.

Sure, she was moody and volatile. And yes, whatever she was feeling, she made sure you were feeling it, too. But that was good. That's what could've made her great — *could've* being the operative word.

I first met Queenie at a movie premiere at the Renaissance Ballroom, over on West 138th Street. The movie I'd soon forget – it was some ill-conceived melodrama – but Queenie I would always remember.

It was a cold day in early February, with patches of dirty ice on the ground and leaden skies overhead. It was late afternoon, an odd time for a premiere, so the event drew few fans and, except for Queenie, mostly B-level talent.

It was a party of gray pigeons and Queenie stood out like a peacock. For a moment, I wondered why she was even there. She was vivid. She was vibrant. And when she found out that I was Lanie Price, *the* Lanie Price, the society columnist, she went from frosty to friendly and started pestering me to see her perform.

"I'm at the Cinnamon Club. You must've heard of me."

Well, I had, actually. Queenie's name was on a lot of lips and I'd heard some interesting things about her. I could see for myself that she was bold and bodacious. I decided on the spot that I liked her, but I couldn't resist having a little fun with her, so I shrugged and agreed that, yeah, I'd heard of ... the *Cinnamon Club.*

Queenie caught the shift in emphasis and was none too pleased. She raised her chin like miffed royalty, pointed one coral-tipped fingernail at my nose and, in her most regal voice, said, "You will appear."

I smiled and said I'd think about it.

The fact was I had a full schedule. A lot of parties were going on those days, and it as my job to cover the best of them. However, I finally did find time to stop and see Queenie one night two weeks later. I called in advance and Queenie said she'd make sure I had a good table, which she did. It was excellent, in fact, right up front.

To the cynic, the Cinnamon Club was little more than a speakeasy dressed up as a supper club, but it was one of Harlem's most popular nightspots. It was on West 133rd Street, between Seventh and Lenox Avenues, what the white folks called "Jungle Alley." That stretch was packed with clubs and given to violence. Why, only a few weeks earlier, two cops had gotten into a drunken brawl right outside the Cinnamon Club. One black, one white—they'd pulled out their pistols and shot each other.

That was the neighborhood.

As for the club itself, it was small, but plush. The lighting was dim, the chairs cushioned and the tables round and tiny and set for two. All in all, the Cinnamon Club seemed luxurious as well as intimate.

It was packed every night and most of the comers were high hats, folks from downtown who came uptown to shake it out. They liked the place because it was classy, smoky and dark. For once, they could misbehave in the shadows and let someone else posture in the light. That someone else was Queenie. The place had only one spotlight and it always shone on her.

Rumor had it that she was out of Chicago. But back at that movie premiere, she'd mentioned St. Louis. All anybody really knew was that she'd appeared out of nowhere. That was late last summer. It was mid-winter now and she had developed a following.

You had to give it to her: Queenie Lovetree commanded that stage the moment she stepped foot on it. Every soul in the place turned toward her and stayed that way, flat out mesmerized and a bit intimidated, too. Only a fool would risk Queenie's ire by talking when she had the mike.

A six-piece orchestra, one that included jazz violinist Max Bearden and cornetist Joe Mascarpone, backed her up. Her musicians were good — you had to be to play with Queenie — but not too good. She shared center stage with no one.

At six-foot-three, Queenie Lovetree was the tallest badass chanteuse most folks had ever seen. She had a toughness about her, a ferocity that kept fools in check. And yes, she was beautiful. She billed herself as the "Black Orchid." The name fit. She was powerful, mythic and rare.

Men were going crazy over her. They showered her with jewels and furs and offers to buy her cars or take her on cruises. In all the madness, many seemed to forget or stubbornly chose to ignore a most salient fact, the one secret that Queenie's beauty, no matter how artful, failed to hide:

That Queenie Lovetree wasn't a woman at all, but a man in drag.

When Queenie appeared on stage, sheathed in one of his tight, glittering gowns, he presented a near-perfect illusion of femininity. He could swish better than Mae West. His smile was dirtier, his curves firmer and his repartee deadlier than a switchblade. From head to toe, he was a vision of feminine pulchritude that gave many a man an itch he ached to scratch.

That night, Queenie wore a dress with a slit that went high on his right thigh. Folks said he packed a pistol between his thighs, the .22-caliber kind. If so, you couldn't see it. You couldn't see a thing. Queenie kept his weapons tucked away tight.

Gun or no gun, he smoked. When he took that mike, the folks hushed up and Queenie launched into some of the most down and dirty blues I'd ever heard. He preached all right, signifying for all he was worth, and that crowd of mostly rich white folk, they ate it up.

During the set, Lucien Fawkes, the club's owner, stopped by my table. He was a short, wiry Parisian, with hound dog eyes, thin lips, and deep creases that lined his cheeks.

"Always good to see you, Lanie. You enjoying the show?"

"I'm enjoying it just fine."

"I'll tell the boys, anything you want, you get."

After Queenie finished his set, the offers and invitations to join tables poured in. He took exuberant pleasure in accepting them, going from table to table. But that night, they weren't his priority. He air-kissed a few cheeks, exchanged a few greetings and then slunk over to join me.

"The suckers love me," he said. "What about you?"

"I'm not a sucker."

"Well, I know that, Slim. That's why you're having drinks on the house and they're not."

He sat down and turned to the serious business of wooing a reporter.

"So, what do you think? Am I fantastic or am I fantastic?"

"I'd say you've got a good thing going."

"You make it sound like I'm running a scam."

I hadn't meant it that way, but given his fake hair, fake eyelashes and fake bosom, I could see why he thought I had. "I'm just saying you're perfect for this place and it's perfect for you. Everybody's happy."

"It's okay," he said. "For now."

"You have plans for bigger and better things?"

"What if I do? There's nothing wrong with that."

"Not a thing. I've always admired ambitious, hard-working people."

"Honey, I ain't nothing if not that." He leaned in toward me. "People say you're the one to know. That you are *the one* to get close to if somebody's interested in breaking out, climbing up. Because of that column of yours. What's it called?"

"Lanie's World."

"That's right. *Lanie's World.*" He savored the words. "And you write for the *Harlem Chronicle?*"

"Hm-hmm."

"You think you can write a nice piece on me?"

"Well," I hesitated. "There *is* some small amount of interest in you, but—"

"*Small?* People are crazy about me. The letters I get, the questions. They want to know all about me. Where I come from, what I like, what I don't, what I eat before going to bed."

I shrugged. "But they've heard so many different stories that—"

"I promise to tell you the whole truth and nothing but."

"Well, thanks."

I'd been in the journalism game for more than ten years. I'd worked as a crime reporter, interviewing victims and thugs, cops and dirty judges. Then I'd moved to society reporting, where I wrote about cotillions and teas, parties and premieres. It seemed like a different crowd, but the one constant was the mendacity. People lied. Sometimes for no apparent reason, they obfuscated, omitted, or outright obliterated the truth. And often the first sign of an intention to lie was an unsolicited promise to tell the truth, "the whole truth and nothing but."

In some areas, of course, I was sure Queenie would be factual, but in others ... It didn't matter. I'd decided to interview him. I was sure to get a good column out of him. I just wasn't sure this was the place to do it.

People kept stopping by. They shook his hand and praised him and begged him to join them. Men sent drinks. They sent flowers and suggestive notes. But they were out of luck that night. After every set, he'd rejoin me, tell me a little bit here, a little bit there.

"I like action," he said, "lots of action, diamond studs and rhinestone heels. I love caviar and chocolate, sequins and velvet. Most times, I'm a lady. But I can smoke like an engine and cuss like a sailor. The men all love me cause I treat them all the same. I call them all Bill. By the way, you got a ciggy?"

I shook my head. "Never took to 'em."

He turned and tapped a man sitting at the next table. "Butt me, baby."

"Sure," the guy said, grinning. He produced a cigarette and lit it.

Queenie flashed a dazzling smile, said in a husky voice, "Thanks, Bill," then turned his back before the fellow could make a play.

"Bill" shot me a rueful look. All I could do was give him a sympathetic smile.

During one of the longer set breaks, Queenie invited me back to his dressing room, "so we can talk without them fools interrupting." He described how at age fourteen, he'd fallen in love with a sailor, who smuggled him on board ship and took him to Ankara.

"He was the greatest love of my life, but that bastard sold me."

"Sold you?"

"Yeah. To a guy in a bar." He saw my expression and said, "But seriously. I'm not lying. And that guy turned around and sold me, again — to a sultan for his harem."

Believable or not, Queenie's tales were certainly fascinating.

He described corrupting wealth and murderous intrigues. Sultan's wives were poisoning each other and one another's children in a never-ending struggle for power.

"For a while there, it was touch and go. I didn't eat or drink nothing without my taster."

"How terrible," I said, with appropriate horror and sympathy.

At the next break, he talked about his further adventures in Europe. When he was nineteen, he said, the sultan sent him off to an elite finishing school near Lake Geneva, in Switzerland.

"Honey, I couldn't take that place. I made tracks the minute they weren't looking. Went to Paris. Got me a nice hookup. Performed at the Moulin Rouge. Would've stayed there, too, but a rich uncle came and found me."

"A rich uncle?"

"Hm-hmmm," he said, with a perfectly straight face. "He's

dead now. But that's okay, 'cause now I've got lots of rich uncles." He gave a wicked wink. "A girl can't have too many, you know."

I just had to shake my head. At my expression, Queenie threw his head back and laughed. His shoulders rocked with deep, raunchy amusement. He laughed so hard, tears rolled down his cheeks.

"Oh, shit," he said, trying to regain control of himself. "I'm ruining my makeup."

I've seen and heard enough to be well beyond what shocks most people. So, it wasn't Queenie's stories that got me. It was the obvious pride and conviction with which he told them. People talk about being larger than life, but it usually doesn't mean a thing. When applied to Queenie, it did. And his tales were as tall as tales can get. Sure, they were hokum. That was obvious, but it was okay. It was more than okay because it would make rip-roaringly good copy.

Back out on in the clubroom, watching him onstage, I mused about his real history. No doubt it was like hundreds of others. He'd been a touring vaudevillian, or had grown up singing gospel in some church down South, then either run away from home or been kicked out. He was a young boy with a pretty face, the kind that would attract certain types of men. Boys like that, out on their own, they get their innocence lost fast. Queenie was no exception.

No doubt, he'd spent years on the circuit, in smaller clubs, dark and dirty. Underworld characters had smoothed his path and a wealthy man or two had taught him to love the finer things in life, men who lived double lives, with women during the day and men at night. Now, Queenie was here, in New York, the big time. It was his chance, and he was going to run with it, milk it for all it was worth. I certainly couldn't blame him.

Queenie liked to flash a big diamond ring. When he sang, the ring caught the light. It was a lovely yellow diamond, set in yellow gold, surrounded by small white diamonds. I had a good eye for jewelry, but at that distance I couldn't say whether it was fake. If it *was* real, then it was worth ten times a poor man's salary. If it wasn't, then it was a darn good imitation and even imitations like that cost a pretty penny.

"That got a history?" I indicated it when he rejoined me.

He glanced at it, smiled. "Honey, everything about me has a history."

"Care to tell me this one?"

He fluttered his large hand daintily and held up the ring for a long, loving look. Then he smiled. His golden eyes were very feline. His husky voice just about purred. "Not this time, sugar. But I will, if you do a good piece on me. If you do it right, then I'll give you exclusive access to Queenie Lovetree. You'll be my one and only and I won't share my shit with anyone but y—"

Gunfire exploded behind us. I jumped and Queenie's eyes widened. Heads swiveled and the music shredded to a discordant halt. Then someone gasped, another screamed and people nearby us started diving under tables.

At first, I wondered why.

But as people scrambled to get out of the way, I could see the club's bouncer, a man named Charlie Spooner and the coat check girl, Sissy Ralston, unsteadily emerge from the area of the entrance. They wound their way past the tables, coming toward us, their hands held high. Directly behind them, a man emerged from the shadows. He wore a big Stetson, a big black one, pulled down low to cover his eyes, and a long, black trench coat, with a turned-up collar.

It was a very sexy look, but the real eye-catcher was the Tommy gun he held on his hip, his black gloved hands firmly grasping the two pistol grips. It looked real; it looked deadly; and he had the business end of it pressed against Spooner's spine.

The bouncer was a good guy, a war veteran of the 19th Infantry. He had war medals and was married, with a kid on the way. He'd been on the job six months, had taken it, he told me, because he could find nothing else. Now his olive-toned skin had turned ashen gray; his usually jovial face was tight with fear. He had survived bombs and missiles and landmines overseas.

Had he gone through all that to die in a stupid nightclub robbery at home?

I knew the Ralston girl, too. That child couldn't have been more than sixteen. She was just a kid trying to earn money for her family. Her father had died the year before and her mother was a drinker. Sissy was the sole support for her seven-year-old brother and six-year-old sister.

There they were, the bouncer and the coat check girl, so terrified they could barely put one foot in front of the other.

Death march. I flashed on stories my deceased husband had told me about the war, stories of both soldiers and civilians being marched to their execution, of whole villages being lined up against a wall and shot. A chill went through me. I tried to think, tried to get hold of the fear and think.

A million questions shot through my mind.

Was this the result of some bootleggers' war? Or was it supposed to be a robbery? If so, would he take the money and run? Or was he the type to kill us all just for the fun of it?

He was covered. That meant he wanted to make sure no one saw him. Did that mean that if no one did anything stupid, just gave up the jewels and the wallets and fancy time pieces, he'd let us all live to tell the story?

I looked out over the crowded room, at the white faces peering out of the smoky gloom, and didn't see a hero among them, thank god.

The gunman shoved Spooner and Ralston to the small open space just before the stage and had them stand side-by-side.

"Everybody, wake up!" he yelled. "Take your seats and show your hands."

But we were all too scared to move.

"I will count to three and then start shooting — for real. One ... two ..."

My heartbeat was pounding a hot ninety miles a minute, but my hands and feet felt cold. From the corner of my eye, I saw Queenie slip his right hand under the table. The gunman saw it too. He swung around and leveled his gun on us.

"Bring it out," he said. "Nice and slow."

Queenie gave him an insolent look and mouthed the word, "No."

I was stunned. I'd talked to Queenie long enough to know he thought he could handle anyone and anything, but what the hell was he thinking of? Okay, so he had pride. He didn't want people to see that he was scared. But this was not the time to act all biggity and try to impress people. He could get us killed.

"Queenie," I hissed, "do as he says."

"No."

The gunman's lips twitched, but he said nothing. He looked Queenie in the eye, made a slight adjustment in his aim, and squeezed the trigger.

Copper-jacketed pistol rounds erupted from the muzzle in a sheet of flame; a shower of shiny brass cases rained down from the breech. The firepower released with the slightest pressure of the gunman's finger would've been enough to kill five men, much less one.

The stream of bullets ripped a trench in Spooner's chest. Blood splattered everywhere. The Ralston kid crumpled in a dead faint. People shrieked. Some ducked down again, but others raced for the door. They were screaming, tearing at each other.

"Shut up and get back here!" the gunman swung around and yelled. "Shut up or I'll mow you down."

The bouncer looked down at himself, at his ravaged chest. He plastered his big hands over his gaping wounds, as if he could hold in the blood. Then he looked up at me, in mute sadness. He stumbled forward a step and his heart gave out. He sagged to his knees and fell, face down.

The gunman looked up from the dead man and pointed an accusing finger at Queenie. "You!" he said. "You made me do that!"

Queenie had gone gray under his elaborate makeup, gray and speechless. He had finally gotten it. This was not one of his tall tales, where he could play the star. This was real.

"Back to your seats everybody!" the gunman yelled. "Get back in your seats and show your hands. Do it, or I'll start shooting. And I won't stop till the job's done."

This time, folks moved. They scrambled to get back in place.

The killer turned back to Queenie and me. "Come over here, the both of you, where I can see you."

We stood up and edged out from around the table, but kept our distance from him.

The gunman was taller than me, but not by much, which made him short for a man. The coat seemed to have padded shoulders, but I had the feeling that he would've appeared broad even without them, that he was built like a quarterback, muscular and stocky.

For the most part, he'd successfully masked his face, but part of it showed above the mask. His eyes had a distinctive almond shape and they were light-colored: blue or gray, I couldn't be sure. The band of skin showing over the bridge of his nose, it was light, too. In other words, this was a white guy. Last, but not least, I detected an accent. European, northern European, perhaps. So, not just any white guy, but a *European* white guy. He'd sure traveled a long way to cause trouble.

"Now, you," he told Queenie, "take the heater out or she's next." He pointed the gun at me.

I half-turned to Queenie to see what he'd do. *Please, don't do anything stupid.*

Queenie slipped his hand through the slit of his dress. And lingered there.

He was going to try something dumb, like shoot from down there. I could see it in his eyes.

Don't do it. Don't do it.

Queenie looked at me and I looked at him. If he pulled a dumb stunt like that and I managed to survive, then I was going to kill him myself. That's what I was thinking and that's what I put in my eyes.

I guess he got the message.

He eased out with a small black handgun and aimed it downward. My lungs expanded and I inhaled big gobs of sweet relief.

"Put it on the floor and kick it over here," the gunman said.

Queenie did as told. He kept his eye on the submachine gun the whole time. I still didn't trust Queenie not to try something and I guess Mr. Tommy Gun didn't either, so I understood why he was keeping his weapon trained, but I was beginning to wonder why he was training it on me.

"Get over here." The gunman indicated the space right before him.

Queenie glanced at me. His eyes held doubt, fear and resentment.

"Do what he says," I whispered. "Please. Just do it."

"Come on," the gunman growled.

Queenie's gaze returned to the gunman. Stone-faced, he held up his gown, then stepped delicately and ladylike over Spooner's body. He stood before the gunman, chest heaving, eyes narrowed and said with tremulous bravado, "Well?"

The gunman slapped him. He was half a head shorter than Queenie, but wide and solid. Queenie swayed under the blow but didn't stumble. He seemed more stunned than anything. His hand went to his lip and came back bloodied. His jaw dropped in alarm.

"My face! You piece of shit! You hurt my face!"

The gunman slapped him again. This time Queenie went down. He tripped backward over Spooner and landed on the floor in a pool of blood. He screeched at the blood, scrambled away from the body, and got to his feet. Blood smeared his hands and dress. From the look on his face, he had finally gotten the message.

The gunman gave me a nod. "You! Come here."

Queenie and I exchanged another glance. Then I took a step forward. The gunman produced handcuffs and tossed them at me. I caught them instinctively.

"Cuff up the songbird," he said. "You," he told Queenie. "Hands behind your back."

If there was one thing I'd always told myself I would never do, it was to be an accomplice to a crime, to in any way assist a kidnapper or killer in harming me or someone else. I had read, and written, so many stories in which the victims had cooperated with their killers. They had done so in the minute hope of surviving, but all they'd really done was make it easier for their killer to get them alone, isolate them and do what he felt needed doing.

I'd always said I would resist. I wouldn't cooperate. I wouldn't make it easy. No me. Oh, no.

But now, here I was, and things appeared differently. They weren't so cut and dry. For one thing, someone else's life was at stake, not just mine.

"Well," the gunman said. "Shall I shoot you or shoot somebody else?" He glanced down at the Ralston girl, still unconscious on the floor. "How about her?" He turned his gun, took aim.

"No!" I pulled Queenie's hands behind his back and slipped on the handcuffs.

He flinched at the touch of cold steel. "Please, no, Slim. You—"

"It'll be all right," I said, trying hard to sound calm.

I snapped the cuffs shut, and when the gunman ordered me to step back, I did.

He made Queenie stand next to him, checked the cuffs and nodded. Then he grabbed Queenie and started backing out. He wound his way to the rear exit, back stage left, and kept the singer in front as a shield.

Queenie panicked. "Oh come on now, people! Y'all ain't gonna let him take me like this, are you? Somebody do something. Please!"

People stayed frozen to their seats. No one was willing to play the hero. Not in the face of that weapon.

Queenie's eyes met mine. "You! Slim, you—!"

The whine of police sirens rent the air. The cops were probably headed to another emergency, but the killer assumed the worst. He pushed Queenie aside and sprayed the room with gunfire. All hell broke loose. People stampeded toward the door. Wall sconces exploded. The room fell dark. Plaster and dust showered down.

I heard screams. I heard cries. I dove under a table and covered my head. Bullets ripped up the floor two inches from my face. I couldn't believe it when they didn't touch me.

"Motherfucker! Get your hands off me!" Queenie cried.

I heard the back door bang open. I heard a scuffle and a scream. Then the door slammed shut and all I heard was the heavy thumping of my terrified heart.

ABOUT THE AUTHOR

Persia Walker is the author of three acclaimed historical novels, *Black Orchid Blues, Darkness and the Devil Behind Me,* and *Harlem Redux.* She is also a contributor to the anthology *Mystery Writers of America Presents The Blue Religion: New Stories About Cops, Criminals and the Chase.* She won the Author of the Year Award by the Go On Girl! Book Club.

Persia has served on the Mystery Writers of America mentoring panel and as a member of the board of the MWA's New York Chapter. She is a former news writer for The Associated Press and Radio Free Europe/Radio Liberty, Inc.

Visit her online at http://PersiaWalker.com or Facebook.com/Author.Persia.Walker.

CPSIA information can be obtained
at www.ICGtesting.com
Printed in the USA
LVOW11s1442181116
513600LV00001B/2/P

9 780979 253874

"IF YOU HAVEN'T DISCOVERED KATHERINE KINGSLEY, YOU DON'T KNOW WHAT YOU'RE MISSING."
—Lindsay Chase

D0001243

"KATHERINE KINGSLEY IS A MIRACLE WORKER, A WRITER WHO UNDER- STANDS THE MAP OF THE HUMAN HEART."
—Romantic Times

"EGERIA," HE WHISPERED, STROKING HER CHEEK. "LOVELY, LOVELY EGERIA. WHO ARE YOU? WHAT TERRIBLE SECRET ARE YOU KEEPING THAT YOU WOULD PUNISH ME SO?"

Lucy shook her head back and forth, back and forth as hot tears trickled from the corners of her eyes, her heart breaking. "I—I can't," she gasped. "Please, don't ask me anymore—"

In answer he bent his head, his warm lips covering hers, cutting her off with a hard kiss, his mouth opening on hers, demanding a response.

She couldn't deny him. God help her, she couldn't deny him. She poured everything of herself into that kiss, her arms twining around his neck as his tongue invaded the soft inner recesses of her mouth, his breath mingling with hers, drinking her in as if he were drinking in her very life, his hands moving over her back, pulling her even closer to him until her body was molded to his, his hips pressed hard against hers.

Lucy's heart pounded so painfully fast that it physically hurt in her chest. She was on fire, lost to everything but his heated touch, his taste, his unique smell, so exciting, so exciting. . . .

Dell Books by Katherine Kingsley

IN THE WAKE OF THE WIND
ONCE UPON A DREAM
CALL DOWN THE MOON

KATHERINE KINGSLEY

Once Upon A Dream

A DELL BOOK

Published by
Dell Publishing
a division of
Bantam Doubleday Dell Publishing Group, Inc.
1540 Broadway
New York, New York 10036

ISBN: 0-440-22076-9

Printed in the United States of America

Published simultaneously in Canada

April 1997

10 9 8 7 6 5

OPM

To Lucy Diana Verey,
Whose irrepressible spirit
makes life a continuous joy
Happy adventures, dear one

Acknowledgments

$\mathcal{I}$'d like to extend my deepest thanks to Brian Polke of Ballycastle, County Mayo, whose gracious assistance helped to give shape and form to this book. I'd also like to thank my dear friend Penny Patterson, who found me my cottage near Downpatrick Head, and her aunt Penny Cavanaugh, who loaned it to me and from which I happily researched the beautiful countryside and fascinating history of Ireland.

Ursie "the Bird" Graham was of great help with the local flora and fauna, as was Pat Kendall, who managed to get hold of two essential books and ship them from England. And without Gina and Geoffrey Verey and their unwavering and unstinting hospitality, despite my moving into their house and plaguing them for endless weeks, I never would have managed to get all the groundwork done. You both deserve medals of valor.

My heartfelt gratitude goes to Francie Stark and Jan Hiland, who were extremely generous with their time, comments, and friendship as they read never-ending pages of manuscript and dispensed excellent advice, as did my husband, Bruce, who also did all the cooking *and* the grocery shopping so that I could complete this book on time. Bless you, all three.

I'm also indebted to Patricia Upzack, Kathleen Menton, and Kurtis Klemm, who literally helped me to keep body and soul together during the long writing process—not an easy task, but they somehow managed it.

My agent, Maureen Walters, never fails to make me laugh, even when I'm under deadline and sure that I've already used up every word in the English language. Most especially I owe thanks to my outstanding editor, Marjorie Braman, who never nagged, even though she only had the vaguest idea of what this book was about. I deeply appreciate her unflagging faith that it would All Work Out in the End, as well as her enormous enthusiasm. I'm not sure how many editors are willing to say "Never mind the details, just give me a wonderful story."

To you, the readers, I'd like to extend a special thanks for all the letters that poured in about *In the Wake of the Wind*, the first book in the trilogy. So many of you asked for Rafe's story, which pleased me greatly since I was in the middle of writing it. Here it is! And so you don't have to ask, yes, Hugo's story is next. I always love to hear your comments, so please feel free to write me at P.O. Box 37, Wolcott, Co 81655. An SASE is much appreciated. Enjoy!

My tiding for you: The stag bells
Winter snows, summer is gone.
Wind is high and cold, low the sun,
Short his course, sea running high.
Deep red the bracken, its shape all gone,
The wild goose has raised his wonted cry.
Cold has caught the wings of birds;
season of ice—these are my tidings.

From a poem written by Irish monks
in the ninth century, translation
by Kuno Meyer

1

Ballycastle
County Mayo, Ireland
April 1821

*M*utton and cabbage *again*?"

Lady Kincaid slammed the cover back on the pot of stew Lucy had just hung over the kitchen fire and shoved her bony hands onto her bony hips with a grimace of disgust. "Can't you for once be a little more original, Lucy? This is the third time this week you've cooked that slop."

Lucy turned from the tub of washing in the sink, wringing out one of her stepsister's nightdresses. "I'm sorry, Aunt Eunice," she said, pushing a damp lock of hair off her forehead with one tired wrist. "A haunch of mutton was all I could find at the market this week that was affordable. There's not enough money left in this month's budget for anything else."

"And whose fault is that, I wonder? Certainly not mine. Certainly not Fiona's or Amaryllis's—my poor daughters have suffered aplenty because of you. You can lay the blame for our troubles at your own door, Miss Lucy Kincaid, and don't you forget it the next time you think to complain."

"Yes, Aunt Eunice," Lucy said wearily. There was nothing else to say, and in any case, she'd heard it all a hundred times before.

Her fault. Her fault that they lived in a ramshackle house on a windswept cliff, her fault that there was hardly enough money to support the four of them, her fault that Amaryllis and Fiona had to make do with last year's dresses and she had to make do with dresses she'd outgrown three years ago. Her fault, her fault, her fault. It was a never-ending litany of blame, heaped on her from morning until night. She bowed her head, wishing she was anywhere else than in this dark, dank kitchen, listening to her stepmother's shrill voice. But that was nothing new either.

"The girls and I are going into Ballina to pay calls," her stepmother said, pulling on her gloves. "We'll be back by six, and I expect the washing and ironing to be done and the house to be spotless. Oh, and Lucy, there's a basket of mending in my bedroom. Be sure you have it completed before we return."

"And my bed linen needs changing, Lucy," Fiona said, prancing into the kitchen. "I spilled my morning cocoa on it." Her long pointed nose went up in the air like a badger's, sniffing, then wrinkling in distaste. "Not mutton and cabbage again! Oh, Mama, I think I'm going to be sick. Can't you *do* something with the girl?"

"Poor darling, I know what a trial she is to you, but I'm afraid that, as usual, Lucy squandered our monthly allowance."

"Typical," Fiona said, plumping up the carrot-red hair that Lucy had painstakingly arranged for her. "She can't do anything right." She put her bonnet on top of the pile and marched over to Lucy. "Tie the bow, and for goodness sake, dry your hands first," she commanded, leaning forward and sticking her pointy chin within an inch of Lucy's face.

Lucy obliged, silently longing to pull the bonnet right down over Fiona's ears. "There," she said, turning back to the washing, wishing they would go and leave her in peace. Peace. That was a joke. She hadn't had a moment's peace since the day eight years before when her stepmother had arrived on her father's arm and turned her life into a living hell. It had only gone downhill from there.

"Mama! Mama, Fiona's stolen my petticoat, the one with

the lace trimming," Amaryllis cried, barreling into the kitchen, her round, pimply face mottled red with rage.

"I did not," Fiona said, turning on her sister. "It's mine, *mine* I say! You tore yours last week, remember, and you sneaked it into my drawer after Lucy mended it, thinking I wouldn't notice that you exchanged them."

"Liar! I did not. It was you who tore *your* petticoat last week. Isn't that right, Lucy?"

"I wouldn't know," Lucy said, disgusted with both of them. Would they never stop squabbling? "They both look the same to me, and what difference does it really make? The tear is virtually invisible now."

"You may think so, but I know it's there," Amaryllis said sulkily. "Look." She hoisted her skirt, showing one plump calf, and stretched out a length of white material. "There's the rip, right there, as plain as day."

Lucy peered at the tiny stitches that bound the flounce to the linen. She could barely see them herself, and she knew exactly where they were, for it had taken her over an hour to painstakingly execute them. Amaryllis had never offered a word of thanks, but then if she had, Lucy would have fallen on her backside in shock. "I'm sorry the stitching is not to your satisfaction," she said curtly. "I'd offer you my own petticoat, but I don't think you'd care for the coarse cotton."

Eunice ignored her, waving her hand at her daughters. "Come along, girls. Time is wasting. Let us leave Lucy to her cleaning or she'll never have it done by the time we return."

She swept out of the kitchen, Fiona and Amaryllis in tow, the sounds of squabbling fading as the front door slammed.

They were gone. "Thank the Good Lord for small mercies," Lucy whispered, glancing up at the clock, already bone weary. Eleven o'clock, and she had at least two days' work to fit into seven hours. But if she was quick and thorough, she'd be able to escape for a walk before they returned. Her stolen time outside, drinking in fresh air and walking over the land she loved, was the only thing that renewed her, that kept her sane.

Oh, for the old days at Kincaid . . .

Once life had been so grand, so glorious, when Kincaid and its people had prospered under her father's tender care. And then it had all fallen apart.

Kincaid. Lucy covered her eyes with her hand, willing away the image of lush trees and rolling green fields cut through by the sparkling blue of the River Moy, willing away the memory of the great stone house where sunshine blazed at the windows in summer and winters were warmed by roaring fires in the grates.

Kincaid, where she had spent her childhood with a mother and father who loved her and gave her a life as free as a bird in the sky. Gone, all gone now, both her parents dead and the house fallen into neglect, the man who had stolen the estate from her father not even caring enough to look after it. Thomas Montagu had been nothing more than a boozing absentee squireen who had allowed his land agent to evict more innocent tenants than she could count and who had brought the very land to ruin from sheer negligence, interested only in enriching himself at the expense of the poor.

She squeezed her eyes tightly shut, willing away the tears that threatened. *She would not cry.* She'd given up crying six years ago, on the day she'd buried her father, the day that her stepmother of only twenty months had boxed her ears and told that she wouldn't stand for tears, that their impoverished situation was all Lucy's fault and she'd spend the rest of her life paying for it. So far she had, and there was no end in sight.

Nothing was ever good enough for Eunice, not that there was money to manage anything else, thanks to the dishonorable Mr. Montagu. But a fat lot of good it did to blame him now, with him six feet under and no way to put the situation back the way it had been.

Oh, she had rejoiced indeed when news had come the year before that Thomas Montagu had broken his filthy English neck on the hunt field. She hoped with everything in her that his black soul would burn in hell for all eternity for what he'd done to her father, although the question now was what further calamity was going to befall Kincaid, now that Thomas Montagu's cousin was the new owner.

Not a word had been heard from him since his cousin had died. What did Kincaid matter to him? What did he care about the suffering of the evicted tenants, whose bellies ached with hunger and whose children had little chance of surviving rampant disease even if they didn't die of starvation?

Lucy glanced out the window of their bleak house on the edge of the peat bog and gazed longingly toward the cliffs of Downpatrick Head where terns and seagulls wheeled freely and unfettered in the overcast sky, beckoning to her.

Hurry, hurry, she told herself. *If you're fast enough, you'll have a good half hour of freedom. A half hour to forget your misery and exhaustion, to forget this prison, a half hour to let your soul fly free, a half hour to dream . . .*

She turned back to the sink and began scrubbing in earnest.

"It's a damned good thing you broke your neck, Thomas Montagu, or I would have broken it for you."

Raphael Montagu, eighth Duke of Southwell, hissed the words out from between his teeth as he stood on a bluff looking down over the sorry sight of Kincaid Court, the property he'd become responsible for on the day his cousin had died. Rafe hadn't received the news for a full six months, the solicitor's letter informing him of Thomas's death following him around the Mediterranean until it finally reached him in Nice just as he was about to embark for England after a year's absence.

Fortunately, his various competent stewards and solicitors

had looked after his assorted properties with solid heads while he'd been away. Nothing untoward had greeted him on his arrival. Nothing, at least, until this moment.

Rafe shaded his eyes and cast his gaze over the house, standing simple and proud in its emerald-green valley, the mottled gray stone reflecting the hazy light as if it had been built for that purpose alone.

Its basic structure was clean, but the dilapidation that had fallen on what once must have been magnificence was in evidence everywhere. Windows were broken, the roof dripped with damp, and grass had grown up in a wild tangle outside what had once obviously been a well-kept courtyard. Now sheep and horses grazed there with abandon.

He'd had a sinking feeling as he rode down the long carriageway that something was badly amiss, for the fields lay fallow and cottages stood empty, shutters and doors hanging loose on hinges. He knew poverty ran rife in Ireland, but he hadn't expected to find such a miserable state of affairs at the great house, not after he'd seen the papers that had documented the condition the estate was in when Thomas had taken it over some six years before.

He turned to the land agent who silently stood ten paces behind him, his cap pulled low over his brow and his arms folded across his chest. "How long has this been going on?" Rafe demanded in icy tones.

"How long has what been going on, your grace?" Paddy Delany replied, shifting his weight onto his other foot.

"This—this travesty," Rafe said. "This complete lack of attention to the estate? I find it hard to believe that in the one year since my cousin's death the property has fallen into such a deplorable condition."

"There was no money, your grace," Paddy said, tugging at the brim of his cap. "No money at all, not to run things the way they should have been," he added.

"No money? It was my understanding that my cousin had

income aplenty from this estate, more than enough to keep it going."

"Had, your grace, that being the point, you see. I'm not wanting to speak ill of the dead, but your cousin was fond of his excesses, if you catch my meaning . . ." He shrugged and smiled, but the smile didn't reach his eyes.

Rafe didn't like the look of antagonism that lay behind them in the least. Paddy Delany might behave as if he were a beleaguered land agent, but Rafe strongly suspected that the story went far deeper. "I see," he said evenly. "And yet it was my understanding that you have been responsible for the running of Kincaid Hall for these past six years. As I said, before that time the estate returned a handsome profit. Where, may I ask, has that profit been invested since?"

Paddy Delany crossed his arms, meeting Rafe's unwavering stare as if he were Rafe's equal, if not his better, an attitude that Rafe was not accustomed to and not appreciative of. "I wouldn't know, *your grace*," he said, his tone barely concealing sarcasm. "As I said, your cousin had his ways, and he wasn't likely to put back profits into the land that he might otherwise put in his pockets."

"What, exactly, are you implying?" Rafe asked, his tone stony.

"Why, nothing at all, your grace. What I'm *telling* you is that your cousin wasn't here all that much, preferring his own country to ours. I had to make do with what I had. And then when he died and there was no money at all . . ." Paddy Delany shoved his hands into his pockets and sighed heavily. "We all suffered, your grace. It's a blessing you showed up when you did, sure it is, or who knows what might have happened? My sainted mother was on her knees in thankful prayer when she heard you were coming, she that close to her deathbed with the cold and barely any peat left for the fire."

"I'm not interested in your sainted mother, Delany, or her supposed proximity to her deathbed," Rafe said impatiently, thoroughly tired of being treated like an imbecile. "I am only interested in what has happened here, and why."

"Well, then, and aren't you just like the rest of your grand countrymen, caring nothing for the plight of the Irish you've robbed and swindled?" Delany said, his tone now cocky. "You show up here asking all sorts of questions, but since you don't seem inclined to hear the truth of the matter, you'll get no more answers from me."

"As far as I'm aware, I haven't robbed or swindled a soul in my life," Rafe said dryly. "And to be perfectly blunt, I find your insinuation insulting."

"And to be perfectly blunt, I find your questions insulting, *your grace.* If you don't trust what I have to tell you when you have no other word to go on, then you're a fool. What do you know of our lives, our miserable conditions, when you yourself have admitted you've never before stepped foot in our country? What do you know of poverty, of hunger?"

He kicked at a clod of grass, sending a shower of earth into the air. "Do you see this? This is good soil that could have fed—and once did feed—at least a hundred people until your cousin demanded it be turned into hunting ground for himself and his friends, and they rarely showed up to use it even for that. And you all but accuse *me* of being responsible for the state of things here?"

Rafe ran his gaze over the land agent's tattered cloth coat, the worn leather of his boots. He nodded, making a silent decision to keep the man on despite his attitude. Paddy Delany might be an insolent devil, but he had a point—Rafe had no one else to rely on.

"You had better show me the most recent books, Mr. Delany. We need to formulate some sort of workable plan. Clearly the estate cannot be allowed to deteriorate further or it will lose what little value it has left."

"Right you are, your grace," Paddy said with a brisk nod of his head, as if to say that he was pleased that his new employer had finally seen reason. "Let's have at it then, although you won't find much there. It was a fight keeping a single penny out of Mr. Montagu's hands, but you'll see that for yourself by the time you're finished."

Rafe unfortunately believed that—he'd known his cousin a little too well and had never had a moment's liking for the man, an undisciplined, profligate bastard with no sense of responsibility toward anyone or anything. If there was one thing Rafe could not tolerate, it was a man who didn't take his obligations seriously.

"What about the family who lived here previously? What happened to them?" he asked, not sure he wanted to hear the answer. Thomas had had a way of leaving destruction in his path.

Paddy cleared his throat. "I really couldn't say, your grace. I know they moved away to a poor showing of a house and one not befitting the station of an Irish baron, but it couldn't be helped. Their leaving had something to do with political troubles, I can say that much, but who doesn't have political troubles in these parts?"

"So I understand," Rafe said shortly, his heart taking a dive even as he spoke the words. He also knew how ruthless Thomas could be, how he'd never let anything stand in the way of something he wanted. And apparently he'd wanted Kincaid. "Where is this house?"

Paddy Delany jerked his head toward the north. "It's that way, outside of Ballycastle, not so far from the sea. Lord Kincaid died six years back, and his widow and the daughters live there alone near the cliffs of Downpatrick Head, that much I do know." He cleared his throat again. "But what would you be wanting with them?"

Rafe asked himself the same question. But the answer wasn't really so difficult or obscure. If Thomas had behaved in his usual fashion, then chances were that he was responsible for their plight. And if that was the case, then it was Rafe's responsibility to find out the circumstances. Tomorrow. He'd see to it tomorrow, for he'd had all he could take for one day.

He walked over to the white gelding grazing nearby that he'd hired from a reluctant blacksmith in Killala, and taking the reins, he mounted it. "We'll continue this conversation tomorrow, Delany. Have the books ready. And in the meantime, open the house. I intend to move in tomorrow."

"Where will you stay tonight, your grace?" Delany asked, his eyes reflecting nothing at all.

"At an inn in Ballina. Surely someone will be willing to take a filthy Englishman's money?"

That remark shook the neutral expression off Paddy Delany's face. "You might try Mulligan's on the main street," he offered, his eyes flashing suppressed fire. "They could use the custom, and their linen is clean and the food decent. At least they won't shoot you in your sleep."

"I thank you. It's a reassuring thought that I might wake to see another dawn. Good day, Mr. Delany."

Rafe didn't bother to wait for an answer. He turned the gelding's head and kicked it into a gallop, wishing only to clear his head by the sea. But first he had to collect his belongings and his valet, Adams, and check into the inn. The Kincaid family and their problems could wait.

An hour later he mounted his horse again and headed north. He finally drew to a halt on the edge of the double-sided cliff called Downpatrick Head and gazed out over the ocean, the waves crashing and spuming against the sheer foot of rock, an impossibly long drop below. He pressed his fingers to his temples as if he could still the pounding that had started in his head when he'd first viewed the desperate wreck Kincaid Court had become.

Ireland. It was a strange country. Something about it disturbed him; perhaps it was the cold, misty light that obscured everything it touched, or perhaps it was the starkness of the wild, windswept wastes and bare cliff faces, so suddenly contradicted by undulating verdant landscapes. Rafe relished clarity; it gave life form and definition. The world was complicated enough as it was without the added confusion of a country that couldn't make up its mind about what it was.

He shook his head. Even the people couldn't decide who they were. He knew all about the constant uprisings, the ongoing fight for Irish republicanism. Protestant, Catholic, neither was happy with the other, nor could they agree on anything, including their mutual national identity. Anglo-Irish were pitted against Gaelic Irish, peasants were pitted against landowners, and Protestants relentlessly squeezed the life out of the Catholics, forcing them to pay tithes to the Anglican church, not allowing them to hold office or even own a decent amount of land.

Everything in this bloody place was a battle. He'd never encountered ruder, more obstreperous or antagonistic people in his life. Even getting the barest civility out of the innkeeper in Ballina had proved impossible, and all he'd done was ask a few simple questions, such as what had become of the Kincaid family. Apparently Paddy Delany wasn't the only one unwilling to talk about them, and he wondered why.

"I wouldn't be knowing anything about Lady Kincaid and her daughters, your grace," Mulligan had said sullenly as he'd handed Rafe his room key, the contempt in his voice barely disguised. "I've worries enough of my own without adding other people's troubles to them. In any case, Lady Kincaid is British and her business is none of mine."

The implication was clear. Raphael was also British and not welcome to information or hospitality beyond what his money bought for a room and meal. Charming. With the exception of Paddy Delany, whose job depended on being marginally civil to his new employer, not a single soul he'd met had anything pleasant to say to him.

"Rafe, my boy," he murmured, shifting in his saddle as he patted his horse's neck, "you are about to embark on the single most foolish act of your life, and may God save your sorry soul."

He rubbed his face hard, then dropped his hands and looked back over the roaring sea. And then a movement on the cliff directly opposite him caught the corner of his eye, and he drew in a sharp breath of surprise.

A woman was walking across the top, a young woman. His gaze narrowed. One didn't see women who walked like that in the drawing rooms of London. There was nothing modulated about this woman's movements; she walked over the land as if she belonged to it and it to her, as if they existed in perfect harmony together. Her dark hair blew liberated of restraint, streaming out behind her, the red cloak fastened around her shoulders beating hard around her body as she moved toward the edge of the cliff, facing into the wind that blew in from the ocean.

She appeared perfectly free, as if she had no constraints, no ties that bound her. Freedom . . . Rafe released a heavy sigh. He couldn't remember the last time he'd felt free.

He couldn't take his eyes from her. Her lithe, sure strides reminded him of one of the ancient goddesses. It was as if somehow she represented everything he was no longer and would never be again. Egeria—that's who she reminded him of, the Roman goddess connected with water who had so wisely advised Numa Pompilius, second king of Rome. Theirs had been a beautiful story, symbol of the human heart's search for an ideal love, immortalized by Byron.

Romantic love was a quest in which Rafe personally had been thoroughly stymied, but there wasn't anything he could do about that unless an Egeria of his own fell across his path, a highly unlikely event at this late date. In theory, one couldn't miss what one had never had, but there was some small corner of his soul that longed for love nevertheless.

His horse tossed his head and let out a soft whinny, and Rafe steadied him with a firm hand.

His eyes hungrily drank in the woman as she halted on

the cliff's precipice and turned her face up to the sky, a smile on her lips. He wished . . . he didn't really know what he wished, only that he might feel as peaceful as she looked in that moment.

And then she began to speak, words called in a soft, musical Irish accent, words he knew by heart, words blown over to him by the grace of a westerly breeze, each one clearly enunciated.

> *There is a pleasure in the pathless woods,*
> *There is a rapture on the lonely shore,*
> *There is society, where none intrudes,*
> *By the deep Sea, and music in its roar:*
> *I love not Man the less, but Nature more,*
> *From these our interviews, in which I steal*
> *From all I may be, or have been before,*
> *To mingle with the Universe, and feel*
> *What I can ne'er express, yet cannot all conceal.*

Something tight squeezed at Rafe's heart, an indefinable emotion that caused him to lean forward in the saddle and grip the reins tighter in his hand. She knew. She understood. The private words she spoke to the wind were Byron's, culled from the fourth canto of *Childe Harold's Pilgrimage,* the poem he had read over and over again in his quest to try to make sense of the Universe, of his life. And she spoke them as if she knew them and their meaning as surely as he did. As if she understood the deep wounds that afflicted a soul and rendered it helpless, as if she too had been wounded by events beyond her control.

Rafe was possessed with a mad desire to kick his horse and try to find a way over to the other side, to find out who she was, where she came from, to tell her that he too understood. But there was no fast way over to her that he could see, not without going a half mile around and back again.

She suddenly turned as if she'd felt his gaze upon her. Her

eyes met his across the expanse that separated them and her body went utterly still, one hand pressed against her throat.

Rafe's breath caught. He could not make out every detail of her features, but there was no mistaking the wild beauty of her face even at that distance, or the spellbound expression in her eyes. The moment stretched endlessly as if time ceased to exist, the two of them caught in a mystical enchantment that bound them helplessly together, neither able to tear their gaze away.

The ocean crashed violently against the edges of the separate cliff faces, but even its roar couldn't drown out the words that pounded in Rafe's ears as if pulled from his very heart, and he wanted to speak them aloud to her in acknowledgment. But the wind blew the wrong way, and he knew she'd never hear.

And then a miracle occurred, for the wind suddenly died down and a silence fell, leaving only the distant crashing of wave against rock as a backdrop.

And so he spoke, seizing upon the immediacy of the moment and taking the opportunity to offer back to her the gift of Byron's poetry, hoping she would hear and know that he did understand, that they stood in the same place, even though they were separated by an abyss. He called the words to her, as loudly as he could, yet they sounded soft in his heart.

> *Egeria! sweet creature of some heart*
> *Which found no mortal resting-place so fair*
> *As thine ideal breast; what'er thou art*
> *Or wert,—a young Aurora of the air,*
> *The nympholepsy of some fond despair;*
> *Or, it might be, a beauty of the earth,*
> *Who found a more than common votary there*
> *Too much adoring; whatso'er thy birth,*
> *Thou wert a beautiful thought, and softly bodied forth.*

A startled look came over her face, and then she took two halting steps backward. And spoke again in reply, staring directly at him, hand gripped to her white throat, her voice filled with emotion—and an anger he didn't understand.

> *There is the moral of all human tales;*
> *'Tis but the same rehearsal of the past,*
> *First Freedom, and then Glory—when that fails,*
> *Wealth, vice, corruption,—barbarism at last.*
> *And History, with all her volumes vast,*
> *Hath but one page,—'tis better written here,*
> *Where gorgeous Tyranny had thus amass'd . . .*

Her voice broke off suddenly and she turned, taking another step toward the precipice. And just as suddenly she fell over the edge and plunged from sight.

Rafe stared, horrified, the breath leaving his body in a great rush. It couldn't be. She couldn't be gone, just like that. He was having another nightmare and any moment he'd wake up . . .

But he knew perfectly well he was awake. And he knew that she was gone, never to return. She had taken her life as he had unwittingly watched.

He kicked the gelding furiously, urging it toward the path that led to the other side of the cliff, galloping at breakneck speed toward the spot where he'd last seen her. A darkness clouded his vision, caused not by the waning light but by a desperation in his soul.

He knew all too well the wrenching despair that led people to such acts of self-destruction. Maybe the freedom and purpose he'd seen in her stride as she'd approached the face of the cliff had been just that—an intent to free herself from the harsh tethers of life, just as his father had freed himself on that awful day twenty years before, taking Rafe's freedom with him.

On that day Rafe's life had irrevocably changed. On that

day a nine-year-old boy had been forced to become a man. On that day Rafe had discovered the meaning of secrets.

He flung himself off the back of his horse, running to the place where she'd last stood. Wincing, he looked down. The ocean swirled far beneath, crashing furiously against the sheer rock edge below, sending great angry sprays up into the wind. A slight ledge jutted out two feet below, but it led nowhere. Nowhere at all.

There was nothing else to be seen, nothing else to be heard. Just the heaving water and the haunting, melancholy cries of the gulls and terns, as if they too mourned her passing. She had been swallowed up by the sea, gone as if she'd never existed. And he'd only just found her.

A harsh cry ripped from his throat as a terrible surge of anguish swept over him. Had she looked at him in her last moments of her life, her gaze unwavering and so eloquent, so full of heart, because she knew it was the last time she would gaze on anyone? And he hadn't even known what her eyes had been telling him, poetry clouding his brain.

. . . *To mingle with the Universe, and feel*
    What I can ne'er express, yet cannot all conceal . . .

It all sounded different now, the words taking on ominous meaning. And later, she had spoken of "the moral of all human tales," of vice, corruption, and tyranny. What had her life been like, to drive her to such an act?

If only he'd realized—had called something to her, done something different, something to let her know that he could have changed everything, whatever it took. He would have done it. He would have done it.

Rafe finally raised his head as dark drew in. He didn't know how long he'd been standing there, only that he was tired, hungry, and cold to the depth of his soul.

He'd felt alone for the majority of his life, but he had never felt as alone and helpless as he did now. So futile and empty. And yet there was nothing to be done. Even in his dismay, he was wise enough to realize that reporting the incident would be a mistake. Feelings ran high against the British, and he didn't need a trumped-up murder charge to contend with along with everything else. Her body would wash up somewhere and someone would claim her.

He was back to keeping secrets. But what was one more secret now?

Poor Egeria. Poor, desperate Egeria.

Rafe mounted his horse and turned its head toward Ballina and the prospect of a solitary meal he no longer desired in front of a roaring fire at his inhospitable inn. He doubted the night would hold much sleep.

"*B*ritish," Lucy muttered, stopping to catch her breath. She bent and rubbed her sore knees, grazed by her tumble on the rough rock. If she hadn't been so upset, she would have watched where she was going, for the hidden path down through the sinkhole that she used as a shortcut home was narrow and dangerous and only to be used with great caution.

She straightened again and planted her hands on her hips. "Wouldn't you just know it? That's what you get for letting your head be turned by fairy tales, Lucy Kincaid. It's a lucky thing you didn't kill yourself."

It was a miracle, really, considering the narrowness of the ledge she'd tripped on, upended by shock and disappointment.

If he'd just kept silent, all would have been well and her lovely fantasy would have stayed intact. But he hadn't. He'd gone and opened his mouth, and out had come the vile accents of an Englishman. An *Englishman,* of all despicable things. No prince at all.

But in all fairness to herself, he *had* looked like a prince of old, sitting on his white horse, with his halo of golden hair and handsome features, his piercing eyes that gazed at her as if she were the princess he'd been seeking in all the four corners of the earth. A prince who had all the right qualifications, for he knew poetry, well enough to quote the correct verse back at her. A prince who had come to rescue her from her miserable life and carry her off on his white charger to a bright future.

What a fool she was. Worse, she was a late fool, and if she didn't hurry, she was bound to hear all about it as soon as she returned home.

She knew better than to linger on the cliffs, but the day had turned so fine, and the sunshine and fresh air felt so wonderful after a long day stuck indoors frantically trying to finish her chores. She didn't know how the time had gotten away from her, only that the prince—no, the *Englishman,* she quickly corrected—had held her enthralled.

It just went to show how true the old adage was that looks were deceiving. If she'd known what he really was, she never would have given him a second glance. Her mistake. And a big one if she didn't get home before her stepmother.

She picked up her skirts and began to run in earnest.

"Where have you been, you odious girl?" Eunice flung the front door open just as Lucy barreled toward it. She took in her stepmother's furious face with a sinking heart.

"I was just out walking, Aunt," she said, ducking as her stepmother's hand swung out, but she didn't move fast enough. The hard slap echoed in her ear and left her cheek stinging painfully.

"Just walking, you say? A likely story. I came home to find the house empty and the stew burning in the pot! And this after I distinctly told you to do your chores!"

"But I did do my chores, every last one of them," Lucy said, covering her cheek with a shaking hand. "The washing and ironing and mending are done and the house is scrubbed spotless, just as you wished. I only wanted a breath of fresh air."

"You know you are forbidden to leave this house on your own," Eunice said, grabbing Lucy and pulling her through to the kitchen so violently that she nearly wrenched Lucy's arm out of its socket. She released Lucy with a sudden jerk that sent her flying onto the floor.

"Look at what your disobedience has caused this time," she spat, pointing accusingly at the pot that now hung sideways on the hook. Its cover lay on the hearth where Eunice had thrown it, and the contents dripped slowly down into the fire, sending up spurts of greasy smoke. The unpleasant odor of scorched lamb and burning fat filled the air.

"I—I'm sorry," Lucy said, staggering to her feet. "I thought I had left enough stock in the pot to keep the stew from burning." And then she realized that in her exhaustion and her haste to get away she had forgotten to add the two extra cups of liquid that she'd set aside for that purpose.

"You're sorry," Eunice sneered. "You're always sorry, Lucy, and I'm tired of hearing it, for your apologies mean nothing, and we both know it." She took two steps toward Lucy, her posture menacing.

"Please, Aunt Eunice," Lucy said, backing away. She didn't think she could bear to be struck again. She knew all too well the extent of pain her aunt could inflict in anger. "I didn't mean any harm, really I didn't. I'll make something else for dinner—it won't take me a moment—"

Eunice caught her by the ear and twisted it. "Oh, you'll make something else indeed, not that you'll be eating any of it. That's the least of your worries, my girl." Her eyes narrowed. "I've warned you what I'd do if I caught you sneaking out to engage in seditious activities and who would pay. It would only take a word from me to the magistrate and your precious O'Reillys would lose their land and their livelihoods, no less than any of them deserve. I am an Englishwoman, and my charge of sedition would be taken seriously, very seriously indeed, especially given the circumstances I have been thrown into because of you."

Lucy's eyes widened in fear. "Oh, please, Aunt—please don't! I swear that I only went for a walk—I saw no one, no one at all. You can't turn in innocent people for crimes they haven't committed—that would be as bad as what happened to us!"

Her stepmother dropped her hand and Lucy clapped her fingers to her burning ear. "No peasant in this despicable country is innocent of subversion, and you least of all," Eunice said. "I know all about the insurrectionist thoughts you still harbor in your heart, despite the calamity you caused. Your father would be alive today if it hadn't been for you."

Lucy closed her eyes and swallowed hard. She could tolerate almost anything at all, even the charge that she was an insurrectionist, but the accusation that she was responsible for her father's death cut more deeply than she could bear, for that much was true. Her stepmother only brought out that particular allegation when she was hell-bent on making Lucy suffer, and Lucy refused to give her the satisfaction of a reaction.

"I made a nice vegetable soup for tomorrow's lunch that you can have for dinner tonight, and I'll cut some cheese," she said, raising her chin. "The bread I baked this afternoon is still warm. I'm happy to go without, and I'll take any other punishment that you wish to give me, but please, do not harm the O'Reillys, for they have done nothing wrong."

Her stepmother smiled coldly. "Very well, I'll spare the O'Reillys this time, since you beg so prettily. Now get on with preparing another meal. The girls and I are famished."

Lucy nodded, grateful that her stepmother had rescinded her threat, or at least for the moment. As soon as Eunice left the kitchen, Lucy immediately went to the stove and heated the soup. Then she quickly laid the table and scoured the scorched stew pot, knowing that if she didn't fulfill her tasks, Eunice would not hesitate to wield the sword she'd been hanging over Lucy's head for six long years.

It was blackmail, pure and simple, but diabolically effective. With one word from Eunice, dear Mr. O'Reilly would be thrown into jail, no questions asked, his wife and children turned out into the streets. These things happened every day. The O'Reillys might be innocent, but that made no difference at all to Eunice. That they were poor, Irish, and Lucy's dear friends was good enough for her. Eunice would surely bring them to ruin if Lucy put one step wrong.

As soon as Eunice and the girls were safely tucked away in bed and Lucy had washed up the dirty dinner plates, her empty stomach growling with hunger, she quietly let herself out the back door and went out to the stables, where she could be assured of some peace.

The moon was nearly full, and Lucy, exhausted, sat down on a bale of hay that rested outside the stable walls, cursing the day that Eunice Gupwell had entered her life.

She would never forget that dreadful afternoon. It had started so well, her father finally due to return from England, where he'd gone to conduct business on behalf of the Irish people. He'd written to say he was coming home and bringing a wonderful surprise with him. The last thing Lucy expected was the surprise he had in mind.

Her father alighted from the carriage and Lucy ran out the door to meet him, filled with happiness. Three long months it had been since she'd laid eyes on his dear face, and at first she saw nothing but him as she wrapped her arms around his back in a fervent embrace. And then a woman materialized behind him, the haughtiest woman Lucy had ever seen, her face sharp, her eyes sharper yet and coldly calculating as they swept Lucy up and down in what Lucy could only interpret as displeasure.

"Eunice, allow me to present my daughter, Lucy. Lucy, my sweet, this is your surprise. Give your new mother a kiss and make her welcome, there's a darling."

Lucy nearly keeled over with shock. *Her new mother?* She shot her father a frantic look, praying she'd misunderstood. Surely he'd meant her new governess? He'd said he intended to find her one, now that she was of an age to be taught the female social graces a man knew little about . . .

"Lucy?" he repeated, nudging her in the back and urging her forward. "Come now, daughter, show some manners to your Aunt Eunice."

Lucy somehow managed to stumble out a welcome and her frozen lips grazed the woman's heavily powdered cheek. In that moment she knew that her father had made a terrible mistake and life would never be the same.

She was right. Her new stepmother made no bones about the fact that she disliked Lucy, although she was careful never to show her animosity in front of her husband, saving it for private when she didn't bother to disguise her distaste for her twelve-year-old stepdaughter, treating her with heavy sarcasm.

"Really, Lucy, I don't think your attitude is pleasing, no more pleasing than your unfortunate appearance. I do wish you would try harder, if only for your father's sake. You might at least tie your hair back in a more seemly fashion, but I suppose with such unfortunate hair as yours, it is difficult to do anything with it. It's rather too bad, that shade of glaring black, but I suppose you inherited it from your mother."

She called Lucy gawky, which Lucy was, not that she could do anything about it. She mocked Lucy's accent, and that did put Lucy's back up, for her accent was pretty, softer and more lyrical than Eunice's ugly clipped British intonation that stripped the charm from the English language. But Lucy soon learned to imitate her stepmother's speech patterns to avoid being needled.

She said Lucy was ignorant, which Lucy wasn't. Her father had educated her himself and done a fine job, but Eunice had no care for that sort of learning. She was interested only in needlepoint and painting watercolors and playing vapid tunes on the pianoforte. Lucy played lovely Irish ballads on the harp, but that wasn't good enough for Eunice either, so Lucy dutifully set about teaching herself her stepmother's preferred instrument and she studiously improved her needlepoint. Watercolors were beyond her, but she worked at them anyway. She tried as hard as she could to please the unpleasable Eunice for her dear father's sake.

At first he seemed contented enough with his new wife, even though she was as different as night to day from Lucy's mother, a gentle woman with a cheerful manner who had run Kincaid with an efficient and loving hand until her death two years before. But where Lucy's mother adored everything about Kincaid, being a woman of old Gaelic blood, Eunice, who had not a drop of Irish blood in her, did nothing but complain about the cold and damp and lack of adequate facilities.

Lucy couldn't think what Eunice found inadequate about Kincaid; it was the coziest, most comfortable house in all of Ireland, with water closets and bathrooms in nearly every bedroom and fires burning in every grate. But nothing satisfied Eunice, who moaned nonstop about Kincaid's isolation, the lack of parties, the rutted roads and the rain, the inferior quality of servants and the even more inferior quality of the food. The only blessing was that Eunice had no idea of how to run the house and no interest in doing so, and so she left the management to Lucy.

Lucy loved the servants, who made her task easy. They were her dear friends, as were the local people whom Eunice called filthy peasants and treated like vermin beneath her feet. And to call the food inferior really was beyond belief: It was the freshest, most wonderful food in the world and there was plenty of it too, and nicely cooked. Just because it didn't come smothered in rich French sauces didn't mean it wasn't of the highest quality.

Lucy really didn't know how she was going to bear life with her stepmother, given Eunice's nagging tongue and overbearing manner. But she didn't say a word to her father, not wanting to upset him—Lucy knew he had married Eunice to give his daughter what he thought was a much-needed mother. Unfortunately for them both, he had unwittingly chosen a harridan for a wife, and as the weeks went by, it became clear to Lucy that he regretted his decision. But he never said a word to her, and Lucy loved him enough to keep her silence on the subject as well.

But the worst was yet to come. Two months later, Eunice's two daughters from her first marriage arrived.

Fiona, a year older than Lucy, had her mother's red hair and sharp features and an even sharper tongue, if that was possible. Amaryllis, only two months younger than Lucy, was a pudding-face who never stopped stuffing it with sweets, and that didn't help her already spotty complexion. Her frizzy mouse-brown hair was rendered uncontrollable by the wet weather, and she spent hours and hours tying it up in tight ribbons while she plastered her face with various smelly concoctions that were supposed to make her skin flawless.

But Lucy tried with them too, once again for her father's sake, even though they were impossibly stupid and couldn't get a sentence out without littering it with malapropisms.

"How many times do I have to tell you that I'm discerning of horses?" Fiona said when Lucy yet again invited her to ride, even offering her own favorite mare as a mount. "If you had any sense you would realize that I have no desire to jilt around on a smelly, sweaty beast and cover myself in hair."

"Lucy, you are such a putrid heathen," Amaryllis said, when Lucy invited her to go fishing. The salmon on the Moy were running high, and Lucy thought she was offering a great treat. "If you ever want to catch a husband, you should be concerting on your appearance," Amaryllis continued, snickering. "There is a great deal of room for improvidence, after all. No man wants to be married to a woman who wears breeches and comes home smelling of slimy fish." More snickering.

And when Lucy went out with the guns for a wonderful day of woodcock shooting, Fiona and Amaryllis behaved as if she were truly beyond the pale and said as much. "You really are a retestable girl. Melding with the riffraff only shows what sort of stock you come from."

There was nothing to be said to that. She was of Irish descent. They were of British. The implication was clear: She wasn't fit for their company. Her relationship with her stepsisters was doomed for failure, just as her relationship with her stepmother was doomed.

Perhaps if events hadn't unfolded as they had, things might not have been as bad. But sadly, events had unfolded as they had, and her father had died, leaving her alone and helpless, consigned to her stepmother's care.

Which was why she was now acting as housemaid, cook, and general dogsbody instead of living the comfortable life of privilege to which she'd been born. She didn't mind so much about losing the comfort or the privilege, not when so many of her friends suffered around her. What she minded most was being forbidden to see the people she'd grown up with and loved with all her heart, regardless of their lower station.

They were Irish. *She* was Irish. That was all that mattered. They shared a common heritage, a common love for land and country. And a common hatred for the English, who had brought about so many of their troubles.

Eunice and her daughters were the crowning example of why the British deserved to be loathed, Lucy thought, leaning her chin into her hands. The British were all the same, thinking they were better than anyone on the face of the earth, as if God had given them some special dispensation. Superior and grasping, they took as they pleased, and never mind whom they trampled in the process.

Rape, pillage, thievery, injustice, it was all in a day's work for the English, and history had proved that they would never change, given that they'd been at it for a good eight hundred years when William the Conqueror had raped and pillaged his way into Saxon territory, seizing the crown. The English hadn't looked back since.

Lucy took a deep breath and raised her face to the shining gold circle of the moon.

"O Lord, if you love me at all, please, please, take me away from all this," she whispered. "I try hard to follow Your path and not to complain, and I know many have suffered and been martyred far worse than I before this in the name of their country and their faith, but a little mercy on Your part would be much appreciated. Only if You think I'm deserving of it, of course," she added fairly.

The moon hung as silent and far away as God, and Lucy sighed. She was beginning to wonder if He ever listened to prayers, for it seemed to her that if He did, there wouldn't be so many hopeless people living hopeless lives. But still, she was probably one of the least deserving of His servants, since she was proud and intractable and her volatile temper was one of her more glaring faults—or at least it had been before the appearance of Eunice Gupwell. Now it lived like a caged beast inside of her.

Lucy shrugged philosophically. "Oh, well, Lord, maybe You found a way to put me in my place, and I suppose I shouldn't be complaining, since I suppose You know what You're doing, and I must deserve this. But I still don't understand why You had to take my father away . . ."

A hard lump formed in her throat and she swallowed against it. Any thoughts of her father, which unfortunately occurred on a regular basis, only brought more misery.

How she regretted her actions that night, regretted believing the semiilliterate message that she found lying on her pillow, imploring her to go to her old friend Nell Bailey who lay ill with a terrible chest congestion that threatened to carry her away before the night was over.

Lucy had gone, of course, taking her bag of medicinal herbs with her. Loyalty and concern compelled her to go, even though her father had warned her that Nell's brother Jamie was deeply involved in the local Secret Society and Lucy was to stay well away from the family. Feelings were running high at the moment and violence could break out at any time.

But her father discovered her disappearance and went after her, knowing what she didn't know—that a rising had been planned for that very night.

It was his great misfortune to be found in the Bailey house at the time of Jamie's arrest, having only just arrived to take Lucy away. Lucy flinched as memory returned in full, explicit detail, each horrible moment forever ingrained on her brain.

She would never forget the terrible shouting, the sound of the door splintering as the British militia broke in, the sharp sounds of gunfire coming from the front parlor as she cowered in the back bedroom with Nell, whom she'd been surprised to discover in perfect health, Nell just as surprised to see her. Nor would she ever forget the feel of Nell's sobbing, shaking body in her arms as her brother was shot dead before her eyes.

But worst of all was the unforgettable sound of Lucy's father's voice calling to her in panic, suddenly cut off by another hail of gunfire.

He'd lived long enough to be carted off to jail, to see his beloved estate confiscated. That Kincaid was the only Protestant household that hadn't been targeted for trouble didn't bode well for him—it only made him look worse, for her father was well known to be sympathetic to the anti-Union cause, and the British weren't prepared to hear his argument that Kincaid had been spared because he was a fair landlord and good to his tenants.

He'd lived long enough to know the misery of being ostracized by friends he had held dear, once he'd been released from prison. Long enough to know what miseries life could hold in a cold house near the cliffs of Downpatrick.

And yet he never once blamed his daughter, not even on his deathbed.

"Look after Eunice and her children," he'd whispered to

her, taking his last labored breaths of life, his fingers wrapped tightly around hers. "They are not used to this life or this country, and they have nowhere else to go, no one to turn to but you. You are Irish and can manage better than they. Sustain them. Sustain them."

He paused for a long moment, then smiled up at her, even though his face was strained with pain. "Be strong, my Lucy, and always stand firm in your beliefs and your love for your country—continue to pray for her freedom. You cannot blame yourself for what happened to me—only Thomas Montagu is responsible, for he deliberately set a trap for both of us."

"But, Papa," she said, her heart breaking, tears of anguish and guilt pouring down her cheeks. "If only I hadn't gone to Nell's on a misguided mission, you would not be lying here now!"

"It was not your fault," he said. "The Lord is taking me to His Kingdom, and I shall be content to be with your mother at last. Do not miss me too much, Lucy, and remember above all that I love you, daughter of my heart." He squeezed her hand weakly. "Make me proud, and most of all be the happy girl you were born to be. Never forget that your mother gave birth to you with a smile on her face. Find a man to love as truly as I loved her, and when you find him, never let him go, for love is God's greatest gift of all to us."

And so he died as he had lived, with love in his heart and hope in his soul.

Lucy had held on to his words with everything she was worth. She reminded herself of them every day and every night, the food that sustained her spirit and kept her rising in the morning, even when she was cold and tired and on the verge of hopelessness.

With the thought of her father firmly in the forefront of her mind, Lucy rose from her bale. She went into the dark stable to check on the horses and make sure they had enough hay and water for the night. And then she slowly made her way back to the house and her much-needed bed.

Lucy's head ached, and every bone in her body felt as if it had been dragged behind a horse for at least two days. The heavy pounding on the door didn't do anything to lift her spirits. Another creditor, no doubt, come to exact payment she didn't have. No one else but demanding creditors ever came to call.

"All right then, keep it down—I'm coming," Lucy called from the kitchen. Cleaning cold ashes from the fireplace suddenly seemed a delightful task, compared to what was probably waiting for her.

She wrenched the door open, not bothering to wipe the cinders from her face or straighten the cap she'd piled her hair up under. "Well then, and what's gotten under your skin for you to be making such an almighty banging at this hour . . ."

The words died in her throat as she blinked into the bright sunlight, taking in the man before her. She stared, utterly nonplussed, her heart pounding painfully in her chest.

It was he. The man from the day before, the man who had stared at her from the other side of Downpatrick Head, the man who for one brief magical moment had made her believe in fairy tales and princes and true love.

She'd even gone so far as to dream about him in her brief hours of exhausted sleep, a sweet dream where he'd held her in his strong arms and kissed her, whispering passionate words of love into her ear. In the dream she'd been dressed like a princess of old, wearing a fine gold dress spun from the thread of a thousand silkworms, a gossamer shawl around her shoulders.

And here he was at her door, even more handsome than she'd realized, now that she could see him up close. His hair, the color of dark gold, blew around his bare head, and his gray eyes, as clear and piercing as a bright winter day, regarded her steadily. But they held no sign of recognition.

She knew she was dirty and that the dim interior light in which she stood had him at a disadvantage, but still her heart fell. *Don't you know me?* she wanted to cry. *Don't you remember the way you looked at me yesterday, your heart in your eyes?* But she steeled herself, remembering that he was not only English, but partly responsible for her current lack of sleep.

"M-may I help you?" she finally managed to stammer.

"Is Lady Kincaid at home?" he asked in his despicable English accent.

"And who might you be?" she demanded rebelliously in a strong brogue, even though she could speak English with every bit as proper an accent as he on the rare occasions that she put her mind to it.

"Southwell," he replied, producing a snowy-white card with a gold crest on it and holding it toward her with long, perfectly manicured fingers. Lucy took it with a shaking hand and looked numbly down at it.

Raphael David Charles Montagu, Duke of Southwell, Marquess of Airely, Baron Montagu, it read.

Lucy swallowed hard over the tight knot of revulsion that formed in her throat. *He* was Thomas Montagu's cousin and Kincaid's new landlord? A duke? And not just a duke, but an arrogant duke with a fancy calling card, fancy string of titles, and fancy dress. The devil himself couldn't have come as a more terrible shock.

She narrowed her eyes, the loathing that she already felt for him building into a righteous fury. "I'm not in the way of knowing how to read," she lied, thrusting the ivory rectangle back at him as if it were poison.

"I didn't mean it for you," he said coolly, ignoring the card directly under his nose. "I meant it for your mistress. You might give it to her and tell her that the Duke of Southwell would be much obliged if she would receive him."

Lucy thrust her chin forward. Her mistress indeed. Who did the man think he was? God Himself? Sure, and she was the chambermaid born to lick his boots, and so he clearly thought, given that he scarcely bothered to look at her. It was little wonder he didn't recognize her when he thought her a mere servant beneath any regard at all. Well, she could play that game with the best of them.

"The lady of the house is not at home," she snapped. That wasn't true, but his holiness didn't need to know that her stepmother was still upstairs sound asleep, even though it was gone past ten. The sooner they were rid of him, the better.

"I see," he said, examining the toe of his gleaming boot as if it held a great fascination. "Then you will please tell her that I called and would be gratified if she would be kind enough to return the call this afternoon at her convenience. She can find me at Kincaid Hall."

"And what would you be wanting with her ladyship?" Lucy asked, unable to help herself.

"I cannot see what business that is of yours," he replied, a slight frown of displeasure marking his brow.

"Well, you can't expect me to be passing on messages from complete strangers," Lucy said, shoving her hands on her hips, wishing him to hell.

"I can certainly expect someone in Lady Kincaid's employ to do the job she's paid to do," he retorted, raising one eyebrow. "And if you don't, you can be sure your mistress will hear about it, for I will return should she not come to me."

Lucy bit her lip. The last thing she needed was another tongue-lashing from Eunice. "Very good, sir," she said, refusing to use his high-and-mighty title. "I'll pass the word on."

He nodded curtly, shot her one last look of disdain, and turned on his booted heel. Lucy watched as he mounted his horse, the large gelding as white as snow, and thundered off into the distance, his back ramrod straight.

"Meacht gan teacht ort, mar gheanna fiane Baile Ui Dhoinn!" she muttered in Gaelic, slamming the door and leaning her head against the wood, delayed shock pounding through her body and leaving her weak at the knees.

If only he *had* been her prince—an Irish prince, of course—she would have thrown herself into his arms and poured out her troubles to him. He would have lifted her onto the back of his white charger and taken her away to a blissful life in a lovely house and together they would have made beautiful children and heaped beneficence upon the people . . .

"Who was at the door, and what was that you just said, Lucy?"

Lucy spun around to see her stepmother standing halfway down the stairs, her dressing gown wrapped tightly around her as she peered through the dim light.

What she'd said was *May you go and not return, like the wild geese of Ballydine,* but she wasn't about to goad Eunice into doling out another punishment for that piece of impertinence. "The gentleman at the door was the new owner of Kincaid, Aunt Eunice."

"The new owner of Kincaid?" her stepmother said uncertainly, one hand clutched at the neck of her wrapper. "Did he give his name?"

"Many of them," Lucy said tartly. "The most significant one was the Duke of Southwell." She knew that would make a big impression on her snobbish stepmother.

Eunice emitted a shriek. "The Duke of Southwell? Good heavens! Oh, my goodness gracious—the duke was calling on *me*?" Her hands flew to her bare head, and she patted her uncombed auburn curls as if that would make a difference to her disheveled appearance.

"He certainly wasn't calling on me," Lucy retorted. "I told him you weren't at home since I knew you wouldn't be presentable."

Her stepmother's cheeks flushed with excitement. "But

he's one of the most eligible men in England, you imbecile girl! Perhaps he heard I have two daughters of marriageable age. Why didn't you detain him?"

"Because he requested that you pay him a call instead," Lucy said. "This afternoon, at your convenience."

"He did? What else did he say?" Eunice demanded, flying down the rest of the staircase. "Tell me everything. Did he ask who you were?" she said, one hand creeping to her cheek in dismay.

"No. He assumed I was the maid and I didn't bother to correct him," Lucy replied wearily.

Her stepmother nodded curtly, but she couldn't hide the quick flash of satisfaction in her green eyes. "Just as well," she said. "Your appearance would have filled him with revulsion if he'd thought anything else." She clapped her hands. "What are you standing about for? Bring up the breakfast trays and hot water and be quick about it. The girls and I will need to start dressing. Perhaps our fortune has changed at last!"

She turned and ran back up the stairs, flapping like a hen chasing after the feed bucket.

Lucy watched her go with a sigh of disgust. Typical. One English duke had spent two minutes on the doorstep and her stepmother was already planning a wedding. It was enough to make a body sick.

She turned on her heel and went back to the kitchen to boil hot water and prepare three breakfast trays.

But her mind was sorely troubled. What did an English duke *really* want with her stepmother? Lucy couldn't shake off a heavy sense of foreboding that the duke was going to turn their lives upside down, and it wasn't a happy thought.

Still, her aunt's absence would give her a chance to pay a surreptitious visit to the O'Reillys and bring them some much-needed food.

"*L*ady Kincaid and her daughters are outside wanting to see you, sir," the maid announced awkwardly, scratching at her cap with one hand and pulling at her apron with the other as she attempted a curtsy that looked more like a duck bobbing under water.

"Thank you, Nancy," Rafe said, regarding her with resignation. He really couldn't expect much polish from a village girl who had been hired only that morning, but she really was going to need some training. "Please, show them in," he prompted. "And straighten your clothes," he called as she vanished again.

Raphael stood, rubbing his tired eyes. He hadn't been able to shake off his troubled thoughts of the woman on Downpatrick Head since he'd left the cursed place. Who was she? Where had she come from, and more important, why had she thrown herself off the cliff to her death? A dozen possibilities had run through his mind, each of them more depressing than the last.

He frowned, wishing that he could turn time back and change the tragic course of events. Wishing the mysterious woman he thought of as Egeria was still alive. Wishing all sorts of things he couldn't have.

"Lady Kincaid and her girls," the maid said, poking her head back into the room like a rabbit inspecting a burrow.

Rafe turned abruptly and regarded the woman who appeared in the drawing room doorway. He instantly regretted his invitation.

She was one of the more unpleasant-looking creatures he'd ever laid eyes on. It wasn't that she was unattractive, more that everything about her spoke of sharpness. Her nose was sharp, her cheekbones and chin were sharp, her eyes, deep set and slightly too close together in her head, were sharp and regarding him rather too keenly.

"Lady Kincaid, may I make you welcome?" His gaze traveled past her to the two girls who stood behind her, and he had to stifle a laugh. Now they really *were* unattractive, one tall and gangly, with hair the color of new rust, the other short and plump as a partridge and spotty to boot. He couldn't think why Lady Kincaid had brought them along, when he'd only requested to see her. Perhaps she was a deluded mother hen proudly parading her half-hatched chicks. He'd met enough of both in his time.

"Your grace, I am delighted to make your acquaintance," Lady Kincaid said, rushing forward and dropping a curtsy. "I cannot tell you how pleased I was to hear that you had paid me a call, although you must excuse the sorry state of my dwelling—it cannot properly be called a house."

Raphael privately agreed with her. He'd been wondering all day why Lord Kincaid had left his wife and stepdaughters in such straitened circumstances. Lady Kincaid's present state of penury only reinforced his suspicion that Thomas's purchase of Kincaid Hall had not been a fair bargain.

"Please, take a seat. Miss Kincaid and, er . . . Miss Kincaid? I beg your pardon for my form of address. I don't know your Christian names, or which is the elder, for that matter."

"This is Fiona, my eldest," Lady Kincaid twittered, gesturing toward the redhead, who simpered and giggled. "And Amaryllis, my youngest," she added, indicating the pudding. "But their surname is actually Gupwell, your grace, as they are the children of my first marriage to Mr. Lionel Gupwell of Sussex. Sit down, girls, sit down, and show his grace your pretty manners."

Gupwell? Rafe thought the name suited them perfectly. There was a certain poetic justice to it. "Tell me, Lady Kincaid," he said, suppressing a sigh at what was obviously going to be a tedious half hour, "you are British, are you not? How did you come to relocate to Ireland?"

"Oh, yes, your grace, I am British through and through," she said, fluttering her hands. "My second husband, the late Lord Kincaid, was of Irish descent, however. We were introduced in England, and he persuaded me to move to the land of his birth upon our marriage." Her face darkened. "I cannot say that living in Ireland has been a happy time for me," she continued, her voice now plaintive. "I pine for my own country more than I can say, but sadly, I have not the funds to effect a change in my pitiful situation or even see to my dear daughters' marriages, for they have no prospects here at all. We are as you see us, stricken by poverty, with no one to turn to."

Both Gupwell girls pulled long, sorrowful faces as if to confirm their mother's words.

Rafe nodded. "I see," he said, not really seeing at all. "It was your husband's death that threw you into these circumstances?"

"Our unfortunate circumstances," she said, emphasizing the word "unfortunate," in case he might have missed it, "preceded my husband's premature death, and certainly hastened it, all thanks to Thomas Montagu. But perhaps I should not speak ill of your relative . . ." She cast a sorrowful glance up at him from under her carefully darkened eyelashes.

"What has my cousin to do with your situation?" Rafe asked cautiously, knowing what was probably coming. Knowing Thomas.

Lady Kincaid clutched her hands in her lap and looked

down at them, the picture of unhappiness. "Do you wish me to be blunt, your grace?"

"I wish nothing else," he said, bracing himself for the inevitable bad news. "Please. Continue."

"Your—your cousin arrived in Ireland looking for a less expensive property than he could find in England but one that would still give him standing as well as comfort. Mr. Montagu visited us at Kincaid Court, claiming a connection through a mutual friend." She sighed heavily and pulled a handkerchief from her reticule, dabbing at her eyes. "Unfortunately, your cousin decided that Kincaid itself would suit him well, and so he seized an opportunity to have it confiscated from my husband."

"Thomas had Kincaid *confiscated*?" Rafe said, his stomach tightening with suppressed outrage. "And how, pray tell, did he manage that? Was your husband a Catholic?"

"No!" she said, as if the very word was an anathema. "Ian's family converted to Protestantism three generations ago to avoid that very problem. It was all lies that your cousin fabricated, your grace," she said, her voice rising as she dabbed more furiously at her eyes. "All lies! My husband had nothing to do with the outbreak of rebellion he was accused of aiding—why would he compromise everything he held dear? It was just that dear Ian was found in the company of one of the insurrectionists directly after violence broke out and your cousin accused my husband of complicity, saying that he had overheard him earlier plotting with the man. Why should Ian have lost his home, his position, his good name over such a miserable mistruth?"

"Poor Mama," the eldest Gupwell girl said, fidgeting with her skirt. "It has been such an ardent time for her."

"Yes," the pudding chimed in, "and she's been so brave in the face of calumny."

Dear Lord, Rafe thought, they can't even speak correctly.

"Oh, my sweet girls," Lady Kincaid said, a tear squeezing out of the corner of her eye. "You have been brave too, always willing to lend a hand and never complaining about our difficulties, even though you must go without pretty clothes and decent food."

"Please, try not to upset yourself, Lady Kincaid," Raphael said gently, seeing her very real distress and knowing all too well that Thomas was easily capable of creating a false scenario in order to implicate Lord Kincaid and steal his property. He'd seen Thomas in action, stepping over anyone in his way to get what he wanted. He'd been like that even as a child, and Rafe had had no tolerance for him then.

"Let me see if I understand you," he continued, rubbing his temples as he tried to sort through the hellish tangle that was Irish politics. "Your husband was accused of treachery to the Crown because he was discovered in the company of someone suspected of anti-Union activities. And Thomas's word alone was enough to convince the magistrate that your husband was guilty? Why?"

"My husband was well known for his sympathies toward the cause for emancipation, your grace," Lady Kincaid said, sniffing loudly. "I told him time and time again how dangerous his political ideology was, but he would not listen to me. But he never had any hand in aiding or abetting the violence that constantly erupts here. My husband was a man of peace and so he preached."

"Yes, of course. And yet my cousin was nevertheless able to implicate him."

"Yes, your grace, that is it exactly. My husband had no defense but his word. It was not enough, for the evidence your cousin concocted against him was strong. And so Kincaid Court was taken away by the government and sold to your cousin for a song. The only property my husband was allowed to keep was the one you saw today, a worthless house on worthless land, and we had only a pittance of income left to support us." She sniffed into her handkerchief. "Ian was wounded in an exchange of gunfire at the time of his arrest and died of his injuries only a few months later, abandoned by his friends, his very heart broken."

Rafe considered this piece of information. When questioned, Paddy Delany had said nothing about the Kincaid family being forced out into the cold, only that there had been political troubles and the widow and her children had relocated to a less desirable property. He'd certainly never expected to uncover such a sordid story of treachery and outright theft.

Now here he was, facing this woman and her daughters who had been impoverished through no fault of their own and through no fault of his. Yet to his way of thinking, they had become his responsibility, as unwelcome a burden to him as Kincaid Court was. All thanks to that miserable toad Thomas.

He had to do something. Perhaps he would even feel better if he did something. He hadn't been able to avert a tragedy yesterday, but he could certainly ease this family's way in the world.

Rafe tapped his fingers against his thigh, thinking hard. There had to be a way to make their lives easier without burdening himself with them in perpetuity. Lady Kincaid had talked about her daughters' lack of prospects. Well . . . perhaps he could do something about that.

"Lady Kincaid, if you had the means now, I assume you would immediately wish to return to England," he said, as pleased with his quickly formulated plan as he could be.

"Oh, yes, your grace," she said, raising her head and nodding vehemently. "I cannot tell you how quickly I would wipe the mud of this godforsaken country from my feet. My daughters and I would be on the next boat." She gave a delicate shrug of one shoulder. "But, alas, that is not to be. It is all I can do to keep food on the table, and that of the poorest quality . . ."

"Perhaps I can do something small to aid you in your time of trouble, for I have been moved by your story." He wondered if his shaken reaction to the horrible scene he had witnessed the day before hadn't caused him to lose his common sense, for Rafe didn't miss the quick calculation in Lady Kincaid's eyes as she sensed a plum about to be dangled.

"Something small to aid us in our time of trouble?" she repeated, leaning slightly forward as if to grab the plum before it disappeared from her grasp.

"I would be willing to stand your daughters to a London season so that they might find husbands," he said. "I can set you up in your own town house, see to proper wardrobes for the three of you, and lend you my patronage. And I can bestow modest dowries on each girl to increase her chances for a suitable match."

The girls squealed loudly in unison, and Lady Kincaid looked as if she might fall out of her chair at any moment. "Your—your grace," she sputtered, her pointed face mottling red. "You are too good, truly too good . . . I never expected such generosity!"

Rafe held up a hand. "There is one provision. If your daughters do not manage to find husbands in this one season, then I assume no further responsibility. Naturally I will do my best to further their cause, but you, madam, will have to see that they are prepared to make the best possible impression." He gave her a meaningful look, reluctant to say anything further in front of the girls.

"Oh, your grace, upon my word, my girls are the best-behaved pets that ever lived! It is only the opportunity to show them to their best advantage that has been lacking. Oh, my gracious, this is a dream come true!"

The Gupwell girls nodded vehemently, clutching each other's hands in wild excitement.

"Perhaps," he said, trying to stifle a feeling of apprehension that he'd just made a terrible mistake. "But be warned. You will live comfortably, not extravagantly, on the stipend I give you. There will be nothing more forthcoming beyond that. And should the season finish without your daughters being spoken for, you will return to Ireland, although you may keep their dowries—which will remain in trust—in order to pursue their marriages in the future. Have I made myself clear?"

"Oh, yes, your grace," Lady Kincaid said, looking alarmingly as if she were bent on kissing Rafe's hand. He forestalled that unhappy prospect by quickly standing and moving over to the window.

"However," he said, a thought occurring to him as to how Lady Kincaid might be of some use, "you could do me one small favor in return."

"Anything, your grace. Anything at all. You are truly an angel of mercy!" she gasped, both hands pressed to her bosom.

"Not in the least. I prefer to think of myself as a reasonable man making a small gesture of apology for my cousin's behavior. Whatever the truth of the matter regarding your husband's misfortune and subsequent death, you were not at fault for what happened."

"You are most kind, your grace. There are not many who would be so generous or so understanding."

Rafe scratched his temple, thoroughly out of patience with the silly woman and her gawking, giggling daughters. "As I was saying, you could help me by telling me what you can about how you managed Kincaid Court in your time. There is much to be corrected here, and I would be grateful for any assistance you can lend me. The land agent has shown me the books, but he has no knowledge of how the estate was run prior to his tenure and no understanding at all as to how the household was managed."

Lady Kincaid offered an uncertain smile. "Certainly, your grace. If you will but permit me to gather my thoughts and try to locate the old housekeeping books, I could return tomorrow if that is convenient."

She looked around her, her brow furrowed as if seeing the house for the first time. The maid had removed the dust covers and done a cursory cleaning, but Rafe could just imagine what Lady Kincaid was thinking and he couldn't help but feel sorry for her obvious consternation. He felt it himself and he didn't have her emotional attachment to Kincaid Court.

"That will do very well," he said. "I shall not take up much of your time, for the books should tell me everything I need to know, and naturally you will want to begin to plan for your departure. I must write some letters and make arrangements for your stay, but with luck you will be in London in a few short weeks. In the meantime, you must make your own arrangements here for dress fittings, as the London season will have started in earnest and there will be no time to see to your wardrobes once you arrive. I will not detain you any further."

Lady Kincaid simpered at him, her eyes sharp with excitement as she rose and curtsied again. "You have saved our veriest lives, your grace. Our veriest lives. You shan't be sorry."

"I trust I won't," he said as the girls executed curtsies nearly as unfortunate as the new maid's and scurried through the door.

Rafe, utterly tired of being "your graced" to death, wondered if he wouldn't be very sorry indeed. But the die was cast, and there was no turning back. At least his generosity might act as a salve to his bruised conscience.

If only he could turn back the clock—if only he knew what had happened to Egeria to make her want to take her life. If only he could have stopped her . . .

"One moment," he said quickly, thinking that Lady Kincaid might be of more use to him than he'd realized. "I don't suppose you happen to be acquainted with a woman who lives in your vicinity? She is young and comely, wears a red cloak, and her hair is dark."

Lady Kincaid stopped abruptly in her grand passage from the drawing room. She hesitated for a moment before turning. "A young dark-haired woman who wears a red cloak, your grace?" she said, frowning heavily. "And where might you have seen her?"

"Late yesterday afternoon on Downpatrick Head," he said. "I hoped that you might know her identity."

"I can think of no one by that description," Lady Kincaid said in a dismissive tone. "It must have been a passerby. Downpatrick Head attracts curiosity because of the rock of Doonbristy that stands off it. It has an old legend attached."

"Oh?" he said, regarding her steadily. "And what is that?"

She shrugged one shoulder. "The Irish are attached to their legends, your grace, and this is a particularly silly one—something to do with a fight between St. Patrick and the Devil that was so violent they knocked a piece of the headland off into the sea."

Raphael had noted the detached stack of rock, but the legend held no significance to yesterday's event that he could see. "I had wondered about it," he said noncommittally. "And I also wondered at a young woman walking on her own so close to the cliff's edge." He waited to see if that might elicit something more.

"Some people have no common sense," she said with a dismissive shrug. "It would have served the girl right if she'd gone right over."

Raphael winced at her casual cruelty, but then she couldn't know the truth. Clearly, the girl's disappearance had not yet been discovered, or perhaps Lady Kincaid was right—Egeria had been from elsewhere and had chosen that isolated spot to end her life for whatever desperate reasons of her own.

"As you say," he replied, showing her to the door. "I'll expect you on the morrow."

As soon as she had gone, Rafe slumped into a chair and put his head into his hands.

Life had never seemed so deplorably cruel. Or so deplorably empty.

* * *

"Lucy! What are you doing here?" Brigid O'Reilly grabbed Lucy's arm and quickly pulled her inside the cottage. "Did anyone see you?" she asked, looking back out the door before she closed it.

"Don't worry, I didn't come across a soul. I had a chance to slip away, so I took it. Oh, Brigid," she said, slipping the basket from her arm and removing her cloak, "you wouldn't believe what has happened now."

"Oh, no," Brigid said, her eyes widening. "Lady Kincaid didn't find out about the food you've been bringing us every month, did she?"

"No, she hasn't the first idea," Lucy said, carrying the basket over to the kitchen table and setting it down. "Look in here—there are eggs, milk, and cheese, and fresh bread, and I also slipped in some salted pork and dried beans. And I even managed a pound of butter!"

"Butter? Lucy . . ." Brigid said, her face spreading in a broad grin. "I can't even remember the last time we had butter for our bread."

"Then enjoy it for all you're worth. It's no less than you deserve."

"Bless you," Brigid said softly, squeezing Lucy's hand. "I know the chances you take sneaking food out of the house."

"Don't you waste your time worrying about me. How is little Colm? Is he recovered from the whooping cough?"

"He's much better, thank you. My ma is just putting him down for a sleep. She'll be right happy to see you, almost as happy as she was that Colm made it to his first birthday, God be praised."

She pulled out a chair at the table and plopped Lucy into it, sitting down opposite and leaning her elbows on the table. "Well then, what's this news you're bringing us? I could do with a bit of gossip."

Lucy smiled fondly at her dear friend. She and Brigid had grown up together, for Mr. O'Reilly had been one of Kincaid's tenants before Thomas Montagu had evicted him. The O'Reillys had done their best ever since to scratch out a living from the poor soil of their tiny leased plot of land outside Ballycastle.

But with eight hungry children to feed, there was never enough to go around. Seeing that they had a little extra food was worth the risk, for without it they would surely starve.

"If it's gossip you want, I can give you that sure enough," Lucy said. "You'll never guess whom I answered the door to this morning."

"Sure, and that'll be the King of England come to pay his compliments to her highness, the Lady Kincaid," Brigid said with a mischievous smile.

"You're not so far off," Lucy retorted. "As it happens it was the Duke of Southwell come to pay his compliments to Her Highness."

"Who in the name of the Blessed Mother is the Duke of Southwell?" Brigid said, frowning.

"Someone who thinks he's next to God," Lucy said. "And he happens to be Thomas Montagu's cousin, and the new owner of Kincaid."

"May the saints protect us!" Mairead O'Reilly appeared from the bedroom, her face pale. "What did he want, colleen?"

"I don't really know," Lucy said, jumping up to give Mairead's cheek a kiss. "He said he wanted to see my stepmother, and as soon as she heard he'd called, she took off out the door like a ball shot from a cannon, dragging Fiona and Amaryllis with her. She seems to think he wants to marry one of them."

Mairead O'Reilly burst into laughter. "She does, does she? And what would a duke be wanting with one of those bad-tempered, pasty-faced girls? He'd be better off marrying my Brigid, not that she'd have him, would you, my sweet?"

"Not on your life," Brigid said, swatting a fly off the table. "I wouldn't let any Englishman within a mile of me, let alone a filthy, titled relative of Thomas Montagu's, may he rot in hell as he deserves."

"Yes, but if he isn't interested in paying court to my step-sisters, then what does he want?" Lucy said, fiddling with the locket around her neck in which hung the miniatures of her parents, always a comfort to her, especially in times of trouble. "He already has Kincaid. There's nothing else to take away."

Mairead O'Reilly scratched her head in perplexity. "It's a mystery to be sure. He didn't say anything to you, Lucy?"

"He just handed me a high-and-mighty calling card with his string of titles on it and said he wanted to speak to Aunt Eunice and would she please attend him at Kincaid this afternoon. Maybe his business had something to do with the estate."

"He didn't ask you?" Brigid said. "After all, you are the proper heir to Kincaid—or would have been, and you ran the house all those years. Who better to ask?"

"And how was he to know any of that? He barely looked at me, thinking I was a servant. I'm surprised he didn't ask me to clean the dirt from his boots while he was at it." Lucy grinned. "Of course, not a speck of dirt would dare to fall on that fine British leather, so there was no need for me to go down on my knees."

"And doesn't that make a change?" Brigid said with a disgusted snort. "It makes my blood boil just thinking about what that dreadful woman has done to you, Lucy, treating you like the mud beneath her feet. God should strike her dead."

"Now, Brigid, don't you go thinking you know what the Good Lord should and shouldn't do, not that I don't privately agree with you," Mairead said gently. "What sort of age is this duke, Lucy?"

Lucy paused for a moment, not that his image wasn't burned into her brain, but she thought she ought to at least give a pretense of considering. "He's somewhere in his late twenties, I'd say. He's tall and fair of hair, and better-looking than any man has a right to be—and I reckon he knows it too, from the way he struts about like an arrogant peacock."

That wasn't entirely fair, for in truth, he hadn't really strutted, but Lucy was still sure that he was mightily arrogant.

"Doesn't sound much like his cousin," Brigid said. "Except for the arrogance part, for never a more arrogant man did I ever come across. Or a crueler man either, throwing innocent people out into the street with no care to what might become of them."

"You can blame that Paddy Delany in equal parts," Mairead said, clenching her red, chapped hands together. "He was happy to enforce Mr. Montagu's wishes, wasn't he? He practically lived in Thomas Montagu's back pocket. I still think he's responsible for the forged note you received that terrible night, Lucy—he had everything to gain and nothing to lose by seeing Kincaid fall into Thomas Montagu's hands."

Lucy stood, not wanting to go over that painful ground again, although she wasn't sure that she didn't agree. "Oh, well, I doubt anything will change at Kincaid. Paddy Delany will continue to do as he pleases, and the duke will probably turn a blind eye to the suffering. I'd better hurry home before there's more trouble. Give my love to Mr. O'Reilly and the others—I miss you all so much."

"As we do you. Let us know when you can what happened between the duke and your stepmother, won't you?" Brigid said anxiously, giving Lucy a hard hug. "And thank you for the food. Look, Ma, what Lucy brought us . . ."

Lucy bid them a tender farewell as Mairead inspected the basket with exclamations of pleasure.

She quickly made her way home to finish the cleaning and washing and start the supper. Her heart felt lighter for having seen her friends and talked over her troubles, but she still couldn't help worrying about the duke's motives.

*   *   *

"Well, Lucy, didn't I tell you?" Eunice said, throwing off her cloak and collapsing into a chair, extending her feet out toward the blazing fire Lucy had laid. "My luck has finally changed."

Lucy glanced from Fiona's and Amaryllis's smirking faces to her stepmother's. "What happened?" she asked tentatively, nervously wondering what made all three of them look like cats in the cream pot.

"Fiona and I are to be married," Amaryllis announced smugly, handing her cloak to Lucy, who hung it up. "The duke is arraigning it."

"More like the duke is arranging his own marriage," Eunice said, tapping the tips of her fingers together. "He now has only to decide which one of you girls will be his wife."

Lucy turned and stared at Eunice, unable to believe her ears. "I—I don't understand," she stammered through her shock. "Did he say as much?"

"What he said was that he is prepared to offer us his patronage so that the girls may find husbands," Eunice said. "Naturally he wasn't going to come right out and announce his intentions, but the implication is clear nonetheless, and just as I thought."

"We're going to London for the season," Fiona crowed. "We will have a town house of our very own and couches to Almack's, and glorified clothes to wear—"

"And invocations to all the best balls, with gentlemen at our beckon call," Amaryllis added dreamily, and then she sat up straight as her mother's words sank in. "Do you really think the duke has it in mind to offer for one of us, Mama? Oh, to be a duchess . . ."

"And why else would the duke go to the trouble of bringing us to London, may I ask? Everyone knows that it is long past time that he marry and produce an heir. And the word is vouchers, Fiona dear, not couches."

"But *surely* you must mean he intends to offer for me, Mama?" Fiona asked, ignoring her mother's correction and shooting her sister a filthy look. "After all, I am the eldest and therefore the overt choice."

"I am not a mind-reader, Fiona. We shall have to wait and see. Now enough talk. Run upstairs, both of you, and change out of your good dresses."

Lucy closed her eyes for a moment as Fiona and Amaryllis dutifully bounded up the stairs, giggling and gossiping. She found it hard to believe that a handsome, eligible, and presumably wealthy duke would be deluded enough to want to make either Fiona or Amaryllis his wife, but on the other hand, why would he go to the expense and trouble to take them to England? It didn't make any sense. On the other hand, she hadn't come up with anything that made any more sense.

"I see," she said, thinking that even if the duke's wits had gone wandering, it was no business of hers, and at least she'd have a temporary respite from her stepfamily. "How very nice for you. I'm sure you'll have a wonderful time. When will you return?"

"I don't plan on ever returning to this dreary country, and I won't have to if the girls marry—that is part of the agreement. And as for you, miss, you will be coming along."

"But—but I don't want to go to England," Lucy said with alarm, seeing that her stepmother was perfectly serious. "I would far rather stay here."

"What you want is beside the point. You will do as you're told. And furthermore, when we do get to London you will stay out of sight." She waved a languid hand in Lucy's direction. "The duke has offered his patronage solely to the three of us."

A wave of misery washed over Lucy. Of course he would. He wouldn't want anything to do with an Irish girl, would he? "But then what possible reason would you have for taking me along?" Lucy said desperately. "I can stay here and look after the house."

"Oh, no. I don't plan to leave you here on your own

where I can't keep my eye on you. You're already too sneaky as it is. Look at your behavior only yesterday, never mind what you did to us six years ago." She pointed a finger at Lucy, her voice rising shrilly. "If it hadn't been for you, we would still be living at Kincaid and your father would still be alive, and don't think I've forgotten it."

Lucy knew she hadn't forgotten it. Eunice made a point of reminding her every two seconds. "But I still don't see why you want me in London, Aunt Eunice, especially if you want me to stay out of sight."

"To put it plainly, you deserve to be ostracized from polite society, and ostracized you shall be for as long as I have anything to say about it. It will do you good to watch your betters take their proper place in society—a place they would have assumed much earlier if you hadn't brought our lives crashing down around our ears."

Lucy didn't bother to defend herself, since her stepmother had always refused to listen to the truth. She looked numbly down at her hands. Ostracized. But then she was ostracized now, so what difference did it really make? "As you wish, Aunt Eunice," she said in a small voice.

"Exactly. As *I* wish. And furthermore, if you make any more trouble for me I shall be sure you regret it. I do not want the duke even to know of your existence, for if he did, my daughters' chances would surely be ruined."

"I don't see why," Lucy started to say, but Eunice cut her off with a furious glare.

"Enough!" she cried, two angry spots of red staining her pale cheeks. "You will not talk back to me. I've had enough of your impertinence to last me a lifetime, Miss Lucy Kincaid, and enough of your pride and disobedience as well. Heed my words, and heed them well: If you do not do precisely as you are told, I shall make good on my threat and turn the O'Reilly family's life into a living hell."

The renewed threat stopped Lucy cold. "Yes, Aunt Eunice," she recited dutifully, the surest and quickest way to placate her stepmother.

Eunice nodded with satisfaction. "And I've decided that as part of your punishment you can make yourself useful. We shall need a maid to look after our personal needs, and you do know how to dress our hair and look after our clothing. It's no worse a position than you deserve, given all the aggravation you've caused me, and it will keep the staff from asking unwelcome questions about your presence." She smiled coldly. "As far as the rest of the world is concerned, you will be the personal maid I've brought along from Ireland. That should knock your pride down a peg or two. You can go by the name of Lucy O'Reilly, which should serve as a constant reminder not to cross me in any way."

"Lucy—Lucy O'Reilly?" Lucy choked in disbelief. "It is not enough that you reduce me to a servant in your house, but you would steal my name as well as my friends'?"

"I certainly don't want anyone thinking that there is a connection between us. And I warn you again, you had better do or say nothing to give the impression that you are anything more than my maid. In fact, it would be best if you kept entirely to your quarters."

"What you really mean is that you intend to keep me locked away," Lucy said dully, thinking of life without fresh air and sunshine. Cruel punishment indeed.

"Not locked away, exactly, but I won't have you slipping out and gallivanting around where anyone might see you," her stepmother said. "House servants keep to the house, to the servants' quarters, to be precise. You will not have the status of lady's maid, for a lady's maid accompanies her mistress about town, and I have no interest in having you accompany me anywhere. No, you will be a simple maid with no privileges at all."

A cold sickness took hold of Lucy, spreading through every fiber of her being. She was to be dragged away from her beautiful homeland, stripped of her surname, and forced to

masquerade as her stepmother's maid? And yet what choice
did she have? She had no money of her own, and she wasn't
of age to be able to refuse. Her stepmother was her legal
guardian and could do with her as she pleased. Even worse,
to punish Lucy, she would do with the O'Reillys as she
pleased. Lucy's hands were tied. She could do nothing but
accept the miserable hand fate had dealt her. "Yes, Aunt,"
she said tonelessly, knowing she was trapped forever.

"Very good. I am glad we are clear on the matter. Now go
make tea. It was a cold drive back from Kincaid, and I'm
frozen through and through."

"Right away, Aunt Eunice," Lucy said, turning toward the
kitchen. Anything to be alone, to have some time to collect
her thoughts.

"Oh, and Lucy, do you have the old Kincaid housekeeping accounts?"

Lucy stopped in her tracks and turned. "The housekeeping accounts?" she said, puzzled by this sudden change of
subject. "Yes, they're upstairs in my room. But why—"

"Never mind why, girl, just fetch the books. I have a mind
to go through them. If I'm to run a proper house in London,
I'd like to have a better idea of how to budget."

Lucy personally thought that was one of the more absurd
ideas her stepmother had come up with—Eunice wouldn't
know how to budget if her life depended on it. "But I could
run the house for you, if you'd like," she said, thinking that
at least would make life more interesting.

Eunice sniffed. "If you think for one minute that I intend
to let you loose with the generous sum of money the duke is
going to bestow on us, you are sadly mistaken. You can't
even manage to run this excuse for a house properly."

"No, Aunt Eunice," Lucy said, wanting to strangle the
woman. She did her best to put decent food on the table and
see that there was enough money left over to keep the horses
in feed and the family in clothes, as well as paying for all the
other odds and ends. But she managed, even if she went

without herself. God forbid she should have a sorely needed new dress when Fiona and Amaryllis might have had a new pelisse or reticule instead.

"Exactly, my girl, exactly. Now see to that tea. I'm fair parched." Eunice heaved a sigh and put her feet up on the stool. "There is a great deal to be done, a very great deal. I don't know how I'm to manage it all in such a short space of time."

Lucy had nothing to say to that. She knew who would manage, and it wouldn't be her stepmother.

She made the tea and served it, made dinner and served that, listening all the while to the three of them chattering about their fine plans for the future.

And finally, finally, when they had retired for the night and Lucy had washed the dishes, she took herself off to her attic room and undressed, shivering in the cold. It was always cold, for there was no fireplace in her room. In any case the cold came more from her heart than from her body tonight, for her future looked bleaker than it ever had.

It was all the duke's fault that her life had come to this, that she was to be dragged off to a filthy city and forced into humiliation. Forced to hide even from him—especially from him.

The awful thing was that she hadn't been able to erase him from her mind. His imposing figure and handsome face had been in her thoughts all day, an unwelcome but persistent intruder into the most private corners of her being. She *knew* he was a bloody Englishman with no good in his heart, but that didn't seem to keep his image at bay.

Lucy finished washing and slipped between the freezing sheets, shivering uncontrollably. She blew out the single candle on her bedstand and turned her cheek into the pillow, willing sleep to come.

But she was not given the comfort of sleep. Instead, the image of a tall man with dark-gold hair and gray eyes swam once again before her mind's eye, gazing at her with single-minded intensity as he had the day before when he had stood across from her on the cliff.

Oh, in those moments, those shining moments when she thought he was a prince . . .

Well. He might be as handsome as a prince, but he didn't even come close to fulfilling any of the other requirements. Princes were supposed to rescue damsels in distress from towers, not condemn them to one.

She sat up and lit the candle again, picking up the book of poems that always soothed her when her mind was troubled. Turning to one of her favorite passages she began to read, losing herself in the gentle rhythm of *Childe Harold's Pilgrimage*, a poem that so well reflected her own sorrow, the prospect of her own desperate future. And yet there was a sad sort of beauty in it too.

> *Egeria! sweet creature of some heart*
> *Which found no mortal resting-place so fair*
> *As thine ideal breast; whate'er thou art*
> *Or wert,—a young Aurora of the air,*
> *The nympholepsy of some fond despair . . .*

But as she read, the printed words were replaced by the memory of the duke's deep voice reciting the words to her across the abyss, the shock of his British accent stripping her of all delight.

She snapped the book closed with a moan of frustration. He'd even ruined her favorite poem, her greatest solace. How could one man cause so much trouble? She flung the book across the room, where it hit the wall with a satisfying thump.

And then, after looking at the volume for a moment, tilted on one side, the pages skewed, she slipped out of bed and retrieved it, climbing back into bed and opening it to the same passage.

Or, it might be, a beauty of the earth,
Who found a more than common votary there
Too much adoring; whatso'er thy birth,
Thou wert a beautiful thought, and softly bodied forth.

"Just so," she whispered, thinking of how beautiful he had looked sitting on his horse. "Too bad you had to be an Englishman . . ."

She drifted off to sleep with the book clasped tightly to her chest as if she were clutching a life raft in a dangerously stormy sea.

4

"*M*y dear boy, how lovely to see you," the Dowager Duchess of Southwell said, giving her eldest son a warm kiss of welcome. "Your business in Ireland must have gone uncommonly well for you to be back so quickly and full of such unexpected plans."

She settled back onto the sofa in the sun-filled drawing room and regarded Raphael quizzically. She'd been awash with curiosity ever since receiving her son's letter informing her that he intended to sponsor Lady Kincaid and her daughters this season and wished his mother's assistance.

Rafe was not prone to taking in strays, so she could only presume that his generosity had something to with an attraction to one of Lady Kincaid's daughters. She had been praying for years that her son would take a wife and produce some grandchildren for her to cosset, but Raphael had never before been prone to showing anything more than polite attention to the women who graced the London drawing rooms when he bothered to grace them himself. She couldn't help but wonder if there was hope at last and had to resist the urge to question him further.

"You're looking very well, Mama," Rafe said, accepting the cup of coffee she poured him, his expression revealing nothing. "What news do you have?"

"Nothing very exciting. Lady Chesterfield has managed to

elicit a proposal for her daughter Frances, quite a coup for Francie's first season, and so early on, but then Francie always was uncommonly pretty, don't you think?"

"I hadn't noticed," Rafe said, glancing at her over the rim of his cup, one eyebrow cocked. "Who is the lucky man?"

"Jarvis," the dowager replied, waiting for Rafe's reaction.

"Good God," he said, choking. "That old man? What could the girl's mother be thinking? He's fifty if he's a day."

"And titled and rich and never married, like someone else I know. If he can be stricken with true love at his advanced age, it can happen to anyone." She smiled mischievously, but her amusement faded at Raphael's suddenly stony expression.

"Enough, Mama," he said. "You know how I feel about the subject."

"Perhaps that's the trouble," she replied tartly. "I don't know how you feel. You are always so controlled, my dear, that one cannot tell what is occurring behind that neutral ducal mask you like to assume."

Rafe frowned and put his cup into the saucer with a clatter. "And how would you have me behave? Like Hugo, perhaps, dashing about challenging people to duels, creating scandals with married women and opera dancers, single-handedly supporting the gaming hells of Paris?"

"Your brother is not my concern at the moment. Hugo will settle down in his own good time—he is still only twenty-five."

"And has created enough havoc to be at least twice the age," Rafe said wryly.

"At least he enjoys himself," the duchess said. "Although I do wish you would relax your ban and let him return to England where he belongs. Three years is long enough in exile, don't you think?"

"I'm sorry, Mama, for I know you miss him, but until Hugo gives some indication that he's grown up and is willing to take on some responsibility, I think it's better if he creates mayhem elsewhere. I haven't the time to constantly bail him out of scrapes, nor the inclination to fund his excesses."

The duchess released a sigh. "I suppose not, and I won't interfere. You are the head of the family, after all, and must do as you see fit. But that brings me back to my original point. You *are* the head of the family, Raphael, and you have a responsibility as such."

"I think I see the unfortunate direction this conversation is headed in," Raphael said with an impatient shake of his head.

"Darling, you have recently seen your twenty-ninth birthday. It is well past time for you to marry and produce an heir."

Rafe stood, shoving his hands low on his hips, his brow drawn down. "Mama, I am very fond of you, but not so fond that I intend to stay and listen to your never-ending litany on the subject of my loins and their duty."

"But, darling, you have to marry at some point. It *is* your duty."

"I have told you many times before that when and if I decide to marry, it will be to a woman of my choosing. I will not tolerate one more season of being forced to suffer the procession of empty-headed misses you produce for my perusal."

"Oh? From the sound of it, you have already organized the season for yourself. You do recall Lady Kincaid's two daughters whom you are about to install at Number Five, Upper Brook Street?"

Rafe rubbed one hand over his forehead. "Oh, yes, I recall. And I thank you, Mama, for arranging the house for them, as well as everything else you have done—and are going to do for me."

"It is my pleasure, darling boy, for you know that I enjoy assisting you in any way I can. But I must confess to curiosity about the girls. I met Kincaid years ago, you know."

"Did you?" Rafe said, his brow clearing. "How interesting."

"He was such a pleasant man and so interesting on the subject of Irish emancipation. He once said—"

Rafe snorted. "I don't want to hear another word about Irish emancipation, thank you. I've had enough of an earful in the last three weeks. Not one Irishman can open his mouth on any subject including the weather without bringing the blasted government into it. My head ached for the full time, and not just from the political fanaticism. It was a miserable experience altogether."

"You do look tired," she said with concern, not happy about the dark circles under Raphael's eyes. He always had worked too hard, putting the welfare of his various properties and tenants ahead of his own. She'd been so pleased when he had taken a year off to travel with his cousin Aiden and Aiden's dear new wife Serafina, sending back long letters of his experiences abroad. But even those detailed missives lacked the zest and enthusiasm for life that once had defined Raphael's nature. His childhood seemed such a long time away to her. But then Rafe had ceased to be a child a very long time ago.

She pushed that thought to one side, for she refused to worry over something that couldn't be changed—or at least couldn't be changed by her. Her only hope for her son's happiness lay with another woman. The only problem was that no woman had yet appeared in whom Rafe showed any interest and she really didn't know what more she could do to push him along the path to his own salvation.

"Tell me, Raphael, how did you find the Kincaid estate? You said nothing in your letter, and I never did understand why Kincaid sold his family home to Thomas, of all dreadful people. I know I shouldn't speak ill of your own father's nephew, but he really was not a very nice boy."

"He wasn't a very nice man either," Rafe said, sitting down

again as he began to explain the details of what he had learned.

The dowager listened carefully, her dismay growing by the minute as her son wove a miserable story about how Thomas had stolen Kincaid away from its rightful family and left them in poverty.

"Oh, dear . . ." she said, when he had finished. "I think I begin to see what prompted you to make such a generous offer. How very kind of you, my dear."

"Foolish is more like it," Rafe said, shaking his head. "I feel as if I made a bargain with the devil, for the brief time I've already spent in Lady Kincaid's company has not been a pleasant experience. She is grasping, and I might have said empty-headed, but the household accounts that she turned over to me show that not to be the case. Kincaid was extremely well managed under her watchful eye." He smiled faintly. "If nothing else, I at least have hope that she will not squander the money I've given her for her daughters' come-out."

"And the daughters?" the dowager said, gently prompting. "Are they as handsome as their father was?"

"Oh—didn't I say in my letter? They're Kincaid's step-daughters, the product of Lady Kincaid's first marriage to a Mr. Gupwell. I cannot think he was particularly fine-looking, considering his progeny."

One hand crept to the dowager's mouth. "Not—not Lionel Gupwell, by any chance?" she said, trying to suppress a choke of laughter. "Oh, yes, I do see, for he was most unfortunate in his looks, and not a very clever man, although harmless enough and tolerably well connected. But how odd."

"What is odd, Mama?" Rafe said, crossing one long leg over the other and regarding her wearily. "That I have offered to sponsor two girls who are as ugly as the backside of a hound?"

"No—only that I thought Kincaid had a daughter of his

own. Perhaps I was thinking of someone else. It is difficult keeping so many families straight."

"But you do make an admirable effort," Raphael said with a tolerant grin. "I've never known anyone who knows more about people's business than they do themselves. However, I can assure you that the Gupwell girls are the only daughters Lord Kincaid could lay claim to—unless he produced a child on the wrong side of the blanket whom I don't know about."

"Really, Raphael!" the dowager said in mock horror, and he laughed, a sound that warmed her heart, for she heard it too rarely.

"Don't you go all proper on me now, Mama. You know as well as I do that bastard children are a common occurrence, even in your elevated social circles."

"Nevertheless, I do *not* think you should put too fine a point on the matter as I cannot approve, no matter how common the occurrence might be. In any case, your social circle is exactly the same as mine, even if you do choose to spend the majority of your time avoiding it." She cocked her head to one side. "I confess to surprise that you are willing to go to the trouble of sponsoring two girls of unfortunate appearance and their avaricious mama. I suppose that, as usual, you feel bound by duty." She tried to disguise her disappointment that nothing more than duty had motivated her son to take the Gupwell girls on. She'd so been hoping that he'd found love at last . . .

"I can hardly feel otherwise. You might be thankful that I can remedy the situation so easily. Just think of the permanent obligation I'd have on my hands if Thomas had left a handful of by-blows behind on top of the rest of the mess he left."

He pushed a hand through his golden hair, ignoring his mother's attempt at a disapproving expression. "But never mind Thomas and his unfortunate habits, for I'd rather get on with the matter at hand. I think we must try to dispose of these girls as quickly as possible."

The duchess nodded. "I hope they do not plan to set their sights too high, for without beauty, charm, or large fortunes they can hardly expect to land more than an impoverished squire."

"I don't care if they land pig farmers," Rafe said, casually examining the back of one hand. "If they decide they are too proud for the lowly offers they'll be lucky to attract, then they'll be right back where they started, in a crooked house on the edge of an Irish peat bog with nothing at all. And I shall wash my hands of them."

"Very sensible," the dowager said, relieved that Raphael had committed nothing further. Given his outsize sense of responsibility, it could have been much worse, she decided. "Well, then. I suppose we should get started, for the sooner you have Lady Kincaid and her daughters off your hands the better. Where are they now?"

"Last heard of, they were putting up at a Dublin hotel, waiting for their wardrobes to be completed. I booked them passage on a boat due to leave two days ago, so I imagine they will be arriving at any time. They are to send word here when they are installed in Upper Brook Street."

"Then I suppose I should arrange for their presentation at court next week, followed by vouchers for Almack's, which will take care of their come-out," the dowager said. "The Southwell name will naturally open all the necessary doors, but they will have to do the rest in terms of making the right impression."

Rafe snorted. "Good luck. I might as well warn you, I don't intend to follow you about while you open all those necessary doors. I hope you don't mind."

"Mind? I expected nothing else. You may be admirably responsible in all other areas of your life, but you've never done more than the absolute minimum when it comes to presenting yourself in society."

Rafe shot her a rueful smile. "I know how my aversion to attending routs and soirées and balls aggravates you, Mama, and for that I am sorry, but you can't change me at this late date."

"I've given up trying," his mother replied. "But really, Raphael—if the family is as unpromising as you say, aren't you concerned about what people will think of your lending them your patronage?"

"I don't give two snaps, and since when have you ever worried about what people think, Mama?" Rafe retorted. "I thought you took great satisfaction from doing exactly as you pleased and letting the rest of the world go hang." He rose and dropped a kiss on the top of her head. "I've always admired you for your complete disregard of other people's opinions. Anyway, you love to rise to a challenge."

He had a point, the dowager privately conceded. And what a challenge. She might actually have fun confusing the polite world by bestowing the precious Southwell patronage on a thoroughly unsuitable family. She could always claim a fast friendship with the late Lord Kincaid, for in truth she had enjoyed their passing acquaintance.

The outcome remained to be seen, but she would try her best to enjoy herself in the meantime. And to redouble her efforts to find her son a suitable wife.

Lucy unfolded the last of Fiona's dresses and hung it in the grand wardrobe in Fiona's grand second-floor bedroom. London was exactly as she had expected—dirty and noisy, crowded with people and carriages and houses that stuck together like limpets on a rock. There was no room to breathe, let alone to think. The only blessing was the window in her attic bedroom that overlooked the back garden. The first thing she'd done was to throw open the sash and let the cool breeze flow in. The park beckoned temptingly only a short distance away, but sadly, that was forbidden ground.

She closed the wardrobe doors on the freshly pressed dresses. She'd never seen so many clothes in her life—between Amaryllis and Fiona and Eunice, they had amassed all that Dublin's dressmakers had to offer. Trunk after trunk had arrived with them, and the better part of Lucy's day had been taken up with putting everything away.

"Lucy, fish me my new shawl," Fiona demanded from her position at the dressing table where she was busily primping, turning this way and that as she admired her profile.

"Which new shawl?" Lucy asked, thinking that Fiona looked like an overfeathered ostrich as it was. Ruffles, bows, ribbons, all adorned her pale-blue, high-waisted dress, and there were more on Fiona's cap, which ended with a great satin sash under her chin.

"The white lace, you idiot. It was made to be worn with my walking dress. Can't you keep anything straight?"

"I do beg your pardon," Lucy said, digging out the required item, which she was sorely tempted to wrap around her stepsister's neck. "Are you going walking, then?"

"One never knows who might come to call," Fiona said, casting her a superior look. "Mama has written to the duke to inform him of our arrival, and he is bound to haul straight over."

"The—the duke?" Lucy stammered, her fingers suddenly fumbling with the scrap of material. Her stomach tightened painfully as her heart leapt with alarm. This was the moment she'd been dreading, not that it had anything to do with her. It was just that—just that . . . she didn't even know. Only that she wished she'd never heard of the man. That he plagued her thoughts night and day, making her life even more of a living hell than it already was. Anyone would think she was as silly as her stepsisters, indulging herself in hopeless fantasies about a man she could never have, and didn't even want when it came to that. What would she do with a duke? And he certainly wouldn't know what to do with her.

"He's coming today?" she managed to ask through a dry mouth.

"Yes, and when he does arrive, he might very well invite

us for a stroll in Hyde Park. Mama says that is where all the fashionable people walk."

"Yes, I know, I've heard all about it," Lucy said, handing her the shawl and untying the cap so that she could dress Fiona's hair. She'd heard everything there was to hear about how the *ton* lived and dined and danced and entertained. The last three weeks had been a nonstop lecture, delivered by Eunice not to her, who was in no need of it, but to Amaryllis and Fiona, who sorely were. Unfortunately, Lucy was subjected to most of Eunice's instructions, for there was no escaping from her constant presence.

She now knew more than she cared to about the habits and mannerisms of those born to British society. How one fluttered a fan. How one curtsied in varying degrees to people of rank. How one did not curtsy at all to those beneath one's regard. How one walked across a room, gave the cut direct or indirect to those one wished to insult, or simpered to those one wished to impress. It was all too silly, Lucy thought, as if one didn't have anything better to do than posture like a peacock and gossip about one's friends and enemies.

She couldn't help but be disgusted by the shameless waste of money on unnecessary items when so many people suffered from poverty and hunger. She'd seen enough of that as they'd traveled through the country, although the level of poverty did not come close to that which abounded in Ireland.

And yet . . . and yet she also couldn't help but wonder what it might be like to move among the very people she disdained, dine at their tables, accept a gentleman's hand for a dance. She would do a good job of waltzing, she reckoned, having been dragged into partnering her stepsisters so that they could practice their steps. But maybe not, since she had been forced to play the part of the gentleman, twirling them around and around, accompanied by her stepmother's loud humming.

"*Da* da da, *da* da da, *move* those feet, girls," while Fiona and then Amaryllis made mincemeat out of Lucy's poor toes.

That had been a sorry picture indeed. She wondered just how long it would be before her stepsisters made laughing-stocks out of themselves. Not that she wished them ill—she didn't, for their success would mean her freedom. Which was why she stood here now trying to make some sense out of Fiona's wild red hair that refused to stay tucked up in neat curls.

"Ouch! You're scabbing my scalp with those pins!" Fiona squealed, clamping her hands to her head and undoing Lucy's best efforts.

"I'm sorry, but if you want to look like a lady, you'll have to put up with a little discomfort. This isn't County Mayo, you know, where no one worries whether every last curl is perfectly in place."

Fiona grumbled but let Lucy finish the job. Lucy placed the cap back on Fiona's head and tied the sash in a wide bow. "There," she said, standing back. "I think that will do."

Fiona stared anxiously into the mirror. "Yes, I suppose I look preventable," she said, worrying at her bottom lip. "Do you think I look prettier than Amaryllis?"

Lucy almost—*almost* felt sorry for Fiona. The two girls had done nothing but bicker about which sister the duke intended for his wife. Personally, Lucy was still convinced that the duke had no such intentions toward either of them, but with Eunice constantly fanning the flame of competition, it was little wonder that they were at each other's throats the whole time. And as she didn't know what the duke really did intend, she couldn't completely rule out the possibility that he was dangling for a wife.

"I think you both look very nice," she said tactfully. "I am sure the duke will too." She had her doubts about that, but it didn't do to voice them.

"What is Amaryllis wearing?" Fiona said, twirling before

the looking glass with an over-the-shoulder glance at the back of her hem.

"Her yellow dress with the silk flowers on the bodice," Lucy said, thinking that the color was an unfortunate choice for Amaryllis's complexion, since it only made her look more sallow than usual. It was a pity that her stepmother didn't have better taste in clothes, but Lucy supposed that couldn't be helped. Eunice had refused to listen to Lucy's opinions, calling them uneducated and unsolicited.

"Oh, *that* one," Fiona said, scowling. "I wanted that one for myself, but Mama said I could have the velvet opera cloak instead."

"And very handsome it is," Lucy said, looking up as Amaryllis came barreling breathlessly into the bedroom, thumping about like a beached whale.

"He's here, he's here, and he has his mother with him!" she shrieked. "Mama is greeting them in the saloon. I declare I think my heart is going to leak from my chest!" She pressed her palms against her heaving bosom.

He's here. Lucy's knees went weak with shock, but she forced herself to control the violent emotions that seized at her heart. She might not be able to control her fantasies, where the blasted duke had free rein to do as he pleased and very often did, but she could certainly control her reactions when she was on guard against her overly fertile imagination. Why should she care if he was in the house? He was *English,* wasn't he? She *hated* the English, didn't she?

"If the duke is here, you had better go and stand at the top of the stairs and wait to be summoned," she said, pulling Amaryllis's bodice up with a tug, for it was showing an indecent amount of *English* bosom. "And where is your fichu? I dressed you in it only half an hour ago."

"Leave me alone, Lucy," Amaryllis said, slapping Lucy's hand away as she tugged her bodice down again so that two trembling mounds of white flesh reappeared. "Baring one's boom is all the rage. I don't need a silly fitchu."

"Fichu. And next you'll be damping down your dress so that you look as if you just stepped out of the rain," Lucy replied shortly. "Have a little modesty, Amaryllis. You'll find it goes a long way."

"What would you know? You're no better than a servant," Amaryllis said, sticking her tongue out. "Even Mama said so."

Lucy didn't reply. Maybe she was no better than a servant in their eyes, but at least she had her pride, as much as her stepmother had attempted to strip it from her. And she had her modesty too. They wouldn't find her standing on her head to impress anyone, from a duke to a dustman, and they wouldn't find her painting her face or baring her breasts just to please the dictates of fashion, not that she had the option to do any of those things.

"Remember," she said, herding her stepsisters out the door, and reciting from Eunice's social litany, "it's 'your grace' to both of them for now. When you're better acquainted, you can address them as 'Duke' and 'Duchess,' but you'd best err on the side of caution until you find your feet and hear how others go on."

Fiona rolled her eyes. "And who are you now, a duchess yourself?" She covered her mouth and giggled wildly. "Yes, your grace, whatever your pleasure, your grace," she mocked, sweeping Lucy a low, lopsided curtsy.

Amaryllis tittered. "Summon her grace a carriage, Fiona. Duchess Lucy wishes to pay the King of England a visit."

"He'd have her head for daring to show her face," Fiona said. "Can you imagine Lucy at court? The entire assemblage would fall into a faint at the sight of her. Have you looked in the mirror recently, Lucy Kincaid? As our mama always says, it's excruciating that a man as handsome as Papa Kincaid managed to produce a daughter as ugly as you."

Lucy felt like dying. Even though she was accustomed to her stepsisters' barbs, they rarely ceased to find their mark. Flushing deep red as Fiona and Amaryllis flounced out of the bedroom, she slowly walked to the looking glass and regarded her reflection.

Her hair fell down her back in a messy braid and the old dress she'd outgrown three years before was soiled, the hem torn where she'd caught it on the corner of a trunk she was unpacking. Her forehead was smudged with a streak of dirt where she must have run a hand over her damp brow. She reached up and tried to wipe it away, but only made it worse.

Lucy had never paid much attention to her looks, but she suddenly felt ashamed of her shabbiness in the face of her stepsisters' grandeur, as overstated as it was.

As much as she hated to admit it, she wished she might be in their shoes, that it was she who was going downstairs to greet a duke and his mother. She wished that it was she they would greet with pleasure, she whom they would take walking in the park in her fine new clothes, she they would bring to their grand house and introduce to their grand friends. She loathed herself for thinking it at all, but if she were to be honest with herself, it did seem a happier life to the one she was leading. And yet there was no good in wishing for what she couldn't have and didn't really want anyway, not deep down in her heart.

Lucy slowly raised her head. She was Lucy Kincaid, daughter of Charles Kincaid, descended from Gaelic lords. She could be proud of her lineage and her country, and be damned to the *English* who had stolen the land and tried to steal the pride away from her people, just as Eunice had tried to steal Lucy's own pride, all she had left to her. To the devil with Eunice and the uppity attitude that she'd passed on with great success to her own daughters.

She, Lucy Mary Katherine Kincaid, would hold her head high and her values even higher. She would not be beaten down. She would not be diminished, no matter how others tried to diminish her. She would make her dear father and mother proud of her, whatever fate dealt her. She would remain true to herself.

She had to escape. She couldn't stay in the same house, knowing the duke was here, knowing she would never see him, never have tea with him, never dance with him. Never kiss him.

Choking back unwelcome tears, Lucy ran upstairs to wash and change into a clean dress, determined to take advantage of the brief respite given to her and take a forbidden walk in the park. She'd wilt without fresh air. A half hour, no more, and no one would see her, for she'd leave carefully by the back.

As a small gesture of pride, she brushed out her hair and put it up every bit as fashionably as she'd arranged her stepsisters' hair.

And then she picked up her red cloak, the only object of clothing she owned that wasn't worn and shabby, the last present her father had given her, the only thing other than her locket left of her old life.

She gathered her cloak around her and let herself out of her room, closing the door softly behind her. As she passed by a window, she caught the sight of her own reflection in the glass. She lifted her chin.

And she wasn't ugly either.

5

*R*afe was about to die from boredom. One more vapid word out of either of the silly Gupwell girls or their mother and he was sure he'd lose his mind. He leaned his shoulder against the mantelpiece and gave his mother a resigned look as if to say *I told you so*.

But his mother ignored him, behaving as if she were enjoying herself. His sainted mother was good at that. She'd probably look as if she were enjoying herself in the middle of a battlefield. He, on the other hand, was growing weary of pretending to things he didn't feel. He'd been doing it for years and the charade was wearing thin.

He tuned out the tedious conversation, wishing he were anywhere but here. Even Ireland would be preferable, and there was a dark irony in that since he hadn't been able to wait to escape from his tormented memories.

But they had followed him even here.

He'd gone back to the cliffs of Downpatrick time and time again, hoping that he'd been mistaken in Egeria's fate, that she would magically reappear and his conscience would be put to rest. But day after day he had walked the cliffs alone.

Not a word had reached his ears about a drowned body being found, not a soul had said anything about a dark-haired woman in a red cloak going missing. Of course, hardly anyone talked to him voluntarily, but still, it was as if she had never existed. He began to wonder if he'd imagined the whole episode, but he knew perfectly well he hadn't. It was burned on his brain every bit as much as her face was burned on his brain and the haunting expression in her eyes burned on his soul.

It maddened him that he couldn't get her off his mind.

She had become a hopeless obsession, hopeless not only because she was gone, but because there didn't seem to be anything he could do to make her memory disappear. He hadn't slept well in years, but now he hardly slept at all.

You could have stopped her, you could have stopped her . . . The thought beat constantly through his head, as illogical as it was, for how did one stop someone from killing herself when she stood across an unreachable vastness?

Deep inside he knew where his guilt came from, but the knowledge didn't make him feel any better. Once before he'd been unable to stop a needless tragedy, and his sense of helplessness and responsibility had never left him.

He had dedicated his life to making sure that everyone around him was content, even if it meant denying his own needs. He had looked after his friends, his family, his estates, his tenants, had performed his duty as a duke and head of the family to perfection.

And yet nothing had filled up the black void inside of him. Nothing eased the anguish left by his father's death, although time had dulled it and he had consigned it to a back corner of his mind. Until three weeks ago when the wound had been ripped open again and he had been re-minded far too acutely of how precarious life was and how easily it could be thrown away, as if it meant nothing at all. As if the people left behind meant nothing at all.

He trusted in God but couldn't help wondering what He made of such an act. Rafe didn't believe that God would not admit such tortured souls to heaven where they needed most to be, for surely someone so devoid of hope as to want to take his own life needed the loving care of his Father more than the usual assortment of lost souls. But he did wonder if God was not disappointed that one of His creatures hadn't made a better showing.

Rafe had talked of his feelings to no one, not his dearest friend, Aiden, not even his minister, and certainly not his mother or brother, for they were the last people in the world he wished to see hurt or shamed. Ignorance in some cases really was bliss, and that was how Rafe intended to keep it, since he was the only one who knew the true story of his father's death. He had guarded it close to his heart for twenty years, twenty long, lonely years, and his heart had not carried the burden lightly or easily.

But just as he had inherited the dukedom, so had he inherited his father's secret, and so it would stay.

He only wished that he knew what demons had driven his father to such despair that he would actually put an end his life. He'd always wondered if there had been a love affair that had gone wrong. Or perhaps his father had had a financial setback, not that he hadn't left Rafe a small fortune when he'd died. But he supposed he'd never know. He'd never know Egeria's reasons either, and there was no point in torturing himself further over either mystery.

Who was he to try to comprehend the secrets of the mind or what pushed people to the point of no return?

He wandered over to the window and gazed out over the park entrance, not really focusing on it. And then his eye caught a flash of red and he looked more carefully. It was a woman. A dark-haired woman in a red cloak whose carefree stride looked hauntingly familiar. He had only ever in his life seen one person move that way. And he had just been thinking about her.

He drew in a sharp breath of disbelief. It couldn't be—it couldn't *possibly* be her. Could it?

"I beg your pardon," he said, already moving toward the door without a thought to the impropriety. "I—I've seen someone I must speak to on an urgent matter. I'll return shortly." And he was gone before anyone had a chance to object.

He tore down the street, ignoring the stares of people passing by, and reached the park entrance in a matter of moments. Pausing, he looked around frantically, scanning the walk ahead. And saw another flash of red on the path in front of him.

His heart pounding in his chest, he dashed toward it, not even thinking about what he would do, what he would say, only that he had to know if this woman was his Egeria, as impossible as it seemed.

"I beg your pardon, miss," he said, coming up behind her, breathing hard. "Please—a moment of your time?"

She turned abruptly, one slender hand going to her throat as she stared at him. As she had stared at him once before, using the same gesture.

"My God . . . it *is* you—" he said, staring at her in return, dizzying relief sweeping over him. He felt as if he were looking a miracle in the face and joy filled his heart. *Not dead. Perfectly, beautifully alive, and even more lovely than he'd imagined.*

He wanted to throw his arms around her, feel her warmth under his touch, the vital beat of her heart against his chest. But he restrained himself, merely grabbing her by the shoulders. "Where did you disappear to?" he demanded.

Her eyes widened in alarm and she tugged away from him. "Unhand me, sir!" She gasped, taking a quick step backward.

"Do you have any idea how worried I've been?" he said illogically, dropping his hands to his sides. "I thought something dreadful had happened to you! I've been looking for you everywhere!"

"You—you are mad," she choked.

"Mad? I'm *furious*. I thought you were dead, for the love of God—there was no other explanation I could think of for your vanishing act. I've barely slept since, and now I find you strolling in a London park as if you hadn't a care in the world."

She frowned. "Oh. Perhaps you are not mad, but you have certainly mistaken me for someone else."

"No. Oh, no, I haven't," he said, gazing into wide eyes, a fascinating shade of cinnamon with yellow starlight around the irises, eyes that were fringed by thick dark lashes. "Are you saying you do not know me?"

"Know you? How could I know you when we have never met?" she said, tilting her chin up at him. He couldn't help noticing that her chin had the tiniest of clefts in it.

"Come now," he said, his voice gentling. "Let us not prevaricate. We spoke to each other on the cliff at Downpatrick Head in Ireland." He reached out and caressed her arm through the wool of her cloak. "You were wearing this very garment."

"But how could we have spoken, sir?" she said, drawing away from his touch. "I've never been to Ireland. And as I am not in the habit of speaking to strangers, I must ask that you take yourself away before I am forced to call for assistance. It is most improper of you to assault an unmarried female in this fashion."

Rafe opened his mouth to protest, but then snapped it closed again, as it occurred to him that her accent held not a trace of an Irish lilt. It was as British as his own. Another mystery.

But it *was* her. He knew it was her. If he didn't know it by the way she looked and from what she wore, he knew it from the way he felt inside, that same sense of enchantment, of deep and perfect affinity with her.

"I beg your pardon," he said, battling with confusion over the change in her accent. "But I am certain it was you."

"I am sorry to disappoint you," she said, her gaze steady. "I do hope you find your friend, for you are clearly suffering from great distress if you have been driven to running after complete strangers in the park. Now if you'll excuse me, I am late for an appointment."

"Won't you at least tell me your name before you go?" he said, determined to discover her true identity before she vanished. Again. "Perhaps you are related to my friend Egeria," he said with a smile. "You are so alike you could be twins."

She paled and her hand jerked at her throat. Rafe knew he had her cornered. She hadn't forgotten any more than he had; she felt the fundamental connection every bit as much as he did. Her hand still rested at her throat where the pulse beat fast. "I do not have a twin," she said. "I am an only child. Furthermore, my name is not Egregia—"

"Egeria," he corrected, his smile broadening at her deliberate mispronunciation. "But if not that, pray tell me what it is, for you are every bit as beautiful as she. Perhaps more so."

She blinked at him as if the sun had dazzled her eyes, then tore her gaze away, shaking her head violently. "I am sure it is not proper for you to talk to me in such a fashion. I—I must go. I am late." And she turned on her heel without another word and ran down the path as if she were escaping from the devil himself, disappearing within moments.

Rafe watched her go with an infinite sense of regret.

He ran a hand over his face, wondering why she was trying to hoodwink him. He'd know her anywhere. But why would she bother to lie to him? Unless . . . unless she was a stickler for convention and refused to acknowledge him until they had been formally introduced. It was a remote possibility, but the only explanation.

But who *was* she? She said she was unmarried, but he felt certain he knew all of the women of marriageable age in London, since his mother had made a point of making sure he did . . . although she might have made her come-out the previous season when he had been absent from the country. Now there was a distinct possibility.

Well, whoever she was, he would find her and solve this

mystery. London wasn't such a large place that she would be able to disappear for long.

A smile tugged at the corners of his mouth. It was usually he who performed the disappearing act, having perfected the art of escaping unscathed from the clutches of predatory females. Never once had a woman tried to escape from him, and he had to admit it made a refreshing if inconvenient change.

His heart infinitely lighter now that he knew Egeria was alive and well and living in London, he headed back to Upper Brook Street to make some reasonable excuse for his bad behavior.

The two Gupwell girls who had only a half hour before seemed such a wretched burden now appeared as a blessing to him, for he would have an excuse to change his usual habit and could willingly attend every last ball and rout he had to in order to find Egeria.

And once he did, one way or the other he would dig the truth out of her.

"Raphael, darling, what on earth came over you to send you flying out of the house in such a headlong fashion?" his mother asked as soon as she had settled herself comfortably in the carriage. "I declare, I thought you'd taken leave of your senses! And I don't believe for one moment that silly story you dispensed about a long-lost friend. You don't have any long-lost friends that I'm aware of, for you keep excellent track of your acquaintances."

Raphael rubbed the bridge of his nose, prepared to make the first move in his campaign. "Mama, you know every family in England of any social standing. Are you acquainted with a young unmarried woman of about twenty years or so who has dark hair, light-brown eyes, but to whom I wouldn't have been introduced in this last year?"

His mother turned in her seat and treated him to a long, puzzled look. "Now I *know* you've taken leave of your senses. You could be describing half the girls in England. And what does this girl have to do with your racing out into the street?"

Rafe shrugged. "It's the oddest thing. I know I saw the very same woman in Ireland only three weeks ago. She was wearing the same red cloak and had the same coloring and the same walk." He shot his mother a sidelong glance, hoping she hadn't seen through him. "And yet this woman does not speak with an Irish accent as she did then, so I have to assume there is some reason for her dissemblance today."

"Good heavens, do you mean to say you actually *spoke* to this poor girl without an introduction?" his mother said, looking even more astonished.

"I did, although this time she was none too pleased about it," he said with a self-deprecating grin. "I know I shouldn't have, but I couldn't help myself. She rang my ears with invective, said she'd never seen me before in her life, and then vanished from sight."

"And very proper of her," his mother said after a long moment. "Well, my dear, I suppose she could be Anglo-Irish, in which case she wouldn't have much of an accent if she was properly schooled, and no accent at all if she put her mind to it."

He simply shook his head. "Oh, well, whatever her reasons for pretending not to know me, I'll find her."

"I see," his mother said, regarding him thoughtfully. "And why, may I ask, are you so interested in this nameless person?"

Rafe tried to look as nonchalant as possible. "No reason, really. I am merely curious to know what she is doing in England. County Mayo is a long way from London."

"Well," his mother said reasonably, "those dreadful Gupwell girls are in London, are they not? They were also in County Mayo only three weeks ago, and furthermore, they speak without a trace of Irish accent. So I do not see why it is beyond the realm of possibility that the girl who has piqued your curiosity wouldn't also adjust her accent whilst in England to better fit in."

"I suppose so," Raphael said slowly, seeing an odd sort of logic to his mother's theory. "Perhaps that is the case, which means that the mystery is solved."

"Is it? You still do not know who she is, but I suppose I can keep my eye out for someone of her description, as vague as you were. The effort is bound to be vastly more entertaining than marching those unfortunate girls you've landed me with around town." She shook her head. "Goodness, did you see their dresses? I declare, I thought I'd walked into a bordello. I can see I have my work cut out for me if I am to make them presentable before their appearance at court."

She chattered on as if she had no more than a passing curiosity in his unusual display of interest over a woman he'd never formally met. Odd in a woman like his mother, he thought suspiciously, who never let an opportunity to leg-shackle her son slip her by.

"Lord above in heaven," Lucy said, throwing her cloak onto her narrow bed and throwing herself down next to it. "When are You going to show a little mercy?"

Her heart still hammered uncontrollably, driven by the remnants of fear. She'd nearly fallen over in shock when the duke had stopped her in the park, the last person on the face of the earth she expected to see. She had no idea why he hadn't been where he was supposed to be, safely ensconced in the drawing room with her stepmother and stepsisters.

But there he'd stood, large as life, a huge smile creasing his handsome face as he'd looked down at her. He'd smiled because of her, because he'd found her again and was pleased.

Lucy hugged the hard pillow to her chest and rolled onto her back, a dreamy smile playing on the corners of her lips. He had recognized her, after all—he hadn't forgotten their magic moment on Downpatrick Head any more than she had, and a thrill went through her at the realization that it had mattered to him—that somehow she mattered to him.

Do you have any idea how worried I've been . . . I've been looking for you everywhere!

A part of her couldn't be very pleased about that, for she'd be in the most terrible trouble if Eunice had the slightest inkling that he'd gone to the trouble of running after her. That he'd actually been searching for her. For her, Lucy Kincaid. The only time anyone ever went searching for her was when she was in trouble.

In trouble—that thought set off another one and her brow crinkled as his words came back. He'd thought her dead? She couldn't imagine why. But thinking about it, she supposed it might well have looked as if she'd fallen over the edge of the cliff instead of just stumbling onto the ledge. Oh, the poor man. He must have been frantic with worry.

A chortle escaped, and then another. Served him right too. Thinking she'd fallen to her death was a just punishment for everything he'd done since, since he'd as good as pushed her over the edge of a different kind of cliff.

She sat up, still grinning. *Egeria*, he'd called her. She thought she'd done a brilliant job of pulling the wool over his eyes, fumbling over the name as if she'd never heard it before. And fumbling over it in her perfectly proper British accent, just as she'd roundly denied knowing him, or ever being in Ireland. That had been a fine touch. Now, there was a delicious irony. She as Irish as could be, and he couldn't tell that she hadn't been born down the street from him.

A lark sang sweetly in a tree outside her open window. Drawn to its music, she went over to the blowing curtains and leaned out, turning her face to the breeze. "So, then, Mr. Raphael David Charles Montagu, Duke of All You Command, didn't I just flummox you? You didn't know whether you were coming or going. You're probably still wondering if you didn't make a big mistake. Or at least I hope you are, or we're all in trouble."

She pulled her head back in and executed a little twirl. Now that the fright he'd given her had faded, she was filled with a sense of exultation. He thought her beautiful. He'd said so, hadn't he? He'd even lost sleep over her.

He might be a filthy Englishman, but he was still a man, and to Lucy's knowledge not a single man had ever thought her beautiful, not to mention losing a wink of sleep over her. How delicious it all was! Right out of a fairy tale.

For the first time in her life, Lucy actually *felt* beautiful. She ran her hand down her cheek, thinking that if she hadn't seen the keenness of his eyesight for herself, she would have thought he was hopelessly myopic. She'd been wondering about that ever since he'd agreed to take on Fiona and Amaryllis.

But if he was myopic, he wouldn't have recognized her at all, would he have, not when to his knowledge he'd never before seen her across a chasm. No, there was nothing wrong with his eyesight, just his attitude, or he'd have recognized her when she'd opened the door to him in Ballycastle. But then he'd thought her only a servant and not worthy of a second look. Just like a Englishman, seeing only what he wanted to see, even when what he was looking for was right under his aristocratic nose.

But still . . . even though he was *English,* and even though she'd probably never see him again, she could dream, couldn't she? That wouldn't be betraying her Irish ideals, for a little bit of dreaming served as a nice escape from her dreary existence.

In her dreams she could still be a princess and he her prince, and no one would be harmed. In her dreams they could quote poetry to each other, gazing into each other's eyes as the rest of the world disappeared. In her dreams he could touch her as he had in the park, the heat of his hands sending shivers of responding heat coursing through her body.

And in her dreams she could pretend he wasn't an Englishman.

Couldn't she?

A heavy volley of rapping started at her door, and then Fiona's voice, breaking into her fantasy. "Lucy? Lucy, are you in there? Come out this minute. We're to go out to a supper this evening, and we need to dress, you lazy girl."

Lucy quickly grabbed up her cloak and hung it on one of the nails on the wall that served as a closet. "I'm coming, Fiona," she called, pulling open the door only to be met by Fiona's flushed face.

"Sleeping, were you?" Fiona said, looking her up and down. "I should tell Mama and get you into trouble, but I'm in too good a mood to truffle with you."

"Then your meeting with the duke and his mother went well?" Lucy asked as if butter wouldn't melt in her mouth.

"You wouldn't have believed it—they were the most pleasant people, treating us as if we were just as grand as they. I'm sure the duke has inventions toward me, really I am," Fiona said, clasping her hands to her bosom. "He was in such a fine temper, smiling and laughing the whole time. He's even coming with us this evening. It's a supper to be held at his mother's house, since we're not firmly out, but there will be lots of people there. I can't wait . . ."

Neither could Lucy, for it occurred to her that she would hear constant stories about Raphael, even if they were secondhand and from her stepsisters' self-aggrandized viewpoint. A little bit of something to feed her dreams was better than nothing at all, and she could always pretend it was she on his arm instead of them.

6

Two months. Two long months and not a sign of her. Raphael was about to go out of his mind with frustration. He couldn't believe that it was possible for anyone to vanish into the bowels of the earth so effectively, but Egeria had managed it. If he didn't know better, he might almost think that she wasn't mortal after all, for what earthly creature could appear and disappear at will, leaving no trace? He *still* couldn't work out how she had performed her vanishing act over the edge of the cliff, although he suspected the narrow ledge had something to do with it. What other explanation was there?

He allowed his valet to help him into his coat in preparation for yet another tedious round of evening fare. Scheduled for tonight was a visit to Almack's Assembly Rooms, the supposed bastion of all respectability, and surely the most boring, yet he'd gone religiously week after week in hopes of seeing her there, just as he'd gone everywhere else, always looking.

He spent most of his time leaning against walls, watching the Gupwell girls make fools out of themselves, saving them from themselves only when absolutely necessary. If he hadn't been so anxious to find Egeria, he might have found the situation laughable. Under any other circumstances he would have bailed out of the social whirl at the earliest opportunity, especially since tongues were now wagging in full force.

The Duke of Southwell was hanging out for a wife—what other reason would he have to be attending every function, given that in the past he'd avoided them like the plague? Or so went the gossip. And he was fed up with it. He was fed up with all of it.

Ah, well, he was stubborn and persistent if nothing else, he thought as Adams adjusted his coat, stuck an emerald pin in his neckcloth, and pronounced him ready. Ready. Rafe wasn't ready, he was doomed.

He marched downstairs to his study, savoring the peace and quiet, knowing it would be the last allotted to him for the next few hours. He poured himself a glass of wine, enjoying the quality of the claret, the best and probably the last he'd have that night. Almack's served only warm lemonade, weak tea, or orgeat, all revolting concoctions designed to turn the stomach, not unlike the company that flocked on Wednesday nights to King Street in droves, waving their vouchers as if they were manna from heaven, given directly from the hand of God.

God in this case might go under the combined names of Sally Jersey, Emily Castlereagh, Therese Esterhazy, Dorothea Lieven, Emily Cowper, and the truly dreadful Mrs. Drummond Burrell, the patronesses of Almack's. With the exception of Maria Sefton, a sweet, kind-hearted woman, they were all top-lofty dragons in disguise who would have asked for the credentials of the Good Lord Himself if He'd tried to gain entrance, and they might very well have turned Him away for lack of breeding.

Rafe laughed shortly. Breeding. It was exactly what most of them did in order to perpetuate their precious lineage, with no thought to love. That was reserved for discreet liaisons after marriage, once the necessary heir was produced. The entire system was based on hypocrisy. He had to wonder if he'd been a product of the same creed, if his mother had ever loved his father, for she had recovered from his death remarkably well. But then she hadn't known anything about the circumstances surrounding it. Maybe that made a difference, maybe that was why she carried on so easily. She felt no blame, thinking his death had been nothing more than an unfortunate accident.

He knew better.

And he also knew that he would never marry without love, not without deep, abiding love. He knew it was possible, for he'd seen it happen—his cousin Aiden had found that kind of love only two years before under the most unexpected of circumstances, and Aiden's life had been turned around as a result. Rafe was delighted for him. At the same time, he didn't expect lightning to strike twice in the same family, and certainly not in the same generation.

He took another sip of wine, reflecting on the capriciousness of life. Two months and he was becoming everything he despised—a man whose sole occupation was to escort highborn misses out onto the dance floor, make polite conversation of no meaning, counting how many quadrilles and waltzes were sufficient before he could take his leave.

And oh *God*, he was sick of it. Sick of the simpering females dangling after him in hopes of becoming the next Duchess of Southwell, sick of the platitudes, the empty flirtations. Sick of the banality of it all. He wanted Egeria and only Egeria, and by God, he'd find her if it was the last thing he did.

Two more weeks and it would all be over. His mother had already held her ball, the usual great success. The last big event of the season was being held at the end of next week by his mother's good friend, the Marchioness of Stanhope, and it promised to have a huge turnout. All the glittering members of the upper one-tenth of the upper ten thousand promised to be there. If Egeria didn't show up then, he was throwing his hat in. He'd go back and stake himself out on the Downpatrick cliffs if he had to.

He would find her.

The only problem was that he'd neglected his other responsibilities for too long. Southwell needed his attention, not to mention all his other properties. He'd learned from his Mediterranean trip that his attention wasn't strictly needed; his estates were competently handled by his various stewards. But still, his primary connection was to the land and its people, and he missed personally administering his own affairs.

This social whirl was not for him and never had been. Yet he suffered it in the hope that he'd find a nameless woman. He suffered it because he wanted to find her more than life itself. She *was* life itself. And still she eluded him, as much as she haunted his sleepless nights. She was out there somewhere.

He would find her, he thought again with grim determination.

"Your carriage awaits, your grace," the butler said with a discreet clearing of his throat just as Rafe finished the last of his wine. "The duchess is in the entrance hall."

"Very good," Rafe said, placing his glass down on the table with a heavy sense of inevitability. "Thank you, Loring. Tell her grace that I shall be out in a moment."

He braced his fingers on the side table for a moment, gathering himself. Two more weeks. And he had no way of knowing if the fortnight left to him would hold happiness or damnation.

Eleanor, Dowager Duchess of Southwell, watched as her son took up his usual position against the wall of the ballroom, arms crossed over his chest, his expression neutral, although she could read the boredom behind it. Boredom and misery.

His eyes were focused on the door as always, as if at any moment his mysterious dark-haired woman might walk through it. Eleanor knew perfectly well the only reason Raphael had religiously attended every event of the season was in hope of finding her, not that he'd uttered another word on the subject since the day he'd gone after her in the park. Being Raphael, he wouldn't, for he had always kept his feelings close to his chest. But a mother's instincts were never wrong, and she knew just how desperately he wanted to find her, as much as he'd downplayed his interest. And that was the most intriguing thing of all.

Poor boy. He was eating his heart out over this girl, whoever she was, and Eleanor wished that she could somehow deliver the child up to him on a silver platter, but she was beginning to lose hope herself. None of her discreet inquiries had borne fruit, and she despaired at this late day that the girl was magically going to appear.

Which led her ask to the question once again—who *was* she, and where had she come from? There was an Irish connection, that much was certain, but what it was escaped her, for the only girls with any association to Ireland this season were the Gupwell sisters and they claimed no knowledge of anyone else from County Mayo who might be in London attending the season.

The Gupwell sisters. The duchess released a heavy sigh. She was so tired of bribing young gentlemen to dance with them, of practically begging invitations from her friends to their various entertainments. Only two more weeks and she would be free of the girls *and* of their mother, who was the worst of the lot as far as she was concerned. She almost felt sorry for the Gupwell sisters, for they couldn't help having a mother pushing them relentlessly forward when they obviously weren't suited to the heights of society she intended for them.

Lady Kincaid was not cursed with her daughters' stupidity—that had come from their father's side, along with their looks. She was far more dangerous, for although she was far from intelligent, she had the kind of superficial but incisive mind that never missed an opportunity to further her advantage. The dowager had seen it in action time and time again.

Vicious and manipulative, Lady Kincaid somehow managed to best those around her who did not see through her disguise of sweetness and civility.

She was probably the only reason her daughters were still in circulation despite their impossible gaucheness, for Lady Kincaid managed to smooth over every mistake with a well-chosen excuse, using the unfortunate circumstances of their upbringing in Ireland during their formative years to elicit sympathy and understanding. And she never missed an opportunity to mention the Southwell patronage to further her cause.

Eleanor had long before decided that Eunice Kincaid was one of those extraordinary women who managed to cow other people through the sheer force of their personality, and she did it exceptionally well. However, she hadn't fooled Eleanor for a moment, although Eleanor had been very careful not to let her know that. It was to her advantage that Eunice Kincaid thought she had the Dowager Duchess of Southwell wrapped around her little finger, for that gave Eleanor the upper hand in all of their dealings.

But a more vile woman Eleanor had never known, and she couldn't wait until the day she could turn her back and walk away, never to lay eyes on the woman again. Poor Raphael. It just showed what sort of trouble his sense of duty got him into. It was a good thing she loved him so much, or she would have wrung his neck for getting her into this impossible predicament.

If nothing else, at least the excuse of squiring the Gupwell girls around had given him a reason to mingle in society again, even if it was for a hopeless cause.

Her train of thought was interrupted as Fiona Gupwell sidled up to her.

"Duchess," the girl simpered, dropping a lopsided curtsy, still no improvement over any of her earlier attempts, despite the duchess's best efforts at correcting her. At least she'd had better success with their wardrobe, passing on strict instructions to their maid to modify them. "I was wondering if you might introduce me to the gentleman who has just come in—I haven't seen him before, and he is most devilish handsome."

The duchess suppressed a sigh of irritation. Fiona Gupwell was the biggest sapscull she'd ever had the misfortune of coming across, her stupidity and garrulousness matched only by her sister's. It was a miracle that the Ladies' Committee hadn't revoked the girls' vouchers after the last fiasco when Amaryllis had dogged the Earl of Chesney all night in hopes of eliciting an invitation to dance from him, a terrible breach of polite behavior. But they hadn't, only as a favor to Eleanor, who would be paying it back for years, no doubt.

"Which gentleman would that be?" the duchess asked as patiently as she could manage.

"That one over there," Fiona said, pointing her finger toward the door. "I'm sure I can make the right interpretation this time if I put my mind to it."

The duchess quickly took Fiona's hand by the wrist and lowered it, then waited a moment before looking. She really didn't know what she was going to do with the girl.

She angled her head toward the door, pretending to survey the crowd, but her gaze halted abruptly on the figure in question. A very familiar figure, and one she hadn't expected to see for some time to come, considering he'd been exiled to the Continent by his brother for unruly behavior.

"Good heavens!" she exclaimed, forgetting all about Fiona Gupwell and making her way through the crowd to his side. "Hugo, my dear boy—what a delightful surprise!"

He turned and treated her to a lazy smile. "Hullo, Mama," he said, bestowing a warm kiss upon her cheek. "Loring told me you'd be here. I'll wager you're surprised to see me."

"Indeed I am, and your brother will be even more surprised. What possessed you to return to London?"

"The lights of Paris were growing dim," he said, grinning

with his usual charm. "I thought I'd come home and see if the weather blew any fairer since my departure. I thought Rafe must surely be over his temper tantrum by now."

"Your brother doesn't have temper tantrums," she said reprovingly. "And he was quite right to send you away. You behaved most abominably."

"Perhaps I was a trifle misbehaved, but three years is a bit long to hold on to a grudge," Hugo answered. "And who is this, tugging on your sleeve?"

The dowager looked over, only to see Fiona grinning like an idiot. "Oh," she said, wishing the girl would vanish, never to return. "Allow me to present Miss Fiona Gupwell, the eldest daughter of Lady Kincaid. Your brother has offered her and her sister his patronage this season. Fiona, my younger son, Lord Hugo Montagu."

She nearly laughed out loud at Hugo's incredulous expression. She could just imagine what he was thinking— Raphael was not in the habit of handing his patronage out, and certainly not to a gangly, hatchet-faced girl with a distinct lack of manners.

"It is indeed a pleasure, your lordship," Fiona gushed, executing another of her unfortunate curtsies. "I did not even know his grace had a brother, but I am sure I am dilated to discover the happy fact."

The slightest of frowns crossed Hugo's face as he made his bow. "How very kind," he murmured.

"And may I also present the younger Miss Gupwell," Eleanor added, for naturally Amaryllis had rocketed across the room the instant she saw that her sister might have snatched up a prize Amaryllis had somehow missed.

Hugo's incredulous gaze fell on Amaryllis's round, pimply face and traveled back to his mother in strong question.

"And their mother, Lady Kincaid," she said, about to burst her corset with glee, as that awful woman breathlessly joined her daughters, having nearly knocked over half the room in her hurry to reach them. "Lady Kincaid, allow me to present my son, Lord Hugo," she said with a poker face.

"Oh! Oh, my goodness—your *son*, Duchess? And what a fine, handsome man he is. My, isn't this a surprise? Who ever would have thought? How fortuitous . . . that is, for you," she added quickly. "Two strapping boys to warm a mother's heart."

The duchess had no trouble reading Lady Kincaid's mind. It had not escaped Eleanor's attention that Lady Kincaid had decided on Raphael for one of her daughters. And now that Hugo had appeared, he would clearly do nicely for the other. And if wishes were horses, beggars would ride, she thought with an inward chuckle.

"Do you enjoy dancing, Lord Hugo?" Fiona slipped her arm into the crook of Hugo's elbow and furiously batted her pale eyelashes up at him. "I enjoy the waltz most prodigally."

"I . . . er, that is, I fear I've strained my ankle," Hugo said, casting his mother an alarmed look that begged for rescue.

Since Hugo had never once asked for rescue in all of his twenty-five years, the duchess was inclined to take mercy on him. "You must forgive my son," she said. "He has made a long journey this very day and only came here tonight to let me know he arrived safely. How is your poor ankle, darling? Are you sure you shouldn't be sitting down?"

"No, no—I'm on the mend, Mama, although I mustn't overtax my strength," Hugo said, his eyes conveying his gratitude to her.

"Overtax your strength?" Amaryllis squeaked, one hand going to her fat cheek. "Have you been dreamfully ill, my lord?"

Hugo inclined his head, eyelids lowering over bright blue eyes that fairly screamed for an explanation of this travesty from his mother. "I won't bore you with the details, Miss Gupwell, but I have not been . . . well. I have come home to recuperate."

"And we must not keep you any longer, my dearest," the duchess said, trying to keep her lips from twitching. "You were most thoughtful to make an appearance, but I think it is best if you take the carriage home before any further mishap should occur. Your brother would be most distressed to find you here, instead of safely tucked away where you belong."

"Rafe is *here*?" he said, looking even more incredulous, if that was possible. "Here, tonight, at *Almack's*?"

"Naturally, darling. Where else would he be?" She shot him a warning look, designed to keep his tongue in check.

"Oh . . . of course. Where else? Where else indeed," Hugo said weakly. "How foolish of me to think him anywhere else. He's always so enjoyed an evening of dancing and gossip."

"Precisely."

The dowager turned with dismay at the sound of Raphael's voice coming from over her left shoulder. "There you are, darling. Look who is here . . ." She held her breath, waiting for the explosion. But to her surprise it didn't come.

"Yes, so I see," Raphael said mildly enough. "Hello, Hugo. How are you?"

"Well enough, brother, thank you," Hugo said, looking unusually unnerved. "I was just taking my leave. My health and all that."

"How wise. One wouldn't want your health compromised, especially in a public place."

"How drawl you are, Duke," Amaryllis twittered. "I declare, you keep me in a constant state of entertainment."

"How very obliging of me," Raphael said dryly. "But lest I provide you with more entertainment than you bargained for, you'll allow my brother to make his excuses and be on his way."

"So soon?" Lady Kincaid said, fluttering her fan in Rafe's direction. "We were only just becoming acquainted with

Lord Hugo. He is such a pleasing young man, although of course we are in sympathy over his recent illness."

The duchess held her breath, wondering what was coming next. She hadn't enjoyed herself so immensely in weeks. Raphael at least looked fully alive and focused for once on something other than the door, as much as he looked as if he wanted to throw his brother out of it.

"His recent illness?" Rafe said, cocking an eyebrow. "Yes. Poor Hugo does have a tendency toward a certain constitutional weakness." He turned toward his brother, as dark as Raphael was fair. "I'll be home early to tend to you," he said, inclining his head toward the door.

"Er, right ho," Hugo said, bowing to the ladies. "See you later, brother dear."

Raphael waited until Hugo had descended the staircase and disappeared from sight before turning to his mother. "A word in private, Mama? If you'll excuse us?"

He took his mother by the arm and led her off to a corner. "What is the meaning of this?" he asked, his voice as smooth as silk.

"I really can't say, darling. Hugo only said that he was homesick, and he hoped that you might have forgiven him by this time."

"Forgiven him? For what? Drunken brawling? Or perhaps you mean involving himself in a duel the last time his feet were on British soil? Or maybe you refer to the scandal he created with Lady Juliet Harrow that led to the duel—"

"Never mind all that, dear," the dowager said, cutting him off. "Your brother is home, and I think you should let bygones be bygones. Hugo may very well have turned over a new leaf."

"Not if the pile of gambling debts I received when *I* returned home is any indication. So you're telling me that you had no hand in Hugo's return?"

"None, although I cannot say that I am unhappy that he is

back. Give him a chance, Raphael, if not for his sake, then for mine."

Raphael expelled a long breath. "Very well, Mama. I'll do as you ask, but I doubt that it will be long before Hugo puts his foot in it again, and this time his banishment will be to a country a great deal farther away, I promise you that."

She patted his arm. "Thank you, dearest. You are a most generous man, as I've said many times." The dowager couldn't resist a smile. "Did you see the way the Gupwell girls and their mama descended on Hugo the minute he appeared?"

"I could hardly miss it, any more than I missed Hugo's cocky entrance. Those girls have the sharpest noses for fresh blood that I've ever seen."

"Honestly, Raphael, what *am* I to do with them? I declare, I've done my best, but not one man has shown any interest, and there's hardly any time left."

"You have fulfilled your obligation admirably, Mama. You cannot be responsible for their lack of looks or of manners."

"I find it hard to believe they are Ian Kincaid's stepdaughters. He was such a pleasant, well-mannered man, although he exhibited a serious lack of judgment in marrying their mother, I must say. I would not have made such an effort toward the girls if I hadn't had the utmost respect for him, but I really cannot tolerate that woman."

Raphael's lips twitched. "I have to confess, if I'd known that she'd turn out to be that monstrous, I never would have undertaken the exercise in the first place. Never mind, we only have to tolerate them for two more weeks. Then they're back to Ireland and good riddance."

"Yes, although I do so hate to admit defeat. I've always prided myself on being able to marry anyone off—present company excepted, that is."

Rafe graced her with a quelling look.

"Oh, well. Maybe I'll pay them a visit tomorrow and go over the matter of correct deportment one more time. There are still a few social occasions left, and one never knows. Miracles can happen."

"I'm counting on it," her son said cryptically and led her back into the throng.

Cold fowl and pigeon pie, followed by roast lamb and potatoes, then salmon and lobster, maybe some cockles. Lucy raised her head from her sewing, thinking hard. What next for her dinner party? Oh, yes. *A nice foamy syllabub, all washed down with two kinds of delicious claret. Served in deeply cut old Cork glass, the table laid with exquisite silver and china on a cloth of snowy linen . . .*

"Lucy? Lucy, where are you, you sloth? Luuuucyyyyy?"

The shrill voices came from below and Lucy lowered the sewing into her lap and blearily looked at the clock. Two o'clock in the morning and they were home—an early night.

She made her tired way down the stairs to the second floor where Amaryllis and Fiona stood in the hallway, giggling away, their mother busily scolding them, her words falling on deaf ears.

"And did you have a fine time tonight?" Lucy asked, rubbing her eyes. "You're looking very gay."

"It was wonderful," Fiona said, spinning in a circle. "I danced one quadrangle with the duke, of course—"

"So did I," Amaryllis interrupted, glaring at her sister, who ignored her.

"And Mr. Beaufort danced a waltz with me," Fiona crowed.

"Yes, dear," her mother said, "but as I've told you before, you mustn't cling quite so hard. And it's a quadrille, Amaryllis."

"I wasn't clinging, I was making intercourse," Fiona protested. "Mr. Beaufort is hard of hearing, so I had to lean close."

"It's no wonder he's hard of hearing, since he's seen at least fifty-five birthdays," Amaryllis said disdainfully.

"I didn't see you dancing with anyone but the duke," Fiona shot back.

"I don't have to dance with anyone *but* the duke. Everyone knows that he has formed a tinder for me," Amaryllis said, sticking her tongue out.

"Then why does he always dance with me too?" Fiona replied smugly. "He's only being kind when he asks *you* to dance."

"Enough, girls, enough—we'll simply have to wait and see which of you the duke has formed a *tendre* for. We have calls to pay tomorrow and the hour grows late. Lucy, see my daughters to bed, then come attend me in my room."

"Yes, Aunt Eunice," Lucy said, turning to follow Fiona down the hall. If she was quick about it, she'd have them all tucked away by three o'clock and could catch a few hours of sleep before it all started again.

"Oh, and I didn't tell you," Fiona said as Lucy pulled her evening dress off. "It was the most exciting thing—the duke has a brother! His name is Hugo, and I think he'll suit nicely for Amaryllis if she'd ever stop eating those chocolates and gain a figure. I will be Her Grace, the Duchess of Southwell, and Amaryllis will be Lady Montagu—only a curtsy title, but a title nonetheless, and not to be sneezed at."

"Lady Hugo, and it's a courtesy title," Lucy said absently, surprised by this latest development. Raphael had a brother? Odd that no one had heard of him before this. "Does he resemble his brother?" she asked.

"No, not really," Fiona said, bending over the wash basin. "He is dark and although as tall as his brother, his eyes are blue. And he is much jollier than the duke, although the duke is much more—ducal." She looked up from her splashing. "The duke behaves in a correctly superior fashion, and of course his patrimony makes all the difference, for *everyone* talks to us in such a friendly fashion . . ."

Fiona prattled on until Lucy had her safely tucked away in bed, then heard much of the same from Amaryllis. But Lucy didn't mind—their accounts filled her head with images, and she was able to edit their silly statements without any trouble. She now had a complete picture of the people of the London *ton*, who they were, what they wore, where they lived, in London and on their country estates.

Every night when she went to bed she played out the evening's scene as if she had been there, as if it had been she who had danced with Mr. Beaufort—he sounded unfortunate—and with Raphael—who was anything but, save for having the fatal flaw of being an English duke.

As she readied her stepmother for bed, treated to the usual stony silence, she tried to imagine Raphael's brother Hugo. Another piece of the puzzle to fit into place. She'd seen the dowager duchess from the upstairs window of the landing on a number of occasions, a handsome woman with a pleasant face—or as pleasant as it could be for an English-woman.

Raphael took after his mother in appearance, for he shared the same fine bone structure and gray eyes, the same elegant bearing. She'd seen him from the upstairs window too, and each time her heart had caught in her throat. But he had never seen her, thanks to all the saints in heaven, for she was careful to watch from behind the curtain. Once he'd looked up with a puzzled frown as if he'd felt her gaze on him, but she'd ducked back just in time, her heart beating in her throat.

"That will be all," her stepmother said, waving her hand at Lucy. "I will need my blue muslin walking dress tomorrow. Be sure it is cleaned and pressed by eleven. I don't wish to be disturbed before then for any reason."

"Yes, Aunt Eunice," Lucy said, dropping an obedient curtsy. "Good night."

She blew out the candles in the hallway and made her way up to her attic bedroom, humming a little tune as she imagined herself waltzing with Raphael, round and round a brilliantly lit ballroom . . .

7

"*L*ook, Ma, it's a letter from Lucy," Brigid cried, breathlessly running in the door, clutching a folded piece of paper in her hand. "It's come all the way from London!"

"Let's hear what it says then," Mairead O'Reilly said, looking up from folding the great pile of laundry she'd just brought in from the line.

Brigid ripped open the seal. "Let's see . . . oh, I do wish I'd paid more attention when Lucy was teaching me to read."

Her mother laughed. "Get on with it, girl, for I have a hunger to know how our girl is getting on. And be quick about it, for I have a meal to put on the table and I could use your help with the cooking, what little there is to go in the pot."

Brigid licked her lips and peered at the letter in concentration, reading haltingly.

My dear Mr. and Mrs. O'Reilly and all your fine children, Brigid most especially,

London is a great big city, larger than anything you could ever imagine, even bigger than Dublin, and that took me by surprise, for Dublin was the largest city I'd ever seen. London is crowded and noisy, but to be fair, I only ever saw it from the carriage on the way in, all the way back at the beginning of May, what seems like a lifetime ago. Still, I feel as if I know all about it, for I hear stories from Fiona and Amaryllis about where they've gone and what they've seen.

There's a place called Vauxhall Gardens, very grand from what I've been told, with all sorts of walkways, and amusements such as outdoor concerts and fireworks and even tightrope walkers. Can you imagine it? And there's somewhere else called Astley's Royal Amphitheatre, with a chandelier that holds fifty patent lamps! They have clowns there, and acrobats and swordfights and pony races. It must be a right old spectacle.

Brigid raised her head, her face a mask of wonder. "Isn't that something, Ma?" she said, shaking her head. "Who would have thought?"

"Go on, lass, go on," Mairead said, the diaper she was folding forgotten in her hands.

Brigid cleared her throat and bent her head back to the paper.

Every week Fiona, Amaryllis, and Aunt Eunice go to the theatre. There are a number of them, the most elegant being at Covent Garden. Sometimes they even go to the opera! Every other night there is some sort of fancy entertainment they rush off to, where fashionable people crush together to see and be seen, dressed in the finest clothes you have ever seen. Why, just my stepmother and stepsisters' wardrobes take up half the house and most of my time. It's a right challenge trying to keep up with their belongings.

I should add that it's a good thing the duke's mother made the girls take off most of the trimmings they started out with, or they would have looked like trollops for certain, but then they wouldn't listen to me when they were ordering their finery. It gave me great pleasure to pull off all those bows and ribbons, I can tell you.

I don't think Fiona or Amaryllis have any real prospects for finding husbands, since no gentleman's name comes up on a

*regular basis except that of the duke's. They are both holding
out their hopes for him, but since he always looks bad-tempered when he arrives, as if he's about to bite into a sour
apple, it is hard to tell his intentions toward them.*

*Of course, I only ever see the duke from the window or over
the balcony of the upstairs landing, since I'm not to show
myself, especially to him—he's not to know I even exist, and
Aunt Eunice would have my head if I poked it anywhere but
into the servants' quarters or the bedrooms.*

"She'd have her head all right, and hang it on the palace
gates if she could," Brigid said with disgust. "Oh, that Lady
Kincaid is a vile one and no mistaking it, just like the rest of
those British."

"Aye, we've all suffered at their hands, but that's nothing
new," Mairead said, wiping her moist brow. "But never mind
that now—what else does Lucy say? I have a feeling that
there's a good deal she's not saying, despite all the brave
words."

"What do you mean, Ma?" Brigid asked, looking over the
page. "It seems to me it's all plainly laid out here."

"Yes, and it's between the lines you need to be looking,
lass. Lucy's always been courageous, a fighter from the day
she was born.

Brigid just nodded. There was only one Lucy, and Brigid
had always stood in admiration of her friend, who had survived through thick and thin no matter what troubles the
Lord had seen fit to send her, and done it with a raised chin.

"Go on then, girl, go on," Mairead said. "If I could read
myself, I'd take the thing away from you. The way you're
going about it we'll be here until Sunday."

Brigid turned her attention back to Lucy's letter.

*I have a little bedroom up in the top of the house. I can see
the garden and a bit of the park from it, and I try to pretend
that I am in the country. I miss walking in the fresh air most of*

all, but every now and then I sneak out into the garden when the others are out.

Reading this over, I realize I sound as if I'm complaining, and I don't want you to worry. It's really not so bad. The other servants are nice enough to me, even if we don't speak much, my being Irish and all. I have three square meals a day that I don't have to cook, and for once someone else sees to the cleaning and scrubbing. The only thing I really have to do is look after my stepfamily's needs. I've taken over the household books again, since Aunt Eunice is as useless as ever and too lazy to do it herself. She only checks to make sure I haven't taken anything for myself, which I haven't, except the money to send this letter, and that she'll never miss.

I hope that Mr. Trefaney kept his promise and is sending you the extra produce from our garden and livestock while he oversees everything until my return. He seemed willing enough to oblige me and keep our secret.

I miss you all more than I can say. Ireland has never seemed more beautiful to me than it does now that I am far away. It's the truth that it is the most beautiful country on the face of the earth, for England cannot compare. I cannot wait to come home.

Until then, I send my love, and hope this letter finds you all in good health and good spirits.

Brigid wiped away a tear. "She signs it 'Your devoted friend, Lucy Kincaid.' "

Mairead sighed, wiping her own eyes. "She's a good, brave girl, her father's daughter to be sure, never thinking of her own good but always of the people around her. It's a crime, that's what it is, that she should have been brought to this state. There's no fairness in the world, but don't we know it."

"That's it, Ma, isn't it, but we're all in God's hands, or so you keep telling me."

Mairead's eyes twinkled. "And if you're referring to Sean O'Dougal, I'm thinking that situation is more in your hands, my girl, for the boy can hardly see straight for wanting you. Looks to me as if you're going to have to do something to put him out of his misery. You've made him wait long enough. Two years can seem endless to a young man of his lusty nature."

Brigid blushed bright red. "I—I didn't think you knew."

"And what sort of mother do you think I'd be if I couldn't see a thing like that right under my nose? I've held my tongue, but I can see which way the wind blows." Her voice gentled. "If you're holding back because you're worried about me, don't you think any such a thing. Lizzie's coming right up under you and can take over your chores. There's nothing worse than a girl pining away for a man she loves, and I can speak the truth about that, for I know how I wanted your father. Better you marry and raise the children you have under God's approving eye than go making any outside of it." She wagged a finger at her daughter.

"Yes, Ma," Brigid said, blushing again.

Tying her apron around her waist, Mairead turned to the stove and put a pot on to boil. "Lucy should be as lucky as you, colleen, make no mistake about it. She deserves a loving man and a house of her own instead of that prison her stepmother's made for her."

"Aye, that's true enough," Brigid said, taking up a knife and starting to peel the potatoes that would make their soup that day. "But where's Lucy going to find a man when she's been locked away for years and it looks as if there's no end in sight?"

"That's where God's hand comes in, Brigid. That's where God's hand comes in." Mairead nodded wisely and sat down at the table to help her daughter with the potatoes.

"I'm sorry, your grace, but Lady Kincaid and her daughters have not yet returned from paying their calls," the butler said at the open door of Number Five, Upper Brook Street.

"Would you care to wait? I expect them back within the hour."

"Thank you, Plimpson," the dowager duchess said, walking into the front hall. "I will wait."

"May I offer you any refreshment?" Plimpson asked.

"No, thank you. As it's such a fine afternoon, I believe I will take a turn in the garden. Do let me know when Lady Kincaid returns."

The butler bowed and led the duchess through to the French doors that opened onto the enclosed garden.

Eleanor stepped outside and paused to admire the burgeoning rose beds, grateful for a few minutes alone to enjoy the peace and quiet. There hadn't been much of that today, with Hugo and Raphael at each other's throats within minutes of Hugo's arrival at the breakfast table. From the sound of it, their private conversation the night before hadn't gone as smoothly as she'd hoped. Her mind wandered back to that morning and her sons' vitriolic exchange.

"What are your plans for today, darling?" the duchess had asked her younger son, who did not look in the best of tempers.

"I think I'll trot along to the bank this morning and deposit my newly acquired fortune in my account," he replied, shooting a dirty look at his brother. "You'll be pleased to hear that I did very well in Paris, Mama, surely more pleased than Raphael was when I gave him the happy news that I'm now a rich man."

"As I told you last night, I have no interest in the recent killing you say you made at the gambling tables," Raphael said, stabbing his fork into the kidneys on his plate, an annoyed expression on his face. "Knowing you, the money will go the same way it always does, and I have no intention of giving you another advance on your allowance or paying another penny of your debts."

"And as I told you, brother dear, I have given up gambling," Hugo replied, buttering his toast with smooth precision. "I made enough in Paris to live on for the next fifty years without any help from you. Why must you always think the worst of people?"

"I beg to differ, Hugo. I do not always think the worst of people unless they give me good reason. In your case, your past behavior speaks for itself."

Hugo glared at his brother. "I suppose you think you lived such a blameless life that you're in a position to judge everyone else. I have news for you, brother. You may be the duke, but you're not God, as much as you might like to think you sit at His right hand."

Raphael wiped his mouth and threw his napkin down on the table. "That's enough, Hugo. I think I have been most reasonable with you, considering that I did not give you permission to return home."

"If I'd waited for that, I'd have had one foot in the grave by the time the summons came. If you'd prefer, I will find my own lodgings, since my presence causes you such obvious distress."

"That won't be necessary. I'd rather have you where I can see you."

"Now, now, boys," the duchess said equitably, looking up from the letters she'd been reading. She'd been playing peacekeeper between them for as long as she could remember, and the role came as easily to her as breathing. "There's no need to squabble. Raphael, dearest, why don't you give your brother a chance? He says he intends to reform, and you should be happy at the prospect."

Raphael pushed his chair back and stood. "I will be in the study attending to business," he said curtly. "Do let me know when the moneylenders appear at the door." He stalked off.

"What is *he* in such a tiff about?" Hugo asked when Raphael was safely gone. "I thought he'd be pleased that I'm trying to change."

"I'm sure he is, Hugo, but your brother is out of sorts at the moment."

"What does he have to be out of sorts about? He's one of the richest men in England," Hugo said indignantly.

"That doesn't necessarily make a person happy, dear. Your brother has a great many responsibilities and he doesn't always take the time to see to his own happiness . . ."

The duchess picked a bright red rose from one of the bushes and lifted it to her nose, drinking in the sweet scent. Poor Raphael. He'd bravely carried the weight of the dukedom on his solitary shoulders for so long, never complaining. He deserved so much more than a life spent looking after everyone else. It would be so nice if he had someone to look after him for a change, someone who could bring a little sunshine into his life.

It was such a shame that the woman he'd been seeking refused to be found. Eleanor had never seen Raphael so downcast, as hard as he tried to hide his despondency from her, and she wondered again at the real story behind his connection with the girl. She very much doubted it was as simple or as casual as Rafe had implied, for his uncharacteristic behavior indicated otherwise.

Picking up her skirts, she started down the ornamental path, her thoughts drifting back to a time long ago when her husband had been alive and Rafe had been a carefree child. They'd been happy then, despite her husband's tendency to bouts of melancholia. But as he'd kept to himself when they came upon him, the children were oblivious of his darker moments. It was his premature death that had adversely affected them, the lack of a father's guiding hand driving Hugo to wildness and rebellion, exacerbated by his resentment toward his older brother who was forced to step in to try to control him.

And poor Raphael, who'd had the misfortune to discover his father's body after the tragic accident, had retreated further and further into himself, the laughter gone from his eyes as he gradually picked up the burden of the dukedom.

If only he and Hugo had managed to remain friends, Raphael would have someone to share his troubles with. But instead Hugo did everything he could to annoy the brother he'd once worshiped, and Raphael gave Hugo every satisfaction. The two had barely spoken, or at least civilly, in years.

Maybe if Raphael had a wife and children of his own to dedicate his time and energy to, Hugo wouldn't consider himself so much under his brother's control or feel the need to cross him at every turn.

She had no idea what to do about the situation. If Hugo really had managed to win a large fortune at the tables, she could be sure that he'd use it in a fashion that would continue to irritate his brother, for she doubted he had any intention of truly reforming. That would give Raphael too much satisfaction.

Ah, well, the only thing to be done was to wait and see and hope they didn't come to blows. In the meantime, she had the Gupwell girls to contend with, and that was a challenge in its own right. Only two more weeks . . .

Her gaze suddenly sharpened as she caught sight of an attractive young woman sitting on a bench in a far corner of the garden, her dark head bent over a book, her expression engrossed as she turned a page. Raphael's words echoed yet again in Eleanor's ears. *A dark-haired girl of about twenty years of age* . . .

But she wore a shabby dress and her hair hung down her back in a braid. No fashionable young lady then, Eleanor thought with disappointment. She'd paid particular attention to every girl with dark hair and a reasonably pretty countenance who had come across her path in the last two months, making sure that Raphael met every last one of them, but with no result.

The girl had to be a member of the household staff, Eleanor decided, although she had personally interviewed all the staff before hiring them. And then she remembered that of course Eunice Kincaid had said that she'd brought her own personal maid with her from Ireland. The girl had an Irish look about her with her ebony hair and fair complexion, although her bone structure was finer than Eleanor would have expected, her neck long and slender.

There was something intriguing about her, not the least of which was that she was reading a book, a skill one wouldn't expect in an Irish servant. Eleanor thought for a moment, then decided to find out more, for her curiosity was aroused, and not just by the girl's looks. She must be the servant who had single-handedly managed to reconfigure the Gupwell girls' fussy wardrobes according to Eleanor's exacting specifications, not an easy task, and one that required an exceptional talent with the needle. No, there was definitely something odd here, and Eleanor was not going to let the matter rest until she had some answers.

Lucy, lost in reading Jane Austen's *Emma,* at first did not hear the footsteps approaching, and too late her head jerked up. To be caught in the garden, reading of all things, was a crime punishable by a full week without supper, and in her alarm the book slipped off her lap and landed on the ground.

Her heart nearly stopped when her startled gaze took in the Dowager Duchess of Southwell. She jumped to her feet with full intent to flee, but the duchess stopped her before Lucy's feet could put thought into action.

"Good afternoon," the duchess said, smiling at her. "Isn't it a lovely day?"

"Y-yes, your grace. Please excuse me, for I have duties to attend to."

The duchess reached out and lightly stayed Lucy's shoulder. "Please, do not run off, for your employer is not due back for some time and I would be happy for a little company. Sit, child, and tell me of yourself. You obviously know that I am the Duchess of Southwell. And you are Lady Kincaid's maid, I believe?"

"I am, your grace," Lucy replied, thinking she surely had died and gone to hell, for that was the only explanation for feeling as if she were burning up with mortification and terror.

"And a very clever girl you are. I cannot tell you how much I admire your work with a needle. Two months ago I thought I would have to hire my own excellent French dressmaker to undo the mistakes made by the seamstress in Dublin, not that the disastrous consequences were her fault. There is no accounting for taste."

"It was nothing, your grace," Lucy said, flushing but secretly pleased that the duchess appreciated her long nights of hard toil. "I only did as I was told, although Lady Kincaid had as much understanding about the reason behind your wishes as a cow does when it's led off to a field of potatoes and told to graze. The cow can't get at the root of the matter, but doesn't miss what it can't see either." Lucy cringed as she heard what she'd said, for she hadn't meant to speak so freely.

The dowager laughed. "A unique way of stating the matter, but I have to agree. Your name?"

"Lucy K-O'Reilly," Lucy said, covering herself in the nick of time.

"Lucy K. O'Reilly. A good Irish name, although I can't help but note that you don't have the broad brogue of a country girl. Tell me, Lucy, where are your people from?"

"County Mayo, your grace," Lucy answered, feeling as if she were sinking into the great peat bog itself.

"Ah, yes. My son has spoken of it. He recently inherited an estate there, a place called Kincaid Court, where Lady Kincaid once lived. Perhaps you're familiar with it—it sits outside of Ballina, near Killala."

Lucy gritted her teeth. "Yes, I'm familiar with it. A lovely place it used to be, but I wouldn't be in the way of knowing anything about it now."

"My son says it is terribly run down," the duchess said, giving Lucy a far too discerning perusal of her person for Lucy's comfort. "Such a pity, for I know how attached Lord Kincaid was to his home. He spoke of it most fondly."

Lucy shot the duchess a look of strong alarm. *The duchess had known her father?* One part of her wanted to ask everything she could about their connection, but the other, more cautious part kept her tongue quiet, for the duchess would be mightily curious about why Lucy was so interested.

"He did indeed love his land, and he was good to the people who worked it," she said, knowing she had to come up with a logical story about her connection to Kincaid before the duchess asked any more probing questions and flushed out the truth. Since she had already offered the O'Reilly name, she borrowed from their history as well. "My parents were once his lordship's head tenants, but they were evicted from the property five years ago, a year after it changed hands."

"Yes. Yes, I see. That was when my nephew bought it. Then I gather it wasn't a happy time for the tenants?"

A happy time? Lucy once again held her tongue, although she was longing to heap forth invective upon Thomas Montagu's sorry soul and tell the duchess all the terrible things he had done. But she really didn't think it would be wise to speak badly of the woman's own nephew. "Indeed, it was not a happy time, your grace," she said instead. "The new land agent was a black-hearted, ruthless scoundrel, intent on lining his own pockets. He raised the rents so high that everyone was bled dry, and he tricked and fleeced us all in every other way he could find. My family ended up with nothing, and this after all the years of sweat and blood my father put into farming the land."

"How terrible for you," the duchess said with heavy sympathy.

"It hasn't been an easy time, but then, one makes do with what one has."

"As you have?" the duchess asked gently.

"As I have," Lucy agreed truthfully. As much time as she'd spent heaping curses on the Montagu family, she couldn't bring herself to dislike the duchess, for she seemed a kind woman who did not scorn those she deemed beneath her.

The duchess bent over and retrieved the fallen volume, and Lucy cringed, knowing that she'd been further caught out. Daughters of tenant farmers in County Mayo did not read. Although Brigid did, she thought with a sudden flash of relief. If she just adopted Brigid's experience for her own, she might be able to flummox the duchess.

"Emma," the duchess said, turning the book over in her hand. "How interesting that you should be reading this. Are you enjoying it?"

"I find it interesting, your grace," Lucy said honestly. "I borrowed it from Miss Fiona, who bought it at Hatchard's but displayed no interest in reading it. I'm sure she wouldn't mind, although I'd be grateful if you wouldn't mention it, or mention seeing me here today."

"Your secret is safe with me. But you still haven't told me, what have you made of the story so far?"

"In truth?" Lucy said, recklessly eager to discuss the book with someone else, even though she knew she should prevaricate.

"In truth," the duchess replied, sitting down and folding her hands on her lap.

"Well, then," Lucy said, also sitting down, for it would be rude to continue to stand. "I find Emma an annoyingly interfering sort of person, always thinking of what's best for everyone else without taking into consideration their needs or wishes. She always seems to get it wrong when it comes to declarations of love. One cannot force others into feeling what they do not, any more than one can stop them from feeling what they do. It is up to the individual to decide his or her own fate." She paused. "Whenever possible, that is."

"True," the duchess said, nodding. "So true. You are wise beyond your years, my child."

Lucy glanced over at her. "Not wise at all, your grace. Perhaps I speak idealistically, for I have no control over my own fate."

"But if you had?" the duchess asked softly. "What then would you do with it?"

Lucy bowed her head, spinning with a million impossible visions. "I would see that people in need had food in their bellies and roofs over their head," she whispered. "I would marry a man who loved me and who would look after me and our children and do it with love in his heart. I would do my very best to ease suffering in any way I could, and I would"—she turned and gave the duchess a halfhearted smile—"I would try to make the people around me laugh from the sheer pleasure of life," she finished. "I must sound delusional, but that is what I would do."

She blinked, realizing how much she'd said without meaning to. For some reason, her feelings had come pouring out, probably because the duchess had offered a sympathetic ear. "I—I'm sorry," she said. "I didn't mean to go on like that."

"Not at all, my dear," the duchess said, patting her hand. "I am touched by what you said. You seem to be a girl of fine sensibilities. And I must add, a girl who has clearly had an education, unusual in a tenant farmer's child. How did you learn to read?"

"Lord Kincaid taught me," she said truthfully. "He believed that education was the only way to get ahead in life, and he was generous with his time."

"That sounds very like him. I cannot tell you the times that he talked about his feelings concerning Irish independence. The Act of Union with Britain was of great concern to him, and I have to agree that I think it was dreadfully unfair to the Irish."

"Oh, yes, your grace," Lucy said, hugely grateful and surprised that the duchess was so understanding. She'd never known that any of the British felt anything but disdain toward the Irish and their difficulties. "It was a terrible day when the act was passed," she said fervently. "My—Lord Kincaid said it was a piece of British chicanery intended to remove all chance of allowing the Irish people to guide their own destiny. And all of William Pitt's promises of Catholic emancipation were nothing but lies designed to push the dissolution of the Dublin Parliament along."

"And for that I cannot be proud of England," the duchess said. "I never did much like Mr. Pitt's ambition, although I must admit that in some other areas he did make a good prime minister, being a strong advocate for parliamentary reform. Of course, you must remember that it was not Mr. Pitt who reneged on his promises for Catholic emancipation, child, for it was the king and Mr. Pitt's own cabinet who stymied him in that proposal, and he did resign as a result."

Lucy hadn't thought of it like that before, and she had to admit the duchess had a point. But nevertheless, whoever the responsible parties were, facts were facts: Ireland was ruled by the British, and the Catholics, who made up the vast majority of the country's population, had hardly any rights at all.

"Perhaps one day you will see Ireland for yourself, your grace," she said. "And when you see the suffering and poverty of the people firsthand, you will better understand how terrible it has been for my people to live under the British yoke."

"Yes . . . I would like to visit Ireland," the duchess said. "And when I do, perhaps you would be kind enough to show me these things of which you speak."

Lucy stared at her in astonishment. "You actually *want* to see the truth of what I tell you?"

"Naturally," the duchess replied. "As you said only a few minutes ago, educating oneself is of utmost importance. I'm a great advocate of justice, and if I believed only what I read or what other people told me, what use would I be in forming an objective opinion of what *is* just?"

Lucy was about to reply, for she too had strong opinions on the subject of justice, when the sound of a carriage pulling up outside the wall caused her to jump to her feet again in alarm. "Please excuse me, your grace—I must go! I'll be in terrible trouble if I'm found out here speaking with you."

"What a pity. I was so enjoying our conversation. Perhaps we can pick it up another time."

When pigs sprout wings and fly, Lucy thought. "I—I don't know about that," she said. "I'm not meant to be seen—that is, I must remember my position lest I lose it. Good day, your grace."

"Wait—don't forget your book, child," the duchess said, holding it out to her.

"Thank you," Lucy said, grabbing the volume. She picked up her skirt and ran toward the servants' entrance without a backward glance.

She didn't see the long, speculative look the duchess gave her as she left, for if she had, she'd have been sure that the great peat bog was about to open up and swallow her whole.

8

*R*aphael's temper was foul. He threw down his pen, unable to concentrate on his work. It was bad enough that Egeria seemed to have slipped through his fingers, but Hugo's unexpected appearance only made his mood worse. Hugo could be depended on to bring trouble in his wake, and Rafe was in no frame of mind to deal with his vexatious brother, not when everything else in his life was falling apart.

"Damn you anyway, Hugo," he muttered, shoving the pile of papers to one side. "And damn you too, Egeria, for having cast a witch's spell over me."

He was getting exactly what he deserved for his impetuosity. He'd learned long ago that there was no room in his life for anything other than measured action and reaction, but in the case of Egeria, that practice had gone straight out the window.

He felt like a callow youth ensnared in a web of his own making, a silly fool consumed by a hopeless yet desperate yearning to find once again the woman who had briefly made his heart soar, who had reminded him of what life was and could be. Only to remind him now of what hopelessness was, what a terrible mistake he'd made in deluding himself that an accident of circumstance could bring him peace and happiness.

Once again Byron had put it perfectly, coupled in the same canto in which he had embraced the perfection of Egeria. Now *there* was a man who had experienced the raw truth of love and its ensuing disillusionment.

He murmured the verse aloud, the words bitter on his tongue.

Few—none—find what they love or could have loved,
Though accident, blind contact, and the strong
Necessity of loving, have removed
Antipathies—but to recur, ere long,
Envenomed with irrevocable wrong;
And Circumstance, that unspiritual god
And miscreators, makes and helps along
Our coming evils with a crutch-like rod,
Whose touch turns Hope to dust—the dust we all have trod.

Dust. That was exactly what his hopes had become. He might as well bury them now and be done with it, turn his attention to getting on with his life.

But oh, the sting of it. His heart felt like an open wound, so stupid, since it had never had the chance to hold real love inside, harboring instead a self-induced illusion of the emotion.

Maybe that was all romantic love was—an illusion, a panacea against despair that had nothing at all to do with the beloved and everything to do with one's own desire to stave off the loneliness of the soul. Maybe he was better off without love, for all that his quest to find Egeria had brought him was an unceasing torment that only pointed out to him how alone he really was.

He looked up as a light tap came at the door. "Raphael? May I come in?" his mother called.

"Please do," he said, standing as she entered. "You're looking very pleased with yourself," he observed, taking in her rosy cheeks and enthusiastic demeanor.

"Am I? I suppose I have had an agreeable day," she replied, walking over to the bookshelves and running her finger along the spines of a row of leather-bound volumes.

"Is there something I might help you find?" he asked, curious as to what his mother was seeking. She was a voracious reader, but usually took her books from one of the circulating libraries.

"No, thank you, darling. I am merely doing a little research on an obscure title. Ah, I've found it," she said, pulling a thin volume from the shelf.

Rafe hid a smile. His mother's reigning passion was genealogy, and she knew more on the subject of aristocratic families and their lineage than most of them knew themselves.

"Anyone I know?" he asked.

"I don't think so, dear. The gentleman in question died some years back in another country." She sat down in the wing chair by the fireplace and bent her head to the book, flipping quickly through the pages, her reading spectacles perched on the end of her nose.

She looked like a bloodhound hot on a scent, he thought with amusement, and apparently she'd successfully tracked down her prey, for in a moment a satisfied smile crossed her face as she honed in on a page, her finger jabbing at a particular passage.

"Just as I thought," she murmured, snapping the book closed. "How very interesting."

"I won't ask," Rafe said as she replaced the book on the shelf. Unlike his mother, he had little interest in the complexities of bloodlines. He knew his own and that was quite enough for him. But his mother hadn't appeared to hear him, lost in thought.

"Darling," she said, suddenly turning to him, "I wonder if you would do me an enormous favor?"

"That depends," he said warily, steeling himself for the subject of Hugo.

"Would you escort the Gupwell girls and their mother to

the opera this evening without me? You know how the girls love to go, not that they understand a word or appreciate a single note, but they do so like to see and be seen, and the royal dukes are expected at the performance."

Raphael, relieved that her request had nothing to do with his brother, was happy to oblige so simple a request, not that it would give him any pleasure to be saddled with the girls on his own. On the other hand, since it was the opera, he wouldn't be expected to dance or make conversation. Mozart's *Semiramide* was playing tonight, one of his favorites, and he would be able to sit back and enjoy it. And there was always the remote possibility that Egeria might finally appear, even though he'd just given up all hope. Or thought he had. Apparently his will was not as strong as he'd like to think.

"Of course, Mama," he said graciously. "But why your change of plans?"

"I think I would like a quiet evening alone. I must confess, I am feeling a bit tired."

Raphael gazed at his mother with concern, for it was most unlike her to admit to such a thing. She had always enjoyed the most robust health and had the energy of a woman half her age. "You are not unwell, I hope?"

"Oh, no—nothing like that," she said cheerfully. "It is only that I feel the need of a little time to myself. The girls are such demanding company, and I still have so many evenings of taking them about before they leave."

A twinge of guilt pricked at Raphael, for it was he who had landed his mother with the awful family to begin with. "I understand perfectly," he said. "Enjoy your reprieve."

"Thank you, dearest; I am sure I shall," his mother said, blowing a kiss in his direction as she drifted out of the room, looking supremely satisfied.

Raphael wished he could enjoy the same satisfaction, but it continued to elude him.

* * *

"Do hurry up, Lucy, or I shall be late," Fiona said crossly as Lucy adjusted the bright red ringlets at the sides of Fiona's sharp face and placed a garland of white damask roses on the crown of her head.

"Which opera is being performed tonight?" Lucy asked, stepping back to regard her handiwork with a critical eye. But there wasn't anything more she could do to improve Fiona's unfortunate appearance. She could only work with the material at hand, and although Fiona's yellow *gros de Naples* evening dress was of fine quality, Fiona herself wasn't so pleasing to the eye.

"I don't remember the name," Fiona said, primping in front of the looking glass. "I think it's by Motsert."

"Mozart," Lucy said, wishing it was she who was going to King's Theatre to listen to the soaring music. She'd never attended an opera, but she was sure the experience would be breathtaking. It was a pity Fiona and Amaryllis were not musical, their lackluster performances at the pianoforte were even more grating when they sang along in tuneless voices.

"That's what I said, Motsert," Fiona retorted with annoyance. "I do wish you'd listen, Lucy."

"I beg your pardon," Lucy said, trying not to let Fiona's stupidity annoy her. She helped her stepsister into long white kid gloves and handed her a fan fashioned from Chinese crêpe. "There. And here is your wrap."

Fiona grabbed it from her. "I think I hear the carriage now. The duke is consorting us alone this evening—I think it is a mark of special favor. Mama is certain he will make his offer any day now." She flounced out of the room, calling loudly to her sister without another glance at Lucy.

Lucy swallowed hard. The thought of Raphael permanently attached to one of her stepsisters and therefore indirectly connected to her was enough to make her feel ill, for she couldn't help but wonder what Eunice planned to do with her if an ill-fated match between the duke and one of her stepsisters did occur.

If Eunice was so hell-bent on hiding Lucy away, she'd have to bury her six feet under to keep the duke oblivious of her existence once he was a member of the family. But then she wouldn't put cold-blooded murder past Eunice.

She sank down into a chair, miserably pondering her fate. She wished more than anything to return to Ireland, for she missed it most dreadfully, but she was beginning to think that the way things were going she'd never see her home again. Eunice had made no bones about her intention of staying in England, and she certainly wasn't going to spend the money to pay Lucy's passage back.

Even if Eunice could manage to find the generosity somewhere in her stingy heart to send Lucy home, she wouldn't do it—she wasn't about to hand Lucy her freedom. That would be *too* benevolent, for she knew what joy it would give Lucy to have a life of her own in the place she loved best with people who felt far more like her family than Eunice and her daughters ever would.

Lucy wearily stood and went to the top of the stairs, leaning over the banister as the sound of voices drifted up to her. The duke's low, measured tones were barely audible over the higher-pitched yapping of her stepsisters and the shrill commands barked by her stepmother to the footman.

"Fetch my cloak, Martin. Girls, straighten up. His grace cannot like slouching . . ."

Lucy strained for a glimpse of Raphael's face to see if there was any affection toward Fiona or Amaryllis reflected on it, but all she could see was his broad back and strong shoulders and the gleam of golden hair, silky hair she had dreamed of running her fingers through.

And then they were gone, the sound of the door closing after them echoing up the stairwell.

Lucy turned away, tears stinging at her eyes. She thought she'd known what loneliness was, but she had never felt as alone as she did tonight.

If only . . . She shrugged off the thought before it could fully form into a list of all her secret longings. If wishes were horses, beggars would ride, she told herself firmly, and went down the corridor to Eunice's room to start cleaning up the spilled powder and stains of face lotion her stepmother always left behind.

The duchess impatiently waited until eight o'clock when she was sure that Eunice Kincaid and her daughters would be safely installed with Raphael in their box at the opera. As soon as the clock struck the hour, she called for her carriage.

She'd spent the last few hours formulating a plan, and although it had a few holes in it, she was reasonably certain her strategy was workable. She still couldn't believe the good fortune that had led her to stumble across the girl whose existence Eunice Gupwell had tried so hard to conceal.

Lucy O'Reilly indeed.

Lucy Mary Katherine Kincaid, only child of Ian, sixth Baron Kincaid, and Laura, née Colclough, the entry from the book of Irish Peerage had read. *Born 1800. Laura Kincaid deceased 1810. Lord Kincaid remarried 1813 to Mrs. Eunice Gupwell, no issue . . .*

The duchess leaned back against the blue velvet squabs of the carriage, mulling over what conceivable circumstances had led Ian Kincaid's daughter to be cast as his second wife's maid. She wouldn't put anything beyond Eunice, but to go so far as to omit any mention of her stepdaughter was beyond the pale. To give her another name entirely and treat her like a servant was truly beyond belief.

She doubted Lucy had any idea how much she'd given away about herself during their conversation that afternoon. It had taken Eleanor only a few minutes to determine that Eunice Kincaid's Irish maid was not only well spoken and well educated but that she was also a girl of good breeding.

Her fine bone structure and elegant bearing had aroused Eleanor's suspicions, and those suspicions were only heightened by Lucy's resemblance to Ian Kincaid. At the time she wondered if Lucy wasn't Ian's base-born daughter, which might explain her position in Eunice's household, but Eleanor's investigation had proved otherwise—and cast her into elation.

And it wasn't just the discovery she'd made regarding Lucy O'Reilly's true identity that gave her such happiness. Twenty years of age. Dark-haired. Light-brown eyes, with an Irish accent that could likely just as easily turn into one that was British. And beautiful too, although Raphael had been careful not to mention that.

Eleanor could easily understand why Eunice was so anxious to hide her stepdaughter's light under a bushel, given her ambitions for her own unattractive daughters, who would have been instantly eclipsed by Lucy's loveliness and artless charm. But that in no way forgave Eunice's despicable actions.

"We shall just see what is what, Miss Lucy Kincaid," she murmured, tapping the tips of her fingers together. "For if you are not the woman my son has been seeking these last three months, I am not worth my salt."

It was not for nothing that Eleanor, Dowager Duchess of Southwell, was known as the greatest matchmaker London had seen in years, and for once she was determined to see that her talents served her own family.

"Lucy, get yourself cleaned up and come downstairs to the drawing room straightaway," the housekeeper commanded, poking her head into Lucy's room.

Lucy slowly put down the iron, wondering what transgression she'd committed—and then, her heart sinking, she remembered the unexpected meeting she'd had with the duchess that afternoon in the garden, where she shouldn't have been at all. Had Mrs. Mead somehow discovered it? "Have I done something to anger you, Mrs. Mead?" she asked with dread.

"Not that I'm aware of yet, girl. Get on with it; you don't want to keep the duchess waiting."

"The—the *duchess*?" Lucy said with horror. Why did she want to see her now? If she'd had any complaints, she could have voiced them this afternoon, but instead she'd praised Lucy's skill. It had to be something else, but *what*? She'd seemed so pleasant, so sympathetic, but Lucy must have displeased her in some way . . .

Lucy swallowed against a lump of panic. "What does she want with me?"

"How am I to know?" the housekeeper said. "The duchess doesn't tell me her business, but I imagine she must have something to say on the subject of the Misses Gupwells' clothing. It's not the first time she's been displeased, although in the past she's been content to pass the message on. You must have done something unsatisfactory with their wardrobes."

Paralyzed with fear, Lucy had to force herself to move. "I'll be right down," she said, hurrying to the washstand and splashing her face and neck with water, then quickly changing into a clean dress.

She checked her appearance in the broken looking glass over the dresser. After piling her hair into a knot at the nape of her neck she secured it, then pinched her cheeks, for they had lost all color.

Her knees shaking so badly that she could hardly stand, Lucy forced herself down the stairs, sure that the end had come and she'd be out on the streets before she knew it, deemed unsuitable to be a future duchess's maid. Yes—that had to be it. And Eunice would throw the O'Reillys into the street right after Lucy, just for spite.

The last thing Lucy expected was the duchess's warm greeting.

"Lucy," she said, rising and walking over to her, taking both her hands. "Do not look so fearful, child; I haven't come to take your head off. Quite the opposite."

"The—the opposite, your grace?" Lucy said, her head spinning with confusion. "I don't understand."

"Of course you don't. But you see," she added gently, "I do. I believe I understand everything, or close to it, and the time has come for us to speak plainly. Come, sit down here beside me."

Lucy's throat had gone dry as the duchess spoke. She stumbled toward the sofa and gratefully sank down onto it, for her knees really wouldn't hold her for another second. "I—I don't know what you mean," she stammered. "What do you wish to speak plainly about?"

"You, child. You, and how you came to be in this predicament."

"What predicament do you mean?" Lucy said, clutching her hands together. "Do you refer to what I said this afternoon about the Irish situation?"

The duchess shook her head with a smile, then reached out and covered Lucy's clenched fists with her hand. "I wonder," she said slowly, "what threat Eunice Kincaid is hanging over your head to make you so determined to hide the truth of your birth. I think I understand why *she* would want to hide it, but your silence is another question entirely."

Lucy stared at the duchess, her heart in her throat and terror in her heart. She tried desperately to pull herself together, thinking of the O'Reillys and their fate if she didn't. "What truth do you refer to? I told you, your grace, I am but the daughter of a simple tenant farmer who once worked Lord Kincaid's land. Lady Kincaid took pity on my plight and hired me to—"

"Enough, Lucy," the duchess said, cutting her off. "We haven't much time, and I have no patience for fabrication. It is not necessary, not any longer. I *know* who you are, you see. I would have to be blind not to see your father's face in yours. I told you today that I knew him."

Lucy squeezed her eyes shut. There had to be something she could say to persuade the duchess she was wrong—

something. Her brain worked furiously as she sorted through possible explanations and then finally hit on one. "I see I cannot deny the nature of my birth," she said, her hands working in her lap. "But I would not disgrace my mother by speaking of it . . ."

The dowager laughed with genuine amusement. "Oh, Lucy, then do not disgrace your mother now, for she would not thank you for it. She married your father in good faith, after all, and although I can see that you are not lacking in imagination, trying to deny your heritage is foolish and no service to either your parents or yourself. I saw the record of your birth for myself just today, and furthermore, your father spoke of you with pride and love when last I saw him. That is what led me to go looking for the record in the first place."

She nodded at Lucy's look of astonishment. "Yes, child. I thought I must have been mistaken in my memory when my son returned home and told me that he was taking on Lord Kincaid's two stepdaughters. When I questioned him he assured me that Kincaid had left no children of his own. But he was wrong, wasn't he? And how was he possibly to know the truth when no one had bothered to tell him?"

Lucy could hardly breathe. All over. It was all over. She was done for. The duchess had somehow ferreted out the truth, and Eunice would hear about it sure enough. And then it was curtains for Lucy and the O'Reillys, and there wasn't a thing she could do about it now except to throw herself on the duchess's mercy and beg her to keep her silence.

"Please, your grace," she said, raising her face. "I cannot deny the truth of what you say any longer. But if you have any heart, remember what I told you in the garden and have a little compassion for the helpless people who will suffer should you speak of this to a soul."

"I think a small glass of brandy would do us both good just now," the duchess said, rising and pouring from a de-

canter on the sideboard. She handed Lucy a glass and resumed her seat. "This is an interesting situation, I must say.
And I begin to think I understand a little of what has made
you keep your silence. That woman who calls herself your
stepmother has threatened you, has she not?"

"She has threatened an impoverished family whom I love
very much," Lucy said, taking a sip of the strong spirit and
coughing from the fumes. It had been a very long time since
she'd tasted alcohol of any sort, not since before her father
had died when they'd always had wine with dinner. But
nevertheless the fiery drink steadied her and gave her courage to speak. "She told me that if I do anything to reveal the
masquerade she will see that the O'Reillys are cast out, accused of dealings they have nothing to do with. Their safety
is in my hands, your grace, and I will do nothing to jeopar-
dize it."

"The O'Reillys," the duchess repeated thoughtfully. "Yes. I
see. They were your father's tenants." She sipped on her
brandy. "Isn't she clever, holding you hostage under such a
terrible threat? But then nothing Eunice does surprises me.
She turns her own weakness of character into a strength."

"But she is strong, make no mistake, your grace. She has a
will of iron when it comes to having her way. For as long as
I've known her she's been like that. There is no crossing
Eunice, not without terrible repercussions. She has held the
O'Reillys' safety over my head since the day my father died,
and if I do not do exactly as she says, they will pay the
price."

"Not if I have anything to say about it," the duchess said,
her gray eyes, so like her son's, suddenly flashing with anger.
"But confrontation is not how we shall go about this business. I have a much better idea. However, you must agree to
play your part."

"My part? What part can I possibly play other than the
one I've already been playing? If Eunice hears anything
about our encounters, everything is finished."

"I have no intention of Eunice hearing anything. To be perfectly honest, I loathe the woman, and although it is unchristian of me, I haven't anything kind to say about your foolish stepsisters either. Their welfare does not concern me. Yours does."

"But, your grace—your son intends to marry one of my stepsisters! You will be a mother-in-law to either Fiona or Amaryllis and therefore cannot afford to put yourself in the middle of this situation."

The duchess stared at her, then burst into gales of laughter. "My dear girl, you cannot possibly be serious. Where did you come up with such a ridiculous idea?"

"But—but Eunice is so certain about your son's intentions, as are my stepsisters," Lucy said in strong confusion. "Why else would he have gone to the time and expense to launch them in society?"

"My son," the duchess said, "has always been a victim of his conscience. Ever since he was a small boy, if he saw an injustice, he would try to right it. In the case of your stepfamily, once Raphael discovered the nefarious means that his cousin used to gain possession of Kincaid Court, he felt a responsibility to make reparation, and launching your stepsisters so they might find husbands is how he decided to do it." Her smile faded. "Had he been aware of your existence, child, I assure you that matters would have gone very differently for you."

Lucy was rendered speechless by the duchess's explanation. It was so simple that she wondered why she hadn't thought of it herself. But then she hadn't ever thought of Raphael as being a man of conscience, convinced that he was painted by the same brush as his cousin—as all Englishmen.

She couldn't help the flood of relief that swept over her at the thought that he didn't intend to marry Fiona or Amaryllis after all. She had pictured far too clearly the image of Raphael standing at the altar waiting for one of them, of Raphael consummating his marriage vows in a large bed with the lights turned low, holding someone other than her in his strong arms. Holding Fiona or Amaryllis, while, instead of her, one of them gasped with pleasure and delight at his passionate touch.

A heated blush covered her from head to foot as she realized the direction her thoughts had taken, and in front of his mother, no less. If the duchess had any idea of the fantasies Lucy had about her son, she would not be looking on her so kindly.

"Do you not believe me, Lucy?" the duchess asked, regarding her curiously. "I assure you, I have told you the truth. My son has no more regard for your stepfamily than I do. He deeply regrets his generosity toward them, for they have made his life a nightmare since they arrived."

Lucy grinned. "That I do believe, your grace. My stepfamily is gifted in that direction."

"So they are," the duchess said with a long-suffering sigh. "But never mind all of that—the question is what we are going to do about you."

"Nothing, your grace," Lucy said quickly. "I appreciate your concern, but as I have told you, if Eunice learns that you've discovered the truth, not only I but the O'Reillys will pay dearly."

"I intend for nothing of the sort to happen," the duchess replied. "As I have told *you,* I have a plan, and it is a perfectly delicious one."

"A plan? What sort of plan?" Lucy took a quick swallow of her brandy, trying to fortify herself. Any plan of the duchess's other than keeping her silence was sure to be a bad one.

"Next week my good friend Sarah Stanhope is giving a large ball. I want you to attend."

It was Lucy's turn to stare. "I—I beg your pardon?" she gasped, nearly choking in alarm. "You cannot be serious!"

"But I am. Perfectly serious. Now listen carefully, for I have it all worked out. If all goes according to plan, your stepmother and stepsisters will never know you were there, but my son certainly shall, although he won't have the first inkling of your true identity, and that is exactly what I wish . . ."

9

$\mathcal{L}$ucy stood in front of the long looking glass in Fiona's bedroom, pins sticking into her everywhere as she submitted to the fitting of the most beautiful ball dress she'd ever seen.

The duchess had cleverly slipped her personal dressmaker into the house that evening while everyone was out, on the pretext of Madame DeChaille seeing to some last-minute changes to Fiona's and Amaryllis's dresses.

Lucy still couldn't believe that she'd agreed to the duchess's proposal, but the two glasses of cognac she'd consumed that night a week before must have addled her brains, for she had. One more day and she would be entering a grand house on Lord Hugo Montagu's arm, to be introduced as Miss Laura Walker from the Isle of Wight.

"You see, Lucy," the duchess had said as she'd proposed her preposterous scheme, "if you use another name and speak with a British accent, no one will be the wiser—and I have reason to believe that you can speak every bit as much like an Englishwoman as I do. Furthermore, Walker is not so unusual a name that anyone would remark on it."

"But, your grace, my stepmother is sure to recognize me, not to mention my stepsisters!" Lucy said, her head reeling with the enormity of what the duchess was suggesting.

"Nonsense. They might think you bear an astonishing resemblance to Lucy Kincaid, but how would Lucy Kincaid ever afford a ball dress, let alone secure a coveted invitation to the last ball of the season? And you will arrive with my younger son, who I assure you will be willing to go along with my scheme if only to annoy his brother. No one will doubt his word that you are whom he says you are—a girl from an obscure but good family to whom he owes a favor."

"But I still don't see what you hope to accomplish, your grace. I will return home and be plain old Lucy once again, if I'm not discovered, that is. If I am, I won't live to see morning."

"But you won't be discovered. Hugo is rather brilliant when it comes to hoodwinking people. I should know. I'm his mother." She stood and refilled their glasses. "Not only will you have a wonderful opportunity to show the polite British world that you're every bit as good as they are, which I know will give you enormous pleasure, but you'll have a wonderful time flying in the face of your stepmother after the way she's treated you." She handed Lucy her glass. "I don't usually force spirits on young women, but I think you're going to need this if you're to hear the rest."

Lucy numbly took the tumbler. "What more could there possibly be?" she said, not able to believe she was listening at all. "What you've already suggested is insanity, begging your pardon, your grace."

"Insanity? I think this is the most sensible notion I've had in a long time. You see, my ultimate goal is for my son Raphael to come face to face with you. It will not be the first time, will it, Lucy?"

Lucy colored beet red. How could the duchess *possibly* know that? She felt as if she had no more secrets left—the duchess had somehow ferreted out even this one. "I don't know what you mean," she lied, utterly flustered.

"Of course you do. You met in Ireland, did you not? And again in Hyde Park. He told me all about it."

"He did?" Lucy said faintly, one hand creeping to her throat in dismay.

"Indeed he did, and he's been looking for you ever since."

Despite her panic, Lucy's heart soared at the thought that Raphael had been thinking about her at all, even though she had been thinking constantly about him. Even if he *was* an Englishman. But he had actually been looking for her all this time? The knowledge surpassed all her wildest dreams. "He has?" she whispered.

"He has. Why else would he break the habit of a lifetime and go traipsing all around London, attending events that normally bore him to death?" The duchess resumed her seat. "I promise you again that it has not been because of any affection for your stepsisters. My son is far happier rusticating in the country, looking after his properties. If there is one thing he cannot bear, it is empty-headed misses hanging out for husbands."

"But—but what leads you to believe that he has been looking for *me*?" Lucy stammered. "Are you sure you haven't confused me with someone else?"

"Someone else whom he saw in County Mayo and later here in London? Someone else of your exact description who can switch accents at ease? Someone else who owns a red cloak, which I believe you must, for he was very certain on that point? It was you, was it not, Lucy, whom he encountered both times?"

Lucy swallowed. There didn't seem to be any point in holding back any more, since the duchess already knew nearly everything. "Yes," she said softly. "It was I. But I still have no idea why he would be seeking me out. We have only had the slightest of exchanges—and one other that he's not even aware of, for he came to the house in Ireland looking for my stepmother." She lowered her gaze. "He thought I was the maid when I answered the door, and he treated me as such."

"He saw what he expected to see, I suppose," the duchess

said gently. "I confess to surprise, however, that he didn't recognize you, considering what an impression you had made on him earlier."

Lucy looked up at the duchess, slightly mollified. "In fairness, I was dirty," she said. "I'd been cleaning out the fireplaces. And it was dark inside, so perhaps his eyes were not adjusted from the sunshine, for it was a bright morning."

"So," the duchess said thoughtfully. "You have been acting as your stepmother's servant for some time now. I thought as much. Did this begin after your father died, Lucy?"

Lucy nodded, willing away the tears that burned at her eyes. "She blamed me for his death, you see—and not just for that, but for everything that happened after it. Afterward there was no money for a servant, and since Eunice didn't have the first idea how to go about the chores or run a house, I did everything myself, until one day I really was only a servant to her." The whole awful story came rushing out, Lucy grateful finally to have a sympathetic ear to pour it into.

". . . And because the O'Reillys were the only people who really knew what Eunice had done to me, she was determined to make sure they didn't talk, so she threatened me with their undoing," she finished, wiping her eyes. She wasn't crying. She *never* cried.

"There, there, child," the duchess said, handing her a handkerchief. "I better understand now how difficult your life has been, and I confess I am livid about how despicably your stepmother has treated you for so long. It is time to put a stop to it, don't you agree?"

"Oh, Duchess," Lucy blurted out, "I would like nothing better than that, but I do not think you have fully grasped the situation! Eunice is my guardian until August when I turn twenty-one, and even then I will have no money of my own to live on. If I did move away, supposing I could find a decent job, she would certainly make the O'Reillys pay for my deserting her and leaving her without help." She mopped her eyes. "I had hoped that Fiona and Amaryllis would marry and Eunice would live with one of them and set me free, but that does not seem likely now, so we will all be back in the same situation. Don't you see, it's no good?"

The duchess fell silent. After a few moments of contemplation she looked over at Lucy. "I believe I've heard quite enough, Lucy Kincaid. If you are to change your situation, you will have to change your attitude. Pick your head up, girl, and seize the opportunity I am offering you. Take up the position you were born to and show your face at Lady Stanhope's ball."

"But what will attending a ball accomplish?" Lucy said, by now exhausted from trying to explain the impossibility of the situation. "Yes, I would derive satisfaction by fooling all the fine people there, which I think I could do, given everything I've learned about them from Fiona and Amaryllis since I've been here. And yes, I would be especially happy to fool my stepmother and stepsisters, but at the end of the day, what would be different? I would have had a taste of what life might have been like for me, but it would all be over in a few short hours, and I would be back here, Lucy O'Reilly, personal maid. And things would seem even bleaker." She ran a hand over her forehead. "In any case, I don't belong in British society. I'm not cut out for it."

"You are cut out for anything you put your mind to," the duchess said firmly. "And you forget that I don't intend for this to be a small piece of diversion, designed to last one brief night. I intend this to be the beginning for you."

Lucy wanted to scream with frustration. "A beginning *and* an end," she said, twisting the fine linen handkerchief into a tight knot. "What good could any of this accomplish? I've told you over and over again, Eunice will take her revenge."

"You forget about my son and his sense of justice," the duchess said quietly. "He is not a stupid man, nor easily bamboozled. I am counting on the fact that after seeing you at the ball he will eventually work out the story for himself, and when he does, you can be certain that justice will be done and your stepmother will answer to him."

Lucy thought that if anyone had been bamboozled, it was the duchess. If her precious son was so fair, with such an almighty eye toward justice, he would have fired Paddy Delany the instant he met him. But that wasn't the case, as she'd learned from Mr. O'Reilly before she'd left.

Paddy Delany was still fleecing the estate for everything it was worth and lining his pockets with the proceeds, just as he had been from the time he'd taken over Kincaid as land agent. And she still wondered if he hadn't been in cahoots with Thomas Montagu, turning in poor Jamie Bailey to the Constabulary, leaving her a letter to go to the Bailey house, knowing her father would follow her and be caught in the same trap. No, there was no way she believed that Raphael saw anything other than what he wanted to see. Why should he? He was a duke, after all, and could ignore what he pleased, just as he'd ignored her at her own door.

"You obviously think highly of your son, which is as it should be," Lucy said. "But he won't be dealing out any justice to me."

"Then prove me wrong," the duchess replied. "Go to the ball and prove me wrong. If you turn down my proposal, then you are not made of the stuff your father was. I never knew him to refuse a challenge, especially if it was for a just cause."

Lucy raised her chin. She was Lucy Mary Katherine Kincaid, and every inch her father's daughter. "All right then, I will," she said, picking up the gauntlet the duchess had thrown down. "I will. But only on one condition."

"And what condition would that be, child?" the duchess asked with a slight smile.

"That you promise not to tell Raphael anything about me—about who I really am, or how I came to be at the ball, or that you ever laid eyes on me before. Without that assurance, I cannot agree, for your son is bound to confront Eu-

nice with the truth, and that I could not abide, justice or no.
I *must* protect the O'Reillys."

The duchess nodded solemnly. "I give you my word.
Raphael will never hear the truth from me."

Which was why Lucy was standing in front of the mirror
being stuck with pins as Madame DeChaille turned and
twisted her, muttering to herself in French the whole while.

Lucy had always been too proud for her own good, and
she was surely now to pay the price, for she honestly didn't
know how she was going to pull off such a huge charade,
despite the duchess's limitless confidence in her.

But what a beautiful dress it was, made to the duchess's
exact specifications, fine white tulle over a white satin slip,
the bodice scalloped with Belgian lace, the sleeves short and
finished with the same lace. The skirt was lined with rows of
silk Persian roses attached by bows of blue satin ribbon, with
a small posy of silk spring flowers sewn onto the front of the
bodice. The whole was finished off by a wide blue satin sash
that fastened in a bow at the side.

"And for your hair, *ma chérie,* you will have a wreath of
French pearl beads and roses woven through it," Madame
LaChaille said, finished with her adjustments. "I will return
to dress you tomorrow as soon as your stepmother's carriage
has left, claiming for the benefit of the staff that I left something behind tonight." The old woman clapped her hands in
glee. "I have not been involved in such a grand adventure
in years! It makes my heart young again to have a hand in
furthering a romantic plot. We will slip you down the back
stairs and out through the garden to your waiting carriage,
and no one will be the wiser."

According to Madame LaChaille, the duchess had told her
that Lucy O'Reilly was not Lucy O'Reilly at all, but a young
girl of good birth whose stepmother had locked her away
from the eyes of society so as not to dim her own daughters'
light. Lucy's going to the ball was all a great secret designed
to foil her stepmother's wicked scheme.

It really did seem terribly romantic when Lucy looked at it from that angle, and despite her fear, she couldn't help but be swept away by excitement. In twenty-four hours she would be Laura Walker, dancing alongside the cream of British society. Maybe even dancing with Raphael.

The very thought sent a thrill of alarm through her— alarm and something else that started in the pit of her stomach and left her feeling all hot and flushed.

In truth, of all the prospects that terrified her, meeting Raphael face to face again terrified her most of all, even though she'd rehearsed her story over and over.

But to have one night dancing in his arms, her dream fulfilled, was worth every risk she was taking—a night of wonder that would carry her through the rest of her life. Should there be a rest of her life, that was, for if Raphael tumbled to the truth, he would surely challenge her on the spot and she'd find herself the cynosure of the entire room, uncovered as a fraud.

He might have been looking for her over the last few months, but if she knew anything about him, he wouldn't appreciate being played for a fool by a snip of an Irish miss.

"Now we must slip this off you very carefully because of the pins, and we will begin to sew together," Madame LaChaille said. "Ah yes, you will look like a princess by the time I am finished."

A princess . . . Lucy Kincaid, princess for a night, if only in her own deluded mind.

"Now, Hugo, darling," the duchess said, tucking her fingers through her younger son's arm as they walked in the park, "I have a little favor to ask of you, and one that I hope you will indulge me in."

She'd waited all week before making her request, for Hugo wasn't very good at keeping secrets, especially when it came to his brother. But this was one request she was certain he would grant her, given that it gave him an opportunity to tease Raphael, one of his favorite occupations.

"What is it, Mama?" Hugo asked pleasantly enough.

"It might sound rather odd, but I wish for you to escort a young woman to Lady Stanhope's ball tonight."

Hugo slowly turned his head and looked down at his mother, his eyes narrowing. "Now, Mama," he began, "you know I do not wish any part of your matchmaking schemes, for I am perfectly content to be a bachelor—"

"No, no, dearest, this scheme is not aimed at you but rather at your brother."

Hugo burst into laughter. "You must be joking! Rafe has even less of a desire to be leg-shackled than I have, if that's possible. You've never had any success at all with either of us, so why don't you finally give it up?"

"But this is different, Hugo," the duchess said, slowly pulling in the line that she'd cast out. "The young lady in question is one in whom your brother has shown considerable interest. But you see, she is a bit of a mystery, and I confess I have been rather naughty in concocting this scheme."

"A scheme?" Hugo said, suddenly looking interested. "What sort of scheme? And what do you mean she's a mystery?"

"It is a rather complicated story, but do you remember that I told you your brother has been out of sorts recently?"

Hugo shrugged one shoulder. "One of your better understatements, I'd say. He's been behaving like a bear with a sore head, snapping at anyone who dares to speak to him."

"Exactly. You see, he has been looking for this particular girl for some time, but he has no idea of her real identity or where she is from."

Hugo grinned. "A mystery indeed. So you think that Rafe's finally been stricken with love?"

"He has certainly been stricken with something, including a severe case of frustration," the duchess replied. "The point is that I have only just discovered her for myself, but Raphael does not know that I have."

"That's hard to believe. I thought there was nothing my dear brother didn't know."

"That is as may be, but I assure you, in this instance he is completely in the dark about a great many things. I believe he does have strong feelings for the girl, for even though he has not said as much, his actions have certainly proved it. You know perfectly well that Raphael is not inclined to attend every possible social event during the season, let alone any of them."

"No . . . so he really must have been hoping to find this mysterious someone," Hugo said thoughtfully.

"Exactly. Therefore, now that *I* have finally found her, I plan to produce her at Sarah Stanhope's ball on his behalf, but I need your help if I am to manage it. Sarah has agreed to my scheme, but she is the only one other than myself, my dressmaker, and the girl in question who knows anything about it."

"Why don't you bring her yourself?" Hugo asked logically. "It wouldn't be the first time you've pushed a match."

"Because," the duchess said patiently, "I do not want your brother to think I had any hand in the matter. Not only would he construe my actions as unnecessary interference, but he would be bound to come to me for information, and that would not do at all."

"And why not?" Hugo said, regarding his mother with supreme curiosity.

"Because I have given the girl my word that I would not. In any case, as I just said, if Raphael suspected me of meddling in his concerns, he might very well turn his back on the entire situation. But if *you* appear with her, then Raphael will go to you for information when she vanishes again, which she will have to do." The duchess paused. "I am afraid you will have to tell your brother a pack of lies about how you did come to bring her to the ball, but it is all in a good cause. Raphael *cannot* know I had anything to do with this."

Hugo stopped dead in his tracks. "All right, Mama, what is really going on here? I don't mind in the least helping you out, but you're going to have to tell me a great deal more before I voluntarily put my head in this particular noose."

"Do you swear to me that you will not tell your brother any of what I am about to tell you? He has to discover the truth for himself or it is no good."

"Very well, I swear," Hugo said. "Now tell me everything."

So the duchess did, not leaving a single detail out, finishing up with exactly what she needed Hugo to do. "And there you have it. Now that you know everything are you still willing to help?"

Hugo gazed at her, his lips trembling and his eyes dancing with mischief. *"Willing?"* He gasped. "I cannot wait. Ah, Mama, you really have come up with a corker this time. Poor Rafe. It's about time he got his just deserts."

He threw his head back and roared with laughter so loud it echoed around the park.

"What are you looking so cheerful about?" Raphael asked, looking up as Hugo trotted into the study in evening dress, a huge grin plastered across his face.

"Do I look cheerful?" Hugo said, flashing his brother a look of innocence that Rafe didn't trust in the least. "I cannot think why. It's just another ball we're attending. Been to plenty of those in my time, and they're all tediously the same."

"And you've misbehaved at most of them," Rafe said. "I hope that in the spirit of your supposed reformation, this time you'll make an effort not to dishonor the family name."

"Really, brother, you do know how to hold a grudge. Actually I plan to behave with complete propriety. Older and wiser, you know. Anyway, I've been away so long that my name is but a distant memory."

"A likely story," Rafe snapped. "The last time you attended a ball you tried to seduce the younger daughter of your host."

"Did I?" Hugo said, widening his eyes in a manner that infuriated Raphael. "It's all such a blur—oh that's right. I placed a bet at White's that I'd get a heated kiss off the ice-maiden Lady Caroline Stuart before the night was out, and I made three hundred pounds off it, didn't I?"

"And cost me another five thousand when I had to pay off her irate father after it went a bit further than a kiss," Rafe said coldly.

"Ah yes, that's right," Hugo said, clapping him on the shoulder. "Most obliging of you. Allow me to repay the debt."

"If I allowed you to repay every debt you've ever incurred, you'd be penniless, despite your new fortune."

"Sorry about that."

Hugo hung his head, but Rafe didn't miss the smirk he was trying to hide and it made his blood boil. "Just watch your step tonight. I am in no mood for trouble."

"From what I've seen, you have enough of it with those Gupwell sisters and their serpent of a mother," Hugo retorted. "Not quite up to your usual snuff in that choice, Rafe. I cannot think what came over you."

"Neither can I," Rafe said sourly. "But that is none of your business. I'll manage the Gupwell sisters *and* their mother, and by the night's end I'll be done with them for all time."

"Will you?" Hugo said, the sly smile returning to his face. "That might be a trick."

"What do you mean by that?" Rafe demanded.

"Only that I've learned that things can appear simple on the surface, when in actuality one has dug oneself in deeper than one realizes."

Tired of arguing with Hugo, Rafe conceded the point, for he really didn't want to think about the tedious Gupwell girls or their dreadful mother another moment. "I suppose you are right," he said as the image of Egeria flashed painfully across his mind. "But then, life is never simple, however hard one tries to convince oneself it is. Still, the agreement is clear in this case. The season officially ends tomorrow and Lady Kincaid has not accomplished the necessary task of finding husbands for her daughters, so they have no choice but to return to Ireland."

"And you, Raphael? Are your hands then clean?" Hugo asked, his gaze sharpening on his brother.

"Clean? What do you mean? I promised them nothing further. I thought I explained the whole arrangement to you when you plagued me about it the other night."

"So you did," Hugo said, pouring himself a glass of sherry. "But again, I'm not so sure you'll be rid of them that easily. Situations like this have a way of coming back to haunt one." He grinned. "I should know."

"Yes, you should," Rafe said wearily. "Let us leave it alone, Hugo, for I do not wish to start the evening badly."

He didn't wish to start the evening at all, but that was no longer in his hands, since he'd agreed to attend the Stanhope ball weeks before. But he'd been in a state of terrible melancholy all day, for with the conclusion of this last night, all hope of finding Egeria was truly gone.

And with it, all hope that the myth of happy endings might actually be true.

"Lucy, do stop fadgeting," Amaryllis said, looking over her shoulder with annoyance. "Anyone might think you had something more important on your mind than getting us ready for the ball. Has your mind gone permanently wayfaring? You are paying me no attention at all, and this is the very night the duke might proposition me. I need to look my best."

Lucy shook herself from her thoughts. Only two more hours. Two more hours and she would be facing either disaster or success, success the least likely scenario.

Her shaking hands refused to steady themselves as she twisted Amaryllis's mousy hair into a cascade of fat curls that did nothing to enhance her equally fat face, but this was the style Amaryllis had favored ever since Georgina Bovill had such success with it, securing the hand and title of Lord Fenwick.

But then Lucy imagined Georgina Fenwick probably had the looks for cascading curls, whereas Amaryllis was better suited to a plainer style. And Lucy was sure that Georgina Bovill's success in finding a husband had much more to do with an engaging personality and pretty face, since, according to Fiona, the girl had hardly a feather to fly with. Amaryllis would have to work very hard to cultivate an engaging personality, not as easy a thing as cultivating cascading curls.

Two more hours . . . Would Raphael look up and see her? Would he even recognize her in her finery? And if he did recognize her, what would he do?

"*Lucy!* Will you pay attention—you're practically burning me with the curdling iron!"

"Sorry," Lucy said dreamily. Would he smile with pleasure upon seeing her as he had in the park, or gaze upon her with the wonder he had on Downpatrick Head when they'd exchanged poetry as if they'd been exchanging hearts?

Or would he look at her with no recognition at all, as he had in the doorway of the house on the edge of the peat bog, as if she were nothing at all to him, nothing to bother looking at? If he did that, her heart would surely break, even if he *was* an Englishman.

"Lucy, you wrench, what is the matter with you?" Amaryllis cried angrily, swatting Lucy's hand away. "I declare, I'll have no hair left on my head with the way you're pulling at it."

"I'm so sorry, Amaryllis. I suppose I was just thinking of the grand time you're going to have tonight and trying to imagine who you might be dancing with."

"I'll be dancing with everyone, you stupid girl, just as I

always do. And by night's end I'll be afficiandoed to the duke, and everyone who's anyone will be paying me court."

"Affianced," Lucy said as absently as she always did when Fiona and Amaryllis mutilated their words. "Wouldn't that be something?" Something indeed, if the duchess had gotten it right, she thought, putting one final twist into Amaryllis's overly curled head.

"Luuuuucy, where is my wrap?" Fiona said shrilly, flying into the bedroom. "You forgot to lay it out! What is the matter with you tonight?"

"I was just saying the same thing," Amaryllis said, shooting Lucy a nasty look as she stood and admired herself in the looking glass.

"It's all right for you, isn't it, Amaryllis, but the duke is going to proposition me, the eldest."

"Your wrap is lying on the end of your bed," Lucy said, her words drowned out by a sudden volley of words between the two sisters.

"He is not!" Amaryllis screeched.

"He is, he is," Fiona said, stamping her foot.

"He isn't—he is going to offer for *me*," Amaryllis screeched, her face a mask of fury. "He danced with me last yesterday evening."

"He danced with me first," Fiona countered just as furiously. "That is far more a sign of fever."

"Stop it, both of you," Eunice commanded, sweeping into the room just as the girls were going for each other's throats. "The duke will make a decision between you tonight, and whatever happens, our lot will be improved. Whoever is left behind will marry the duke's brother if you play your cards right, and that is no dishonor. Now pull yourselves together and come downstairs."

She cast Lucy a disparaging look. "As for you, do not expect us back before three at the earliest. There is bound to be a celebration announcement and therefore the festivities will run late. My daughters will need some extra settling when we return. Be sure to have hot milk at the ready."

Lucy inclined her head, her secret huge inside her, never more glorious than now in the face of her stepmother's cold disdain. "As you wish, Aunt Eunice. Enjoy your evening."

"Be assured that we shall. And you, my girl, make sure that everything is in readiness for the morrow, for we will be parading around London, one my daughters celebrating the catch of the decade."

More likely one way or the other I'll be dealing with temper tantrums from the three of you, Lucy thought, but she smiled brightly. "I'll say a prayer that everything goes well tonight," she said, planning to say that prayer on her own behalf.

"Never mind your prayers. Just see to your duties. Come along, girls. The duke and his mother will be arriving any moment."

Lucy watched them go, knowing that the next time she saw them, it would be in a brightly lit ballroom, and she'd be wearing a crown of roses and pearls on her head and white satin slippers on her feet.

10

"*Ah, ma belle,* your appearance surpasses even my wildest hopes." Madame DeChaille stood back, her work finished. "Perfection. Sheer perfection. Come, see for yourself."

She took Lucy by the elbow and led her over to the cheval glass. "*Et voilà!*" she said with a flourish, as if uncovering a masterpiece.

Lucy had to force herself to look, terrified of what she would see, that she would not be worthy of such a beautiful dress. But instead she drew in a long, wondering breath, for she hardly recognized the woman who gazed back at her.

The Lucy Kincaid she was accustomed to seeing had disappeared, replaced by a stranger. A fine, elegant stranger whose eyes and cheeks glowed, whose hair was piled high on her head in an intricate arrangement, red roses and white pearls woven through it. The only thing left of the old Lucy Kincaid was the locket she wore around her neck with the pictures of her parents inside.

"Is it really me?" she murmured in astonishment, unable to believe her own eyes.

"Yes, *chérie,* it is really you," the old woman said, her face wreathed in a broad smile. "You truly look like a princess. The duchess will be so very pleased when she sees you."

"I—oh, *thank* you, Madame," Lucy said, impulsively giving the dressmaker a hug.

"Seeing your happiness is all the thanks I need," Madame DeChaille said, returning the embrace. "You will be the brightest light in all the room tonight. And now you had better hurry, for his lordship awaits you in the carriage." She handed Lucy a pair of long white kid gloves and a circular ivory fan. "Come, I will make sure no one sees you as you leave."

Lucy looked in the mirror one last time, just to be sure she hadn't turned back into her old self, but the same stranger still gazed back at her, looking far more serene and composed than Lucy felt. "Oh, my goodness," she said breathlessly. "Oh, my goodness gracious. Who ever would have thought . . ."

Madame DeChaille laughed merrily. "I had some idea, as did the duchess. It was only you who doubted that we could transform you so completely."

Lucy smiled uncertainly. "I suppose since I hardly recognize myself, there's little danger anyone else will recognize me." And that was all to the good. Wasn't it?

Her heart pounding frantically, she followed Madame DeChaille down the back stairs and slipped out the door into the garden.

The night was balmy, a gentle breeze blowing, and the moon hung half full in the sky, casting a soft silvery light over the grass. Lucy turned and gave one last wave of her hand toward the dressmaker, who stood watching in the doorway, her small round figure backlit by lamplight.

Taking a deep breath, Lucy picked up her skirts and ran down the path and out through the garden door onto the street.

A large carriage waited only a few yards away, a liveried coachman sitting on its box, his hands loosely holding the reins of four perfectly matched white horses. Two footmen dressed in blue and gold stood at attention behind.

Her steps halted and she drew in a sharp breath as a tall, dark-haired man moved out into a pool of moonlight, his well-built figure clothed in formal evening attire. He walked toward her, a smile hovering around the corners of his mouth, his gaze brushing over her with something she couldn't define. Surprise, maybe? Or perhaps it was dismay. She couldn't be entirely sure.

But one thing she was sure of, and that was that he was a very handsome man, although as different from his brother in looks as night was to day.

For Lucy knew he could only be Hugo Montagu, and he was here to take her to the ball. A part of her still couldn't believe it was really happening. A fine coach-and-four waiting for her, complete with a handsome gentleman—even if he *was* British—to escort her. She, Lucy Kincaid, was about to go to a ball. She felt as if she was surely dreaming, for such things didn't happen in real life—or not in her life, anyway.

"Good evening," he said, taking her gloved hand and bowing over it. "You must be Miss Lucy Kincaid—or perhaps I should say Miss Laura Walker, if we're to begin the charade. I am Hugo Montagu." He smiled down into her eyes, looking not the least bit nervous, which made her wonder if he had an ounce of sense in his handsome head.

"I—that is, I am," she stammered. "It is very nice to make your acquaintance. Oh, dear," she said, abandoning all pretense of composure. "It's no use my trying to behave like a fine lady. I'm afraid I'm about to collapse right here on the pavement from nerves."

He laughed. "You don't want to do that and soil your pretty dress—my mother would never speak to me again. Here, take my arm. I'll keep you steady."

"Thank you," she said, grateful for the support as he tucked her trembling fingers into the crook of his arm.

"Not at all. I know this situation is new to you," he said conversationally, as if he were discussing nothing more earth-shaking than the weather, as if he escorted untried and inexperienced Irish girls pretending to be seasoned English gentlewomen to balls every day of the week. "My mother told me all about your predicament, and I am completely at your service this evening. Here, mind your step."

Lucy climbed into the carriage, trying her best to look graceful, not an easy task when she had a fine dress to manage. It was one thing doing it in her head, something else altogether in practice.

"Oh," she said on a long breath, looking around in awe at the blue velvet squabs, the lamps on the inside—on the inside!—and the parted blue velvet curtains at the windows. "It is very grand, isn't it?"

"Not as grand as some. This is my mother's personal carriage, and she dislikes opulence."

"Well, it's surely as opulent as anything I've ever seen," Lucy said, fingering the soft material of the cushions. She glanced shyly over at him. "This is very kind of you—to take me to Lady Stanhope's, I mean, and risk my making a fool out of both of us."

Hugo tapped the roof with his cane, then crossed one leg over the other as the carriage clattered off down the street. "I had wondered, naturally, what I was taking on when I agreed to the charade, although my mother usually exhibits sound judgment. I think I can safely say that I am looking forward to the experience."

"I find that difficult to believe," Lucy said, clutching her hands together in her lap. "As you must know, Lord Hugo, the possibilities for disaster are endless."

"I don't see why," he said comfortably. "As long as we both stick to the script, we should be safe. You speak as most of my acquaintances do, and your appearance is exactly what it should be, down to your satin slippers. No one other than my mother will know you, with the exception of your own family, but my mother seems to think that they will see what they are meant to see."

"And what is that?" Lucy asked, nervously toying with her fan.

"What else but a young woman named Miss Laura Walker from the Isle of Wight who bears a passing resemblance to someone they cannot quite place." He grinned. "It really is the most wonderfully cunning ruse. Were I a gambling man, I should bet five thousand pounds that you will have no trouble convincing all of the *crème de la crème* that you are exactly who you say you are."

Lucy shifted in her seat to regard him full on. "May I ask you one question, my lord?"

"Please, you must call me Hugo, for we are in this together, are we not? But what is your question?"

"Why are you doing this for me?" Lucy said directly. "I am a complete stranger, and although you might be acquainted with my circumstances, you are nevertheless putting yourself in a precarious position that might very well work out badly for you."

Hugo smiled, and for the first time she saw a cynical edge beneath his easy humor. "If for some reason it all went wrong I doubt that anyone would blink an eye in my direction," he said. "Did my mother not tell you? I am the black sheep of the family, recently returned from the Continent to my brother's infinite regret. I am incorrigible and will always be incorrigible, as well as being a blight to my family."

Lucy matched his smile, appreciating his honesty and his desire to put her at ease. "Then we are in accord," she said, liking him more by the minute. "For although our circumstances might be vastly different, I too am a blight to my family. And never a bigger blight than I will be tonight, should they find me out."

"I think you might be an even bigger blight to them if they do not find you out," Hugo said. "I am marginally acquainted with your family, you see, and I have every reason to believe that your arrival is going to cast them into despair.

I do not like them, Lucy, and I cannot be sorry for what is about to happen."

"What is that?" Lucy said, frowning, for she had no idea what he meant.

"You will have to wait and see for yourself," he said cryptically. "Just remember three things. The first is that should my brother ask you to dance, you must accept. The second is that no matter what happens, you must not waver from your story under any circumstances. And the third is that you must leave by midnight."

"By midnight? Why?" Lucy asked, thinking that was only three short hours away. Three short hours in which to live her entire life.

"Because if you don't, you might not be home before your stepmother and stepsisters, and as my mother pointed out, that might well cast suspicion on you as well as getting you into trouble that you don't need. It's not worth the risk."

"Oh," Lucy said, seeing his point. "Yes, all right."

"In any case," Hugo continued, "if you stay any later, my brother will have too much time to avail himself of information. Trust me when I tell you that he is a master at wearing a person down."

Lucy shivered. She knew that well enough after his relentless grilling in the park. But she could pull the wool over his eyes. Of course she could. She had before, hadn't she? And then another, more alarming thought occurred. "Why do you care about what your brother might think? He has no reason to take any interest in me at all."

"Does he not? You forget, Lucy, that my mother told me everything, right down to his trying to hunt you down all over London," Hugo said bluntly.

Lucy paled. "She did?" she said faintly.

"She did, which leads me to believe that my brother has a vested interest in finding you. You might fool everyone else with your new appearance, but I mightily doubt you will fool him, not if I know my brother. Be warned, Lucy. If you do not wish him to learn the truth, then you must play your cards carefully and close to your chest."

"How carefully?" she asked through a dry throat, terrified all over again.

Hugo tapped his finger on his knee in emphasis. "Dance with him once, twice if you must, for to refuse him would look suspicious. Speak to me, to my mother, once I pretend to formally introduce you, speak to whomever else you wish, but do not allow my brother any private time with you, for to do so really would be courting disaster. Unless, that is, you want him to discover your identity."

"But I don't!" Lucy cried in alarm.

"Then heed my words. For I promise you, should you slip in any direction, Rafe is the one who will spot it. The less time you spend in his company the better."

Lucy nodded, feeling sick with a combination of excitement and dread. Rafe. His brother called him Rafe. Hearing the familiarity made him seem even more real—positively human.

Three hours. Three hours to live an entire lifetime. Three hours forced to pretend to be someone she wasn't, but she didn't care. She would dance in Raphael's arms if she was lucky. To be held by him if even for a few brief moments was all she wanted.

The carriage pulled up in front of the largest house Lucy had ever seen, lights glowing from every window, the muted sounds of music and laughter drifting into the street as the footman opened the carriage door and helped her out.

"So it begins," Hugo murmured softly into her ear, taking her hand. "Remember, you have nothing to fear, for my mother and I will back up everything you say, and *no* one would dare question my mother. Except Rafe," he added as an unnecessary reminder.

Lucy's knees knocked together, but she squared her shoulders. She was Lucy Mary Katherine Kincaid, and she was about to take on all of London society and show them she was every bit as good as they were. Even if she did have to pretend to be British.

Raphael had arrived at the Stanhope ball tediously early. They always arrived tediously early, the Gupwell girls terrified that they might miss a single opportunity to catch a husband, not that there was any chance of that.

He'd made the best use of his time, dancing with his hostess Lady Stanhope, who seemed in a particularly fine humor and had teased him relentlessly about his unmarried state. Her merry jesting about finding the woman of his dreams hadn't done anything to improve his own humor, not when it cut so close to the bone.

Then he had danced with the usual assortment of misses, including the Gupwell sisters, of course—and thank God *that* was nearly for the last time, for neither his toes nor his tolerance could take much more of a pounding. One more dance with Fiona and he'd be finished. He'd be happy never to dance again.

He was now content to stand back against the wall and lazily converse with acquaintances, observing the proceedings from a distance. And watching the staircase that led down into the ballroom.

He was so damned tired of endlessly watching doors and staircases in hope that Egeria would appear. He was a fool, and a deluded fool at that, to be wasting his time in this manner when he had far better things to do.

"Southwell, where have your thoughts wandered?" Freddy Lyndhurst said. "I was asking if you'd heard anything from your cousin Aubrey. He's been abroad a rather long time, hasn't he? But then I suppose he is caught up with dancing attention on his new wife. What was her name—Serafina? Rather an unusual girl, but pretty, and he seemed to be over the moon about her when I last saw him."

Rafe brought his attention back to Freddy. "No, I haven't heard a thing in some time, but it takes weeks for letters to arrive from that part of the world. I left them in Cyprus, where Aiden was doing some shipping business. I imagine they'll be home shortly."

"Excellent. I had a question for him regarding one of his stallions that I'd like to breed to a mare of mine. I have an idea that the cross will be a good one."

"Oh?" Raphael said absently. Horse breeding was a subject on which he was particularly well versed. "Which stallion did you have in mind?"

"I was thinking of the black out of Phantom Night and Sunshine's Promise. I saw him run as a two-year-old last year at Ascot and he made a fine showing."

Raphael was about to answer when his gaze caught his brother appearing at the top of the staircase, a beautiful dark-haired woman dressed in white at his side.

Rafe's gaze sharpened and he very slowly straightened, shock waves racing through him as he drank in her familiar features, features that for so long he had seen only in his mind.

Oh, dear God. Egeria. It was Egeria, at long last.

"Lord Hugo Montagu and Miss Laura Walker." The announcement boomed down to him as they moved off the top of the stairs.

Laura Walker? That was her name? He wanted to crow with happiness. He not only had a name, but the woman who belonged to it, and she was right here in front of him, delivered like an answer to a prayer.

But what in the name of *hell* was she doing hanging on his blasted brother's arm, of all miserable people? What connection could she possibly have to Hugo, who had been out of the country for three full years? Well, he would find that out soon enough.

He didn't take his eyes from her as she floated gracefully down the grand staircase. He'd never seen anyone so beautiful. *Thank you for this chance, Lord, this last precious chance . . .*

He was vaguely aware of the sudden hush that came over the room, not unlike the hush that had come over his heart, and he realized that he was holding his breath. He slowly released it, wondering what she would do when they came face to face. Deny him yet again?

"Who is that girl?" Freddy said, his voice full of wonder. "I have never before laid eyes on her, but by God, I swear she has already cast an enchantment over me."

"She's obviously a friend of my brother's," Raphael said shortly. He wasn't about to share her with Freddy. He wasn't about to share her with anyone, especially not Hugo. "Excuse me."

He moved away from the wall, carefully considering his next move as he walked toward them. Now that he had her within his grasp, he would take his time. If she wanted to play games, he would play along. But only for so long, for once he had her alone, he would find out exactly what he wanted to know. *Exactly* what he wanted to know.

For the first time in his life, he was delighted to be a duke with all its attendant privileges, and he would exert every last one of them without a twinge of conscience.

Lucy couldn't believe she'd negotiated the interminably long staircase without tripping over her own feet. The huge room was a blur of lights and colors, and in her daze she couldn't pick out a single face in the throng. She only knew that all eyes were on her, and she had no idea whether she was being stared at in polite interest or in supreme displeasure. Just at that moment being swallowed up by the great peat bog seemed positively inviting, far more inviting than being swallowed up by this crowd.

"Oh, Hugo," she whispered, "I don't know if I can do this. They're all looking at me as if I'd just stepped into the middle of a circus ring."

Hugo squeezed her fingers. "You're doing beautifully. Keep your chin up and tell yourself that you're better than the entire lot of them put together. I dare say it's the truth too. We're going to have a roaring good time duping the entire *ton*."

Lucy doubted that, but she did as she was told and kept her head level and her gaze straight ahead . . .

Only to see Raphael coming right for her, his gray eyes boring directly into hers. Her fingers jerked on Hugo's arm and her heart started pounding in earnest.

"Oh, no," she choked. She wasn't ready—she couldn't possibly be ready. But he looked so wonderful, so handsome in his black tail coat and snowy white waistcoat and neckcloth, his golden hair gleaming under the lights of a dozen crystal chandeliers.

"He didn't waste any time, did he?" Hugo said, sounding amused. "All right, princess, here you go. He's almost on us. Give it your best."

"Good evening, Hugo," Raphael said, coming to a halt directly in front of them. "I wondered when you were going to arrive."

"I had to collect Miss Walker," Hugo said blithely. "She is staying on the other side of town. Miss Walker, may I present my brother, the Duke of Southwell?"

"Miss Walker?" he said in his deep, rich voice, his face betraying nothing as he took her hand and bowed over it, the heat of his fingers burning right through her glove into her palm.

"How do you do, your grace?" she said, astonished the words came out smoothly, as if she spoke them all the time, as if his touch wasn't making her weak at the knees.

"I am extremely well, thank you," he said, releasing her hand. "Better than I have been in some time. And you, Miss Walker? How are you? Or perhaps I needn't ask, for you are looking very well. The veriest picture of good health."

"I—thank you," she said, raising her startled gaze to his. This wasn't how the script usually went, was it?

"No need to thank me," he said. "It was a mere observation. The London air does not agree with many people—all the smoke, you know. It can become so thick that it swallows a person right up."

Lucy wanted to kick him. So. He wanted to play cat and mouse, did he, couching his words with hidden meaning? Well, two could play at that game. "Smoke has never troubled me, your grace, unless it is blown directly into my face off the end of a gentleman's cheroot. But then a man who would blow smoke into a lady's face is no gentleman, is he?"

Raphael smiled lazily. "I gather you put a great deal of stock in a gentleman's behavior, Miss Walker?"

"Naturally," she replied, actually beginning to enjoy herself—she'd always liked a good challenge. "Isn't a man's behavior the measure of the man himself?"

"I have always believed that to be the case. And that said, I have been remiss in my own behavior by neglecting to ask you to dance. The orchestra is just striking up a waltz. You don't mind, do you, Hugo?"

"I don't mind in the least, if Miss Walker does not."

Lucy realized that she'd just been skillfully caught in her own trap. But hadn't she been dreaming of this moment for months? "Thank you, your grace," she said, curtsying. "I would be honored."

Still, as much as she wanted to dance with Raphael she wasn't so sure she was ready to be exposed to the entire room just yet. Suppose Eunice and Fiona and Amaryllis were out there watching, even though the duchess had promised to spirit them into another room as soon as she arrived? But she'd brave it.

Raphael took her by the hand and led her out onto the dance floor, turning toward her. Out of habit Lucy's right hand drifted toward his waist, her left raising upward.

Raphael quickly caught her right wrist and neatly slid his hand up into hers, looking down at her quizzically. "If you don't mind too terribly much, I think I will take the lead tonight. Surely you will allow me that much?"

Lucy wanted to drop through the floor. *How* could she have made such a foolish mistake? "I beg your pardon," she said, trying to cover her error as Raphael's other hand came lightly around her waist to rest on her back. "I have small sisters, you see, whom I have recently been teaching to dance," she said, a sudden trembling taking hold of her body at his touch.

"Ah," he said. "Small sisters. And as you have not been out and about this season, you have had little practice in the correct position, is that it?" He swept her around as he spoke, skillfully guiding her in wide circles.

"Yes, that is it exactly," she said, grateful that he'd accepted her explanation so easily.

"Then tell me where you have been, Egeria," he asked softly.

Lucy nearly stumbled. "Laura. My name is Laura," she insisted. "I see you still mistake me for your missing friend."

"Good, we are making progress if you do not deny our meeting in the park."

"Why would I deny it?" she replied, nervously peeking around his broad shoulder for any sign of her stepmother or stepsisters, but thank goodness they were nowhere in sight. She relaxed slightly. "We may not have been formally introduced, but my memory is perfectly intact."

"Is it? I wonder. Falls sometimes impair the brain."

"I do not recall falling," she said, feigning puzzlement. "Perhaps it is your brain that has been impaired, for you attribute a great many actions to me that exist solely in your own fertile imagination."

Raphael slanted a smile down at her. "Do I now? I begin to think that if anyone should be applauded for possessing a fertile imagination, it is you, my dear girl."

"My imagination is adequate, but not exceptional," Lucy said as he spun her around the room again. "I am really rather uncreative when it comes to making up stories."

"Then why don't you tell me the truth for once and enlighten me as to where you have been hiding these last two months?" he said flatly. "Surely you have not spent all your time teaching your younger sisters the waltz?"

The conversation was not going as smoothly as Lucy had hoped. Hugo was right—his brother was ruthless when it came to extracting information. But she was prepared, the story ready on the tip of her tongue.

"If you must know, my father has been ill, your grace, and although we came up to London for the season, I have been obliged to look after him since he took ill, as well as looking after my sisters who are not yet out. Does that answer your question?"

Raphael raised one eyebrow skeptically. "Partially. But if that is the case, how is it that you came to be here tonight in the company of my brother?"

"Your brother is a friend of my father's," she said, reciting the story the duchess had gleefully concocted. "Hugo very kindly paid him a call to inquire about his health, and when he heard of my predicament, he offered to escort me here tonight, since my father has been unable to go out and I have had no one else to act as chaperone."

Raphael burst into laughter. "And your father thought Hugo a suitable chaperone? He really must be ill indeed."

"I *like* Hugo," Lucy said, glaring at him. "He is kind and thoughtful and at least *he* behaves like a gentleman."

No, this was not going at all as she had anticipated. What had happened to her lovely fantasy of being swept around a dance floor by a dashing prince? Raphael Montagu was nothing more than an irritating pest, ruining all of her fine dreams in one fell swoop. She should have had the sense to expect it. After all, he was nothing but a filthy *Englishman,* and his true colors were showing.

"You like Hugo," he repeated, his brow drawing down. "And why not? He probably whispers sweet nothings into your ear and empty promises of a glorious future, while his mind is bent on nothing but seduction. A gentleman indeed."

"Oh, will you be quiet?" she said furiously. "This is my only dance of the season and I'd like at least to enjoy it. Do you always yap on in such an irritating fashion?"

Raphael gazed down at her, his expression suddenly indecipherable. "If you would like silence, silence you shall have," he said, pulling her imperceptibly closer, his fingers tightening on her back.

Lucy was suddenly aware of the strength he held in check, his arm like a steel band around her, his hand gripping hers, but not so tightly that it hurt. Only so tight as to remind her who was in control.

The heat of his body radiated into hers, and his scent, masculine and heady with faint overtones of sandalwood and lime, was impossible to ignore. For the first time she understood the meaning of the phrase *the male animal*. Dangerous. Powerful. Not to be toyed with.

Lucy shivered. This was more like it—as long as he didn't open his mouth. That had been his downfall from the very beginning and she should have remembered it. But quiet, holding her like this, everything was right with the world. In fact, the world had all but disappeared. She felt safe, even though she knew she wasn't. She felt loved, even though she knew she wasn't.

But what did it matter? All she'd asked for was a night of illusion and it had been given to her. If she had to settle for a few minutes of bliss instead of a few hours, so be it. Being in Raphael's arms felt lovelier than anything else she'd ever experienced, even nicer than Ireland in the spring when the sun came out and the trees and flowers bloomed and lambs were born all fresh and new, just as she'd felt reborn a few short hours ago.

She drank in the experience, every second of it, as if she had never drunk of anything else, as if this were the first taste of water on her tongue, the first touch of hands on her body, the first of everything. And the last, which made it all the more bittersweet.

The music ended, but Lucy didn't notice. It was Raphael who drew away. "The dance is finished, Miss Walker. I hope you didn't find it too excruciating."

Lucy, still lost in her dream, smiled mistily up at him. "Oh, no, your grace. It was lovely."

An expression of some powerful emotion Lucy couldn't define flashed in his eyes, but it was gone so quickly she thought she must have imagined it.

"I am delighted you at least do not find me lacking in my dancing skills, although I seem to disappoint you in every other area," he said, leading her off the floor.

"Not in *every* area," she replied, then belatedly heard herself. "What I mean is that I am not accustomed to being interrogated by a perfect stranger," she amended quickly.

"Is that what I am? A perfect stranger?"

"How can you be anything else? We have only ever exchanged a few casual words."

"Odd that I don't consider the words we exchanged to be the least bit casual, but I suppose that is a matter of personal interpretation. As is your accent."

Lucy's happy haze vanished as she snapped abruptly back to reality. He really was the most infuriating man. "Do you now object to the way I speak, your grace? It seems to me that it is I who displease you in every regard."

"You could not be further from the truth," he said quietly. "But I do not like being lied to, Miss Laura Walker. The charade is wearing thin."

Lucy's eyes widened in alarm. Had he seen through her already? "I don't know what you mean," she said, relief flooding through her as they finally reached Hugo, who was engaged in close conversation with his mother. Safety at last, and the duchess finally there to protect her. She released a quick breath.

"You know very well what I mean, but now is not the time

to discuss it," Raphael said in an undertone, then raised his voice to conversational level. "Hello, Mama. Hugo, I am returning Miss Walker to you."

The duchess turned. "Ah, Raphael, there you are." She bestowed a warm smile of welcome on Lucy. "Miss Walker. How very nice to meet you, my dear. My son has spoken so fondly of your father. I am delighted you were able to come out tonight." Not a single flicker on her face betrayed that she knew Lucy perfectly well.

"Thank you, your grace," Lucy said, dropping into a low curtsy. The duchess was very good at this, she thought as she rose again.

"And how is your father? I understand he was taken ill when he arrived in London. So unfortunate."

"He is much improved, thank you, although I think he will be happy to return home. He much prefers the sea air." Lucy was uncomfortably aware of Raphael's eyes boring into her, and she knew he was weighing every word she spoke.

"Quite understandable," the duchess said. "You live on the Isle of Wight, I believe? Hugo said that you made your come-out there last year."

"Yes, your grace, although it was a very quiet affair, just a small dance at our house, since my mother had died the year before and anything more lavish would have been unsuitable." She smiled brightly.

"Ah, yes. That explains why I have not had the pleasure of meeting you before. Is this your first time in London?"

"This is my first time ever away from home," Lucy said pointedly. *That* should get Raphael. "I feel a bit lost in such a big city, but what little I have seen of London has been exciting. It is very different from my small town."

"I should think so. Perhaps next season you will come up again and see all that you missed. I would be happy to take you about, my dear." She turned to Hugo. "What a charming girl, darling. I am so happy you were able to bring her along this evening so that her trip to London was not an entire loss."

"I was happy to do her father the favor," Hugo said smoothly. "He was most distressed that he was unable to give his daughter the season she had hoped for."

"I didn't mind," Lucy said. "My father needed me far more than I needed a season."

"A very pretty sentiment. And speaking of pretty, your dress is lovely," the duchess said. "My own modiste couldn't have done a finer job."

Lucy had to bite her lip to keep from laughing. "Thank you," she said, her eyes dancing. "It seems as if I have waited forever to wear it." She felt like an actress on a grand stage, with everyone playing their parts to perfection. Surely Raphael had to be convinced by now that she was Laura Walker from the Isle of Wight?

But just as the satisfied thought passed through her head, the corner of her eye caught the alarming sight of three people careening toward their little group.

Lucy's heart leapt in terror, for they were none other than her stepmother, Fiona, and Amaryllis, and they looked as if they were on a mission, with her as their objective.

11

Something was wrong. Rafe couldn't put his finger on exactly what it was, but a number of things didn't ring true to him. He had the strong feeling that Miss Laura Walker was still trying to flummox him. Not only did she now claim to have sisters when she'd told him in the park she was an only child, but she said she'd never been away from home before? Indeed.

He knew perfectly well that she had been in Ireland back in March, and not on the Isle of Wight as she claimed. But why the dissemblance? What was she hiding? And why was she claiming to be from the Isle of Wight at all, where people most definitely did not speak with soft, lilting Irish accents, as she had done on Downpatrick Head when she'd thought no one was listening?

Hugo was bound to be up to his neck in this fiasco, although for the life of him, Rafe couldn't think how. Hugo hadn't been back in the country long enough to have involved himself in much of anything.

He was about to ask just how Hugo knew Mr. Walker when he spotted Lady Kincaid and her two daughters barreling across the room toward them. His mother spotted them at the same time.

"Hugo, dear," she said quickly, "why do you not take Miss Walker over and introduce her to her hostess? Lady Stanhope was so kind to offer the invitation, after all, and I think this might be a good time. I see that dreadful woman coming and I really do not think Miss Walker needs to be subjected to her or her daughters."

"An excellent idea, Mama," Hugo said. "Miss Walker?" he said, taking her by the arm and practically dragging her away, although she looked thrilled to be going.

Raphael could hardly be surprised, given that she pretended to want to have nothing to do with him. But he knew better—she had given herself completely away during their dance. She wasn't the only one who had been undone, although he hoped he'd done a better job of hiding his feelings.

No, Miss Laura Walker wasn't going to get away from him so easily. He'd deal with her later, and his brother as well.

"Duchess, Duke—there you both are," Eunice Kincaid said breathlessly, Fiona and Amaryllis bumping into each other as their mother halted abruptly. "Goodness, what a crush it is tonight!" She patted her scrawny bosom. "It took forever just to cross the room."

"Yes," Raphael said, irritated that their arrival had kept him from asking the questions that burned at him. "The room is becoming more crowded by the moment."

Eunice's gaze traveled after Hugo's retreating back and the woman on his arm. "Who was that with Lord Hugo just now?" she asked, the venom in her eyes belying the smile on her face. "I do not believe I have seen her about this season."

"That was Miss Walker," the duchess said, not elaborating any further. "A beautiful girl, is she not?"

"She'll do, I suppose," Eunice snapped. "Is she a particular friend of Lord Hugo's?"

"Not a particular friend, although my son did escort her here tonight," the duchess said coolly. "Why do you ask?"

"I merely wondered. I saw the duke dancing with her as I came out of the dining room. I thought she looked vaguely familiar, but I couldn't place her."

Raphael's eyes sharpened with interest. He wished the Gupwell girls would cease their loud whispering to each other so that he could concentrate. Lady Kincaid lived in Ireland. Did she recognize Egeria—or rather Laura—from there, perhaps?

"I can assure you that you do not know Miss Walker," his mother said before he had a chance to speak. "She was just telling us that she has never before been away from the Isle of Wight. This is her first night out in London society."

"I see. But I certainly am not acquainted with anyone from the Isle of Wight," Eunice said in a condescending tone. "It is not a fashionable location, after all. I am surprised she is here in such rarefied company at all."

"I can imagine," the duchess said. "Raphael, darling, I see Lord Delaware over there near the windows. Would you be so kind as to take me to him? I have been meaning to ask him about the progress he has made with his marvelous gardens—and perhaps he can tell us if he has heard anything from his son."

"Certainly, Mama," Rafe said. He too wanted to know if there was any word from Aiden, not that he wouldn't relish any excuse to be away from Lady Kincaid and her daughters. "If you will excuse us?"

"But, Duke," Fiona said in an irritating whine, "I need a dance partner. I was explicitly hoping you would ask me for the next quadrangle."

"Fiona, really," the duchess said brusquely. "How many times do I have to tell you that you must *wait* to be asked? My son is busy at the moment with other obligations."

Amaryllis dug her elbow into Fiona's ribs, her pudding face as smug as could be.

Raphael couldn't wait to hand them their tickets for their passage home, and he'd do it first thing in the morning.

He swiftly took his mother off across the room. For the next two hours his gaze followed Egeria's progress around the ballroom. He watched with annoyance as she danced with Hugo, and then watched as she danced—twice—with Freddy Lyndhurst, then with Hugo again, and then with three other of his acquaintances, chatting away the entire time as if she hadn't a care in the world. As if she'd given not another thought to him, for she didn't look his way once.

Well, fine, he thought as Hugo led her out for a third time. He would get her alone at some point. All he had to do was bide his time. And then he would find out everything he wanted to know, whether she wanted to tell him or not.

Lucy was having the time of her life. Her nervousness had vanished, for not so much as a single person had questioned her with the exception of Raphael, and he seemed content to leave her alone. Still, she was keenly aware that he watched her like a hawk.

She ignored him as best she could, taking Hugo's sound advice to keep her distance. As for her stepmother and stepsisters, it wasn't difficult to avoid them in a room filled with so many people.

"So, Miss Laura Walker, what do you think of your grand success?" Hugo asked, leading her off the dance floor. "You are the toast of the evening."

"I don't know about that," Lucy said cheerfully, "but I must confess that I'm enjoying myself immensely. I never thought going to a ball would be so much fun! Everyone has been so nice to me."

"And why shouldn't they be nice to you? You are jolly and amusing and pretty as can be, and you don't bother with airs and graces."

Lucy colored with pleasure. "Thank you," she said. "But perhaps I should be putting on airs and graces if I'm not to stand out like a sore thumb."

"Absolutely not," Hugo said. "You have no idea how refreshing you are—especially since you've suddenly appeared at the end of a long and trying season when all the same people have said all the same things to each other at all the same occasions. You are a breath of fresh air, and I daresay you could have the pick of the room tonight if you wished to marry."

"No, thank you," Lucy said vehemently. "I won't lie and tell you that I haven't enjoyed every minute, but I could never marry an Englishman, for it would go against my every belief." Lucy suddenly realized what she'd said, and blushed. "In any case, tomorrow morning my life will go back to what it was. Fairy tales are meant to be just that—a brief respite from reality."

Hugo grinned. "I should take offense at what you said about Englishmen, seeing as I am one, but I am enjoying your company too much to quibble with you. It's not every day that I have an opportunity to take a fairy princess to a ball. I'm the envy of every man in the room."

"It's kind of you to say so. And even kinder of you to have looked after me so well tonight, introducing me to your friends and keeping me well away from my stepfamily *and* your brother."

"Believe me, it has been entirely my pleasure. And as I don't see either of the despised parties anywhere in sight, I think I can risk getting us some well-deserved refreshment. Champagne?"

Lucy clapped her hands together in delight. She'd never tasted champagne, had only dreamed of what it might be like, but this was a night of firsts. "Yes, *please*," she said, her cheeks glowing with pleasure. "I've the most fearful thirst—I mean, I am dreadfully parched," she said, correcting herself, for her Irish had slipped out unbidden in her enthusiasm.

Hugo laughed. "Whichever way you put it, it sounds as if you could use a glass. Good. Stay here—I'll be right back."

Lucy nodded, watching as he made his way through the throng. Life was indeed grand. Here she was, dancing in the finest dress she'd ever seen, conversing with the high-and-mighty British as if she were one of them, fooling them all, and she was about to drink champagne—it truly was the stuff of dreams.

She released a happy sigh. She couldn't wait to tell the O'Reillys every last detail, for they'd never believe it. She'd been busy storing up all of her impressions so that she could not only tell them about it, but also so that she could pull out her cherished memories when she needed them in the years to come.

And she had so many! Talking horses with Lord Lyndhurst, speaking of fashion with Lady Stanhope—and wasn't she the most pleasant of women, even if she was English? She'd even debated politics with Lord Wentworth, who was a right silly fool but kind nonetheless. So many memories to hold close.

But the most special one, her very favorite of all, was dancing with Raphael. Once he'd shut his handsome mouth, that was. No man in the room compared with him. No other man had danced with the same grace or held her with the same strength. No other man was so clearly intelligent, a quality she held in high esteem. Who else did she know who could quote Byron off the tip of his tongue, and quote it not only correctly but from the right section of the right poem?

Lucy closed her eyes and sighed, remembering the feel of her fingers resting in his, of his hand pressing against her back, the dizzying sensations of being swept round and round again, his face only inches from hers, his breath warm on her cheek.

She blinked dreamily. But her eyes shot wide open as she saw Fiona and Amaryllis and their ever-present mother only yards away, heading straight toward her.

They'd seen her. They'd seen her, and they weren't going to leave her alone, she could see that much. It was curtains for her if she didn't move quickly. She looked wildly around for an escape and suddenly saw it behind her and off to the left.

There was a door. A lovely, wide-open double door that

led to the outside. She didn't waste a moment, swiftly disappearing through a large group of people, excusing herself as she pushed by them, Amaryllis's shrill voice coming from too close behind.

"Where did she go? Who does that Laura Walker think she is, showing up uninvited and Napoleonizing Lord Hugo's attention like that? I'll see to her, I will."

"If anyone sees to her it will be me," Fiona said. "I saw the retestable way she danced with the duke, looking as if she thought she was going to march off with *my* prize. How dare she?"

"Neither of you will see to her," Eunice said in reply. "I will deal with the upstart. No one snatches what is ours from under our very noses, especially that little nobody. She'll be very sorry she showed her face once I'm finished with her."

Lucy rushed out onto the deserted veranda, but that wasn't nearly far enough if they decided to pursue her. And knowing them, they would. They'd somehow find her out, and the only solution was to vanish before they could speak to her.

Picking up the hem of her dress, she ran swiftly down the steps and out across a large garden whose beckoning darkness promised to cover her and give her shelter. The moon cast only a dappled light, easy enough to avoid. Her breath coming fast now, she frantically looked around for a hiding place.

And the good Lord gave it to her, a large gazebo appearing out of nowhere, the shadow of a large oak tree protecting it from sight. The music and the noise of the crowd was now only a soft undertone in the distance, drifting intermittently over to her on the breeze. Like the garden in Upper Brook Street, its perimeter was surrounded by a wall with a door to the outside street, but Lucy didn't have the strength to go any farther.

She stepped into the gazebo and sank onto one of the benches, her head lowered as she tried to catch her breath.

She knew it had all been too good to be true. Even in a crowd of a thousand people she still couldn't hide from Eunice. The woman had the instincts of a mother fox when it came to anything that might compromise her children's success and the nose of a badger when it came to sniffing out Lucy's transgressions.

She wanted to cry, but she was too tired, and anyway, she didn't cry. Ever. Not even in her worst moments, and this surely had to be one of them.

If Eunice somehow discovered the truth, Lucy's beautiful dream would be shattered, her lie exposed, for Eunice would go straight to Raphael with her suspicions and tell him everything, embellishing her story so that Lucy would sound wicked and deceitful. She would tell him that Lucy was her Irish maid, masquerading as a lady. That Lucy must have stolen money to buy her dress. That Lucy was nothing more than the dirt beneath his feet. And he would believe Eunice. What reason would he have to believe anything else? He was already convinced that he'd seen her in Ireland, despite her repeated denials.

She couldn't possibly go back inside, now that she knew Eunice was hot on her trail and wouldn't let the matter rest.

The ball was finished, at least for her.

She thought her heart might break, and she lowered her face into her hands, wishing her life was over, that it might have stopped in the moment that Hugo had left her, when she was still a fairy princess . . .

> *Here didst thou dwell, in this enchanted cover,*
> *Egeria! thy all heavenly bosom beating*
> *For the far footsteps of thy mortal lover . . .*

Lucy very slowly raised her head as the disembodied words floated to her through the soft night, words so familiar, the deep voice even more so. She was surely dreaming, for it couldn't really be him. How could he possibly have found her all the way out here?

Silence fell, and she rubbed her eyes, peering into the blackness. No, she'd imagined it, for there was no one there. All she could see was the empty stretch of garden and the house beyond.

And then a shadow shifted among the other shadows under the oak tree and emerged into a patch of light. Lucy pressed back against the railing as a shock of panic kicked through her, her palms flattening against the cool wood of the seat as if she could brace herself. Protect herself.

He stood not ten feet away, the moonlight catching on his head and shoulders as he watched her steadily. He spoke again, his voice low.

> *The purple Midnight veil'd that mystic meeting*
> *With her most starry canopy, and seating*
> *Thyself by thine adorer, what befell?*
> *This cave was surely shaped out for the greeting*
> *Of an enamour'd Goddess, and the cell*
> *Haunted by holy Love—the earliest oracle . . .*

His voice trailed off and once again he fell silent, his body completely still, bathed in shimmering moonlight. Golden. He was so golden, golden as an archangel, she thought illogically.

Her hand slipped to her throat where the pulse pounded rapidly beneath her fingers. *That's it—he is a ghost,* she thought wildly, desperately trying to gather herself. *Oh, please, Lord, let him be a ghost. I don't think I can deal with the man.*

But he walked forward in a most unghostly fashion, his footsteps muted by the thick carpet of grass, but definitely real. He paused, one foot resting on the step of the gazebo, his fingers wrapping around an upright post.

"Egeria. What troubles you so that you felt the need to escape?"

"Raphael?" she asked uncertainly, gripping onto the railing so hard that she drove a splinter into her palm, but she hardly felt it.

"Who else? Were you expecting Freddy, perhaps?"

"Who is Freddy?" she said in confusion, not sure of anything any longer, only that he was there and he was very real. And he was regarding her with that keen gaze she'd come to know so well, the gaze that never failed to unravel her, just as it unraveled her now, leaving her breathless and trembling like a leaf.

"Never mind. It's not important. Why did you disappear?"

"I—I wanted to be alone," she said. "I needed some fresh air."

"It's a long way to come for a breath of air when the veranda would have done just as well. Were you running away from me?"

She blinked. She wasn't about to tell him that she'd been escaping from her dreadful stepmother, but she wasn't going to lie to him either. "No," she said truthfully. "I wasn't."

"Then why?" he asked, stepping into the gazebo and sitting down next to her.

Thoroughly unnerved by his nearness, she pressed her hands against her eyes, trying to regain a semblance of control.

"Something has happened to upset you," he persisted. "Even in this light I can see that you are as white as a sheet."

"It was nothing," she said, lowering her hands into her lap, deciding to tell him the partial truth before he wrenched the whole thing out of her by sheer force of will. "Just something unpleasant that a woman and her daughters said about me that I overheard."

Raphael groaned. "Not a sharp-faced witch and two exceptionally ugly and uncouth girls?"

Lucy's lips trembled with the beginning of a smile. "How

did you know?" she said, longing to hear what else he would say about them.

"Because I have been subjected to their company and their excruciating conversation and manners for nearly the whole of the season," he said. "That would be Lady Kincaid and the Misses Gupwell, and I have yet to decide which of the ghastly daughters is the more unfortunate."

Lucy's smile widened. "I do think the girls could use a lesson in vocabulary," she said, finding to her surprise that she had started to relax. "I didn't hear much, but I did hear enough to wonder how it is possible to mangle the English language so thoroughly."

"That is not all they mangle," he said dryly. "My feet have been subjected to their not-so-tender administrations for weeks. There is nothing subtle about the Gupwell sisters, including their performance on the dance floor. So what did they and their hellcat of a mother say that cast you into despair?"

"It was nothing really. Only that they were going to chase me down and give me the sharp side of their tongues for daring to show my face tonight. And daring to dance with you." She glanced over at him with an impish grin. "I gather that you are considered a great matrimonial prize and both sisters are determined to have you."

Raphael snorted. "You are right on both counts, but I promise you, I have no intention of proposing anything to them other than they take the next boat back to Ireland. And they will have no choice but to go, for our arrangement is clear on the point."

"Ireland?" Lucy said, stiffening with excitement. On the next boat? She would be back home in no time! But her heart fell as she realized that would mean not ever seeing Raphael again.

Raphael leaned back against the railing and regarded her speculatively. "Yes. Ireland. A country with which you are familiar, I believe?"

"Oh, please," she said quickly, "let us not go back into that again. I *told* you—"

"I know what you told me," he said, picking up her hand and gazing down at it. "And I don't believe a word. I have no idea why you are so determined to lie to me and pretend to be someone you're not, but I do intend to find out." He looked up, meeting her eyes. "You might make it easier on both of us and just tell me the truth."

Lucy pulled her hand away, panicked all over again. "I do not understand why you persist in this notion that I am someone else—this Egregia creature."

Raphael threw his head back and laughed. "Oh, no you don't. You're not going to try to fob me off with that one, not again. It didn't work the first time, and it is certainly not working now, any more than your protestations that you've never set foot off the Isle of Wight are working." He folded his arms across his chest. "So, Egeria, why the pretense?"

Lucy didn't know what to do, what to say. He had her cornered. It was just as Hugo warned—if he got her alone, he would dig the truth out of her one way or the other. But she wouldn't let him. *She would not let him.*

"I don't know what you're talking about," she said, clenching her hands together in her lap. "And even if I did, I don't have to answer to you, your grace."

"Raphael," he said, running his finger over the back of her hand, his voice as smooth as silk. "You called me Raphael earlier. How did you know my name?"

"Your brother used it. How else?" She jerked her hands away, and to keep them well away from him, she sat on them.

"Really? My brother generally calls me Rafe," he said, looking down at her with a half smile. "But never mind that. Tell me, how does Hugo know your father?"

"He—that is, your brother met my father at the races some years ago," she said, relieved to be back on rehearsed territory. "My father gave him some useful tips."

"And is your father a gambler too?"

"Certainly not," she said indignantly, forgetting for a moment that Mr. Walker was only a fiction of her imagination. "He is a horse breeder."

"An Irish horse breeder?" he said, resting his arm on the edge of the railing.

"An *English* horse breeder," she said, acutely aware that his hand was only inches from her neck. "You certainly are preoccupied with the subject of Ireland."

"Perhaps," he said. "The memory is not easy to erase."

"What happened to you there, I wonder? This Egeria of yours must have exerted a powerful influence over you."

"Oh, yes," he said, his finger lightly brushing away a wisp of hair from the side of her throat, leaving a trail of fire behind. "She did indeed. How could she not? A beautiful, wild Irish girl in a crimson red cloak, her hair streaming in the wind as she recited Byron's poetry from a cliff's edge? I'm sure I don't need to draw you a picture."

Lucy shivered. The picture was already clear as day; it was his description that was new—and utterly enthralling. "How very romantic," she said faintly.

"Exactly," he said, his fingertips resting on her pulse, which beat like a caged bird. "Rather soul-stirring, actually, until she fell off the cliff to her death. I was not very happy, as you can imagine. I assumed she had deliberately jumped, especially when she'd just finished speaking about the moral of all human tales in the same breath as treachery and corruption."

Lucy drew in a sharp breath. He thought she'd actually *killed* herself? She'd only been speaking about British barbarism. She felt horribly guilty for the anguish he must have suffered. "How awful for you," she whispered.

"Yes, it was," he said, stroking the hair off her forehead. "It's not much fun being witness to a suicide. I spent the next three weeks asking about her, looking for her everywhere, going back and walking the cliff over and over, praying that I'd been mistaken, that there was some other explanation. But she didn't appear again, and I could only think the worst."

"But surely someone must have known whom she was when you asked about her," Lucy said, powerless to move away. His touch felt so wonderful—so gentle and so masculine all at the same time. She wanted to melt into it. "Wasn't she reported as missing?" she asked through her haze.

"No one knew a thing. Of course, my being British didn't help. The Irish have a tendency to close ranks when they think an Englishman is snooping about in their business."

"I—I see. And then you saw me in the park and thought I bore a resemblance to her, since my cloak was red. And you hoped against hope that she was alive after all, which is why you said all the odd things you did."

"Yes," he said. "That is why. And that is why I have continued to look for her." He stood and held out his hand. "Listen. Do you hear? They're playing another waltz. Dance with me?"

"All right," she said, swallowing hard, unable to resist this last opportunity to be held in his arms. One last time. One last time.

She took his hand and let him draw her to him. Now that they were away from the ever-watchful eyes of society he held her close, his cheek resting on her hair as he moved her in slow circles around the gazebo, his hard chest pressed against hers, his arm wrapped tightly around her waist, and she savored every moment.

"Tell me," he murmured, his breath warm against her cheek. "Do you believe in love at first sight?"

"Yes." She sighed, then realized what she'd said and how he might interpret it. "I mean—I mean no, of course not. Do you?"

"I didn't until two years ago when my cousin Aiden met a young woman in a clearing in the woods near his home. He fell in love with her on the spot, with no idea of who she was. He married her the next day."

"He did?" Lucy said, thinking that was the most wonderfully romantic thing she'd ever heard. "Are they happy?"

"Blissfully so. Still, I never thought the same thing would happen to me—to be honest, I never really hoped to find love at all. But I did, that day out there on the Downpatrick cliffs."

Lucy's heart nearly stopped. He actually *loved* her? *That* was why he'd been looking for her? If only things were different—if only she could tell him the truth. If only. If only . . . But even if there had been nothing else standing in her way, he was still English. She couldn't possibly love an Englishman. Could she?

"You—you fell in love, just like that?" she choked.

"Yes," he said quietly. "Just like that, only I don't think I realized it until tonight. Odd, isn't it, falling in love with someone you don't know at all, yet feel as if you've known all your life. Only to have her vanish as if she'd never been."

"Maybe—maybe she didn't really vanish," Lucy said, hot tears pricking at her eyes. "Maybe you'll find her again someday." Impossible. It was impossible. She couldn't afford to contemplate such a thing—she couldn't afford even to dream about it. She could never be a part of his life. "And even if you don't, maybe you will find someone else to love," she said, the very thought cutting her to the quick.

Raphael's steps slowed and then stopped. He took her by both shoulders, holding her slightly away from him as he gazed down into her eyes, his own eyes clear and filled with question.

Somewhere in the distance an owl hooted, the only sound in the still night as a long, heavy silence stretched between them.

"But I have found her," he finally said, his voice hoarse. "The problem is that she doesn't want to admit I have. She would rather I think that I have lost her forever. A bit cruel, don't you agree?"

Lucy closed her eyes, unable to bear the pained honesty she saw in his. She hadn't fooled him after all. He'd known it was she all along.

"Egeria," he whispered, stroking her cheek. "Lovely, lovely Egeria. Who are you? What terrible secret are you keeping that you would punish me so?"

Lucy shook her head back and forth, back and forth as hot tears trickled from the corners of her eyes, her heart breaking. "I—I can't," she gasped. "Please, don't ask me any more—"

In answer he bent his head, his warm lips covering hers, cutting her off with a hard kiss, his mouth opening on hers, demanding a response.

She couldn't deny him. God help her, she couldn't deny him. She poured everything of herself into that kiss, her arms twining around his neck as his tongue invaded the soft inner recesses of her mouth, his breath mingling with hers, drinking her in as if he were drinking in her very life, his hands moving over her back, pulling her even closer to him until her body was molded to his, his hips pressed hard against hers.

Lucy's heart pounded so painfully fast that it physically hurt in her chest. She was on fire, lost to everything but his heated touch, his taste, his unique smell, so exciting, so exciting . . .

He finally raised his head, cupping her face between his large hands. "That answered rather a lot," he said, his voice rough, his thumbs caressing her cheeks. "Will you tell me the rest of the truth now?"

"I have to go," she said in a blind panic, on the verge of pouring it all out.

"Go? It is early—only midnight. Listen—the bells are just starting to toll."

Midnight? Already? "I promised my father I would be home

by now!" she cried in alarm, pulling away. If she didn't go, not only would she be late, she'd be lost. She was no proof against his persistence, certainly no proof against his seductive touch.

"Your ailing father is probably tucked up in bed and sound asleep," he pointed out. "If indeed there is an ailing father. You haven't been able to make up your mind whether you have sisters or are an only child."

"You are impossible! Nothing I say pleases you."

He smiled down at her. "That is not entirely true, although I would prefer honesty at this point. Egeria, my love, give up the charade. Let me help you with whatever trouble you are in."

"I am in no trouble at all," she lied, desperate to get away. She'd be in real trouble if she didn't get home before the others, and now that she knew there would be no celebration of a marriage proposal, they might be home early and in terrible tempers. "Really I'm not." *Yet,* she thought frantically.

"And I wonder why I don't believe you."

"Believe what you will," she cried. "It matters not at all to me."

"I think it matters a very great deal. As much as it matters to me. Please. Do not vanish again, for I don't think I could bear it."

Lucy shook her head. "I must go."

"Wait," he said, restraining her with one hand, his fingers resting on the curve of her neck. "Don't go at least without telling me where I can find you."

"No! Leave me be—I don't want to be found!"

Lucy violently wrenched away from him. One more second and she'd be undone. And late. She picked up her skirts and ran as fast as she could toward the garden door that led to freedom.

She didn't even look for the carriage, dashing around the

corner as she reached the safety of the street. She ducked into an alleyway, breathing hard.

The pounding of his footsteps echoed down the pavement as he chased after her, his voice frantically calling her name. "Egeria? For the love of God, come back!"

She clung against the rough wall, waiting for the sound of his voice to fade away. Eventually it did, silence falling.

She wearily left the safety of her alley and started the long walk home, her heart aching for lost love and lost opportunity. Her heart aching for him.

The fairy tale was over. She was back to being Lucy O'Reilly, not even Lucy Kincaid, and tomorrow her life would hold only the ashes of one night of wonder.

Rafe returned to the gazebo and sank onto one of the benches, leaning his head into his hands, feeling emptier than he'd ever felt before. She was gone, somehow vanished into the night. And now he was alone. Utterly, profoundly alone.

He'd been so close. He'd finally found her. He'd held her safe in his arms. Had kissed her, had reveled in her response, for she had kissed him back in full measure—there was no mistaking her sweet, impassioned response, everything he might have hoped for. She loved him in return, he was as sure of it as he could be.

And yet she had left him. Left him without a hint as to how to find her again.

He looked down at his palm where a small gold locket rested, the chain broken. It had come off in his hand when she'd twisted away from him. Maybe—maybe it held some clue as to who she really was, for he no longer believed that her name was really Laura Walker. A woman who kept secrets, who didn't want to be found didn't give her real name. That would make tracing her far too easy.

But if she didn't want to be found, why had she come to the ball tonight? And *why* had she come with Hugo?

Hugo. His eyes narrowing, he stood, slipping the locket into his pocket. He'd examine it later. Right now he had something much more important to do.

12

"What do you mean she's gone?" Hugo said, glaring at his brother. "I've spent the last hour looking for her!"

"She's gone," Rafe repeated, biting the words out. "She ran away."

"From you, I assume," Hugo said with disgust. "What did you do, try to seduce her?"

"That's enough!" Rafe snapped. "It's not important why she left. I want to know where she went to."

"How should I know?" Hugo said, shrugging. "I'm not her keeper."

"You will damn well tell me where she lives, and you'll tell me now or I'll tear you to pieces."

"I think not, brother dear. If you frightened the girl so badly that she took off into the night, I'm not about to deliver her back into your hands."

"Oh, dear," the duchess said. "You must have said something to upset her, Raphael. The poor child—she is not accustomed to society, after all. From what she said, she has lived a very sheltered life." She frowned. "What do you want with her anyway, darling? It is most unlike you to chase after shy young girls."

"That's exactly what I'd like to know," Hugo said, shoving his hands on his hips. "Her father will have my head for this night's work. It will be a miracle if he doesn't have another heart attack when she arrives home with no escort, and most likely in tears. If she arrives home at all. A woman out on the streets by herself at night is not safe."

"I assume she took a hansom cab," Rafe said shortly. "Now enough of this nonsense. I don't know what game you are playing at, Hugo, but I do know you've handed me a pack of lies about Miss Laura Walker. You will tell me who she really is—and I want the truth this time."

"What on earth do you mean?" the duchess said. "Raphael, I am beginning to think your brain is fevered. Why would you say such a peculiar thing? The girl seemed perfectly innocent to me."

"Or she was until my brother got his hands on her," Hugo said, his eyes flashing. "I'm not going to tell you a thing, brother. You have no right to any information at all, especially given the way you've behaved—and you accuse *me* of bad behavior?"

"Damn you, I want that girl!" Rafe roared.

"And what am I now, your procurer?"

It took every ounce of control Rafe had not to plant his fist in his brother's smirking face. "Very well," he said. "I'll find her myself. I don't need your help. But I swear to you, Hugo, when I do discover the truth—and I shall—you will be very sorry you crossed me."

Hugo took the duchess's arm. "Come along, Mama. Let Rafe work off his bad temper on someone else."

Rafe glared after his brother, more furious with him than he'd ever been in his life. Oh, yes. He'd take care of Hugo.

But first he'd find Egeria.

Tomorrow. He'd start looking tomorrow. There wasn't a stone of London he'd leave unturned.

"Hugo, dearest, you were absolutely marvelous," the duchess said, beaming at her son. "You handled the situation brilliantly."

"Thank you, Mama. So did you," Hugo replied. "It's all

going exactly according to plan. Clever of Lucy to have taken my advice and left by midnight—Rafe must really have given her a grilling, but he obviously didn't get anything much out of her, just enough to confirm his suspicions."

"As I expected. Good. He will only be that much more determined to go after her."

"I have no doubt. And when he discovers that he's right and there really is no Laura Walker from the Isle of Wight, he'll be forced to go to back to Ireland, since that is his only other point of reference. He really must be besotted with her to be driven to the behavior he exhibited tonight."

"I do believe Raphael is in love, dear. Is it not wonderful?"

"I don't know about that—I can't help but feel sorry for Lucy. He's not the easiest man."

"Don't be silly, Hugo. She is just as much in love with him. From the look of things, I think Raphael is all she wants in this world, although it might be some time before she admits it to herself." The duchess sighed heavily. "You must remember that she is Irish and not predisposed to feeling very friendly toward the British."

"So she told me, although she didn't seem to object too much to dancing with half the British aristocracy."

"She had a point to prove. Well. So far, so good. But you will have to stand firm, dear, for your brother is very angry with you and he won't let the subject go easily."

"Don't worry about me—I can handle Rafe. I'm actually enjoying my predicament, almost as much as I'm enjoying his," Hugo said, taking two glasses of champagne from a tray and handing one to his mother. "I think we should drink a toast to our resounding success."

"Why do we not drink a toast to Raphael's finding Lucy and putting matters right?"

Hugo grinned. "If she'll let him. But as you say, to Rafe and Lucy. May they eventually be very happy. And may that bloody Kincaid woman live miserably ever after."

The duchess raised her glass. "Amen."

* * *

Lucy quietly slipped in through the servants' entrance and tiptoed up the stairs on sore feet. Fortunately she hadn't had a difficult time finding her way from Curzon Street back to Upper Brook Street, once she'd thought to find the park and follow it along. But satin slippers were not designed for walking a distance.

She pulled them off one by one and massaged her toes, looking sorrowfully down at the soiled satin. With shaking fingers she took off her crown of roses and pearls and laid it on the bureau. And then she reluctantly reached behind her and began to unfasten her dress, not an easy job with so many buttons to undo.

After slipping out of it, she laid it on the bed, then stood back and gazed down at it numbly. A beautiful dress fit for a princess.

But she was no princess. No princess at all.

She sank down onto the mattress and lovingly stroked her hand over the fine material. Here was where Raphael had touched her—and here. Here was where his hand had rested on her waist, and later, here was where his arms had embraced her. Arms that would never embrace her again.

Her hand slipped to her neck, seeking the comfort of her locket. But her fingers met nothing but skin.

Lucy sat up straight, frantically searching in the bodice of her chemise. Nothing!

Jumping up, she grabbed the ball dress and shook it out, praying the locket had caught in the material when she'd taken it off. But no luck. It was gone.

Lucy pressed her hands against her face with a low moan. She couldn't have lost it—she just couldn't have. It was the only thing she had left of her parents, the only reminder of their beloved faces, of the happy life she had once led.

She walked over to the window, forcing back bitter tears, and looked out over the dark night. Gone. It was all gone. Not just her locket, but all of her foolish dreams as well.

Gone in the blink of an eye, leaving her with nothing but an empty future. And now she didn't even have her locket to give her solace.

Turning away, she walked back to her narrow bed and picked up her dress. She hugged it to her tightly, thinking of the brief night of happiness it had brought her, then carefully folded it.

Pulling her small case out from under her bed, she laid the dress on the bottom, gently smoothing out the material. She placed her slippers on top, along with her wreath of flowers, and finally covered everything over with a layer of tissue paper, just to be safe. She never knew when Fiona or Amaryllis or even her stepmother might go prying into her few belongings.

And then she slowly closed the case as if she were closing a chapter of her life.

But the night wasn't over yet, nor could she tuck her memories so safely away. She still had to wait for her stepmother and stepsisters to return, and she was bound to hear all about the ball, bringing everything back in vivid, painful detail.

She put on her old dress and went down to Fiona's room, settling in a chair and steeling herself for the inevitable disaster.

An hour later the front door slammed and a volley of shouting erupted in the front hall. Lucy went to the top of the stairs and listened.

"It was all your fault!" Amaryllis cried. "If you hadn't pushed yourself on him in that notorious fashion, he wouldn't have changed his mind about marrying me!"

"It was nothing to do with me," Fiona sobbed. "It was that wicked girl's fault. If she hadn't shown up and murmurized him, everything would have been different."

"For heaven's sake, it's mesmerized!" Eunice snapped. "Can't you get anything right? And she didn't mesmerize him, she waggled herself under his nose like a bitch in heat.

Of course he was going to respond to such a wanton invitation."

"Yes, but look how angry he was when she disappeared—he hardly spoke a word on the way home except to tell us that we have to return to horrible Ireland tomorrow," Fiona said with a thick sniffle. "Now our lives are ruined!"

"Go upstairs immediately, girls," Eunice said, her voice containing suppressed fury. "The duke wouldn't have had his head so easily turned by a strumpet if you'd done your jobs properly."

Lucy, surprised that Eunice had spoken so sharply to her daughters when she usually only used that tone to her, stepped back from the banister as Fiona and Amaryllis came stomping up the stairs, sniveling loudly.

"Hello," she said, forcing a smile to her lips. "How was the ball?"

"Oh, stumble it, Lucy," Fiona snapped rudely, her eyes swollen and red. "I do not wish to discourse it."

"Only because you made such a fool out of yourself and ruined both our chances," Amaryllis said.

Fiona slapped her sister hard across the cheek and Amaryllis screamed. "Mama! Mama, Fiona hit me!" she cried, bursting into tears.

Eunice came swiftly up the stairs, her eyes snapping with cold fire. "Stop it this instant, both of you! I've heard enough. I was counting on you to change our miserable lives, do you hear me? But you let me down, didn't you?" She glared malevolently at both girls, who stopped their howling to stare at her in stunned surprise. "Now we are forced to return to that dreadful, filthy country filled with dreadful, filthy people and nothing to show for ourselves but new wardrobes and your pathetic dowries that I can't even touch. How could you have been so stupid as to throw away our chances for riches and glory? All I ever asked you to do was to make suitable marriages so that I could rid myself of the odious place!"

"B-but, Mama," Amaryllis gulped, "we did everything we could to coerce the duke. We behaved just as you said—"

"Be quiet, you odious child! You're both as dimwitted as your father was, and I thought that was impossible! But you've managed it, as well as inheriting his looks, for they certainly don't come from *my* side of the family."

She turned on her heel and stormed off down the hallway to her bedroom, the door slamming loudly after her.

Lucy looked back and forth between Fiona and Amaryllis, their expressions crushed, and her heart went out to them. It might be true that they were both stupid, and they certainly couldn't be called anything close to pretty, but that wasn't their fault, any more than they were spoiled and selfish.

They may have inherited their lack of brains and looks from their father, but Eunice's hand alone had formed their characters. And now she was paying the price of her own handiwork.

But to turn viciously on her own children in such a fashion was too cruel. Lucy knew well enough how it felt to be on the receiving end of Eunice's savage tongue.

"Come, Fiona, and bring your sister," she said gently. "I have milk heating over the fire in your room, and I think it might help to soothe you both. You have clearly had a trying night, and if we're to leave on the morrow you must get some sleep."

She led them to chairs by the fire and sat them down, handing them each a cup of warm milk. "Tell me what happened, then."

"It was awful," Amaryllis sobbed, her plump shoulders shaking. "A woman apparitioned out of nowhere—no one had ever seen her before—and it was so unfair, because she was wearing the most beautiful dress, one that would have trapped anyone's eye—"

"And the duke instantly asked her to dance with him, and you could tell that he was bestowed with her, not just from how he looked at her, but also because he never took his gape off her all night," Fiona interrupted, rubbing a balled fist into one puffy eye. "How were we to combat with someone like her? She was—she was beautiful, like a princess out of a fairy tale!"

"No, she wasn't," Fiona said sullenly, blowing her nose on the handkerchief Lucy offered her. "Mama said she was nothing more than a curtsy-stand." She frowned. "Although I cannot think what that means . . ."

"A courtesan," Lucy said, thinking that only Eunice would say such a wicked thing. "It's another word for a lady of the night."

Her stepsisters stared at her in horror. "Do you—do you mean one of those fallen women who takes money for her services?" Amaryllis gasped.

"Yes, but I doubt very much that was the case. Courtesans are not allowed into the sort of places you have been attending, and even if they were, dukes would not acknowledge them in polite company, let alone dance with them."

"Oh. Well, whatever she was, she shouldn't have been there at all. Mama said so. She ruined everything."

Lucy felt nothing but relief that her stepsisters hadn't the first clue that the woman they were discussing was herself, but she couldn't help feeling a stab of guilt that she'd inadvertently caused her stepsisters such distress. "Oh, dear. I'm so sorry," she said.

"I don't know what you are sorry about," Amaryllis said. "It's not as if you know anything about what it is like to be ejected by a duke."

"No, you're right, of course." Lucy had to turn away to hide her amusement. For once Amaryllis had gotten a word right. They'd been ejected, no question about that. "What happened next?" she asked, unable to help herself. Their account of the evening, far from being a painful reminder, was so far from the truth that it was laughable.

"Well, the curtsy-stand vanished, and then the duke vanished after her, and then he finally repaired and in the worst of tempers because she really *had* vanished."

So, Raphael had been in a foul temper? Lucy smiled sadly. It was little wonder, given how she'd left him. She could only hope that he would recover quickly. Probably far more quickly than she would, if she ever did. "Where did she go?" Lucy asked, wondering what else Raphael had said, if anything.

Fiona sniffed loudly. "Who knows? But he didn't have a kind word to say to either of us, or Mama either. He just said that we were to cluster our belongings, for he was taking us home. And then he told us in the carriage that we'd had our chance and made nothing of it so he was sending us back to Ireland posthumously, and we weren't to trouble him again for he was cleansing his hands of us as of that minute." She burst back into floods of tears. "I so wanted to be a duchess."

"So did I," Amaryllis wailed. "I wanted to wear fine jewels and have everyone bow and chafe to me and call me 'your grace,' and eat as many chocolates as I wanted."

Fiona shot her a look of disgust. "Is chocolate all you ever think about? Well, that's all too bad, isn't it, for we're going back to that pigsty of a country, and no real gentleman will ever gawk at us again."

"Ireland is not a pigsty," Lucy said indignantly. "It's a lovely place. And as for gentlemen, there are lots of good, decent Irishmen, if you'd just remove your blinders and take a sharp look at what's in front of you. You still have your dowries, after all, and there are plenty of men in need of those, as well as being in need of good wives."

She pulled up a chair and sat down. "Your mother may have filled your heads with all sorts of grandiose ideas, but isn't it better to marry a simple man who will truly love you and look after you than to marry a titled man who has nothing to offer you but an empty heart?"

Both girls stared at Lucy as if she'd lost her mind. "You cannot be sensuous," Fiona said, forgetting her tears. "I wouldn't marry an Irishman if he were the last man on earth."

"Your mother married an Irishman," Lucy pointed out gently.

"And look what happened to *her*," Fiona retorted. "Mama says marrying an Irishman was the worst mishap she ever made, for look what befouled us—she says all she wanted from the horrible matrimony was position and money, and even then her promised riches were snitched from her grasp."

Lucy swallowed hard against the sharp retort that burned in her throat. It was no news to her that Eunice had married her father for money and a title, certainly not for love. But it still hurt to hear the words actually voiced by Eunice's own daughter.

"So obstreperously," Fiona continued, "no Irishman could afford to deluge me with jewels and favors and make me an important lady with lots of houses and servants to commend."

"That's right," Amaryllis added. "Irishmen are all poor and live in hotels. If I can't have diamonds and chocolates I don't want to marry at all. Why should I suffer that disgusting Act of Martial Duty if I don't get beautiful things in return?"

Lucy just shook her head, seeing that there was no way she was going to convince them that titles and riches and grand houses did not automatically bring happiness. Without love to fill up one's heart, marriage would be a miserable thing. Eunice and her father's marriage was clear testimony to that.

"Drink up your milk and let me get you into your nightclothes," Lucy said, rising. "A sound night's sleep will do you both good, and we have a long journey to start tomorrow."

Lucy finally got them both settled down and into bed. She took a deep breath, steeling herself to deal with her stepmother. She went down the hall to Eunice's door, tapping lightly. There was no answer.

She tapped again, then carefully cracked the door open. "Aunt Eunice? I've come to prepare you for bed."

Lucy ducked just in time as a slipper winged past her and hit the wall with a thud.

"Go away, you loathsome girl!" Eunice cried, hunched over her dressing table, her face red with rage, one fist clenched on the glass top. "I do not wish to deal with you tonight. I have enough troubles without being reminded me that I wouldn't be in this position at all if it wasn't for you."

Lucy paled. *Did her stepmother know the truth?* Was she simply biding her time before exacting a horribly cruel punishment, torturing Lucy by leaving her to wonder?

"Don't just stand there gaping at me, girl. I am sure you are pleased as can be that my daughters failed."

"No—no, of course not, Aunt," Lucy said, her heart in her throat. "I had hoped that they would find husbands, and I am sorry that it did not work out for them."

"A likely story," Eunice snapped. "You have been hoping all along that it would end exactly like this so that you could go home to your beloved Ireland." She spat the word out as if it were a bad taste in her mouth. "If I didn't need you to help in my house I'd leave you here to fend on your own, just to teach you a lesson."

Lucy expelled a long breath. So Eunice still didn't know it had been Lucy at the ball—she was just in a bad mood because things hadn't gone according to plan. "Yes, Aunt," she said, feeling as if she'd just been given a reprieve from a fate worse than death. "When will we be leaving?"

"You just cannot wait to go, can you? What is the matter, Miss Lucy Kincaid? Did you not enjoy your stay in the servants' quarters?" She smiled nastily.

"I cannot deny that I will be happy to be back home," Lucy said, lifting her chin. "But I am nevertheless sorry for your daughters' misfortune. I know they both had their hearts set on marriage to the duke."

"The duke," Eunice said, slamming her fist down on the

table so hard that the bottles jumped. "I never want to hear his name again, do you understand? He is nothing but a cold-hearted reprobate, leading us to believe that he had honorable intentions. But, oh no—the minute a pretty piece of skirt showed her face, he forgot all about us, dancing like one besotted, as if we were nothing—nothing to him! He even went so far as to disappear outside with her on some salacious assignation. What kind of behavior is that, may I ask?"

"But—but perhaps you were mistaken all along in his intentions," Lucy said, pointing out the obvious. "He said that he was extending his patronage so that your daughters might find husbands, not that he intended to make an offer himself."

"What would you know of it?" Eunice screeched, her face a mask of fury. "Were you there to hear what he said? No, you were not! You know nothing of anything, but as usual you like to poke your nose where it doesn't belong."

"I beg your pardon," Lucy said, trying to sound contrite when what she really wanted to do was set her stepmother straight once and for all. It was *she* whom Raphael had danced with under the brilliant chandeliers, *she* whom he had gone after in the garden. *She* whom he loved. But she kept her silence, just as she always kept her silence.

"Are you sure you don't wish for me to help you ready yourself for bed?" she asked.

Eunice picked up the second slipper, and Lucy swiftly backed out, closing the door just as the shoe struck on the other side.

Numb with exhaustion, she went upstairs to her little bedroom and undressed, quickly washing in the cold water of her basin.

She crossed to the bureau and picked her brush up, running it through her hair with rhythmic strokes, hardly registering what she was doing, staring blankly ahead. And then her gaze focused as she caught a glimpse of her reflection in the cracked mirror. She slowly lowered the brush and leaned forward, looking more carefully, trying to see what Raphael had seen.

A beautiful, wild Irish girl, he had said.

But all she saw was a woman with a pale, haunted face and hollow eyes.

Lovely, lovely Egeria.

But she was not Egeria, she was only Lucy Kincaid. Plain old Lucy Kincaid, nearly twenty-one years old, but who felt at least a hundred.

She took the mirror off the wall and placed it facedown on the bureau. And then she padded across the cold floor and slipped beneath the thin sheet, staring dry-eyed at the shadows on the ceiling, her heart an aching bruise inside her chest.

Do you believe in love at first sight?

Yes—oh, yes! her wounded heart cried.

Egeria, my love . . . please do not vanish again, for I don't think I could bear it.

And the truth had been in his eyes. She had seen not only the love there but his desperation. And there wasn't a thing she could do about any of it.

She'd known all along that there would be a price to pay for living one night of a dream. She just had never expected it to be quite so high.

13

*I*reland. Lucy had wanted to cry when she saw the first sight of land, her shining emerald island beckoning to her, from the deck of the boat. *You're home, Lucy. You're back where you belong,* the breeze had seemed to whisper.

But something was missing. She'd been home for a full fortnight, but she felt as if she had left a large piece of herself behind in England. She wasn't the same Lucy Kincaid she'd been when she'd left for London. She didn't know *who* she was anymore.

Raphael David Charles Montagu had seen to that.

Once she'd been a girl who believed in dreams, in endless possibilities. She'd been a child, wishing on a star. The irony was that when she'd wished on that star, she'd wished for love.

She couldn't complain—she'd gotten exactly what she asked for. Maybe she should have been more specific and wished for an *Irishman* to love. She certainly hadn't counted on his turning out to be an English duke.

She wrung out a sheet and hung it on the drying line, stabbing the clothespins onto the corners. It wasn't fair. It just wasn't fair. She'd done everything she could to convince herself that what she felt for Raphael was infatuation, that all the fantasizing she'd done about him had caught up with her that night of the ball, that the passionate kiss they'd shared had addled her brains.

All to no avail. For she did love him—she knew that now. She loved him hopelessly and most of all, she loved him foolishly.

It was over. Finished. He was in England where he belonged, and she was in Ireland where she belonged. They clearly didn't belong together, not with all of their essential differences. Why, then, did her heart feel as if it was breaking?

So much for love. And dreams.

Raphael. Lucy bent back over the washtub, willing herself to think of something—anything else. He was ever-present in her thoughts, his face ingrained on her mind, the memory of his voice, his touch with her always. But the memories she thought she would cherish only brought her pain and a terrible emptiness.

She moved through her life like a shadow, not really seeing or sensing, just . . . existing. Although her life had held no real happiness for her in years, she no longer took enjoyment from the simple things that had always sustained her. The song of a bird through an open window, the sight of a rainbow after a cleansing rain, the plaintive bleat of a lost lamb looking for his mother, none of those made her stop in her chores and smile in pleasure at God's gifts.

Even Amaryllis and Fiona had stopped needling her, as if they sensed that she really didn't hear them. Of course nothing stopped Eunice, who had been in an ungovernable temper since their return, but Lucy didn't hear her either.

The only time she had felt marginally like her old self was the afternoon she managed to slip away to the O'Reillys, when Eunice took the girls into Ballina to complain to friends about the ill treatment she had received at the hands of the duke.

But even then something was missing.

The O'Reillys had been delighted to see Lucy, full of questions about her time in London, begging for details. Lucy told them what she could, but where she had once been longing to pour out every last thing, she now found it difficult to speak of her time in London at all. When it came to the subject of Raphael, she found it nearly impossible.

"I have no idea what the duke is really like," she lied, when Mairead O'Reilly asked about him. "I've only ever heard about him from Fiona and Amaryllis, and one can't take anything they say seriously. But he must have some common sense if he washed his hands of them. He won't be darkening our doorstep again, that's for sure." And how the thought hurt—never to see his face again, never to see his smile, hear his laughter, feel his arms holding her . . .

"That seems to be the only sense he's exhibited so far," Mairead said with a shake of her head. "I don't know why he bothered to take them on in the first place, unless it was purely a show of British solidarity. He probably thought he'd make a grand gesture and rescue the poor things from Ireland, if you see what I mean."

"I don't know," Lucy said, pressing a hand against her aching forehead. "I don't care." And that was the biggest lie of all.

Mairead gave her a strange, searching look. "You're appearing peaked, Lucy Kincaid. It's looking to me like the English air did nothing for your health, although it's hardly surprising seeing as you were cooped up inside all the time, dancing attendance on those spoiled girls and their mother. What you need is a bit of Irish sunshine."

"I reckon you're right," Lucy replied, giving her a wan smile. "Forgive me for not being more entertaining. I think I must still be tired from the journey and my stepsisters' non-stop tears. I can't help but feel sorry for them—they are terribly crushed that their plans didn't work out, and their mother has only made them feel worse."

"What, and now you're saying that Lady Kincaid, such

that she is, has actually criticized her darlings to their faces?" Brigid asked, her face a picture of disbelief.

"She's done worse than criticize them. She's holding them accountable for every last disaster, even when it was she who coached them in their behavior every step of the way. She doesn't stop from morning until night, harping on each unfortunate mistake they made."

"And doesn't that sound about typical," Mairead scoffed. "She never has taken responsibility for any of her actions, always pushing the blame onto others. Look at what she's done to you, Lucy, and you being your father's daughter. It's a disgrace, that's what it is. I don't know why she married an Irishman to begin with if she so despises our country and our people."

"She married him because he had money and a title, even if it *was* Irish, and money and a title are all she's ever wanted," Lucy said. "But never mind her," she added, too tired and despondent to go any further into the subject of her stepmother's conduct. It was hard enough having to live with it. "She won't change, and there's nothing to be done about it."

"And that's God's unfortunate truth," Mairead said. "But, colleen, you turn twenty-one next month—is there not a way to be done with her once and for all? Surely you can pack your bags and leave, find somewhere else to go?"

"Where would I go? What would I do?" Lucy replied. "I'm not fit for much of anything."

"You could teach," Brigid said. "You taught me to read and write—why couldn't you teach others? You taught Nell too, and she got a job in a shop."

"And how would anyone afford to pay me? I could try to get a job as a governess in a good household, but one way or another Eunice would make it impossible. You know she would. Maybe *I* could get a job in a shop, though . . ."

A job in a shop. Lucy had been thinking about it ever since. She scrubbed a hand over her forehead, then straightened, rubbing her aching back. It was true—she could try to get a job in a shop, but who would hire her?

Everyone in the villages around knew her situation, but as much as they might feel sorry for Lucy, her association with Eunice would put them at risk. Eunice could turn on any of them at any time, and she wouldn't hesitate, just to get back at Lucy. The O'Reillys would only be the first step in Eunice's vindictive retribution should Lucy rebel.

There was nothing to be done but stay where she was. And try not to dream of Raphael.

Rafe had had it. He'd spent a full week scouring London. Nothing. No one knew of a Laura Walker. He spent the next ten days visiting the Isle of Wight, but just as he anticipated, Laura Walker had never been heard of there either, or her horsebreeder father for that matter.

Having just returned from that fool's mission, he now sat dejectedly in the drawing room at Southwell, declining his mother's offer of wine. If he thought life was empty before, he'd had no idea of what emptiness it was capable of holding, not since he'd held Egeria in his arms and realized how very much he loved her.

"I simply do not understand, dear," his mother said, sipping on a cup of tea. "You insist that you have looked everywhere for this girl and she is not to be found. Why do you persist in this hunt? If she does not wish to be located, for whatever reason, why continue searching?"

"Because I want her," Rafe said, rubbing the space between his eyebrows with his thumb. "I want her. You saw her for yourself that night, and you cannot possibly have missed the resemblance between the woman I described to you last May and the woman you met at the Stanhope ball."

"I did wonder," the duchess said equitably. "It was the only explanation I could think of for your peculiar behavior. But I really do not see how she can be one and the same person, given that she said she has never before been off the Isle of—"

"She lied!" Rafe cried in frustration. "Can you not get it through your head that she lied? I don't know why—God in heaven, I wish I did, but I don't! There's something she's hiding, although I cannot imagine what it might be. Why would she say she lived on the Isle of Wight when they've never heard of her there—and why would she deny being in Ireland when I *know* she was? And furthermore, I heard her accent with my own ears—an accent that miraculously disappeared when she was here."

"If it means so much to you, darling, why do you not go back to Ireland and look for her there?"

"Don't you think I looked the first time around?" Rafe roared. "I spent three full weeks looking, with absolutely no success. I thought—well, that's irrelevant. The point is that I now know she is deliberately trying to evade me."

"And that should tell you something," the duchess said. "Are you sure you would not like a cup of tea or some wine, dear? You look most upset."

"I *am* bloody well upset! Wouldn't you be if you'd finally gone and fallen in love with someone and couldn't do a blessed thing about finding that person again? It is *not* a pretty picture."

"Oh, my goodness. You hadn't mentioned love."

Rafe hadn't meant to mention it, and he silently cursed himself for blurting it out, but he couldn't change that now. "Well, it's the truth," he said curtly. "And I'm not about to explain to you the circumstances of how it happened or why, so don't bother asking."

"I would not dream of it, but that does change things, does it not?" The duchess tapped the tips of her fingers together. "I think you had better catch the next boat to Ireland, dear. If you are so sure this is the same girl you saw there, then it stands to reason that is where she would be now. She does not seem to be anywhere else."

Rafe flung one leg over the other. "And where do you suggest I start looking? I just told you that I combed the length and breadth of County Mayo and came up with nothing."

"I would comb again if I were you. You never know what you might find, and you are not accomplishing anything here. In any case, I have been thinking about Kincaid Court."

"What about Kincaid Court?" he said with annoyance. "What does that have to do with anything?"

"I know you loathe me to interfere in your affairs in any way, but I cannot help but be deeply troubled by what your cousin Thomas did. If he was so unconscionable as to steal Ian Kincaid's home away from him and leave the family in such dire straits, goodness only knows what he did to anyone else connected to the property."

"What do you mean?" Rafe asked, paying closer attention.

"Surely there must have been tenants who depended on the land for their livelihood? And yet you said everything had fallen into disrepair—that the fields lay fallow and the outlying houses empty. What do you think happened to those poor people?"

Raphael frowned. "I honestly don't know. I assumed they took up leases elsewhere when Thomas turned the fields over to hunting ground."

"But do you not think you should find out, dear? After all, they were no more responsible for Thomas's actions than Ian Kincaid was, and yet they might have suffered terribly as a result of them."

"I'm only aware of what the land agent Paddy Delany told me—that Thomas took the annual profits of some twelve thousand pounds a year and put them into his own pocket instead of back into the land."

"Exactly. And I have to wonder what this Mr. Delany did to compensate for the loss of income. It is rather difficult running an estate with no money. He might have raised the rents impossibly high to compensate, don't you think?"

"It's a possibility," Rafe said, scratching his cheek. "I had a look at the most recent books, but they were rather difficult to interpret—unfortunately, Delany is not thoroughly literate. And I probably need a better understanding of the Irish system of land management."

"Nonsense, darling. Land management is the same everywhere and you have a brilliant grasp of it. Look how successful all of your holdings are—you have increased your income tenfold since your father's time. Every single property turns a handsome profit."

"Every single property has an excellent steward looking after it," Rafe pointed out. "I don't think I realized just how excellent my stewards were until I came home to find that I hadn't been missed in the least. Everything was in perfect order. Such efficiency makes a man feel a bit redundant."

His mother smiled. "Trust me, darling, you are anything but redundant. Your sound advice will always be needed by us all."

"Thank you, Mama, but there's really no need to butter me up. I am not cast into despair over the matter. I'm just not as urgently needed as I had imagined."

"Perhaps not. But it does occur to me that although you might not be urgently needed here, you are needed elsewhere. I have a notion that Paddy Delany might be a rascal, especially if Thomas was responsible for hiring him."

Rafe thought that over. It was true that he'd had an uneasy feeling about the man from the beginning, but his hands had been tied by necessity at the time. He'd left Delany with a list of detailed instructions and money with which to act on those instructions.

Maybe that hadn't been such a clever thing to do . . .

"I believe you have a point," Rafe said slowly. "Maybe it would be a good idea if I went back to County Mayo and had a good look at the situation."

"You have always been such a reasonable man," the duchess said serenely. "And your returning to Kincaid would put my mind at ease, for I know that you will right any wrong you might find."

"I will certainly do my best," Rafe said. "Thank you for bringing the matter to my attention. I admit I've been rather distracted the last few months."

"Never mind, dear—love will do that to people. I remember well how buffle-headed I was when your dear father was courting me. I could not keep two thoughts together for more than a minute."

Rafe regarded her curiously. "It was a love match, then?"

The duchess looked at him in surprise. "Naturally it was. I adored your father from the day I met him until the day he died. Did you think I married him only for position?"

"I honestly didn't know," Rafe said, greatly relieved to hear that wasn't the case. He couldn't help but remember the times his father would lock himself away for days on end. He would have to admit there were times he thought his father's behavior was due to an unhappy marriage.

"We had our ups and downs, but all marriages do over the course of time," the duchess said. "I would say that on the whole we were very happy together. Your father did occasionally suffer from melancholia, which made life difficult for him, but you were so young that you probably do not remember."

Rafe stared at her. "Melancholia?" he asked in a low voice. *Dear God, but here might finally be an explanation . . .*

"Yes, dear. It happens in the best of families. We weathered the storms when they happened, and then the sun would come out again and all was well."

All was well . . . until the day his father put a shotgun to his head in a deserted field and pulled the trigger, never knowing that his nine-year-old son watched in horror from the woods.

He pressed a shaking hand to his forehead, quickly forcing the memory away, refusing to let the demons take hold. They belonged to the dark, to the nights when his guard was down and they slipped across the uneasy borders of sleep to wreak their vengeance on his unprotected soul. He'd be damned if he let them anywhere near him in daylight.

"Raphael? You are suddenly looking pale. Does the knowledge that your father had an illness upset you?"

"Upset me?" he said faintly, attempting to recover his equilibrium. "No. I'm glad you told me. It—it explains some things."

"Oh? Such as what, darling?"

"Nothing important," Rafe said. He might have an explanation, but his mother still didn't need to know the truth about her husband's death. There had been enough suffering.

"I see," the duchess said, regarding him with concern. "Perhaps you remember more than I realize."

A great deal more than you realize, Mama. "I do remember bits and pieces," Rafe said out loud. "But let us not discuss it any further. If I'm to leave for Ireland, I have arrangements to make. Where is Hugo, by the by?"

"He is in London as far as I know," his mother said, her expression clearing. "Why? Are you still very angry with him?"

"Furious. But then I've been furious with Hugo for years, so what difference does it really make? I only wondered if I'd have an opportunity to kill him before I left."

The duchess laughed. "You have been threatening to do that since you both were boys, and as far as I know, you have never harmed a hair on his head."

"There is always a first time," Rafe said, standing. "I'll leave tonight, I think. There's no point in delaying."

"What a good idea," the duchess said. "Do keep me informed of your progress, will you?"

"Of course. I don't know how long I'll be gone, but certainly long enough to make sure everything is running smoothly."

"I shall miss you, but don't hurry back on my account," his mother said cheerfully. "And who knows, maybe you will find your mystery woman while you're there. She's a lovely girl and would make you a fine wife."

Rafe didn't know whether to strangle his mother or hug her. "Thank you," he said, not doing either. The gut-wrenching truth was that he privately agreed.

And a hell of a lot of good it did him.

14

*R*afe closed the last of the Kincaid books with disgust. He'd been over every transaction made in the past ten years, having finally found Ian Kincaid's original accounts stuffed away in the attic gathering dust.

His mother was right. Paddy Delany was a rascal, all right, and a thief to boot. Rafe had been none too pleased to arrive and discover that not a stroke of work had been done on the house or the land and Paddy himself as drunk as a lord, ensconced in the drawing room as if he owned the place, a bottle of good Irish whisky dangling between his fingers.

Rafe had been right in his decision not to send any warning of his arrival this time. If he hadn't been so angry, he might have been amused by the startled expression on Delany's face when he walked in.

But he hadn't been amused, not at all. Nor was Delany when Rafe gave him an ear-splitting lecture and sent him away—for the time being.

This time he was going to see that it was for good.

Thirty families evicted for failure to pay an exorbitant rent, a rent that had tripled in the first year of Thomas's ownership. Thirty families pushed out to starve, thirty houses left standing deserted, the land wasting away while Paddy Delany fiddled the books and pocketed a good portion of the profits.

He shoved his hands through his hair, almost as angry with himself as he was with Delany. He must have been even more upset than he'd realized the last time he was here, or he surely would have seen the inconsistencies all around him and asked far more questions. But he hadn't—his mistake.

Delany must think him as big a fool as Thomas had been, content to take his land agent's word that things were as Delany said. Either that or Thomas had been in cahoots with Delany all along, which wouldn't surprise Rafe, save for the fact that Thomas had hardly been around to take notice of anything.

He pushed back his chair and stood, determined to confront Delany immediately and see him straight off the land.

Things were going to change. Things were definitely going to change.

"Oh, it's you, your grace," Paddy Delany said, turning from a group of laborers he was instructing to till the south field for a late planting of hay. "What might I be doing for you?"

"I want a word with you, and you can walk over here with me so that I may have it," Rafe said bluntly.

"All right then," Paddy said, following Rafe a few paces away. "But make it quick—I don't trust these men to do anything right unless I'm standing over them."

"You need not stand over them any longer, Mr. Delany. To put it plainly, I find myself no longer in need of your services."

Paddy Delany stared at him, his color fading. "Begging your pardon, your grace, but have you taken leave of your senses? How do you think anything is going to get done if I'm not around to see to it?"

"I have not taken leave of my senses, Mr. Delany. If anything, I've taken hold of them after going through a decade's worth of books with a fine-tooth comb. You are an embezzler, and even worse, you are a heartless, self-serving tyrant, preying on innocent people unable to defend themselves."

Delany stared at him, his mouth hanging open in shock. "What—what is that supposed to mean?" he choked.

"You dared to stand in front of me three months ago and spout off about the plight of the Irish, about how they'd been robbed and swindled by my countrymen while you were busy doing exactly that—and to your own people, no less." Rafe's mouth tightened. "You spoke eloquently of poverty and hunger while you were driving people to it. You spoke sorrowfully of the good soil that once fed over a hundred people, while you were deliberately forcing tenants off that very soil."

Paddy Delany's face turned brick red. "You really have taken leave of your senses to level such accusations against me. I don't know what bee's gotten into your bonnet, but if it was the drink you saw me having the other day, I swear that was a one-time thing. I was tired and frustrated with the delays."

"Finding you drinking in my drawing room is the least of my worries, but do you really think me so stupid that I would believe anything you say at this point?" Rafe said, folding his arms across his chest. "I have the proof in black and white, Delany, and a mind to take it to the authorities. Oblige me by permanently removing yourself from the premises, however, and I might reconsider."

"I—I am sure I can explain everything to your satisfaction, your grace," Delany stammered. "You must bear in mind that your cousin was a spendthrift. It was everything I could do to try to keep him in check, and virtually impossible even then."

"Yes. My cousin was a spendthrift. He was also a fool, which explains why he hired you. I don't know and I don't really care how much of a hand he had in this atrocity with you, for he never had any ethics to begin with—a shining example being how he stole Kincaid away from its rightful owner. But you, Delany, are ten times more despicable than my cousin ever was." He pointed toward the carriageway. "Begone. Do not let me see your face here again, for if I do, I can promise you that you'll be very sorry. Jail is not such a comfortable place."

"You'll be sorry for this day's work, that you will, *your grace*. You'll pay and you'll pay dearly," Delany said, his face now black with rage. "You don't go pushing people like me around and get away with it. Your cousin learned that sure enough."

"Did he? How very interesting. Thank you for that piece of information. Now get the hell out of here before I call the militia and have you hauled away."

Paddy Delany spat on the ground, then turned on his heel and stormed off, shouting a string of curses as he went.

"And good riddance," Rafe muttered. He walked back over to the group of workmen who were gaping.

"Mother of God, your lordship, but you just crossed a dangerous man," one of them said. "Nobody messes with Paddy Delany and lives to tell about it."

"Watch me," Rafe said. "And starting today, your wages are doubled. A man couldn't feed a family of two on what you're being paid."

"Bless you, sir," another man cried, and then they all joined in with a chorus of thanks, their tired faces wreathed in astonished smiles.

"Do not thank me for what is only fair," Rafe said. "What someone *can* do, however, is tell me where I might find a family by the name of O'Reilly. They used to be the head tenants here, and I plan to bring them back if they'll come, along with as many of the other cotters who were evicted—if I can find them."

Rafe could hardly hear through the answering roar of information and cheers. He learned what he needed to know, then went to saddle up the white gelding he'd bought from the blacksmith in Killala. He wasn't about to waste another minute. Justice would be restored to Kincaid as soon as humanly possible.

Lucy walked down the road toward Ballycastle, swinging her empty basket in her hand. It was market day, the one day she was allowed out on her own to do the shopping. With luck she might even run into Brigid.

She turned her face up to the sun, but even its radiant heat didn't ease the chill that ran through her bones. Nothing had. Probably nothing would. Nothing except Raphael. He was her sun now, and without him she felt as if she'd never be warm again.

Odd. It was her twenty-first birthday, supposedly her hour of liberation, but she felt nothing. It was a day like any other, a day without hope. All she had to look forward to was finding the best value for money at the market and then cooking whatever she found over the next week.

The hustle and bustle of the marketplace filled her ears as she approached, but she had to force a smile to her lips as she greeted the various stall-keepers. "Lovely day," she called, not really meaning it. "How are the children, Mrs. Murphy?" she asked, wanting to know but not really hearing the answer.

She poked around in the vegetable stands, hating having to haggle. If she'd had money to burn she would have spent it in every last place to help out the poor beleaguered farmers, but she didn't have an extra penny, did she? Eunice was as tight-fisted as ever, expecting Lucy to bring home quality and quantity on only pennies. She even went so far as to search Lucy's basket when she returned to make sure that she hadn't spent anything on something frivolous for herself.

What would Lucy do with a useless ribbon? She only bought those for Amaryllis or Fiona or Eunice herself on command.

"Lucy?" Brigid's voice shook her out of her reverie.

"Brigid," she said, happy to see her dear friend but having to gather the energy to welcome her warmly.

"How much time do you have left?" Brigid asked, her face alive with excitement. "I have something important to tell you, but I don't want to make you late."

"Not that much," Lucy said. "Aunt Eunice is off with the girls again, but she was only going to Killala, so she won't be gone that long."

"I'll be quick then." Brigid took her arm and led her off into a corner away from the stalls. "Lucy—I didn't want to say anything to anyone other than Ma and Dad before I told you." Her eyes danced with happiness. "Lucy, my darling Lucy, I am engaged to be married!"

"Married?" Lucy said, knowing she should be surprised and delighted for her friend but feeling nothing. Fancy that. Brigid, married. And why shouldn't she be? Brigid had been pining after Sean O'Dougal for the last two years and he after her. Lucy was sure that Brigid would be blissfully happy. Someone ought to be blissfully happy, even if it couldn't be her.

She hugged Brigid tightly. "I am so pleased for you. All the best of luck, dear friend. I know you love him fearfully."

"Oh, I do, Lucy, I do. I've waited the longest time, wanting to be sure Ma could do without me, but she gave me her blessing back in June, and so I went ahead and flirted with Sean for all I was worth so he'd know his attentions were finally welcome. And here we are." She squeezed her hands together. "The date is set for September. Will you stand beside me? I know it's a lot to ask, your being Protestant and all, but it would help knowing I have my closest friend to hold me up when the time comes."

"You know I will," Lucy said, wondering how she was going to manage to smile through a wedding of all things. Not that she could ever have married Raphael, even if he'd wanted her to. She might love him, but he was still English, and that would never change. "The only trouble is arranging a time I can get safely away without Aunt Eunice knowing," she said, pushing the sorry thought of Raphael's tainted blood away.

Brigid nodded thoughtfully. "I hadn't thought of that, but we can come up with something to be sure. Just let me know when your stepmother plans to be away and we'll work it out from there."

"I'll do my best," Lucy said. And she would too. She'd do her utmost to be happy for her friend, even though her own heart was breaking. But she couldn't think about Raphael. Not now. One didn't think about the heated touch of a man's hands on one's body, or the feel of his mouth descending in a ravishing kiss either, not in the middle of the marketplace. "I'd best get on with the rest of my shopping, for I have a hundred chores to do at home," she said, forcing her mind back to practicalities.

"Of course you do. I'll see you here next week then?"

"Yes. I expect you will." Lucy went back to pinching lettuce and cabbages, feeling as if she were the only person in the world who knew the face of love but would never experience its full glory.

Rafe rode down the coast road, his gaze scanning the countryside for the cottage that the workmen had described. But his attention was distracted by the sight of the cliffs of Downpatrick Head standing in the distance, the sea glittering behind. He drew his horse to a halt and gazed at them, memory flooding back in full force. Egeria, standing just there, softly reciting poetry. He, watching, losing his heart to her in only a matter of moments.

Perhaps after he had concluded his business with the O'Reilly family he would ride out there, although he couldn't think why he wanted to subject himself to another onslaught of pain. She wouldn't be there, and he'd be left with nothing but a aching heart. Again.

He slipped his hand into his pocket for the gold locket he

had carried with him since the night of the Stanhope ball and pulled it out, looking down at it for the hundredth time. It still told him nothing. Engraved on the back was a date: August 6th, 1800. He assumed that was the date of her birth, and he realized with a jolt that today was the sixth of August. She'd be twenty-one.

He wondered if she was happily celebrating, wherever she was. He wondered if she ever thought of him, if her heart ached as badly as his did. Easing the locket open, he gazed at the two portraits inside. A man and a woman—surely her parents, for he could see a resemblance in their faces.

This was all he had left of her. One locket containing two portraits whose likeness served only to remind him of the woman he had lost.

The wind moaned around him, a lonely, haunting sound, and he sighed heavily. He was so tired of hurting, so tired of the emptiness in his heart, tired of endlessly yearning for what he couldn't have. So many sleepless nights, his body hard with wanting.

Would he ever be able to erase her from his mind, be able to forget how she'd felt in his arms, the tremors that had run through her body as she'd ardently opened her mouth under his, her breath shuddering as he invaded her with his tongue . . .

Rafe squeezed his eyes shut against an acute stab of longing that hurt not only in his heart but in his loins as well. "My sweet Egeria," he whispered. "Come back to me. Please come back to me."

Looking down at the locket one last time, he clasped his hand tightly around it. Maybe, just maybe if he showed it around someone might recognize the portraits, although the chances of that were also next to none. But it was worth a try. Anything was worth a try.

He replaced the locket in his pocket and picked up the reins, urging his horse forward into a canter, forcing himself to concentrate on the matter at hand.

The O'Reilly cottage wasn't difficult to spot, sitting as it did by itself, sheltered by a bluff. It reflected the poverty of the people who lived there, for the roof was badly in need of repair and the whitewash on the exterior walls was flaking and streaked with dirt.

A pretty dark-haired woman stood outside hanging up washing, a toddler on her hip. She looked tired, he thought, worn down by struggle and futility, all hope gone for a better future. But he would see what he could do to change that.

She looked up, shielding her eyes with one hand as he rode through the broken gateway.

"Mrs. O'Reilly?" he asked, pulling up on the reins.

"Yes," she said, her expression wary. "I'm Mairead O'Reilly. And who might you be?"

"I am Raphael Montagu," he said, deliberately omitting his title so as not to intimidate her. He swung off his horse and looped the reins over the gatepost. "If you don't mind, I'd like to have a word with you and your husband."

She took a step backward, the wariness on her face replaced by fear. "My husband is inside, having his noon meal. What would you be wanting with him?"

"Mrs. O'Reilly, I fully understand why you would be suspicious of me," Rafe said calmly. "My cousin treated you very badly. But I assure you, I have not come to cause you any trouble. If you would allow me to come inside, I can explain."

Mairead nodded abruptly. "All right then," she said, standing back. "Enter if you will, but I'll ask you not to upset Seamus. He's had a hard time of it lately and he doesn't need any more worries."

"I understand," Rafe said, removing his hat and ducking under the low doorway.

A weathered man sat at the table, spooning porridge into his mouth. His hand halted as he took in Rafe and the spoon clattered into the bowl. He pushed his chair back and slowly stood. "Good day to you," he said, but his eyes said something else entirely.

"Good day, Mr. O'Reilly. Forgive me for disturbing you in the middle of your meal, but I think you might want to hear what I've come to say. I am Thomas Montagu's cousin and the new owner of Kincaid."

Seamus cleared his throat. "You're the duke then," he said, scratching his neck. "And what do you want with me? I haven't had anything to do with Kincaid in five years, not since your cousin's agent evicted me for failing to make the payments. If you've come for back rent, you've wasted a trip—I'm already a month behind on this place."

"May I sit down?" Rafe said, not surprised by O'Reilly's bitterness. He had every right to it.

"Suit yourself." Seamus grunted, pointing at a chair. "You'll forgive me if I eat while you talk. We can't afford to waste our food around here."

Rafe pulled out the chair and sat down, folding his hands on the table. He waited as Mairead came in and sat down next to her husband, settling the toddler on her lap.

"Well, then," Seamus said, taking a gulp of ale. "Say what you've come to say and be done with it."

"This morning I finished reading through ten years of estate accounts," Rafe said, going straight to the point. "When I was done, I fired Paddy Delany on the spot."

They both stared at him speechless, as if he'd just announced that he'd fired the King of England.

"He wasn't very happy about it, seeing as he's had six lucrative years of robbing Kincaid blind, not to mention ruthlessly squeezing the tenants dry until they could no longer afford their leases. He certainly wasn't very happy about what I had to say regarding his character."

"I can imagine not," Seamus said with a disdainful snort. "Paddy Delany doesn't take kindly to hearing the truth about himself. But what does any of this have to do with me and my family?"

"It's really very simple. I'd like you to come back to Kincaid as head tenant. I need someone who knows how things were once run. I won't be hiring another land agent for some time, not until I better know what I need."

Mairead gasped, then covered her mouth with both hands, tears starting to her eyes.

"It's a kind offer, your lordship, but I'm afraid that I cannot take you up on it," her husband said. "As I just told you, I can't even manage the rent on this miserable place. How do you expect me to come up with the money for a lease at Kincaid?"

"But I'm not asking you to pay rent—at least not for a full year. That should give you time to get back on your feet. Furthermore, at the end of the year all rents will be what they were before my cousin took over. And naturally I'll pay you for whatever services you perform for me."

Seamus O'Reilly's jaw dropped open. "I'm dreaming," he whispered. "Sure, that's it—I've fallen asleep over my ale and I'm dreaming." He slapped the side of his face.

"No dream," Rafe said with a smile. For the first time he was beginning to appreciate the unique charm of the Irish. "It's a fair offer and one I don't think you can afford to refuse."

"Refuse?" Mairead wiped away the tears streaming down her cheeks. "He won't be hearing any refusals, will he, Seamus?" she asked, turning to her husband.

"I don't see it," Seamus said, shaking his head in disbelief. "What's in it for you?"

"The land is no good to anyone the way it is, and if there's one thing I cannot abide, it's wasted land," Rafe said. "It's to my advantage to see that it is made profitable again, and I can afford to wait for a return on my investment." He leaned forward. "I will give you the funds outright to buy what you need in terms of seed and materials this year and ask only that you put your own hard work into bringing in a late crop."

"Merciful Jasus, I can't believe what I'm hearing," Seamus said, wiping his brow with his forearm. "I've prayed and prayed for a way out of this hell, and you're the answer to my prayers, your lordship, that you are."

"I don't know about that," Rafe replied. "The way I see it, you could very well be the answer to mine, for I've been stumped as to how to turn such a desperate situation around. But I haven't finished yet—all the tenant houses will be done up at my expense, providing that you can help me to bring the other cotters back to Kincaid. Without them my plan is useless."

"Done!" Seamus roared, pounding a fist on the table. "They'll listen to me right enough. Whoever would have thought an Englishman would turn out to be so decent?"

"We're not all scoundrels," Rafe said with amusement. "My cousin may have left a bad taste in your mouth, but then I suppose if I judged all Irishmen by the likes of Paddy Delany, I would think they were thieves and villains."

"True enough. Er . . . there's only one thing that I think you ought to be knowing. I, um, I can figure well enough, but I'm not so good in the reading and writing department, and there's quite a bit of that to be done in the course of looking after things." His face darkened. "It's just that education was forbidden to the Catholics until the Relief Acts were passed, you see, and by then I was already helping my da work the land, so I missed out on that part of things."

"Ah," Rafe said, appalled that any of the Irish had ever been forbidden an education just by virtue of being Catholic. But there was apparently a great deal he didn't know about their suffering under the hands of the British. "I wouldn't let your lack of reading or writing trouble you," he said lightly. "I'll think of something to get around that."

"Bless you, your lordship," Mairead said, drying her eyes. "You cannot know what this means."

"I can guess," Rafe said quietly. "As I'd like you to come as soon as possible, I am prepared to give you the money you need to pay off your debt here." He reached into his pocket and pulled out a small bag of coins, pushing it across the table. "That should cover your rent amply. Take it as an advance on your salary," he continued, realizing their pride would allow nothing else.

"Thank you a thousand times over," Mairead said, taking the pouch. "But look, your lordship, there's something of yours caught in the string."

Rafe realized that the locket must have become entangled. "Thank you," he said, holding out his hand as Mairead unraveled the chain.

She was about to hand it to him when she suddenly stopped and looked at it more closely. "Good Lord above, Seamus, look! It's Lucy's locket! She's never without it—she must have dropped it somewhere."

Rafe's heart almost froze in his chest. Dear God above— could it be that Mairead O'Reilly actually *knew* the girl? His pulse leapt frantically in the base of his throat at the thought that he actually might have stumbled across a real clue to Egeria's real identity at last.

"Where did you find this, your lordship?" Mairead asked curiously. "Lucy must have lost it somewhere around here, for she never goes far from this place."

"Actually, I found it in London," he said, forcing himself to speak calmly. Lucy. Her name was Lucy, and she lived somewhere nearby. "I was hoping to find the owner so that I could return it, but there is no name inscribed on it, just a date. And there are two portraits inside—I assume they are of her parents."

"London? You found it in London?" Mairead said nervously, suddenly looking guarded. "How odd . . . well, never mind that. I'll be sure she gets it back, since it means the world to her. It's all she has left of them."

Rafe reached over and took it from Mairead's hand. "I'd rather return it myself, if you will tell me her full name and where she lives."

Mairead shot a panicked look at her husband, who only shook his head as if he didn't know what to say. "I don't know that I can do that, your lordship," she said uncertainly. "I don't want to cause her any trouble."

Rafe looked down, then met Mairead's eyes squarely. "I have reason to believe she is already in trouble," he said very softly. "If you will trust me with the truth, I'd like to help."

"What makes you think she's in trouble?" Seamus asked cautiously. "You've never even met her."

"To the contrary. Lucy was wearing this locket at Lady Stanhope's ball only a few short weeks ago. I should know. I danced with her. She lost it then."

"But—but that's impossible," Mairead gasped. "Absolutely impossible! Lucy wouldn't have been attending any ball."

"Why not?" he asked, toying with the chain.

"I—I can't say. I shouldn't have said anything at all to begin with," Mairead stammered. "I must be mistaken in the matter. Mayhaps it's someone else's locket."

"Mrs. O'Reilly, I can see that you are trying to protect the girl. Your intentions are obviously good, but I believe them to be misplaced." He ran a hand through his hair, carefully measuring each word, desperate for the answers that were finally within his reach. "Please, let me help. I promise you no harm will come to her, but I have to know the truth."

"He's helped us, hasn't he, Mairead?" Seamus said. "I think he can be trusted to help Lucy."

"I don't know," Mairead cried. "I just don't know . . ."

Rafe was about to explode with frustration. He pressed the clasp and opened the locket, exposing the portraits. One last try. He'd give it one last try before he shook the truth out of her. "Who are these two people? Will you at least tell me that much?"

Mairead swallowed hard, then finally nodded. "Yes, all right then. It would be a crime to keep the truth from you if you really do want to help."

"Believe me when I tell you that I do," he said, excitement quickening in his chest. At last, at long last . . .

"That's Lord Kincaid there on the right," Mairead said, pointing a finger. "And on the left is his first wife Laura, and a sweeter soul you never could find, other than Lucy. She got both her brains and her kind nature from them."

Rafe stared at her, shock coursing through his veins. "*What?*" he whispered raggedly, the breath leaving his body as forcefully as if he'd been physically struck. "Dear God in heaven, are you telling me that they had a daughter? And that daughter is named Lucy?"

"Yes," Mairead said, twisting her wedding ring around on her finger. "She is. We love her dearly too, so don't you go upsetting things for her. She has enough troubles."

Rafe gripped the edge of the table so hard that his knuckles showed white. "I don't believe it," he said in a voice so low it was hardly audible. "I don't bloody well believe it."

His mind worked furiously as he tried to put the pieces together. Eunice Kincaid had made no mention of her. *Why?* And what had Lucy been doing in London? Why had Eunice not said a word, even when Lucy appeared at the ball . . . but under an assumed name? He frantically thought backward—Lucy in the park, desperate to get away from him, denying even knowing him—denying ever being in Ireland. Lucy on the cliff, suddenly disappearing, impossible to find.

And his last memory of her, pulling out of his arms, begging him not to ask her any more questions. Terrified. *Why?*

He looked up, fury raging through him. "What in the name of *God* has been going on here?" he demanded, his voice harsh.

Mairead got to her feet and crossed the room to a table. She opened the drawer and pulled out what appeared to be a letter. "I think this might explain better than I can," she said, handing it to him. "It's from Lucy. She wrote it from London for my daughter to read to us."

Rafe took the sheets of paper and began to scan the pages,

his fury growing by the moment as the story became crystal clear, told in Lucy's own words. Words that described an intolerable situation, a life of servitude and isolation meted out at the hands of an insufferable stepmother.

. . . I hear stories from Fiona and Amaryllis about where they've gone and what they've seen . . .

Fiona and Amaryllis, those two stupid girls, walking and dining and dancing in places where Lucy should have gone, would have gone, had he only known.

I only ever see the duke from the window or over the balcony of the upstairs landing, since I'm not to show myself, especially to him—he's not to know I even exist. Aunt Eunice would have my head . . .

So. Lucy had been aware of his identity all the time. Of course she had—she'd have known it almost from the beginning but had been unable to acknowledge him. And he'd been completely unaware of her identity, fool that he was.

I have a little bedroom up in the top of the house. I can see the garden and a bit of the park from it . . . I miss walking in the fresh air most of all . . .

And so she had been forced to slip secretly out to the park, a brief respite from her attic prison. He set his jaw and read on.

The other servants are nice enough to me, even if we don't speak much, my being Irish and all. I have three square meals a day that I don't have to cook, and for once someone else sees to the cleaning and scrubbing. The only thing I really have to do is look after my stepfamily's needs . . .

She had been cooking and cleaning and scrubbing for them on top of everything else? He gritted his teeth against a cry of outrage.

I've taken over the household books again, since Aunt Eunice is as useless as ever and too lazy to do it herself. She only checks to make sure I haven't taken anything for myself . . .

He knew he'd recognized the hand—it was the same fine, precise script he'd seen in the carefully kept Kincaid housekeeping books Eunice had claimed were her own handiwork.

He slowly lowered the letter to the table, shaking his head back and forth. The whole thing seemed impossible, but there it was in black and white. No wonder she'd behaved as she had. No bloody wonder . . . Poor Egeria. Dear *God,* but what her life must be have been like.

And he hadn't known. She'd been right under his nose the entire time and he'd been utterly oblivious. If only he'd realized—if only he'd known who she was from the first day. But Eunice Kincaid, damn her black soul, had made sure that he didn't. He'd kill the woman. But first he'd find Lucy.

When he was finally able to speak again, he had to fight to control his voice. "Thank you," he said, abruptly standing. "I have a birthday present for Lucy Kincaid. If you'll excuse me, I think I'll go deliver it."

He left without another word.

15

"Lucy, get the door," Eunice commanded as a rapid series of knocks sounded on it. "Come along, be quick about it. And if it's a tradesman, send him away. I do not wish to deal with him."

Lucy looked up from the sitting room fireplace where she'd been cleaning out the grate. She got up off her knees with a sigh and brushed off the front of her dirty apron, only leaving more streaks of soot behind. It would be nice if Eunice could put down her needlepoint and answer her own front door for once, or Fiona or Amaryllis for that matter, since they were doing nothing but squabbling over a game of cards.

She impatiently pulled the door open. And froze.

Raphael?

It wasn't possible. The sun was playing tricks with her eyes, that's what it was. She blinked, but he still stood there, his arms folded across his chest, his golden hair glinting in the sunlight.

She rubbed her eyes and looked again, sure that it must be someone else, that her constant longing for him had scrambled her brains. It had to be someone else. Raphael was in England, safely pursuing his life as a duke.

"Is Lady Kincaid at home?" he asked, looking directly at her without a single sign of recognition.

"I—I . . ." Lucy swallowed hard, her head spinning. She'd been here before, done just this—it was as if no time had gone by, yet everything in the world had changed since then. *What was he doing here?* she thought in panic.

"Who is it, Lucy?" Eunice called.

"Tell her it's Southwell," he prompted, as if she hadn't a brain in her head. And she truly felt as if she hadn't. "The Duke of Southwell," he added as she stared at him.

"It's—it's the duke," she stammered, stumbling back a pace.

"The *duke?*" Eunice gasped. She jumped to her feet. "Let him in, you stupid girl!"

Lucy stood away and Raphael strode past her into the room. She stared after him, one hand slipping to her throat. He didn't know her—he didn't even know her. And yet it was just as well . . .

Her gaze traveled to her stepmother, who had apprehension written all over her face. "Good day, Duke," Eunice said coolly enough. "This is a surprise to be sure."

"I can imagine," he said, nodding politely toward Fiona and Amaryllis.

"You're back!" Amaryllis squealed, the cards in her hand spilling to the floor. "Oooh, I knew you'd come. You must have missed us drastically."

"How simply speculative to see you again," Fiona added with a simper.

"And you," Raphael said with no change of expression, turning back to Eunice. "If you don't mind, Lady Kincaid, I would like a private word with you. Perhaps you could send your daughters upstairs?"

"Oh, Mama," Fiona said plaintively. "Must we?"

"Upstairs this minute," Eunice snapped. "And do not come down until I summon you." She spread her skirt out and sat down, graciously extending her hand toward the opposite chair as Fiona and Amaryllis sulked up the stairs, grumbling under their breath.

Eunice seemed to have forgotten all about Lucy, who was pressed back in the shadows against the wall, her eyes wide with alarm, her breath coming in short, painful jerks. To see him again should have made her heart sing with happiness. Only she knew that he hadn't come for her—he'd looked straight through her, hadn't he? His business was with her stepmother—and she couldn't imagine what it could be. Instead of thrill, her spine pricked with fear.

"To what do I owe the honor of your visit?" Eunice asked, echoing Lucy's own thoughts.

"No honor at all," Raphael said, sitting down and crossing one long, muscular leg over the other. "I believe a complete lack of honor is more the point."

Eunice folded her mouth into a tight smile of satisfaction. "So. You have finally come to your senses," she said.

"I regret only that I did not come to them sooner," he replied smoothly.

Eunice nodded, one quick downward jerk of her head. "It is about time," she said. "I can only assume you have come to make an offer."

Lucy held her breath in agonizing anticipation, waiting to hear his answer, praying it was not what Eunice expected. It couldn't be—Raphael loathed her stepsisters.

Raphael ran a thumb over his chin. "No, not an offer. A demand."

Lucy frowned in puzzlement. A demand? What sort of demand? Did he want his dowry money back?

Eunice's fingers fluttered at her throat. "A demand? Do you expect me to refuse you?"

"Not at all. I expect you to acquiesce with all speed. The terms are not negotiable."

Eunice shrugged one shoulder. "I daresay I will not quibble. Which of my daughters do you intend to speak for?"

"If you will allow *me* to speak, I am sure it will all become clear. I do not appreciate being rushed, Lady Kincaid."

"No, of course not," Eunice said quickly. "You must forgive my anxiety—it is only that I have been waiting so very long for you to make a declaration. La! sir, but you have kept us all hanging in suspense."

Lucy was about to expire from suspense herself. He couldn't *possibly* mean to marry one of her stepsisters. Could he? She couldn't endure the thought. She pressed a shaking hand against her mouth, stifling a rush of nausea. Not Raphael, who had said he loved her. Her—not Fiona or Amaryllis. But she had disappeared from his life, hadn't she? What was he supposed to do—live out the rest of his life as a bachelor?

"Hanging," Raphael said thoughtfully, examining his fingernails. "An apt word, and a just one under these circumstances."

Lucy wondered why he looked as if he'd like to slip a noose around Eunice's neck. He certainly didn't appear like a man about to propose marriage.

Eunice inclined her head. "I bear you no grudge in the matter, especially seeing as you had a difficult choice to make."

"I had no trouble at all. It was merely a matter of biding my time."

"But you gave no sign!" Eunice exclaimed. "I must admire your *sang-froid*. You led us a merry dance, indeed you did."

"My *sang-froid,* as you say, has been sorely tried, especially in this moment. And if anyone has been led a dance, it is I, although I would not describe it as merry. I would go so far as to call it deeply disturbing."

"Ah, yes, I can imagine," Eunice said with a sympathetic sigh. "But I applaud your sensibility, for you realize that in choosing one daughter, you must therefore reject the other. I am on tenterhooks to hear which of my girls you have chosen."

So was Lucy, although it really made no difference. He was lost to her, but he'd never been hers to begin with—

only in her dreams. She wanted to slump to the floor in heartbroken misery.

Raphael rubbed his finger over his lower lip. And then he turned his head and looked directly at her, a smile playing around the corners of his mouth, reaching all the way into his eyes. "Lucy," he said. "I intend to marry Lucy."

Lucy stared back at him, the blood draining from her cheeks. This wasn't happening. She'd fallen asleep on the hearth and it was all just a dream. He didn't even know who she really was—how could he? Even now he thought she was Eunice's servant. And dukes didn't marry servants.

"*Who* did you say?" Eunice whispered, her face paling.

"I said Lucy," he replied quietly, turning his gaze back to Eunice.

Eunice fumbled with her shawl, her eyes frantically darting around the room and finally fixing on Lucy. "No!" she cried, her eyes flashing with fury. "You despicable girl, what have you done?" she said, her voice rising to a shriek. "You schemed this, didn't you? You schemed this all along, you treacherous little serpent! Oh, you shall be sorry. Very, very sorry indeed."

Lucy couldn't speak. Her nightmare was coming true— her entire world had crashed down around her and she couldn't even speak. She shook her head back and forth, back and forth, trying to force something through her tight throat, but she couldn't think clearly enough even for that.

Raphael spoke for her. "If anyone schemed, it was you, Lady Kincaid," he said, biting out the words. "Did you really believe that you could shove your own sorry daughters in front of my nose and expect me actually to offer for one of them?"

"I—I assumed you had an interest, yes," she stammered, her face white as chalk.

"And so to ensure that I would not look elsewhere, you tried to hide Lucy from me, knowing that she outshines your own pathetic brood by far—"

"You would marry my *servant*?" Eunice cried. "Have you lost your mind? A stupid Irish girl you have seen but twice before? What did she do, raise her skirts for you out there on the cliff that day?"

Lucy wanted to die from mortification. How did Eunice even know about their encounter on the cliff? But to imply in front of Raphael that she would . . . She turned her head away, pressing her cheek against the wall.

"Enough!" Raphael stood, towering over Eunice and she cowered away from him. "You will not speak of Lucy in this offensive manner, do you understand? You lied to me even back then, didn't you, when I asked you if you knew the identity of the girl I'd seen. You denied any knowledge of her. You denied her very *existence,* Lady Kincaid."

"I—I don't know what you mean," she replied, looking truly frightened now.

"I think you know exactly what I mean," he said, his eyes snapping with anger. "What you have done is contemptible. I offered you my goodwill with full explanation that it was because your husband had been unfairly treated at the hands of my cousin. I made no mention at any time that I intended anything else, certainly not marriage to either of your daughters."

"It was a reasonable conclusion to draw," she said plaintively.

"And I suppose you thought it was reasonable to hide the extremely pertinent fact that Ian Kincaid had a daughter of his own? A daughter whom you have been treating as an unpaid servant for years?"

Lucy stiffened with shock, She couldn't breathe, couldn't think, couldn't move. He *knew*? Oh, God in heaven, he really did know the truth. But *how*? She'd been so careful. This was worse than anything she could have imagined. The poor O'Reilly's—one English duke had managed to undo all of her efforts to protect them, for Eunice would surely make them pay now.

"No!" she cried, taking a halting step into the room. "No, Raphael—you must stop this now. You're wrong." She covered her face with her hands. "I'm not—oh, you don't understand," she moaned. "You don't understand anything."

In three quick strides he was at her side, gently grasping her by her shoulders. "Lucy," he murmured. "It is too late for lies now. I know the truth." He cupped her chin and raised her face up, looking down into her eyes with such tenderness that she wanted to throw herself into his arms and beg for his protection. But she couldn't do that.

"Please," she whispered. "Don't take this any further. You might have somehow uncovered part of the story, but you really don't know what you're dealing with. I beg you—if you care for me at all, let it be!"

"But I can't. I'm already involved." He slid his hands down her arms. "Lucy, I *know* you are Ian and Laura Kincaid's daughter. I know that you have been living under Eunice's cruel yoke, hidden away and treated like dirt under her feet. The only thing I don't know is why."

Lucy tore her gaze away, shaking her head frantically.

"Oh, so you want to know why, do you?" Eunice said, her voice sharp with malice. "Then I shall tell you—because she is a vile, wicked girl who is fully responsible for the state you find us in now. You cannot believe anything she says, for she lies at every turn—my poor husband would be alive today if not for her."

Lucy couldn't bear to hear another word. She ripped herself out of Raphael's grip and stumbled to the door, wrenching it open and tearing through it, running as fast as she could away from the house as if she could outrun the demons that pursued her.

But her legs were too shaky to hold her for long, and she collapsed onto a rock, breathing heavily.

She didn't even know where she thought she was going. She had no money—she had nothing. Nothing at all now, for Eunice would never let her back into the house, not after everything that had just happened.

Raphael. He'd said he wanted to marry her, but that was impossible. He must have said it as a way to get at Eunice. But even if he had meant it, it made no difference. She couldn't marry him. He was still an Englishman, no matter how much she loved him.

She supposed she really could try to get a job in a shop if anyone would take her on, although nothing there had changed, either. Everyone would be too afraid of Eunice to risk crossing her.

Especially after Eunice took out her wrath on the O'Reillys and saw them dispossessed.

Lucy bowed her head into her hands and wept in true despair.

Raphael watched Lucy go, torn by a strong desire to run after her and the need to finish his conversation with Eunice before she had a chance to gather her wits about her.

But now that he knew who she was, and where he could find her, he felt safe in letting her go—for the moment. His business with Eunice wouldn't wait.

He turned around, anger pounding through every vein. If ever he had murder in his heart, he had it now. "I think you had better explain yourself, Lady Kincaid," he said tightly. "Not that I think there is any acceptable explanation you can possibly offer, but I'd like to hear what you have to say."

"There is a good reason I kept Lucy's existence from you, your grace," Eunice said, pressing back against the cushion of her chair, her hands squeezed to her bosom as if she could fend him off. "She cannot be trusted."

"She cannot be trusted? Implying that you can? Do you expect me to believe anything you say after all the lies you have told me?"

"I never lied," Eunice protested tearfully. "It is true that I did not reveal the full facts, but as I said, I had good reason."

"Which is?" Rafe asked, folding his arms across his chest, thoroughly disgusted with the woman.

"I—I told you that my husband was betrayed and lost his home, but I did not tell you that it was his own daughter who betrayed him, who led him directly into the lap of the insurgents. *That* was why he was implicated. *That* was why he was fired upon and then jailed, and why we lost our home. And *that* is why he died." She lowered her head. "You must believe me, for it is the truth."

"Even if I did believe you, which I don't, I can see no reason for your unconscionable treatment of your step-daughter. Not only did you force her to cook and clean for you here, you went so far as to deny Lucy her very birth-right. Instead of bringing her to London to make her come-out and take her proper place in society, you brought her to be your maid, locking her away in an attic bedroom, even refusing her the fresh air. How much crueler could you possibly have been?"

"It was everything she deserved." Eunice sniffed, blowing her nose into her handkerchief. "How else was I to treat her after everything she'd done to me and my daughters? She turned our lives into an endless misery."

"And you haven't managed to make hers far worse? You are a despicable, evil woman, Eunice Kincaid, and I have no sympathy for you. None at all."

He leaned over her, his hands grasping both arms of the chair. "I am taking Lucy away from this place this very after-noon. I will marry her and make her my duchess."

"I won't permit it!" Eunice screeched, her face turning bright red. "I am her guardian and you will not do anything of the sort. She is underage and cannot marry without my consent."

"You seem to have lost track of time." He straightened. "Your stepdaughter turned twenty-one years old today and no longer needs your consent."

Eunice stared at him in disbelief. "No," she whispered. "No—it cannot be."

"Yes. You will have to find someone else to be your unpaid slave. From now on Lucy will have the life she so richly deserves—at my side."

Eunice jumped to her feet, her fists knotted at her side. "Then you are a fool, for the baggage has filled your head with a pack of lies, working upon your sympathies. She went to you and poured her troubles out, didn't she, persuading you that the only way she could escape was if you married her?" White lines of rage ran from her sharp nose to the corner of her thin mouth. "She wanted you for herself, not because she cares anything about you—how can she?— but because she wants to be a pampered duchess. You will regret your decision for the rest of your life, I promise you that, once you find out what you have really married."

"Not another word!" Rafe roared. "Lucy did *not* come to me. She said nothing at all, although I wish to hell she had. I pressed her hard enough for the truth, but she was too frightened to give it to me. And I do not wish to marry her because I feel sorry for her, I wish to marry her because I love her."

"But—but *how*?" Eunice wailed. "How can you? I refuse to believe that all of this happened in one brief afternoon on Downpatrick Head."

"All of this happened over a period of months, starting that afternoon on Downpatrick Head and continuing through your months in London," Rafe replied wearily.

Eunice gaped at him. "London? But—but that's impossible."

He smiled coldly. "I know you recall the beautiful girl who came to the Stanhope ball with my brother, the girl I danced with who later vanished so abruptly. You thought she looked vaguely familiar, did you not?"

Two spots of red flared in Eunice's hollow cheeks. "No . . . no, it can't have been," she said, sinking back into her chair, her fingers working at the material of her dress with little jerks. "Surely not—not Lucy?"

"But it was. And you saw then how the land lay, did you not? You might not have realized she was your stepdaughter, but you certainly realized that I had strong feelings for her."

Eunice looked as if Rafe had struck her. "How dare she," she cried. "How dare Lucy disobey me like that? How dare she ruin my daughters' chances?"

"Your daughters, madam, never *had* a chance, not with me, and obviously not with anyone else. But that is your problem, not mine. Still, despite how disgusted I am with you, your daughters should not have to pay for your mistakes. They may keep their dowry money—with one provision."

"What—what provision is that?" she asked with alacrity, stumbling over the words in obvious anxiety that the money might slip through her fingers as easily as Lucy had.

"You will stay away from Lucy," he said, his tone ominous. "As of today you will relinquish all claim to her. Should malicious gossip of any fashion reach my ears, I will know exactly where to come."

She licked her lips, then nodded soundlessly.

"I am pleased you understand me. I'll fetch Lucy now to pack up her belongings. I expect you only to say farewell to her and wish her well, and not a word more. Is that clear?"

"Perfectly," Eunice said, gripping her hands together in her lap, her face tight and colorless.

Rafe nodded curtly and went directly to the front door, breathing a heavy sigh of relief that all had gone according to plan.

He closed it behind him, scanning the distance for Lucy, wondering if she hadn't run off to the cliff.

But he spotted her easily, sitting very still on a rock a little way down the road, her head bowed forlornly, her braid hanging over her shoulder. She looked so young and alone, so vulnerable, and his heart squeezed painfully in his chest.

God, how he loved her. He'd never known anyone so brave, so incredibly strong of spirit. Anyone else would been broken long ago, but she had survived. And not only survived, but exhibited extraordinary forbearance and grace in the face of a seemingly insurmountable difficulty.

He would never let her be hurt again if his life depended on it, he vowed. Never again.

16

*E*ven through the depths of her misery Lucy sensed a presence nearby. Her head jerked up, the breath jerking from her body at the same time.

Raphael stood only a few paces away. His gaze locked with hers and the intensity that blazed in his eyes nearly knocked her off her rocky perch.

A horrified exclamation escaped from her throat as she realized the precarious position she was in. She had to get away—and quickly, before he confronted her and started pressing her for answers she wasn't prepared to give him.

She jumped up and started running blindly down the road, panic driving her foolish flight.

Foolish, because only moments later his strong hands grabbed her from behind and pulled her to an abrupt halt, holding her in a gentle grip.

"And I wonder where you think you're off to now?" he murmured, his breath warm against her cheek.

Lucy shuddered, breathing raggedly, and not just because she'd been running. His touch burned into her skin all the way through the thin material of her dress. "I—I don't know," she said honestly. "Oh, God, I don't know. I don't know anything anymore."

He relaxed his hold and turned her around. "I'm sorry," he said, his voice very low and soft. "I hated having to do that to you back there, but I couldn't think of any other way to confront Eunice."

She slowly dragged her gaze to his face. *"Why?"* she asked on a choked sob. "Why did you have to do it at all? I told you not to come looking for me."

"What else do I seem to do these days?" he said, a hint of amusement in his voice. He glanced around. "Odd. This doesn't look like the Isle of Wight. I should know—I was just there."

Lucy colored furiously. "Oh," she said, desperately trying to steady herself, not easy when he looked down at her from only inches away, his gray eyes impenetrable.

"Oh? That's all you have to say?" He cocked one eyebrow.

"What else is there to say? You found me." She swallowed hard.

"Didn't I just?" he replied, still holding her, and far too close for comfort. "It only cost me another three weeks of sleepless nights and a few hundred miles of travel. But what are those small inconveniences in the grand scheme of things?"

"I don't know why you bothered," she said, her voice shaking as furiously as her body. "It's only going to cause trouble—terrible trouble."

"I have something I thought you might want returned." He let go of one of her shoulders and dangled a gold necklace in front of her face.

"My locket!" she said, grabbing for it, immense relief sweeping through her that she finally had it back. "Thank goodness! I thought it was gone for all time." She clutched it tightly against her chest as if it could offer her protection.

"And you probably thought I was gone for all time as well," he said, not smiling now. Not smiling at all.

"I did, yes," she said, gulping at his grim expression.

"Hmm. And I wonder how you feel now that I'm here?"

"I don't see that it's any of your business," she said, her nerves so on edge that her teeth chattered.

"I think it's very much my business," he said, his fingers tightening on her shoulder. "And you just heard me say why."

The blood drained from her face. "I—I don't know what you mean," she said in a small voice.

"Lucy. I don't know what is behind any of this—your fear, even why you ran away earlier and again just now. But nothing has changed as far as my feelings for you are concerned." He caught her hand up in his and stroked its back with his thumb, sending heated shivers through her. "I meant what I said to you that night in London, you know. It wasn't just the moonlight or the magic of the moment. And I meant what I said to Eunice. I want to marry you."

She looked down, her heart tearing into shreds. "Raphael—don't. Please don't. The situation is impossible."

"Not so impossible." He reached his hand out and tenderly drew a finger down her cheek. "Not anymore."

"But there are so many things you don't understand, so much you don't know." She swallowed back tears, her throat aching with the effort.

"What more do I really need to know other than that your real name is Lucy Kincaid and your stepmother has been treating you cruelly for years? Everything made sense when I learned your identity—everything you've said and done since I first laid eyes on you. I was enraged beyond belief to realize what that witch has done to you, but that's over now."

"But it's not over!" Lucy cried. "That's what I mean—you have no idea what you've done by meddling in something that doesn't concern you."

"Doesn't *concern* me? Dear God, Lucy, haven't you been listening to me? I love you. What could possibly concern me more than that?" He frowned. "You're not still afraid of Eunice, are you?"

"I'm afraid of what she will do," Lucy said, forcing herself to ignore the declaration of love that tugged at her heart and made her want to throw herself into his arms. "You don't know her—not really. You have no idea what she is capable of."

"Do you honestly think I can't handle a woman as pathetic as Eunice? She might be vicious, but she is no match for me. I left her a babbling wreck back at the house, after extracting a sworn promise she would not come near you again."

"It's not myself I'm worried about so much," Lucy said, biting her lip, thinking that Rafe might think himself all-powerful, but he had no idea of what he was really up against.

"You're surely not worried about those unfortunate step-sisters of yours?" He flashed a sudden grin at her. "I'm sorry—I shouldn't be making light of matters after all the terrible way Eunice has treated you, but oh, Lucy, your brain—your poor, poor brain, forced to listen to those two imbecilic girls day in and day out. I don't know how you've managed to keep your sanity."

Lucy couldn't help smiling in return, finding it very difficult to resist him when his eyes lit up with the laughter she remembered so well. "One adjusts," she said.

"You would say something brave, wouldn't you?" He stroked a lock of hair off her cheek.

"It's not brave," she said, wishing he wouldn't touch her like that, for he made it very hard for her to think clearly. "It's just that there are some things you can't change, and Fiona and Amaryllis's limited comprehension is one of them."

Raphael's grin broadened. "How generous of you to put it like that."

"They're not so bad, not really," she said in their defense. "They can't help themselves. It's not their fault that they were born with only half a brain each. At least they understand each other perfectly well, even if no one else can make any sense of them."

"It's good to hear the Irish back in your voice," he said with a chuckle. "I missed it."

"You did?" she replied, startled. "I thought you much preferred the strangled accents of your countrymen."

"Oh, you do that very well too, but this suits you better." He expelled a soft breath. "Ireland suits you, Lucy. I'd much rather see you like this, being yourself in the place you belong. It is how I first saw you. Why I first fell in love with you."

Lucy's eyes welled with sudden tears. "I don't seem to belong anywhere any longer, thanks to you."

"Nonsense," he said. "I know exactly where you belong."

Lucy wasn't about to go back over that treacherous ground. "How—how did you find me out?" she asked in an attempt to divert him. "I thought I'd covered my tracks so well."

"You did," he replied. "Too well, for I was beginning to think I'd never see you again, and I wasn't very happy about that prospect. I found you by sheer luck. I went to speak to some old Kincaid tenants today—not to ask about you, but on estate business. They recognized your locket when it became caught in something I was giving them."

"My locket?" Lucy said, puzzled. "But who would even know about—" She pressed a hand against her cheek in sudden comprehension. "Not . . . not the O'Reillys? *They* told you the truth?" She couldn't believe the irony. Here she'd been doing her best to protect them and they had gone and led Raphael straight to her and their own downfall.

"Exactly. The O'Reillys. Don't be angry with them, for it was I who insisted they tell me."

"Why am I not surprised?" Lucy said darkly. "You have a way of insisting that wears a body right down."

Another smile curved his lips. "Years of practice," he said. "But even then the O'Reillys didn't actually say very much. Instead Mairead gave me a letter you'd written to them when you were in London. It explained a great deal."

"She gave you my letter?" Lucy said, her heart sinking even farther, right into the old bog itself. She remembered what she'd written far too clearly. It was no wonder that he was so well informed. "Oh."

"Oh, indeed." He looked down at her, two fine lines drawn between his brow. "Lucy, please believe me when I tell you that if I'd known about you, I never would have allowed Eunice to treat you so. You would have been out with your stepsisters, beautifully dressed, having a wonderful time."

"Over Eunice's dead body," Lucy said shortly. She raised her chin. "And who said I wanted fancy clothes or that I had any interest in London society?"

His frown deepened. "Then what were you doing at the Stanhope ball? And speaking of that, how and why were you there with my brother? And I'd appreciate the truth, not another one of your farfetched stories."

Lucy's mouth opened and then quickly snapped closed. She didn't have the first idea what to say, but she had better come up with something other than the truth, for she didn't want to get the duchess or Hugo into trouble when they'd only been trying to be kind to her.

"I met your brother in the park just as I met you," she said, thinking fast. "I pretended to be Miss Laura Walker, and he felt sorry for me and invited me to the ball. I accepted because I thought it would be interesting to see for myself how the other side lived—just for curiosity's sake, you understand."

Rafe rubbed the bridge of his nose. "Lucy, do you really take me for so much of a fool?"

"I'm sure you're a very intelligent man," she said, squeezing her fingers together.

"Then *why* are you forever trying to pull the wool over my eyes?" he said with exasperation. "It hasn't worked once yet, has it?"

She colored, seeing that she hadn't succeeded this time either. "I suppose not."

"Let me make this easy for you. I sense my mother's hand in this—she's a master schemer. Now that I think about it, there are all sorts of odd things she said and did that don't add up any other way." He slanted a searching gaze down at her. "She said she knew your father . . . yes, and I remember now—she once mentioned that she thought he had a daughter. I didn't pay any attention at the time. My mistake."

"You mean to say you make mistakes?" Lucy said dryly. "How very human of you."

"Isn't it though?" he replied with a wry smile. "But don't think you can distract me with insults. My mother came roaring home one day hell-bent on looking up someone's pedigree, and the next thing I knew she'd excused herself from the evening's activities, which is most unlike her. I assume she went directly to you. Would you care to fill in the rest?"

She shook her head, not saying a word.

"No, of course you wouldn't—that would be out of character, wouldn't it?" he said with black humor. "All right then, I'll do it for you: Having worked out how despicably Eunice had been treating you, my mother conceived a wild plan to present you at the ball, right under your stepmother's nose, and much more important, right under mine." He rested the side of his fist against his mouth, then gave a smothered laugh. "Yes. I think I see the whole thing now."

"You do?" Lucy said, amazed by his acuity. She watched him in fascination as he gazed off into the distance, his eyes narrowed in thought.

"Mmm," he said after a moment. "My mother then enlisted Hugo's help, and Hugo was thrilled to provide it—oh, let me tell you, he was beside himself with glee. He played his part to the hilt."

"He was very good, wasn't he?" Lucy said with a grin, seeing there was no use denying anything anymore.

"You should have seen him *after* you took off into the night. Outraged indignation over my behavior battled with righteous fury, and my mother stood there and fed the whole thing without the bat of an eye while I did my damndest to wring the truth out of him—to no avail, I might add."

Lucy had to struggle not to laugh. She could just imagine Raphael's frustration when his brother refused to tell him what he wanted to know. "Are you very angry with them?"

"Let me put it this way. They both got exactly what they wanted—Hugo succeeded in making me look like a blithering idiot, and my mother managed to head me in your direction without giving a thing away. She is the world's most indefatigable matchmaker."

"M-matchmaker?" Lucy stared at him. "What on earth do you mean? That's not what she had in mind at all!"

"You don't know my mother," he said mildly. "However, since she knows that I cannot bear her interfering in my life, she decided to send me on a wild goose chase instead, knowing that eventually it would bring me here to you."

Lucy peeped a hesitant look up at him. He didn't *look* angry that he'd been so thoroughly hoodwinked, but she'd learned that he was very good at disguising his feelings when he wanted to. "What are you going to do now?" she asked, nervously chewing on the end of her finger.

"I'm going to marry you. What else?"

"You can't marry me," she said, shaking her head adamantly.

"Why on earth not?" he asked, not looking the least bit perturbed. "It's the obvious solution, isn't it? I have to get you away from Eunice, and marrying you is the fastest and easiest way I can think of. Besides, I *want* to marry you."

"But that's not what I meant. I don't want to marry you," Lucy said frantically, her hands pressed against her flushed

cheeks. "I *can't* marry you." Oh, if only things were different . . .

"Why not?" he asked, regarding her curiously.

"Because you're—you're *English*," she cried. "I can't marry
an Englishman."

He stared at her as if she had lost her mind. "You cannot
be serious."

Lucy clenched her hands by her sides. Why did he always
make everything so difficult? "Yes, I'm serious. I think you're
very handsome, and you can even be nice at times, but
you're still English."

Raphael gazed down at her, a smile playing on the corners
of his mouth. "Would you marry me if I were a Chinaman?"

"No. And don't tease me. Even if you weren't English,
how could I marry someone whom I hardly know?" she said,
throwing another obstacle into his determined path. "We've
only ever spoken to each other four times before this."

"Three," he corrected. "Believe me, I've counted."

"Four," she repeated firmly. "We spoke the day after I saw
you here on the cliff, when you came to the house looking
for my stepmother."

Raphael grabbed her arms, his fingers crushing her flesh
as he glared down at her. "That was *you*? Of course it was
you—how bloody stupid of me not to have put it together
before this. You little witch!" He shook her, his eyes blazing
with anger. "You could have put me out of my misery then
and there! One word from you would have saved me anguished weeks of thinking you'd gone and leapt to your
death. *Why?* Why didn't you say something when you had
the chance?"

"If you hadn't been so busy being a condescending duke,
you would have seen the truth for yourself," she said, scowling at him.

"How? As I remember, your face was covered with black
soot, and I could barely make out two words of what you
were saying through the thick Irish brogue you put on! And

furthermore, you told me you couldn't read, and the girl I was looking for had been fluently spouting Byron at me the day before."

"I wasn't spouting it at you, I was talking to myself," she replied indignantly. "You were eavesdropping."

"I should thrash you, I really should," he said through clenched teeth. "Do you know how much trouble you would have saved us both if you'd only told me who you were then?"

"How could I? You didn't ask, and I wasn't about to volunteer the information, especially when I found out who you were. An English duke who happened to have the family name of Montagu didn't inspire me with confidence. I'd had enough misery heaped on me by your wicked cousin."

He released her abruptly. "Very well, I'll concede you that point, but you still could have told me your name in the park when I asked you point-blank. You must have known then that I intended your family no harm. Why did you lie?"

"You know why," she said in frustration, rubbing her sore arms. "You weren't supposed to know anything about me. Eunice threatened to do something awful if you ever laid eyes on me. I was already in enough trouble."

"She threatened you, did she?" His eyes narrowed. "Now we come to the crux of the matter. Just what did she threaten to do to you?"

"Not to *me*—she couldn't do much more than she already had. She said she would accuse the O'Reillys of sedition and that would be an end to them."

Raphael briefly squeezed his eyes shut. When he opened them again they held pure, raw rage.

Lucy shivered. She'd never seen anyone look so dangerous. "Now do you see why I couldn't say anything?" she asked, rather pleased with his savage reaction.

"Yes, I see," he said, his voice shaking with anger. "And something tells me that this wasn't the first time she'd made that threat to you."

"No. She'd been saying it for years to keep me in line. It worked very well."

"I've heard enough," he said, raking a shaking hand through his hair. "I'm going to murder the woman, I really am."

"No! You're not going to say anything at all. Don't you understand? She'll probably act on her promise anyway, and if you anger her any further it will only make things worse. The O'Reillys will already pay a high enough price."

"I don't think you've heard a word I've said," he snapped. "Eunice Kincaid will be silenced for once and for all. She won't lay a finger on the O'Reillys or on you ever again."

"How can you say that?" Lucy cried. "You might be a duke, but you're not God. Even you can't stop her from going to the authorities. The O'Reillys will lose everything!"

"I think not. The O'Reillys will be living at Kincaid under my protection. That was my business with them today."

Lucy couldn't believe she'd heard him correctly. She blinked. "Wh—what did you say?"

"You heard me. Seamus O'Reilly has agreed to take up his old lease, rent free for a year. Furthermore, he's going to be helping me run Kincaid, and he'll be handsomely paid for his trouble."

"But—but what about Paddy Delany?" Lucy said, her head spinning with confusion. "He'll never stand for it. He hates the O'Reillys."

"I fired him this morning," Raphael answered curtly. "He won't be back."

Lucy stared at him. Gone? Delany was gone? And the O'Reillys were safe? "Praise be to all the saints in heaven," she whispered, dizzy with relief. "It's over. It's finally over." Free. They were free.

"Yes, it's over, and partly thanks to you. You must have said something to my mother about Delany's true character, for she put the idea in my head that things were not as they should be at Kincaid. That's what brought me back so quickly." He released a heavy sigh. "It's all going to change, Lucy, I swear it to you. It will be the way it was in your father's time."

"Thank you," she said, her eyes filling with tears of gratitude, loving him with all her heart.

"Don't thank me. Marry me. Let me bring you back to Kincaid where you belong."

She shook her head with a shaky smile. "No. I am more obliged to you than I can say, but I cannot marry you. You're still English."

"Oh, for the love of God!" Raphael roared. He took two steps toward her and roughly pulled her into his arms, crushing her body to his, his mouth coming down hard on hers in a bruising kiss.

Molten fire leapt in her belly and she moaned low in her throat as his tongue drove deep into her mouth, demanding a response. Her hands slid up over the taut muscles of his chest, his heat branding her through her dress, and her body curved into his as she feverishly answered his demand with everything in her.

But somewhere in the very back of her mind, one last shred of sanity tugged at her through her dizzied senses. She couldn't—she couldn't surrender to him like this, or she would end up giving him the answer he wanted and sacrifice all of her principles.

Summoning up the tattered fragments of her will and strength, she twisted her face away, pushing at his chest with all her might.

Taken off guard, Raphael staggered backward. He quickly regained his balance, but not his composure, for he stood staring at her as if she'd just attacked him with a pole-ax. "What did you do that for?" he asked hoarsely, his breath coming hard and fast.

"Why do you think?" she cried, wishing her racing heart would behave itself. "Just because you're English and a duke doesn't mean you can take what you want when you please!

That's just how you British have been behaving toward us Irish for generations, plundering without a thought as to what we might want!"

"Don't try to tell me you didn't want that as much as I did," he said with a frustrated laugh. "You plundered right back."

"I did not—you caught me by surprise, that's all," she said, planting her hands on her hips and glaring at him.

"You're a proper hellion, Lucy Kincaid," he said, rubbing the back of his neck. "All right then. Tell me this—if you don't marry me, how in God's name do you think I'm going to get you away from Eunice and back to Kincaid? You do want to come home, don't you?"

"Of course I want to come home," she said, wanting that more than anything, almost as much as she wanted Raphael to kiss her again. She shoved that perilous thought away abruptly. "But I can't. Not if it means having to marry you."

"And how else do you think you're going to manage to come back to Kincaid?" he asked, one eyebrow rising in pointed question.

"I'm not. There is no other way, and I won't surrender my ethics just to come home. There are certain things I simply will not do, no matter how much I might want to."

"Such as?" he asked with an infuriatingly wicked grin.

"Don't you *dare* play the rogue with me now," she cried, understanding his meaning perfectly. "And it's no use trying to bully me by hanging the temptation of Kincaid over my head."

"Then what *do* you intend to do? Where else do you have to go? You can't possibly go back to Eunice."

"I—I know," she said softly, wondering the same question for the twentieth time. "Maybe the O'Reillys will take me in, now that they are going back to their farm. There's not much room, or even enough food for ten people, but if I help them work the land . . . No—that would still be too much to ask of them. I don't know," she said, kicking at a clod of earth. "I'll think of something."

"Actually," Raphael said slowly, "I think I might have an idea."

Lucy looked up at him in question. "An idea that doesn't have anything to do with marrying you?" she asked suspiciously.

"Nothing at all. Why don't you come and be housekeeper at Kincaid? The place is in an awful mess, and you did manage it at one time, after all. Who better than you?"

Who better indeed? Lucy thought, her heart suddenly racing with hope. She could still be at Kincaid, but her principles would stay intact. "I don't know," she said hesitantly. "People might talk."

"Talk about what?" he asked. "It makes perfect sense. I think it's a perfect solution, and there's nothing inappropriate about it. A large house needs a housekeeper, and who knows more than you about running the place? And furthermore, you can help Seamus O'Reilly with his book work, for he'll have a hard time managing Kincaid without some assistance."

"True," Lucy said, her expression growing thoughtful. "You do need a housekeeper and Seamus O'Reilly will definitely need help . . . and my father taught me all about running the estate." It did sound like a perfect solution, now that she'd thought about it for all of thirty seconds. But still . . .

"Look at it this way: I can also use your help, and my proposition gives you a roof over your head and wages in your pocket so that you can be independent. Speaking of which, do you have a wage in mind?"

"Oh—I suppose twenty-five pounds a year would be fair," she said, casually throwing out the outrageous sum. A wage—a real wage, to spend as she pleased.

"Twenty-five pounds? I'll give you eighteen and no more, and that's extremely generous of me."

"Done," Lucy said with surprise that he'd agreed so easily. That she'd agreed so easily. But eighteen pounds seemed like a fortune to her, and she *would* have her independence. "I do have to insist on a free hand with the running of the house," she added, just to be sure he thoroughly understood her terms.

"You can run the damned house any way you please. But I have to insist that you take your meals with me and sit with me in the evenings. We might not be able to share the full benefits of marriage, but I refuse to be denied your company."

Lucy didn't mind that stipulation at all. The thought of eating with Raphael and sitting with him in the study after dinner, sharing the news of the day, was a cozy one. It would *almost* be like being married, wouldn't it? "Agreed," she said.

She was thrilled with how matters were turning out—with a little luck not only was she finally going to be free of Eunice, but she also would have a good job in her very own childhood home, with Raphael for company. She felt as if all her dreams were about to come true. Or almost all of them . . . It was a pity about the kissing part, but she'd have to live without it.

"When do I start?" she asked, breathless with excitement.

"Today. And let's not waste another minute. Is there any reason that you need to go back to the house?"

Lucy blanched at the thought. "I do have some things to collect—not much, since I haven't many belongings, but there are some personal items I don't want to leave behind. But . . . but what about Eunice? She's bound to fly into a rage."

"Not to worry. I'll protect you from Eunice while you gather up your things. As I told you, I've already taken care of her. You are free to come with me."

Lucy slowly raised her face to his. "Really? Just like that?" she asked, her voice trembling.

"Just like that. Eunice will never trouble you again."

A tear slid down Lucy's cheek and then another. "I—I cannot quite believe it," she murmured thickly.

He took his thumb and traced it down the wet trail. "Believe it," he said. "Don't cry now, sweet girl. It is time to be happy, for this is all going to be behind you in another few minutes."

"I am happy," she said, rubbing her nose. "And I'm not crying. I never cry."

"Don't you? Then you must have something in your eye."

"Yes. It must be the chalk blowing off the cliff," she said, grateful that he hadn't pushed the point.

He held out his hand and she took it, his fingers wrapping around hers, so warm and solid. He would protect her. Of course he would protect her. Even if he *was* an Englishman.

But still, she stopped abruptly outside of the front door. "Raphael?" she asked tentatively.

"Yes?"

"Are you absolutely sure?"

"That Eunice has been felled? Yes. I am."

"That you want me at Kincaid," she replied in a small voice.

He caught her to him in a hard embrace, his hands smoothing over her hair. "Oh, yes. Yes, I am. Very sure."

She quickly pulled away from him. "And none of that either," she said firmly, even though she longed for his caresses with all her heart. "I am your housekeeper, nothing more."

Raphael grinned down at her. "You're the most enchanting housekeeper I've ever seen. But I'll do my best to behave myself."

"Is that a promise?" she asked solemnly.

"That I'll do my best? Yes," he said, his eyes dancing with laughter.

"Then I am ready," she said, straightening her back and raising her chin. "Take me inside. And then take me home."

17

In the end it was nothing, considering all of the possible scenarios Lucy had imagined. Raphael took her into the house and straight up the stairs, ignoring Eunice, who said not a word.

He sat in her small bedroom, protecting her as he'd promised as she gathered her belongings together.

His gaze flickered slightly as she smoothed out the ball dress in the bottom of her case, but he said nothing, quietly watching as she laid out the rest of her meager belongings and finally shut her little case.

She cast one last look around the room where she'd lived for the last six years, six long years of listening to Eunice's abuse, of having her will, her very spirit, crushed by the lash of her stepmother's tongue and the back of her hand. Six long years of interminable servitude to a woman she hated.

But maybe God had shown her some mercy at last.

She stole a glimpse over at Raphael's profile and her breath caught in her throat. He was so handsome, his body so strong and powerful even as he sat there on her narrow bed, gazing out the tiny window. And he was kind too. But most of all she loved him.

Even if he was an Englishman.

Eunice stood as they came down the stairs, her eyes conveying nothing, her frozen posture saying everything. Lucy looked directly at her, Raphael's hand giving her strength where it rested around her back, his gentle pressure against her waist reminding her that she was safe with him.

"Good-bye, Aunt. Please tell Fiona and Amaryllis that they are welcome to visit whenever they please." *But not you. Never you.*

"I wish you a happy life," Eunice returned, not meeting her eyes, her cold fury tangible to Lucy, its tentacles threatening to reach out and ensnare her once again. Lucy's heart began to pound in earnest, for she could already feel Eunice wrenching her from Raphael's safe hold, boxing her ears, and sending her first to the ground and then back to the kitchen.

Raphael must have sensed her panic, for he tightened his grip on her waist. "The hour grows late," he said. "It is time to go, sweetheart."

She looked blindly up at him. "Yes," she choked. "Please."

He paused only for a moment. "You will, of course, remember everything we discussed, Lady Kincaid? I would be so disappointed should you forget, and I imagine you would be as well. And there is one last thing: If you think to deliver any kind of retribution against the O'Reilly family, think again, for I have taken them under my protection." His gaze drilled into hers. "Do not forget my position; my word is far more powerful than yours. You will be left not only penniless but without a shred of reputation, what little of it you have left."

"Oh, begone with you both!" she cried. "I will keep my end of this pitiful bargain, and I will also be deliriously happy never to see either of your faces again!"

"I believe we both feel the same," Raphael said, quickly ushering Lucy out the door.

"All right?" he asked, carefully examining her face once they were out in the front garden, the door shut safely behind Eunice's rage.

Lucy, more shaken than she cared to admit, tried to smile and failed miserably.

"Never mind," he said gently, untying his horse. It shook its head and whinnied softly in welcome. "Pegasus, meet Lucy," Rafe said, leading the horse over and stroking his white muzzle as Lucy looked on numbly. "You are going to carry us both back to Kincaid, and I ask you to be fleet-footed. Sprout wings if you can, for we both need to be rid of this loathsome place as quickly as possible."

He grasped Lucy's waist and lifted her up onto the front of the saddle in one easy motion, springing up behind her, placing her case in her hands.

"Ready?" he murmured against her hair.

"I've never been more ready for anything," she replied, taking one last long look at the stark, ugly house that represented her captivity. She turned her head away, never so glad to see the last of anything in her life.

And turned her face to the future as Raphael kicked his horse into a canter, sweeping her away, one arm holding her fast around her waist, his strong chest supporting her back.

A half hour later, the arched stone entrance way of Kincaid came into view, the wrought-iron gates standing open, the fields and pastures and woodlands of the demesnes visible beyond. Lucy drew in a sharp breath. She hadn't laid eyes on her home for so long—it seemed like a lifetime, and yet at the same time it seemed like only moments ago, as if the intervening years of banishment had never been.

Raphael slowed Pegasus to a walk and turned through the arch, passing the empty gatehouse. Lucy looked around her, drinking in every last tree, every last flower, every last blade of grass. It was all so beautiful, so perfectly wonderful.

And yet there was a sad air of shabbiness that permeated everything. She'd heard from the O'Reillys how matters stood, but it was still a shock to see the depressing truth with her own eyes.

But the biggest shock of all was the sight of Kincaid Court

itself. Her family house, her beautiful family house, had fallen into semiruin. As Raphael pulled Pegasus to a stop, her gaze slowly traveled over the gray three-story structure with its two square wings that stretched out on either side. With dismay she took in the broken windows, the overgrown grass, the untrimmed ivy that crept in tangled disorder over the entire stone facade.

She turned and stared in wide-eyed despair over her shoulder at Raphael. "How—how could things have come to this?" she whispered raggedly.

"I know," he murmured, drawing her back against his chest, his arm holding her tight as if he could buffer her shock with his body. "What my cousin and Delany did between them is a crime." He brushed her cold cheek with his warm lips. "But as I said, I'm going to see to it that everything returns to the way it once was."

She numbly shook her head, gazing back at the house. "How? It will take a fortune to put it to rights."

"Lucy, you forget that I am a duke," he said, his chest rumbling with laughter. "That may not be much in your eyes, but it is useful when it comes to spending money."

"I hope you are a rich duke, because you're going to be spending a lot of it," she said wryly.

"A very rich duke," he replied. "And a hungry one as well. Come, let's go inside and get you settled. It will be dark soon and only a few rooms are furnished with candles."

He dismounted, and taking her case, he lifted her down, looping the reins over Pegasus's neck and leaving him to graze.

Lucy walked through the doorway, glancing briefly up at the Kincaid coat of arms etched high above in the arch of stonework. She could barely make it out through the overgrown ivy. But it was still there, and the sight gave her courage. At least Thomas Montagu hadn't destroyed that along with everything else he'd laid his filthy hands on.

Her eyes slowly adjusted to the dim light that permeated

the great hall through the dirty windows and her gaze swept around, looking for familiar pieces of furniture, the family portraits that had lined the walls all the way around and up the great wood staircase.

The furniture was still in place, but many of the portraits were gone—or at least the most recent ones. Apparently Thomas Montagu hadn't wanted any reminders of the previous occupants.

Raphael came up beside her and wrapped his free arm over her shoulder, drawing her close against his side. "I can imagine what you must be thinking," he said quietly. "But nevertheless, welcome home, Lucy Kincaid."

She looked up at him with a bleak smile. "It's a far better home than the one I've just come from," she replied, taking comfort from his closeness.

"That's my girl," he said, giving her a squeeze. "Now if you can bear the mess upstairs, let's go and find you a bedroom."

"Where are you sleeping?" Lucy asked nervously, thinking that wherever it was, she had better be as far away as she could get.

"In the master bedroom at the top of the stairs." He gave her a searching look, his eyes flashing with something dark and dangerous. "Why? Do you wish to share it with me, Egeria?" he asked very softly, his fingers slowly and deliberately caressing the nape of her neck.

Lucy colored furiously and she abruptly pulled away from his seductive touch. "Of course not," she said, heated images of herself lying entwined in Raphael's arms racing unbidden through her mind, causing her pulse to jerk wildly at the side of her throat.

"Really," he said, a wicked smile tugging at the corners of his mouth. "Why don't I believe you?"

"Don't start playing games with me, Raphael Montagu," she snapped. "Our arrangement is perfectly clear."

"Oh, yes," he said, hell dancing in his eyes. "Perfectly. I

am at your service, Miss Kincaid, and apparently you are at mine."

"I am not *at* your service, I am *in* your service. There is a large distinction between the two," she said tightly.

"Is there?" he replied, all innocence. "Perhaps you would care to explain it to me." He cocked his head to one side in expectation.

"You are impossible!" she cried. "Must you always twist my words around to suit yourself?"

"My dear Lucy, if anyone is a master at twisting words around, it is you. Come along before I pick you up and haul you upstairs over my shoulder."

Lucy didn't waste another minute. She ran up the stairs as fast as she could, deciding that her old room would do very nicely, being on the far end of the corridor and across the hall.

Her hand paused on the cool doorknob and then, taking a deep breath to steady herself against a flood of memories, she turned it and pushed open the door.

A squeal of shock escaped from her throat. She couldn't be in the right room—she *couldn't* be.

Her mouth hanging open, she slowly looked around her, at the scarlet velvet curtains at the window, the equally scarlet hangings on the bed, the plush scarlet upholstery on the chairs.

Where was the lovely blue silk that had been there before? And what were those things tied to the bedposts—they looked like cords, but for what function? And what were all those strange objects on her bedside table? She couldn't think what purpose they might serve either.

Raphael came in behind her. "What the devil . . ." he said in a suffocated voice.

"My—my room," she stammered. "What has happened to it?"

"*Your* room? My, what an interesting little girl you were."

Lucy ignored him, marching over to the bedside table and

picking up a picture book that lay there. At least it appeared to be a picture book, but she couldn't exactly work out what the pictures were of. She leafed through the first few pages. They seemed to be figures of people in very strange positions—

"Oh, no you don't," he said, snatching the book out of her hand and snapping it shut.

"But what is it?" she demanded. "I've never seen anything quite like it."

"I am relieved to hear it," he said, shoving the book under the pillow.

"What are these things?" she said, picking up an odd-shaped piece of glass that looked something like an elongated hourglass.

Raphael took that away from her too and thumped it down on the table, next to a string of wooden balls.

When she looked at him in question, she saw that he'd turned a deep red, matching the bed hangings nicely. He didn't look at all like his composed ducal self, she thought in bewilderment, her gaze traveling back to the hourglass.

"I think we had better find you another room," he said abruptly, taking her forcibly by the shoulders as she curiously fingered one of the cords wrapped around the bedpost. "Now," he said, turning her smartly around.

"Wait," she protested, craning her head over her shoulder. "I want to understand what all this is."

"No," he said. "No waiting, no arguments, and certainly no understanding. If I'd bothered to look in here before, I would have locked the door." He pushed her out of the room and slammed the door behind them, as if he were shutting out the devil himself.

A little smile of dawning comprehension crept across her face. "Oh . . ." she said, thoroughly enjoying his discomfiture. "I see. This is where Thomas entertained his harlots."

Raphael choked violently. "Lucy—"

"Do you think I do not know about harlots? You forget

that I haven't been a well-sheltered girl," she said, teasing him unmercifully. "The servants in London talked about harlots all the time when they thought I wasn't listening. Lord Everleigh keeps a stable of them in his—"

"Enough!" he roared, practically dragging her down the hallway. "Here," he said, shoving another door open. "You will sleep in here where I can keep an eye on you."

Lucy blanched. It was the room next to his own—her mother's room, and one that thankfully her father had not allowed Eunice to use, consigning her to the bedroom on the other side against Eunice's strong protestations.

This room had a connecting door. "I—I can't," she stammered. "Stay in here, I mean."

"Why in God's name not?" he said, pushing both hands through his hair, still looking thoroughly shaken.

She pointed at the door between this room and his. "Because of that," she said.

He followed the direction of her finger. "Don't be a bloody idiot," he said shortly, looking back at her. "If I wanted to ravish you in the middle of the night, I could just as easily use the outside door. Unpack your belongings, and not another word out of you." He strode over to the long windows and pulled the curtains back, letting a golden stream of evening light in.

Lucy grinned impishly. "You'll tell me, you know. You can't keep me in the dark forever."

"Tell you what?" he said, throwing open a window, looking as if he'd like to toss her right out of it.

"What all those—those *things* were."

Raphael glared at her menacingly. "I do not wish to hear you mention the subject again. If you do, I will take your slender neck between my hands and wring it until you turn blue."

"You won't," she said, laughing and dancing away from him as he stalked across the room toward her. "You've worked too hard to find me. Oh, *Raphael*, it is grand to be home."

He stopped dead in his tracks, his expression suddenly changing to one she couldn't read at all. "That's good," he said. "Get settled, Lucy. I'm going to put Pegasus in the stables. I will see you downstairs when you are done."

He turned on his heel and left without another word, not even bothering to close the door behind him.

Raphael dismissed the groom for the evening, wanting to see to Pegasus himself. He needed something to do to take his mind off Lucy. Dear heaven, but she was a handful, he thought, rubbing the horse down vigorously, the work giving him an outlet for his restless energy. He had a sinking feeling that she wasn't going to be as easy to manage as he'd hoped.

Nor was his own physical response to her, which seemed to be entirely out of his control every time he was near her.

He'd just about expired when he'd seen the room Thomas had done up for his decadent idea of fun and games, but when Lucy had started thumbing through the pillow book, frowning as she tried to make out the erotic pictures, he'd been utterly undone. And when she'd picked up the dildo, innocently examining it as if were some curio . . . he should be shot for the images that had flashed through his mind.

Rafe groaned and rested his forehead against the gelding's neck. He'd never in his life been ruled by anything but his head—certainly not his loins. He'd had mistresses aplenty, kept discreetly at a distance, women who knew how to enjoy the pleasures of the flesh and had the good sense not to expect anything more from him. But Lucy was a different matter entirely.

Lucy was all tangled up in his heart.

She had done nothing but upset his well-ordered life from the first moment he'd laid eyes on her. She was completely unlike any woman he'd met before, a contradictory mixture of innocence and wisdom, of artlessness and passion, of stubbornness and surrender, equally as sweet as she could be contentious. She was as capable of eloquently quoting ethereal poetry into the wind as she was of spouting off about harlots with nary a blush.

And yet she had blushed violently when he'd made mention of her sharing his bed. And hadn't that been a satisfying moment, the feel of her nape so soft and fragile under his fingers, her cinnamon-colored eyes with that tantalizing burst of yellow starlight gazing up into his in wide alarm. And beneath the alarm, a desire as obvious to him as his own.

He raised his head and gave Pegasus a sound pat. "It won't be long," he murmured, walking over to the feed bin and scooping out an extra measure of oats. "Not long at all before Kincaid has a mistress and I have wife."

Pegasus whinnied softly, and Rafe laughed. "I'm so glad *someone* agrees."

He walked back to the house feeling more composed and went upstairs to wash and change for dinner. When Adams had finished with him, Rafe pressed his ear against the connecting door, listening for signs of Lucy moving about on the other side. But there was only silence.

He went downstairs and poked his head into the drawing room, and then the library. Nothing.

He finally found her in the kitchen, chatting up a storm with the maid Nancy as if they were old friends.

She looked up with a smile from the pan they were both bent over. "Nancy and I are just putting the final touches on dinner," she said. "We're having sauteed trout, followed by a haunch of venison, and all sorts of lovely garden vegetables. Oh, Raphael, you have no idea how wonderful it is to have proper food to cook!"

Raphael swallowed. So far the fare Nancy had served up had been overcooked and tasteless, and it was all he could do to force the muck down his throat. He doubted if Lucy had any more of a clue how to cook a decent meal than Nancy had, but he sincerely prayed there might be some slight improvement. He hadn't had a decent meal yet in Ireland, and his palate was suffering along with his stomach.

He smiled bravely at her. "It sounds delicious," he said, visions of dry trout and charred venison dancing before his eyes.

"It will be. Go and sit down at the table and pour the wine. I found a nice claret in the cellar."

Rafe obediently did as he was told, taking a sip of the wine, which at least slid down smoothly. Only minutes later Lucy came in, pulling off her apron. "There," she said, lighting the candles. "Doesn't the table look nice?"

He hadn't noticed until that moment, accustomed to well-laid tables, not that he'd seen one of those in Ireland either, now that he thought about it. She'd put out a snowy linen tablecloth and set the whole with shining silver and china. "Very nice," he said appreciatively.

"It took forever to get the tarnish off the silver—it obviously hasn't been used in ages," she said, taking her place next to him and spreading her napkin onto her lap. "Now don't growl at Nancy when she comes out, Raphael. She hasn't had any proper training for serving at table, but I'll take of care of that, starting tomorrow."

"I don't growl," Rafe said indignantly. "I politely request. It's not my fault that she slops food all over the table."

"No, but one person's polite request is another person's growl. You can't help being English, but you might try a friendly manner. Nancy is absolutely terrified of you, which doesn't help her to keep a steady hand."

"I don't see what she has to be terrified of," he protested. "I have made an effort to be perfectly pleasant despite her mistakes."

"You're a duke," Lucy pointed out, as if he were unaware of that salient point.

"I realize that I'm a duke," Rafe said, suppressing an irritated sigh. "It's hardly something I'm likely to forget, but you needn't remind me of my position every five minutes. It's not as if I carry a flag with my crest emblazoned on it everywhere I go."

"No, of course not, but you do have a manner about you that announces your rank for you, and some people find it intimidating."

Rafe frowned. "Are you rebuking me, Miss Lucy Kincaid?"

"Oh, dear, you really must be hungry," she said, grinning at him. "Never mind, the trout will be out in just a moment."

That's what Rafe was afraid of, but he kept his mouth shut. Moments later Nancy came barreling in through the door and plopped the platter on the sideboard. "Here you go, Miss Lucy," she announced. "I did it just like you said."

Lucy went over to the sideboard, showing Nancy how to neatly debone the fish. "Here, like this, just down the middle," she said, adding something unfathomable in Gaelic with a merry laugh.

Rafe watched her with fascination, vaguely aware that there was something different about this Lucy.

She was . . . happy, he realized with a little jolt. He'd never seen her so light-hearted, so much in command. And there was something else, that sense of freedom he'd sensed in her when he'd first seen her walking on the cliff, as if she belonged to the land and it to her.

That was it. Lucy was finally back where she belonged, and it showed in every movement, every word, every gesture.

He leaned his chin on his fist, wishing with all his heart that it was he who had put the light back in her eyes, but he knew perfectly well it was Kincaid that filled her heart.

No wonder she hadn't given two figs about marrying him. What she'd wanted was her home—not him at all. He had merely been a means to an end, a convenient person to remove her from her stepmother's tyranny.

Rafe muttered a curse under his breath. How was he ever going to convince her to marry him if all he was to her was window-dressing? She didn't want to be a duchess. Why should she, when she had everything she wanted right here? He was nothing more than a despicable Englishman, an unwelcome intruder in her country. In her home.

He scowled, his temper growing filthier by the moment as he listened to her gaily conversing with Nancy, not paying him the least attention. She bent over to take something out of the sideboard, her ripe bottom neatly outlined as her dress pulled tight.

Rafe squeezed his eyes shut, digging his fingers into his forehead as he broke into a cold sweat. Oh, *God.* She had to marry him. She just had to. He hadn't been in the same house with her for more than two hours and he was already going out of his mind with need.

Lucy straightened and turned. "We're ready—Raphael? What is wrong? Does your head ache?"

He glanced up. "Not my head," he muttered.

"What then? You look very uncomfortable," she said, sliding a plate in front of him.

"My—my back," he lied. "It must be sore from sitting so far back on the saddle." *With you pressed directly against my loins, thank you very much,* he added privately.

"Oh . . . I'm sorry. Maybe I can rub it for you after dinner."

Rafe averted his gaze. She could rub it all right, but it wasn't his back he had in mind. "Mmm," he said indistinctly.

"Do eat your fish before it grows cold," Lucy said, sitting down again, a slight frown of concern creasing her forehead.

Raphael picked up his knife and fork and began to cut his trout without paying much attention. But the first taste jerked him back to his faculties. It was—it was delicious.

He looked down at the trout then up at Lucy in disbelief.

"How did you *do* this? I haven't tasted anything so wonderful in—well, in some time," he finished tactfully.

"Just a little butter, with a touch of wine and lemon to deglaze the pan at the end, and a final sprinkle of parsley," she said, her eyes shining with pleasure. "Do you like it, then?"

"Yes. It's absolutely delectable, moist and fragrant, and the juices are sweet and delicate." *Lord help me,* he groaned to himself. *Get a grip on yourself, man. You're only eating a piece of fish.*

"I'm so glad it pleases you. Wait until you taste the next course."

Raphael couldn't bring himself to think about the next course. He concentrated on finishing his fish, thinking of unobjectionable words like scales and gills.

But when the venison came, rich and flavorful, its flesh tender and succulent, he was at a complete loss to describe it to Lucy without falling completely to pieces. "Very good," he said, smiling feebly at her.

"I hope you like your meat undercooked. I don't yet know your tastes, although I'll do my best to learn quickly what you enjoy. You must be sure to tell me your preferences."

Rafe's eyes teared up. He had a strong desire to burst into wild hysterics. "Yes," he choked. "Yes, I'll be sure to do that." He wiped his eyes with his napkin and took a very large swallow of wine, hoping maybe that would dull his screaming senses.

"There is an apple tart to come," Lucy said, regarding him with bafflement. "Raphael, what *is* the matter with you?"

"The matter with me? Nothing. Why would you think anything was wrong?" he asked, desperately trying to get a hold of himself.

"Because you're behaving in a very peculiar fashion."

"Am I?" Raphael drew in a deep, steadying breath. "Lucy, would you mind if I asked you a personal question?"

"I don't think so," she said, touching her bottom lip with

her finger, unnerving him all over again. "I owe you some answers after everything you've done for me."

"Do you hate me?" he asked, watching her intently for her reaction, trying to gauge just how hopeless his position was.

"*Hate* you? Raphael, why on earth would you ask such a thing?" She slowly lowered her knife and fork to her plate, a perplexed expression on her face.

"Because you said earlier that you wouldn't marry me. You said it was because I am English. Does that really trouble you so much?"

"Oh . . ." Lucy said, dropping her gaze to her hands. "Oh," she said again, faintly coloring. "As I said, you can't help being English, but—it's just not a good idea for Irish people to marry British people, that's all."

"Why the hell not?" he roared, losing all semblance of control. "I love you, Lucy—isn't that bloody well good enough for you?"

Lucy stared at him, her face paling.

"I'm sorry," he said more quietly, seeing that he'd upset her badly. "It's just that I don't understand."

Lucy bit her lip. "I know. But you're not in my position, are you?"

"And what position is that?" he said, pushing his plate away, his appetite gone. "Do you mean that you see yourself as housekeeper to me, a blasted duke? Or do you mean that you're a stiff-necked Irish girl who hates the British on principle?"

"I mean that—oh, I don't know what I mean," she cried. "Why can't you just be content to leave things as they are?"

"Because I do love you," he replied, draining his glass. "What am I supposed to do about that? Forget it? Pretend that I feel nothing for you at all?"

"N-no," she stammered, tears filling her eyes. "I don't know what you're supposed to do. But you can't just go falling in love with people you happen to see on the edge of a cliff, even if you do think they've gone and jumped off it. It's not logical."

Rafe looked sideways at her, playing with the stem of his glass. "I never said it was logical. I only said it was true."

Lucy wrapped her arms around herself. "You still can't go falling in love with people you don't know anything about."

"Why not? It's done. It's not going to change, and in any case, I know everything about you I need to know. For the love of God, Lucy, stop being so damned logical and allow yourself a little feeling."

"Oh," she said, coloring angrily. "You think I have no feelings, do you? You think that I haven't thought about you for every minute of every day, that I haven't dreamed about you too, and for months on end? Let me tell you something, Mr. Duke," she said, poking a finger in his direction. "I have, but dreams are just that. Dreams. They have nothing to do with the realities of life, and you seem to be forgetting that, lost in some fantasy of ideal love you've conceived. This is not a fairy tale where you can come riding in and sweep me off my feet to some fine castle."

Rafe gazed at her speculatively. "Really. I thought that's exactly what I'd done."

"Precisely!" she said. "That's what *you* thought. You might be in a position to command as you please, but you cannot command *me,* regardless of what you think." She stood, pushing her chair back so hard that it tipped over backward. "I might not be a duke like your high-and-mighty self, but I have a mind of my own," she said, planting her hands on the table and leaning over them until her nose was in his face. "I've been pushed around for nine years, told what to do and how to do it, and I've had enough of it! And if you don't like my attitude, then I'll go and get a job in a shop."

Raphael grinned, his heart infinitely lighter for her impassioned speech, which had told him worlds about how she felt. And that she had a hot temper as well. "No need for that," he said, pouring himself a second glass of wine. "It suits me to have you here."

"And it suits me to look after your house," she said, straightening. "But that's all I'll do, your worship. If you so badly want to find someone to marry, go and—go and marry Fiona."

Rafe burst into laughter. "Now, there would be a dream made in heaven. Stop being so damned stubborn, sweetheart, and admit you love me as much as I love you. Why don't you just marry me and put us both out of our misery?"

Lucy glared at him, her small bosom heaving with emotion. "Don't call me sweetheart," she said, clenching her fists by her sides. "You can drink your wine and eat your apple tart without the benefit of my company." Storming to the dining room door, she suddenly stopped and turned. "And I won't marry you."

"Why not?" he asked, trying to keep a straight face. Lucy in an impassioned rage was a sight to behold.

"Because you are *still* an Englishman!"

She stalked out and Rafe watched her until she vanished from sight.

"And I still love you," he murmured, leaning back in his chair.

He ate his apple tart in thoughtful silence, and as soon as he was done, he rose and went into the library to pen a detailed letter of instruction to his mother.

18

$\mathcal{L}$ucy stood at the window of her bedroom, brushing her hair as she watched night draw down. Night at Kincaid. She never thought she'd see it again, the sky streaked with fingers of red and purple, the River Moy gleaming from across the distant fields.

The only thing that marred her pleasure was the argument she'd had with Raphael. But she couldn't tell him the truth—that she loved him in return. That would only make him more persistent in his foolish quest to marry her.

She didn't really see why he wanted to marry her anyway—she'd make a terrible duchess. What would he say to his friends? *This is my wife Lucy, who hates the lot of you on principle.* Oh, that would go down very nicely.

A light tap came at her door and she turned, pulling her shawl more closely around her nightdress. "Who is it?" she called, assuming Nancy had come up to speak to her about something.

"It's Raphael. May I come in?"

Lucy's hand crept to her throat and she swallowed hard, wondering what he wanted. "Yes," she said hesitantly, wondering if that was such a good idea. Raphael and bedrooms didn't mix well.

He opened the door, but instead of entering, he leaned against the door frame, his arms folded across his chest. He'd removed his coat and neckcloth and opened his shirt at the collar. He looked thoroughly male—and unbearably handsome.

"I don't think you should be here," she said, heat rushing to her cheeks.

"I know I shouldn't be here. I probably shouldn't be anywhere near you." His gaze raked her up and down, his expression impenetrable.

"You shouldn't? Why not?" she asked nervously. "Are you very angry with me?"

"No. Actually, I wanted to apologize to you for my bad mood at dinner. You didn't deserve the sharp edge of my temper."

"Oh," she said, her lips parting in surprise. "Actually, I was going to apologize to you. I don't usually go off like that, but I think I must be tired. It's been a long day."

"It has indeed," he agreed. "And you've been through a great deal. I shouldn't have pushed you to say things you weren't prepared to say."

"Thank you," she said softly. Her fingers tightened on the edge of her shawl. "Why *were* you in such a bad mood? Have you—have you changed your mind about wanting me here as your housekeeper?"

Raphael sighed. "No, Lucy. I am happy to have you here."

"What then? Was the meal not to your liking? You said you enjoyed it, but perhaps you were just being polite."

A half smile tugged at his mouth. "The meal was wonderful. You have no idea how much I enjoyed it. It's only that . . ." He raked both hands through his hair, looking acutely uncomfortable.

"It's only what?" she said, confused. "Please, don't keep me in suspense. You're usually much more articulate."

"It's not easy being articulate when I'm standing in your bedroom and you're wearing nothing more than a nightdress," he replied dryly, running a finger over the side of his mouth.

She blushed hotly. "Oh. I'm sorry. I was about to go to bed."

"You needn't be sorry, although I can't say that I think very much of the little you are wearing. Don't you have anything nicer?"

Lucy looked down at herself, embarrassed. She'd darned the coarse cotton shift so many times that it was one big patch. "No," she said quietly, her gaze fixed on the floor. "I'm sorry I don't meet your ducal standards, your grace, but this is all I possess in the way of nightwear."

Raphael straightened abruptly, then walked directly over to her and lifted her chin with his finger, forcing her to meet his eyes. "It was an observation, not a criticism, Lucy. There's no need to be so prickly."

"And what would you have me wear? Nothing at all?"

He laughed softly. "I don't think I should answer that. Actually, if you'll wait a moment, I have an idea." He strode across the room to the connecting door and disappeared through it.

Lucy, not at all sure what he had in mind, put her hairbrush down and padded curiously across the room on bare feet, peeking through the open door, only to see him rifling around in a drawer. She chewed on her lip, wondering if he kept a supply of ladies' nightdresses on hand for those spontaneous occasions when they might come in handy. She found she didn't like the idea at all.

He pulled something out and came back to her, handing her a folded piece of fine white linen. "It's one of my shirts," he said in explanation.

Lucy stared down at it. He wanted her to wear his *shirt*?

"You'll find it far more comfortable than that scratchy-looking thing you're wearing. Go on, put it on."

"Now?" she said, unnerved.

"Now. I don't trust you not to toss it out the window the minute I'm gone," he answered with amusement. "I'll turn my back. You have to the count of ten, and you had better be wearing it by then or I won't answer for the consequences."

Lucy didn't waste a second. She dropped her shawl, pulled her nightdress off, and lowered the soft folds over her head. The shirt fell around her, well below her knees. The fabric was lovely next to her skin, so silky and delicate. Not a single scratch to be felt. "I'm done," she said, smoothing her hands over the linen.

He turned around again and gave her a long, appraising look. "Much, much better," he said thickly, his gaze lingering on her breasts. "In fact, I'd say absolutely lovely."

Lucy gasped and looked down in horror. The material was practically transparent, the dusky pink of her nipples showing right through it. She quickly bent down and grabbed up her shawl, wrapping herself tightly in it.

Raphael grinned. " 'Kindled he was, and blasted, for to be thus, and enamored, were in him the same,' " he quoted. "Ah, Egeria, you do not make it easy on a man."

"I don't—I didn't mean to . . . oh, you are impossible!" she cried, thoroughly flustered.

He laughed. "Only human. Here, hold out your hand and let me roll up the sleeve."

Lucy cautiously poked one hand out, the other keeping a fast grip on her shawl. He cuffed the linen at her wrist, and when she grabbed hold of her shawl with that hand, he did the same to the other. "Thank you," she said, regarding him warily.

"My pleasure. If you're not too tired, would you mind if I sit down?" he said, nodding toward two armchairs set side by side in front of the gently blazing fireplace. "You didn't keep your agreement to sit with me after dinner, and I haven't said all of what I wanted to say."

"Please. It is your house, after all," she said curtly, wondering what was coming now. Was there no escaping him?

"Perhaps, but it is your room," he said, taking a seat. He stretched his long legs out toward the fire, crossing one ankle over the other. "Of course, if you married me, it would be your house too."

"Raphael," she said on a warning note. "I have *told* you . . ." She sat down, curling her bare legs up under her catlike to keep them warm.

"I know what you told me. I just thought I'd remind you of the practicalities, since you're such a practical girl." He tapped his finger against his mouth. "Although I wonder how practical you really are at heart," he said, picking up the book that lay on the table between them and examining the title. "*Childe Harolde's Pilgrimage*. My, what a surprise."

"Just because I enjoy poetry doesn't mean that I don't have a firm grip on reality," she said, shooting him a daggered look.

"Most people who enjoy poetry do not commit large portions of cantos to memory, especially cantos that address the quest for ideal love. Byron writes so stirringly about life being ruled by blind fate, does he not?"

"He also writes about being faithful to one's essential character," she countered.

"And about how, at some point in life, it is possible to begin again. I have to agree with him."

Lucy spotted an opening and leapt. "And do you also agree with the strong stand he takes against British imperialism? He states very clearly that England's repression of other countries—like Ireland, for example—goes directly against the traditional ideals of freedom and liberty which supposedly form the fabric of your society."

Raphael grinned. "Touché. So, my clever girl, where did you get such a fine education? There are some who might call you—God forbid—a blue-stocking."

"My father taught me," Lucy said proudly. "He, like Lord Byron, believed in man's right to individuality, and he considered a good education a cornerstone in that pursuit."

"He did a fine job," Raphael said quietly. "You must miss him, Lucy. You were—what? Fourteen when he died?"

The fire crackled and hissed in the grate, the flickering flames highlighting the strong bones of Raphael's face and casting shadows deep into the room. "Yes," Lucy said, a sharp knife of pain stabbing at her heart. "I was fourteen. And I miss him very much."

"You loved him, then?"

She frowned. "Of course I loved him. He was a wonderful man, kind and gentle and good."

"And it was he who instilled these ideas about the monstrous British in your head?" Raphael asked, gazing into the fire, his expression perfectly neutral.

"He loved his country," Lucy said carefully, looking for the trick, for this line of questioning was surely leading to some point. She'd never known Raphael to ask an idle question. "And he taught me to love the concept of freedom."

"I can see that freedom means a great deal to you, and so it should," he said, turning his head to regard her steadily. "But you are free now. You may come and go as you please, do as you wish."

"Yes," she said, "and I thank you for that. Before today, freedom was only a distant memory."

"You thank me, and yet you still despise me for the circumstances of my birth, which I had no control over."

Lucy saw the trap too late. Bishop to king's pawn. "I do not despise you," she said, trying to recoup her position. "All I have said is that I cannot marry you *because* of the circumstances of your birth. My father married an Englishwoman, and look how badly *that* turned out."

He smiled bitterly, looking back at the fire. "I'm hardly surprised, although I don't really see what Eunice's unfortunate temperament has to do with us."

"It's not just her temperament," Lucy retorted hotly. "It's the English blood that runs in her veins that makes her loathe and demean the Irish."

"And so you naturally assume that since the same English blood runs in my veins, I must feel as she does." He pinched the bridge of his nose between his fingers. "Obviously my being an English duke doesn't help matters in your mind, not that I asked for that, either."

"Oh, *Raphael*," she cried in frustration, "don't you see? It's not what you asked for or didn't ask for. You have the hand you were dealt, just as I do. But those two hands were dealt from two entirely different chessboards—I mean decks. We can't change the facts to suit ourselves."

"I don't see why we need to change anything except your attitude," he said, leaning his head back against the chair and turning it sideways to gaze at her, an odd, intent expression in his eyes. "I can no more help my birthright than I can the way I feel about you." The corner of his mouth twitched. "I wish to God I could—maybe I wouldn't be in so much physical pain."

"Oh," Lucy said guiltily. She'd forgotten all about that. "I'm sorry—your poor back."

"My back?" he said, looking puzzled. "There's not a damned thing wrong with my—oh, yes," he said with a wry smile. "Well, I lied. Lucy, are you so innocent that you don't know anything about a man's anatomy?"

She colored furiously. "Of course I do. That is, I've changed little boys' nappies before . . ." She trailed off uncertainly, not happy with the way that had come out.

Raphael shook his head with a snort of laughter. "That was decidedly not what I was referring to. Little boys aren't afflicted with this particular problem."

Lucy touched a finger to her lower lip. "I don't understand you," she said uneasily. "What else is there to know?"

Raphael covered his eyes with one hand. "Oh, merciful God in heaven," he mumbled. He rubbed his hand down over his face, then loosely dropped it onto the arm of the chair, his fingers curling into his palm and then relaxing. "Your father neglected some of the finer aspects of your education, but I'm hardly surprised. This is the sort of explanation you need a mother for."

A mischievous smile flashed across Lucy's face as she finally comprehended his meaning. She'd felt the hard evidence for herself that very afternoon, and she shivered in memory. "Oh, you mean *that*," she said, seizing on a way to get back at him. "I had no idea it was painful, though. *I'd* always heard that men thought it very grand. But maybe that's just Irishmen."

Rafe slowly sat up straight and stared at her. "You bloody little vixen . . ."

Lucy burst into helpless laughter. "No wonder you've been behaving as if you had St. Vitus' dance," she gasped. "I hear the prolonged condition is worse than a bad rash—or at least that's what my friend Brigid says about her Sean."

In a flash Raphael was on his feet and bending over her, both hands gripping onto the sides of her chair, his face hovering only inches away. His eyes blazed into hers without a shred of humor. "Do you think to toy with me, Lucy? I assure you, it's a dangerous game."

The laughter faded from her face. If anything looked dangerous, it was Raphael. Her spine tingled as his hand lifted and brushed her cheek, his breath soft and seductive on her skin.

"Oh . . ." She sighed, melting back against the chair, her lips parting without conscious thought as silence pounded between them.

His mouth closed hard on hers, and he slid his hand roughly behind her neck, drawing her up toward him as he plundered her mouth with his tongue, giving her no respite, taking her like a pirate taking a willing victim—without question, already knowing the answer.

Lucy's blood hummed wildly in her veins, excitement flowering in her belly and spreading to the juncture of her thighs, flooding her with moisture as his hand slid down to the side of her breast, then over, cupping its weight in his palm, stroking and teasing the taut peak of her nipple with his thumb until she writhed underneath him with excited little moans.

He shuddered and bent his head, his breath a blazing heat through the fine linen as he pulled her erect nipple into his mouth and tugged on it, catching it between teeth and lips.

Hot pleasure flowed through every limb, weakening her as a fierce throbbing started deep and low inside her body. Her hands slipped around his neck, savoring the feel of corded muscle and the soft hair that brushed against her fingers as his hand slid down her body and slipped soft linen up her thigh, his fingers trailing fire in their wake.

"Oh, dear God, Raphael . . ." She gasped as he brushed the soft moist curls between her legs, her entire body jerking with the sweet agony of his touch.

A groan tore from his throat and he broke away, standing abruptly, his fist pressed to his mouth. He turned his back abruptly, his breath coming in rough pants. "I trust you understand what frustrated desire is like a little better now."

Lucy drew in a long shuddering breath and released it. "Yes," she murmured, forcing the words from a dry throat. "I believe I do."

He spun around, his face taut, the veins in the side of his neck strained. "Then do *not* play with me," he said, his voice shaking. "God knows I want you, but I want you as my wife, Lucy. I may be a blasted duke, but I'm no saint. Don't expect me to behave like one forever."

He gave her one last long look, then crossed the room in five quick strides. Pausing at the connecting door, he turned. "By the way, happy birthday."

The door shut solidly behind him.

Lucy stared at it, her trembling hands pressed against her mouth. *Happy birthday.* She wished she'd never been born.

She lowered her head onto her knees and burst into tears of helpless longing.

* * *

"We've finished planting the west field," Raphael said, striding across the courtyard, his shirt sleeves rolled up on his forearms. "If the weather holds we should have a good late hay crop."

Lucy looked up from her position in the flower beds where she was busy weeding and pruning. She wiped a strand of hair off her cheek and smiled up at him, taking in his tousled hair and the dirt that streaked his damp shirt. He looked less like a duke by the day and more like a simple farmer who enjoyed working his land.

"Wonderful," she said. "That and the turnip yield will help with wintering the animals."

"I certainly hope so. I have a load of sheep coming in next week, and I'm thinking about restocking the stables." He rubbed his wrist over his forehead. "I'm going up to wash. I'll see you inside for luncheon."

"I'll be in shortly. I'm just going to finish up this bed," she said, watching his retreating back with a wistful sigh.

It was all coming along so well—they'd been working from dawn to dusk, but their efforts were paying off. The house looked more like its old self, the broken glass replaced and the ivy trimmed. The tenants were back on their farms, the fields plowed and furrowed.

Kincaid was a changed place from the day she'd ridden up three weeks ago, decay permeating everything, a heavy silence in the air. Now it thrummed with activity and purpose. The house was fully staffed with people Lucy had chosen herself, a lively and good-tempered group, happy for the work and the fair wages. The tenants came and went freely, bringing their concerns to Raphael as soon as they realized that he had an open and willing ear and was committed to bringing prosperity not just to himself but to them as well.

All in all it was a happy, peaceful picture, she and Raphael working side by side to keep everything running smoothly—the perfect picture of domestic tranquility. Looking at it, no one would have guessed that tranquil was the last word to describe their relationship.

They were perfectly pleasant to each other, taking their meals together, Raphael consulting her on various matters to do with the estate. They sat in the library every evening, sometimes reading, sometimes playing chess, which Lucy had discovered Raphael played as well as he played cat and mouse.

He hadn't once mentioned marriage, nor had he mentioned what had passed between them that first night in her bedroom—he hadn't come near her bedroom again, or near her, for that matter.

But he didn't have to. She felt his piercing gaze on her as she walked into a room or left it. She felt the tension coiled in him like a spring, and it was wound so tight in her that sometimes she thought she might explode. It was all she could do to keep a smile on her face and lightness in her voice, to pretend that she didn't notice a thing.

But she noticed everything he did far too acutely—every look, every gesture only served to remind her of the unspoken, unsated desire that raged between them.

The irony was that her hunger for him only grew worse with time. Lucy had foolishly thought that if they kept their distance, behaved amiably toward each other, the physical longing born in a fantasy would fade, replaced by simple friendship as they grew to know each other as they were in reality.

Unfortunately, the opposite had happened. The more that Lucy learned about Raphael, the more she loved him for the man he really was. She didn't think of him as an unreachable duke any longer, or even as a flawed prince from a fairy tale, but rather as a man of infinite complexities. His keen intelligence was balanced by dry, self-deprecating humor, his innate authority by compassion and consideration. He could even be charming when he put his mind to it.

But what she liked most was the way he treated the Irish

as his equals, working side by side with them, laughing at their jokes, their light-hearted teasing that was an inherent part of the Irish character. He took the banter in his stride, replying in kind. They liked him for it and gave him a margin of acceptance.

Even if he was an Englishman.

Such a pity, Lucy thought, standing and brushing her dress off. It was made of lovely pale-blue muslin, only one piece of an entire wardrobe Rafe had insisted on having made for her.

He'd ignored her halfhearted protests just as he ignored everything else she said that was contrary to his own opinion. In this case his rationale was that she was his housekeeper and should look the part.

Lucy didn't think that most housekeepers had beautifully made dresses and undergarments fashioned of the finest fabrics, but by the time the dressmaker had delivered Lucy's new wardrobe, it was too late to do anything but thank Raphael for his thoughtfulness. And in all truth, she hadn't really minded. She took a secret pleasure in wearing pretty things again, and she liked the simplicity of Raphael's taste, for it was he who had chosen everything.

Naturally. She'd never known such a man for having his own way. Well, he could have it in everything else, but when it came to marrying her, he was fresh out of luck.

She didn't understand God at all. It seemed very perverse of Him to have answered her prayers and sent her a man to love whom she couldn't fully have. In her innocence she hadn't thought to add the part about a man whom she could climb into bed with at night, who would take her in his arms and do all sorts of passionate things to her—

"Oh, dear," Lucy murmured, wrapping her arms around herself. "Don't go thinking about *that* again or you won't make it through the next hour."

But in truth, the memory of Raphael's scorching touch on her body was never very far away. She'd never imagined that anything could feel so wonderful, and the appalling thing was that she didn't have a lick of shame about what they'd done. All she wanted was more, greedy, sinful girl that she was.

It was a good thing she wasn't Catholic, or she'd be confessing for all she was worth, and the priest would be stuffing his fingers into his ears to block her unbridled enthusiasm out.

She couldn't help but wonder if Brigid had gone beyond letting Sean kiss her, if Brigid had let Sean's hands and mouth ravage her breast with sweet fire, if Brigid had any idea how lucky she was that in only one week she would be gasping and moaning in Sean's bed. With a wedding ring on her finger and God's blessing on her soul.

Lucy was beginning to think an eternity in hell might be worth one blissful night with Raphael, one single night of glorious passion. Just to know what it was like, of course— God wouldn't begrudge her that much, would He? Maybe one night would only equate to some time in the Purgatory Brigid was always going on about. But still, it was far too dangerous a thought to entertain. One night would turn into two, then three, and then she'd be in his bed for good, a condemned women, even if a happy one. She knew herself too well. And if she caved in, she really would burn in hell, for God wouldn't be that forgiving.

Lucy shivered, even though the day was blazing hot. She quickly ran inside and up to her room to splash cold water all over her face and neck. She peeped into the looking glass to see if she looked composed, and decided that it probably didn't make any difference. Raphael had a way of seeing right through her, no matter what she did or said.

She quickly rebraided her hair and went downstairs to face another dance with the devil.

* * *

Raphael had just sat down to his meal of cold pigeon pie, wondering what was taking Lucy so bloody long when she came dashing through the door, a bright smile on her face.

He knew that smile. It was the one she put on when she didn't want him to know what was really on her mind. It wasn't much of a stretch to work out what it was. Her cheeks were flushed, and not from the sun. Good. His silent campaign of tormenting her was paying off. Lucy was as much of a physical wreck as he was.

His gaze traveled deliberately down to the curve of her soft breasts, lovely high, round breasts with rosy nipples that tightened into hard little peaks when aroused. He lingered there a moment, then deliberately raised his eyes and smiled at her in return, delighted to see that her mouth had parted slightly and her breath had quickened. "Hungry?" he asked innocently.

"Famished," she said, then blushed even more deeply. "I—I didn't have time for anything but a piece of toast this morning."

"I know," he said. "I was there. You might as well sit down and eat, since I plan to pay a visit to the O'Reilly farm this afternoon to go over the books, and I thought you might want to ride with me." He'd bought her a mare two weeks before, and he enjoyed riding around the countryside with her. He'd discovered that Lucy was an accomplished horsewoman, happy to leap any obstacle in her path without turning a hair. He'd discovered all sorts of things about her, and with each new revelation, he realized more and more what a perfect wife she would make him.

She was brilliant at running a household and had an easy touch with the staff, a real bonus. She was extremely well versed in matters not only of farming but also of horseflesh, two excellent qualities for a man in his business. She had an admirable brain in her head, which made conversing with her a genuine pleasure and mentally sparring with her a delight.

And he already knew how she would respond in bed, an equal partner there as well. Yes, Lucy was going to make him a fine wife. She just didn't know it yet.

"I'd like that," she said, digging into her pigeon pie, unconsciously answering his private thought. If only he could get the same answer out of her to the real question.

"Good. I think they're always more comfortable with me when you're around."

"Only because I've known them for years," she said. "All they have to be grateful to me for is having brought them extra food when they were close to starving. You, on the other hand, have turned their entire lives around and given them back hope. I think they regard you as some sort of god."

Rafe chuckled. "I doubt that—they're rabid Catholics. There's no room in their thinking for anything but the Holy Trinity."

Lucy glared at him. "Do you have a problem with their religion? It has given them solace in times of terrible suffering."

Rafe grinned, raising both hands up in front of him. "Don't you go jumping all over me, Lucy Kincaid. I don't give two figs what religion a person practices as long as it's not shoved down my throat. If they want to be bound to the church hand and foot, being told what to think and how to think and when to think it, that's their business." He shrugged. "Personally, I'd rather have a little leeway in what I think about the Almighty."

"And I suppose you'd like the same leeway in what He thinks about you," Lucy retorted.

"I doubt He gives me much thought at all," Raphael said, enjoying the feisty sparkle in her eyes. "He has better things to think about. That's the beauty of the Anglican church, you see. One attends on occasion, just to remind God that you're there, and then you're free to go about your business."

Lucy took the bait as he had hoped. "You are impossible!"

she said. "That's what comes of being a duke. You think you can do as you please with no thought to the consequences."

"I didn't say that. I simply feel that my business with God is between Him and myself. I don't need a priest standing there telling me that he's a few steps closer to the Almighty than I am."

Lucy leaned her arm on the table and gave him a quelling look. "You forget the sacrifices priests have made in this country in the name of the Catholic religion. During the penal laws priests were forbidden training in Ireland, and any priest who came back from foreign soil was hunted down and hung, drawn, and quarterd. And by whom? The Protestants," she said with satisfaction.

"And you forget that in this country religion and politics have been closely tied together for a good two hundred years," he returned. "Anyway, the penal codes have gradually been repealed."

Lucy's eyes shot fire straight at him. "The laws still prevent Catholics from bearing arms, holding public office—"

"The Relief Act allows them to practice law," he said reasonably.

"Yes, all right, one more little Relief Act. But what about total emancipation? What about the Catholics being forced to pay tithes they can't afford to a church they despise?"

"I don't say that I support the suppression of Catholic rights, Lucy," he said patiently. "But you must look at the larger picture, which is basically all wrapped up in political wrangling for land ownership and economic dominance. I hold a seat in the House of Lords, and I sit there listening to the battle waging—"

"And what do you do about it?" she cried. "Do you stand up and speak in support of emancipation not only for the Catholics but for all the Irish? Emancipation from Britain? The repeal of the Act of Union?"

Rafe belatedly realized that mentioning his seat in the House was probably not a good idea. "I confess I am not a political creature," he said, treading cautiously, for he could see that he'd unthinkingly touched a raw nerve. "I rarely attend parliamentary sessions, being busy with other matters. But when I do, I listen carefully. And what I hear is that England is a long way away from giving up her stranglehold on Ireland. It may not be fair, but it is a fact."

Lucy put her fork down so forcefully that it clattered onto her plate and bounced off. "Is that all you care about? *Facts?* Let me tell you something, your supreme dukeship. You are in a position where your voice would be counted. You now own land in Ireland, you work with the people, you see their terrible difficulties—"

"Which I've tried my best to alleviate," he pointed out. "I can't move the earth, Lucy, I can only try to make the best of any given situation. If I stood up in the House of Lords and started spouting off my personal views to seasoned politicians, I'd be laughed out of the place. My title means very little in that particular arena."

"Every action taken, every speech made against this atrocity is a step in the right direction," Lucy said adamantly. "Oh, *Rafe,* can't you see that you could make a difference?"

He drew in a sharp breath, forgetting all about the point he'd been about to make. Rafe. She had called him Rafe, the familiar name only his close friends and brother used. It fell like sweet music on his ears, felt like a clear, sharp drink of water to his soul. If she privately thought of him like that, then there was hope. There was real, tangible hope.

"Why are you staring at me?" Lucy asked, frowning. "It's not such a preposterous suggestion."

"No. Not preposterous," he said, smiling at her. "The next time I'm in London, I'll be sure to stand up and speak my piece."

Lucy's face lit up with pleasure and surprise. "Why don't you go right now?"

He laughed. "Because Parliament doesn't sit again until January, my sweet radical. In any case, even if it did, I have work to do here right now. Don't you think that should take precedence over a speech?"

She thought for a moment, then nodded. "Yes. You're right. But do you promise that the first chance you have, you will go and speak for us, Raphael?"

"Rafe," he said. "Call me Rafe. If you do, I promise I'll speak for you, although you're going to have to lecture me day and night until I have every last fact absolutely correct."

Lucy leapt up and danced over to him, leaning over his back and throwing her arms around his neck with abandon. "I'll call you anything you please! Oh, thank you! Thank you, Rafe—you have no idea what it means to hear you say it. Wait till I tell the O'Reillys. They'll be calling you a saint for sure."

He ran his hands down her forearms, clasping them to his chest, relishing the feel of her touch. "I don't care what they call me," he said, his voice slightly hoarse. "I only care that you are happy. If my making a speech means so much to you, I'll shout it from the rooftops." He summoned every ounce of control, for he was sorely tempted to pull her into his lap and take every advantage of the situation. "Now, finish your meal," he said with a monumental effort. "We have business to attend to—and, Lucy, do me a favor. Don't say anything to the O'Reillys or anyone else about our agreement. If they're going to accept me, I want it to be because of what I do here, not for the privilege of speaking in the House that my title brings me."

Lucy relaxed her hold and straightened, her arms sliding away, leaving him feeling empty. "I'll keep my peace," she said solemnly, taking her seat. "But I think you're a very fine man for standing up for the cause."

Rafe grinned. "I hope you'll still think that when I'm done making an ass out of myself."

Lucy opened her mouth to reply when a commotion started in the hall just off the dining room. Rafe looked over his shoulder to see what had happened when the butler, if he could properly be called that, appeared in the dining room. When Lucy had hired the household servants, she hadn't worried about their skills, only about who needed the work most, reasoning that she could train them after the fact.

"Begging pardon, yer grace," Dooley said, tugging at his cap, "but there are two English misses at the front. Gupwell's the name, and they say they've come to see Miss Lucy. I told them they weren't even going to enter the gates of heaven until I'd consulted you first."

Rafe shot a startled look at Lucy, who looked as surprised as he felt. "It is your decision," he said, watching her closely.

"Is there an older woman with them?" she asked, her expression wary.

"No, miss. Just themselves and poor wee Tommy Fingall from Ballycastle driving the carriage, and he looks just about done in. And if you don't mind my saying so, they look about as done in as he is." He held out his hands helplessly. "I hope you don't mind, miss, but I asked Tommy in for a wee drink of poteen, whether you'll be entertaining the ladies or not. It's not right that a body should be subjected to such a screeching earful."

Lucy smiled in a manner that told Rafe she knew exactly who poor Tommy Fingall was. "A fine idea," she said. "If Tommy's had to bring his charges all the way from outside Ballycastle with their mother not there to silence the girls, he'll probably need an entire quart of poteen to steady his nerves. However, I suggest you limit him to a single glass if he's to return them in one piece."

Dooley grinned. "Does that mean I should be showing the harpies in, Miss Lucy?"

"Indeed it does," she said. "And you had better stand back, for they move very quickly without looking for obstacles in their way."

Dooley tugged on his cap again. "Right as rain you are, for they practically ran me over in their haste for the door. And all I was trying to do was get their names, just as you told me. Mother of Jasus, it's not an easy thing to be blocking the entrance to those two. They could probably talk Saint Peter into surrendering the gates of righteousness from sheer volume alone."

Rafe looked back and forth between Lucy and Dooley, enjoying every moment of their exchange. There was something so colorful and infinitely descriptive about the Irish version of the English language that far surpassed the usual understated British usage he was accustomed to.

"You're sure you want to do this, Miss Lucy?" Dooley asked, looking doubtful. "They're English, you know." He suddenly colored as Rafe raised an eyebrow in his direction. "Begging pardon, yer grace."

"Surrender the gates," Lucy replied, shooting Rafe a look of amusement. "They are my stepsisters, and I will not turn them away, despite their unfortunate manners."

Dooley gave her one last questioning look, but he went to do as instructed.

"Are you very sure?" Rafe asked her softly as she deliberately folded her napkin and placed it on the table. He couldn't help but be concerned about the reason behind the bloody Gupwell sisters' unexpected visit. "I'd be happy to send them away."

Lucy met his concerned gaze evenly. "Very sure," she said. "My argument is not with them. And I confess, my curiosity is piqued. I cannot think what aim they have in mind or why they have gone to such lengths as to hire Tommy Fingall to bring them all the way out here."

"Nor can I," Rafe said. "But I believe we are about to find out."

19

*F*iona and Amaryllis came barreling through the door and Lucy stood, forcing a smile of welcome to her mouth. Seeing her stepsisters again reminded her all too sharply of the hell her life had been only three short weeks ago.

"Lucy, oh, Lucy!" Fiona cried, glancing uncertainly at Rafe, who greeted them politely enough. "How we have missed you, you have no idea!"

"Mama has been in the worst temper," Amaryllis added, adjusting her bonnet. "And the new girl can't cook at all, or do anything the way you can. It annoys Mama exorbitantly to have to pay her."

"I can imagine," Lucy said shortly, thinking of Eunice's perpetually sour face as she was forced to dig into her purse. "But please, do sit down. We were just finishing our meal. Are you hungry? There is plenty of pigeon pie if you'd like it."

"Pigeon pie?" Amaryllis shrieked, her face lighting up with greedy delight. "Oh, yes, please. I've starved since you left."

Lucy laid places for them and cut them some pie. "So tell me," she said when they had settled down to their meal. "What brings you all the way out here?"

"Well," Fiona said, chewing noisily, "we wanted to come to see you before this, but Mama wouldn't relent until today, and even then she didn't want to give us the money to pay the driver, so we had to use our leftover pin money from London. We never go anywhere anymore. All Mama ever does is sit by the window looking diggers out of it."

"Daggers," Lucy corrected automatically.

"That's what I said," Fiona replied with annoyance. "Anyway, Mama looks diggers out the window and goes on and on about how you considerately stole the duke away from us."

"Did you?" Amaryllis said, scowling. "It didn't seem like something you would do, but Mama is quite sure you schemed the entire thing."

"No. I didn't scheme to steal him away," she said, glancing over at Rafe, whose face was completely expressionless. "It just happened that when he came back to Ireland he discovered that I was your stepsister, and he wanted to bring me back to my family home where I could be of some help to him."

"Oh. I suppose that's not so bad. But Mama says you think he's going to marry you when he isn't," Fiona said with an uncertain frown. "She says he only pretended to want to marry you to get you away to Kincaid."

Lucy, furious that Eunice would say any such thing when she was nothing more than a simple housekeeper, opened her mouth to protest. But Rafe's hand caught hers under the table and squeezed it hard.

"What else did your mother say?" he asked, cold steel in his eyes.

Fiona waved her fork in the air. "She says you only want Lucy as your curtsy-stand."

"My—my *what*?" Rafe said on a choke.

"Courtesan," Lucy replied under her breath. "I imagine she actually said something much worse, but I think that's the only word for the profession that the girls have in their vocabulary, such that it is."

Rafe's face had gone black with rage. "You may tell your mother that she is very wrong about my intentions toward

Lucy. And you may also remind her of our agreement. One more piece of slander against her stepdaughter or myself and she will be very sorry indeed."

"She's already sorry," Amaryllis said, stuffing another piece of pie in her mouth. "She's sorry she didn't lock Lucy away entirely and hurl away the key."

This time it was Lucy who squeezed Rafe's hand tightly, for he looked as if he were going to leap across the table and take out his ire on poor Amaryllis.

"I'm not surprised that she feels that way," Lucy said. "But never mind that. How has she been treating you?"

"She hadn't been at all nice," Amaryllis said with a pout. "She screams at us all the time and says that we are a waste of her time and energy and she wishes she had never married our father, for all he gave her was two stupid, ugly girls." Her face crunched up as tears threatened. "We're not stupid or ugly, are we, Lucy?"

"Of course you're not," Lucy said, feeling genuine sympathy for them. Eunice really was a contemptible woman, taking out her anger on her defenseless daughters. "Your mother only says such hurtful things because she's disappointed things didn't work out as she'd hoped."

"She says she wishes she'd never married your father either," Fiona added. "She says all *he* gave her was a useless title and a wicked stepdaughter who ruined her life, and she hopes that one day you know what it's like to be a wrenched window with horrible children who stab you in the back."

"Do you mean a wretched widow?" Lucy said, thinking that only Eunice would wish such an unhappy fate on her, but there was nothing new in that.

"That's what I said. I wish you would stop correcting me, Lucy. You make it very difficult to keep my thoughts together when you're always jumping in."

"I think I've heard enough," Rafe said, standing abruptly, one fist clenched at his side. "I'm going to the O'Reillys. Are you still coming, Lucy, or do you wish to stay here with your stepsisters?"

Lucy didn't want to leave Fiona or Amaryllis in such an unhappy state, but she didn't want to miss seeing the O'Reillys either. A compromise occurred to her, although she didn't know what Rafe would make of it. "Well, actually," she said, smiling up at him hesitantly, "would you mind terribly if we took them along? They have come all this way, and it might be nice for them to get out and meet people. Eunice *has* kept them cooped up all this time, which must be awful for them, considering her state of mind."

Rafe shot her a look of complete frustration. "As you wish," he said, looking as if he wanted to strangle her. "I suppose I can drive their carriage over there while Tommy Fingall drinks his poteen. Someone around here might as well enjoy himself."

"Thank you," Lucy said, loving him for acquiescing so readily. She knew he only did it to please her, for she was well aware of his strong distaste for the girls.

"Consider it a favor you'll owe me," he said, smiling at her with a private intimacy that made Lucy's spine tingle. He held out his hand to her to help her up. "Come along, sweetheart. The afternoon is getting on."

Lucy took it, surprised by both the overt physical contact and the endearment, both of which he'd been avoiding. She supposed he was trying to make some point in front of Fiona and Amaryllis that would go straight back to Eunice—and his tactic was successful, for the girls were goggling at them both in astonishment.

"Would you like to come to the O'Reillys?" Lucy asked. "Their farm is only three miles down the road, and Mrs. O'Reilly has the sweetest children."

"We're going to visit a *farm*?" Fiona asked, her mouth dropping open in horror.

"It's a very nice farm," Lucy said. "I think you'll like it, and it's something to do, isn't it?"

"Does Mrs. O'Reilly have chocolates?" Amaryllis asked hopefully.

"Oh—I'm glad you reminded me," Lucy said. "You go ahead to the carriage. I'm just going to run into the kitchen and put a basket of food together, if that's all right with you, Rafe."

"Naturally," he said as Fiona and Amaryllis jumped up and ran out of the dining room, giggling loudly. "Did you think I hadn't realized that you've felt compelled to feed half of County Mayo from the Kincaid kitchen?"

"Oh," she said in dismay, for she hadn't thought he'd known. "Are you very cross?"

"Do I look cross?" he said, his eyes filled with laughter. "You needn't ask, Lucy. I told you that the house is yours to run as you please. I hardly think a few baskets of food to help the needy is going to put a serious dent in my pocketbook." He squeezed her fingers lightly. "With a little time and luck, the cotters won't need our help, and think what a nice day that will be for them."

Lucy gazed up at him, thinking once again what a kind, generous man he was. "A fine day indeed," she said very softly. "Thank you for understanding. And thank you for letting me bring Fiona and Amaryllis along today."

He lightly stroked a finger under her chin, and Lucy drew in a shaky breath at the sensual touch. "It did occur to me that maybe it would be good for them to see how the tenants live," he replied. "It also occurred to me that they'll tell Eunice all about visiting the O'Reillys, and she will be reminded not to be tempted to try anything foolish. With luck they'll also tell Eunice that we're blissfully happy together, on the very verge of matrimony."

Lucy frowned. "But, Rafe, we're not on the verge of matrimony at all—why pretend we are, when I really am only your housekeeper? That seems innocent enough."

"Because what you are and what I want Eunice to think you are two entirely different matters," he said, dropping his hand. "If Eunice believes we are affianced, she is far less likely to spread damaging gossip among her friends. You may not have any regard for the proprieties, but other people do, and I won't have your reputation slandered." He flashed a smile of unholy amusement at her. "You don't really want people calling you a curtsy-stand, do you?"

Lucy burst into laughter. "God forbid. You have to admit, my stepsisters aren't entirely unlovable."

"Your opinion, and a generous one at that. But I will say that I do feel sorry for them, now that I know how Eunice has been treating them. No one deserves to be subjected to her malice, not even your sorry stepsisters." He sighed in resignation. "I suppose we should do something to help them out, so if it doesn't trouble you to have them around, I'll give poor wee Tommy Fingall a tidy sum to drive them out here regularly."

"You might have to give wee Tommy Fingall more than a tidy sum," Lucy said, grinning. "I have the feeling that it will take a king's ransom to convince him it's worth his trouble."

"He can have all the poteen he likes on top of steady employment. Shall we say twice-weekly visits? I honestly don't think I could bear to have them around more than that."

"Nor I," Lucy said fervently. "I'll offer the invitation to the girls, and we'll see what they say."

"They're bound to say something painful like: 'We'd be simply ravished to oblige.' "

"You have it exactly," Lucy said, her shoulders shaking with mirth. "I think you've been reading *The Gupwell Girls' New and Improved Lexicon for the English Language.*"

Rafe rolled his eyes. "If you only knew some of the things that have come out of their mouths in the midst of polite company, you'd be appalled. Even Hugo was appalled, and Hugo is rarely taken aback by anything other than a shocking loss at the gaming tables," he said, glancing toward the door. "I suppose I'd better go attend to them before they unsettle Dooley any further."

"I won't be but a minute," Lucy said, still smiling. She went to the kitchen to prepare the basket, surprised to find that she was actually looking forward to seeing how the rest of the afternoon with her stepsisters was going to unfold. Fiona and Amaryllis always managed to make an impression wherever they went, even if it wasn't the impression they were hoping for.

She imagined the O'Reillys would enjoy their visit hugely, for they had only heard Lucy's outrageous stories about her stepsisters. Actually meeting them in person would certainly give them something to smile about.

And Rafe was right. It would be good for Fiona and Amaryllis to see how other people lived.

Rafe pulled the carriage up in front of the O'Reillys' large cottage, where Seamus O'Reilly and his eldest son, Fergus, were up on the roof busy rethatching with the help of the strapping Percy twins, who had moved on to the adjoining farm that had been their father's before Delany had forced him out. Mr. Percy had died only two years later from pleurisy, his will to live gone.

It did Lucy's heart good to see his boys, now young men in their early twenties, back where they belonged and full of purpose.

She waved gaily at them and they waved back. "How are you keeping, Lucy?" Eamon called down to her—or at least she thought it was Eamon. It might just as easily have been his brother Conor, for they were as alike as two peas in a pod.

"Well, thank you," she called back. "How are the pigs doing?"

"The sow's about to drop her litter," Eamon said, taking his cap off and wiping his brow. "Looks like it's going to be a grand brood, God be thanked, and his lordship too for providing the extra feed." He touched his finger to his brow and saluted Raphael, who raised a hand with a smile.

"Old Daisy is as plumped up as can be, and every last teat is already starting to fill," Conor added, sticking his head over the side of the roof. "She'll have enough milk to feed twenty piglets, so we shouldn't lose a one, providing we get them all through the birthing. But then Daisy's nice and wide in the hips, so there shouldn't be any trouble."

"What good news!" Lucy cried, turning to see what Fiona and Amaryllis had made of that piece of earthy information.

But their faces weren't twisted up with disgust at all. Instead, they were staring wide-eyed at the Percy brothers, their mouths hanging open in what appeared to be thunderstruck wonder, their hands clasped tightly in each other's as if they were in complete agreement about what they were seeing.

Lucy blinked in astonishment. Conor and Eamon were good-looking young men with hair the color of ripe wheat and eyes as blue as the sky, it was true. But they were Irish farmers, and as far as Lucy knew, neither Fiona nor Amaryllis had ever given a second glance to any Irishman, certainly not to two cotters who raised pigs for a living.

She turned and looked at Rafe to see if he'd noticed. He had, of course, since nothing ever seemed to escape his attention. He raised both eyebrows at her as if to say he was as surprised as she was.

"Lucy! Your Lordship," Mairead exclaimed, coming out of the cottage, wiping her hands on her apron. "I was wondering whose carriage had come visiting us in the middle of the day. And who might your friends be?" she said, regarding Fiona and Amaryllis with open curiosity.

Lucy grinned. "Allow me to introduce my stepsisters," she said, relishing Mairead's look of astonishment. "They came to visit me at Kincaid, and I thought I'd bring them along. I hope you don't mind."

"Mind? It's a fine day indeed, Lucy Kincaid, when you're

bringing your stepsisters to meet me," Mairead said with an impish smile. "Come in, come in and make yourselves comfortable. I'll put on a nice pot of tea."

"Thank you," Rafe said, reaching up and taking Lucy by the waist, easily swinging her to the ground, then passed her the basket of food with a little smile. He held out his hand to help down Fiona and Amaryllis, who had both gone unusually quiet.

Lucy made the proper introductions and they followed Mairead inside to the spotlessly clean kitchen.

"You've done a fine job in putting everything back in order," Lucy said, admiring the sparkling windows that poured bright light into the room—a far cry from the dark kitchen of their last dwelling.

"Aye, it's been hard work getting it back to the way it was, but joyful work. We're overflowing with blessings at the moment, what with being back home again and Brigid getting married next week."

"Is she here?" Lucy asked, hoping she was.

"She's not, lass, and she'll be sorry to hear she missed you, as will the rest of the children. Lizzie's taken the young ones to play with the O'Malley brood so that I could get some chores done, and Brigid's off getting her marriage instructions from Father Cloony, although I don't know that he needs to be telling her how to be a good wife," she said with a merry laugh. "Sean O'Dougal is a lucky man to be marrying our Brigid, for she'll see to all his needs just as a proper Irish wife should."

She filled the pot with boiling water, then counted heads and laid out nine mugs and nine spoons. "Get the sugar from the cupboard and the jug of milk, will you, Lucy? I'm going outside to call the men down off the roof."

Lucy jumped up to fetch the requested items. She glanced over to see Raphael watching her steadily, his cheek resting on his fist, a smile hovering around the corners of his mouth. "What?" she asked uncertainly. Sadly, she didn't have the same gift of reading his thoughts as he did hers.

"I imagine Sean O'Dougal knows just how lucky he is," he said, folding his hands together on the table. "Or at least I believe he does, given the way I've seen him looking at Brigid."

"She looks at him the same way," Lucy said, color rushing to her cheeks. The way Raphael was looking at her was enough to make her knees go weak.

Fiona and Amaryllis started giggling. "I think love must be in the air," Fiona said, digging her elbow into her sister's ribs.

Amaryllis squirmed in her chair. "Who are the twins on the roof, Lucy?" she asked, her plump cheeks pink.

"Eamon and Conor Percy," Lucy replied, doing her best to ignore Raphael, whose smile had broadened into a wicked grin. "They farm the land just down the road."

"They're very handsome," Fiona said with a gusty sigh.

Raphael smothered a laugh, and Lucy had to fight to keep a straight face. "They're very nice as well," she said. "I've known them since I can remember. We used to play together down by the river. Conor can tickle trout right out of the water—he tried to teach me the trick, but I never quite mastered it."

"Tickling trout? What is that?" Fiona asked, for once not wrinkling her nose in distaste at the mention of something that might dirty her hands.

"It's a way of catching trout without using a rod," Lucy said, picking up the pot and starting to pour the tea. "You lie very still on your stomach with your hands in the water and wait for a trout to come along to investigate. And then you tickle it under its tummy and toss it out of the water. But as I said, I never mastered the skill."

"How very clever," Amaryllis said. "I wish I could do something like that."

"I'm sure if you ask Conor he'd be happy to show you—

that is, if you can figure out which one of the two he is. I've never mastered that trick either."

Fiona nodded happily. "I am sure I can work it out," she said. "Did you really mean it about our coming to visit twice a week, Lucy? Because if you did, I am sure there are all sorts of things I can learn to do if I put my mind to it."

"If you like, you can help us pull Kincaid together. There's lots of work to be done both at the house and on the farms." Lucy waited for shrieks of protest, but instead Fiona and Amaryllis exchanged a look of excitement.

"Oh, indubitably," Amaryllis said. "We'd like to help, wouldn't we, Fiona?"

Fiona nodded vigorously and then suddenly went very still as Seamus O'Reilly and Fergus came in, followed by the Percy brothers.

"Look, Seamus, here are Lucy's stepsisters, Fiona and Amaryllis Gupwell," Mairead said, indicating each in turn. "And isn't that nice?" She handed mugs all around.

"Very nice indeed," Seamus said, pulling off his cap. "Welcome to you. This here is my son Fergus, and our neighbors Conor and Eamon Percy, come to help us out with our roofing."

"How do you do, then?" the twins said in unison.

"How do you do?" Fiona and Amaryllis said in equal unison, looking as if they were about to fall off their chairs in delight.

"You'll be Lady Kincaid's daughters, I'm thinking," one of them said. "And I'm Conor, just to set you straight, for the world has a hard time getting us right. I have this little beauty mark right here over my cheek," he said, pointing at it with a grin. "It's what gives me an edge over my brother with the girls."

"It's very nice, I'm sure," Fiona said, blushing furiously. "You're the one who tickles trout then."

"Sure, and who taught me but my ma, God rest her soul. Now, she had the gift, even if her tongue was like a yard of vinegar when you crossed her. But the trout didn't know that, did they now, and they came to her like they were bees to a honey hive."

"How captive-making," Fiona said, her eyes shining.

"Captive-making," Conor said, scratching his head. "I never thought of putting it like that, but it's the truth sure enough, and you're a clever girl to know it, Miss Fiona. She surely did capture them, and an hour later we'd be sitting down to dinner and stuffing our bellies with the finest fish you ever did taste."

"Was your mother a good cook?" Amaryllis asked, her gaze traveling up and down Eamon as if he were more delectable than an entire box of chocolates.

"Was she a good cook?" Eamon said with a hearty laugh. "I'm not after bragging, but our ma was the best cook this side of Killala, and I myself am not far off. Conor might have learned from her sainted self about trout tickling, but I learned about cooking, right from the time that I could stand knee-high to her, and she wasn't a tall woman at that."

"Lawks," Amaryllis said, looking ready to swoon with happiness. "I am very proportioned to a good meal myself."

"Well, then," he said, looking at her plump figure with open appreciation, "you'll have to be coming along to our place and bringing your sister, for I think I can promise not to sour the cream."

Lucy shot a look of glorious amusement at Raphael, who looked as if he might slide under the table at any moment in silent hysterics.

"You just let us know when," Fiona said, looking about to explode. "We have the use of a carriage twice a week—but it will have to be in daylight hours," she added primly. "Our mother is very firm about observing the properties, and she says that after nightfall anything can happen."

Conor nodded solemnly, regarding Fiona as if she had great common sense, a prized virtue to a farmer. "And a fine rule it is. Property rights are not a thing to be sneezed at," he said, sipping at his tea. "It's a nice thing to know your ma understands the need to stay vigilant. Come night, any thief can slip in and take as he pleases if you don't keep your guard up."

Lucy couldn't listen to another word, not without breaking down completely. She abruptly excused herself, saying that she wanted to admire the flowers Mairead had put in that week. Rafe was fast on her heels and the O'Reillys not far behind.

Lucy made it as far as the front garden before collapsing in tears of laughter. "Who would have thought?" she gasped, wiping her eyes. "The Percy brothers and my stepsisters?"

Rafe slid an arm around her shoulders, his grin half splitting his face. "Stranger things have happened, I suppose. Ah, Lucy, do you think it's possible? Do you think there might be two matches in the making?"

She looked up at him, tears rolling down her cheeks. "I don't know. I honestly don't know, but there's promise. And if those two silly boys are inclined to court them, I'm certainly not going to stand in their way."

Seamus grunted. "Conor and Eamon could use wives to help them out and they know it, but they're not in the way of being able to afford to court any lasses. It's everything they can do to keep their heads above water as it is without adding the burden of a family."

"Perfect," Rafe said, clapping Seamus on the back. "You might put a word in their direction that each of those girls comes with a dowry. That might help to sweeten the pot."

"Aye, and I think I might be asking a commission from the boys if I have a hand in getting those girls to the altar with them," Seamus said with a broad grin. "What's the take, then?"

"Five thousand apiece," Rafe replied. "That should buy plenty of livestock."

"Five *thousand*?" Lucy said, gasping in shock. She couldn't even imagine such a sum. "Rafe, you must have been mad to settle that staggering amount on them!"

"Not mad, just desperate," he said, giving her shoulder a light squeeze. "And even that sum brought no takers, or at least not in England. What do you think, Mairead? You have an eye toward these matters, and you know the Percy boys. Do you think there's any chance they might really be interested?"

Mairead considered, her head cocked to one side. "I'll say this much—I've never seen either one of them look seriously at a lass before, but they both seem to be as intent on looking now as they are when they're examining a hog in the marketplace, and that's saying a mouthful."

Rafe roared with laughter. "You couldn't have put it better. Well, let them look and hope they'll buy. I can't think of a more perfect solution. I'll pray for more weddings in the near future."

Mairead looked from Raphael to Lucy and back at Raphael again. "I think I'll be praying for more weddings as well. It's never too soon, not when the feeling is there and leading to God only knows what."

"I couldn't agree more," Raphael said cheerfully.

Lucy wanted to die with mortification, for she realized that Mairead saw straight through her and was probably thinking the worst. "It's a little early for that sort of thing," she said hastily, trying to redirect her. "They've only just met."

"It doesn't take long to fall into sin," Mairead replied sharply, refusing to be diverted. "Best have the priest before it does."

Seamus cleared his throat, heading his wife off before she could go any further. "Why don't I send the four of them off on a walk while we go to work, your lordship? Fergus can accompany them, and I feel sure they'll be safe enough. We'll only be two hours at the most, what with Lucy to help."

"A good idea," Rafe said, not looking the least disturbed

by Mairead's pointed remarks. "Tell the Percy brothers that I wish them to take a look at the southern corn crop, and I'd be obliged if they entertained Lucy's stepsisters while they do it so that we might concentrate on the business at hand. That should take care of any possible awkwardness."

The Percy brothers were all too happy to oblige, and Fiona and Amaryllis certainly posed no objections, practically dragging the twins out the door. When they returned two hours later, the girls looked as if they'd died and gone to heaven, and Conor and Eamon had gone straight there with them.

Fergus looked done in and disappeared immediately, shaking his head.

Fiona and Amaryllis didn't stop talking all the way back to Kincaid, prattling on about every last word that had been exchanged between the four of them.

". . . And Eamon said the corn is ripening this year the grandest he's seen it," Amaryllis said. "He said it is all thanks to you, Duke, that he's never known such a man for bringing propriety in his wake."

"Yes," Fiona chimed in. "And Conor said that you will rape your well-deserved reward by autumn. Isn't that good news?"

Raphael choked, his fingers tightening on the reins. "Just what I wanted to hear," he mumbled, looking thoroughly rattled.

Lucy covered her face, her shoulders shaking helplessly. Poor Raphael—it wasn't hard to imagine what he must be feeling. "I think you mean he will reap his reward," she gasped when she could speak again.

"That's what I said. I don't know what you think is so amusing, Lucy. *I* thought it was a very nice thing for Conor to say."

"Indeed," Lucy said, wiping tears from her eyes. "I'm glad you had such a nice time. But I think it might be wise if you don't mention anything to your mother about meeting Conor and Eamon."

"We wouldn't think of saying a word," Amaryllis replied, looking appalled at the very idea. "She might not ever let us come back again if she knew we'd been talking to farmers, even though they're most obligating people we've ever met."

"Exactly," Rafe said, his composure marginally back in place. "You might say, however, that Lucy and I plan to introduce you to some eligible young men. That should help to persuade her to let you visit us regularly." He looked as if that was the last thing in the world he wished.

"Oh! What a very good idea," Fiona said, clapping her hands together. "Mama is sure to like the sound of that."

Rafe pulled the carriage up in the courtyard and helped Lucy down. "Stay here and keep them out of trouble," he said in an undertone. "I'm going to find Tommy Fingall. He can't drive this carriage away fast enough."

Only minutes later Lucy and Raphael stood side by side, watching the carriage barrel down the drive, Fiona and Amaryllis waving and shouting at them until the carriage disappeared from sight.

Lucy turned to Rafe, her eyes dancing with laughter. "Did you enjoy yourself then?" she asked, gazing mischievously at his stormy face.

"Not a word," he snapped. "Not one more bloody word." He turned on his heel and stormed into the house, leaving Lucy doubled over in merriment.

Oh, life really was grand.

20

The Catholic church was small and simple for a supposed cathedral, but still the largest building in all of Killala and filled to overflowing with friends and family who had come to see Brigid O'Reilly marry Sean O'Dougal.

The dim interior light was brightened by the candles at the altar where Brigid stood in her simple white dress and lace veil, a wreath of wildflowers on her head and a smile of pure happiness on her face.

Rafe could just imagine why—she was probably thinking of where she'd be in a few short hours and what she'd be doing. His gaze traveled over to Lucy, who stood to one side, a posy in her hands and a wistful expression on her face as her friend exchanged her marriage vows.

He scowled. It could just as easily be Lucy standing at an altar if she'd only back off her ridiculously stubborn position and agree to marry him. He squeezed his hands together in his lap, stifling a throb of frustration. He really didn't know how he was going to hold out much longer.

He glanced over at the Percy twins, sitting next to Fiona and Amaryllis. Even they had made more progress than he had, he thought, looking down at Fiona's hand secretly nestled in Conor's.

Impossible but true. It looked as if the Gupwell girls really were going to make matches with those two pig farmers.

And here he was, a duke, with everything in the world to offer Lucy, and she didn't want any of it.

Mairead sniffled happily into her handkerchief in the pew directly in front of him as Sean slipped a gold band onto Brigid's finger.

With this ring I thee wed, with my body I thee worship . . .

Rafe wanted to scream. *I'd worship your blasted body if you'd give me half a chance.*

He'd done everything he could to show her what a fine couple they'd make, how perfectly suited they were. But to no avail. Lucy wouldn't budge. One would think he'd committed a crime by being British, as if there were something he could do about that.

His gaze ran over Lucy again, who wore an enchanting yellow dress, the exact color of daffodils in the spring, one that he had chosen because it matched the golden starburst around her irises. He couldn't help but admire her slim shape as his eyes took in the tantalizing curve of her breasts, the indentation of her waist, the gentle swell of her hips, the outline of her long, shapely legs. He finally raised his gaze back to her sweet face and settled on the full curve of her rosy mouth.

A mouth created for kissing.

Rafe suppressed a groan. He really couldn't go on like this—he barely slept at night, knowing she was only a room away. She on the other hand probably slept like a baby, secure in the knowledge that he wasn't going to ravish her in the night.

Yet.

The music swelled and everyone rose and watched the newly married couple make their way down the nave, stars in eyes of both. Lucy walked gracefully behind. She glanced over at him and smiled softly. Rafe forced an answering smile to his tight mouth. He felt much more like crying.

"It was a lovely ceremony, wasn't it?" Lucy said outside the church as the bridal party readied itself to return to the

O'Reilly cottage for the wedding feast. "Brigid was in such a state of nerves this morning when we were dressing her, but she settled down once she saw Sean waiting for her inside."

"And you?" he asked, not the least interested in Brigid's premarital jitters. "How were your nerves?"

Lucy looked up at him, her gaze puzzled. "They were fine. What reason would I have to be nervous?"

"Any mention of marriage seems to make you jumpy as a cat," he said. "One would think you were against the institution entirely."

Lucy gave him a long, hard look. "I think marriage is a fine thing as long as two people have the same background in common, which Brigid and Sean do."

Rafe expelled a harsh breath of impatience. "I don't suppose it has occurred to you that you are the child of a peer as I am. The only difference between us that I can see is that I was born on the other side of the Irish Sea. The wrong side."

Lucy grinned. "I think you are finally grasping the point."

Raphael had a strong urge to throttle her. "I am not in the mood for your games, Lucy."

"And I am not in the mood for your black humor or your needling," she shot back. "This is Brigid's wedding day, and the least you can do is behave as if you're happy for her."

"I am happy for her. She had the good sense to marry the man she loves. You, on the other hand, haven't the sense God gave you to see what is right under your nose and do the same."

"Oooh," she said, planting her hands on her slim hips, her eyes flashing fire. "And I suppose you know all about it, do you then? I never said I loved you, Raphael Montagu, so don't you go putting words into my mouth."

"They're there. You just refuse to speak them," he retorted curtly. "You're the hardest-headed woman I've ever had the misfortune to meet. There's no pleasing you, Lucy Kincaid. God help me, but I'm sorely tempted to throw you over my shoulder and carry you off to the nearest vicar. I'll thrash the damn vows out of you if I have to."

Lucy's hand slipped to her mouth, her eyes wide. "You wouldn't dare."

"Don't tempt me," he said, thinking it sounded like a fine idea, the best he'd had in some time—if his mother would just show up with the special license he'd requested her to acquire on his behalf, a license that would allow him to marry Lucy at any time in any place. He wished he knew what was taking his usually efficient mother so bloody long.

Lucy backed away a pace and then another. "You can thrash me to within an inch of my life, but I still won't marry you."

"We'll see about that," he said dangerously, taking a step toward her, pushed to his limit.

Mairead appeared just at that moment and laid a hand on each of their arms. "Saints above, it looks as if the two of you are about to kill each other," she said with a chuckle. "But whatever you're sparring about can wait. It's time to leave, and it's a merry party we'll be having to celebrate, so leave your differences behind. I'm sure they'll wait."

Rafe drew in a deep, steadying breath. "They'll wait," he said, glaring at Lucy. "For the time being."

He turned abruptly and went to gather up Fiona and Amaryllis, who were sequestered in a corner with the Percy twins.

At least putting the Gupwell girls and their swains on a leash gave him something to do other than murdering the woman he loved.

Lucy's blood boiled with fury all through the party that went on until nearly ten o'clock that evening. She was so angry with Raphael that she could hardly think straight, but she made a deliberate effort to dance and sing and generally carry on in true Irish style—as much to annoy Rafe as to please the O'Reillys.

Much to her astonishment, Raphael did the same. She watched him surreptitiously as he danced his heart out with half the neighborhood, not a shred of his usual reserve in place. He drank, he ate, he talked a blue streak. If she hadn't known he was a filthy Englishman, she would have thought he'd been born down the road.

And the people—*her* people—responded in kind, slapping his back, laughing uproariously at his jokes, dragging him out again and again to leap wildly about with them.

Lucy wanted to kill him. She wanted to kill her friends too. Why couldn't they see that he wasn't one of them, that he was the enemy?

And yet in her heart of hearts she had to be honest with herself. He wasn't the enemy, not really. He had somehow managed to insinuate himself among them, sharing their troubles, alleviating those troubles when he could, and they knew it and responded with grace and gratitude by treating him as one of their own.

"What troubles you, lass?" Mairead asked, coming over to Lucy's hiding place in the little back garden where she had retired to take a break and nurse her indignation.

"What makes you think that anything troubles me?" Lucy said testily.

"Come now, colleen. Are you thinking that I don't know you at all, that I can't see what is inside you?" She patted Lucy's shoulder gently. "You're pining away for the man, and he for you. It's been going on for some time, hasn't it? Since before you even left for England."

Lucy stared at Mairead, thinking she must be some kind of witch. "How did you know that?" she asked in an anguished whisper. "I didn't say anything . . . nothing at all."

"You didn't have to, not from the first time you showed up on our doorstep and told us about his arrival. Your feelings were written all over your face, not that I have any idea what could have passed between you. But those feelings have been growing in you ever since, haven't they?"

Lucy nodded, dropping her head onto Mairead's comforting shoulder as the older woman drew her into her arms.

"There, there, child. There's no need to cast yourself into such a state of unhappiness. It's not as if he doesn't feel the same."

"He's an English duke." Lucy sobbed bitterly. "I can't marry an English duke, Mrs. O'Reilly. It wouldn't be right, not after what his people have done to us. I'd never be able to hold my head up again."

"So he wants to marry you, does he? Well, it shows a sense of honor, at least. I wondered what he had in mind all these weeks of keeping you at Kincaid. My heart has been sorely troubled about the matter."

"Raphael has been nothing but honorable," she said in his defense, raising her head and wiping her eyes. "I am the one who refuses to marry him."

"Why, wee lass?" Mairead asked simply.

Lucy stared at Mairead in true shock. "How could you even ask a question like that?"

"Because although I understand your position, and rightful enough though it is, I can still see that you care deeply for him and he for you. There are always exceptions to a rule, child."

"No," Lucy said adamantly. "No exceptions, not to this rule. I know he's been good to you, and he's been good to me too, but that doesn't mean that I can cross the line. Our children would be born with mixed blood, their loyalties split. Our eldest son would be an English duke in Raphael's stead."

She shook her head, going back over territory she'd thought of time and time again over the last month, concerns she hadn't dared to broach to Raphael. "Can you not see what would happen? Our son would inherit all of Raphael's lands and business affairs in England, his enormous power. Why would he choose Irish interests over those of England? We'd end up a family divided, and it would break my heart to see that happen."

Mairead stroked her hair. "It's not that I don't understand your worry. But the man doesn't seem like the usual Englishman, even if he is a duke. Look at him now," she said, nodding in Rafe's direction. "He's happy here, colleen, and that happiness is largely due to you, just as sure as the same unhappiness that's eating at his soul is due to you. Would it be such a great sacrifice to give him what he needs?"

"I—I can't," Lucy said, her throat so tight she could hardly swallow against the ache. "I don't know how to give him up, but I have to somehow find a way to forget my feelings for him. I would be dishonoring my father if I did anything else. He would never forgive me for marrying into the family that destroyed him."

"Oh, your father, is it? I think I begin to see." Mairead rubbed Lucy's arm. "Forget your troubles for now, lass, and come and join the celebration. You don't want people thinking that you've deserted them, and those wanton stepsisters of yours need an eye on them."

Lucy struggled to smile. Twice already she'd dug Fiona and Amaryllis out of impassioned embraces in the shrubbery. "Yes, all right then," she said glumly, and followed Mairead back to the party with a distinct lack of enthusiasm.

Raphael was thoroughly sick of pretending to be happy and gay when he felt anything but. He'd put every ounce of energy into the charade for Lucy's sake, but she didn't appear to notice, avoiding him at every turn in favor of her friends. Her precious *Irish* friends, damn her anyway, he added, staring down into his glass of whisky.

He looked up, wondering for the tenth time where she'd disappeared to, when she came around the side of the house with Mairead. His eyes narrowed as he took in her pale face and miserable expression in the brief moment before she raised her chin and forced a smile to her lips.

So. Lucy had been playing a charade too. Somehow that made him feel better. He put down his glass and walked directly over to her, determined to clear the air between them, now that his temper had cooled.

"Where did you go?" he asked, looking down at her with a little frown. "I was worried about you."

"I—I was doing something for Mrs. O'Reilly out back," she said, not meeting his gaze.

"Lucy, I'm sorry," he said, lightly touching her shoulder. "I don't wish to argue with you. I was upset earlier and I shouldn't have taken out my temper on you."

"I don't wish to argue with you either," she replied, still looking down at the ground.

"Then let's not. Come and dance with me. The fiddler is just striking up another tune."

She shook her head. "I have to go find Fiona and Amaryllis."

Rafe grinned. "Don't worry about Fiona and Amaryllis. I sent them inside to cool off after I found them starting off down the road for a little private groping. Your stepsisters have absolutely no regard for their reputations."

"And here I was thinking that it was *my* reputation you were so worried about that you threatened to drag me off to be married against my will," Lucy said tightly.

Rafe counted to five before speaking. "I suppose I deserved that."

Lucy finally looked up at him, her eyes snapping with anger. "Yes, you did. I'll do with my reputation as I please, and I don't need you trying to bully me into doing something I have no desire to do."

Rafe's temper flared again, and he rarely lost his temper, Hugo being the shining exception to the rule. To lose it twice in one day was infuriating, and he was even angrier with her for goading him into it. "So what you are telling me is that I should have no regard at all for your reputation, is that it?" he said through gritted teeth.

"That's it exactly. You can order me around your house, but you cannot order how I think or how I feel. Or insist I feel something I don't," she added, twisting the knife even more savagely into his gut.

"Fine, Lucy," Rafe said lazily, refusing to let her see that she'd hurt him deeply. "We'll play by your rules and see how you like it."

"What's that supposed to mean?" she demanded.

"You'll just have to wait to find out," he said, not sure what he meant himself, but certain that once he figured it out he would teach her a well-deserved lesson for her pig-headed attitude. "It's time to go home. Get your things and I'll get the girls," he said, not bothering to wait for an answer. She could damned well do as she was told for once.

Lucy couldn't sleep. She'd tried everything—reading, counting sheep, pacing around her bedroom, but nothing worked. All she could think of was Raphael's stormy face when he'd curtly said good night to her and gone upstairs, the slam of his bedroom door echoing down into the hall where she stood, staring helplessly after him.

She'd never seen him like this, so silently grim, anger caged like a dangerous beast inside of him. Thinking about it, before today the only other time she'd seen him truly angry was a month ago when he'd learned of Eunice's threat to her and the O'Reillys. But then his rage had not been directed at her. This was a different experience entirely, and it made her feel small and sick inside.

She hadn't meant to enrage him—she'd only been speaking her mind, although to be fair, she could see that she had perhaps not been as reasonable as she might have been. Still, the truth was the truth, and that was that she wasn't going to marry him. He had no right to keep pressing the point.

The private concerns that she'd revealed to Mairead were an inalienable fact. She'd learned at an early age that only trouble came out of mixing one's feelings with the harsh realities of life. Her father would still be alive today if it hadn't been for her impulsive actions that awful night of the uprising. And the Good Lord only knew what would happen if she caved in to her impulses now and agreed to marry the man she loved. No matter how strong that love might be, trouble was sure to follow: husband pitted against wife, children against mother, betrayal and heartbreak inevitable.

It had happened too many times before over the course of her country's history, and it would surely happen again. Her dear father hadn't brought her up to be a fool and walk headlong into certain disaster—and he would turn over in his grave if she deliberately married into the family that had ruined him. No. No good could possibly come of a marriage between them.

Rafe would thank her in the end. Wouldn't he?

Turning from the window where she'd been gazing sightlessly out into the night, she wrapped her shawl more closely about her delicate cambric nightdress and rubbed both hands over her face, thinking that maybe a glass of brandy would help to calm her thoughts and her raging emotions. Nothing else had.

Crossing the room, she pressed her ear against the connecting door to be sure that Rafe was asleep, for she didn't want him to hear her going downstairs and come after her. She couldn't bear another confrontation, not that she thought he was in any frame of mind to even want to look at her, let alone talk to her.

There was no sound.

She opened her door cautiously and, picking up a candlestick, slipped quietly down the stairs to the library, where she knew Rafe kept the decanter.

The door was open a crack and she pushed it wider, surprised to see that a gently glowing fire crackled in the hearth. She thought she'd checked to be sure all the grates were cold, but given her distracted state of mind when she'd gone to bed, she might have missed just about anything.

And then she saw the powerful body silhouetted in the wing chair on one side of the fireplace and froze, her hand jerking on the candle so hard that it sputtered and dripped hot wax onto her hand.

"Ouch!" The cry escaped her throat involuntarily as she blew onto her scalded skin.

Raphael sat up abruptly and turned, his gaze searing into her, far hotter than any dripping wax. He looked like the devil himself, his hair disheveled, his shirt unbuttoned all the way down to his waist and gaping open to expose his muscular chest, firelight dancing over his powerful physique.

She tore her gaze away, not knowing what to do. Flee? That would look silly indeed, as well as betray her panic. Stay? That would be even worse punishment. Maybe she could just back out slowly.

"What the bloody hell are you doing here?" he demanded.

"I—I couldn't sleep," she said on a frightened gulp, placing the candlestick on the mantelpiece with trembling fingers.

"Odd," he said in a queer, strained voice. "I couldn't sleep either. Why do you suppose that is?"

"I have no idea," she replied, her own voice stifled and weak, as weak as her poor shaking legs. Oh, *Lord,* but he was beautiful, an angel of darkness, his hair a golden halo around his head, his strong, chiseled features half cast in the flickering light of the fire.

"What made you think you could sleep better in here?" he asked, the words slashing like a whip through the stillness of the room.

"I thought a glass of brandy might help," she replied, feeling like an idiot.

"At least pouring a glass of brandy is *something* I can do for you." He pushed himself to his feet and stalked over to the table that held the decanter and glasses, looking thoroughly dangerous.

It was a simple glass of brandy, Lucy told herself with a shiver. Nothing more.

He poured two glasses, then turned and held one snifter out to her. "To your very good health and happiness," he said, holding his own glass up with dark irony in his eyes.

"Thank you," Lucy answered, snatching the snifter from him as if it might burn her fingers. She took a cautious swallow of the strong spirits, trying to steady her frayed nerves.

He sipped from his glass, regarding her over the rim with an intensity that made her toes curl. "I'm not entirely in my right senses tonight," he said in a voice so low it was barely audible. "It might be best if you took yourself away."

Lucy bit her lip in determination, not about to be intimidated by him now. If she let him frighten her, he'd only think he could do it again. "I suppose you mean you're half-seas over," she said, forcing lightness into her tone. "Hardly surprising, when you consumed enough good Irish whisky tonight to put a bull to sleep."

"It didn't seem to work on me though, did it? And yes, I'm dead drunk. I give you fair warning."

"Of what?" she asked, biting on her lower lip, trying not to stare at the massive span of his bare chest, trying desperately to stifle the desire to reach out and run her hands over the taut muscles.

"That I have half a mind to put your challenge to the test, to play Pompilius to your Egeria. This is no sacred grove, but I cannot think you care any more about that than you do your reputation."

Lucy took a large gulp of brandy to save herself a reply to that alarming statement. She choked, the fiery liquid burning her throat. Her eyes filled with water and her nose stung painfully as she tried to catch her breath.

"Do you find the idea so daunting, Lucy? Or perhaps it is only that you enjoy keeping me in torment. And why wouldn't you, since you say you have no feelings for me at all." He raised his glass high and quoted softly into the heavy silence, not taking his eyes off her.

> *What deep wounds ever closed without a scar?*
> *The heart's bleed longest, and but heal to wear*
> *That which disfigures it; and they who war*
> *With their own hopes, and have been vanquish'd, bear*
> *Silence, but not submission: in his lair*
> *Fix'd Passion holds his breath, until the hour*
> *Which shall atone for years; none need despair:*
> *It came, it cometh, and will come,—the power*
> *To punish or forgive—in one we shall be slower.*

He sighed, a deep ragged breath. "I wonder which it will be, Lucy. Do I face eternal punishment, or forgiveness for what I cannot control?"

Lucy shook her head, hating the raw pain on his face, pain she was responsible for causing him. "Don't," she said, her heart breaking all over again. "Please don't."

"Don't? Don't tell you how I feel? Don't tell you that my heart aches and my body burns for what I cannot have?" He moved toward her and lifted his hand, sliding it behind her neck, his fingers gently stroking her nape. "For this, Lucy. And for this," he said, moving even closer and lowering his head, his breath warm at the corner of her mouth as he brushed his lips over her cheek and up her temple.

Lucy moaned softly at the seductive contact, her hand slipping up without conscious thought to caress the side of his face, her fingertips trailing down over his cheek and the strong line of his jaw.

He shuddered, burying his mouth in her hair. "God help me," he whispered. "I want you so badly I could die."

His gentleness and restraint were her undoing. She couldn't hold out against him any longer, not when she felt his anguish and need in the very depths of her soul. Not when she felt the same and had it in her power to give them what they both so badly wanted.

Just one night . . . and a few hundred years in Purgatory.

Her decision made, Lucy moved away from him and put her glass down on the table, then took his snifter out of his hand and placed it next to hers.

He watched her, a slight frown drawn between his brow. "Was it what I just said?"

"Yes," she said, turning to him, her heart pounding furiously with a combination of fear and anticipation. She held out her hands to him, letting her shawl slip off her shoulders to the floor.

"Yes. It is exactly what you just said. Take me upstairs, Rafe. Take me to your bed."

21

$\mathcal{R}$afe stared at her, disbelief freezing him to the spot. And then comprehension sank into his dazed brain. He didn't waste another second, springing forward like a tiger suddenly uncaged.

He pulled her into his arms, his mouth descending on hers in a frenzied kiss of hunger and relief and infinite gratitude. Lucy pressed against him in heated response, her soft body pliant and willing as she opened her mouth to his, accepting everything he had to give her.

Himself. Only himself. All of himself. *Thank you, God.*

He scooped her up into his arms, her weight no more than a feather to him, but he trembled anyway. "Egeria," he whispered as he blew out the single candle, cradling her head against his shoulder as her arms twined around his neck. "My sweet Egeria," he said hoarsely, his voice breaking from the very effort of speaking. "At long last."

He carried her up the stairs, dropping kisses on her hair, her brow, pausing only to awkwardly reach for the handle of his bedroom door, refusing to put her down even for a moment.

He swore softly, fumbling with the knob, and the door finally swung open, closing solidly behind him as he kicked it with his foot once he was safely on the other side.

So close now . . .

He looked down at her face, her eyes only half open and gazing up at him dreamily, a soft smile parting her lips. She was ready, so ready. He'd never seen a woman more ready or more open to her own desire. And his. Oh, God, and his.

He thought he might burst with it. He laid her down on the great four-poster bed, moonlight spilling over her, bathing her in gold. A goddess. She really was a goddess, her dark, silken hair falling loose over her shoulders, her slender form clothed only in a sheer white gown, her cheeks flushed with promise.

It took him only a moment to strip off his shirt and come down to her, the weight of his lower body pressing her back against the soft linen of the sheets. "So lovely," he murmured, stroking her hair back off her smooth brow and spreading his fingers through it. "So perfect." His hand slid recklessly down over her hip as he captured her lips in a searing, driving kiss that only made his blood boil hotter.

Control, he thought wildly, impatience burning in him like wildfire, a desperate urge to possess her pounding through his veins. He forced himself to slow his breathing, to steady his pace, but the feel of Lucy's hands wandering all over his chest and shoulders made that very hard. He thought that the amount he'd had to drink that night might have numbed him slightly, but it hadn't made a single dent on his raging senses, only on his befuddled brain.

He captured her wrists with one hand and raised them above her head, the movement only inflaming him more, for it brought her small high breasts directly against his chest. He lowered his mouth to one lovely swell of flesh and tongued her nipple through the fine material of her nightdress, his teeth gently nipping and suckling at the taut peak, an ardent groan coming low in his throat as Lucy writhed and arched beneath him in helpless need, tiny moans slipping from her throat.

It was a simple thing to lift the flimsy material from her and pull it over her head, letting it float to the floor, to bare her flesh to his gaze, to cover one breast with his hand and mold its soft shape to his palm, a simple thing to remember how long and how often he had wanted her in this way.

His mouth replaced his hand and he lightly touched her bared nipple with his tongue, then drew it into his mouth, tugging and suckling on one hard bud and then the other until she dug her fingers into his shoulders, her breath coming in short, sweet pants.

Her skin felt like silk under his fingers as he skimmed his hands down her fragile rib cage and over her hips to her thighs, thighs that quivered under his touch. He ran his fingertips up and down over her soft inner flesh in a slow caress, watching her face as she closed her eyes and drew in a sharp little breath.

"Oh," she whispered, her thighs parting as he brushed his fingers over the downy curls at the juncture of her legs, curls that were warm and damp with desire.

"God, how I love you," he said, his voice shaking as he slipped his finger between the folds of her silky wet cleft and stroked, back and forth in a persistent rhythm, finding her delicate nub and slowly circling it with his thumb until desperate little cries of pleasure tore from her throat.

Her neck arched back and he drove his finger deep into her hot, slick inner flesh, running his tongue down the line of her throat. Lucy's hips lifted to draw him deeper, and her hands pushed down over his flaming skin, moving to the waistband of his breeches with impatient, fumbling movements. "Rafe," she pleaded, a faint, desperate whisper. "Come to me?"

"You're going to have to wait for just a moment," he said with a strangled laugh, for she was only making the situation worse, her fingers an agonizing torture as they brushed over his engorged shaft.

Shifting to release the painful confines of his trousers, he jerked the restricting buttons open until he was free. He rolled to one side, impatiently stripping off the material, then came back to her, as naked as she was, and more than ready to take her fully.

Only to find her gazing down at his erection, her eyes wide. "Oh, my," she murmured, touching her tongue to her upper lip. "I had no idea."

Rafe grinned at that piece of foolishness. "I thought I explained it to you in detail. Lucy—you're not frightened, are you?" he asked, suddenly remembering through his drink-fogged brain that she really didn't have any idea what to expect. "I don't want you to be frightened of me, ever. I couldn't bear it."

"No," she said, smiling mistily up at him, her fingers twining into his hair. "I'm not frightened of you—I was just surprised for a moment. I *want* you to make love to me. I've wanted you for so long, even though I tried to pretend I didn't."

"And I've wanted nothing more than to make love to you, sweetheart," he said raggedly, relieved that her acceptance of his male proportions had come so easily, because he was about to explode.

He stroked his hands over her face, loving her even more for her simple honesty. He bent his head to kiss her again, his tongue plunging in and out of her mouth, setting a rhythm that he couldn't wait to follow with his hips.

Lucy sighed and pulled him closer, and he didn't waste another moment. He spread her legs with his knees and poised his tip at her entrance, gently pushing into her, stretching her to accept his length.

Despite her tightness she didn't resist him, arching her hips up against his, her entire body shuddering with need. It was all the invitation he needed. He thrust hard, breaking through the fragile barrier of her maidenhead and sheathing himself fully in her.

His breath caught in his throat and he crushed his mouth against her hair as wild sensation poured through him. He stiffened, holding himself completely still for a few seconds, about to lose his last shred of control.

Oh, God. He'd never felt anything like this, not like this. Lucy. She was life itself, the sun that drove the dark nights of his soul away, the wind that blew happiness into his lonely heart, the rain that made hope blossom in his chest like flowers spreading over a wasteland. His joy went far beyond physical pleasure, an elation of love found and claimed.

He began to move in her, driving hard and deep as if he could brand himself on her, and Lucy met him thrust for thrust, her legs twining around his back, her fingers working frantically over his back, his buttocks, sobbing his name over and over until the sobs became frantic cries and she writhed under him like a woman possessed, her pulse beating wildly in her neck against his mouth.

He raised himself up on his elbows to watch her face, her head moving back and forth on the pillow, her eyes closed and her brow furrowed as if she were concentrating deep inside herself, searching for something unknown but just within her grasp.

He gave it to her, plunging into her and holding deep.

A long, wordless cry broke from her throat as her body trembled and then convulsed around him, throbbing in powerful spasms of release that drove him to his own.

He moaned in exquisite agony, the simmering fire in his loins bursting into raging conflagration as he poured his life into her, the pleasure unbearable. He was dying, he was sure of it—the intensity of the blaze would reduce him to nothing but ashes. He vaguely registered the distant cry of his voice, her name on his lips as the last of his senses swirled away into a blackness so profound he couldn't breathe.

With a superhuman effort he managed to suck air into his lungs before collapsing onto his side, drawing her with him, his deep, labored gasps muffled against her damp hair.

"That was extraordinary . . ." he murmured when he could finally speak again. "Truly extraordinary."

Lucy snuggled up against his side and smoothed her mouth over his slick shoulder. "Thank you for making it so special," she said very softly.

"Oh, I think I can do much better than that," he said with the trace of a smile, exhaustion pulling at the corners of his mind, dragging him toward sleep. "After all, I was drunk and desperate, and it was your first time." He yawned and wrapped his arms around her. "Maybe later I'll show you what I mean."

He drifted off, contentment settling over him. Life had never felt so rich and full. Tomorrow, when his head was clearer, he would set the date for their wedding . . .

Lucy waited until Rafe's breathing had deepened into sleep. She carefully removed herself from his embrace and sat up, gazing down on his face. His thick eyelashes lay dark on his cheeks, his strong face softly lit by the moonlight streaming in through the window. He looked peaceful. And vulnerable too, like a child whose cares had been washed away.

But there was nothing childlike about Rafe. He was the strongest, most controlled man she'd ever known, and to-night he had proved to her just how much of a man he was, taking her to heights of passion she'd never imagined in her wildest dreams, showing her the truth of his love with every caress, every word, every exquisite thrust of his body in hers until she thought she'd break apart with love and excite-ment.

A tear slipped down her cheek, followed by another, drip-ping onto her clenched hands. She felt like dying. He'd spo-ken of their lovemaking as if it were only the beginning, rather than an ending. Did he really think that it was that simple, that she would move into his bed with no thought to the consequences?

Still, it was her fault. All her fault, for it was she who had opened the door, she who had practically begged him to make love to her. She could have stopped him at any time—

or at least she thought she could have, not that she'd wanted him to stop. Not for one second.

Lucy released a shuddering breath, covering her face with her hands, her shoulders shaking with silent sobs. She didn't regret her impulsive action one bit, for she'd had a glorious night of love and the memory would last her the rest of her life. She would grow old and frail, but no matter how old or how frail, she would never forget what it had been like to be loved by Raphael, to feel his strong arms around her, his body in hers.

But despite that, she had a terrible feeling she'd made a monumental mistake, for Raphael clearly had a different idea of how things were going to be, and she didn't know how she was going to explain to him that she wouldn't—couldn't be his mistress. That would be an even worse sin than marrying him.

Her gaze wandered over the powerful lines of his body, the sheets tangled around his legs, leaving one muscular buttock exposed. One masculine *British* buttock, she reminded herself, snatching her hand back as it involuntarily crept out to stroke the deep hollow just below his lean hip.

It was a good thing her monthly course was about to start, or she might really be in trouble. That was all she needed— his baby planted in her belly. He'd never let her go.

Best she went now, before he woke up and ravished her all over again.

Lucy quietly slipped out of bed, suddenly aware of the wetness dripping between her legs. She reached down to touch it and pulled her hand up, looking down at the smear of blood mixed with his seed. Her virginity gladly given along with her heart. And that heart hurt sorely, for he could never know how completely it belonged to him.

"Oh, Rafe," she whispered, her eyes filling with renewed tears of anguish. "If only . . . if *only*."

She crept out of his room, knowing if she stayed she'd be

lost. She cast one last look in his direction, then made her way to her lonely bed.

Rafe opened his eyes, the morning light dazzling and painful in his eyes. His mouth felt like the inside of a rubbish bin, his senses blurred. A hazy image of a sweet body held in his arms vaguely penetrated his haze, and he shot upright as full memory returned.

Lucy. He'd made frantic love to Lucy. Oh, *God*. What had he done? What in sweet hell had he done? Sharp needles shot through his skull as he went back over each moment from the time he'd spotted her from his wing chair to the last thing he remembered. Embracing her in his arms, that was it, after an explosive encounter of lovemaking.

And oh, dear Lord, but what an encounter it had been. He certainly remembered every moment in full, exquisite detail. It had been the most enchanting night of his life.

He pressed his palms against his pounding temples. He wasn't accustomed to drinking to excess and the whisky had taken its toll on him. But a good breakfast would help alleviate the worst of the aftereffects.

Much more important was to find Lucy, who must have slipped out of bed earlier and gone to start her household work. He felt terrible for having passed out on her—not a very gallant thing to do, especially after taking her virginity, so sweetly given.

And he'd had no right, not before marrying her. The drink and his own stormy emotions had clouded his judgment, stripped away the self-control he prided himself on.

He'd have to arrange their wedding as soon as humanly possible, since it was entirely possible that he had gotten her with child. He grimaced, praying that wasn't the case. He would much prefer that any child they were blessed with was conceived in holy wedlock.

But still, he couldn't be too terribly sorry, for Lucy had

finally seen reason, and that was worth a very large prayer of thanks.

Lucy stared down at her plate of kidneys, pushing them around with her fork. Her usually hearty appetite had deserted her, her stomach in knots. She dreaded the inevitable confrontation that was coming, but the sooner she explained her position to Rafe, the sooner she could stop worrying.

"Good morning, Lucy. I trust you slept well?"

Lucy started, dropping her fork. Her gaze shot up to see Rafe standing in the doorway, looking as if he didn't have a care in the world, a smile hovering on his mouth.

She shot a quick glance at Nancy, who was clattering around at the sideboard, putting out a fresh pot of coffee. Lucy wished she'd be done with it and disappear. "I—I slept very well," she lied. Her eyes hadn't closed all night. "And you?"

"Like the dead," he said, taking a seat. He scratched his temple, watching her with an unfathomable expression. Nancy poured him coffee, then went back to the sideboard and filled a plate, taking what seemed to be forever. She finally slid it in front of Rafe. "There you are, your grace. Nice kidneys, and eggs fresh from the hen this morning. And you'll be having a dish of fowl for your lunch today, just the way you like it, with mushrooms and—"

"Thank you," he said, cutting off her culinary diatribe. "I am sure it will be delicious, but that will be all, Nancy. Miss Lucy and I do not wish to be disturbed."

Nancy bobbed a curtsy, shooting Lucy a look of open curiosity before she vanished back into the kitchen.

Rafe took a sip of his coffee. "You look tired," he said, a hint of laughter in his eyes. "Did I wear you out?"

Lucy blushed hotly at so blatant a reminder of what they'd been doing only a few hours before. "No," she said. "But I need to talk to you about that."

Rafe chuckled softly. "I'm sorry I fell asleep so quickly. It won't happen again, I promise."

"No. That's just my point. It won't happen again," she said through a tight throat, gathering her courage.

He nodded, then released a heavy sigh. "I agree. I'm sorry, sweetheart, for although I can't really regret what passed between us, I shouldn't have taken advantage of you like that. I'd had too much to drink and wasn't thinking clearly."

Lucy stared at him. She couldn't believe it was going to be so easy. "I—oh, Rafe, *thank* you for understanding," she said with a rush of gratitude. "I didn't think you would, especially since it was I who started it all. I shouldn't have, I know that, and I was sure that you would be very annoyed with me today for telling you that I—that we couldn't . . ." She trailed off in confusion, twisting her napkin in her lap.

Rafe flashed a smile of amusement at her. "Are you saying that you took advantage of me when I was in a compromised state?"

"No—well, yes," she said, utterly flustered. "It's just that I so wanted . . . oh, dear," she said, covering her hot cheeks with her hands. "I'm not making myself very clear."

Rafe burst into laughter. "You didn't compromise me, Lucy. It was the other way around, but as I said, you needn't worry, for I have no intention of letting it happen again—or at least not until you have a wedding ring on your finger."

"A—a wedding ring?" she said, her hands freezing on the linen. "But I—but I'm not going to *marry* you! I thought you understood that!"

Rafe's amusement abruptly faded. "What in sweet hell do you mean by that?" he said, his brow snapping down. "Of course you're going to marry me. Do you think I would have made love to you if I thought anything else?"

"But I *told* you over and over again," she cried desperately, horrified by his easy assumption. "I can't marry you—you're English!"

"And I might very well have planted an *English* babe in

your belly," he roared. "For the love of God, Lucy, what kind of man do you think I am? I would not dishonor myself or you by doing anything other than marrying you. What were you thinking last night?"

"Only that I wanted to give you what you asked for, just that once," she said, terrified by the black rage on his face. "And it was wonderful, and I'm not sorry, and anyway, you haven't planted a babe in my belly, so there's no harm done."

"And how can you possibly know that?" he said icily. "I assume you are aware of how babies are made? You can't possibly be that naïve."

"Of course I'm not," she said with annoyance. "But it's the wrong time of the month."

Rafe slammed his hands onto the table, glaring at her. "It's never the wrong time of the month, you little fool. Dear God, but I ought to throttle you! You will marry me whether you like it or not, because I will not stand for anything else—I've thoroughly compromised you."

"No one has to know," she said in a small voice.

"Don't you think people are going to wonder should your belly start to swell? And if you think for one moment that I'm going to allow you to bring my bastard child into the world—"

"There won't be any child," she cried. "I wish you'd listen for once instead of issuing commands right, left, and center. You never think to ask what a body wants, do you?"

"I don't have to ask what your body wants," Rafe said, his eyes glittering. "I know perfectly well, and in explicit detail. Are you really silly enough to believe that you won't eventually end up back in my bed? How do you think you're going to stay away, now that you've had a taste of what it's like?"

Lucy's temper snapped. "You are nothing more than an arrogant bully," she hissed. "I can do anything I put my mind to, and furthermore, I wouldn't place even one toe near your bed again if my life depended on it, so there!"

"Did I disappoint you so much?" Rafe asked in a silky voice. "As I remember, you seemed to be rather pleased with my attention at the time."

Lucy jumped to her feet, wanting to throw something at him. "You can remember what you like, but I'd thank you to keep your inflated opinions to yourself, since I have no use for them."

"Or for me, apparently," Rafe said, his eyes flashing cold fire. "Which makes you nothing more than a—"

"Don't say it," she said, on the verge of bursting into tears. "Don't you dare say another word, Raphael Montagu, or I swear I'll never speak to you again."

"One reaps what one sows, Lucy, and I think you would be wise to bear that in mind in more than one regard."

"My goodness, it seems I've come just in time," came a well-modulated voice from the doorway, a voice Lucy recognized all too well. She spun around to see the dowager duchess standing there, Hugo at her shoulder, both of them regarding Lucy and Rafe with fascination.

"Y-your grace," Lucy stammered, appalled by what they might have overheard. She shot a quick look at Rafe, to see he was equally appalled.

"Hello, Lucy," the duchess said. "My son wrote to say he had found you and installed you in your family home at long last. Hello, darling. Heavens, it is a long journey to get here."

Rafe slowly rose to his feet, looking thoroughly shaken. "Mama," he said, and Lucy could tell he was trying desperately to regain his control. "I wondered how long it would be before you arrived. What's Hugo doing here?" he added with supreme displeasure.

"And well met to you too, brother," Hugo said, looking stung, but his face quickly shuttered.

"I specifically asked our mother to come, not you," Rafe snapped.

"Really, darling, you could not have expected me to come all this way without an escort? Hugo was kind enough to offer to accompany me. The least you can do is make him welcome."

Rafe pushed both hands through his hair. "Please, do sit down. Would you care for something to eat or drink?"

"Thank you, but we broke our fast at the inn where we stayed last night," the duchess said. "I would be happy for a cup of coffee, though."

Lucy quickly fetched a cup for her and one for Hugo, wanting to drop through the floor with mortification. Of all times for the duchess to show up, why did it have to be just then?

The duchess launched into a long, amusing story about her journey, giving both Rafe and Lucy time to collect themselves, which Lucy was sure was exactly what she intended.

"Never mind all that now," Rafe finally said, interrupting her impatiently. "Did you bring the document I asked for?"

"I did indeed," the duchess said merrily. "Naturally I had go all the way to Canterbury, but once I explained, the dear man was happy to oblige. He sent you his best regards."

Rafe nodded curtly, and Lucy couldn't help but wonder what document Rafe needed so badly that he'd sent his mother first to Canterbury and then all the way to Ireland to hand-deliver it. But he didn't say anything further on the subject, and neither did his mother.

"I would be so grateful if you would show me up to my bedroom, Lucy," the duchess said. "I am longing for a wash, and my maid will be anxious to unpack my trunk."

"I would be happy to," Lucy said, thrilled with an excuse to escape from Rafe's stifling presence. "If you and Hugo will come with me, I'll take you straight up."

"Marvelous. And then I would so like to see the rest of Kincaid, darling Raphael, if it is not too much trouble. I have tried to imagine it many times, but the little I have seen is so much more attractive than I had anticipated."

"If you'll forgive me, I have work to do. I'll leave that pleasant task to Lucy," Rafe said with a singular lack of enthusiasm. "I'm sure she can explain *everything* to you in great detail."

"It would be a pleasure," Lucy said, seized with a strong desire to pour the contents of her cup over Rafe's head. "I'd be happy to explain anything at all."

Rafe shot her a poisonous glare as she stood and led the duchess and Hugo from the room, but she ignored him, chattering gaily away as if she hadn't even noticed.

That ought to get him, she thought triumphantly. If there was one thing Raphael hated, it was being ignored.

22

$\mathcal{R}$afe could cheerfully have shot Lucy. He couldn't understand her for the life of him—how could she *possibly* still stand on her idiotic pride and refuse to marry him after what had happened between them? She didn't have an iota of common sense in her head, never mind any regard for his feelings.

He was truly beginning to wonder if she loved him at all, for even in the heat of lovemaking she had never mentioned the word. Not once. She behaved as if losing her virginity was of no consequence to her.

And she had the nerve to talk about principles to him.

He rubbed his aching brow, then bent his head, struggling to concentrate on the paperwork in front of him.

But it was no good. All he could see was Lucy—Lucy as she had looked in bed last night, a goddess, her face flushed with passion. Lucy as she had stood before him today, a harridan, her face just as flushed, but this time with anger as she rejected every last reasonable argument he'd given her for why she had to marry him.

She couldn't possibly be pregnant, she'd said. As if she knew anything about it at all. By God, she'd be sorry if the day came that she realized she was wrong. But she'd be married long before then—now that his mother had arrived with the special license they could be married in an instant.

And would be, no matter what Lucy thought now. If he could only find a way to get through to her . . .

He threw his quill down and shoved his face into his hands with a groan. The hell of it was that he loved her so damned much. He wanted her to marry him of her own free will, not because he'd forced her hand. Or just because he'd seduced her.

Rafe winced, cursing himself for his own stupidity.

And as if that wasn't enough, his mother and Hugo—Hugo, of all bloody people—had managed to arrive right in the middle of a heated argument. God only knew what they had overheard or what they had made of it. Marvelous.

His life was a catastrophe, all thanks to Lucy and her high-minded ideals that had absolutely nothing to do with reality.

"Yer grace?" Dooley asked, poking his head through the door without even bothering to knock.

Rafe looked up wearily. "What is it now?"

"Mairead O'Reilly's here to see you, sir, and she looks as determined as a hellcat, bent on getting her way. I told her—"

"Get you out of my way, Liam Dooley, before I swat you," Mairead said impatiently at his shoulder. "His lordship doesn't need to hear any of your yammering."

"Please come in, Mrs. O'Reilly," Rafe said, thinking there was no end to what people wanted from him. "What may I do for you?"

"I'd thank you to give me ten minutes of your time and let me speak my bit," Mairead said, marching into the room.

"By all means," Rafe said, not in any mood for dealing with other people's problems. "Perhaps you'd like to sit down while you do it. What's this all about?"

"It's about Lucy, your lordship," Mairead said, taking the chair on the opposite side of the desk.

"What about Lucy?" Rafe said with a frown, wondering just how much Mairead had divined. If she intended to deliver one of her lectures on morality and God, he'd see her away faster than she could run.

"The lass is sorely troubled, and I've been struggling with my conscience about whether to tell you about it, for Lucy won't thank me for divulging her confidences. But I've been in a state of worry over her, and it seems maybe there's some explaining to be done that she's not going to be doing herself."

Rafe's gaze sharpened. "What sort of explaining?" he asked, hoping against hope that Mairead might actually know something he didn't.

"Well, sir, I've seen with my own eyes that you and Lucy have strong feelings for each other, and she told me herself that you want to marry her. But she won't, will she now? And there's good reason for it, no matter how much she loves you."

"But there lies the rub," Rafe said bitterly. "She doesn't love me in the least."

"Nonsense," Mairead replied. "She told me just how much she loves you while she was sobbing her troubles onto my shoulder last night, her wee heart breaking."

Rafe gripped his hands together, fighting to keep a neutral expression when what he really wanted to do was jump up and leap around the room like a madman. Lucy loved him— he hadn't been wrong after all. Thank God. Thank *God*.

He cleared his throat. "I see," he said evenly. "And what troubles are these?"

Mairead caught her bottom lip between her teeth. "Like I said, I shouldn't be betraying the confidence at all, but I don't know how else to make things better."

Rafe knew this territory well—he'd been there before when Mairead had hovered on the edge of offering information about Lucy. "Then I suggest you go ahead," he said, stifling his impatience. "Lucy and I are at a stalemate and I haven't the first idea of what to do to break it."

"Well, you might have a powerful grip over her, sir, but

her past holds her even more powerfully in its grip. It's going to take everything you can do and say to make her see matters in a different light, for she struggles mightily with her pain."

"I'll do anything," Rafe said, leaning forward. It seemed that once again, Mairead O'Reilly, simple farmer's wife, held the key to his salvation. It was a humbling thought. "Please. Tell me everything you know."

Mairead nodded. "I can't be absolutely sure of all the details, but it begins years ago with Paddy Delany and your cousin, Thomas. They plotted together for Thomas to gain claim to Kincaid, and one terrible night they put their devilish plan into action . . ."

Rafe listened carefully as Mairead slowly and thoroughly unfolded an appalling tale of deception, Ian Kincaid as the main target, Lucy used as the pawn in their unconscionable game. The story he'd heard from Eunice, which he completely discounted as a lie designed to paint Lucy in a bad picture, began to make horrifying sense, only in Mairead's version, Lucy had acted in complete innocence, responding to a forged letter—but nevertheless had not only brought about her father's disgrace but also his eventual death from the wounds he suffered that night.

He could well imagine the pain and guilt she carried. He should know. He carried a similar burden of his own.

". . . So you see, sir, Lucy thinks she cannot marry you, for you happen not only to be British but you are also a Montagu, and therefore in her mind her father's enemy. The girl has carried the weight of her father's disgrace and death on her shoulders for so long that she cannot see night from day, nor separate the kindly acts of one Englishman from the sins of another."

She regarded Rafe earnestly. "She's tried to make up for her mistake in every way she could, going so far as to let her stepmother make a slave out of her, but nothing gives salve to her conscience, and I fear she will bear the weight forever.

Unless—and I beg your pardon for being so forward—unless and not until you can find a way to ease her pain. She does love you so." Mairead bowed her head as if the speech had exhausted her.

"Thank you for disclosing all this to me," Rafe said quietly, leaning his forehead into his hands. So many things explained. So very many things—Lucy's reluctance to speak of the past. Her adamant stand against the British, but most particularly against him, who just happened to be a Montagu.

His family had betrayed hers. And to Lucy's mind there was nothing worse. Nothing. He saw it all so clearly now, and just a little too late.

It was a miracle she'd allowed him into her heart at all, but no little wonder that she'd struggled so hard against her love for him. Incredible that she'd even allowed him to claim her body and soul, if only for one night.

"There's one last thing, your lordship," Mairead said, giving him a keen, knowing look. "Lucy worries that if she did give in and marry you, your children, and in particular your eldest son, would spurn this country, and you would end up a family divided, her on one side, you and your children on the other."

"What in the name of . . ." Rafe slowly raised his head and stared at her. "Where did she get a bird-witted idea like that? She already knows my position—she's bloody well *seen* what I'm trying to do here, and not just for her."

"Yes, but you forget that Lucy has had the experience of seeing a family shattered by a British stepmother who hates and slanders the people she lives among. You'd do well to take that into consideration."

"I will take everything you have told me into consideration, Mrs. O'Reilly," Rafe said as calmly as he could manage, which was not a very impressive showing. "I cannot thank you enough for your candor."

"I can only pray you'll know what to do with it. Poor Lucy

has never been able to prove that she had nothing to do with the events of that night, any more than she could prove that Mr. Montagu or Paddy Delany did. It's eaten away at her, poor child, what with losing Kincaid and then her father and being blamed for the entire mess by her stepmother."

"I'll see what I can do about that," Rafe said, his mouth tightening. "The larger difficulty is somehow convincing Lucy that I would never turn my back on her or this country. I only want to marry her, Mrs. O'Reilly, not ruin her life."

Mairead smiled gently. "And I believe you, sir. But it's Lucy you need to be telling, not me. You have to find a way to show her you can be trusted—trust doesn't come easy to a girl who's been through what she has."

"I understand." He understood all too well.

"Well, then, I'll be on my way, for I have work to do." She paused at the door. "Oh, and your lordship, a word of advice. We Irish have a saying: The best way to get an Irishman to refuse to do something is by ordering it." She laughed. "You might have a little more success with the lass if you bear that in mind. I heard a bit of what the two of you were shouting about outside the church, you see."

Rafe rubbed the back of his neck, thinking that Mairead might have a good point. "I'll take that into consideration too," he said, feeling a little ashamed of himself. Perhaps he did have a tendency to command rather than ask. Lucy had accused him of that very thing only an hour ago.

"Good day to you then," Mairead said. "And good luck to you also." The door closed behind her.

Rafe sat in silent thought for a few minutes, then pulled out a sheet of paper and wrote out a full page, covering everything Mairead had just told him about the night of the insurrection.

When he was finished he went to get his pistol. He loathed firearms and only kept a gun for protection, but in this case it might be useful for another purpose.

He and Paddy Delany were going to have a little talk and Rafe was going to get some answers, whether Delany wanted to supply them or not.

"And this is the formal garden and cascade," Lucy said, walking the duchess and Hugo over the property. "The garden is not yet up to snuff as you can see, but we've been concentrating on practicalities like repairing the dairy and stableyard, and the main house, of course."

"Nevertheless, it is all as lovely as can be," the duchess said. "Soon enough everything will back as it was. Tell me, what is Kincaid's total holding?"

"Two thousand one hundred acres," Lucy replied absently, her thoughts still back in the dining room with Rafe. "The whole demesne is enclosed by walls, so you can imagine how much limestone it took to build them. I would estimate that about half the land is woodland and park, and until recently the rest lay fallow, but Rafe has turned much of it back to crops such as corn, turnips, and hay. And potatoes, of course."

"And he has leased much of that land out to tenant farmers?" the duchess asked. "I gathered from Raphael's letter that the O'Reillys have returned."

Lucy, pleased that the duchess remembered, nodded. "Yes, along with most of the other tenants. As it happens we attended Brigid O'Reilly's nuptials yesterday. Your son dances a fine Irish reel."

"Rafe danced an Irish reel?" Hugo said in disbelief. "*My* stuffy brother?"

"He danced a number of them, and as well as any Irishman," Lucy said, already out of patience with Hugo, who had done nothing on their walk but aim barbs at his brother. "And he's not stuffy, not in the least. I think it's very unkind of you to say he is."

"Why? Rafe's never been anything but a high-stickler with

me. The way he goes on, you'd think he was some kind of a saint—perfection itself."

"Stop it, Hugo," Lucy said curtly. "Your brother doesn't consider himself anything close to perfect. The way you talk, you'd think he was inhuman and unfeeling, and he's anything but."

As upset with Raphael as Lucy was, she didn't think he deserved Hugo's scorn. Hugo hadn't gotten down on his hands and knees and planted potatoes, had he? Or stripped off his shirt to hammer shutters back together and mend leaking roofs.

Lucy shoved that last memory to the back of her mind, thinking it would be best if she didn't dwell on how handsome and virile Rafe looked with a bare chest—or how wonderful the powerful muscles of that chest felt under her hands. She didn't want to think at all about the warm, salty taste of his skin and the hot sweetness of his tongue tangling with hers.

She squeezed her eyes shut against a sharp pang of longing, her unruly body betraying her yet again.

"Lucy, dear, you are not unwell, are you? You are looking rather flushed," the duchess said with concern. "Perhaps the sun is too hot for you."

"N-no, I'm perfectly fine," Lucy said, passing a hand over her brow. "Just a little tired."

"Naturally you are, after all the excitement of last night."

Lucy nearly choked. "We—we did not get home until very late," she said, wondering frantically just how much the duchess really had overheard.

Hugo smirked. "Kept Rafe up past his bedtime, did you? It obviously affected his temper."

"Hugo, why do you not walk ahead?" the duchess said. "I would like to have a private word with Lucy."

"I'm sure you would," Hugo said with a wicked grin. "Don't concern yourself with me in the least. I can entertain myself." He loped off, whistling a little tune between his teeth.

"Tell me, Lucy, now that we are alone. How are you really going on here at Kincaid? You and my son did not look very happy with each other when Hugo and I first arrived."

Lucy wanted to die right there on the spot. "We were only having a small disagreement about—about harvesting," she said, desperately searching for a reasonable explanation. "Raphael has an exaggerated idea of the yield from a certain planting." Oh, Lord, but she hoped that would cover anything the duchess might have heard.

"The yield. I see," the duchess said, nodding thoughtfully. "And he thinks he knows more about it than you do."

"Rafe always thinks he knows more about everything than anyone else," Lucy snapped. "I've never known such a man for wanting his own way."

The duchess smiled. "I suppose that my son has carried the responsibility of the dukedom for so long that he is accustomed to having his word obeyed. But you are not saying that he has treated you badly in any way, are you?"

"Oh, no," Lucy said, belatedly realizing that she'd said more than she'd intended. "He is nothing but kind and considerate to me. It is only that there are certain matters we do not see eye to eye on, and so we occasionally argue."

"I understand that your position here at Kincaid is that of housekeeper," the duchess said, pausing to admire the view.

"Yes," Lucy said, peeping a glance at the duchess's serene profile. "It seemed the most practical solution. Once Raphael tracked me down he didn't want me staying with my stepmother any longer, and I thought I could be of service to him here." She blushed furiously, for that hadn't come out right either. "I used to manage the house and the accounts for my father," she added quickly.

"And your stepmother? How did she react to my son's discovery of your identity? I cannot think she was very pleased to have him take you away."

"She was furious," Lucy replied. "But there was nothing she could do. I had reached my majority, and Rafe didn't give her any choice in the matter."

"No, he would not," the duchess said. "Although I confess I am surprised he told her he intended to make you his . . . housekeeper. I would think your stepmother would have kicked up a great fuss about that."

"Well . . . he didn't exactly say that," Lucy said, digging the toe of her half boot into a clump of soft earth. "He told Eunice we were to be married."

The duchess turned her head, the incisive expression in her gray eyes so like her son's. "And are you to be married?" she asked quietly.

Lucy realized that she'd just been neatly cornered—unfortunately, a physical resemblance wasn't the only family trait the duchess shared with her son.

"No," Lucy said just as quietly. "We are not."

The duchess gazed back over the view with no change of expression. "Is that his choice or yours, child?"

"It is mine," Lucy said, seeing that there was no escape. She bet the duchess played a fine game of chess too.

"A great pity. I had every hope that you would bring my son some well-deserved happiness. He has been alone for so long." She sighed. "Ah, well. I am not usually wrong in these matters, but I suppose I must have misread your feelings. I was quite sure you were very much in love with Raphael, and I know he is in love with you, for he told me so in no uncertain terms—not that I couldn't see it with my own eyes."

Lucy blushed fiercely. "He—he *told* you that?"

"Indeed he did, child. Has he not told you for himself?"

"Yes . . ." Lucy said, unwelcome tears welling up in her eyes. "Yes, he has, but it makes no difference."

"No *difference*?" the duchess exclaimed. "No difference that he loves you with all his heart and wishes to make you his wife? Do you really care so very little for him?"

"I care for him above anything, but there are too many insurmountable obstacles between us," Lucy said, gulping back a sob.

"No obstacle is insurmountable when there is also love between you," the duchess said. "Bear in mind that my son has never given his heart before, Lucy. He is not a frivolous man, but rather one who feels things very deeply, as much as he doesn't wear his emotions on his sleeve. If he loves you, you can be sure that he would never betray that love." She touched Lucy's shoulder gently. "You will not find a better or more loyal man anywhere. Please—do not make up your mind against the marriage until you are very sure there truly is no way to resolve your differences."

Lucy couldn't reply, her throat thick with unshed tears. Oh, if *only* . . .

"I'll leave you now. You would probably like some privacy."

Lucy just nodded, her face turned away. As soon as she was sure she was alone, she sank to the ground and let the tears come as they would. They poured through her fingers and dripped onto the earth as she wept for lost love and shattered dreams, bitterly watering the soil of Ireland with her anguish as so many before her had done.

Raphael found Paddy Delany at his house in Ballina, a large, handsome stone structure on the outskirts of the town—a house that Paddy would never have been able to afford had it not been for the large profits he'd made during his tenure at Kincaid.

So much for his sainted mother dying of the cold and no peat for the fire.

Rafe didn't bother knocking. He pushed the door open and strode in, finding Paddy slumped in a chair in the sitting room, a bottle of whisky on the table next to him, a full glass in his hand.

No surprise there, either.

"Sit up, Delany," Rafe said, cocking his pistol and pointing it at him.

Paddy shot up in the chair, his mouth falling open as he took in Rafe and the gun barrel aimed at his chest all in the same moment.

The glass slipped from his fingers and fell to the floor, splashing whisky everywhere. "What in the name of Jasus . . . Have you gone daft, man?" he spluttered, his fingers gripping onto the arms of his chair as the color washed from his ruddy face.

"Not in the least," Rafe said coolly. "I've come for some answers, Delany. I trust either you'll give them to me or you won't, in which case, you will end up with a bullet in your chest."

"Now, see here, your grace, don't you be pointing that thing at me. We're two grown men and can discuss our differences without the use of force."

"Can we?" Rafe lowered the pistol. "In that case, you can tell me exactly what happened six years ago, the night that Lord Kincaid followed his daughter to the Bailey house, the same night of the uprising when Jamie Bailey was shot to death for his involvement—and Lord Kincaid was also shot and then arrested for treason."

"Why, just that, your grace," Paddy replied, his bleary eyes growing wide with innocence. "I don't know anything more about than you do. How could I? I wasn't there, was I?"

"You might want to reconsider that ill-advised statement, Delany. You and my cousin were well known to be as thick as thieves. Isn't it ironic that both you and Thomas should gain everything you wanted from Ian Kincaid's unfortunate misadventure that night?"

"Like I said, it wasn't anything to do with me," Paddy said with a shrug. "Your cousin was the one with his eye on Kincaid. It wouldn't surprise me to hear that he did something to help his luck along, being the sort of man he was, but it's the first I've heard of it."

"I see," Rafe said, realizing that Paddy was too drunk and too stupid to see just how much trouble he was in. Or maybe he simply assumed Rafe was such an idiot himself that he could be easily duped. "Perhaps I was mistaken, in which case, I beg your pardon," he said, carefully changing tactics. "But perhaps you can still help me."

"Sure, your grace, although like I said, I don't know much."

"Then allow me to enlighten you about what happened that night," Rafe said. "Lucy Kincaid found a letter in her bedroom that said Nell Bailey was deathly ill. Lucy had been forbidden to visit the Baileys by her father because of the unrest and his suspicions that Jamie was involved in a plot to burn a number of Protestant holdings, but she went anyway, concerned for her friend."

"There's nothing new in what you're telling me," Paddy said, retrieving his fallen glass and refilling it from the bottle. "That's all common knowledge."

Rafe smiled coldly. "Perhaps. But it is odd, is it not, that upon arriving at the Bailey house she found Nell in perfect health, with no knowledge of any letter? And even odder that my cousin, a house guest at Kincaid, should have gone to Lord Kincaid in deep concern, claiming to have seen his daughter slipping out of the house late at night—and in the company of a man who perfectly fitted Jamie Bailey's description. Naturally Lord Kincaid went after his daughter."

Paddy knocked back the contents of the glass. "I always heard that the girl was up to her neck in plotting with the troublemakers," he said. "She probably made up the story about the letter to save her skin after everything went sour."

"Really? But try looking at it in another light. Suppose Lucy was innocent after all, and somehow Thomas had prior knowledge of the uprising. Suppose he planted the letter himself, or had someone else do it, and then he removed the evidence after Lucy had left but before going to Lord Kincaid with his story?"

"I don't see what purpose that would have served," Paddy said, suddenly looking wary.

"Oh, it served his purpose perfectly, for Lord Kincaid was exactly where Thomas wanted him when the militia came for Jamie—and already accused of complicity, for the militia didn't give him a chance to speak before they shot him too, although not to kill."

"It could have been a stray bullet," Paddy protested.

"I don't think so," Rafe said. "You seem to forget he was tried for the crime of sedition and his land confiscated—and delivered directly into my cousin's hands."

Paddy shifted uncomfortably in his chair, but he said nothing.

"But there are two things that puzzle me," Rafe continued. "The first is this: Jamie would never have returned home if he thought his involvement in the uprising had been discovered, so someone must have turned him in to the militia— and if not Thomas, then who? And the second question is how Thomas knew that the uprising was going to occur that night. I doubt he was in on the plans, being a British Protestant."

"You're contradicting yourself," Paddy said with supreme confidence. "You can't have it both ways. Either Thomas knew about the plans or he didn't know. The way you put it, I don't see how he could have known anything at all."

"Not unless he had an inside informant, someone who was an Irish Catholic—someone who had access to the information and who also had as much interest in seeing Lord Kincaid ousted as Thomas had," Rafe said, springing the trap. "There is only one possible person who fits that description, and that is you, Delany."

Paddy crossed his arms. "You're dreaming," he said, his lip curling. "I keep myself to myself. The first I heard of any uprising was after the fact."

"A pity," Rafe said, shaking his head sadly. "I was beginning to think you were going to see reason. You see, Delany, I hold all the cards. I can go to the militia now and present my case, and I have tenants aplenty to back me up in my suspicions." He weighed the pistol in his hand. "You'd probably hang."

"For what?" Paddy scoffed.

"For complicity in defrauding an Irish peer. For conspiracy in a heinous crime. Of course since Thomas can't be tried, being dead, the full weight would be on your shoulders."

A sweat broke out on Delany's brow and his eyes darted back and forth as if looking for an escape.

"On the other hand, should you agree to sign a full confession, which I happen to have drafted for you, I might reconsider and let the matter go. All I wish is for Lucy to have the comfort of knowing that she and her father are both fully exonerated. The confession would stay safely at Kincaid, out of the hands of the magistrate, providing you cause no further trouble."

Delany's lips pulled back over his teeth in a snarl. "Damn you," he hissed. "Damn you for a cheating, lying Englishman."

"Or I could just shoot you now," Rafe said, raising the pistol and pointing it directly at Delany's chest. "Believe me, I'd derive great satisfaction from the act, given everything you have done. And since I'm a lying Englishman, I'll claim self-defense and get away with it with no trouble."

"You're bluffing," Paddy said, still as arrogant as a rooster, even though perspiration poured down his cheeks, the acrid stench of fear filling the room.

"Am I?" In a flash Rafe crossed the room and grabbed Paddy by the collar, dragging him to his feet and jabbing the barrel of the gun under the tender flesh of his jaw. "Outside with you then. You're finished either way. You can hang, or you can die like a man. Your choice."

"You haven't the nerve," Paddy said, sneering up at him. "You're nothing but a lily-livered British aristocrat, puffed up with self-importance. You're no better than your cousin, for you've taken Kincaid over with no argument, haven't you? If you cared so much about justice, you'd return it to its rightful owner, wouldn't you then?"

"Spare me the lecture on Irish nationalism, for you've no right to it, Paddy Delany. You've taken what you had no right to take and left suffering in your stead."

"I did the best with what I had!" Paddy cried, trying to wrench away to no avail.

"You did indeed," Rafe said, tightening his hold on Paddy's collar. "And you profited well, did you not? But never mind that. We have a separate issue today, and it's one I'm inclined to kill you for. Shall we go?"

"I'm not going anywhere with a miserable Englishman— I'd rather die here on the spot."

Rafe shrugged. "Fine. Personally, I'd rather shoot you and get it over with, but I'm just as content to see you first rot in jail before you're hanged, drawn, and quartered and your head stuck on a pike outside of Newgate. Because you see, if you choose the magistrate's route, I have no compunction in changing the story and telling him that you were instrumental in the plot to begin with and only changed your tune after Jamie was killed and you saw a way to save your skin. And you know what the government thinks about that sort of behavior."

"They'd never believe you," Paddy spat out.

"Wouldn't they? I really don't think the sworn word of a British duke would be called into question, especially if that British duke is maligning his own cousin in the bargain. And don't forget that you've made sworn enemies out of the Kincaid tenants. I know for a fact that to a man they would be willing to say anything I tell them to say." He leaned his face into Paddy's. "But as I said, I'd be just as happy to oblige you and shoot you here and now."

Paddy looked as if he was about to soak his pants. His legs shook so badly that he would have collapsed if Rafe hadn't kept him upright by sheer force.

"Get—get that thing away from my throat," he whispered.

Rafe lowered the barrel, still maintaining a firm grip on Paddy's neck. "I assume you would prefer to sign?" he asked.

"G-give me—give me the accursed paper," Paddy jabbered. "I'll make my mark on it."

Rafe produced it from his coat pocket, along with a pen.

Delany grabbed both from him and scribbled his name at the bottom, his hand trembling so badly that his signature was barely legible. He shoved the paper and pen back at Rafe.

"There and be gone with you." Every muscle in Paddy's body shook as he spoke, his face now a bright red. "I swear you'll regret this day as long as you live."

"I doubt that very sincerely," Rafe answered, tucking the signed document securely in his pocket. "But I will tell you this, Paddy Delany. Cross me one more time and you will regret the day you were born—this piece of paper will go directly to the magistrate. I hope we are perfectly clear."

"Perfectly, *your worship*. Most perfectly. I only wonder who's going to have the most regrets."

"I can answer that for you very easily. It will not be me."

Rafe released Paddy with a violent shove and turned, leaving without another word.

His only goal now was returning to Lucy with the signed proof of her innocence in hand—and somehow managing to convince her that it made all the difference in the world to them both.

23

$\mathscr{L}$ucy spent the afternoon in the rath that contained the Kincaid family graveyard. The ring of trees on the rim offered her physical shelter, and the graves of her mother and father that sat side by side offered her sore heart a measure of comfort. Or if not comfort, at least she didn't feel so completely alone in the world.

She knelt by her parents' headstones, pulling up the overgrown weeds, softly singing Irish ballads that her mother had taught Lucy at her knee, sweet ballads of love, sorrowful ballads of loss.

When the graves were finally tidy, she sat back on her heels and ran her fingers down the cool stone of her father's marker, tracing the lettering of his name, the dates of his birth and death, the epitaph: *His banner over me was love* . . .

Lucy dropped her hand, thinking how true it was. Her father had always held love in his heart—for his family, his country, for peace and for justice. Even though justice had been denied him.

And yet even then he had not let hatred into his heart, reaching instead for renewed determination that Ireland should be free.

He had died with those words on his lips: *Always stand*

firm in your beliefs and your love for your country—continue to pray for her freedom. And she had. Oh how she had.

But he had said something else too, just before he drew his last breath. *Make me proud, and most of all be the happy girl you were born to be . . . Find a man to love as truly as I loved your mother, and when you find him, never let him go, for love is God's greatest gift of all to us.*

"Oh, Papa," she said, drawing in a deep, shuddering breath. "I have found a man to love, a wonderful man and a good one. But he's British, Papa. He's British and he's a Montagu. How can I love him and still stand firm in my beliefs? I'm so confused . . ."

She buried her face on her knees, her shoulders shaking with dry sobs. Raphael. Where was she ever going to find the strength to give him up?

Lucy.

The word came drifting to her on the warm breeze, a whisper barely heard. She slowly raised her head and looked around, but there was no one there. She was alone—just she and the dead inhabited the little rath.

And then another murmur came, as soft as the rustling leaves. *Be of good heart, child, and give your love where it belongs. It is God's gift, not His burden that He lays on you . . .*

Lucy drew in a startled breath, pressed shaking hands to her mouth. She imagined it. Surely she imagined it. She didn't believe in fairies or leprechauns, or the dead coming back to speak to the living, either. Did she?

She pushed herself to her feet, blinking up at the sky. "Papa?" she whispered uncertainly. But there was nothing more. Just the sighing of the wind and the sound of birds chirping in the trees. "God?" she asked even more uncertainly. No. It couldn't be God. She was sure He didn't refer to Himself in the third person, nor would He bother talking to Lucy Kincaid. It had to have been her imagination.

More shaken than she cared to admit, Lucy cast one last

long, wondering look at her father's grave, then made her way back to the house.

As Lucy changed for dinner, she could hear the murmur of voices coming through the connecting door—Raphael talking to Adams, a quiet, unassuming man who kept well out of the way when he wasn't attending to Rafe's needs. She had a feeling that he was lost in the company of so many Irish, but maybe the duchess and Hugo's arrival with an English maid and valet would make him feel as if he had an oasis of home around him.

She knew how it felt to be alone and isolated in a strange country and she couldn't help but feel sorry for him.

Her hands paused as she was putting her hair up. For the first time it occurred to her that maybe Rafe too had felt alone and isolated all these weeks, the only Englishman other than his valet in a sea of Irish faces. And yet he hadn't said a thing about missing England.

He had quietly gone about the business of restoring Kincaid, never complaining, never saying an unkind word against any of her countrymen. He seemed like the sort of man who could make himself comfortable anywhere. But something his mother had said just that morning drifted back to her.

I had every hope that you would bring my son some well-deserved happiness. He has been alone for so long.

Lucy wondered what the duchess had meant by that. As far as she knew, Raphael had never been alone. He'd always had his mother and his brother, and as far as she knew, he'd had a father for a good long time too.

She frowned, thinking that Raphael never talked about his childhood. In fact, he'd never mentioned his father at all. And the implication behind the duchess's words was that Rafe had not been happy, that he *had* been very much alone.

She thought back to the first time she'd seen him, sitting on his horse, gazing at her across the abyss.

There had been something about him then, as if he understood the sorrow she had been feeling, as if he felt it too and wanted her to know that he understood. And so he had quoted the words of Byron back to her to tell her that very thing.

But had she really been listening to the meaning behind the words? Had she ever once taken into consideration *his* feelings, what he was trying to tell her about himself? What had he said to her just last night? She gazed toward the window, drawing the partial stanza from memory.

> *What deep wounds ever closed without a scar?*
> *The heart's bleed longest, and but heal to wear*
> *That which disfigures it; and they who war*
> *With their own hopes, and have been vanquish'd, bear*
> *Silence, but not submission . . .*

Lucy bit her lip. He had not been talking about passion, not then. *The heart's bleed the longest, and but heal to wear that which disfigures it.* She wasn't even sure that he'd been talking about her.

What could have wounded him so deeply? It hadn't been a woman—his mother had said that he had never given his heart before. Odd in such an attractive man. He must have had opportunity aplenty to fall in love. And yet he'd said himself the night of the ball that he'd never hoped to find love, not before that day on the Downpatrick cliffs.

Why? Lucy pressed her fingertips into her brow, trying to think back over everything he'd ever told her about himself. And the more she thought, the more she realized that he'd actually said very little. He let his actions speak for him. And poetry—someone else's words, not his own. Also odd in one as eloquent as he was. It was as if Rafe didn't want to reveal his innermost feelings, as if there was a secret he held deep inside himself.

And yet he had chosen her to love, had chosen her to let

his guard down in front of. And what had she done but rejected him out of hand, and all because he was an Englishman.

Lucy squeezed her eyes closed against a sharp stab of guilt. She'd been so busy fending him off that she'd never told him how precious his love was to her—how precious *he* was to her. She'd taken the gift he'd given her and thrown it back in his face, denying she felt anything. Denying him.

She'd gone so far as to let him make love to her, not once considering how he might feel when she refused to marry him even then. Dear God in heaven, how she must have hurt him. He never would have said the things he had to her that morning if his pride hadn't been deeply injured.

For he was a proud man, she knew that now. But he didn't wear his pride like armor. It was she who did that, she who was so sure of her principles that she'd never bothered to look beyond them to what was really important.

. . . *Be of good heart, child, and give your love where it belongs. It is God's gift, not His burden that He lays on you* . . .

"Oh, Papa," she whispered. "What have I done in the name of Ireland? What terrible thing have I done?"

Rafe suffered through dinner in near silence, letting his mother and Hugo carry the conversation. He hardly heard what they were saying—even Hugo's barbs went nearly unnoticed.   Lucy was as quiet as he was. She kept her gaze lowered, not once meeting his eyes, her face too pale for his liking.

He was hardly surprised after what he'd said to her that morning. He still cursed himself for losing his temper with her, although she'd given him plenty of provocation. But that was still no excuse for nearly calling her a . . . He shoved the word away, refusing even to form it in his mind.

It was he who had pushed and pushed her at every opportunity, never once asking her what she wanted and finally taking what he needed. Which made him nothing more than a selfish, self-serving bastard.

"Raphael? Darling? Did you not hear me?"

Rafe looked over at his mother, struggling to remember what she'd been talking about, but to no avail. "I beg your pardon," he said. "What were you saying?"

"Goodness, but you have been wool-gathering this evening. I daresay I have never seen you so distracted. What can be on your mind?" She smiled at him as if to say that she knew perfectly well but was far too polite to bring it up.

"Just a small business matter," he replied, not willing to give her even a speck of satisfaction.

"You must have been worrying about your crop yield," she said. "Lucy mentioned that you were concerned about what might come of the planting."

Rafe nearly choked on the sip of wine he'd just taken. "Did she?" he said, wanting to kill his mother and Lucy both. He shot a quick look at Lucy, who had paled even further. And she damned well should have, feeding his mother a line like that.

"Been sowing the seed again, have you, Rafe?" Hugo said with a wicked gleam in his eye. "Never did know a man so fond of tilling the earth. You should have been born a farmer with your proclivities. Dukes are supposed to keep their hands clean and leave the dirty work to others—or at least that's what I always thought."

Rafe added his brother to the list. "Don't push me, Hugo," he said in a low snarl. "You're already in my black books for the stunt you pulled in London."

"Do you mean escorting Lucy to the ball? I cannot think why you'd be annoyed about that. She deserved a little fun after everything she'd been through."

"I'm referring to your refusal to tell me the truth when I asked you for it outright."

"Oh, that. I didn't want to foil our mother's carefully laid plan. But I can see that you've worked our little ruse out for yourself."

"That and a few other things," Rafe said, being deliberately obtuse. He'd talk to Lucy later, and not just about Delany's confession.

"Then you should thank us both," Hugo said cheerfully. "If it hadn't been for us, you probably wouldn't have worked anything out at all. Instead, here you are, exactly where you wanted to be."

"Where I want to be or do not want to be is none of your concern," Rafe said tightly. "I'd thank you to keep your nose out of my affairs."

"Your affairs are your own," Hugo replied with a grin. "I wouldn't think to intrude. It was just one innocent night, after all, or at least on my part."

Rafe nearly sprang out of his chair and lunged for Hugo's throat, but his mother's hand on his shoulder restrained him.

"Now, now, boys, let us not have any of your bickering in front of Lucy. She looks exhausted, poor girl, and it is little wonder, after your keeping her up half the night, Raphael."

Rafe stared first at his mother and then at Lucy in complete disbelief. Lucy hadn't—she *couldn't* have . . .

"I gather Irish weddings are unusually vigorous," his mother continued blithely, and Rafe breathed again. "I think an early night would be in order for all of us. It was a lovely dinner, Lucy. You must give my compliments to your cook."

"I will," Lucy said, looking as if she wanted to disappear under the table with embarrassment, which gave Rafe some small measure of satisfaction. "I am so pleased you enjoyed Nancy's efforts, Duchess," she added faintly. "Would you care for tea in the drawing room?"

"No, thank you, my dear girl. I too am tired, but in my case it is from so much traveling. I think I will go up now. Hugo? Will you light my way?"

"Certainly, Mama. I am ready for my bed as well." Hugo

stood and flashed Rafe one last mischievous smile. "Sleep well, brother. And you also, Lucy. Don't let the bedbugs bite. Or anything else."

Rafe glared at him, but Hugo just chuckled in the face of his brother's wrath. "Come, Mama. Let us leave Lucy and Rafe to discuss their crop failure—or success, as the case may be."

Rafe breathed a sigh of relief as the door closed behind them. "I'm sorry about that," he said to Lucy, who sat frozen in her chair. "Actually, I'm sorry about a great many things, but my brother's acid tongue is one of his more unfortunate qualities."

"Do you—do you think they know about last night?" Lucy said in a strangled voice.

"I have no idea, although I think Hugo might well have guessed. My mother is a little more difficult to read. I can't always tell what she knows and what she doesn't. But neither of us has any way of divining how long they were standing there this morning. They might easily have heard only the very end."

"I tried to put our argument in a different light, just in case," Lucy said, looking up at him miserably.

"I gather that you did," he replied, his heart going out to her, for she really did look mortified. "But really, Lucy—*crop* yields?"

"It was the only thing I could think of that made any sense," she said, twisting her napkin around in her fingers. "Your mother asked me directly what we'd been arguing about, and that was the first thing that came to my mind."

Rafe couldn't help the laugh that escaped him. "I suppose I can see the logic. But never mind that now. I truly am sorry about some of the things I said."

"And I," she replied, a flush spreading over her pale cheeks. "I didn't mean to upset you so badly."

"Nor I you. I've had all day to think about it, and I've

come to the conclusion that I was unnecessarily brutal in my statements."

"Oh, no—" Lucy said quickly. "You were not brutal in the least. It was I who goaded you, and I shouldn't have done. Please, Rafe, let us not argue anymore, for it distresses me so."

"Does it, sweetheart?" he said, smiling softly at her. "I am glad to hear that you are not entirely indifferent to me, even though that is the impression I believe you tried to leave me with. But let us drop the subject just for a moment, for I have something important to talk to you about—and you need not worry. It has nothing to do with you and me. Or at least not directly."

Lucy clutched her hands together, anxiety written all over her face. "What is it?" she whispered. "Surely not Eunice?"

"No, not Eunice. This is about how your father lost Kincaid six years ago."

"How—how he lost Kincaid? But you know how it happened," she said, her expression wary now.

"I only knew a part of what happened. I wish you had trusted me enough to tell me the whole story before this."

"Then Eunice *did* say something to you," Lucy said, looking away. "I thought she must have done, but you didn't bring the subject up, so I prayed she had kept her silence."

"When has Eunice ever kept her silence?" He shook his head. "I heard her version of events the afternoon I confronted her, but I discounted it as a pack of lies. However, today I learned that there was a margin of truth to it."

Lucy bowed her head, one shaking hand moving to her throat. "I suppose you must hate me now," she said after a long moment.

"*Hate* you? Why on earth would you think that?"

"Because you believe that my antigovernment activities led my father to his betrayal and his death," she cried. "And why shouldn't you? I've done nothing but go on and on about the

Irish cause. You probably think I would do anything, however extreme, to win that cause over."

Rafe rose, moving around the table to where Lucy sat. He lowered himself onto one knee and gently turned her to face him. "I think nothing of the sort," he said quietly. "I heard a very different story today, a story about a young girl who was led in all innocence into a trap designed for her father. I learned that she witnessed terrible things that night and that she was blamed for everything that happened afterward." He sighed heavily. "I believe that she in turn blamed herself for something that had nothing to do with her, and so took on an impossible burden of guilt—and because of that guilt she allowed herself to be very badly used by her stepmother."

Lucy trembled under his hands, her head lowered so far that he couldn't see her face.

"Sweetheart. Look at me?"

She shook her head. "I c-can't," she said, her voice so strained he could hardly hear it. "It's all true—I did go to the Bailey house, and my father followed me. He was dishonored because of what I did. He *died* because of what I did. But I didn't mean for it to happen, I swear it, Rafe. I didn't mean for it to happen."

"I know. And I have proof of your innocence," Rafe said, reaching into his coat pocket. "Dry your tears, Lucy, and look at this. Look, my love," he insisted, taking her chin and forcing it up, pushing the paper into her hand.

"What—what is it?" she asked on a gulp.

"It's Delany's full confession, saying that he and my cousin planned the entire fiasco as a way to steal Kincaid from your father—I wrote it all out first, then forced him to sign it. Look: it says that Delany wrote the letter and Thomas planted it in your bedroom, that Thomas then went to your father to tell him you'd disappeared and to imply that you'd gone off with Jamie Bailey."

Lucy looked down at the sheet of paper, quickly reading over it, then slowly dragged her gaze to his. "But how?" she asked, her voice breaking and her eyes flooding with tears. "How did you put all the pieces together?"

"Mairead came to me this morning and told me the story as she understood it. It wasn't too difficult to fill in the blanks, knowing Thomas as I did and having had a good dose of the way Delany's mind works. And yours," he added with a little smile.

"But how did you ever convince Delany to sign it?" Lucy said, tears trickling down her cheeks.

"It was nothing that a few strong words and a pistol at his throat couldn't do. It's finished, sweetheart. It's finally finished. You are absolved of any wrongdoing."

"Thank you, Rafe. I thank you with all my heart." Lucy shook her head, staring down at the page. "I cannot believe it," she said, her voice thick. "I cannot believe it, after all this time . . ."

"Believe it. And you say you never cry," he murmured, handing her his handkerchief.

"I don't," she said, wiping her eyes. "Or at least I never used to. I don't know what's gotten into me lately."

"Hmm," he said. "Maybe it has something to do with not having to be brave every waking moment. You don't, you know. You have me to protect you now."

A smile trembled at the corners of Lucy's mouth. "You like protecting people, don't you? I think you like it almost as much as ordering them around, but I suppose that's what comes of being a duke."

"Lucy," he said on a warning note. "I did apologize for my behavior this morning." He couldn't believe she was still throwing the damned dukedom up in his face when all he'd tried to do was to make her life a little easier.

She nodded. "Yes, and I didn't mean it like that. I just meant that you have a way of commanding things so they turn out as you want them. I think you must have learned it from your father."

Rafe flinched, the unexpected mention of his father catching him off guard and leaving him feeling raw and exposed. He stood and walked over to the window, looking out over the night. A full moon was rising in the sky, its golden light cascading down over the lawn and reflecting on the gleaming surface of the river. At least something in his life looked calm and ordered.

He released a harsh breath. "I doubt my father has anything to do with my own behavior," he said. "He died when I was very young."

"Oh, Rafe," Lucy said from behind him, her voice heavy with sympathy. "I'm so sorry—I didn't know. How old were you?"

"Nine," he said shortly, having no intention of pursuing the subject. "But never mind that. There's something else I'd like to ask you." He leaned his hand against the cool windowpane, giving them one last chance. One last heart-wrenching chance to change both their futures. "Do you really think of me as your enemy?" He braced himself for her answer.

"My—my enemy?" Lucy said in a shaky voice. "Why would you ask me that?"

"Don't beg the question," he said curtly. "It's simple enough. You have said time and again that you will not marry me because I am British, but it occurred to me today that perhaps my greater sin is in being a Montagu." He glanced over his shoulder at her, praying to see absolution in her face.

Lucy stared at him, her face ashen. "Rafe . . ." she whispered, her fingers clutching on the edge of the table. "I—I don't—I mean . . ." She trailed off.

"Never mind," he said tightly. "You've answered my question."

"But you don't understand," she protested. "The least you can do is hear me out. It's *complicated*."

"I've heard enough. I honestly don't think I can bear to hear any more," he replied, his heart feeling as if it were shredding into a hundred bloody pieces. It had become chillingly clear to him that no matter how Lucy might feel about him, she was obviously never going to let go of her grudge or her blasted principles. Maybe the only way to make her happy was to hand Kincaid over to her and disappear from her life.

He looked back out the window at the bright night, his grip on his control stretched to the limit.

He suddenly stiffened. "Dear God," he whispered, realizing that the night *was* bright—far too bright. "Oh, dear God!"

"What is it, Rafe?" Lucy asked in a puzzled voice.

"Fire—the whole bloody west wing is on fire!" he cried. "Raise the alarm, Lucy—get everyone out—and then ring the stableyard bell for all you're worth! We're going to need all the help we can get."

He tore out the door without another word.

24

$\mathcal{L}$ucy didn't hesitate. Her heart pounding with fear, she somehow managed to get everyone out of the house within minutes.

"Get all the buckets you can find and start filling them at the well," she commanded the group, then flew to the stable-yard and grabbed the bell rope, pulling on it with all her strength.

A furious ringing broke out into the night, sending the alarm to the cotters.

"Please hear it," she prayed desperately, looking over her shoulder at the terrible sight of flames shooting out of the ground windows of the west wing—the one wing that was still closed off, thank God. If anyone had been in there they would have been burned alive . . .

She heard Rafe shouting directions to the men, could see people running in all directions.

Oh, her house, her beautiful, beautiful house. It couldn't burn, it just couldn't. Rafe would protect it—Rafe would know what to do, she thought desperately.

The duchess appeared at her shoulder. "Give me the rope, child. I'll take over. You are of far more use back at the house. See what Raphael needs."

Lucy nodded and handed the duchess the rope, then tore back to the west wing. Rafe had already organized a line of people from the well to the house. They passed buckets along furiously, one to the other and finally to Rafe and Hugo, who stood side by side, emptying buckets onto the flames as fast as they could grab them.

"What can I do?" she panted, reaching Rafe's side. The heat emanating from the fire seared into her skin and she had to take a step back.

He barely spared her a glance. "Get away," he barked. "Just see the water keeps coming."

"Be careful," she pleaded. "Please be careful, Rafe."

"There's no time to be careful," he said, grabbing another bucket from Dooley, who stood right behind him. "If the roof goes up the whole house is finished. Get the hell out of here, Lucy. Get out now!"

Lucy swallowed hard, but obeyed him instantly, dashing back to the well to help draw the water.

In what seemed like an hour, but was probably only about fifteen minutes, the first of the tenants started to arrive, the O'Reillys in the lead.

"Holy Mary, Mother of God," Mairead said, taking in the scene as she reached Lucy. "What happened?"

"I don't know." Lucy gasped, her back burning from heaving the heavy buckets. "There were no candles lit in the west wing, no fires in the grate. I just don't know." She paused to wipe the dripping sweat off her brow. "I can only think it was deliberately set."

"But by whom? And why? No one has a grudge against the duke," Mairead said in bewilderment, taking a bucket from Lucy.

Lucy straightened as a blinding flash of comprehension struck her. "I can think of one person," she said, fury grabbing hold of her and burning as hot as any fire. "Oh, I can indeed, and his name is Paddy Delany."

"Paddy Delany . . . Aye, you could have the right of it," Mairead said slowly. "But I don't know how you're going to prove it. He's a sly one, he is, and good at covering his tracks."

And then all conversation ceased as they focused on their strenuous task. Whenever Lucy had a chance she'd search the crowd for Rafe, and every now and then she'd catch a glimpse of him, or hear his voice barking out orders, reassuring her that he was still safe.

Time lost all meaning. One moment it seemed as if they had the fire under control, and the next it would break out somewhere else, and they would have to redouble their efforts. Every muscle in Lucy's body ached, but there was no stopping, not for a minute.

"Lord have mercy—what is that crazy man doing?" Mairead suddenly exclaimed.

Lucy looked over to where Mairead was pointing. Hugo had wrapped a rope around his waist and was scaling the outside wall, climbing toward the roof.

"Oh, no," Lucy cried. "He'll kill himself for sure!"

That seemed to be Rafe's opinion as well, for he was shouting up at his brother, a volley of violent curses interspersed with orders to come down. They did no good— Hugo ignored him.

He reached the roof, then untied the rope and tossed it down. "Stop your bloody tirade, Rafe, and tie a bucket on the end," he called, his voice coming faintly from three stories up. "I'm going to damp the roof down."

"You're going to break your damned neck if I don't break it for you first," Rafe shouted back, but he tied a bucket onto the rope anyway.

Hugo hauled it up, and splashed it out, then sent the rope back again. Time and time again Rafe sent a bucket up, watching, his head tilted back with a desperate expression on his face. She could just imagine the terror Rafe was feeling as his brother balanced precariously on the rooftop, his feet slipping and sliding on the wet surface as he moved around to each new area.

She could hardly breathe through her own fear.

She didn't know when it was that she realized the flames had been extinguished, only that there was a slow cessation of movement, a murmur of relief that went through the crowd.

Through her numbness she was dimly aware that the tension in her body had started to uncoil and she could breathe again. Someone took the bucket out of her hand and led her over to a patch of grass, gently pushing her down.

It was Mairead. "Sit here and catch your breath, lass. The danger is past."

Lucy rubbed one hand over her face, then looked back up at the roof, where Hugo stood grinning down at his brother, his hands planted on his hips.

"Try not to call me a hero," he called down.

"A bloody idiot is more like it," Rafe replied sharply. "Now get down from there before anything else happens."

No sooner were the words out of his mouth when a great crash sounded and the portion of the roof where Hugo was standing gave way.

A cry ripped from Rafe's throat and he leaped forward, pushing away the hands that tried to restrain him.

"You can't go in there—it's not safe, your lordship," Seamus O'Reilly insisted. "I'll go—me and Fergus."

"Get your damned hands off me," Rafe roared. "I'm going after my brother and you're not going to stand in my way. And you're not coming in with me either. As you said, it's not safe."

He ran toward the door and wrenched it open, choking as acrid smoke swirled around him, burning at his nose and stinging at his eyes. He blindly made his way up the staircase, pushing away charred timber as he went, calling for Hugo the whole time.

All that met his ears was silence, broken only by the hissing of hot, wet wood.

God. Oh, God. Not Hugo. Not Hugo—he'd die himself if anything happened to his brother—the little brother he'd sworn to keep safe from harm.

He reached the third floor and looked up, seeing the sky through the great hole in the roof, the moon casting a blessed pool of light onto the floor. "Hugo! For God's sake, answer me!"

"ver here." Hugo's voice came weak and strained from ..der a pile of beams and rubble. "I'm over here, Rafe." He moaned in pain.

Rafe crossed the room in three strides and dropped to his knees, frantically clawing at the debris until he had cleared Hugo's face. "Dear God, are you badly injured?" he asked, looking down at his brother with deep concern. Hugo's face was white as a sheet.

"I think my ribs are broken," Hugo croaked. "There's a beam or something pinning me down. I can't breathe very well."

"I'll have you out in a minute," Rafe said, pushing aside timber until he saw the beam that had trapped Hugo.

He somehow managed to get his hands underneath it, and with a strength that came from some deep reserve in his exhausted body he lifted it and rolled it off his brother's chest.

"Ah, that's better," Hugo said, pulling in a cautious breath of air. He tried to sit up, but fell back again with a sharp grimace.

"Steady there, little brother," Rafe said. "I think you've done enough for one day." He slipped his arms under Hugo's back and lifted him up, supporting his brother's weight against his chest. "Can you walk?"

"I think so," Hugo said, as Rafe pulled him to his feet. "Oh. Then again, maybe not." He gasped as he collapsed against Rafe.

"Never mind," Rafe said, scooping his brother up into his arms. He staggered back against Hugo's weight, which matched his own. "Let's get out of here before the whole damn thing falls in."

Hugo looked up at him, his blue eyes dull with pain. "Thanks, Rafe. I don't know why you didn't just let me suffocate after all the aggravation I've caused you."

"Because I love you, you bloody fool. I don't know why you can't get that through your thick head."

Hugo smiled faintly. "Maybe because you never bothered to tell me."

"Why bother when you never listen to anything I say? Why the *hell* didn't you come down off the roof when I told you to?"

"I couldn't—couldn't let Lucy's house burn down. Wetting the roof seemed the best way to save it," he said with a weak cough. "Damnation, but that hurts."

"I'll send for a doctor to look at you as soon as we get out," Rafe said, breathing hard with the strain of carrying his brother. It took him a good ten minutes to negotiate the staircase, between having to pick his way over rubble and stopping to rest for brief intervals.

He'd just reached the open door when another ominous rumble started and the rest of the roof caved in with a thunderous roar, sending up clouds of dust and smoke.

"Oops," Hugo said, his eyes closing and his head rolling back on Rafe's shoulder as he fainted.

It was just as well, Rafe thought, taking him out into the fresh air. Hugo was going to be in serious pain for a few days, and the less of it he was awake for the better.

He dimly registered the relieved exclamations of the gathered crowd as they emerged from the wreckage, thinking only of getting his brother to a safe place where he could lay him down.

Lucy and his mother appeared at his side as he gently stretched Hugo out on the grass and collapsed next to him.

"Hugo—how is Hugo?" his mother asked, her voice tight with fear. "Raphael, tell me he is not—"

"He'll be fine," he said, struggling to pull air into his lungs. "He's broken some ribs, but I don't think there's any worse damage. He's breathing fairly easily, so I doubt he punctured his lungs."

"Thank God," his mother said, her voice thin with strain. "When the rest of the roof went, I thought . . . well, never mind what I thought. You are both safe and that is all that matters."

Rafe rubbed his hands over his face. "There's never a dull moment when Hugo's around."

He glanced up at Lucy, who hadn't said a word. "Are you all right?" he asked, taking in her dirty, torn dress, her obvious exhaustion, for she was shaking like a leaf.

"I'll be fine," she said, pushing her hair off her soot-streaked face. "But—but there's blood all over your shirt." She pointed a trembling finger at him.

He looked down with a frown. "So there is," he said, lifting his hand to a shoulder he only just realized was throbbing with pain. His' fingers found a rip in his shirt and a deep gash beneath. "I must have cut myself on something when I was getting Hugo free," he said, wincing at the contact.

"Getting him free?" his mother asked, paling again.

"He was trapped under a beam," Rafe replied. "Lucy, call for a doctor, will you? Hugo could use some looking after."

"Hugo's not the only one," Lucy said, her eyes suddenly flashing with anger. "Oh, *Rafe,* you could have been killed!"

"We saved your house, didn't we? What else could possibly matter to you?"

Lucy looked as if he'd slapped her. She abruptly turned on her heel and walked away, her back stiff.

"Really, darling," his mother said reprovingly. "The poor girl has been through enough tonight. I do not think you should be taking out your temper on her."

"Leave it alone, Mama," he snapped, thoroughly out of patience. Trying to save people from themselves was a thankless job. All he had to show for it was a shattered heart and a ripped shoulder.

For the first time in his life he began to understand why his father might have decided to give up on the whole damn world and take himself out of it.

But still, it was a course of action that Rafe could never follow, mainly because he cherished life and honored the people he loved—although in that exact moment he really couldn't imagine why.

Lucy stormed toward the house, looking for Dooley to fetch the doctor. She was filled with anger and hurt that Rafe had just treated her in such a cold-blooded fashion, behaving as if she meant nothing to him, or he to her. Sometimes she didn't understand him at all.

Why, for example, had he suddenly turned into a glacier after dinner when she'd innocently mentioned his father? Why had he asked her a question—an important question—and then refused to let her give him an answer? And why had he just lashed out at her when all she'd done was to voice her concern about his welfare?

"Lucy—Lucy! Wait up a moment, will you?"

Lucy stopped and turned as Eamon Percy ran up to her, covered from head to foot with dirt and perspiration.

"What is it, Eamon?" she asked curtly, in no mood to talk to anyone.

"I think we found the culprit who did this, but since I don't think his lordship is in any state to be dealing with the situation, I thought it best to come to you."

"You found the culprit? *Where?* Who is it?" she asked, her gaze snapping to his face.

"It's Paddy Delany. Conor tripped across him in the stable when he went to check on the horses—they tend to become panicked when fire's about, you know."

"Yes, I know," Lucy said impatiently, wishing he'd get on with it. "And?"

"And there Paddy was, nearly passed out in the hayloft, for Conor went up to get the horses a bit extra feed, you see. He was mumbling about revenge and the like—Paddy, not Conor that is, and Conor thought that it only made sense that Paddy had come to torch the place, since the duke had dismissed him just like that. Everyone heard Paddy threaten the duke with trouble that same day." He scratched his head. "What do you think, Lucy? Conor and Seamus O'Reilly have him by the throat, and we need to be doing something constructive with him."

A slow smile spread across Lucy's face. "Like murder him?"

Eamon grinned. "It'll do sure enough, but I'm thinking that calling the magistrate might be more the trick. Paddy's kicking and screaming up a fuss something fierce, and with each word he's digging himself deeper into his grave."

"Then go for the magistrate," Lucy said. "Tell him everything that happened here tonight and that the duke will explain everything to his satisfaction when he arrives. There's a lot more to this than you realize. Oh, and Eamon, while you're on your way, stop at the doctor's house, since it's on the main road. The duke and his brother have both sustained injuries and could use his skill."

"Will do, Lucy. Uh—since I've got you here in private, do you think there might be any chance that Conor and I can address our intentions to your stepsisters? We're both keen on marrying them. That is, Conor wants to speak for Fiona and me for Amaryllis. Can we dare to hope?" he asked, his Adam's apple gulping up and down. "We'd look after them very well."

"I think there's every hope, and the sooner the better," Lucy said with a tired smile. "I know the duke will give his blessing to the marriages. It's only their mother to get around now, and knowing Raphael, he'll see to that too. Now get on with you, Eamon Percy. There's no time to waste."

"Right you are," Eamon said, swiftly taking off into the darkness.

Lucy stood still for a moment, stiffening her resolve, then went straight back to Rafe. He needed to know about Delany. And then he could go hang.

"What is it now?" Rafe said, looking up at her as she came to a halt directly in front of him. "Have you come to read me another lecture?"

Lucy glared at him. "I've come to tell you that Conor found Paddy Delany in the stable. He's three sheets to the wind and apparently doing a fine job of implicating himself for setting the fire. I've sent Eamon for the magistrate."

Rafe pushed himself to his feet with a grunt. "I thought as much. Well, that's good of him, isn't it, delivering himself right into my hands—it saves me the trouble of going after him and thrashing the truth out of his miserable mouth."

"I suppose he couldn't resist watching his handiwork," Lucy said with a shrug. "We can only be thankful that he didn't manage to do more damage—and that no one was killed," she added, giving him a withering look. "But then what does it matter to me?"

Rafe glared right back at her. "Don't start, Lucy. I warn you, I'm in no mood."

"Oh, and you think I am? You're not the only one who is exhausted, Rafe. And you're not the only one who is upset and angry either, although for the life of me, I don't know what *you* have to be upset or angry about."

"Then you're a bloody little fool," he said in a low voice, looking sideways at her in the darkness, a savage frown marking his face. "I'm going to deal with Delany. I strongly suggest you keep your distance from me, because I will not answer for my actions."

"I'll keep my distance, all right. I remember all too well what happened the last time you said that," Lucy shot back.

He stiffened, a flicker of some undefinable but powerful

emotion crossing his face. "As you say, Lucy," he replied, suddenly sounding incredibly drained.

His mouth set in a grim line, he strode off to the stable-yard without sparing Lucy another glance.

Rafe finally finished with the magistrate, who was only too happy to take a loudly protesting Paddy Delany off to jail. Rafe had handed over Paddy's confession and the magistrate needed nothing more by way of proof of Paddy's guilt—in more than one matter. Paddy Delany would be locked up for a good long time.

Rafe tried to derive some satisfaction from the thought, but he couldn't seem to feel anything at all. It was as if all the life had drained out of him, leaving him nothing more than an empty shell. And yet underneath his numbness a terrible pain raged.

As soon as the doctor had finished examining Hugo and binding his ribs, he attended to Rafe's shoulder.

"Your brother's a lucky man, your grace, that he is," the doctor said, stitching up Rafe's wound. "Three cracked ribs is a small price to pay for falling the way he did."

"Are you sure that he'll make a full recovery?" Rafe asked, clenching his teeth against the sharp burn of the needle piercing his flesh.

"Quite sure," the doctor said, tying off the thread and cutting it. "Just make sure he stays quiet for a few days. I've given him something for the pain and it ought to make him drowsy enough to keep him in his bed. There you go, your grace. You'll be as good as new. I'll be back in the morning to look in on you both. Try not to put any strain your shoulder."

"Thank you," Rafe said as the doctor applied a bandage over his neat line of stitches. "I appreciate your coming out to Kincaid so promptly."

Rafe gave himself a thorough wash and changed his clothes, his sore arm a nuisance. Despite his exhaustion he knew there was no way he was going to sleep. He needed to find somewhere to be utterly alone with his thoughts and he could only think of one place.

He quietly let himself out of his bedroom and went down the hall to Hugo's room. He was happy to find Hugo sound asleep, his breathing deep and even.

"That's good, little brother," he murmured, looking down at him. Hugo looked so young and vulnerable, his eyelashes dark on pale cheeks, almost like the small boy Rafe remembered so well—before everything had gone wrong. "You sleep fast."

He smoothed Hugo's hair off his forehead. "I do love you, you know. I always have—I'm only sorry I haven't let you know it better."

Hugo's eyelashes fluttered. "I love you too, big brother," he said, his voice thick with sleep. "Sorry about everything . . ."

Rafe smiled softly. "There's nothing to be sorry for," he said through a tight throat.

"It was nice working together tonight," Hugo murmured. "Almost like the old days . . ."

"Yes, almost like the old days," Rafe agreed, struggling against tears.

"You're dressed for riding," Hugo said, turning his head on the pillow and hazily regarding Rafe's doeskin breeches and boots. "Going somewhere?"

"I need to clear my head," Rafe said. "I'm going out to the coast. Sleep, little brother. I didn't mean to wake you."

"Mmm. I think I will." He reached his hand out and clasped Rafe's in his. "It's Lucy, isn't it? Never mind, it will all come right . . ." He yawned.

"I doubt it," Rafe said heavily. "But it's not for you to worry about. I'll see you in the morning."

"Right. The morning." Hugo's eyes closed again.

Rafe gave his brother one last long look, then left, closing the door softly behind him. He headed straight for the stable to saddle up Pegasus, planning to ride him hard and fast, his throbbing shoulder be damned.

Lucy's head lifted as a tap came at her door. She knew it couldn't be Rafe—he wanted nothing to do with her. She slowly stood and pulled her shawl more closely around her nightdress, trying to gather her badly shattered composure. She prayed it wasn't the duchess wanting to talk to her again about Rafe—she didn't think she could stand it.

"Hugo!" she exclaimed as she opened the door to see him leaning against the wall, one hand wrapped around his bandaged chest. "What on earth are you doing out of bed?"

"Doing you a favor," he said on a labored breath, looking as if he might keel over at any moment.

"I don't know what favor you think you can do me, but I'm taking you straight back to your room," Lucy said with exasperation. Didn't any of the Montagu men have an iota of sense in their heads? "Here, lean on me." She slipped an arm around his waist and took the brunt of his weight against her side, leading him down the corridor and helping him back into bed.

"Need—need to talk to you, Lucy," he said faintly as she pulled the covers up over him.

She had to lean over to hear him properly. "Can't it wait until morning?"

"No . . . it's Rafe. He said he's going to the coast, and I don't think he should be alone. He's hurting, Lucy, and I think you're the only one who can help."

"He's gone all the way to the *coast*?" Lucy said in horror. "At this hour, after everything he's been through? Is he mad?"

"Not mad. Just . . . badly upset. I've never seen him like this before, not since our father died." He winced as he tried to shift.

"Hugo—I'm sorry to be asking you difficult questions now, but how *did* your father die? Rafe refuses to talk about him at all, and I don't understand why. He seemed so angry earlier when I brought the subject up."

"Shot—shotgun," Hugo murmured. "An accident. Rafe found him."

"Oh, dear God," Lucy said, stunned. "He was only nine!"

"I know. Terrible thing. I was too young to be able to remember much about it, but I . . . I remember that day and Rafe's devastation. He needs healing, Lucy, and you're—you're the only one who can give it to him. I'd try, but I've been nothing but trouble to him and he hasn't deserved it. And I think . . . I think tonight brought too much back." He flinched with the effort of the long speech. "Sorry—can't talk anymore."

"Don't say another word," Lucy said, straightening abruptly, panic racing through her at the thought of Rafe alone with his pain. "I'll go after him, Hugo, don't worry. I think I know exactly where he's gone. And thank you—thank you for coming to get me."

"I owe him," Hugo said succinctly. "Look after him, Lucy. Don't let him do anything stupid." And on that last alarming statement, he promptly passed out.

25

Lucy couldn't dress fast enough. She didn't bother with anything but a dress and a pair of half boots, and it took her only another ten minutes to reach the stable and saddle up her mare.

She kicked the horse into a furious gallop and headed straight down the coast road to Ballycastle, whispering a prayer for Raphael's safety the entire way.

He wouldn't do anything stupid. Would he?

Finally reaching the approach to the cliffs after what seemed a lifetime, she slowed her mare, her gaze frantically combing the landscape for a glimpse of Rafe. But he was nowhere to be seen.

She breathed a sigh of relief when she finally spotted Pegasus, grazing placidly among a scattered flock of sheep. So she'd been right. Rafe had come to Downpatrick Head after all.

And she thought she knew exactly why.

Quickly dismounting, she tied up the reins and let her mare loose to graze with Pegasus, tearing up the path past the statue of St. Patrick that stood watching guard over the sheep. The moon hung full and bright in the night sky, safely lighting her way.

She mounted the grassy rise and stopped abruptly.

Rafe sat on the edge of the cliff, his golden head lowered,

his hands tangled in his hair. She could sense the anguish emanating from him even from this distance.

She walked very quietly up behind him and knelt. "Raphael," she said, kneeling, her hand gently touching his shoulder.

He started, his head jerking up, and for one brief instant she saw the savage pain on his face before he quickly disguised it. He couldn't so easily disguise the tears that streaked his cheeks.

Rafe—so controlled, so busy always looking after everyone else—and he'd been crying. The realization broke her heart.

"What are you doing here?" he asked, his tone about as welcoming as a brick wall.

"I knew you'd left the house and taken Pegasus. There was only one place I could think of that you might go."

"Damn you, Lucy," he said, rubbing one hand over his face as if he could erase the evidence of his tears. "Could you not leave me alone even now?"

"No," she said softly. "I could not. Not when I knew that you were this troubled."

"Troubled." He laughed harshly. "Yes, I suppose you could put it like that. But don't worry yourself about me, dear girl. I'll muddle through somehow. Englishmen do that. They learn it in the cradle and every day thereafter. We're taught never to show our feelings, and apparently for good reason."

"Rafe . . . please, don't torture yourself like this," she said, wanting nothing more than to throw her arms around him and show him how much she loved him. But she knew he wouldn't allow her to comfort him. Not now. Not after everything she'd done and said.

"Torture myself? Is that what you think I'm doing?" he said, his eyes glittering. "You might want to reconsider that statement. I don't believe I am the party doing the torturing."

"Rafe—I'm sorry. I know I've hurt you, and I didn't mean

to, I really didn't. If you'd only listened to me tonight I could have explained."

"I've heard enough of your explanations. Although there is one more I would like to hear." He gingerly pushed himself to his feet. "Show me," he said, turning to her.

"Show you what?" Lucy answered in confusion.

"Show me how you did it. How you vanished that day. Where you went."

"Oh," she said, relieved that at least that explanation was easy. "Come over here and look down." She led him to the sinkhole, a great opening in the grass that dropped straight through the middle of the cliff to the sea.

He glanced over at her in question.

"There's a path that skirts around inside it," she said. "If you go down on your stomach and look over you can just see it. It's not very wide—the ledge starts just below the edge of the outside cliff and winds in from there. The path comes out on the other side."

Raphael dropped down flat on the ground and poked his head over the sheer drop, staring down. Lucy stood next to him, her gaze following the huge waves that surged violently in and out of the cavern far below. It wasn't hard to guess what Rafe must be thinking.

"So," he said after a moment. "It never occurred to me to look down here. It's a good twenty feet away from the edge." He shoved himself upright and walked over to the face of the cliff, gazing down onto the narrow ledge.

He turned his head to look at her. "You might easily have killed yourself," he said, his face pale and strained despite the calmness of his voice.

"I might have done," she replied. "I wasn't being as careful as usual that day."

He closed his eyes for a moment and expelled a long breath. "Thank God you didn't fall. That ledge is impossibly narrow. You can understand why I thought the worst."

"I'm sorry," she said, and she really was. It must have

been a terrible moment for him. "I can imagine how you must have felt."

"Can you? I wonder," he said tonelessly. "Actually, I doubt it. I doubt you understand anything at all." He looked back over the heaving sea.

"How can I?" she cried helplessly. "How can I understand when you refuse to tell me anything? Rafe, you hold secrets inside yourself that I can't begin to divine unless you choose to tell me."

"Secrets? If anyone has kept secrets, it's been you."

"That's not what I mean," she said with frustration. "For instance, Hugo told me how your father died. And yet you've never talked about it—not once."

He snapped his head around. "Hugo hasn't the first idea how our father died," he said in a tone so low she could barely hear him.

"But . . . but he said it was a shooting accident." Lucy was thoroughly confused. Surely Hugo knew how his father had died? "He said that you found your father's body."

"That much is true," Rafe replied, his expression as hard as stone. He paused, looking as if he were waging a private battle with himself, although Lucy couldn't imagine what it might be.

She gathered her courage up, refusing to let him leave it there. "Then what is it that Hugo doesn't know?" she persisted. "What more could there possibly be, Rafe?"

He squeezed his eyes shut, his brow knotting. And then he opened his eyes again and looked directly at her. "What Hugo doesn't know—what no one knows—is that it was no accident," he replied. "It was deliberate. He shot himself, and I watched him do it."

Lucy stared at him, the blood draining from her face. "*What?*" she whispered.

"You heard me," Rafe said harshly. "Will that do, Lucy? Is there anything else you'd like to drag out of me?"

Lucy swallowed, utterly appalled by what he'd just told

her. He'd only been a small boy. What it must have done to him, to witness such a horrendous act . . . "But why?" she cried. "Why would he take his own life? And why in front of you? That seems cruel beyond belief!"

Rafe pushed a hand through his hair, his face etched with lines of pain. "He didn't know I was there. He took his gun that day as he often did—he liked to go shooting in the fields and he usually took me along. Only on this day, he didn't call for me." Rafe helplessly shook his head. "I saw him go and I ran after him. But before I could reach him, he put the gun to the underside of his throat and he pulled the trigger."

Lucy pressed her hands against her mouth, the dreadful picture he'd drawn crystal clear in her mind. "No—oh, no . . ." She wanted to cry for him, finally understanding so much. It was little wonder that he was always trying to protect people, little wonder that he kept so much buried inside. "Rafe, I'm so sorry."

"So was I," he said, the massive understatement telling her everything. "He died instantly, of course, his brains blown to kingdom come." He looked away, his face desolate, his shoulders hunched in misery. "If only I'd been faster—or had called out to him earlier, I might have been able to stop him. I've never—I've never forgiven myself." He covered his face with one hand.

"But it wasn't your fault. You were just a little boy, Rafe. You can't carry the entire world on your shoulders, you know, especially not a burden like that."

He rubbed his neck. "I never told another living soul before this," he said, his voice tight. "I couldn't. If anyone had known he'd killed himself, he wouldn't have been allowed to be buried in consecrated ground."

"So you, at nine, let everyone think it had been a simple accident and took it all on yourself?" she asked, wrapping her arms around her waist, wishing she could wrap them around him, but knowing he wouldn't welcome the gesture.

Nine, only nine, and he'd borne the responsibility and the heartache ever since. It was a miracle he'd kept his sanity.

"What else was I to do?" he said, walking a few paces away, his back turned to her. "Tell my mother her husband had intentionally killed himself? Tell Hugo his father hadn't loved him enough to work through his despair, that he didn't care enough about either of his sons to want to watch them grow up? I wonder if the man ever took that into consideration before he pulled the trigger," Rafe said bitterly. "He left us, Lucy—without a single goodbye, with no explanation, not even a note. He just left, and I never knew why."

"But he had to have had a reason—people don't kill themselves unless they're truly desperate," she said, frowning. "He must have been driven by some terrible distress. Was there nothing you could find? Something in his papers?"

Rafe shook his head. "There was nothing. Believe me, I looked when I was old enough to take over his affairs. I did recently discover from my mother that he suffered from melancholia, and perhaps his despair was so great that he felt he couldn't go on. But I suppose I'll never really know what was in his mind."

"No . . . I suppose not," she said, finally understanding why he had reacted as he had when he thought she'd thrown herself off the cliff, why he'd been so desperate to find her and so relieved when he had. He thought he'd witnessed another suicide that he'd been helpless to stop. Oh, God—if she hadn't been such a little fool, she could have saved him so much anguish. He'd already suffered more than most people did in a lifetime. She searched inside herself for words of comfort, but Rafe didn't need words. And he didn't seem to want what she could give him. "I'm sorry," she said again, feeling utterly helpless. "It must have been terribly difficult for you all these years."

"I've done my best to honor the responsibilities my father left me," Rafe said with a shrug, "although I don't think I've done a very good job, Hugo being a shining example. My brother has resented me at every turn, and I suppose I deserve it. Instead of guiding him, I've commanded him. It's little wonder that he goes out of his way to aggravate me."

"Would it help you to know that it was Hugo who dragged himself out of bed to ask me to go after you? He was deeply concerned about you, Rafe. He didn't want you to be alone."

Rafe turned and stared at her. "But I—I left him sleeping."

"Perhaps that is what he wanted you to believe. Nevertheless, he came to my room to tell me that you had gone and that he was worried. I think it says a great deal about how much he wants to put things right between you—and how much he cares about your welfare."

"Yes." Rafe turned his face away for a moment, his voice hoarse. "Yes, I suppose it does. I only wish he'd had a father to guide him instead of a brother who was only a few years older than he. I wouldn't have minded having a father myself, but it's no use wishing. What's done is done."

"My poor dear love—what all this must have done to you," Lucy said, her voice breaking along with her heart. "I don't know how you've managed to endure so well."

Rafe's gaze shot back to hers. "*What* did you say?" he asked on a whisper.

Lucy looked at him, surprised by the suddenly fierce expression in his eyes. "I said I don't know how you managed to endure so well."

"Not that—what you just called me."

Lucy blinked. "What I called you? Oh . . . that." She'd gone and put her foot right in it—he was bound to curse her up one side and down the other for even daring to speak the word after everything she'd done to him.

"Yes, that," he said, an unreadable expression on his face. "Dear God, Lucy, does it take confessing the inner reaches of my soul to wring a single word of love out of you?"

"It helps," she replied with an uncertain smile. "It's not

easy telling a man you love him with all your heart when he won't let you past his own front door—"

He closed the distance between them in a single second and roughly silenced her with his mouth, kissing her with hot, savage sweetness until her legs nearly buckled underneath her. He finally raised his head, his breath coming short and fast, his eyes blazing down at her, his fingers gripping her shoulders.

"Did you honestly mean that?" he asked.

"Of course I did," she said shakily. "I wouldn't have said it if I didn't mean it. I—I know I owe you an explanation, but the best I can do right now is to say I'm sorry. I know I've hurt you, and I wish I could change that—"

"Lucy. Lucy, I can't go on like this," he said, releasing her abruptly. "I love you, God knows I do, and it means more than I can say to know that you feel the same. But I can't change the fact that I'm a Montagu. And since you can't seem to find a way to accept me in spite of that, I think the only thing I can do to keep from going stark, raving mad is to leave—to go back to England."

"Go—go back to England?" she said, panic seizing her, turning her blood to ice. He was *leaving* her? "No! No . . . Oh, Rafe, don't go—please don't go."

"What else am I to do?" he asked bleakly. "If I stay, you and I both know what will happen. I refuse to dishonor you again."

"You didn't dishonor me to begin with," she said, tears welling in her eyes. "I *wanted* you to make love to me. I knew I shouldn't, but I couldn't help myself."

He gently stroked her cheek. "I know," he said softly. "Any more than I could help myself. But that's what I mean. You and I—we've been drawn to each other from the first moment we laid eyes on each other. I'm powerless to change how I feel. And I'm equally powerless to change your conviction that we are wrong for each other, as much as it kills me to say it."

"No, you don't understand," she said, hot tears filling her eyes. "That's what I wanted to explain to you earlier tonight, but you wouldn't listen, and then the fire happened."

"What are you talking about?" he asked with a puzzled frown. "I asked you a question point-blank and you as good as told me that you wouldn't change your mind."

"But I didn't!" she cried. "I didn't say that at all—I was only trying to find the right words. Something happened today, Rafe, something important. I can't explain it exactly, because it probably wouldn't make any sense to you—it hardly makes any sense to me."

"What in the name of God are you talking about?" he asked, raking both hands through his hair.

"I realized that I've been a complete fool." She drew in a deep breath, taking the first step to close the abyss she had created between them. "I couldn't see beyond my love for my country to what was really important. I stood on my pride and—and I made an issue out of our differences because I was frightened of what would happen if I allowed you to know how much I loved you."

"And what did you think would happen?" he asked very quietly.

She wiped her tears away, looking up into his beloved face, so strong, so filled with love. "I thought you would take me away from everything I held dear—I didn't understand that without you my life means nothing. But I know now that my life is not about the ground I stand on or the air I breathe, or even about the ideals I hold dear, it's about what is in my heart. And you *are* my heart, Rafe. Without you nothing else makes any sense."

He released a long, ragged breath. "Do you know what you're saying?"

"I'm not *complete* fool," she said with a tremulous smile. "I'm saying that I don't care if you're a Montagu. I don't even mind that you're British. Or a duke. I love *you*, Rafe, and therefore I have to love everything that has made you what you are."

"Then will you please, please marry me, Lucy Kincaid?" he said, his face strained.

She threw her arms around his shoulders and held him tightly to her. "Yes, I'll marry you, Raphael Montagu," she said on a choked sob, her heart soaring with happiness finally to be able to speak the words she'd held back for so long. "I'd be honored to marry you." And *oh,* how she meant it. She felt as if a great weight had been lifted from her shoulders.

He groaned and lifted his hands to hers, easing her grip. "I—I'm very gratified," he said with a muffled laugh. "But try not to kill me before you get me to the altar. My shoulder's a little sore."

Lucy gasped and pulled her hands away. "I'm so sorry— did I hurt you?"

"Not as much as thinking you wouldn't marry me did. Lucy. Lucy, are you absolutely sure?" he asked, gazing down into her eyes, his own filled with question. "I don't want you to marry me just because your compassionate heart is bleeding over something that happened long ago. I never would have told you at all if you hadn't caught me at a bad moment—Hugo's near miss brought everything back just a little too close for comfort."

"Now who's being the idiot?" she asked, rubbing her streaming nose. "I would have agreed to marry you hours ago if you'd only listened to me. But I'm glad you told me about your father, Rafe. I don't want you to keep things from me. Love is about sharing sorrow as well as joy, despair as well as dreams."

"I want to share my entire life with you," he said, drawing her back into his arms. His mouth descended on hers in a fierce kiss, his tongue driving deep into her mouth, his blood radiating hot against her skin through the linen of his shirt.

Lucy arched toward him, seeking more of his touch as her loins melted with the pure heat of desire.

His hand tangled in her hair as the other slid down over her shoulder to cup her breast in his palm. Lucy shuddered at the contact and Rafe groaned. "I'm sorry," he said, lifting his head and staring up at the moon. "I can't seem to keep my hands off you."

"I don't want you to," she whispered against the corner of his mouth, all reason fleeing in the face of his impassioned touch. "I don't want you to at all."

"Hussy," Rafe said with a choked laugh. "Are you saying you want me to make love to you here and now?"

"Yes," she whispered. "Here and now. It somehow seems fitting to seal our vow in the place where it all began."

"Tomorrow," he said, pressing his warm mouth against her temple. "Say you'll marry me tomorrow and I'll seal anything you like."

"But—but what about the banns?" she said, thinking she really couldn't bear it if she had to wait another three weeks for Rafe to make love to her.

"We don't need the banns; I have a special license. My mother brought it today," he replied, tugging at the bodice of her dress. "Tomorrow morning?"

"Oh." She gasped as he loosened the bodice of her dress and slid it down over her shoulders to her waist, exposing her breasts and back to the cool night air. "Oh, yes, tomorrow morning would be perfect."

"I think I finally know . . . how to bend you to my will," he said, drawing her down to the ground. He lowered his mouth onto the swell of her breast, pulling her nipple between his lips and tugging on it until she writhed with pleasure, her hands spreading over his chest, bunching the linen of his shirt between her fingers as she arched her back toward him.

"Wait," he murmured, shifting. "I can't support my weight like this." He rolled onto his back, taking her by the waist and twisting her so that she straddled him. "You're going to have to do the work tonight," he said with a wicked grin. "I'm injured, remember?"

Lucy chuckled. "I'd be happy to have my way with you," she replied, a surge of excitement racing through her at the feel of his arousal pressed between her naked thighs. She boldly reached down and covered him with her hand, her fingers exploring his hard length through the soft material of his breeches.

Rafe drew in a sharp breath of air. "Ah, God, Lucy," he said thickly as she worked the buttons and freed his sex. She shivered as his bared flesh met hers, sliding against her silky curls, hard, velvet steel meeting the soft, damp flesh of her womanhood.

She leaned over, pressing kisses along the underside of his jaw, down his neck, her trembling fingers undoing the buttons of his shirt. She pushed the linen apart and lightly touched the white bandage on his shoulder, thinking of how frightened she'd been when she'd seen the blood staining his shirt. "Did the doctor have to stitch you?" she murmured, pressing a kiss there too.

"Mmm," he said, restlessly moving his hands up and down her back. "Twelve of them. I counted every last one." He slid his palms over her rib cage and ran his thumbs over the underside of her breasts. "Nice," he whispered, his voice hoarse. "So soft."

Lucy closed her eyes as he lifted his hands and shaped the swell of her flesh with his hands, teasing her nipples until wild tremors shook her body.

She smoothed her hands down over the planes of his chest, tracing the taut, masculine shape of muscle and sinew under sleek skin, relishing the involuntary tightening of his body under her touch. She bent her head and suckled his hard nipples, wondering if he would take the same pleasure as she did when he did it to her.

He did. Oh, how he did. He shuddered and impatiently

pushed her dress up over her hips, his thumbs reaching down between them to seek out her cleft, rubbing in little circles until Lucy moaned, eager for him to take her.

Rafe opened her, his fingers slipping deep inside her, and Lucy pulled in a jerky breath as he moved them slowly, at the same time capturing the peak of her nipple, pulling and sucking on it until she shook with helpless whimpers. The pounding of the ocean far below matched the pounding of her heart as he sent her spiraling upward in exquisite agony, her breath coming in short, desperate pants.

"I want you." He gasped. "Now, Lucy." He grasped her by the hips and lifted her onto his hard shaft, pressing her down so that she sank onto him, slowly taking his length.

"Oh, *God,* that's good," he said on a groan, driving up into her, and she welcomed his penetration, adjusting to the feel of his shape inside her. There was no burning this time, only a gradual stretching of her flesh to embrace his dimensions.

He cupped her buttocks, his eyes closing as he began to move in her, helping her to find her own rhythm, the position that would give her the most pleasure.

She threw her head back, reveling in aching sensation, each of his deliberate thrusts building her need until she thought she'd explode with it.

"I love you," he whispered hoarsely. "God, how I love you," he said again, his clear gray eyes fierce with the truth of his words, his hands stroking up over her waist, her back, wrapping in her hair, pulling her down to kiss him.

The movement drove him even more deeply inside her, and she gasped, pushing back against him to take everything he had to give her, greedily, hungrily, as if she could take him into her very heart.

He led her faster and faster, sliding her down on his shaft again and again until desperate little cries tore from her throat. She couldn't breathe, the fierce need inside her blossoming into unbearable pleasure as she reached for release, her hands clutching at his forearms as if he could deliver her.

And he did—oh, he did with one great powerful thrust of his hips. Darkness and light met in a shattering explosion of sensation and she sobbed his name as violent tremors of ecstasy racked her body.

His fingers pressed convulsively into the flesh of her buttocks, and he drove into her with throbbing force, his body erupting in hers as a harsh cry ripped from his throat. Life, she thought joyfully. His life and her life mingling together. As it was meant to be. As it had always been meant. A true gift from God to them both . . .

Lucy lowered her head, her breathing ragged, her palms outstretched on his chest, steadying her shaken body. She was only just now aware of the tears that slipped down her face, trickling one by one onto his slick skin, joining the rivulets of his sweat.

He must have felt them, for he reached his hand for hers and clasped her fingers. "What is it, sweet girl?" he asked, his other hand cupping her chin. "What makes you cry?"

"Happiness," she said on a little gulp. "Oh, Rafe, I never thought it was possible for dreams to come true—not really. I feel as if I've been a dark place for so long, and suddenly the sun has come out to light my way home."

Rafe smiled softly, twined his fingers around a lock of her hair. "You are home, beloved. You're home with me. Wherever we happen to be, know I will always look after you, keep you safe." He pulled her down against him, cradling her head against his good shoulder, gently stroking her hair.

"But where will that be?" she asked in a muffled voice, one last concern pricking at her. "Will you take me away from Ireland, Rafe?"

"I'll never take you away for long," he replied, his hands sliding up and down her back. "I have to go back to England every now and then, but there's no reason why we can't spend a good half of the year here. Will that suit you, Lucy? I don't want you to be homesick, but I can't avoid my responsibilities elsewhere."

"I only want to be with you," she whispered. "But I do want our children to know and love both their countries. Do you think that's possible?"

"Of course it is," he said, caressing her shoulder. "I swear to you I will never stand in the way of that—how could I? I think I've fallen in love with Ireland every bit as much as I've fallen in love with you. The two seem inextricably bound together."

Lucy smiled against his neck. "I think Ireland's fallen in love with you too. And after your heroism tonight you really *might* have sainthood conferred on you."

A rumble of laughter sounded in his chest. "I'll pass, I think. It's hard enough simply being a man."

Lucy pushed herself up on one elbow and looked down at him with a mischievous grin. "There's nothing simple about you, Raphael David Charles Montagu, Duke of Southwell, Marquess of Airely, Baron Montagu." She dropped a kiss on the place where his heart still thudded.

The smile faded from his face. "Thank you," he said quietly.

"Thank you for what?" she asked, puzzled.

"Thank you for taking me as I am, titles and all. Thank you for being able to see past all of that to the man I am beneath."

She drew in a sharp little breath, her heart catching painfully. "I think I saw past everything the first time I saw you," she said in a small voice. "I stood just over there and saw a solitary man on a horse, his heart in his eyes and poetry on his lips. I saw the other half of myself and for the first time in my life I felt complete. And yet I turned the gulf that physically separated us into a gulf that separated us on the inside, all because I was afraid to believe in my dreams."

Rafe shut his eyes. "Dreams," he murmured. "I never had any dreams, not until I met you. You made me understand about hope, Lucy, about the endless possibilities of hope. About the endless possibilities of love."

Lucy smiled softly. "Then I should thank you too, for you've taught me the same thing." She brushed a lock of golden hair off his brow, her heart brimming with that love. "And neither of us will ever be alone again."

"No," he agreed, capturing her hand and drawing it to his chest. "We'll neither of us ever be alone again."

26

$\mathcal{L}$ucy woke to dazzling sunlight and the feel of someone nuzzling her cheek. She sleepily opened her eyes to see Rafe bending over her bed fully dressed, a tender smile on his face.

"Time to rise from your bower, Egeria. It's gone ten already. Have you forgotten your promise to me?"

Lucy stretched lazily. "What promise was that?" she asked mischievously. "I promised you a good many things last night."

"And I plan on taking you up on every last one of them," he said, dropping a kiss on her hair. "But the first one you're going to fulfill is to marry me. I've already spoken to the vicar. He'll be here at noon."

"But—but that's only two hours away," Lucy said in alarm. "I have to find something to wear . . ."

"I don't see why," Rafe said with a chuckle. "I rather like you just as nature made you."

"That's a very pretty sentiment, but somehow I doubt the vicar would agree with you."

"Pity," he said, grinning. "By the by, I hope you don't mind being married here rather than in a church, but I wanted Hugo to be in attendance, and I don't think he'd make it that far."

"Oh—how is Hugo today?" Lucy said, feeling guilty that

she hadn't asked about him immediately. She was so filled with joy that she could hardly think of anything else.

"He's sore but happy. I had a long talk with him earlier, Lucy. I think we sorted out a lot of things. I promised to stay out of his affairs and let him lead his life as he sees fit, and he promised to stop seducing married women and fighting duels with their husbands just to annoy me."

"Oh, dear," Lucy said with dismay. "I knew Hugo was a scoundrel, but I hadn't realized he was quite so wicked."

"Not wicked, just contrary," Rafe replied. "He no more wanted me to play his father than I wanted the job. Now that we understand each other, I think we have a chance to go back to the relationship we had before my father died. We were actually very close once."

"They say fire can be cleansing," Lucy said softly. "Maybe the west wing burning down did some good after all, if it brought you and your brother back together."

"The next time I need cleansing, I'll do it in a bath, if it's all the same to you." He picked her hand up and kissed her fingertips. "Don't worry about the west wing, sweetheart. We'll rebuild it just as it was before."

"Thank you," she said, gazing solemnly up at him. "That means a great deal. But are you sure you can afford to rebuild? You've already put so much money into Kincaid."

"But just think of the small fortune I can save by not paying you a wage. I'll be a rich man again in no time."

Lucy threw a pillow at him in answer and he caught it with a pained grimace.

"Oh, Rafe—" she said in quick remorse. "I forgot about your shoulder. Does it still hurt you?"

"It will work well enough for what I have in mind later," he said with a light laugh, running his fingers over her exposed throat.

Lucy grinned, arching her neck. "I don't mind weighing you down in the least."

"You'll never weigh me down, my love," he said, drawing

her head against his chest and stroking her hair. "If anything, you do the opposite. But no more malingering, and
certainly no more talk of intimacy or we'll never leave the
bedroom. I'll see you downstairs when you're ready."

"Rafe—do you think we could be married outside?" Lucy
asked, peeping a hesitant look up at him. "It's such a beautiful day."

"You may be married anywhere you please. Do you have a
particular spot in mind?"

"Yes . . . I thought maybe out on the rise behind the
garden. It's such a pretty view."

"And you want to look at all of Ireland while you marry
an Englishman, is that it?" he asked with amusement.

"It's just that it was one of my father's favorite places on
all of Kincaid. It just seems fitting. I think he'd be very
pleased, Rafe—he would have liked you, and you him."

"I know I love his daughter," Rafe said softly, brushing a
kiss over the corner of her mouth. "And I will do everything
in my power to make her happy. The dark years living under
Eunice's harsh control will be as if they never existed."

As soon as the door had shut behind him, Lucy jumped
out of bed and danced over to the window, pushing it open.
She rested her palms on the sill and leaned out, breathing in
the air, the lovely fresh air of Kincaid. Her home. And Rafe's.
Together they would make it a happy one and fill it with
their children. And those children would grow up knowing
they were loved. She didn't care a fig anymore that those
children would be half British—they would be Rafe's and
that was all that mattered.

A light tap came at the door and Lucy crossed the room to
open it. The duchess stood there with a pile of material in
her hands.

"Good morning, Lucy," she said with a warm smile. "Is it
not a lovely day for your wedding?"

Lucy smiled widely. "It is indeed. And thank you for your

wise words yesterday, Duchess, for they helped me to see everything more clearly."

"Then I am pleased, for I can think of nothing more gratifying than seeing you marry my son. I have brought you something from Madame LaChaille. She made it for you especially for this day and asked me to send you her warmest regards and best wishes." She walked over to the bed and spread the material out.

Lucy drew in a breath of wonder. The dress was made of white silk, the bodice ornamented with white satin and pearls, the puffed sleeves banded with satin bows. A white satin sash went around the high waist and tied behind. She had never seen anything so lovely, not even the ball dress she'd worn in London.

"It's—it's magnificent," she said, tears pricking at her eyes. "I cannot believe it . . . but how did you know I would need it? Oh," she said, remembering what Rafe had said the night before. "Of course. The special license you brought."

The duchess laughed merrily. "I came prepared with everything you might need. Look," she said, laying more items out. "Here is the family wedding veil, as well as satin slippers and white kid gloves."

Lucy shook her head. "Raphael was very sure of himself, wasn't he?"

"He wrote to me as soon as he found you, Lucy. I only know that he was hoping you would agree to the marriage. And his foresight was rewarded, for here you are, about to become his wife. You have made him very happy, child."

"Rafe's happiness is all I want, Duchess."

"I wish you would call me Mama," the duchess said with a fond smile. "I always did want a daughter, but my husband was taken away from me before that dream was realized. And now after all this time, my wish has finally come true."

Lucy's tears welled up and spilled over, trickling down her cheeks. "Thank you," she said, her voice choked. "I would be honored to call you Mama."

The duchess reached her arms out and Lucy walked into them, holding Rafe's mother in a tight embrace. A family. She was finally going to be part of a family again. God really had heard her prayers, for all of her dreams were finally coming true.

The duchess gently released Lucy. "Now we must concentrate on practical matters. I've asked for hot water to be sent up, for I know you would like to bathe. How clever of your father to have installed bathrooms in the bedrooms—so much easier than having hip baths taken up and down the stairs."

Lucy was grateful for the duchess's calm, matter-of-fact manner, for it gave her time to collect herself. For someone who never cried, she'd turned into a proper watering-pot. "A bath would be lovely," she said, drying her eyes.

"I will send my maid up afterward to help you dress. Oh, and Lucy—I have a present for you." She reached down to the bed and drew a square box out from under the lace veil. "These were given to me by Raphael's grandmother on my wedding day. I think it fitting that you should have them on yours."

She opened the box and handed it to Lucy.

Inside lay a long, gleaming double strand of milky pearls, perfectly matched, and earrings with diamond bows attached. Lucy stared first at the pearls, then up at the duchess, her mouth parted. "But I—you can't possibly want to . . ." She trailed off, too stunned to speak coherently.

"Of course I do. Not only are you to be Raphael's wife, but you are to be his duchess. These have been passed from one duchess to another and now to a third. And when your eldest son marries, you can give them to his wife." She wagged her finger. "You cannot refuse me, Lucy. I have waited a long time for this moment."

"Thank you," Lucy said simply, afraid she was going to start crying again.

"Then I will leave you to make your preparations. I have

things to organize downstairs in preparation for the wedding. Goodness, Raphael gave me hardly a moment's notice, but I believe that he is wise not to delay."

She patted Lucy's shoulder, then vanished through the door, looking extremely pleased with herself.

Lucy's hands slipped to her hot cheeks, knowing the duchess had seen right through both of them. Oh, well, she decided with wry humor, at least after the ceremony she and Rafe could spend all the time they wanted in each other's arms, and no one would look askance.

And maybe God would even spare her the time in Purgatory, since she was marrying Rafe so promptly and for all the right reasons.

"So that is the O'Reillys, the Percy brothers, Brigid O'Dougal and her husband, the Larkin family and the Carneys," the duchess said, ticking off her list. "According to you, Raphael, that's about twenty people you've invited, plus the staff, of course. Is there anyone else other than ourselves and the rector who might be coming?"

Rafe laughed. "Knowing the Irish, the news of the wedding will already have spread and we'll have a good hundred more people on our hands. It makes no difference, Mama. Whoever comes will be here to support Lucy, and that's all that matters."

"Darling, do be practical," his mother said, removing her reading spectacles and fixing him with a firm gaze. "You do realize that we have to feed all these people?"

Rafe, in no mood to be practical, just shrugged. "We'll give them what we have, and likely enough they'll bring what they can, so it will all work out. The important thing is the marriage. This isn't England, where people put stock in what kind of show one puts on."

"I know that, dear, but you do not want your guests going hungry. Never mind, though, for there is nothing we can do about it now. Let me see—Hugo has your grandmother's wedding ring to hand to you at the appropriate moment, and I must say, darling, I think it is a lovely thought that you asked him to stand up for you."

"Providing he can stand up at all," Rafe said dryly. "He's feeling much better this morning, but he's still a little wobbly."

"Your lordship?" Dooley poked his head into the drawing room, and Rafe glanced over at him, wondering why he looked so perturbed.

"What is it?" he asked, praying it wasn't trouble. He wanted this day to be perfect for Lucy.

"It's those Gupwell girls," Dooley hissed, "but this time they have their mother with them, and she's a screaming maniac, insisting on seeing you, sir."

"Oh, no," the duchess said, frowning. "Not that dreadful woman, on this day of all days? Do send her away, darling."

Rafe plowed his hands over his face. Eunice Gupwell was the last person he wanted to see, but he was well enough acquainted with her to know that she wouldn't go away peacefully. He already had a fair idea of what she had come to say. "It's best if I see what she wants, or she'll be outside kicking up a fuss for hours. Send them in, Dooley."

Dooley rolled his eyes, but he tugged on his cap in reluctant obedience.

Only a moment later, Eunice came flying in the door, hauling her weeping daughters into the room by the wrists. "You black-hearted devil!" she shrieked without preamble. "How could you—how *could* you? I knew you and that vile stepdaughter of mine were up to no good, inviting Fiona and Amaryllis to visit you. Ruined, that's what they are!" She released the girls, who stumbled forward, sniffling loudly.

"Good morning, Lady Kincaid," Rafe said coolly. "I trust you remember my mother?"

Eunice ignored him. "You plotted to disgrace me—you must have taken great satisfaction in concocting a scheme to humiliate me even further than you already have. And so you dragged my daughters down into the dirt—the veriest filth."

"I beg your pardon, but I'm not sure I understand your meaning, Lady Kincaid," Rafe said, knowing perfectly well that she was referring to the Percy twins. "And I decidedly do not like your tone."

"My tone?" she sneered. "My *tone* is the least of your worries. I will have you arrested, your grace, and your precious harlot with you for conspiracy to destroy two innocent young girls."

Rafe stood, his face black with fury. "I have told you before that you will not speak of Lucy in such a manner," he said, ready to wring the woman's scrawny neck.

"I'll speak of the trollop any way in which I please," Eunice cried. "She has thoroughly ruined my life, and now she plans to ruin my daughters' lives—and with your help."

Rafe rubbed his thumb over his chin. "I assume this has something to do with Eamon and Conor Percy. Your daughters have told you about the attachment they have made?"

"Oh, Duke," Fiona wailed, her eyes red and swollen, "I know we weren't supposed to say anything about Eamon and Conor, but Mama underheard us talking and she thought we had done the worst. And she beat us and made us go to bed without supper last night, and—"

"Shut your mouths, you pathetic girls, or I will do much worse!" Eunice snapped viciously.

"Now she says she will lock us away forever and ever," Amaryllis said with an impassioned sob, clutching her sister's hand as she gazed at Rafe imploringly. "She says that we are nothing more than whorls and we deserve to be whipped to death for our premonitory behavior. But we did nothing wrong, did we, Duke?"

Rafe smiled, amazed that he had actually learned to decipher the Gupwell girls' language, and equally amazed at the unexpected and unbidden instinct he felt to protect them. "Nothing at all, Amaryllis," he said. "Furthermore, I saw the

Percy brothers earlier this morning and each in turn asked for your hands in marriage. I see no reason why you and Fiona should not accept."

"Accept? Are you mad? They are pig farmers!" Eunice bellowed, her eyes wild. "You would see my daughters married to *pig* farmers?"

"They earn a decent living," Rafe said mildly. "And they are kind and decent men, who are genuinely fond of your daughters. What more would you want for your children?"

"Aaaahhhhhh!" Eunice screamed, clawing at her hair, which was already half falling down around her face. "I forbid it! I forbid it!"

"I don't believe you *can* forbid it," Rafe said, regarding Eunice with sudden concern. She really did not look like a woman in her right mind. "They are of age—or nearly. Fiona is twenty-two, and if I remember correctly, Amaryllis turns twenty-one shortly."

"Next month," Amaryllis said with a finger in her mouth, regarding her mother with large, frightened eyes.

"I believe that makes your daughters independent, Lady Kincaid, and able to marry whom they please. The dowry money is theirs, not yours, and as I have jurisdiction over its disposition, it will go where I see fit. I happen to think Eamon and Conor Percy are perfectly suitable matches for them."

"Wicked!" Eunice cried, sinking into a chair, her fingers tearing at the material of her dress until it shredded under her nails. "Vile and wicked. Evil!" She shook her head from side to side, her lips working soundlessly.

"I beg you, Lady Kincaid, you must take hold of yourself," the duchess said, moving over to the chair where Eunice sat. "Think of your daughters. Surely you do not wish to alarm them?"

Eunice looked up, her lips pulled back in a feral snarl. "You're no better than your son," she hissed. "You were in on the plot from the very beginning. Oh, I know when there is a conspiracy afoot against me. There has always been a conspiracy afoot—first my parents marrying me off to that imbecile Lionel Gupwell because they thought I could do no better. Little did they know." She ripped another fold of her dress. "And then . . . then, when I finally ensnared that blind, romantic fool Ian Kincaid and had my fortune made, look what happened—just look! His spiteful, self-centered daughter destroyed it all for me!"

"Lady Kincaid," Rafe said carefully, realizing with a terrible jolt that the woman was truly mad. "I think it might be best if you—"

"If I did *what*?" she asked, springing to her feet, her eyes unfocused. "If you have your way, you will see my daughters married into a pigsty. I will be left with nothing—no money, no comfort in my old age, no one to see to my needs. *Nothing,* do you understand? And this is all your doing!"

To Rafe's utmost regret, Lucy appeared in the doorway at that moment.

"What . . . what is going on here?" she asked, her gaze flickering back and forth among Eunice, Fiona, and Amaryllis, finally settling on Raphael in alarm. "I heard the shouting and thought I had better come down."

"Your stepmother is a little—unsettled," he said, unable to help drinking in the sight of Lucy in her wedding finery. But he couldn't afford the luxury of dwelling on Lucy and his love for her at that moment, because in the same instant Eunice saw her and leapt forward, her hands outstretched like claws.

"You little witch!" she shrieked. "You actually think to *marry* him? You—you wretched harlot!"

Rafe instantly moved to restrain her, his arms going around her sides, pinning her hands to her struggling body. "Lucy and I are to be married within the hour," he said into her ear. "You will not say another word, Lady Kincaid, for if you do, I really will throttle you. I think we will all be best served if you go quietly upstairs to a place where you can gather yourself. And then, when you are calm, we will talk about your future." Bedlam would do nicely, he thought.

"I know of a nice place in England which will suit you very well," the duchess said, crossing the room and removing Eunice from his grip, taking her twitching body gently by the shoulders. "It is a quiet house where you will be well looked after and you needn't worry about anything."

Eunice instantly stopped struggling. "England?" she said, gazing at the duchess with a sudden childlike smile.

"Yes, dear. England. Now that your daughters and your stepdaughter are to be married, you have no more responsibility to any of them. Just think, you will have people to attend to your every need, and you will never have to return to Ireland again. Is that not a happy thought?"

Eunice nodded. "England . . . I would like that."

"Then we will arrange it as soon as humanly possible, but you must cooperate and come upstairs with me. What you need is a nice rest, for your nerves are overset. You need not worry about your daughters, as my son will see to their future. You have no one to think about now but yourself."

"No . . . no one but myself," Eunice said, then giggled. "Oh, lovely, lovely day," she said, clapping her hands together. "Yes, dear Mama, take me upstairs. I feel most dreadfully tired. Perhaps you would make me one of your nice lavender compresses to put on my aching brow."

"Of course, dear," the duchess said, steering her out of the room with one quick backward look over her shoulder. Rafe met his mother's gaze, and he gave her a smile of infinite gratitude.

"Fetch Hugo's laudanum," she said in an undertone. "And call for the doctor."

He nodded. As always, his mother was a blessing in a time of crisis, easily taking charge. He watched as she led Eunice away, speaking soothingly into her ear.

"Lucy, my love, I'm sorry you had to witness that," Rafe said, quickly walking over to her and taking her into his arms in a reassuring embrace. "But don't worry. It seems my mother has the situation under control. She obviously has a sanitarium in mind, which is where Eunice clearly belongs, I'm afraid."

Lucy raised her face to his. "I've always wondered if Eunice was entirely in her right mind," she said in a low voice, her complexion pale. "I think this incident proves she isn't. But it's the girls we need to worry about now. You see to your mother's requests, and I will look after them."

"I think it's best if you don't explain too much," he murmured. "Try to comfort them—you might distract them with the thought of their upcoming weddings. That should do the trick. But are you all right, sweetheart? That must have been a very disturbing scene to walk in on."

Lucy smiled up at him. "I'm fine. Don't worry about me. I'll take care of everything here."

His heart overflowed with love for her. Lucy, even in the midst of catastrophe, always managed to keep a level head, not unlike his mother. "Your self-possession is one of the qualities I love about you," he said tenderly.

"I'll remind you of that the next time we have an argument and you're tempted to toss me out the nearest window," she replied with a grin. "Go on, help your mother, or we'll never be married, and I cannot wait another minute, let alone an hour."

He touched a finger to the smooth underside of her chin. "Nor can I. And by the by, you're looking stunningly beautiful. If I hadn't been so preoccupied with Eunice I would have told you so on the spot."

She blushed lightly. "Thank you. Did you see what your mother gave me for a wedding gift?" She touched the pearls with her fingertips.

"I did indeed, and they suit you to perfection, as does your dress and the family veil. You're a vision, my love." He meant it with all his heart—he'd never seen anyone so beautiful, and he was awed and honored that she was his.

"Thank your mother. I feel like a proper bride, Rafe—your bride."

"And my duchess, darling girl. And you will be both, as soon as I see to your stepmother. I'm already expecting the doctor at any moment to look in on Hugo, so he can attend to Eunice then. I think it would be best if he takes her away and puts her somewhere under medical supervision until we can arrange for her transport to the sanitarium."

"Oh, Rafe—poor Eunice. It does seem sad that she has come to this."

He smiled wryly. "Ah, well. Eunice always did say that her heart's desire was to live in England again."

Lucy burst into laughter. "I don't think she meant it to be under these circumstances, but you're right. She's getting exactly what she asked for."

"She is indeed, and in more ways than one." He dropped a kiss on Lucy's nose and released her reluctantly. "I'll see you out on the rise. Good luck with Fiona and Amaryllis."

He strode out of the room, thanking his lucky stars for Lucy and the love she gave him so unstintingly. He really never would be alone again, from this day forth.

As soon as the door had shut behind Raphael, Lucy turned to her stepsisters, who were huddled together, drawing silent comfort from each other. Lucy realized for the first time that Fiona and Amaryllis, as different as they were in looks, were as much alike in nature as Conor and Eamon were. They'd be four peas in a pod, living happily alongside one another in the same house. She couldn't think of a happier ending for her stepsisters.

"Well, then," she said, straightening her back and assuming a cheerful expression. She walked over to them, drawing them both into her arms in a quick hug. "Isn't this the best of days? You have marriage proposals from the men you love and no objections from any direction."

"But—but Mama said the most dreadful things . . ."

Fiona wiped the back of her hand under her nose. "You don't know, Lucy! She beat us white and blue after she heard Fiona and me talking. Why do you think she has changed her mind?"

"Don't you worry about that," Lucy said in a comforting voice. "Your mother is happy enough to be going back to England now that the duke has explained everything and she knows you will be taken care of. She was just a little upset at first."

"She was bad enough before, but she has been horribly disarrayed since she heard us discoursing the Percy twins," Amaryllis said, sniffling miserably.

More like horribly deranged, Lucy thought privately, but she wasn't about to tell Amaryllis that. "She was only concerned for your welfare," she replied. "But now it's all settled and you'll be married in three weeks. Just think how much we have to do! You'll need wedding dresses, and we must arrange for the guests and the flowers and the food."

"I'd like a chocolate cake," Amaryllis said, her face brightening. "A very big chocolate cake."

"And you shall have it." Lucy wondered just where she was going to find enough chocolate on such short notice to suit Amaryllis, but she imagined she would think of something. "I hope you don't mind *too* much that your mother won't be there, but I think it's best for everyone if she goes back to England very soon."

"I don't ever want to see her again," Fiona said crossly. "She hit me and sent me right across the floor. I was bruted purple. I can show you if you like," she said, starting to raise her skirt.

"No, that's quite all right, Fiona," Lucy said quickly, staying her hand. "I know well enough what you mean."

"She said horrid things, Lucy," Amaryllis added with a scowl. "I don't think she likes us at all. You've always been much nicer to us. I'd much rather stay here until we can marry our true loves and they take us to live in divan bliss."

"And so you shall," Lucy said with an internal sigh, wondering what Rafe was going to make of being forced to spend three solid weeks with the Gupwell girls under the same roof. Oh, well. He'd asked her to comfort them, and she really couldn't see any other solution. She certainly couldn't send them back to the house by the cliffs to cope on their own.

"Really, Lucy?" Amaryllis squealed in excitement. "Do you mean we can live here until our darlings walk us down the easel? Oh, heaven!" She turned to her sister. "Did you hear that, Fiona? We can eat roasts and cakes and puddings and my stomach will never growl again!"

Fiona nodded thoughtfully. "It seems a good solvent to me," she said. "I will have to speak to Conor to make certain he agrees with the culpability of the situation, but since he holds the duke in high regard, and since you *are* marrying the duke, Lucy, instead of being his curtsy-stand, I do not think Conor will object."

Lucy had to smother a laugh. *Oh, dear heaven,* she thought silently, *I do hope the Percy brothers know what they're doing by taking these two on.* "I am sure Conor and Eamon both will be pleased with the arrangement," she said out loud. "I do have one request of you, though. Since I am about to be married, and since you are my closest relatives, would you agree to stand next to me?"

Fiona and Amaryllis both stared at her. "Really and truly, Lucy?" Amaryllis asked breathlessly.

"Really and truly," Lucy said, meaning it. "I'd like that above anything. If you go and ask one of the staff, they'll see that you have garlands for your heads and posies for your hands."

Fiona and Amaryllis exchanged looks of wild excitement, then dashed out the door before Lucy could say another word.

Lucy sank down into a chair, pressing her hands against her face, smothering a laugh of frustration. It appeared that although Eunice might finally be out of their lives, Fiona and Amaryllis were going to be firmly planted in it, living only five miles down the road. It would be an interesting challenge to deal with them in their new circumstances, for she was certain they would constantly be on the doorstep. Six months of the year in England was beginning to look positively enticing.

She only wished that Eunice had not come to such a bad end, but there again there was nothing any of them could have done to prevent it. Eunice had obviously been badly flawed from the beginning, given everything Lucy had just heard her say, and maybe in some ways she'd be happier now in her madness, retreating to childhood where life had been easier for her.

But Eunice was no longer Lucy's concern. Raphael was about to become her husband and her future, and that was where her responsibility lay now. She would give him everything she had to give, knowing that he would show her everything she could be. And in turn she would do the same for him, knowing he would receive it gladly.

Well . . . knowing Rafe, he might not receive it gladly, but he'd receive it all the same, mainly because she'd see to it. *That* was how much she loved him.

Lucy rose, fully composed now, prepared to make her vows and mean every last word.

She walked toward the rise, holding a bouquet of red roses, Seamus O'Reilly at her side to give her away in her father's place. Rafe had thought of everything. He really *had* thought of everything, she thought with astonishment as she took in the crowd of people standing on the hill.

All her friends were gathered there, young and old—it looked as if half of Ireland had come to see her marry Raphael, and they looked very happy about it, if the smiles that wreathed their faces were anything to go by. Mairead looked as satisfied as Lucy had ever seen her, and it occurred to Lucy that Mairead O'Reilly and the Dowager Duchess of Southwell had a great deal in common when it came to matchmaking skills. She owed them both a debt, for without their help, she doubted she would be here now, about to marry the man of her dreams.

He stood on the edge of the hill, his head bare, the soft breeze ruffling his golden hair, the sun back-lighting it like a halo. She was reminded of the first time she'd ever seen him, for he watched her with the same piercing intensity in his gray eyes. A prince looking at the princess he had sought in all the four corners of the earth and finally found . . . and was now claiming for his own, for ever after. For *happily* ever after.

She smiled at him, a smile of pure joy, as she stepped to his side and he returned the smile as he took her hand in his.

The vicar cleared his throat and began. "Dearly beloved, we are gathered together here in the sight of God, and in the face of this congregation, to join to together this man and this woman in holy Matrimony . . ."

". . . I, Lucy Mary Katherine, take thee, Raphael David Charles, to my wedded husband . . ." Lucy's eyes swam with tears of happiness as she swore to love, honor, and obey Rafe.

And then he took a heavy gold band from Hugo and slipped it onto her finger. "With this ring, I thee wed, with my body I thee worship, with all my worldly goods I thee endow," he said in his deep, rich voice, looking as if he meant every word and then some.

When the final blessing had been said and the vicar pronounced them husband and wife, Rafe took her in his arms, his heated kiss showing her exactly how much he had meant them.

A great cheer went up, but Lucy barely heard it through her singing senses as she returned Rafe's kiss in full measure.

"I love you," he murmured as he finally drew his mouth away.

"I think all of Ireland knows the truth of that now," she said with a shaky laugh, then turned as they were surrounded by their friends and family, who heaped mountains of congratulations and good wishes on them. Lucy had never been kissed so much in all her life, but she treasured every single embrace, every last generous word.

The wedding party began in earnest, and Lucy was astonished by the amount of food and drink that had appeared out of nowhere, much of it brought by the guests, she knew, for the larder and storehouses hadn't held nearly this much.

Wee Tommy Fingall produced a fiddle, as did Dary Larkin and his brother Miles, and they played all the familiar airs and reels of Ireland as the company danced and sang along with great enthusiasm.

Lucy finally took a break from the festivities and walked over to Hugo, who was comfortably settled in a chair that had been brought out for him.

"And what do you think of Irish weddings then, Hugo Montagu?" she asked, a smile on her face as she watched Fiona and Amaryllis dance a lurching reel with Conor and Eamon, treading all over the twins' toes without their seeming to mind in the least.

"It's a fine show, I'll give you that," Hugo said, taking a sip from his glass of beer. "Lucy—I'm glad you came over. I want to thank you."

"Thank me?" she said, looking sideways at him. "For what?"

"For making my brother so happy," he said. "He deserves every last bit of happiness he can get. I never thought to see him like this, so carefree and merry, and it's all due to you."

Lucy slipped her hand into Hugo's and gave his fingers a light squeeze. "It's not all due to me, Hugo. Your willingness to put your differences aside meant a great deal to him."

A sudden grin lit up Hugo's face. "I didn't promise to

entirely reform, you know, just to stop doing things to *deliberately* aggravate Rafe. There's a big difference. You can't expect me to change my spots completely."

"As long as you keep those spots to yourself, I doubt Rafe will mind too much," she said with a merry smile. "Anyway, your brother is going to be too busy trying to keep me in line to pay much attention to what you get up to."

"He'll make you a good husband, Lucy, and he'll be a fine father to your children. I don't think I ever took the time to appreciate what a fine man my brother is."

"What are the two of you talking about?" Rafe asked, appearing at Lucy's side and slipping an arm around her waist.

Lucy and Hugo exchanged a quick look of complicity. "The weather," Hugo said. "Lovely weather for a wedding, brother."

Rafe snorted. "Likely story, but I won't pry. Let me know if you get tired, Hugo, and I'll help you back to the house."

"Not on your life," Hugo said. "I wouldn't miss a moment of this celebration. Watching the Gupwell girls is high entertainment all by itself."

"It's interesting," Rafe said, his expression thoughtful. "In London they were complete misfits, but here they seem to be in their element, and no one seems to mind having them around. Maybe everything really has worked out for the best."

Lucy pressed her cheek against Rafe's solid shoulder. "Not five months ago the three of us were living miserable lives in a ramshackle house on the cliffs, with no prospect of happiness. And then you came along and changed everything, Rafe. Whoever would have thought that we'd be here today, all of us with happy futures ahead? It never could have happened without you."

"I think God had a great deal more to do with it than I did," Rafe said, his arm tightening on her waist. "I told you a long time ago that I believe in destiny. I think we're exactly where we were always meant to be, sweetheart. God may have given us some burdens to carry early in our lives, but he also gave us each other to make sense of them."

Lucy raised her face to his. "I love you, Raphael Montagu," she whispered.

"And I love you, Lucy Montagu. Now come and dance an Irish reel with your besotted husband."

He took her hand and led her back into the midst of the wild crowd, where Lucy knew he belonged every bit as much as she did.

The full moon hung low and golden over the treetops, rising slowly and gracefully into the night sky. Lucy stood in her nightdress at the window of Rafe's bedroom, dreamily watching its progress into the starry heaven as she counted her many blessings. *Starlight, star bright . . .*

She heard the door open and softly close, and Rafe's footsteps cross the room. His arms slipped around her and he nuzzled his lips against her ear. "What are you thinking about?" he murmured.

"Hope," she said softly. "And dreams. The wonder of stars that make those dreams come true."

His hands stroked up her arms. "If you come to bed, you won't need stars to make your dreams come true, Egeria."

She laughed low in her throat as he traced a path along her temple with his mouth. "Are you trying to seduce me, your grace?"

"Yes," he said simply, his fingers trailing over her throat.

"Oh, good," she said, covering his hands with hers and twining her fingers through his. "Rafe?"

"Hmmm?" he murmured, his mouth tugging on the lobe of her ear, sending shivers down her spine.

"Now that we're married, will you tell me what those strange things were in my old bedroom?"

She felt his body stiffen slightly against her back. "Absolutely not," he said with a muffled laugh.

"But why not?" she asked, turning in his arms to look up

at him, only to see his face filled with unholy amusement. "My father always said a good education is the cornerstone of—"

"Never mind what your father said," Rafe retorted, kissing her nose. "I don't think that was the kind of education he had in mind. However, wife, if you're so hell-bent on an education, there are a number of things I have in mind to teach you."

He pulled her over to the bed and drew her down onto it, wrapping her in his arms, his hands tugging at her nightdress. "And I believe I know exactly where to start . . ."

*If you're looking for romance, adventure,
excitement and suspense, be sure to read
these outstanding romances from Dell.*

— ❋ —

Jill Gregory
- [ ] **COLD NIGHT, WARM STRANGER**   22440-3 $6.50/$9.99
- [ ] **NEVER LOVE A COWBOY**   22439-X $5.99/$7.99
- [ ] **CHERISHED**   20620-0 $5.99/$7.99
- [ ] **DAISIES IN THE WIND**   21618-4 $5.99/$7.99
- [ ] **FOREVER AFTER**   21512-9 $5.99/$7.99
- [ ] **WHEN THE HEART BECKONS**   21857-8 $5.99/$7.99
- [ ] **ALWAYS YOU**   22183-8 $5.99/$7.99
- [ ] **JUST THIS ONCE**   22235-4 $5.99/$7.99

Katherine Kingsley
- [ ] **THE SOUND OF SNOW**   22389-X $6.50/$9.99
- [ ] **CALL DOWN THE MOON**   22386-5 $5.99/$7.99
- [ ] **ONCE UPON A DREAM**   22076-9 $5.99/$7.99
- [ ] **IN THE WAKE OF THE WIND**   22075-0 $5.99/$7.99

Joan Johnston
- [ ] **THE BODYGUARD**   22377-6 $6.50/$8.99
- [ ] **AFTER THE KISS**   22201-X $6.50/$9.99
- [ ] **CAPTIVE**   22200-1 $6.50/$9.99
- [ ] **THE INHERITANCE**   21759-8 $5.99/$7.99
- [ ] **MAVERICK HEART**   21762-8 $5.99/$7.99
- [ ] **OUTLAW'S BRIDE**   21276-2 $5.99/$7.99
- [ ] **KID CALHOUN**   21280-4 $5.99/$7.99
- [ ] **THE BAREFOOT BRIDE**   21129-8 $5.99/$7.99
- [ ] **SWEETWATER SEDUCTION**   20561-1 $5.99/$7.99

Connie Brockway
- [ ] **M-CLAIREN'S ISLE:
  THE PASSIONATE ONE**   22629-5 $6.50/$9.99
- [ ] **MY DEAREST ENEMY**   22375-X $5.99/$7.99
- [ ] **A DANGEROUS MAN**   22198-6 $5.99/$7.99
- [ ] **AS YOU DESIRE**   22199-4 $5.99/$7.99
- [ ] **ALL THROUGH THE NIGHT**   22372-5 $5.99/$7.99